I0744825

For my most ardent readers who lift me up with their own words.

This volume is dedicated to: Pat, Candy, Jon, Susan, Kanyon, Steve, Texas, and Paula.

For Harold Trammel whose friendship and support I have come to cherish, not to mention his acerbic notes which often have me laughing out loud (I have learned not to read his notes when drinking tea, especially if I want my keyboard to last).

For Janice Harris who drops everything to cast her critical eyes over my books, and who is on a one-woman mission to teach me the grammar that I was never taught at school.

Thank you for reading so passionately and for taking both myself and these girls into your hearts.

TWISTED MAGIC

1: WHAT DOESN'T KILL YOU

JO HO

ONE

Becky Stevens wanted to die.

The sun had set hours ago leaving the sky a purple-black haze and it could stay that way forever for all Becky cared. If she never saw daylight again it wouldn't be a bad thing.

At least then she wouldn't have to listen to the snickering of those around her, laughing as her world was rocked, and her dreams shattered.

Music blared out from the speakers inside Tonic. The new local hotspot had recently been voted the most popular student hangout of the year but the place seemed too loud tonight, the flashing lights headache-inducing. She felt suffocated by the closeness of the heaving club goers.

She couldn't move without being pressed up against a sweaty stranger. Despite what her well-meaning friends thought, this really was the last thing she needed.

All she wanted was to veg out in her pj's in front of Netflix, but they had dragged her out against her will. She had to show *him* they had said! She couldn't give him the satisfaction of letting him know how he had broken her.

He was her boyfriend Mark.

Well, technically, he was her ex-boyfriend now.

Earlier in the day she had caught him with his tongue down another girl's throat. It wasn't what she had expected to see. Especially that early in the morning during her daily coffee run. The two of them had been together since high school where they were crowned prom queen and king. Dubbed the most popular couple, the two had graduated to the same private college together. As far as she had known, they were a team and Becky had fully expected to live happily ever after with him. They had decided where this amazing life would happen — in California among the palm trees and sunshine. They even knew what they would name their kids: Gemma for a girl, and Logan for a boy.

Why would he do that? Why would he encourage talk like that, getting her hopes up if he had no intention of making any of it happen?

As if the cheating itself wasn't bad enough, as if *seeing* him do it wasn't bad enough, it had to happen as Becky stood blindsided, surrounded by a group of her friends all out getting their breakfast shakes. Her humiliation wasn't complete it appeared unless it was witnessed by *everyone*, which was probably why they had insisted on this unfortunate night out. Her friends had figured a few drinks and some twerking later, and Becky would have forgotten all about him.

But although she had tried to enjoy herself, had tried to wipe that picture of him kissing someone else from her brain, there was no hiding that her heart was broken.

She didn't want to be here.

What she needed was a good cry and to drown her sorrows in a tub of Ben & Jerry's.

Pushing past the dancers, Becky reached the exit and turned around to wave goodbye to her friends. They shouted something at her, but Becky couldn't make out what they were saying above the singing of Bruno Mars.

Getting the gist of it though, she shrugged apologetically, mouthed "next time," and made her way outside.

Becky shivered, unaccustomed to the sudden chill, as the fresh air hit her. They had been experiencing an unseasonably warm summer so the abrupt cold was a shock to the system. She clutched her cardigan closed over her chest, wishing she had worn her favorite one with the buttons. Shelby had insisted on this skimpier one. It came with a waterfall opening that didn't hide her assets and that was a good thing, apparently.

Although no amount of cleavage had kept Mark faithful, Becky thought bitterly.

Picturing her warm bed, Becky hurried towards the dorm she called home. It was only a few blocks away and if she wasn't wearing these stupidly high heels, she could probably get there in half the time. Unfortunately, everyone knew the price of beauty. The four-inch shoes gave her legs the illusion of length even if they pinched her toes and made balancing an Olympic art form.

Making her way across the square, Becky left the music behind and quickly found herself swallowed up by the silence. As she walked, she noticed that there was something different about the air tonight. She couldn't put her finger on it. There was a heaviness to it that was almost palpable. She could feel it weighing down on her.

Or maybe that was just the sudden realization that she was single again.

She'd have to date again. She'd have to go through all the uncertainties that came with meeting someone new, but this time, it wouldn't be as easy as finding him in the same class. Becky was already in her second year at college and she knew the talent — or lack of it — that existed there. The thought of having to be more social, of having to regularly hang out at places like Tonic filled her with dread. While some lived for going out, partying all the time just wasn't for her.

Her ghostly reflection appeared on the glistening

black glass as she approached the John Hancock Tower. She looked away when it creeped her out too much. Her friends always laughed at her for being so jumpy. Becky had grown up with a superstitious mother who always warned her it was best not to look at yourself on shiny surfaces at night, because you might not like what you find there.

It wasn't like she was five or believed in monsters anymore.

Realizing how ridiculous she was being, Becky mentally shook herself. If she hurried up, she could still catch a few old reruns of Gilmore Girls before bed. That show was what she liked to describe as Hug TV. It was the kind of show that always made you feel better after you experienced it — just like a hug — and a hug was exactly what was required right now.

It was as she was clearing the building that Becky heard a footstep behind her.

She noted it in her mind but kept moving, expecting the person to keep their distance or to move away, respecting her personal space.

But more footsteps came… Closer this time.

Too close for comfort.

She stopped, spinning around to see who it might be. A gang of local kids had taken to water bombing passersby lately. Becky was not going to be amused if this was them now, especially not in this cold. Scanning the area quickly, she could see no one. Still, she felt the hairs on the back of her neck rising, one by one. She couldn't shake the eerie feeling that someone was watching her. Tentatively, Becky called out.

"Who's there?"

There was no answer. No other sound.

Just the tap-tapping of her heels, picking up the pace.

Nervously, Becky fumbled for her bag, hoping to take her phone out. She wasn't sure who she would call, she just knew she would feel better with it in her hand, but in her haste, the bag slipped from her shoulder dropping to the ground. Makeup, and her Tennerson keyring fell onto the sidewalk, sounding as loud as gunfire in the silent night. Having fallen from her bag, her phone lay on the ground a little distance away.

Even from a few feet away, she could see a large crack spider-webbing across the dark screen.

"No, no, no…"

Dropping down to the ground, Becky scrambled for her phone, punching the home button, hoping desperately for it to come on but it stayed stubbornly off. Her fingers reached round to press the two buttons that she knew would reset her phone when…

Something *moved* in the reflection of the glass building.

Startled, her head snapped up to look at it.

What she saw there filled her with such terror that she froze, unable to move…

<h1 style="text-align:center">TWO</h1>

COPLEY SQUARE, 1692.

With none of the historical buildings that the world would come to know in existence yet, the square was a large expanse of flat land covered with grass as a young woman drew her cloak around her, hurrying under the light of a blood moon.

She tossed a nervous look over her shoulder. There was nothing behind her but the inky blackness, a giant mouth of darkness that engulfed anything within reach. Still, it was possible that someone or *something* was following her…

And the thought filled her with a terror so strong that fear constricted her throat.

She was warned not to be out here at night, but she hadn't listened. She had thought the blood moon was only a story to scare young children into behaving, but there it hung now, low in the sky.

Impossible to miss.

The sun will turn into darkness, and the moon into blood, before the great and terrible day of the Lord comes.

Unbidden, the familiar Bible verse flashed through her mind but what horror did it prophesize?

She moved fast, wading through knee-high grass, hitching up her long skirts so she could cover more ground, ignoring the sharp blades as they whipped against her bare legs, slicing into them. They were only cuts and cuts would heal, but if the warnings were true, then nothing would save her.

Nothing would save any of them.

As she continued through the field, she heard the distinct sound of someone behind her, but there shouldn't be anyone out here at this time of night. Only she was desperate enough to work so late, ever since her father had fallen ill, and they had fallen behind on payments. There was no other choice. It was either this, or they would lose everything they had worked so hard for.

A low rasping of breath cut into her thoughts.

She was right, someone was following her!

Swallowing her fear, she broke into a run, not caring who saw her panic now. Trees blurred past, but she didn't look back, instinctively knowing that if she did, she would be lost.

If she could just get past this field, into a more built up area, maybe she could seek help. She knew of a healer who lived nearby, who kept their doors open throughout the night for emergencies. If she could just remember which direction she should head in… Was it… West? Seeing a faint glow of a lamp up ahead, relief washed over her.

There! A house!

As she ran towards it, she felt a forceful tug then found herself flying backward into the night until she landed awkwardly on her rump. Stunned, she didn't react at first but then pain exploded, sending her senses on fire. It felt as if she had broken every bone in her body. A metallic taste flooded her mouth as she realized she must have bitten her lip in the fall.

What had happened?

Even as the question flashed across her mind, she felt another insistent tug on her cloak. Next came the arms, wrapping around her vice-like until the breath was squeezed out of her.

And still, she couldn't see who her attacker was.

She tried shouting for help but her words came out a thin, hoarse cry. "Let go of me! Help! Someone, please!"

She flailed, desperate to escape, but the arms were like steel and she couldn't get free. Feeling hysteria claw at her throat, she opened her mouth to scream when her attacker wrapped thick hands around her neck...

...and *snapped it*.

She dropped to the ground with a thud.

COPLEY SQUARE, PRESENT DAY

Becky lay on the ground, her glassy eyes staring blindly across the empty square.

Her face was contorted into an expression of terror that would remain in place when the medical examiner took her back to the morgue to examine her for the cause of death. It didn't take long for a diagnosis to be made as it was clear for all to see: Becky had died of a broken neck.

When it was time for the mortician to take over the body, he did the best he could to hide the damage but there was no amount of paint or makeup that could disguise that face which would go on to haunt him for the rest of his life.

Becky's tortured expression stayed the same throughout her closed casket funeral service, where, in front of her family and friends, Mark had sobbed through the entire ordeal having come to the realization — much too late — that it was Becky he loved. The other girl had meant nothing to him. He had only wanted to experience something new, but when he had gotten his chance, only then had he realized just how lucky he had been to have already found the love of his life.

His dreams were now buried with Becky, six feet under the ground, where her face would stay frozen in that awful twisted expression, until the worms and insects came, and the earth would claim her back as one of its own.

THREE

The sun shone down on the gothic monolith that was Blackville University.

Nestled in the picturesque grounds of Walnut Hill overlooking the crystal blue waters of the reservoir, an army of students hurried to their assigned dorms, assisted by their anxious parents, seeing off their kids for the first time.

Among them, Marley Gray hoisted a box against her hip, hoping that she wouldn't drop the contents all over the floor. Relying on the clean slate that she knew she had here, she was determined not to make a spectacle of herself like she had done, so many times before in the past. Here, Marley was going to have a blast being a normal student, doing normal studenty things. Here, no one was going to find out about her terrible secret.

Not if she could help it.

"You're sure this is the way?"

Her dad, Paul followed close behind, precariously balancing several boxes of his own, peering at her over the top of them. He was tall and dark-haired. Most women considered him handsome — they were particularly drawn to his being a single parent. It seemed that little fact worked better than a Tinder profile in attracting interested parties, although in the thirteen years he had been single, Marley hadn't known him to date. He wasn't able to leave her alone long enough to try, so moving here from San Francisco to let her live in a dorm without him? This was a *big* deal.

"Yes, Dad. It's just around the corner," Marley replied, trying not to roll her eyes at him.

Just because she loved him dearly, it didn't mean he couldn't drive her to distraction with all the constant questioning. It was something that had started when she was young, after her mom had left them. On a seemingly normal day, she had gone with only a terse note behind as an explanation. Paul had been crushed although he'd kept it together for Marley's sake.

At first, it had been pretty tough going.

Five-year-old Marley hadn't understood why Daddy couldn't just bring Mommy back. Why didn't he just get into a car and go after her?

After a few months, the pain began to lessen as Marley became accustomed to having only one parent to call on. After a year, her absence became the new normal, as was ignoring the fact that she had ever existed at all. For most of her life, it had been just the two of them. Marley was pretty OK with that.

Moving past a window, she caught a glimpse of herself in the glass. Her long dark, almost black hair was caught up in a long braid down the side of her face so it wouldn't get in the way of the moving. She had only bothered with basic make-up today, some mascara to give her lashes more oomph, and a little tinted lip balm to keep the dryness at bay. She was lucky that she didn't need much help to look decent, her good genes being the one thing her Asian mom had passed onto her.

Marley was tall, five foot seven, with a slim but curvy build which all came from her Caucasian dad's side. She had the almond eyes and small button nose like her mom. Those who didn't know her would consider her a hottie, but that was only until they got to know the real girl. When that happened, when they discovered the truth about her, it didn't matter what she looked like.

"Thomas Jefferson Hall," Paul said, reading from a plaque on the side of a wall. "You were right, here it is."

He wedged open a door with his foot, leaving space for Marley to go by. Marley smiled at him as she squeezed through, making her way down a hectic corridor, scanning the numbered doors as she went. Students hurried past them, holding up maps looking confused as their parents carried the bulk of their belongings behind them.

"Twenty-two, this is it," Marley said as she opened the door to find her new roommate already inside, standing next to Hugh Jackman.

Marley did a double take and blinked at him before she realized that it wasn't the movie star as she had first thought, but a man who looked very much like him. Seeing her, Hugh-alike beamed and leapt forward to assist with her box.

"You must be the roommate! Let me help you with that," he took the box out of her hands before she could reply and set it on the bed by the wall.

"This is my daughter, Cassie." He gestured at her, encouraging her to greet Marley. "We hope you don't mind, but Cassie has chosen the bed closest to the bathroom, but we can swap if you have any objections?"

Marley shot the other girl a smile. She was rewarded with one of her own, although it was weak. The girl couldn't seem to keep her eyes on Marley, dropping them quickly to the carpet.

"Hi, I'm Marley," Marley said as Cassie mumbled something back, which may or may not have been words.

"That's fine, I'm good with where I am," Marley said, trying not to frown as she studied the other girl. She had ginger hair that wasn't quite straight and thick glasses that made her eyes look owlishly big. She was dressed in jeans and a sweater that swamped her small frame doing nothing good for her. Beyond the fashion crisis, Marley could see that Cassie was uncomfortable. She would have thought it was only first day nerves until she noticed that she seemed particularly nervous around her parents.

Why? Who would be nervous around their own parents?

A woman, Cassie's mother, had been hidden away from view behind a wardrobe door but she stepped around it now… It was all Marley could do not to gasp out loud.

Cassie's mom was *beautiful*.

Like Gisele Bündchen stunning. Everything about her screamed *model*. She even moved with an effortless grace that seemed to glide over to Marley.

"I'm Cassie's mom, Angie, and this is my husband Tom," she said, stretching out a hand to Marley.

"Nice to meet you all," Marley said as she took her hand she noticed how incredibly soft her skin was. Marley made a mental note to remind herself to ask Cassie what her mom's skincare regime she used.

Between Tom and now Angie, Marley found herself slightly blinded by their beauty. Glancing at the awkward looking Cassie, she felt an instant pang of compassion for her. It must be tough when she looked so well, normal, and her parents seemed to have stepped out of the cover of Vogue. With his usual impeccable timing, Paul came into the room just then but stopped dead at the sight of them.

"Oh, OK. Didn't expect to see you here. I've loved all of your movies, by the way, even that bad one," he said to Tom as the other man laughed.

"Everyone says I look like him, but I just don't see it myself."

Angie slipped her hand in his gazing at him adoringly.

"You are much better looking, dear."

While Paul smiled at them, Marley snuck a look at Cassie — for some reason, despite the sweet display her parents were putting on, the other girl looked like she wanted to be swallowed up by the ground. Paul dumped his boxes by Marley's bed taking a walk around the room, checking it out.

"This is nice. You girls get to have your own bathroom."

"Well, no, we have to share," Marley replied, showing that there wasn't another one in the room.

"I meant you don't have to share with the rest of the floor."

Tom shot a wry look at Paul. "It's amazing what perks you can get when you donate a ton of money to the school."

"Well, on my behalf of my daughter, thank you very much for your donations." Paul replied.

Tom smiled as Angie went back to helping her daughter unpack. Paul moved to help Marley, but she gestured "away."

"I've got this. You don't need to help."

Paul looked as if he wanted to argue but knew better than to do so.

"I'd step away if I were you," Tom joked. "I've learned never to mess with a woman's clothes."

Taking his advice, Paul joined Tom at a table next to the window. The two sat and chatted about nothing interesting. Somewhere between sports and politics, Marley zoned out of their conversation, focused on setting up her new home until she had things mostly where she wanted them. There were still a few unpacked boxes containing her course books and stationery, but the bulk of the work had been done. Looking over to Cassie's side, she saw it was the same for her.

Angie opened an oversized Chanel bag that had been sitting by the window next to Tom and fished out a gift-wrapped box which she handed to Cassie now. Surprised, Cassie took it.

"What is this?"

Angie smiled at her and gestured for her to unwrap it.

"A big part of the Cuthbert tradition."

Wondering what it was, Cassie opened the box to reveal a beautiful pair of peep-toed shoes inside. There was a fabric flower stitched onto the front of each shoe, but even from where she was standing, as pretty as they were, Marley could see that the shoes were not new. Cassie, however, couldn't be more delighted.

"Really Mom, you're giving these to me?" Her eyes were wide with shock and rapidly filling with unshed tears.

Angie smiled, beaming with pride.

"Your grandmother wore them when she was married, I wore them when I went on my first date with your dad, then again when we were married, and now I am passing them on to you."

"But, I thought they were only for those kind of occasions?"

Angie shook her head. "They are for landmark occasions and I can't think of a bigger one than the first woman in our family to go to college. We are so proud of you, honey."

Cassie could barely contain herself as she hugged her mom tight.

"Thanks, mom, I promise I'll look after them."

Marley smiled at the two of them even as she felt a small ache in her heart, knowing that this was something she would never experience. She had no mom, and there would be no shoes or anything else that would be handed down to her.

She looked away from them and caught her dad looking at her. She saw from the expression on his face that he knew exactly what she was feeling. He didn't say anything but gave her a wink to see if she was OK. She nodded that she was fine.

Cassie carefully put the shoes away onto the top of her wardrobe as Angie pulled out her cell and held it up high so that the camera looked down on them. As soon as Cassie saw what she was doing, she moaned and flung up her hands to cover her face.

"Just one Cass! It won't kill you!" Angie pleaded, but Cassie kept shying away from the phone.

"I don't want to, Mom. Can't we just get through this without you posting anything on Instagram?" Cassie asked, obviously used to this kind of request.

"But my fans have been looking forward to this for weeks, honey. They've been hearing all about my only child going off to college. They've watched you grow up on my timeline, you can't deny this bit of joy for them. Please, dear, I only want the one picture?"

From his seat at the table, Tom called over.

"You know she won't leave until you say yes, sweetie. You should just get it over with."

"Come on Cassie, I just gave you the shoes, can't you do this tiny thing for me?" Angie asked, batting her lashes at her. "I just want to record this momentous occasion."

Sighing with feeling, Cassie looked up at the camera sullenly.

"Fine," she said as Angie smiled gratefully and instantly adopted a sultry pose. There was the sound of a camera click and then the swoosh of a picture being posted to Instagram. Staring at her phone intently, Angie suddenly beamed.

"My gosh, it already has three thousand likes! All these people know you're here and wish you well!"

"Yay," Cassie replied without any enthusiasm. Tom must have finally noticed how agitated Cassie seemed or he simply felt sorry for her. He got up from the table and went to his wife, picking up her bag from the floor.

"Honey, I think it's time we left our daughter alone so she can get to know her roommate," he said. As soon as the words left his mouth, Angie became anxious as her brilliant blue eyes began to shine with tears.

"You'll call if you need anything, right? Anything at all?"

Faced with their imminent departure, Cassie suddenly didn't look as sullen, in fact, Marley noticed she seemed unsure.

"Even if I don't need anything, I'll call you guys once a week, OK, to let you know how I'm doing?"

Tom enveloped her in a hug. "You better."

As Angie folded Cassie into her arms, Paul approached Marley, his eyes wrinkled with concern and uncertainty. He kept his voice low as he spoke to her.

"If this doesn't work out, you know you can leave at any time. Or even if you just need a break from it all. I've got a room ready for you in the new apartment."

Marley nodded.

When Paul had learned that Marley had been accepted at Blackville University, the first thing he had done was to quit his job. He was a history professor and was certain that he could find something in the Boston area. Despite Marley assuring him that she would be fine, Paul would not hear of her moving to the East coast by herself. As luck would have it, BU needed someone with his skill and experience, so the two had made the move from out West a few weeks ago. Paul had found an apartment to rent on Zillow and had made sure that there was enough room for Marley. Whenever she decided to go home, she would have her own space.

Marley's shrink had made it clear that it was important she have that.

"I'll be fine, dad. Stop worrying," Marley said.

He looked as if he had a lot more to say but casting a quick glance at the other family, decided against it. Wrapping her in a bear hug, Marley clung to him, breathing in the familiar sandalwood that came from the wooden beads he wore on his wrist. They had been a gift from her mom, back before things had imploded. Marley was always surprised that he still wore them, so many years later, but the only explanation Paul had ever given for that was that their relationship hadn't always been bad, and despite everything, she was still the only woman he had ever loved.

"It's not like you're going very far, is it?" Marley grinned suddenly, lightening the mood.

"That is true," Paul replied. "I guess I'll see you around."

Marley watched as Paul waved then left. Cassie's dad had a harder time dragging his wife away, however, as Angie clung to Cassie suddenly, tears streaming from her eyes.

"You've got all your cards, and we've given you cash to tide you over," Angie said between sobs.

"I've got plenty of money, Mom, don't worry," Cassie said. Eventually, Cassie was able to detach herself. She gave her parents a watery smile of her own as they finally left.

And then it was just the two of them.

"They seem kind of attached to you," Marley began, trying to engage Cassie in conversation.

The look Cassie shot Marley made her uncomfortable. She hoped she hadn't said anything wrong. Cassie raked her eyes over Marley, from top to bottom until she couldn't help but feel as if she were assessing her critically.

"Only child and all that," Cassie finally replied.

"Same here."

"Where's your mom?" Cassie asked, looking nervous as if she wasn't used to holding conversations with anyone other than her parents.

"Gone. She left when I was little. It's no big deal. I got over it a long while ago," Marley finished quickly before the sympathy came. She didn't need anyone feeling sorry for her. She was just fine. Cassie must have sensed her reluctance to talk about it further as she changed the subject.

"So what's your major?"

"Journalism. I'm hoping to be a reporter. I love discovering stories, finding things out, especially about people. One of my favorite things to do is people watch in a coffee bar. How about you?"

"Creative writing. I like to read." Cassie broke eye contact suddenly, cheeks flushing red with embarrassment. Marley stared at her curiously wondering what her deal was. Why was she so… awkward?

"Hoping to be the next J. K. Rowling?"

"Something like that," Cassie mumbled, turning away. And just like that, it seemed their conversation was over as Cassie focused on rearranging her things.

Great.

And people thought *she* was weird.

FOUR

Across the hall, Tyler Jones was also unpacking her things, but unlike the commotion and noise that seemed to be everywhere, in here there was only an oppressive silence.

Through the hallway, Tyler could see a girl being hugged by her movie-star-good-looking parents as they bid her goodbye… and the sight was like a knife in the heart. The pain was so intense that she almost gasped. It was only a hug, so how could it affect her like this?

Whenever this happened, whenever the pain came, and as she had done so for the last six months, Tyler focused on her breath. Breathing in, she counted…

One… two…. Three… Four… Five…

On six, she exhaled. She repeated the meditative exercise she had found on YouTube until the stabbing pain lowered into a dull ache.

How much longer was she going to feel like this?

Looking at the only box she had brought with her, Tyler took out her things. There were a few pairs of jeans, tank tops, button-up shirts and sweaters, but other than underwear, all she had left were her study things. The only personal item she had brought with her lay in the bottom of the box. Her sole possessions in the world fit in this one box.

She didn't know whether she should be amazed or sad.

To think there was a time when she had had so much stuff that there wasn't room for it all. Reaching in, she carefully fished out the framed photograph.

In it, she beamed out at the world, her arm around her younger sister, Ally. The photograph had been taken a few years ago when Ally was only seven, and Tyler, fifteen. They shared the same cheesy grins, the same green eyes and glossy chestnut hair. Speckled across Ally's nose were a handful of freckles, but where Tyler's hair was cut into a neat bob, Ally's hung in two longs braids on either side of her face that she kept tied with matching ladybug bands. It was her fascination with the tiny creatures that had earned her the nickname "Bug".

They sat posed on top of their ponies, Oreo and Cookie, on yet another of their weekly rides in the countryside. Each day was one great big adventure and had brought such joy and happiness that neither of them had had a care in the world.

Until one simple text message had changed everything.

The ponies were gone now as were the cheesy grins. And Ally… God, Ally. Tyler hoped desperately that she was OK. It was at least a week before she would get to see her again.

Being away from her cherished sister hurt almost as much as losing their parents had.

From the time she had been born, Tyler was devoted to her sister. The two were thick as thieves. They did everything together; the eight years between them meant nothing. Tyler wasn't one of those girls who craved attention from boys or needed to go out partying. She was perfectly happy staying at home. For her, family was everything.

Which was why, when her parents were killed in the car crash, her entire world was destroyed.

All it had taken was one careless moment on the phone. One glance away from the road. The boy who had killed them — and he was a boy, only seventeen years old — had been busy texting a girl when he had rammed headlong into Tyler's unsuspecting parents' car. Her mom had died instantly, but her dad… her strong, superman of a dad, had clung to life for days.

When he finally died, Tyler hadn't even been in the room.

After not sleeping, eating or showering for over forty-eight hours, the nurses had convinced her to take a break. They said she would feel better when she was clean that she didn't need to be glued to his bedside. Stupidly, Tyler had taken their advice — they went through this kind of thing on a daily basis, surely they would know what they were talking about?

It was while she was showering that her dad had died. She only discovered this when she returned and found Ally lying beside their flat-lining dad on his bed, inconsolable. Her poor sister had been alone when it had happened. Ally had screamed for Tyler until her voice went hoarse from the tears, but Tyler had been too far away to hear her. She never got to say goodbye to her dad. She hadn't been there for her sister.

Some days she couldn't get out of bed from the guilt.

It had taken everything she had to go to BU. To continue her studies like her parents had wanted her to. They had been so proud when she had been accepted. Their daughter was going into pharmaceuticals! She would save her sister and the world with her medicine they had bragged to any who would listen.

Tyler's choice was incredibly poignant to the family as Ally suffered from Chronic Kidney Disease. They didn't know exactly how she had gotten it, but to help her kidneys perform the function they couldn't do on their own, Ally had to have regular dialysis sessions at home. The family had all been willing to donate one of their own kidneys to her, however, in a cruel twist of fate, for whatever reason, they weren't a match. Ally had been on the national donor list for a year now but there was still no sign of a match.

So to help her sister and in her parent's honor, she would do this.

For them. For Ally. Despite how she wanted to crawl into a hole and never come out again, Tyler would do this for her family. She would do whatever was necessary to save her sister and be reunited with her.

A knock sounded on the door, startling her from her thoughts.

A guy stood there with curly black afro hair and dark caramel skin. He was a few years older than Tyler and carried himself with an air of gentleness. Dressed in an old leather biker jacket that seemed slightly too large for him, he shot her a quick smile that lit up his face and made his hazel eyes sparkle.

"Hey. I'm Si. Looks like my sister is going to be your roommate." His voice was rich and deep and filled with a warmth that Tyler found herself instantly intrigued by.

"Hi, I'm Tyler," she replied as Si's eyes ran across her neat unpacking.

"Wow, a girl who packs lightly. Thought I'd never see the day."

Tyler smiled but didn't respond, not really sure what to say. It wasn't like she was going to go into her whole sad story. Si looked away as his sister arrived. Having met the brother already, whatever she had expected his sister to be, she was wrong. Tyler found herself staring at a younger, female version of Si, except this girl had a big mass of corkscrew curls and wore dark, almost black lipstick. Her hair was dyed a harsh, unnatural black with red tips that looked almost like blood, and she was dressed in dark clothing popular with Goths. Tyler had to blink twice at her, having never seen a Black Goth before. She came into the room — reluctantly Tyler thought — took one look at her, then the room and immediately spun around.

"Oh hell no. I'm not staying. Not here and not with her."

She pointed a black painted finger towards Tyler and abruptly left, leaving Si gaping after her.

"Eve! Come on, give it a chance!" He called after her, but it seemed she wouldn't be coming back. Si turned back to Tyler, face full of apology.

"I'm sorry, she's not usually like that. She's been a bit stressed," he finished lamely.

"Right," Tyler replied, not bothering to fill in the awkward gap that followed. Personally, Eve being so rude to her face, she hadn't particularly liked the look of the other girl either! Tyler felt herself brimming with anger only controlling it for his sake since he had been so nice to her.

"I'd better go after her, see if I can get her to come back."

Don't be doing that on my account, Tyler thought, pissed.

Si shot her an apologetic look then took off after his sister.

Alone again, Tyler thought.

Figured.

FIVE

Marley spent the next few hours sorting through her things and finding new homes for them.

Technically, she would be considered a messy person, though she liked to point out that it always started off neatly. She just wasn't able to keep it tidy for long. She was one of those people who had a hap-hazard filing system and always ended up putting things in a "safe place." It was just unfortunate that she never remembered exactly *where* that safe place was.

While Marley carefully stacked her piles of journalism and history books, she noticed that Cassie was fast disappearing under a mound of cosmetic and weight loss products. She also owned more beauty magazines than school books by the looks of things. Marley watched in some amazement as Cassie erected a giant make-up mirror on her desk. Plugging in the cable, she flipped a switch and the numerous bulbs around the mirror flashed on, bathing the room in its warm amber glow.

"That's a pretty hardcore piece of gear you've got there."

Cassie stared shyly at her in the mirror.

"Yeah, it's a professional mirror. It was given to my mom after a shoot, but when she saw how much I wanted it, she passed it on to me."

"You're really into this stuff, huh?" Marley was determined to get to know her new roommate and to put her at ease. Part one of her "becoming normal" plan was to find some real friends, and naturally, that had to start with her roommate.

"I guess," was Cassie's only reply.

Determined not to be put off by her lack of response, Marley continued. "Have you done much research into the college?"

Cassie tilted her head to one side, thinking. "Just the basic stuff on the courses and dorms."

"So you don't know that this place is drowning in fun facts?"

"Like what?" Cassie asked, looking interested for once.

"Like how Kylerman Hall used to be a hotel, and the study lounge on the top floor used to be a pool, so there are some great views from up there."

"That is pretty neat."

"Right? And they do amazing food here. They even have a lobster night! Can you imagine? I LOVE seafood. My dad and I are waiting for that one."

"Your dad?" Cassie frowned, confused.

"He's going to be a history professor here."

"Well, that'll be nice for you to have him so close."

"Yeah, I need to see about that. I love him but he can be a little overprotective."

"That's probably because he's a single parent," Cassie said before her face started flushing red with embarrassment. "Sorry, I didn't mean to sound like I know it all, it's just that mine can be overprotective too. As much as they mean well, sometimes I just need some air, you know?"

"Absolutely," Marley replied. Truthfully, she was enjoying the fact that Cassie was coming out of her shell.

Was it possible that things would turn out OK after all? *That would be a first for sure.*

"Wait! I almost forgot the best one! Did you know a famous playwright died in our halls? Jacob Samuelson. They say it's haunted by him. Apparently, when he's out walking, the lights flicker on and off, and sometimes people can hear footsteps approaching but they can't see anyone."

Cassie shuddered. "Well, that's not creepy at all, thanks."

"You're welcome," Marley replied cheerfully, not the least bit concerned. Picking up the jacket she had left on the bed, she found a small shoebox of her own lying beneath it. The sight of it made her wary, and she shot a look at Cassie to see if she was watching, but, Cassie was focused on lining up her millions of lipsticks and arranging them on a scale of light to dark.

Quickly she flipped open the box, double checking the contents. Inside lay several bottles of prescription meds with her name on them. Her shrink had wanted her to have enough to cover her for any emergencies. School could be a trying time, and they weren't sure how Marley would cope with the pressures on her own, so it was decided to front-load her with an arsenal of meds, should she need them.

Closing the lid, Marley hid the box under her bed and pulled several pairs of shoes in front of it.

If she was lucky, Cassie would never even know it was there.

SIX

Storming away from the dorm, Eve made fast work of losing her brother amongst the crowd. She could still hear him calling out after her, but Eve didn't stop for fear he would catch up to her.

She didn't need to hear what he had to say; she already knew what the gist of it would be: he was disappointed in her for not giving the dorm or her roommate a chance, especially after she had promised him that she wouldn't do this exact same thing (Eve had a bad habit of running away and sticking her head in the sand), but at the end of the day, he wasn't the one who was going to have to live here, sharing every night with a complete stranger in such close quarters. Some people might have found the room cozy, but for Eve who had grown used to her space, it was claustrophobically small.

And then there was the roommate herself.

But Eve didn't want to think about her right now. She knew she couldn't go home as Si would make a beeline there. Needing a place to camp out, she headed to the Coffee Bean, the on-campus java establishment of choice.

When she had been a freshman here last year, The

Bean was Eve's favorite place to hang out. It wasn't just that they served a mean espresso, but all the cute guys had seemed to flock there. Eve was given more numbers waiting for her drink than anywhere else on site. It seemed it was still super popular today, however, given the long line of students that waited in front of her. She stood impatiently behind a group of chatting girls as she searched for her money — which could be in any number of the many pockets she had.

In the past, Eve had dressed only for maximum impact on guys, but she had since learned the futility of that exercise. Looking down and rifling through her pockets, Eve didn't see the girls in front of her turn around but she heard the snickers immediately.

"Oh look, is it Halloween already?" a girl said.

"If all the new intakes look like that, we're not going to have any competition this year," another laughed loudly.

Rage coursing through her, Eve — not one to take abuse lying down anymore — raised her head, meaning to cut them down to size, but she froze dead when she saw who they were, shock radiating through her.

She knew these girls.

More than knew them.

The girls' insulting looks changed too as recognition set in.

"Eve?" Carly, the overly made-up blonde and ring-leader of the group gasped. "Why do you look like that?"

Swallowing her shock, Eve's sensibilities came back to her in a rush. The blood pounded in her head as she was finally confronted with the girls she had not seen for almost a year.

"This is how I look now. You'd know that if any of you had bothered to find out," she snapped back bitterly.

Grace, a brunette wearing a super short skirt and a low cut shirt that showed a distasteful amount of her push-up bra, shot her a disdainful look.

"It's not our fault you disappeared out of school. A phone works both ways, you know."

Knowing that she had never meant anything to them was one thing, but actually experiencing it now still managed to hurt, even after all the time had passed. Despite the fury raging through her, Eve also felt tears prick the backs of her eyes as she glared at them.

"I told you about my problem but none of you cared enough to help me."

Carly sighed dramatically and spoke as if she were speaking to a child.

"We told you what to do, but you didn't, so you can't really blame us for not listening. At some point, don't you have to own your own actions?"

"Besides," Grace said, tossing her long hair as if she were in a commercial. "It's not like we were best buddies or something. We just felt sorry for you."

"Yeah," another of the girls agreed. "You were always so desperate for our attention."

"Well, I certainly don't need that anymore," Eve snapped as she spun on her heels and hurried away before they could see how upset she was.

SEVEN

A few hours later, Marley stood beside Cassie with the other students in her dorm in the common area known as The Lounge.

Ahead of their first scheduled dorm meeting, Marley had watched as Cassie had tried on, then discarded several outfits before finally deciding on an olive green dress. Marley had said that they didn't need to change clothes to meet with their Resident Advisor but Cassie had wanted to. She had also spent a good hour touching up her makeup and struggling to tame her unruly hair. If Marley found it bewildering, however, she kept it to herself, not wanting to make Cassie even more self-conscious than she already was.

Staring around the room, Marley noticed that all except one student were paired up. People were naturally standing beside their roommates but there was one girl, a quiet-looking brunette with a cool bob who didn't speak to anyone and stood off to one side.

To assist them in getting to know each other, their RA had given name badges for the students to wear, just while they had this social gathering. Marley could see the girl who stood by herself was called Tyler. For whatever reason, she didn't seem to have a roommate with her.

Their RA was named Rhett and she thought he was quite the hunk. Judging by the captivated faces from the female students, the rest felt the same. He wasn't that tall, maybe five ten or so, but he carried himself in such a way that he seemed much bigger. His brown hair was trimmed into a neat crewcut, and there was a hint of stubble around his jawline that made him all the more attractive. Intelligence shone from his blue eyes as he took in the room, watching for the last stragglers to arrive. Rhett gave off an air of confidence yet also seemed approachable, which Marley found comforting — if they had any problems living here, he would be the first port of call.

He spent a while going through the ins-and-outs of living at the dorm. Marley tried to take it all in but was beginning to suffer from information overload, it didn't help that he was distractingly good-looking so she was glad when he finally changed the subject.

"Now that we've gone through basic housekeeping here at TJ Halls, I need to switch gears and talk to you guys about something you need to be aware of."

Rhett's voice had lost the friendly vibe he'd had just moments before and now took on a serious tone.

"You might have heard already, but a student was found dead the other night. She was from a neighboring college and she was killed only a short distance from here."

Gasps could be heard around the room. Marley had somehow missed this news, only learning of it now. She found herself chilled and shared a horrified look with Cassie.

"How did she die?" asked a girl with red hair. Her voice cracked at the end, clearly spooked by the revelation.

Rhett hesitated, struggling to decide just how much information should be relayed. Finally, he spoke again. It looked like it was a struggle for him to stay calm, Marley noted.

"Her neck was snapped."

As more gasps sounded, Rhett raised his hand for silence.

"The thing is, our campus is very secure — all the colleges are — but once you are off-site, you run the same risks as everyone else. While police are investigating the murder, it's probably best to be cautious when leaving the grounds. I'd advise you all against going out at night alone. If you see anything suspicious, there are phones that are connected to campus security dotted around everywhere. Do not hesitate to use them, even if nothing has happened but you just feel scared, especially you girls. Women so often don't listen to their instincts only to regret it later so trust yourself and be safe."

A tall blonde raised her hand. When Rhett nodded, she spoke.

"What college was she from, the girl who was killed?"

"I don't know if that information is being released just yet. While we want you to be safe, we also don't think a culture of fear and paranoia will do you any favors. It's best if you all just help each other out, particularly as you are all freshmen, and make sure that none of you are alone when you go anywhere. At least for the foreseeable future."

"Wait, wasn't someone else killed recently? Another young person?"

It was a black guy who had spoken this time. Rhett hesitated before answering.

"Yes, but we don't know if the two are connected."

Rumbles rose through the ranks as the ramifications of a possible connection chilled Marley to the core. *If the same person killed both victims, wouldn't that mean there was a serial killer on the loose?*

"Who knew it'd be safer back in Englewood, Chicago than here," someone said but the joke fell flat. No one laughed, unable to see the funny side to any of this. Rhett walked up to a whiteboard and wrote a number on it.

"Save this emergency number to your phones. This is who you call if you are not near a campus phone and something happens."

The room was suddenly filled with the familiar sound of multiple musical phone keys being pressed. Marley saved the number and watched as Cassie did the same.

"I'm sorry to put such a dampener on your first day. I've been here two years and in all that time, nothing has happened until now, so this is probably a one-time thing and we're being over cautious for nothing. Still, it's better to be safe than sorry. Just remember, safety in numbers."

Rhett turned as if to leave but stopped, then went over to his bag to fish out a pile of booklets from inside.

"Wait, I almost forgot. So we don't end our first meeting with so much doom and gloom, here's some local information for you guys. We've listed the best places to eat, shop and hang out so you should check them out."

Done with the talk, Rhett suddenly found himself swamped with anxious students needing reassurance though Marley couldn't help but notice nearly all were female. Cassie reached the pile of booklets and grabbed two from the top, handing one to Marley.

"Thanks," Marley said.

"No problem," Cassie replied, her cheeks flushing pink again making Marley wonder how long it would be before Cassie wasn't embarrassed by just talking to her. As Marley began flicking through the booklet, she noticed Tyler standing beside them.

"Hey, I'm Marley and this is Cassie," she began.

Tyler gave the two a smile. Though she seemed friendly, there was an air of sadness around her that Marley immediately caught.

"I'm Tyler. I have the room opposite you two." Tyler turned and gestured to Cassie. "I saw your parents saying goodbye to you earlier."

"Right," Cassie replied lamely, instantly wishing she could say something cool for once.

"That meeting was slightly terrifying wasn't it? Wasn't expecting that when I signed up for classes," Marley said, hoping to lessen some of Cassie's shyness and embarrassment.

"Yeah. It's a conversation starter for sure. Not sure how I'm supposed to take his advice though, since I don't have a roommate to buddy up with."

"We noticed you were standing alone. Where's your roommate?"

"Gone. She took one look at the room, then me, then apparently decided she didn't want anything to do with either of us," Tyler said without a hint of malice.

"Seriously? That's both rude and weird," Marley replied.

"Yeah," Tyler shrugged. "I'm not too cut up about it though, kinda like the fact I'll have my own room but it doesn't help with any of what Rhett just said."

"You can hang with Cassie and me, right Cassie? We'd love an extra friend," Marley spoke for the two of them, hoping Cassie wouldn't have any issues with that. To be honest, Marley wasn't sure she wanted to be alone with Cassie too much. The girl was so awkward, it was painful to watch and interact with her, but more than that, it wouldn't exactly help Marley's mission to seem normal. At least Tyler could speak without tripping over her tongue.

Cassie nodded but did the thing again where she couldn't meet the other girl's eyes. If Tyler noticed, she didn't let on.

"It's still pretty early, why don't we check out one of the places recommended in here?" Marley suggested.

"Sounds good," Tyler said.

"Yes," Cassie agreed.

And just like that, Marley had made her first two friends in a long, long time.

She hoped they would still stick around when they found out the truth about her.

EIGHT

A wall of colorful fruit greeted any who came into Fresh and Wild, a trendy smoothie and juice bar overlooking the common (and one of Rhett's recommendations).

The girls sat at a booth near the busy counter where they could catch all the action as they pored over the varied menu. Sia's latest track played on the radio as hectic servers raced around, trying to keep up with demand. Apparently, they weren't the only students who had decided to give this place a try.

"God, there are so many, how am I going to decide?" Marley exclaimed, overwhelmed by the selection. It seemed as though there were hundreds of drinks to choose from. Tyler didn't seem to have the same problem. Her eyes skimmed over the menu fast as lightning, quickly deciding on her choice.

"I'll just have a carrot juice."

"Really? Don't you want a Colada Surprise or Passion Friday? They sound amazing." Marley asked, surprised by the boring choice.

Tyler shrugged. "It feels wrong to pay almost ten

bucks for juice, not when I can cook a whole meal for the same price."

"Firstly, you cook? I've been known to even burn toast. Second, well, yes, sure, but as a once in a while treat…" Marley suddenly felt a bit of a heel for not even looking at the prices. Though she didn't consider herself rich, she and her dad had never really struggled either, not to the point where she couldn't get a drink without checking out the price first.

"That's OK, I can get it," Cassie piped up suddenly. There had barely been a squeak out of her on the walk over, so Marley had almost forgotten she was there, and she felt immediately bad about that.

"I'm fine with carrot..." Tyler began but Cassie cut her off.

"Please. It's a treat, for my new friends." As if to prove she meant it, Cassie took out a fifty dollar bill from her purse. Tyler gaped at it.

"Do you always carry such large bills?"

"Not always," Cassie replied but Tyler didn't know whether to believe her or not. As Cassie had taken out the money, Tyler was sure she had seen more fifties in there and had found herself instantly hit by a wave of jealousy. If she had that kind of money, she'd hire the best lawyer in town and get Ally back in no time.

Thinking of her sister, Tyler took out her cell and sent her a quick message. *Hey Bug, I'm sitting in a hipster juice bar, thinking of you. What're you up to? And have you decided what you want for your birthday yet? xoxo*

"So, what are you having?" Cassie prompted.

"Sorry, I was just sending a message to my little sister," Tyler said. "I guess I'll have the colada drink then, thank you."

"Marley?" Cassie asked, with more excitement than Marley had seen in her since they'd met. Funny how buying them drinks could make her feel like that.

"Same," Marley said. "I love coconut anything."

Cassie smiled and took off to the drinks counter.

"How old is your sister?" Marley asked.

"She's turning ten next week. Still hasn't made up her mind about what she wants for her birthday though," Tyler smiled.

"I've always wondered what it'd be like to have a sister. I'm an only child," Marley explained.

"I can't speak for anyone else, but I'm super close to mine. Especially since our parents died recently," Tyler wasn't sure why she brought that up but there was something about Marley that made her feel that she would understand. There was just something about her manner.

"Oh wow, I'm so sorry. What happened?"

"It was a car crash," Tyler answered in a monotone. She found that even after six months of saying it, it only became easier if she said the words but tried not to feel them.

"Who has your sister now?" Marley asked, hoping she wasn't intruding too much.

"Foster mom. She's a tool," Tyler said suddenly, gritting her teeth. "I don't know how she still has a license to foster any kid, she's totally unfit for the job. I have plans to get Ally back, to become her legal guardian but I'll need good grades and a steady income to do it."

"But if she's that bad, why hasn't her license been taken away from her?" Marley asked.

Tyler shrugged. "Red tape? One troubled kid's word against another? Maybe there aren't enough foster parents to go around so they can't be too choosy about who they accept, who knows?"

"You don't have any other family who could take her?" Marley couldn't fathom what it must be like to be ripped away from those you loved, only to be living under the roof of someone negligent — or worse — abusive.

"No. My grandma's in care for Alzheimer's and my only aunt lives in Holland. She's a kind of free spirit. She doesn't work, and moves around, living with whoever her latest boyfriend is. My mom said she was irresponsible and didn't get on with her. I haven't seen her for years."

Marley was rocked by what Tyler was revealing. Not only had she lost her parents, but she had so much more to deal with than the average student, she made her own issues seem tame by comparison.

"Well, if I can ever help with anything, let me know," Marley finished, hoping they didn't sound like empty words. She meant them. The pain that seeped out from Tyler was palpable.

A beep sounded on Tyler's phone making it vibrate on the table. It was a reply from Ally. She picked up the phone and read the message.

You said you hated hipsters! Not doing much today, had my dialysis earlier so doing homework now. Heepie Jeebie's at the hairdressers. And I think I want that bag I told you about, the one shaped like a ladybug! Is it next week yet? Why is it so far awayyyyyyyyyyy? xoxoxo

Heepie Jeebie's was the nickname Ally had given to her foster mom, Cheryl Heep. The two thought it suited her brilliantly.

"Here they are!" Cassie said suddenly, back with their drinks — and a whole lot more. The tray she carried contained a mound of brownies and cookies. "I wasn't sure what you guys liked, so I got some of everything." She handed out the drinks with gusto as Tyler tried not to gasp at the total on the receipt. Cheap, this place was not.

"So, I heard of a private party happening tonight. This cute guy over by the counter was handing out flyers. He even gave *me* one. It's at a bar! We should check it out," Cassie said happily.

"We're not exactly legal yet," Tyler began, but Cassie shrugged off her hesitation with a wave of her hand.

"The host has hired the place out and they're not serving alcohol so it's all fine."

"Then sure I guess," Marley responded. Tyler looked as if she didn't want to go but Marley gave her an encouraging look.

"Might help to take your mind off things," she said simply. Appreciating her discretion, Tyler nodded.

"OK, sure. I'm in."

Smiling, Marley took a sip of her drink and leaned back happily.

"This is so good. Thanks, Cass."

Sunlight filtered in through the large trees dotted around the common. Enjoying her drink, Marley watched the leaves swaying in the breeze and the shadows dancing in the light. They moved in such a way that they seemed to form the figure of a woman. As Marley watched, the outline became clearer until it *was* a woman she was looking at. She wore an old-fashioned dress but there was something large wrapped around her neck that she couldn't make out. Squinting her eyes, Marley stared through the black shadows that seemed to have suddenly appeared. When it finally sank in what it was she was looking at, she gasped.

The thing around her neck was a noose, and the woman was hanging from a giant elm tree.

The surrounding air seemed to change. Marley could feel her hair turn static. All sound faded until the creak of the noose swinging in the breeze took over everything else. It was so loud, that it could have been right next to her.

Then the dead woman started to move.

Her head lifted from her chest as her dark eyes pinned themselves onto Marley. Slowly, her right arm began to rise until she pointed a finger at Marley.

And then she screamed.

An awful, piercing sound that made Marley jump and lose her grip on her smoothie, though the rest of the world couldn't hear it. This horror was for Marley's ears only.

The smoothie hit the table, spilling its contents over the food and all over Cassie's pretty dress. As her glass landed on the table and rolled off the edge, all sound came crashing back to her. The chatter of the juice bar, the glass as it bumped a table leg before finally stopping, and Cassie's shocked gasp.

Marley jumped up, feeling awful.

"I'm so sorry!" she said as she scrambled for napkins to help Cassie. Seeing the large wet stain soak into her dress, Cassie uttered a cry of dismay before tearing off towards the restroom, leaving Tyler staring at Marley while faces turned to watch them, wondering at the sudden commotion.

"What the hell happened?" Tyler asked.

"I thought I saw something… it doesn't matter."

"It looked like you did that on purpose," Tyler said uneasily, staring at her with that uncomfortable expression Marley knew only too well.

"Did what, throw the drink on Cassie? No, that's not what happened…" Marley wanted to explain, but how could she? How could she tell her what she had just seen without Tyler thinking she was crazy as well?

Tyler seemed to stare at her for an indeterminate age before she finally spoke again.

"You clear up here, I'll see if I can help her," Tyler said, hurrying off after Cassie.

Alone, Marley waited until Tyler had disappeared out of sight before quickly diving under the table to find her bag. Fishing out one of the medical vials she had hidden under her bed, Marley popped a pill and swallowed it quickly, stealing another glance at the elm tree.

But the hanging woman had vanished.

NINE

W ith Tyler and Cassie ensconced in the restroom, Marley made a quick call. Her dad picked up after only two rings.

"Missing me already?" His familiar voice broke through the panicked haze Marley found herself feeling again.

"Dad… I… I just saw something."

They had been through this enough times that he didn't need any clarification on what she meant. She heard his intake of breath followed by a silence as her words sank in. When he spoke again, his voice was warm and calming which wasn't that surprising — he'd had years of dealing with her particular problem after all.

"Did you forget to take your meds?"

"I don't think so. I took one just now though, just in case," Marley answered, keeping her eyes fixed in the direction of the restroom.

This was a conversation she did not want the others to hear.

"What did you see?"

"A woman. She was dressed in old clothing, like

something from the 1600s… and she was hanging from a tree in the common." Even as she spoke the words, the horrific image flashed up again in her mind sending a chill down her spine. She shook herself mentally, to clear it away.

"That's new. Usually, it's regular people you see."

"Well, that's just great, the hallucinations have up-graded," Marley said.

"It's probably the stress of this all. Not only are you starting a new school, but you'll be living away from home for the first time, and now you'll be sharing a room. It's a lot, but Dr. Ellis and I wouldn't have approved this if we didn't think you could handle it."

Marley frowned, not expecting this from him.

"Wait, you're the guy who kept telling me *not* to move out."

"Because I didn't want you to. But that doesn't mean I don't think you can handle it. You've been through so much already, this is just first day jitters. Just remember to take your pills, and I'm sure you'll be fine."

Marley knew he was right, just like she knew what she saw wasn't real but a figment of her condition. Although knowing it and feeling it were different matters entirely.

She first started having her "episodes" a little after her mom had left. She would hear and see things in the night that had her screaming for her mom, but she never came. Lisa was long gone.

At first, they thought she was just acting up, but it wasn't until Paul found her hiding under her bed because the boy who lived in her closet kept pulling her blanket off her when she slept, that Paul realized his daughter needed professional help.

Throughout her childhood, Marley had endured test after test, but they were all inconclusive. Reluctant to drug his young daughter, Paul had opted for the holistic route. They had tried aromatherapy, and meditation, while Paul prayed every night for God to help his daughter. And it seemed for a while that he had heard them as Marley's hallucinations disappeared.

Until one day, at school, Marley found herself crushing on a fellow student called Jeffery.

They talked regularly, but he never seemed to want to take things further. Marley didn't have his number or know where he lived. Their sole relationship consisted of them bumping into each other at school and talking, until finally one day, Marley confronted him, demanding to know whether he liked her or not. He admitted he did, that he felt the same way as her, so Marley told him they should make an actual date outside of school.

On the day of the date — which would be Marley's first date with a boy — with equal parts nerves and excitement, Marley had ended up spending four hours getting herself ready. When she turned up at the Dairy Queen, however, Jeffery never showed, and he never called to explain why. Crushed, Marley went home and stayed in her room all weekend, pretending to be sick so Paul wouldn't bother her. When Monday came around, and Paul wouldn't allow her to stay home from school, she eventually found Jeffery in the cafeteria and yelled at him in front of the whole school. How could he do that to her? How could he stand her up?

Which is when Jeffery had vanished right before her eyes.

One minute he was there, and the next, it was just her, standing in front of the rest of the school, as her classmates and teachers watched her screaming at thin air in astonishment.

After that incident, Marley was dubbed psycho girl. The new school pariah, one by one, her friends dumped her, not wanting to be associated with her. Her reputation ruined, Marley pleaded with Paul for help. It took many sessions of therapy and tests, but eventually, a diagnosis was reached. As long as Marley took her meds, she could live a fairly normal life — at least, that is what she was told.

Whether that was true, remained to be seen.

"You know, instead of hiding your condition, maybe if you at least told your roommate, you could get some much-needed support," Paul's voice gently intruded into her thoughts.

"Or she could ruin my life here before it's even started by telling everyone."

"At some point, you're going to have to trust someone with this Marl," Paul said.

"Maybe, but not yet. It's only my first day. This is my one chance to be normal. I don't want anyone else to know."

"Whatever you decide, honey."

From the corner of her eyes, she saw Cassie and Tyler leave the restroom. Having done the best they could, they were returning to the table. Cassie had a huge stain on the front of her dress and she held the wet fabric off of her chest, looking utterly miserable.

"I've gotta go, call you later," Marley said quickly before hanging up and rushing over to Cassie.

"Cass, I really am sorry. It was a stupid accident."

Cassie looked at her, her eyes bright with humiliated tears. "Is everyone looking?"

"What? No... no one cares. We can just go back and get you a change of clothes." Marley started unbuttoning the shirt she wore over a tank top. "Here, you can wear this over your dress for now."

But Cassie shook her head. "No. It'll only get wet too and it's too long to get back to the dorm... I need a new outfit now," Cassie said as she reached for her purse.

"We passed a nice looking shop on the way here, I'll bet they have something you'll like inside," Tyler offered.

"Let's go." For once, Cassie's voice sounded firm and left no room for disagreement.

"I can't... my dad needs to see me about something,"

Marley began, feeling terrible for dumping her friends, especially after what had just happened, but shaken by her hallucination, she didn't want to be out here anymore.

"That's OK, I'll go with Cassie," Tyler said.

"I'll see you both back at the dorm." Marley smiled at Cassie but it was barely returned. She watched as the two left before shooting one last look at the elm tree.

She felt a small wave of relief when she saw that it was still empty.

TEN

The library was a historical wonder with its towering stained glass windows and stone columns that had admirers coming from miles around to study in awe — but Eve wasn't one of them.

She sat at a desk in the corner with her back to the windows and their amazing rainbow colored views, two of her laptops running.

Needing to regroup, she played World of Warcraft on one laptop, while she worked on her own game, a puzzler that relied on the laws of gravity and physics, on the other. Her hope was to finish it before she graduated and upload it to Steam for sale.

Many other indie game developers had gotten their start to the industry in the same manner, and Eve was determined that it would be the same for her.

Whenever she was coding or gaming, she was in her happy place. Alone with only her laptops and virtual friends for company, all of whom she didn't know IRL (In Real Life), she didn't have to deal with people and their "funny" looks or judgment. Online, she could just be.

And she'd needed to recover after bumping into those girls.

They were the reason why with just one look at Tyler, she had known they couldn't be roommates: Tyler was a rich white girl, just like her ex-friends.

Yes, she'd only had the one box with her at the time, but the rest were obviously on their way or being shipped from God knows where. She knew it in Tyler's designer fringe and lowlights, distressed hipster clothing and the latest slimline MacBook that she saw on the bed which Eve could only dream of owning. It had only come off the line earlier in the year and could power several of her RAM busting apps in parallel, but Tyler would never know what it was capable of as Eve knew she would only use it for word processing.

She looked like every one of those girls Eve had been desperate to be friends with before, the popular girls she had allowed to torture and demean her just so she could breathe the same air…

And the very ones who had dropped her when she had needed them the most.

She was tired of trying now, she already knew where that road would take her. It was especially pointless as the whole "living in a dorm" thing had been Si's brain-child. He wanted her to experience regular school life again, especially after the thing-that-happened that had caused her to flunk her first year. Wasn't it enough that she was willing to redo her school year? Why did he need her to come out of her shell and be her old self again, no matter how much Eve told him that that girl was dead.

She had died last summer.

She was hiding out at the library now, not wanting to deal with Si's anger at home. Eve figured she'd give him a few hours before heading back, right around the time he would be leaving for the bar where he worked.

Whenever they had a blow up like this, Si just needed time to cool down. Sometimes Eve thought he took the

idea of being the man of the house a little too literally —
he was, after all, only a few years older than her — but
those three years might well have been ten for all the differences between them.

After three decades of living in Boston struggling to
make a living running a catering truck selling Jamaican
food, their parents had retired and moved back home to
Jamaica two years ago. It wasn't their original plan to do
this. Eve's grandmother had gotten sick and her parents
had gone back home to look after her. But sadly, she
passed away after only a few months. Her parents had
stayed on to deal with the legalities only to discover that
she had left her house and life savings to them. It wasn't
much, but it was enough for them to quit their business in
the States, pay off their mortgage and Eve's tuition. Si had
always been mature for his age and the two got along
well so her parents weren't at all concerned about leaving
their two adult kids behind.

But if they ever found out about the thing-that-happened after they had left, they would have been on the
first flight back.

As the sun dipped behind a cloud outside, Eve caught
her reflection in the laptop and startled. Although the
Goth style suited her new, "keep out" vibe, it still startled
her on occasion to see the heavy black makeup that now
covered her features. It wasn't always this way. She used
to wear the latest trends and was considered one of the
prettiest girls around. Inundated with dates, she was even
known to be a little loose with her affections.

All that had changed when Eve had fallen in love…
and started living a daily nightmare.

Shivering from the chill that came over her whenever
her mind wandered to that dark place, Eve focused on the
in-game chat in WOW. She'd been playing the game now
for most of the day to kill time. A random player had just
sent a message her way wanting to trade weapons. Glad
for the interruption, she was typing an answer when a

shadow fell over her. Then she felt the presence of someone watching over her shoulder.

"You're a Warcraft fangirl?" asked a voice from behind her.

Eve looked up to see a girl around the same age as her. She had Asian features but was obviously mixed race. Expecting the usual crap she received whenever other girls saw her interests, Eve had to stop the urge to slam her laptops closed, though the girl hadn't sounded like she was mocking her?

"I know it's an older game, but I like how familiar it is," Eve said, half expecting the other shoe to drop.

"I'm more into consoles myself," the girl continued. "I've never been able to play with a mouse and keyboard. It just feels alien to me."

Blinking, Eve realized she was being genuine then felt some of her tension lessen.

"It does take a while to get used to. Which console do you play?" Eve asked carefully, half waiting for the other shoe to drop.

"PlayStation mainly, though I haven't had one for a few years now. The last one broke and we just never replaced it."

"Shame, there are a lot of cool games out now."

"I know. I'd be on it all the time though then I'd never get any work done, so it's probably for the best. Games are such a time sink. You know The Last of Us? I completed it three times before I figured I had a problem. Come to think of it that's around the time that my PlayStation "broke". Maybe I should have words with my dad..." she laughed.

"I'm Marley by the way."

"Eve."

"So, I know this is going to sound a bit presumptuous but all the computers are taken here and I need to look up something quick. Can I use one of your laptops? I'd use my phone but I'm close to maxing out my data and I've honestly no idea where my laptop charger is." Marley asked hopefully, but Eve caught a sense of something underlying the friendliness, and it felt a lot like desperation. Ordinarily, she would have turned her down, but there was something about her that made Eve less cautious than usual. She had to admit it was nice to talk to a friendly girl for once, especially after her recent run-in.

"Sure," she replied gesturing to the one with Warcraft running on it. Eve minimized the game and opened up Google.

"Thanks," Marley said gratefully as she took a seat in front of the computer. She sat in such a way that Eve couldn't see what she was looking up. Realizing that it wasn't any of her business anyway, she turned back to her app and continued working away at it. Caught up in her work, she didn't know how much time had passed in silence until Marley tapped her on the shoulder.

"Hey, thanks for letting me use it. I'm done now."

"Did you find what you were looking for?" Eve asked.

"Yeah," Marley replied, unable to hide her worry. It was on the tip of Eve's tongue to ask what was troubling her, but she had never been the type to overshare and she didn't want to start now. If Marley was looking for a sympathetic ear to listen to her woes, she'd have to find it someplace else.

"See you around," Marley said, her eyes already clouding over as her thoughts took her elsewhere.

"Bye," Eve managed before Marley walked away, head hanging down as if the whole world sat on her shoulders. Wondering what might have caused her to feel that way, Eve slid over to the laptop Marley had used and found herself looking up Marley's searches in the address bar. While she knew this amounted to spying, Eve reasoned that it was fair game since it was her computer.

But there was nothing listed other than Eve's own searches. Marley must have gone incognito mode.

Curiouser and curiouser.

Luckily Eve knew how to get around that. Using her advanced tech skills it was a simple matter to pull up Marley's searches and previously closed windows…

And what she discovered proved an interesting — if morbid — find.

Windows flooded the screen with depictions of women hanging in trees in Boston Common. As part of the witch trials that were popular in the 17th century, the accompanying text explained how the trees were used to hang women accused of being witches. One particular tree kept coming up in the searches, a giant tree that stretched over sixty-five feet high which had been known as "The Hanging Elm". Eve shuddered as she read about the many women who were killed on that one tree alone.

Looking up, she glanced in the direction Marley had disappeared off to.

Why on earth had she been googling this stuff?

ELEVEN

Tyler watched as Cassie tried on a million outfits.

At least, that's how it seemed.

They had been in the boutique going on an hour now, long enough that Tyler was beginning to regret offering to accompany the girl. Just how many dresses could a person try on before making up their mind?

Tyler had watched as Cassie modeled each one, waiting for Tyler's comments. Truth was, Tyler thought Cassie looked decent in nearly all of them but Cassie had found something wrong with every one.

This one made her look fat (something which Tyler had snorted at since Cassie was such a tiny thing. She had been genuinely troubled and really believed that she was overweight). Another made her already small chest look even flatter (Cassie's own words). Another was too short, showing how dumpy her legs were. All of these issues Cassie had with herself Tyler was sure were in her head. She had just met the girl and didn't feel it was her place to correct her, although she did try to let her know that she didn't agree with her negative assessment of herself.

Bored with how long she had been waiting for

Cassie to make up her mind, Tyler found herself perusing the rails herself. It had been a long time since she had gone shopping for fun plus they did have some nice things in here. Picking up a simple maroon colored dress, Tyler went into the dressing room trying it on.

The empire waist, color, and flared skirt were a perfect fit showing off her fair complexion. She came out of the room to show it to Cassie. When the other girl laid eyes on her, she looked stricken.

"You look so good in that Tyler! That color makes your skin pop and the cut of the dress makes your waist look so small. I wish I could look like you," Cassie exclaimed miserably.

"Are you kidding? You look good in that dress yourself Cassie. I think it's time you decided on one. If any of them looked terrible, I would have told you. They were honestly fine. I wish you'd just trust me on this," Tyler finished, a little more impatiently than she wanted to sound.

Cassie hung her head low. "I'm sorry, I just hate shopping you know? It's always so stressful for me, trying to find things that will fit right and not make me look horrendous."

The way she looked now, Tyler knew Cassie meant it, that she wasn't just being a drama queen. Cassie had some real issues with her appearance that no dress would ever fix.

"Honestly Cassie, that dress looks great on you."

She must have finally heard Tyler as she studied herself critically in the mirror, turning this way and that.

"I guess it doesn't look too bad…" she conceded. "OK, I'll get it," she suddenly said to Tyler with a grin. "Are you getting yours?"

"I think so," Tyler said. "I haven't had something new in a while. Think I'll treat myself."

Cassie looked slightly confused. "Wait, you wouldn't

spend a few bucks on a drink but you'll spend this much for a dress?"

"A drink is just a drink, but a dress I can wear over and over again."

Tyler went back into her cubicle to change into her own clothes while Cassie stayed in her new outfit. Moments later, she joined her at the checkout where Cassie had already paid for her dress and had her "ruined" clothes put into a bag. The sales assistant rang up the dress. when the final amount flashed up, Tyler tried not to flinch. Fourty-five bucks wasn't *that* much, but it was still a lavish purchase, seeing as it wasn't essential… but it had been so long since Tyler had bought anything for herself, surely this was OK?

Handing over her debit card, Tyler waited as the cashier swiped it in the machine. Instead of going through, it beeped. The sales assistant smiled reassuringly.

"Don't worry, this just happens sometimes. I'll try again," she said.

Tyler nodded as Cassie looked on. Sliding the card through the reader, the machine beeped again. This time a message flashed up. The sales assistant, a girl not that much older than they were, gave Tyler an apologetic look.

"Sorry, it looks like there's a problem with your account?"

"What is it?" Tyler asked, concern beginning to flood her body whenever anything money related was mentioned now.

"I don't know, you'll have to call them to find out. You can make your call over there while I serve the next customers," she said, gesturing to a quiet corner. Embarrassed, Tyler nodded and quickly called her bank. As she waited to be connected to the right department, she shot a look at Cassie but she seemed oblivious to her concern, holding up a pair of earrings to her face, checking her reflection in a mirror.

Her call was answered shortly by a bored male voice. Tyler went through several security checks before she discovered why her card was frozen.

"What do you mean I've only got thirty dollars in my account? There should be a lot more than that. Hasn't my financial aid come through?" Tyler lowered her voice to a low whisper, hoping nobody could hear her.

"Let me check for you Ms. Jones," the phone assistant said. Tyler could hear him tapping away on a keyboard.

"I'm sorry, the financial aid isn't showing on your account yet, and while you do have two hundred dollars in your savings account, your debit card draws from your checking account."

"Wait, what?" Tyler gasped. "It's not there? But they said it should be by now."

"I'm afraid I'm not privy to that information. I suggest you give your loan company a call."

Reeling, Tyler mumbled in agreement as she hung up. Numb, the blood draining from her, Tyler turned around to look for Cassie only to find her at the checkout again. Even in the midst of her shock, disbelief rose to the surface. Was the girl shopping *again*?

Forgetting all about her dress, Tyler moved to the door in a daze.

Two hundred dollars.

That was all she had to live on. If there was a problem with the loan, what was she going to do? She needed it for her room, for her food and everything else. Seemingly oblivious to her stress, Cassie bounced over to her swinging two shopping bags. When she reached her, Cassie presented one of the bags to Tyler.

"Here," Cassie said grinning. "I got it for you."

Blinking, and barely able to comprehend what she was saying, Tyler frowned at her.

"Got what?"

Cassie gestured at the bag. "The dress! I heard you

saying your financial aid hadn't arrived, so I decided to buy it for you."

Tyler gaped at her stupidly, conflicting emotions running through her. On the one hand, she was pleased to have the dress for nothing, but, it felt wrong to accept such a large gift from someone she had just met. It left a strange taste in her mouth.

"You didn't have to do that."

"I know, it's no biggie. It's not like I couldn't afford it," Cassie said carelessly.

"But…" Tyler began as Cassie stopped her.

"Seriously Tyler, just take it. It's a gift to celebrate our friendship. It's no problem, honestly. I want you to have it. It's the least I can do for making you wait here for an hour while I tried on everything in the shop."

While Tyler was grateful for her generosity, something about the lavish gift felt wrong. Like she would be taking advantage of her if she accepted. She glanced over at the checkout, the thought of returning the dress entering her mind, but Cassie must have sensed what she was thinking as she frowned, looking upset.

"If you return my gift, it would be like a slap in the face for me."

Tyler could see that she meant it. Swallowing her pride, she smiled her appreciation.

"I'll keep it. Thank you, it's a lovely present."

Happy, Cassie slipped her arm through Tyler's as they headed back to dorm.

"I can't wait until they see us at the party. It's going to be the best night ever!"

TWELVE

Try as she might, Marley couldn't stop the horrific images from assaulting her.

She'd been in the dorm for a little while now, but on the long walk back from the library, all Marley could imagine were the hundreds of women, hanging from trees.

And the one specific one who had pointed at her and screamed.

Ordinarily, when Marley had a hallucination like this, it bore no relation to reality so this was something new entirely. Many women like the one she had seen, had been murdered on that very tree. Wasn't that too big a co-incidence… What did that mean exactly? Could Marley see things that others couldn't? Could she see the past… or was it worse than that? Could she see… dead people?

The thought filled her with dread.

Taking out her laptop — which had run out of juice long before she'd even set foot on BU — Marley went through all of her things until she finally found the charger, buried inside a mound of socks. Why she had packed it with them was anyone's guess.

Plugging it in, she waited impatiently for her laptop to get enough power to turn on. Glancing at her bag, she took out the meds, studying the label on the bottle. She'd been taking the pills for so long now that it had become as second nature as her daily vitamins, but now the doubt was setting in. If what Marley was seeing was real, it meant that her diagnosis wasn't correct… and that she wasn't *and had never been* crazy.

Which would mean that everything she thought about herself and everything she knew, was wrong.

Turning the bottle around in her hands, Marley contemplated calling her shrink, wondering what she would say if she told her this latest information, when Cassie and Tyler appeared at the door, back from their shopping trip. Startled, she shoved the vial under her pillow, hoping that neither of them had noticed it.

Cassie came inside and immediately presented herself to her.

"What do you think of my new dress?" she asked, unable to hide the desperate tone in her voice. From her anxious manner and the way she held her breath, Marley knew she wasn't just fishing for compliments. For whatever reason, she needed Marley's approval, and after what had transpired earlier, Marley was only too happy to oblige.

"You look great. That color and cut really suit you," Marley said genuinely.

Cassie smiled and let out her breath in relief.

"Really? I mean, I thought it did, but sometimes I get it wrong."

"Well, you were right this time." Marley paused before speaking again. "By the way, can I just say I'm sorry again, for spilling the drink on you? I honestly didn't mean to."

Cassie shrugged her small shoulders, letting her know it was water off a duck's back. Across the room, Tyler took in their things, specifically Cassie's make up area.

"I can't believe how professional this all looks." Tyler picked up a small tube of something, waving it around. "Like, what exactly is this for?"

"Contouring," Cassie replied, but when Tyler looked confused, she took the tube from her. Twisting the lid, she squeezed a blob of skin colored cream onto the back of her hand and dabbed it onto Tyler's forehead, nose and cheeks, leaving white streaks in those areas.

"I don't think it's the right color for me," Tyler began hesitantly but Cassie made a shushing noise. In her zone now, she quickly and adeptly smoothed out the color with a sponge, working away at Tyler's face until her cheekbones became more prominent and her nose, slimmer, all while looking seemingly natural.

"That's amazing! You really know what you're doing," Marley said in admiration. "Do me next!"

Giggling, Cassie started on Marley. She dabbed foundation over her face, then brushed her eyelids with a bronze powder that emphasized the uniqueness of Marley's eyes. She worked over their faces with all the tricks on her table until all three were fully made up and looking fantastic.

Cassie glanced at her watch. "It's almost seven, the party should be starting soon. We should get going."

"Let me get changed, I'll be right back," Tyler said, heading to her room.

"I've gotta freshen up, but we can head out when Tyler gets back," Marley said, disappearing into their adjoining bathroom.

Alone for a moment, Cassie started tidying up her makeup but her eyes strayed to Marley's bed… and her pillow.

Shooting a quick look at the closed bathroom door, Cassie darted over to Marley's side of the room. Slipping her hands under Marley's pillow, her fingers scrabbled around until they found what they were looking for. She *knew* she had seen Marley trying to hide this very thing when she had come into the room! Picking up the medicine bottle, Cassie read Marley's name on the label. Turning the bottle, she came to the name of the meds.

Thorazine.

Inside the bathroom, the toilet flushed followed by the sound of running water as Marley washed her hands. Hurriedly, Cassie shoved the bottle back under the pillow and ran back to her side of the room as Marley emerged.

"You ready to go?" Marley asked.

"One sec. I'll meet you in Tyler's room in a bit," Cassie replied a little breathlessly, hoping that Marley would take the bait.

"Sure," Marley said as she left the room. As soon as she was gone, Cassie took out her phone and Googled Thorazine. Hundreds of hits flooded the screen but Cassie clicked on the first, the Wikipedia entry.

Within moments, she found the answer to her question.

Eyes wide with shock, Cassie glanced across the hallway, to Tyler's room where Marley stood, admiring Tyler in her new dress as if nothing was wrong.

Although Thorazine could be prescribed for nausea and vomiting, in this dosage it was usually used as a treatment for schizophrenia.

Cassie swallowed, her mouth suddenly dry.

Not only was Marley mentally ill, but she was hiding it from them.

THIRTEEN

Heavy rain blanketed the streets, but it wasn't enough to stop Marley and the girls from attending their first college party.

They looked good, and they were ready for fun. Even Tyler had warmed to the idea of a night free from complications or worry. Tomorrow, she would figure out what she needed to do for cash, but tonight she would enjoy student life and be with her new friends.

Darting into the bar to escape the rain, the girls were instantly swallowed up by the crowd. The music was thumping and loud enough that it made conversation difficult — which wasn't a bad thing in Marley's mind.

She wasn't sure what had happened, but the walk here had been a little weird. She kept catching Cassie sneaking looks at her, but whenever she asked what was up, Cassie just replied that nothing was wrong. And Tyler? She was acting as if she was present but it seemed like her mind was someplace else.

Thinking that Cassie might still be holding a grudge for what happened earlier, Marley decided it was time to make up for it. Gesturing "drink," she pushed her way to the bar but the busy bartender didn't even look her way.

"You've got to be a lot more aggressive than that if you want her attention."

Marley turned to see who had spoken to her and found herself standing next to a guy. He was good-looking… if you liked the smug type. He wore the jersey of BU's football team and had the kind of physique that spoke of regular workouts. Marley was sure that many girls fell for him. There was something about the arrogant sneer of his lips, the puffed up way he stood that put her on edge.

"Oh yeah?" she replied, enough to be polite but not really trying to engage.

"Yeah. She's harder on the girls, but has a liking for studly guys, if you know what I mean," he said, winking at her.

Marley cringed inwardly. Did he really think this would work on her? He waved at the bartender who immediately came over, so apparently, this act did work on some.

"What can I get you?" the bartender asked, somewhat breathlessly. Marley hoped it wasn't for this idiot's benefit. The jock — as Marley knew he was — looked at her, eyebrow raised in question.

"Three cokes, please," Marley answered.

"Three cokes," he repeated loudly. Moments later the drinks were set on the counter but as Marley went to pay, the jock stopped her.

"Let me," he said cheerfully. Marley didn't want to accept his offer, but then again, she didn't know how to turn him down without sounding rude. It was one of life's big puzzles. She grabbed the drinks.

"Thanks," she said as she started heading back to the girls. Unfortunately, the jock followed.

"I'm Trip," he said, shouting above the music to be heard. "Trip Rockwell."

"Marley," Marley replied, hoping somehow that maybe she would lose him on the way back to the girls. No such luck, however, as he followed closely behind. When she arrived back, she found Cassie standing awkwardly alone. Handing her a drink, she asked, "Where's Tyler?"

Cassie pointed a little distance away to where Tyler stood chatting with an older guy. "I think he's the host of this party." Suddenly, Cassie's eyes went wide as she looked over Marley's shoulder, then her cheeks starting flushing bright red. It took a moment before Marley realized that the blush was Cassie's reaction to seeing Trip. Was there something in the water? What could they all see that she couldn't?

"Trip, this is Cassie. Cassie, Trip paid for our drinks just now."

Cassie took hers from Marley as if she were handing her something of major value.

"Thanks…" Cassie managed to stammer back. Trip took one look at Cassie then turned his back on her, focusing on Marley again. Marley caught the move and frowned, not liking his rudeness, but Cassie seemed to take it in her stride. At least, that's what Marley hoped. She for sure didn't need any more reasons for Cassie to have a problem with her.

"So… cool party huh?" Cassie said, trying to engage Trip in conversation. Apparently, she hadn't gotten the memo that he didn't want to speak with her.

"It's lame, but it beats being back at the dorm," he replied still looking at Marley. Marley fidgeted on her feet, beginning to feel uncomfortable by both his interest in her and his treatment of Cassie.

"Which dorm are you in?" Cassie asked innocently.

Trip finally turned to her and looked her straight in the eyes.

"Why, thinking of stalking me?"

"No…" Cassie stammered, mortified. "I was just making conversation."

He gave her a look as if she was something nasty stuck to the bottom of his shoe and fixed his attention back on Marley.

"Well, now that you have your refreshments, do you want to dance?" he asked hopefully.

"I don't dance," Marley replied. "But maybe Cassie would like to?" She meant it to be kind as Cassie obviously had a bit of a thing for him but Cassie's eyes went even wider than they already were if that was possible. She started shaking her head wildly from side to side, gesturing that she didn't know how to dance.

She didn't need to worry, however, as Trip's smile froze. He stared into the crowd, fixing on something across the room. "You know what? I actually see my buddy over there that I need to say hi to. Next time maybe."

Without waiting for a response, he left quickly leaving Cassie embarrassed and Marley fuming inwardly. She looked at Cassie, not knowing what to say. No matter how she tried to be nice to her, it just kept backfiring.

"It's OK," Cassie said finally, lowering her eyes to a point on the floor. "I'm used to it."

With those four simple words, Marley suddenly understood how Cassie's life might have been in the shadow of her parents, two physically blessed people. It hit her how cruel the world was to those who weren't considered "good-looking." She wanted to break the ice that had suddenly descended on the room, but she didn't know what to say. She was finally saved by Tyler gesturing at them.

"Oh hey, Tyler's calling us over."

Marley lead the way through the dance crowd as Cassie followed close behind, trying not to spill her drink. As they reached Tyler, the cute guy she was talking to smiled at Marley.

"Hey, I'm Josh. Welcome to my party."

Marley smiled back. "What's the occasion?"

Josh grinned. "I'm free and single and ready to mingle?"

Cassie laughed loudly — a little too loudly — causing several raised eyebrows to look her way. It probably wouldn't have drawn too much attention to her but then she snorted. Embarrassed, she slapped a hand over her mouth but the damage had been done. Someone in the surrounding group snickered.

"Who invited Miss Piggy?"

"Miss Desperate, more like," came the answer from another faceless body in the crowd. "You see that dress?"

Looking mortified, Cassie visibly shrank in front of their eyes. Already feeling bad for her after Trip's behavior, Marley couldn't believe these people were attacking her friend. They didn't even know her! She spun around, eyes blazing, ready to take on whoever had spoken but only blank faces stared back at her. She wasn't able to locate the owner of the insults.

Tyler too had overheard the comments and was searching for the culprits herself. When she couldn't place them, she met Marley's eyes with a rage of her own. Josh, meanwhile, acted as if he hadn't heard anything wrong.

"So which of you two ladies wants to be my date for the night?" He stressed the word "two," glancing between Tyler and Marley.

Feeling like she wanted to die, Cassie started backing away from them, knowing that she wasn't included in the invitation, but someone grabbed hold of her waist, stopping her from leaving.

"Hey, where are you going? Someone around here must be drunk enough to get with you."

Cassie shook him off and managed to free herself from the guy — a pimply faced teenager. She didn't know if it was her first night away from home that made her brave, or that it was the last in the long line of insults, but she suddenly knew she didn't have to take this from him.

"Shame the same can't be said for you," she snapped into his face.

Not expecting any retaliation, he turned red with anger and shoved her — hard. Cassie went flying through the crowd and hit the floor. The music stopped as Josh signaled the DJ and there were suddenly a million pairs of eyes staring at her. Her heart racing in her chest, Cassie slowly pushed herself up from the floor, blinded by the blinking lights that dazzled her eyes. Confused, she couldn't understand what all the lights were. As she waited for her eyes to right themselves, she heard the snickering first.

Without the music playing, she couldn't *not* hear them.

Finally, her eyes readjusted only for Cassie to realize that the lights came from the many phones that were pointed her way, as people recorded her humiliation for the world to see.

Horrified, she couldn't stop the sob from bursting out. Once that started, the tears followed. Staggering up to her feet, Cassie ran blindly towards the exit even as the crowd laughed at her misfortune. She pushed through people openly taunting her, the only thing on her mind was to get out of this hell hole as fast as she could. She thought she heard someone calling out her name. Cassie couldn't stop now, she had to get away.

Reaching the door, she flung it open and crashed through into the dark square outside. The neon lights of the bar flashed at her, illuminating its name Tonic, but Cassie didn't care if she never came here again. Crying, she wanted nothing more than to be back in the safety of her dorm, but stupidly she realized she didn't know the way.

She almost laughed at how pathetic she was.

Gulping down her sobs, she saw a light in the church across from her and made a beeline for it. At least it would be warm in there.

And empty.

She hurried across Copley Square…

***

Flipping up her collar to protect her neck from the sudden cold, Eve walked quickly towards home.

Si would be at work by now so she wouldn't have to avoid going home any longer, which was just as well. Those chairs in the library weren't the most comfortable things in the world. She was dying for a burger, maybe some fries. Since it seemed like she was going whole hog, she might as well throw in a shake. She was one of those lucky girls who could eat whatever she wanted and never gain a pound. It was something that Si had always been jealous of — he had to work out constantly to look as good as he did. But Eve, on a good day she could give Beyonce a run for her money.

Her stomach rumbled, signaling that it had been too long since she'd last eaten so she picked up the pace. Reaching a road sign, Eve froze when she read the name.

Copley Square.

Taking in her surroundings, Eve suddenly stopped, recognizing the area from a news show she'd watched earlier over breakfast.

This was where the female student had been killed.

She stared at the ground in front of the black building twisting up against the night sky. Nothing was there now. Eve still felt a shiver of fear run down her spine, thinking of the poor girl who had been murdered and left there. All that remained of the crime scene now was some yellow plastic tape.

What were her last thoughts as her neck was being snapped?

Eve wasn't able to stop the morbid question from entering her mind.

She was jolted out of her thoughts by a desperate shout that came from across the square.

"Cassie! Come back!" someone shouted.

Eve looked ahead to see Marley and… wait, was that her would-be roommate? They were chasing after another girl, who looked distressed. The girl was sobbing as she ran into Trinity Church, the other two following close behind. They were only a few feet from her as they disappeared into the building. As Eve was heading that way herself, she reached the church doors and couldn't stop herself from peeking inside curiously.

What she saw made her stifle a scream.

FOURTEEN

Hoping that there wasn't a service being held, Marley crashed into the church, Tyler hot on her heels. There wasn't, but what was inside, what they saw and did next…

Would change their lives forever.

Cassie stood a few feet ahead of them, a look of utter horror on her face, her own issues immediately forgotten as she watched two guys viciously fighting in front of the altar.

One of the guys, the blond, the taller of the two pummeled the short dark haired guy with punches that had Marley wincing. The smaller guy fought back, but he wasn't as physically strong as his attacker. As if he knew this, the blond picked up the other guy and threw him into the altar.

Candles tumbled down, flying across the floor as the cross which sat on top of the altar rocked unsteadily before crashing to the ground, shattering into several pieces.

Marley caught a glimpse of another figure running in behind them. There was something familiar about the big curls and the heavily made-up face. Through the shock and fear, it sank in that it was Eve from the library, but her attention was drawn back to the fight, as the blond leapt onto his victim. Reaching into his pocket, he pulled out an antique-looking knife.

The edge caught the bright flame of a candle, glinting wickedly in the light. The world slowed to a crawl as all four girls realized what he intended to do with it.

"That must be the killer, the one who murdered the student the other night!" Tyler gasped.

"How do you know?" Cassie asked, fear making her breath come in short bursts.

"We don't have time to discuss this, he's going to kill that guy if we don't do something about it!" Marley said urgently.

Knowing that she was right, the girls swallowed their fear rushing forward to stop him from killing another person.

"NO!" Eve yelled.

"Get off him!" Marley screamed.

Suddenly the air around them changed, humming with a strange electricity.

Marley felt her hair become light and float around her as if it were being suspended in water. She could see it was the same for the other girls: they each wore identical expressions of shock and confusion on their faces.

Unsure of what was happening, Marley forgot about the men for a moment as she felt her body resonate with an answering vibration that she could feel deep within her bones. Suddenly, a halo of light surrounded the girls, growing bigger until it engulfed the room, blinding everyone inside.

Almost like a nuclear bomb, it exploded outwards blowing away a chunk of the roof.

Stunned, everyone stopped.

The only movement came from the bits of rubble from the explosion that fell down. The rain was now pouring in through the hole in the roof.

The blond reacted first, double-taking at the sight of them.

He looked straight at Marley. She felt a wave of shock course through her.

His name was Christian.

Although she had never seen him before, she knew this without a shadow of a doubt. There was something about his green, golden eyes that were familiar, as was his strong jawline and the stubborn bend of his nose. His gaze held her rooted to the spot. She didn't know how long she would have stayed like that until Tyler sprinted past her, her hand outstretched.

Then all hell broke loose.

***

Sprinting forward to stop Christian, Tyler yelled out something incomprehensible, her hand stretched out in front of her. The air seemed to twist in on itself as the rain turned suddenly solid…

Then slashed down in *shards* as sharp as glass.

They dropped down on him, slashing his bare arms to shreds. Blood welled from the cuts, dripping from his arms and mingling with the glass rain on the ground.

Desperate to protect himself from their vicious onslaught, Christian backed away from his victim, dropping the knife which clattered to the ground. Shock radiated from Tyler as she tried to comprehend what she had just done. Whatever it was, however, it was already stopping as the glass shards were turning back into rain.

Realizing this, Christian snatched up his knife and went back to fighting with a vengeance. Grabbing his victim by the throat, he whipped back his hand with the knife, preparing to slash down…

When a dark and ominous mass appeared obscuring Eve for a moment before launching off of her to reveal hundreds of *moths* that swarmed around him, blocking his view.

He fell back, swiping at the moths, trying desperately to clear a path so he could see again. There was a sudden movement beside him as someone appeared up close. Like a mirage, Christian could see his victim standing next to him now, but he was wearing different clothes. Christian blinked, confused, as he saw his victim now wore a dress… Cassie's dress.

With Christian distracted by Cassie — who Marley realized was now wearing the victim's face — she saw her chance at saving the other guy.

Ignoring the questions flooding her stressed mind, she rushed into the cloud of moths. She meant only to push Christian away but in the chaos, she wasn't able to see more than a few inches from her face. When she finally reached him, they stared straight into each other's eyes. He shouted something at her, but Marley couldn't make out what he was saying.

Shoving out her hands blindly, Marley saw Christian's expression abruptly twist in pain. The blood drained from his face and he froze, looking at her. Marley didn't know what was happening but she could feel something pulsing in her hands. Not exactly sure why, she squeezed until the pulsing stopped.

Christian gasped out loud as Eve's moths flew away.

And suddenly Marley saw with crystal clarity that her hands were *inside* of Christian's chest.

She had squeezed his heart until it stopped.

Christian stared deep into her eyes, pain and shock seeping out of him.

Then he fell to the ground.

Dead.

FIFTEEN

Despite his bruised and battered body, and the shame that would come from losing a fight to a Guardian — of all creatures — Michael had to choke down his laugh.

He had been searching his entire life it had seemed for the return of the mythical Four and here they had come crashing into the church to save *him*. Who could have guessed that it would be his very own life that would be the catalyst to bringing them back? He couldn't have planned it better himself. Now, not only did he know who they were, they had also killed the one person sent to help them.

They had just made his life so much easier.

Having seen the circle of light, Michael knew the girls had only just come into their powers. Judging by the confusion and fear he saw on their faces now, they had no idea what had just happened.

That suited him just fine.

Without the Guardian around to help them, the girls were on their own and easy pickings. If they had training, if they were able to learn who they were, what they could do, they would be the biggest threat to their plans. It was their fear of the girls' powers that had sent him into this place to sniff them out, but never in his wildest dreams could he have imagined that it would be this easy.

Melting away into the darkness, he let their faces sear into his mind, memorizing them so he could seek them out later.

Look at them! They were like lambs!

Nothing like the powerful beings they had warned him about. Disappearing from view, he smiled to himself, a new goal in mind now.

To destroy the girls before they learned the full extent of their powers.

SIXTEEN

"Is he… dead?" Marley asked, unable to look at the body by her feet.

For the first time in her life, Marley hoped that what she saw was a figment of her mind, that it was her sickness playing its evil tricks on her again, but looking at Tyler and Eve, then Cassie — who still wore the victim's face on her body — Marley knew it wasn't the case.

Tyler bent down to examine Christian's body. When there was no rise and fall of his chest, she backed away.

"I think so."

Eve shared a stricken look with Marley.

"You just killed him."

Marley stumbled backwards, terror making her stammer.

"But how? I don't know how that happened. It was an accident! You all saw right? First, the rain that turned to glass…"

"Then the moths that came from Eve, and Cassie's face…" Tyler finished quietly. "Yeah, we all saw it."

"What about my face—?" Cassie managed to ask before slapping a hand over her mouth in horror. The voice that had come out of her wasn't her own. It was the low, rumbling voice of a man. Her fingers ran across her face, feeling the unfamiliar features.

"Oh my God, what's wrong with it?" she shrieked, panic making her new man-voice rise by several octaves. Diving into her handbag, she retrieved a compact and held it up to the light. When she saw what she looked like, she turned white.

"No! This isn't possible."

"Nothing that happened here was," Eve said.

"Do you think we're suffering from a mass hallucination or something?" Tyler asked, blinking at Cassie's new face until she turned away.

Marley suddenly gasped, remembering something. "Those drinks at the bar, I didn't pay for them, that guy did." she began. "The jock."

"You think he put something in them?" Tyler asked, eyes round by the possibility.

"But that doesn't explain why I saw the same things you did," Eve said quietly. "I wasn't at the bar."

They fell silent, each trying to find a reason that just wasn't there. Trying to clamp down on her own panic, Marley looked around the place when something caught her attention.

"Wait, where's the other guy? The one he was attacking?"

They looked around the immediate area but there was no sign of him.

"He's gone," Cassie said in her own voice. She checked her reflection in the mirror again, breathing out a sigh of relief when her own face stared back at her. Whatever had happened to her face, it was over.

For now, at least.

Tyler reached for her phone, but Eve stopped her from dialing.

"Who are you calling?" she demanded.

"The police," Tyler replied.

"You can't," Cassie gasped. "How will we explain any of this to them?"

"They'll arrest Marley and we can't let them do that," Eve said, earning Marley's gratitude. She shot her a look of thanks that Eve acknowledged.

"No they won't, how can they? There's no physical proof of what happened is there? I know we all saw what she did with her hands, but look at his shirt — there isn't a mark on him."

"They'll think he had a heart attack," Marley said suddenly, picking up on Tyler's thoughts.

"Exactly. Besides, we can't not report this. We can maybe leave out some of the more unexplainable details though."

Looking spooked, Eve picked up her bags that she had dropped on arriving in the church.

"No. I don't want to speak to them. I'm getting out of here," she said, heading for the door.

"Wait!" Tyler called after her. "You can't go, you're a witness!"

"They already have you three, what more can I add?" Eve answered a little panicked Marley thought. For some reason, the thought of speaking to the police scared Eve almost as much as what had happened there tonight.

"Please Eve. We're all scared, but will you stay with us for this?" Marley asked quietly.

Eve glanced at the exit, contemplating her escape for an eternity it seemed. Marley could almost see the doubts racing through her mind before she eventually came to a solution that didn't make her any happier. She sighed and dumped her bags onto a pew.

"Fine. But don't expect me to be holding anyone's hand through this."

Twenty minutes later the place was flooded by the presence of police.

Having called them, the girls had waited outside the church for the cavalry to arrive so it came as a shock, when, after repeating a trimmed down version of events, they were given the news that Christian's body had disappeared. They stood around the broken altar now, staring down at the spot where they had left him.

"He was right there," Marley said.

"Yeah, right where those pieces of the cross are, that's where he was," Tyler agreed.

Detective Saunders, a redhead with the air of a commanding officer, and her partner, Detective Brooks, a man in his early thirties stared them down, obviously not buying any of their stories.

"Listen," Saunders began, her voice hard and unwelcoming. "I've been working two nights straight because of rush week pranks like these. I'm tired, I'm cranky, and I just want to go home and play with my dog who has been waiting all day for me with only the radio for company, so how about you girls tell me what really happened? How is there a hole the size of Texas in the roof of this church? A historical church by the way, and the one where all the members of my family were baptized."

Marley looked at the others as each of them shrugged, one by one.

"You're seriously not giving me anything?" Saunders exclaimed in frustration.

"We did!" Cassie said suddenly. "We told you what we know but you won't believe us!"

Brooks stared at them over the top of his leather notebook. "It's a little hard to believe your story when there isn't any sign of either of the men you mentioned."

"Other than the mess everywhere," Eve snapped, apparently over the grilling they were receiving. "Or do you honestly think we blew a hole in the ceiling then started smashing up the place?" She grabbed one of Cassie's hands suddenly, showing it to them. "Look at her nails — they're immaculate. Not a single chip in the polish. You really think we could have done this without her even chipping a nail?"

She eyeballed the cops, unwilling to break the stare until they finally broke it themselves. Feeling emboldened by Eve's stance, Marley spoke up.

"Are you arresting us or can we go?"

Saunders gave her a withering stare but nodded reluctantly.

"You can go, but we'll be watching you," she said not bothering to hide the threatening tone.

The girls left quickly before they could change their minds.

SEVENTEEN

Moving away from the chaos surrounding the church, Eve scrolled through the apps on her phone.

"Are you coming back to the dorm with us?" Marley asked her.

"Yeah, you do have a room there you know," Tyler pointed out. Eve flushed, looking slightly ashamed from her earlier treatment of her, but still, she didn't want to be with them. It was all too confusing and frightening. Seeing the police, Eve had broken out into a cold sweat. It was all she could do not to run away from them.

They brought nothing but bad memories for her, ones she would rather leave buried in the ground.

She shook her head, shaking off their invitation.

"No. I just want to go home."

"But it's not safe," Cassie said, worry causing frown lines to appear on her face.

"I'm not walking. I'll grab an Uber," Eve said. "I just need to set up an account with them and I'll be good to go."

Cassie shook her head. "I have one already, use mine."

Quick as a flash, she had her phone out, and the Uber app running. "I just need your details."

Normally super private, Eve hesitated to give out her address before she swallowed a laugh. They had already shared a murder, what harm was knowing her address going to do? She took Cassie's phone and typed it in. Within seconds, by the wonder of technology, her car was on its way.

"You don't have to wait with me," Eve said but Tyler shook her head.

"It's going to be here in less than three minutes. We're fine to wait, aren't we?" she asked the others to their agreement. Not used to this kind of thing, Eve didn't know what to think. Aside from her brother, she'd been alone for so long now that it was strange to have other people care about her safety, particularly when the friends she'd had before weren't anything like this. She shrugged, trying not to make the wait as big a deal as it felt to her.

"Where do you think he went?" Cassie asked quietly, shooting furtive looks around them to make sure they weren't being eavesdropped on.

"Christian?" Marley said without thinking. "I don't know."

"Wait, you know him?" Tyler asked, her eyes wide. "Why didn't you say anything?"

Marley swallowed the lump in her throat, unsure of how she was going to explain herself to them. "I don't know him, but when I saw him, it just felt like I did. And his name, Christian came to me."

"I thought he was looking at you funny!" Cassie said. "You were staring at each other like no one else existed."

Her comment made Marley self-conscious. She shrugged, helplessly, unable to explain any of it.

"Are you psychic?" Tyler asked suddenly.

Marley shook her head. "No. I've never been before."

Feeling a set of eyes on her, Marley turned until she found Cassie staring at her, openly curious.

"But you've seen and heard things before, right?" Cassie asked.

Marley gave her a hard stare, hoping that she didn't know what she was talking about, but her knowing expression spoke volumes. Neither Tyler nor Eve were following the conversation, however, each looking as confused as the other.

"What things?" Eve asked.

"Nothing," Marley said firmly, giving Cassie a look which she hoped the other girl would acknowledge. Luckily, she was saved from anything else as a black Prius pulled up to the curb. The driver wound down the window and spoke with an accent.

"Car for Cassie?"

Eve opened the door to the backseat and tossed her bags inside. Climbing in, she wound her window down.

"Hold on," Marley said to the driver, pulling out a notebook and pen. Scribbling something down, she tore the page out of the book and handed it to Eve through the window. "That's my number. Text me when you're back so we know you got home safe."

Blinking, Eve felt the prick of tears in the backs of her eyes. All that time she had spent with her previous friends, and they had never, ever worried over her safety like this yet here were these girls, who she had only met today, who showed more care for her than almost anyone she had ever had in her life. The thought brought a lump that she had to clear before speaking.

"See you around."

Before they could respond, the driver pulled away. Marley's number gripped in her hand, Eve watched the girls recede in the rearview mirror until they were nothing more than shadows in the night.

EIGHTEEN

Marley couldn't even remember walking back to the dorm.

The last thing she could clearly recall was Eve's Uber taking off. After that, the rest was a blur.

Tyler sat with them, in her room, as they each tried to come to some understanding of the events of the night.

Cassie switched on her giant flat-screen TV, flipping it onto a local news channel where a camera crew had already set up outside the church. Holding their breath, they waited for the newsreader to mention the murder but the news story only discussed the act of vandalism at the church which had caused a piece of its roof to have blown off.

Whether or not it was his name, Christian's body had vanished, and so had his victim.

Feeling a throbbing in her head and knowing that a migraine was on its way, Marley stepped out of the room, leaving Tyler and Cassie to discuss amongst themselves everything that had happened. Feeling suddenly claustrophobic, Marley was desperate for some air and silence.

"I'll be back," she said to the others and headed down the hall before they could stop her.

She passed by the RA's room and saw Rhett through the open door, reading in an armchair. He didn't look up as she walked by and she was glad. She knew she was going against his warnings by stepping outside alone, but she was only going to be on the other side of a door. She wasn't intending to leave the campus.

Holding her phone in her hand, Marley reached the exit and pushed the button on the wall. The automated door swung outwards, and she stepped out into the blessed coolness, letting the breeze wash over her. Trees creaked, reminding Marley of the elms in the common, but the ones here were oaks and they seemed less threatening somehow.

Probably because they weren't used to murder hundreds of innocent women.

The campus was quiet, with only the odd cricket chirping into the night. Something flew overhead. *Hopefully not a bat*, Marley thought, shuddering. She knew they wouldn't harm her, but there was something about their faces that made them the stuff of nightmares.

Stepping under the glow of a streetlight, Marley unlocked her phone and hit number one on the speed-dial. It rang a few times before the call went to voicemail and her dad's comforting voice came over the line.

"I'm not around right now, but leave a message and I'll get back to you."

The beep sounded but Marley found herself unable to speak. What could she say that would make her seem any less crazy than the world already thought she was? Without leaving a message, she hung up the call… and froze.

Someone had walked up behind her.

Marley knew it the second it happened. Even if she hadn't heard the *footsteps* snaking behind her, she could feel the charge in the air, and the hairs on the back of her neck lifting. The streetlamp above her flickered then blinked out *completely*.

And suddenly all of Rhett's warnings smashed into her head.

She was standing out here, in the dark. Alone.

Stupid Marley, stupid!

Her heartbeat spiked as Marley steeled herself, gathering her hands into fists. Whoever was there, she wouldn't go down without a fight, that was for sure. Whirling around, she faced her would-be attacker, ready to give him everything she had until she saw those green eyes with golden flecks, staring at her again.

But this time, they weren't intrigued by the sight of her as they had been when they had last met. Oh no, this time, they were *incensed*.

Marley shook off her confusion and lowered her fists.

How could this be happening?

Christian stood in front of her, but there was something different about him. The air around him shimmered and his skin seemed almost translucent. She could see the blood pounding in his veins and rushing around his body. He glared at her with all the fury of the world.

"Of all the stupid things you could do... killing me was probably the worst."

And with that one sentence, Marley knew, life as she had known it was over.

TWISTED MAGIC

2: BEWARE THE SIGNS

JO HO

NINETEEN

All that was left of the shattered streetlamp now lay on the grass as the moon painted the surrounding area in an eerie silver glow.

Marley kept her eyes fixed on the crumbs of glass hoping that the mundane act would somehow bring her out of her head where she was desperately trying to tune out *his* voice. The voice that she shouldn't be hearing at all.

Marley was having an episode again.

She knew she must have lost it big time because standing in front of her, incensed beyond all reason, looking better than he had any right to, was the guy she had just accidentally killed.

Christian stalked around, waving his arms, yelling at her about how stupid she had been though Marley couldn't hear his words anymore. She couldn't hear them above the loud buzz of panic that reverberated in her mind. It had started the second he had said his first words to her.

It was only her first day of college; she was sup-posed to be partying and learning to live without a parent for the first time... so how had any of this happened?

Although it had only been a few hours since the attack at the church which had led to Christian's untimely demise, every second that had passed since seemed like forever. Was this how murderers felt? Was she a murderer? Marley could feel the hand of a ticking clock, moving towards her capture. At any moment, the police would discover what she had done and arrest her. She'd be thrown into prison, never to see sunlight again.

Although they had been cautioned not to leave the dorm at night on their own, she was standing just outside the building. Feeling stifled and needing time alone, Marley stepped out to make a call. She wanted to speak to her dad, to hear his familiar voice and be comforted by that. Even if she knew she couldn't tell him what had happened.

Suddenly the streetlamp above had exploded, raining glass around her before Christian had appeared looking somehow different then when she had seen him.

She couldn't hear what he was saying her stressed out mind wouldn't take any of it in. Deep down, Marley knew that what she was seeing wasn't real. The doctors and shrinks had been right. She was schizophrenic after all, and Christian — ghost or not — wasn't there.

Why then did he seem so real?

Despite his rage, she could see the golden flecks in his green eyes that made it seem as if they were almost glowing. While she had thought his hair was originally blonde, close up, she could see the roots bore more of a bronze shade. He wore a white shirt with the first few buttons unbuttoned. Just beneath the shirt, Marley caught a glimpse of the top of an intricate tattoo on his chest. Drawn to the sight of it, she had to shrug away her immediate instinct to reach out and touch it. If he was a figment of her sick mind, surely he wouldn't be quite this detailed?

"Are you even listening to me?" Christian demanded, cutting into her thoughts.

"What?" Marley replied somewhat defensively, unable to help herself.

"I asked you why you killed me!"

"It was an accident, I didn't mean to," Marley replied, trying to decide whether she wanted him to believe her innocence more or for him to just disappear. Although her subconscious knew he couldn't really be there, the sight of him standing before her filled her with the kind of stomach-twisting fear that seeing someone who wasn't real always did, though this sick scenario was much worse than any other she had experienced before.

"You stuck your hands into my chest and squeezed my heart until it stopped. I'd say that's a pretty big accident. Some might even call it murder."

"I have no idea how I did that. I've got no idea how any of this is happening!" She wished she didn't sound quite as out of control as she felt.

"Oh, so you just happened to be in that church, right when I was putting a stop to Michael. You and your friends just turned up and used your powers to stop me?" Contempt turned his eyes dark.

"I guess, yes. That's what happened," she finished, knowing she sounded lame even to her ears.

He stared daggers at her, not giving an inch. "How stupid do you think I am? You're obviously working with him, but what I want to know is why? Do you have any idea what kind of person he is?"

It was all too much. Her head felt like it was going to implode. Marley threw up her hands as frustration, fear, and exasperation all mixed into one big emotion. "No, I don't know what kind of person he is BECAUSE I DON'T KNOW WHO THIS MICHAEL IS! Can you get that into your thick skull?" She gulped in a lungful of air, hoping it would help with the sensation of drowning she was feeling. She felt as if she were treading water but try as she might, she was unable to stay afloat. At any moment, the water would wash over her but she would welcome it. Anything to stop what was happening here.

Christian must have sensed she had reached her limit for crazy as he finally fell quiet, staring at her with those intense eyes. Marley squeezed her temples, trying to make sense of everything. "I miss the days when it was just hanging women I hallucinated," she mumbled to herself. Unfortunately, Christian caught it and was apparently unwilling to let the comment slide.

"I'm not a hallucination! I'm as real as you are. At least, I was," he said before letting loose some choice expletives about her idiocy.

"Oh yeah? Let's see what the others have to say about that," Marley snapped back, unable to bear it anymore. Wincing at his continual tirade and terrified at what the others might say yet knowing she couldn't hold if off any longer, she started back inside.

Sliding her keycard into the reader, she stepped through the automated doors. She didn't even look behind her, not particularly interested in how Christian might enter the building knowing that the laws of physics probably didn't apply to figments of a sick imagination. Hurrying back upstairs to her room, she found Tyler and Cassie still in the same positions as when she had left them. They looked up at her appearance, relieved to see her.

"We're no closer to any answers if you were wondering," Tyler began.

"Can you see him?" Marley interrupted, pointing at Christian as he followed her through the doorway. Tyler and Cassie turned to stare in his direction but saw nothing unusual. They looked back at Marley, their eyes dark with confusion.

"See who? There's no one there," said Cassie.

"You can't see Christian?" Marley asked. Even though

she already suspected what the answer would be, she had to make the point clear, for herself if no one else.

"Er, no," said Tyler her eyes wide and round, her puzzlement almost palpable.

"Wonderful. It seems you're the only one who can see and hear me," Christian said glumly.

"That thought doesn't exactly fill me with glee either," Marley snapped back, sick of his attitude already. Tyler and Cassie watched her, growing increasingly more concerned by her bizarre behavior.

"Let me get this straight, you can see him?" Tyler asked.

"Yes. Standing right in front of the desk. He practically jumped me when I was outside and hasn't shut up since," Marley replied.

"Jumped you? Please, you're not my type," Christian said. "I like my girls strong and silent."

"Deaf and dumb, more like. That's what they'd have to be to put up with you." She might have killed him, but Marley wasn't going to let him get away with talking down to her all the time.

"Well, this is weird," Tyler said. "It's like I'm watching a show where I can only hear the punch line." She looked over at Cassie to see if she agreed with her assessment of the situation but was surprised when Cassie didn't reply. The other girl gripped her hands together, fidgeting uncomfortably as if she were fighting an inner battle with herself. Her brow furrowed into a frown as she struggled for the right words. When she finally spoke, it was to Marley.

"Are you sure he's there?" Cassie said carefully. "I mean, could he just be in your head?"

Something about the cautious manner she used had Marley on edge. She had heard this tone before, many times. Whenever she saw or heard something nobody else could see, they would adopt this careful and slow manner of speech when they questioned her, as if they were speaking to a child. It drove Marley mad to hear it and reminded her of all those times she would be made to feel stupid — or worse… *insane*. That she heard it in Cassie's tone now meant only one thing.

She knew.

It didn't seem that Cassie was very good at hiding her thoughts as she snuck a look at the pillow on Marley's bed, where one of the vials of her meds was hidden.

"You've been snooping through my things!" Marley gasped. Though they hadn't known each other very long, what they had already been through in that short space of time had brought them together — or so Marley had thought — so the betrayal cut deeply.

Cassie paled, unnerved by the accusation, but she didn't dispute it.

"I only did it because I saw you hiding things from us and it made me concerned! You should have told us about your condition, Marley, especially me. I'm your roommate, I'm the one who has to live with you!"

Having no idea what either of them were talking about, Tyler tried her best to calm things down. She reached out her hands, gesturing for peace.

"I'm sure whatever it is, it's not as bad as it seems. What condition do you have?" she asked Marley.

Faced with the question, Marley opened her mouth to respond when her throat went dry. She couldn't speak even if she wanted to. If she didn't say the actual words, it made the whole thing seem less terrible somehow.

"She's schizophrenic," Cassie finally finished for her, torn by needing to tell the truth while also desperate to remain her friend. Her voice dropped lower, anxious now about exactly how much she should reveal. "She's on Thorazine for it." Finished with her reveal, Cassie chewed on the end of a finger.

Whatever she might have expected to hear that wasn't it. Tyler gaped at them, staring at Marley as if she should be able to see her disease. Marley stood in the center of the room, feeling awful and small. This was like all those times in the past. Just when she thought she'd made a few friends, as she began hoping that things would work out, her dark secret would be exposed and she would become the school pariah. Tears rushed to her eyes that she tried to blink back. Christian, who she had all but forgotten about, had been listening throughout their conversation but now spoke up.

"Perhaps not Marley. What you see and hear could be part of your gift. Your power."

Marley snapped her head at him, a flare of hope rising in her chest.

"My power? I have powers?"

"Well, you're the only one who can see and hear me aren't you?" Christian said. "Look, I might be able to explain some of what's happening here but I'm not going to do it twice. Where's the other one?"

"The other who?" Marley asked.

"The other girl, the Black one with all the makeup?"

"I'll think you'll find it's African American and her name is Eve," Marley retorted, bristling.

Unable to make sense of what was happening in front of her, Tyler couldn't stop the question from leaving her mouth.

"Wait, what about Eve?"

"Christian says he can explain some of what's happening but he won't do it until we're all together. And that includes Eve."

"Even if what you are saying is real," Tyler began hesitantly, "it's not like we have a way of contacting her."

"No, but we have her address," Cassie suddenly supplied. Taking out her phone she opened the Uber app and tapped on the last job. A map appeared with an icon above Eve's location.

"So you believe me now?" Marley asked with more bite than she actually intended. Though she understood why Cassie had exposed her, she didn't have to like it.

"I don't know, but I do know I need to find out what happened, and if this is the only way we'll get any answers..." Cassie answered honestly.

"Well, I hope Eve likes uninvited guests," Tyler said.

Marley shot an irritated look at Christian. "If I have to deal with them, so can she."

TWENTY

Deathly silence hung like a cloud.

Though they wanted nothing more than to plague Marley with questions, the girls mutually decided it would have to wait until they were at Eve's house and didn't have a witness who could overhear them. As it was, their Uber driver kept shooting curious glances at them, wondering why it was so quiet in the car, obviously not used to this odd behavior from three girls. Christian was gone, apparently meeting them at the location somehow. No one knew how that would work, least of all Marley. In the end, they had decided how he — if indeed he were real at all — would get there was the least of their concerns.

They arrived in the area known as the South End. Marley took in the colorful grocery store displays catering to its Irish, Jewish, African American, Asian and Greek customers.

A Chinese store whizzed by as Marley found herself staring at the promotional posters on the windows with their alien writing. Though she was half Chinese, Marley didn't feel connected with that side of herself at all; when her mother had left, she had taken that part of the culture with her too.

As a reaction to her mom leaving, Marley found herself fiercely against anything Chinese, to the point where she couldn't even eat the food, deriving no joy from it whatsoever. When a martial arts movie came on the television, she would change the channel. When everyone else celebrated Chinese New Year, Marley always stayed at home so she wouldn't have to fake enthusiasm for the festival or answer any personal questions. Most of all, however, she stayed home so she wouldn't have to deal with the idiots who would come up to her on the street asking "ni hao?" — Mandarin for "how are you?" which she'd only learned after typing it into an online translator.

She turned away from the store, noting that the car was slowing down, pulling up to a rundown house.

Peeling paint and windows with weathered frames cried out for attention. The two-story Victorian house had clearly seen better days and was now lacking in love. A light was on in one of the front rooms upstairs, though the rest of the house was shrouded in darkness.

Piling out of the car, Marley lead the way up the overgrown front path to an old wood door set with two distorted glass panels to give privacy. A rusty bell sat in a half-rotten frame. She pushed it with a finger and waited. Nothing happened. She stabbed it again, harder, but still, there wasn't any sound from inside.

Guess the bell isn't just old, but broken.

Seeing an iron knocker above her, Marley grabbed it and knocked three times, cringing at loud it seemed in the otherwise silent night.

Moments later a light came on in the hallway as footsteps approached the door. A shadow fell over the doorway, hesitating on the other side of the glass.

"Eve, it's Marley. Tyler and Cassie are here too. Open up!"

The muffled sound of a curse came from the other side

of the door followed by what could only be Eve reaching for an excuse to slink away. When she couldn't come up with a believable one, the door finally opened until the security chain that was latched onto it stretched taut. Eve's face appeared in the crack though it was now devoid of makeup. Without it, Marley was struck by how pretty she was. She was also hit by the thought that she looked vulnerable too somehow.

"What the hell are you all doing here?" Eve demanded, that vulnerability Marley had thought she had seen vanishing immediately.

"We need to talk."

That might well have been the understatement of the year. Reading their tense expressions, Eve saw immediately that something else had gone down.

"I barely left you half an hour ago, what else could have happened?"

"Plenty," Marley said. "Let us in."

Eve hesitated, reaching desperately for an excuse but her thoughts were one big cloud of fog. Reluctantly, she unchained the door, allowing them inside.

They followed as she led them into the living room where they sat on a frayed but comfortable couch covered in a faded sunflower print. Above the open fireplace were framed photographs of Eve and her family. Marley saw what must have been her older brother and parents. They stood in front of this house and a catering truck painted with the Jamaican flag.

There were pictures of Eve and her brother at various ages when they were little, playing in a park, helping their parents in the truck. At the end of the row, a new photograph stood, leaning up against the wall. This didn't have a frame of its own yet. It showed Eve's parents relaxing on a tropical beach beneath a grove of coconut trees.

"I know you didn't come all this way to stare at my family pictures, so what's the deal?" Eve said, clearly uncomfortable at having all of them there. She kept fid-geting with her curly hair and tugging at her clothes — which consisted of a tattered sweater and some lounge pants that had been worn so much that the bottoms had frayed. Despite the low key outfit, Cassie found herself staring at Eve, startled to see that beneath all those layers of makeup, she was beautiful with skin that practically glowed.

Only Cassie had the misfortune to look the way she did.

"Christian is here, and he said he can explain some of what happened tonight," Marley began, cutting into Cassie's appraisal.

"What are you talking about?" Eve asked. Just because they had experienced that madness earlier, it didn't make them BFF's. She found her earlier soft-heartedness rapidly disappearing along with her patience.

"It seems Marley is able to see his ghost," Tyler ex-plained. "He's here right now, but she's the only one who can see or hear him."

Eve blinked, staring at them in astonishment.

"You came all the way here to play some stupid prank on me?"

"It's not a prank," Marley said, annoyed she would even think that. "I can see him."

"Yeah?" Eve replied, a challenge to her voice. Folding her arms over her chest, she lifted her chin defiantly. "Prove it."

Marley looked to Christian for help. "I don't know how."

"Maybe I do," he replied as an idea came to him. He gestured. "Give me a minute." Then vanished without fanfare, leaving Marley with all eyes focused on her.

"He's gone," she explained as a deep flush colored her cheeks. She knew how insane this all sounded. It took every inch of self-resolve not to mumble. "He'll be right back."

"Uh huh," Eve replied, clearly not buying a word of it. She tapped a flip-flopped foot on the scratched wooden floorboards, the black polish on her toes catching the light. They waited without speaking, the only sound the chiming of an ancient clock that lived in the hallway outside. Tension so thick, it covered the air like a heavy blanket. Cassie found her mind wandering, wondering when would be a good moment to ask Eve about her skincare routine. After what seemed like hours — but was only minutes — Christian reappeared.

"Finally!" Marley exclaimed.

"So what's he got?" Eve asked, fully expecting nothing to come out of this futile exercise except to prove that Marley was full of it.

Christian smiled at Marley smugly.

"Ask her who xXIDaBestPlaya420Xx is and why he thinks she'd want to meet him in Dalaran."

"Dial-a-what?" Marley asked, not sure if she'd heard him correctly.

"Da-la-ran," he repeated. "Just say it."

Not understanding any of what she was about to say next, Marley turned to Eve. "He said, who's xXIDaBestPlaya420Xx and why does he think you'd want to meet him in Da-la-ran?"

Eve gasped, the smug look wiped from her face immediately. "How do you know that? There's no way you could know that!"

"Can someone please explain what's happening right now?" Tyler asked a little plaintively as Cassie nodded behind her.

"I went up to her room and saw she was talking to someone in a video game. That's what they were saying in the chat box," Christian explained. Marley repeated what he said to stunned silence.

"Is that true?" Cassie asked, finally breaking the silence.

"Yes," Eve replied. "And there's no way she could

have known that unless she's seen my computer upstairs."

"Tell her, I'm also surprised by some of her decor, Goth's aren't traditionally into Hello Kitty," Christian finished. Marley repeated his words again, much to Eve's embarrassment.

"That stuff is old… I haven't gotten around to throwing it out," she explained quickly as Tyler looked on in amusement. With the truth staring them right the face, Cassie squirmed with embarrassment as her mistake started to sink in. Realizing there was something she needed to say, she turned to Marley.

"I think apologies might be in order… I'm sorry for doubting you," she apologized.

Marley's eyes fixed on Cassie as she studied the other girl silently. She knew it couldn't have been easy for her to admit she had been wrong — no one ever liked to think that they were. She shot her a nod, graciously accepting the apology.

Christian clapped his hands together impatiently, startling her and making her jump.

"Now that they actually believe I exist, do you think I can start talking now? Staying on your dimension is costing me a ton of willpower that I'm not sure I have."

"You need willpower to be here?" Marley asked.

"Apparently so. I feel like I'm being constantly pulled elsewhere. It's exhausting."

"Talk quickly," Marley demanded.

And so he did.

TWENTY-ONE

"I'm a Guardian. We are a secret society that was created centuries ago to assist in the protection of the world from supernatural evil," Christian answered. "I have trained my whole life for this one sole purpose."

"So it's a pretty big bummer that Marley killed you then, huh?" Eve quipped, but no one laughed, unable to find the humor in the situation. Reminded of her own unfortunate actions that resulted in his death, Marley wished she could sink into the ground.

"That's one way of putting it," Christian replied, shooting her a hard look that made Marley feel even crappier.

"So supernatural things, they really do exist?" Cassie couldn't help asking, feeling a chill run down her spine. Did that mean all those monsters they had read about in books and watched in movies… were they all real too?

"Yes," Christian replied simply. "And since you all have a gift, I'd argue that you belong in that category too."

The girls went silent as his words fell over the room. Cassie looked down at her hands, to see if she could see the magic coursing through her, but all she found was a chip in the pale pink polish of her little finger.

"What magical powers do you have?" Cassie asked the air where she thought Christian was standing, though he had actually moved over to the window. Marley didn't think it necessary to correct her, however, as where he stood in the room seemed of no consequence.

"I don't have any, not exactly. But I can't be killed by supernatural evil. I'm protected from that," Christian revealed.

There was a pause in the conversation as the others found themselves looking surreptitiously at Marley. With a sinking heart, she finished the one thought he didn't express.

"But not from me."

"The magic is meant to ward off evil, and apparently *only* evil," Christian said.

Marley could see that he was far from accepting his fate. He paced the room, running his fingers through his short hair in agitation. She closed her eyes, not wanting to see him for the moment. The sight of him constantly sent her mind reeling, her emotions see-sawing from horror to shame. He had been protected from evil, but whatever that magic was, it hadn't been able to stop *her* from killing him.

"Well, at least that proves we're the good guys," she said, fighting to find remain optimistic when all she really wanted was to be back home with her dad in San Fran. Life there seemed like a dream compared to her troubles here, and it was only her first day. *Why had she insisted on coming here? Why did she think school would be the best experience of her life?*

If she expected an answer from Christian, she found none. He kept his eyes fixed on the ground, studiously avoiding her gaze. She didn't need to be a detective to know there was something he wasn't telling them.

She knew it immediately but couldn't summon up the

courage to confront him. With so much confusion in the air, whatever this other thing was, it could wait for another time.

"The guy you were fighting, who was he?" Eve asked.

"His name is Michael," Christian replied. Feeling relieved at the relatively simple task, Marley went back to translating. At least while she was doing that, she wouldn't have her own disturbing thoughts to consider.

"Whenever something suspicious happens, we — my mentor Eric — and I investigate to see if there are any supernatural influences at play."

"And if there are?" Tyler asked.

"If there are, we put an end to them." He stopped, letting his meaning sink in. A dry lump formed in Marley's throat that she tried to swallow.

"We first learned of Michael a few weeks ago, when the first young murder victim was found in Boston with their neck snapped. You must have heard about it in the news. There were several magic sigils on the dead body that ordinary people can't see, but we could."

"You saw them *through* the television?" Cassie asked in amazement.

Christian gave her a level look before answering. "No. We saw the sigils when we broke into the morgue and examined the bodies."

Cassie blinked, trying not to recoil in horror as Christian continued. "We knew immediately that the murderer was killing the victims and using their deaths for something, but the trail went cold until a few days ago, when Becky Stevens, the Tennerson student, was killed in Copley Square. We tracked Michael down, but when he realized who we were, he paid some human low lives to attack us." Christian's voice broke. He stopped, his eyes turning bright with tears.

"Eric was killed, but I got away."

The girls gasped, horrified, taking in his pain even though they couldn't see or hear him. Marley found herself wishing she could touch him to offer some small semblance of comfort. He looked so lost at losing someone obviously close to him that she felt her complicated feelings melting away, leaving only compassion.

"I followed some leads of my own until I found Michael again at Trinity…" He trailed off, not knowing how else to continue.

"And that's where we came in," Tyler finished for him. "But what are we exactly? And why do we have these powers? What are they?"

Christian hesitated. Marley could almost see his mind working over the question. His eyes slid to the floor as he mumbled a response. "Well, that I don't know yet."

The hopeful feeling that had been in her chest now plummeted. A lead weight settled in her stomach. "Wait, you don't know what we are or why this all happened?"

"No. It can't be a coincidence, you all turning up to the church at the same time. Or even that three of you live across the hall from each other. I just don't know what the wider story could be."

"Four," Eve said quietly suddenly. "It was meant to be four of us living across the hall from each other."

Marley and Cassie looked confused until Tyler chimed in. "That's right! Eve was supposed to be my roommate."

"Eve is the girl who took one look at you and left?" Marley asked without thinking, drawing an embarrassed cough from Eve.

"Yeah," Eve replied simply, though her jutting chin challenged anyone who dared to call her out on it. No one did. The three other girls each found her pretty intimidating. Marley let the news sink in as as she considered Christian's lack of helpful knowledge and had to resist the urge to scream. She was back to nothing making sense again.

"When you said you had things to tell us, I thought, that you know, you had things to tell us. Instead, it pretty much sounds like you don't know what you're talking about," Eve said to Christian.

"I do know what I'm talking about, I just don't know why the four of you came into your powers like that tonight," Christian snapped back, annoyed. "You are obviously powerful, or have the potential to be…"

He turned to stare directly at Marley. "And since you have powers, one thing I do know. You need to find out what Michael is up to and stop him," Christian finished firmly.

TWENTY-TWO

"Say what now?" Tyler asked. "You want us to go after and stop this Michael guy?"

"And by "stop" he means kill," Cassie supplied helpfully.

The whole thing hit Eve like a truck just then, the ludicrousness of the situation. A laugh burst out of her and once it left, she couldn't stop, not even when tears streamed down her face. She held her sides, gasping for a breath that wouldn't come. The others watched on in bemusement, unsure of what to do when the front door slammed shut. When the figure stepped in, the room fell into a sudden silence.

"What's so funny?" the guy asked. *This must be Eve's brother*, Marley thought, recognizing him from the photographs on the mantelpiece. He had similar features to his sister, though where Eve's face was heart-shaped his was more angular with a strong jawline that hinted at a stubborn streak. Seeing Tyler, he gave her a small smile, shrugging out of his leather jacket and slinging it over the back of an armchair.

"Are you having a sleepover?" he asked Eve, looking confused.

Eve fidgeted, suddenly extremely nervous.

"No, because we're not five," she finally managed.

Si shot a quick look at the watch on his wrist, frowning at the time. "It's not like I'm not happy you've made friends on your first day, but isn't it kind of late?" he asked, channeling their absent parents perfectly.

"Yes, they were just leaving," Eve said quickly, already trying to get the girls out of the house.

"No! We have more things to discuss," Christian began, but Marley didn't bother to translate for him as Eve grabbed her arm, steering her towards the front door.

"You need to go," she hissed under her breath at them. "I don't want him involved in any of this."

"But we literally know nothing," Marley said quickly.

"I'll meet you tomorrow, at one. In the food court. We'll talk then," Eve replied, flinging the front door wide open. She shoved the girls out, slamming the door behind them. Christian who was still inside the house, stepped *through* the door then shivered violently.

"That's possibly the strangest experience I've ever had in my life, and I've had a few of those lately," he said to no one in particular. Seeing the girls trooping down the steps, he ran in front of Marley.

"You can't seriously be going back to the dorm?" he exclaimed. "We need to find out what Michael is up to…"

Having reached her threshold, unable to take any more, Marley held up a hand to silence him.

"Christian, stop! It's been a really stressful day, and that was even before all the weirdness began. Can you just give it a rest for now? You heard what she said, she'll meet us tomorrow. We can talk about it then," she pleaded, looking suddenly wary and tired.

Christian paused. There was so much he needed to find out from them. The clock was ticking and it wouldn't wait for anyone, no matter how tired they were. He opened his mouth to speak, to plead for them to see sense…

And then he vanished.

***

It was almost midnight by the time Marley came out of the bathroom, ready for bed.

She knew Christian had more to say to her when he had suddenly vanished. Like the video games she used to play, he must have run out of whatever energy he needed to stay on their plane with them. What had he called it? Their dimension.

She knew she should have been worried about him disappearing like that, but truth was, she was actually super relieved. At least now she could just sleep and forget everything that had happened. Sleep could always be relied upon to provide relief.

The drive back had been even quieter than the ride to Eve's if that was possible. It was also filled with a deep sense of unease that hadn't been there on the first journey. Though they knew a little more about their predicament, it felt as if they were in a more precarious position. They still had no idea what they were and why they had any kind of power at all.

To think all she had to worry about before was how to keep her mental illness at bay. That seemed like a snap in comparison to how complicated her life had become now.

Wearing her usual sleepwear of an old t-shirt and shorts, Marley caught Cassie studying her. She sat on the edge of her bed, not even trying to hide what she was doing. It felt as if she was taking in every little detail of her appearance and filing it away into her head. It made her extremely uncomfortable, and she wished she'd quit it.

"What a day," Marley said, climbing into bed hoping a talk would stop the scrutiny.

"Yeah," Cassie replied. "Couldn't have imagined any of this when I signed up for classes."

"Especially when we haven't even started school yet. I thought that was going to be the big killer."

Cassie laid down, took off her glasses then reached for a silver case sitting next to her. Snapping it open, she took two small objects out that Marley couldn't make out from her side of the room.

"What are those?" Marley asked.

"Earplugs," Cassie answered. "I'm a light sleeper so I can't do without them." Settling herself, Cassie looked over at Marley then hesitated. It seemed as if she had more to say until a buzz sounded on her phone. Picking it up, Cassie saw that she had a notification on her Instagram account, the one her mom had set up.

Great. Just what she needed.

Cassie looked at the new comment. Someone she didn't know had posted a YouTube link to her page. Steeling herself, Cassie clicked on the link, expecting this to be another of her mom's fans, filming the model while she was out and about. For some strange reason, people loved to tag Cassie on videos of her, as if she found her mom's day-to-day activities as exciting as they did.

The YouTube link loaded up. Cassie watched the blurry video which seemed to have been shot somewhere pretty dark. Loud music played, the sound distorted by the phone's proximity to a speaker. On the screen, a hazy figure appeared huddled on the ground. Abruptly, the picture became clear. Cassie felt nausea rise in her mouth as she realized the person she was staring at on the ground... was herself.

The video was shot at Tonic and captured her whole humiliating ordeal. Whoever had filmed her had loaded the video onto YouTube, where this terrible person had recognized her before deciding she needed to be humiliated some more.

Stabbing the stop button with a finger, she slammed her phone onto the side table facedown.

"Goodnight," she said curtly to Marley, pushing the plugs into her ears, turning away from her, from the rest of the world. Tears filled her eyes as she swallowed a sob. Why couldn't they just leave her alone? What had she ever done to anyone that they needed to be so cruel to her?

Oblivious to what Cassie was going through and relieved that she wouldn't have to make small chat or deal with her weird scrutiny anymore, Marley laid down, feeling a wave of exhaustion so great that it made her whole body ache. Closing her eyes, she willed her brain to switch off. Some rest, that was what she needed. It would all seem better with rest.

However, sleep would not come.

Worrying thoughts and faces assaulted her mind, one face in particular.

A face with green eyes and blond hair, whose very gaze made her squirm with guilt.

Sighing, Marley's eyes flicked open. Staring through a crack in the curtain at the moon outside, she hoped tomorrow would bring better news.

It sure couldn't be worse than today.

TWENTY-THREE

ESSEX COUNTY, MASSACHUSETTS, 1693.
The urgent message had come in the middle of the night.

The Four were known healers who traveled the country helping those in need. They took no payment for their services, only asking for food and shelter at the homes of the people they helped. This night they made their beds in a stable that belonged to a local farmstead.

A cat had sat watching them curiously from his position on a hay bale bathing his paw as they turned in for the night, when the distressed father had sought them out. His elderly horse had been on its last legs, its frail body trembling from the hard ride here. Ever loyal, she had managed to bring her owner to his destination before collapsing to the ground in a quivering heap.

With her strong connection to nature, Esther had knelt by the horse, taking his head into her lap. She used her power to ease as much of his pain as she could, but there was just too much damage done. Even with her talents, she could not save him. The horse wheezed out his last breath then passed, the life disappearing from his eyes. The Four said a quick prayer, easing its spirit into the next life then prepared to escort the father — who, like their host, was a simple farmer — back home.

Mary clutched her cloak together, shivering at not only the bitter cold that seemed to have befallen the town, but the Blood Moon, hanging low in the sky. As they crossed the fields to his home, they knew it was a portent of terrible things to come, but what?

The father sagged in his saddle, now riding one of the farmer's horses they had borrowed and would have fallen if not for Tabitha who reached out to steady him. It was his daughter that had caused him to ride across the towns in search of them. She was in a terrible way he had explained. Their village healer wasn't adept enough to cure whatever ailed her, and he needed someone with their skills to save his beloved daughter.

The Four rode quickly through the night, their horses kicking up dust behind them. They rode silently through cornfields, over hills and dirt paths using only that Blood Moon for light, each of them praying that they would get there in time. As dawn broke over the horizon casting its pink glow over the father's simple home, they finally arrived.

He had a large family, some nine or so children, all gathered around the still figure of their sister, their small faces haunted by her condition. Their sucked faces and general unkemptness spoke of the struggles this family had endured. Mary could see too, even if she couldn't already sense, that with his gaunt expression and frail bones, the father suffered from a sickness of his own. She pursed her lips, knowing how the family must be struggling with their sole provider out of work. It strengthened her resolve to help his daughter.

She tossed a glance at her sisters. From the expressions on their faces, she knew they felt as she did. It was for these very families that they had dedicated their lives to helping others. They would do that until their dying breath.

His wife, a slight woman cradling a baby with one arm while a toddler with impossibly large eyes clung to her skirts, approached them desperately.

"Please help our daughter, she's the apple of our eyes. We can't lose her."

Tabitha, the most empathetic of The Four gave her a comforting smile. "We will do our best. Can you please take your children to the next room?"

The wife shot her husband a quick look as they nodded, urging the children away. Alone, without the family observing their every move, The Four could speak and work in confidence. They knew from experience that their methods of healing could frighten at times and thus had decided a while ago that they would only work in solitude.

Catherine moved towards the girl who lay covered and resting on the bed of hay. The family were so poor that they couldn't even afford beds for their children. Feeling her sympathy surge, she reached out and pulled back the blanket that covered their daughter…

The Four gasped, horrified by the sight before them.

There was nothing they could do to help their daughter. There was nothing anyone could do for her… for she was already dead.

Her glassy eyes stared up at a terror they would never know, her lips already turning blue. Her fingers were bent into claws, the nails torn and ripped. Mary trembled, swallowing her pity. The poor girl had put up a struggle before her death.

"Her neck was broken," came Tabitha's angry voice, echoing what they could all see.

"Look," Catherine said, pointing at the area above the poor girl's body.

There was a cloud of black that shimmered above the girl's hands. It pulsated, growing from small to big then back again and was a sign that none of them ever wanted to see.

"Black magic," Mary gasped, the words stuck to her throat.

She looked at her sisters, stricken by the knowledge.

"It was black magic that killed her."

TWENTY-FOUR

Cassie's phone woke her at exactly six AM.

Knowing that she wouldn't hear it otherwise, she relied on the vibration feature on her phone as her morning alarm. Yawning, she blinked up at the unfamiliar ceiling, momentarily confused by the sight of it. Even without her glasses, she could tell it wasn't the ceiling she had spent almost two decades looking at. The one she grew up with had glow-in-the-dark stars that her dad had stuck on when she'd gone through a period of night terrors as a kid. They had left the stars there, even when she'd grown older and didn't suffer from the nightmares anymore. Her distressed face flashed into her mind suddenly as last night's YouTube discovery reared its ugly head. *Great*. She'd managed only thirty seconds before feeling humiliated all over again.

Maybe she should have asked her dad to put the stars on this ceiling too.

Pulling the plugs from her ears, she heard Marley's soft breathing from the other side of the room. Slipping on her glasses, Cassie peered at her sleeping form.

How does she look so pretty even when she's sleeping? How was that fair?

The sun peeked in through a small gap in the curtains that seemed to illuminate her perfectly, highlighting all those features Cassie would kill for.

Well, maybe not kill, Cassie thought to herself as last night's events came crashing back to her.

Cassie wanted to know more about their powers. Between Eve's denial and Marley's guilt, it hadn't seemed like there had been a right moment to ask. Questions were burning a path inside, however. She couldn't wait until they found out more.

After feeling so awful her entire life, it was such a relief to finally know that she *was* special, that she could do things normal people couldn't. A smile broke out across her face as she sat up, flinging the covers off herself. Maybe they just needed a bit more time to accept things. Despite the horrors they had faced last night, she liked that she would be indelibly connected to these girls. For someone who was regularly bullied and a loner, it was nice to be part of something, even if that something was potentially dangerous.

Slipping out of bed quietly so she wouldn't wake Marley, Cassie padded barefoot to the bathroom. Shutting the door, she turned on the shower, waiting for the water to become hot. Moving to the mirror, she looked at her face and was disappointed by what she saw there. Despite constant tweezing, she could never seem to get her brows under control. Her eyes managed to be too small and too wide apart for her face — which was always greasy, making her break out in zits all the time. Her lips were thin, her teeth had a gap right in the front. Put together, it made for one giant mess which, though she'd had eighteen years of seeing it, she was still disappointed with when she saw her face each morning.

Even when she was little, it was obvious she hadn't inherited her parents' good looks. The kids at school delighted in telling her she must have been adopted. They said it so much that they even convinced Cassie of this.

On her eighth birthday, after a week of continuous torture from her cruel classmates, Cassie had run away to look for her "real" parents. With only the clothes on her back, she went as far as she could which ended up being only a few blocks away, as this being the first time she had gone out on her own, she had gotten lost. As the sun had set across the city, her parents had found her hours later, sobbing in the park by the swings. When she explained why she had run away, they had been truly horrified. Cassie was their real daughter! They loved her and told her she was beautiful.

Cassie knew they were lying.

Luckily, there were things she could do to help herself to prepare for her first official day of school. She had a lot of work to do and it would start in the shower. Stripping out of her clothes, she climbed under the hot spray then washed, exfoliated, and buffed her entire body using a sea salt that she shipped in from the Dead Sea. It was her mom's favorite, something she used every day. When that was done, she creamed every inch of herself; Mom had always insisted that hydrated skin was happy skin.

Next came the hair, which had a habit of turning frizzy if she didn't follow an exact routine. She washed then conditioned it, combing it out while it was still wet. After the tangles were gone, she worked a smoothing serum through the ends and let the hair dry naturally, which would take another few hours. It was uncomfortable to have wet hair hanging on her back for so long, but it was the only way she could stop the mad explosion that would occur if she used a dryer. After her body and hair were done, it was finally time for the face. When Cassie was fully made-up, it was already eight-thirty.

She stood in front of the bathroom mirror, turning to inspect herself. The outfit she had finally decided on was a pretty jumpsuit she had acquired from her mom, though it'd had to be taken in to fit her, as Cassie didn't have the legs or boobs her mom did. She felt good in it even if she didn't look how she had pictured she would in her head. Worried that Marley wouldn't have long to get ready, Cassie stopped by her bed, agonizing over whether she should wake her or not. Finally deciding to, Cassie shook her shoulder until Marley blinked up sleepily at her.

"What's going on?" Marley asked groggily.

"It's eight thirty already," Cassie said.

Marley blinked again at her, not comprehending then suddenly bolted upright.

"It's what?!" Marley gasped.

"Eight-thirty," Cassie replied.

Seeing Cassie's full get up, Marley knew immediately that she had been up for hours.

"Why didn't you wake me earlier?!" she demanded.

Cassie shrugged. "I didn't know if you wanted me to. We could have different schedules, besides, I figured you'd set an alarm…"

"After everything that happened last night, I obviously forgot. Jesus, Cass, I can't believe you didn't wake me when you've been up all this time."

Marley jumped out of bed, hurriedly pulling on a pair of jeans. She took off her t-shirt, tugged on a tank top then shrugged into a shirt. Grabbing a brush, she started running it through her long hair as she ran into the bathroom.

Cassie stared after her for a few moments, her mind racing before going back to her own wardrobe. Pulling out some clothes, she changed into another outfit, dumping the discarded jumpsuit onto her bed. Hearing the taps turn on in the bathroom, she hesitated, wondering if she should say goodbye to Marley. Remembering her irritation, Cassie grabbed her textbooks and left the room in silence.

Cupping a handful of water, Marley was splashing her face when she heard the dorm door close and knew Cassie had left.

Good. She was furious!

It was obvious Cassie had spent ages making herself ready for class; she couldn't believe how selfish she had been, not waking her. As if yesterday hadn't been bad enough, she had barely slept at all last night, plagued as she was with nightmares of Christian's face, which wouldn't quit haunting her. Now, thanks to Cassie, it looked like she might be late for her first day of class.

Things really weren't going as planned here.

Feeling uncomfortable in her skin, she shot a longing look at the shower, still glistening from Cassie's earlier use of it. She either had time for a wash, or some food. It was one or the other, it couldn't be both. As if to help her decide, her stomach issued a loud rumble.

She would have to cope with being unclean for a little longer.

Brushing her teeth, she slapped moisturizer on her face then hurried into the bedroom. As she had expected, Cassie had already left. There was one change to the room, however, since her exit. A jumpsuit now lay hastily dumped across Cassie's bed. Recognizing it, she had only a moment to wonder why Cassie had changed as she ran to the food court where she gulped down a bowl of cereal in record time before racing to her Intro to Journalism class, managing to get lost in the maze of corridors and buildings on the way. It was a full ten minutes later when she finally made it to class, out of breath, sweating uncomfortably from the effort.

As luck would have it, the only free seats were in the front row.

Feeling all eyes on her, Marley hurried down the room until she reached the front row. Sliding into a free space, she hoped that it would be the last embarrassment of the day.

"Late on your first day. Do you take anything seriously?" came Christian's voice.

She cringed inwardly. Of course she couldn't have a normal first day at school. Why break the habit of a lifetime? Determined not to give him any attention, she focused on her professor, a young woman in her thirties, as she talked through the course schedule in a pleasant voice. She found his outrage pretty astounding considering he had done a disappearing act on them the night before. As if they weren't trying the best they could under the circumstances.

Anger simmered under her skin. He could try to be a little more understanding since these were extenuating circumstances. Keeping her eyes fixed on the front of the room, she concentrated on her professor's clothes, on the crisp cream shirt she wore tucked into a knee-length skirt. Maybe if she could focus on her, there would be a way to drown Christian out.

"It's pointless you wasting your time in here. With Michael running loose doing God knows what, you probably should have saved your tuition fee."

Marley shot him an irritated look out of the corner of her eye but kept her head fixed on the front of the room. *Just keep looking at the professor. At some point, he'll get bored when he doesn't get anything out of you...*

"What's that Christian?" he said, putting on a ridiculously shrill voice that wasn't remotely close to how she sounded. "Did you say a big evil was out there killing innocent people, people who spent their entire lives fighting to protect the vulnerable and will probably kill more? Why, yes, Marley, if you don't GET OUT OF THIS CLASS AND DEAL WITH IT!" he suddenly yelled into her ear.

The anger that had been bubbling away now spilled

over as Marley span around in her seat, slamming her fist on her desk.

"Why don't you just get lost?!" she hissed, much louder than she had intended to.

Thinking Marley meant the comment for her, her professor stopped mid-sentence, shooting her a shocked look as Marley felt students turn to watch her, their eyes burning into her back. She felt a wave of panic engulf her.

This can't be happening again so soon.

"Do you have a problem with what I'm saying?" her professor asked, eyebrow raised in challenge. It was amazing how quickly her voice had lost its pleasantness and was now laced with ice. Tension blanketed the room as everyone waited for her response.

"No, sorry," Marley replied quietly. "It was... an accident."

"That's what I thought. Now, if you don't mind, I'd like to continue with my lesson without any further interruptions."

Marley nodded, hoping desperately for the ground to swallow her. Realizing she wasn't going to leave any time soon, Christian issued an annoyed sigh then vanished. Marley slid down lower into her seat until she was almost horizontal.

This is only your first day, it has to get better.
Right?

TWENTY-FIVE

L unch couldn't come fast enough.

Although Christian didn't bother her again, Marley found it impossible to focus on the syllabus at hand. While she knew other girls might be filled with excitement over having a power — whatever it might be — she knew it was taking her even further from her goal of becoming normal.

She followed the signs to Union Court, BU's food hall, which turned out to be an enormous space containing ten or twelve well-known franchises as well as a few unfamiliar ones. There was a Panda Express *(yeah, they wouldn't be getting too much business from her)*, Starbucks of course, a salad place named Loose Leaf's as well as some others. It was kind of hard to make much out, packed to the brim as it was. All the students in the world were here it seemed.

Her eyes searched the crowd for familiar faces, wondering if she'd actually find them when she saw the girls waiting for her by the entrance. Back in Goth gear, Eve was the easiest to spot. Even from a distance, Marley could see that her face was hidden away again under the heavy layers of makeup she liked to wear. Although it wasn't her place to say anything, she found it a shame as Eve was a naturally pretty girl. What had happened that made her feel she had to hide her real face away?

She saw Cassie next but noticed with a shock that she wore an almost identical outfit to hers. Why would she change out of her designer jumpsuit to wear a more ordinary outfit? If it was first-day impact she had wanted, which Marley assumed was the case since she had taken so damn long in the bathroom, she would have gotten it with the jumpsuit. It was with some relief that Marley saw Tyler looking pretty much as she expected her to look, her tolerance for surprises rapidly dwindling.

"We thought you weren't coming," Tyler said in greeting.

"I just keep getting lost in this place," Marley explained.

Leading them to a place called Coco's Chow, Eve grabbed a meat sub and a bottle of water. "You'll get used to it in a few weeks. Happens to everyone."

The place was so packed, Marley had to squeeze past a group of students to get to one of several refrigerated units.

"I don't think we should talk in here, seems like we'd be overheard anywhere we sit," Cassie said concerned, her eyes flitting around the place nervously.

Moving to the checkout, Eve tossed her a look over her shoulder. "We're not staying here. I know a place we can go that'll be more private. We can talk there."

"You seem to know your way around already," Marley said, envious of her knowledge. It would be great to be able to get around without having to consult a map every five seconds.

"I've been here before," Eve answered before thinking. She stopped quickly, but not before the others caught what she had said.

"You have?" Cassie said.

"When?" Tyler asked.

Her stomach plummeted as she saw them look at her, waiting for an explanation. Knowing that she couldn't hide the truth forever, Eve sighed. "Last year. I dropped out for personal reasons."

"Like what?" Cassie asked again seemingly with no filter.

Eve shot her a hard look. "Do you not know what personal means?"

Cassie's mouth snapped shut at her tone. An awkward flush started over her cheeks. Silence fell as Cassie tried to find a way to apologize. Marley reached for something to say, anything to defuse the situation. Nothing came to mind.

"I didn't mean to pry, sometimes I just speak without thinking…" Cassie finally stammered.

Eve's only response was a sharp nod of her head. "Grab your food. I'll meet you back at the entrance," she said, moving away.

Stung by her curtness, Cassie looked at Tyler and Marley.

"Do you think she hates me now? I'm always messing things up."

"Of course not," Tyler answered, surprised she would even think such a thing. "You just mentioned a sensitive subject is all. Why would she hate you for something so small?"

Cassie didn't answer but her eyes slid over to Eve as she watched her disappearing into the crowd.

***

Moments later the girls followed Eve through several connecting wings until they stepped into a pretty courtyard outside. A stone fountain of an angel formed the center of the small space. The bubbling water provided more than just a pleasant backdrop to their conversation, however. It also doubled to hide it from anyone who might otherwise overhear their unorthodox conversation.

Marley, Eve and Tyler unwrapped their sandwiches, then watched in astonishment as Cassie opened a large box of sushi, a seaweed salad and a fruit salad as she sipped from a green juice. As if that wasn't enough, she also had a large wedge of cheesecake.

"Where do you put all that food?" Tyler said, asking what all the others were thinking.

Unwrapping a pair of chopsticks Cassie shrugged self-consciously. "Oh, I don't eat it all. I just pick at it. I like the variety. Eating one thing's so boring," she said without thinking before looking immediately horrified when she took in their lunches.

"Sorry, I didn't mean…" she started but Tyler cut her off.

"Listen, I used to eat like that too. You've got nothing to apologize for. Enjoy your lunch."

"Help yourself to anything you want," Cassie said in earnest. "I really can't eat all of this on my own."

"Could the four of you be any more ridiculous?" came Christian's voice from above. He sat cross-legged on the hedge beside them.

"Great," Marley said. "You'll all be happy to know that our so-called Guardian frenemy is back." She nodded glumly above her, knowing any chance of a peaceful lunch was now thrown out of the window.

"You said we need to find Michael, but how are we supposed to do that?" Cassie asked first, surprising the others with her bravery. She seemed like she was about to burst from all the questions she had for him.

"When magic is used, it sometimes leaves a trace of itself that other magical beings can sense. Or you could use your powers. That should work too."

"How, when we're not even sure what we can do?"

Marley tried to still her shudder as visions of her hand squeezing Christian's heart flooded her mind.

"There's not a simple answer to that. It's not like you're a superhero with a clear-cut power. You need to discover what they are and what you can do. Once you know that, you can utilize them against him."

"You keep saying we need to go after Michael, but he's clearly dangerous. What makes you think we can go against him when you and your mentor couldn't?" Tyler asked. She didn't want to anger him yet the point needed to be raised.

"It does sound like he's more concerned about this Michael guy than he is about our lives," Cassie said, twisting her chopsticks anxiously.

"This is ridiculous," Eve said suddenly, slamming down her sub. "You want us to give up our lives to fight this guy on only your hearsay when we can't even see or hear you ourselves!"

"Are we back to this again?" Christian roared.

"You can't blame us for being upset," Marley started to say, but she never got to finish. Christian jumped down storming up to her until his face was almost pressed into hers, or would be, had he been alive.

"Don't you talk to me about being upset! I had a life! I wasn't just a Guardian, I had dreams, but you ended them all! You think this is how I wanted to die? In a stupid accident right when I was this close to avenging Eric! The least you could do is to stop this pity party you've got going on, accept your responsibilities, and go after the monster who killed the man who was the only father I ever knew! God, the four of you are so irritating, yapping about food or clothes when there is so much at stake! I can't bear to be around you!"

Without another word, Christian disappeared.

Rather than repeat him — and frankly, she was getting pretty tired of having to parrot his every word — Marley choose to give the gist of his thoughts. Despite how she tried to spare them, however, they were left feeling pretty small.

"I think going after that guy is the wrong thing to do. We don't know how to use our powers — or even what they are," Tyler said.

Cassie nodded in agreement. "Don't you think we should try to practice somewhere, figure out exactly what it is we can do?"

"Yeah. That seems like a better use of our time," Eve agreed to her surprise and relief. It seemed she wasn't holding a grudge against her after all.

"Let's meet somewhere after school. Where can we go that's quiet, where no one is likely to go?" Marley asked. Having only moved to the area recently, she didn't have much idea of what was around.

"I know the perfect place," Eve said. "Give me your numbers, I'll text you all directions."

They nodded, agreeing to the plan as they exchanged numbers. Marley felt a little better knowing they were taking matters into their own hands. They would figure this out without Christian's help.

"He's right you know," Tyler said suddenly, cutting into his thoughts. "He died, and no one knows or even cares about that apart from us. With Eric gone, it doesn't sound like he has anyone else left."

"Christian's life ended without fanfare and now he's back. It must mess with him mentally. It would me," Eve said.

"Do you think… should we give him a funeral service of some kind?" Cassie raised tentatively.

"Like the whole shebang, with the coffin and wake?" Eve asked disbelievingly.

"No, just a small thing. With just the four of us present. And Christian of course. Do you think it would help him?"

"It certainly couldn't make him any angrier could it?" Tyler said.

"But wouldn't we need his body to do that?" Cassie asked.

"Speaking of which, where is his body? I assumed Christian knew where it went but he hasn't said anything about it," Tyler asked.

"No," Marley agreed, suddenly wondering about it herself.

Where was Christian's body?

TWENTY-SIX

"How inept are you, that you can't kill someone who's already dead?"

Across town, several feet below ground level, deep inside the dark, dank sewers of Roxbury, three figures huddled over a body.

The only source of light came from a newly-bought crank light, of the type used for camping. One of the three figures stepped out of the shadows into the light. It was Michael. He stared down at the body lying on a concrete slab with barely concealed rage.

"I'm trying boss," said Pike, one of his cronies, an eerie-looking hunchback. His eyes were too wide for his face, which was hideously disfigured by millions of scar-like depressions. His teeth were filed to points, at least that was how they seemed. In reality, they were fangs, similar in form and function to those found on big cats, and great for ripping his prey to shreds. He wasn't that bright, but he was easy to command and very dangerous.

Just how Michael liked them.

His other little helper was a different matter entirely. Smart, with a sadistic streak that matched his own, Fink was abhorred by his community because of his taste for deep-fried girl-meat. He had struggled to find an employer who would turn the other cheek for this particular culinary quirk of his. That Michael did not care who he ate so long as it wasn't someone he needed, well, it was a match made in heaven. Holding the hilt of a knife, he approached the Guardian's body. His mouth twitching as he licked his lips in anticipation, having never tasted one before. Raising the knife overhead, he swung the blade down, but the knife bounced harmlessly off the Guardian's body, flying across the room.

"What the hell?" Fink exclaimed. "It's like I'm trying to stab a piece of metal."

A fury burned inside Michael. They had not carried the body all the way here only to be unable to destroy it. He snatched the can of gasoline from Pike's hands, approaching it himself.

"If you want something done…"

Unscrewing the cap, he poured the acrid smelling liquid over Christian's body, watching it soak into his clothes, turning them several shades darker. Moving a safe distance away, he struck up a match, flicking it onto him. Flames exploded, their fingers blooming to the ceiling as the fire spread along his body at lightning speed. Michael waited for the smell of burning flesh.

But it never came.

Though the flames danced high, singeing Pike's hair until he was forced to jump out of the way or risk having his face melted, Christian's body and clothes remained intact.

Michael stifled a howl, hurling the empty can against a wall.

"Do something!" he yelled at Pike, who nodded, hoisting a heavy chainsaw into his arms. Pulling the cord, the engine burst to life, the blades whipping wickedly fast, causing a horrendous noise.

Moving towards Christian, Pike lifted the chainsaw

high above his head, slamming it down with all the force he could muster. Like the knife, however, it simply bounced off his body, taking him with it. He lost his grip on the weapon sending the chainsaw spinning across the ground, out of his control, only stopping at a gesture and word from Michael.

Summoning up his power from within, Michael channeled a ball of pulsing energy into his hands hurling it at Christian. Though the body bucked from the contact, it remained intact.

"How is this possible?" Fink asked, awed.

"I'll tell you how," Michael said angrily. Reaching across, he ripped open Christian's shirt to reveal the maze of tattooed sigils that glowed across his body, protecting him.

"Magic."

TWENTY-SEVEN

Scientific apparatus sat on the benches surrounding Tyler.

As her professor droned on explaining the various experiments they would be conducting over the course of the term, Tyler found her focus drifting to the bottles of chemicals lined up inside a cabinet beside her.

Even as a child, Tyler had loved the certainty of science, that if you put two hydrogen atoms together with one oxygen one, you would make water. No matter where you were in the world, this was the same. Science was reliable in a way nothing else was.

This was the first time she had set foot in a lab since her parents had died, and she found herself desperately craving more of that certainty. Life had been so simple before… Feeling the pain well inside her chest again, she squeezed her eyes closed for a moment.

No, not here. Not in class.

She could not burst into tears in front of the whole class on her first day. She would not be known as *that* girl. She had to keep it together.

Focusing on the student in front of her, Tyler studied the back of her head, hoping that the activity would draw her attention away from her debilitating thoughts when something vibrated in her pocket — her phone. It had been set to silent so it wouldn't ring in class, but she'd left the vibrate option on, in case there was an emergency. Now that she was the only family Ally had left, Tyler made sure she could always reach her if she needed to. With all of Ally's medical needs, this was doubly important.

She took out her phone and hid it behind a course book. Hoping her professor wouldn't see, she unlocked it to find a message from the girl herself:

I've finally figured out what I want for my birthday!!!!! Xoxoxo

After the message came a link leading to a bag shaped like a ladybug. Of course. It was exactly the kind of thing Ally loved, and she knew immediately it would get a lot of use. When she saw the price, however, she felt the beginnings of worry.

If this had been before, she wouldn't have blinked at the price — it wasn't exactly expensive — but it was more than she could reasonably afford right now, at least until she had a chance to speak to the loans office to find out what the hold-up was there. As her money issue raised its ugly head again, a wave of resentment came crashing over her.

Why did this have to happen?

Hadn't she gone through enough already? Why was there now added money pressure on top of her fight to reunite with Ally *and* the whole supernatural being thing? She had always been raised to believe in God and had believed in him since she was a child actually, but if there was one, why was he punishing her like this?

Feeling her rage building, she suddenly noticed that

the air had that same heaviness that had been present last night at the church. She could feel the static in her hair, and with it came the knowledge that something unnatural was happening. Terrified of a repeat of last night's events, she tried to clamp down on her own emotions but saw with horror that the solutions in the glass bottles around her were starting to bubble as if they were held over a powerful flame.

She froze, panicked, looking towards her professor, but she could not see what was happening from her vantage point at the front of the room. Tyler turned back to see the solutions were making their way up the spout of the bottles. She steeled herself knowing the bigger cause of concern came not from the solutions themselves, but from the actual glass bottles.

If glass was heated too quickly, it would shatter.

That was another certainty of science. She looked around, hoping her neighbor could see what was happening and do something about it, but his nose was immersed in a textbook, oblivious to the surrounding danger.

She turned back to the bottles and saw that in her split second of hesitation the solutions had reached boiling point. Reacting out of pure instinct, she shoved the student next to her out of harm's way as the bottles exploded, raining glass and chemicals around them. Her would-be lab partner fell off the stool he had been sitting on, landing on the ground in an untidy heap. Students spun around, shocked, as the professor stopped mid-flow a look of first puzzlement then shock spreading over her face.

Something landed on the arm of her cardigan. Tyler glanced down to find whatever solution had landed on her eating a hole into the fabric. Shrugging out of it quickly, she threw it to the ground as the rest of the cardigan smoked and burned. Running to the nearest sink, she shoved her arm under the tap, washing off whatever the solution had been as her professor rushed over to help her. Tyler stared blankly ahead as her professor checked over her, one thought running through her head.

She could have killed someone.

TWENTY-EIGHT

Light danced prettily across the blue water.

The reservoir wasn't popular amongst students and was considered the least exciting area of water in Boston. There were much prettier parks too for dog walkers, which is why Eve figured it would be safe for them to practice their powers here.

Staring at her reflection in her compact mirror, Cassie focused on her face, willing it to change. Eve sat cross-legged on the grass, hands touching the blades closest to her. Her black-ringed eyes were closed as she chanted something wordlessly. Marley knelt before a log, trying to push her hands through it, though it seemed nothing more than an exercise in futility. Sighing, she threw up her hands in frustration. "I've been trying this for an hour now, it's not working!"

Eve opened one of her eyes, giving her a look, the kind of look a mother gives a child having a silly tantrum. "It's been ten minutes, drama queen." She was interrupted from her next words by Tyler's arrival. Her eyes were wild, hair disheveled. Any irritation she felt at her lateness was immediately replaced with concern as it was impossible to miss the alarm she exuded.

"Are you OK?" Marley asked.

"No," Tyler said, unable to hide the panic from her voice. "I accidentally heated up the chemicals in the lab and caused them to explode."

The girls gasped as one. "Did you get hurt?" Eve asked.

"Glass and chemicals went everywhere, but my cardigan got the worst of it."

"At least you weren't injured," Marley said, relieved.

"Apparently I'm the girl who changes or affects molecules. Like the rain that turned to glass last night? I made the solutions heat up until the bottles they were inside exploded."

"At least one of you is paying attention — finally," Christian said, having appeared behind them.

"Is that right?" Marley asked him. "Is that Tyler's power?"

Christian shrugged. "Possibly."

"I don't want any powers!" Tyler blurted out suddenly. "I just need to get some money and get through school. Ally needs me! I can't have all this weirdness mess things up for me. Look what happened today, I could have killed someone!" Tyler said without thinking. Seeing Marley visibly flinch, she was immediately apologetic. "I didn't mean… What I meant to say was…" she began only for Marley to cut her off with a wave of her hand.

"It's the truth. You don't have to apologize every time you bring it up."

"This is why I've been telling you that you need to focus," Christian said. "With great power comes great responsibility. You must learn to hone your powers to fight Michael and any like him."

"What if I don't want to?" Eve said suddenly.

"You don't get a choice," Christian snapped as Marley

repeated him, word for word. She even repeated his tone so the others could fully appreciate what she had to put up with, with him in her head all the time.

"Of course I do! Nobody makes me do anything I don't want to, not anymore!" she yelled back at him. Even though she couldn't hear him, she knew he could hear her.

"You stupid girl!" Christian shouted back, having lost all composure. "This is bigger than what you want, how can you not understand that? Do you not care that people have died, that more people will die?"

"No, not really," Eve replied, shocking them all. "All I know is that my life has been hard enough without all this added to it, so I don't want it, you hear? I don't want any part of this!" She stamped her foot, emphasizing her point.

At that exact moment, ripples danced across the water as something moved below the surface. Marley caught it first but didn't know what it was. Cassie, closest to the water, craned her neck for a better look. Lowering her face to the water, she peered into the blackness where something moved inside. Squinting, she tried to make out what it was when crabs launched out of the water onto the banks of the reservoir, waving their pinchers, swarming around them in the hundreds.

Cassie screamed, running back towards the others. They stood huddled in a group as the crabs circled Eve.

"What the hell is going on?" Eve cried.

"I think this is your power," Christian answered. "Your command of nature. They come when you are in danger or feel threatened in any way."

Eve gaped at Marley, her mouth opened in horror.

"Moths and crabs? What kind of twisted power is that? I don't want any part of this. I'm done."

Stepping over the ring of crabs, she stormed away, unable to hear Christian yelling after her. Determined not to have anything more to do with them, she continued on her way, disappearing over the crest of the hill. Without her to protect, the crabs scampered off in different directions until none were left.

"How Eve feels isn't important. She's in this now, whether she wants to be or not. Nothing else is important, only stopping Michael is."

"For you maybe," Tyler spoke up suddenly. "But I've got a sister who needs me and other pressing things to contend with. I don't actually have time for this." She took one last look at Marley and Cassie, shrugged, then she also went her own way. Stuck in the middle, Cassie didn't know what to do. She shot Marley a helpless look then spun on her heel, following after her.

"Tyler, wait for me!"

Shaking his head, Christian vanished, knowing better than to try to get Marley to see his side leaving Marley sinking down onto the grass, not recognizing her world anymore.

Marley didn't know how long she had sat there. Staring across the body of water, she felt the enormous weight of all they had learned in the last forty-eight hours. Yes, killing Christian had been an accident. She would still have to deal with the guilt for the rest of her life, something which might have been easier if he wasn't becoming such a regular fixture.

She watched the sky become dimmer as the sun sank lower into the horizon. The wind picked up, whipping leaves in a circle around her. It probably wasn't a wise idea to stay out here but quiet time was becoming so rare. She'd needed this moment of calm, and the water provided a peace she couldn't otherwise feel.

Knowing she should get back, she was rising to her feet when her senses became suddenly alert. She knew immediately that she wasn't alone anymore. Sighing, she steeled herself for the inevitable confrontation. "I just wanted a moment alone, OK? Things are getting to be a bit much," she said to Christian, turning around.

Except it wasn't him.

It was a woman.

Though the wind blew, her long black hair didn't move, neither did her dress. It was as if the wind didn't affect her at all. She stood several feet away, but Marley could see the noose around her neck from here.

It was the woman from the Hanging Elm!

In the second Marley realized this, the woman blinked away only to reappear inches from her face! Frozen with fear, Marley could do nothing but stare at the ghostly visage with the terrible darkness in her eyes. The woman moved her mouth as if she were trying to speak. Close to her now, Marley saw with growing horror that her lips had been sewn together. She stumbled back, desperate to get away from her when the ghost clamped her arms around Marley's shoulders, holding her there.

Marley's skin burned from the touch as she struggled to free herself. She twisted this way and that, but the ghost was too strong. She came even closer until Marley couldn't escape that awful stare.

Then she screamed a howl of utter rage and terror.

Marley felt the world start to spin as the ground came rushing up to greet her.

One minute she was standing, the next she felt the cold grass against her face before blacking out completely.

TWENTY-NINE

He should kill them himself.

Christian raged inside Marley and Cassie's room, wishing he were able to do the deed. Instead, he had been rendered next to helpless, those years of training all for nothing. If Eric could see him now, he'd lose it.

Christian could picture it well.

As much as Eric had raised him since he was a boy, he had quite the temper and was known to punch a wall or two, leaving a hole in the wake of his fist. Many's the time they'd had to call a builder to fix their "demolition" mistakes. Christian swallowed the curses he could feel welling up inside although it wouldn't have been a problem to let loose. It wasn't as if the others could hear him. Oh no, that gift only belonged to the one who had killed him.

The universe had a perverse sense of humor.

He watched now as Tyler and Cassie discussed what they should do. They were worried about Eve and Marley being alone when what they should be worried about was Michael and whatever plan he was working on. To his knowledge, Michael had killed several people already, but that was only for starters; he knew the deaths were to fuel some darker motive.

He didn't want to think what that could be.

"Should we call them?" Cassie asked, staring out at the black sky. "I know they wanted to be left alone, but look how dark it is out there."

Nodding, Tyler took out her phone and dialed Eve's number, setting the call on speaker so Cassie could hear. The rings continued indefinitely, however. Hanging up, Tyler tried Marley next. They waited, counting the rings, but she didn't answer either, the call going to voicemail instead. At the tone, Tyler spoke into the phone.

"Hey Marley, it's Tyler and Cassie. We're worried. It's late and you're not back yet. I'm sorry I stormed off but could you call or message us so we know you're safe?"

Ending the call, Tyler looked at Cassie.

"Neither of them are picking up."

"Can't say I'm that surprised by Eve not answering, just didn't expect Marley not to," Cassie revealed. "It doesn't seem like the sort of thing she'd do."

"I know," Tyler said, worried. "I shouldn't have left like that. It's just too much, you know? It's not like I don't have a ton of problems already. I didn't need anymore."

"Do you want to talk about them?" Cassie offered shyly, a hopeful glint in her eyes.

Tyler looked at her as if she was considering doing just that until she shook her head. If she started talking, she might never stop. Cassie tried to quell her disappointment. She knew Tyler had spoken to Marley before about some of her problems, but apparently, she wasn't good enough to confide in. She shouldn't be surprised by this, but it still hurt. It seemed that all her life, people never really wanted to trust her or get to know her. They took one look at her and knew that there was nothing good inside, so they just didn't bother. Feeling herself deflating, she sat down on her bed, hugging a pillow to her chest.

"I'm fine. We should just focus on getting in touch with the others," Tyler finally said.

"Why? They're probably just off sulking," Christian griped, though he knew they couldn't hear him. Still, it was pretty dark out there he conceded glancing outside. It did seem strange that Marley wasn't answering her phone given everything that had happened. Maybe he should go check it out himself. Since he'd last seen her at the reservoir, he pictured it in his mind, holding it there. He felt a pull inside his body, then what could only be described as a sunken feeling. When he opened his eyes again, he was back at the water.

There, he found Marley on the ground out cold.

Seeing her still figure, Christian felt a great hammer of fear in his gut. If she'd been attacked under his watch, while he had been having his hissy fit back at the college...

He left the thought there, unable to finish it.

Sprinting towards her, he took in her pale face. Unconscious, she looked so vulnerable that it tore at his heart. What an idiot he had been to leave her here. He was supposed to know better!

He checked over her body, eyes searching for a wound, relieved when he could see none. He reached for her wrist to feel for a pulse but his hand went straight through her. Letting out a hiss of frustration, Christian watched her chest, hoping to see it rise and fall. He was rewarded by the tiniest movement.

She was alive!

Leaning close to her, Christian placed his hands on the grass, yelling into her face. "Marley! It's Christian! Wake up!"

There was no change in her condition. Raising his voice, he called out her name, over and over, until his voice cracked. He began to despair if she'd ever regain consciousness. Terror raced through him as he considered the ramifications of her not being able to fight Michael.

Without her, the others wouldn't be able to hear him. Without her, they were lost.

It was as he pictured the end of the world in his mind that Marley groaned. Her head moved to the side as she winced from whatever she felt there. Thrilled that she was coming to, Christian leaned closer to her. "Marley, wake up! You need to open your eyes now!"

She moaned, flinching away from him, not liking his loudness. He was rewarded by a flicker of her eyes as she opened them. She blinked up at him in confusion.

"Where am I?"

"You're still at the reservoir. Are you OK? I found you passed out on the ground."

She looked up at him with those hazel eyes with such confusion that Christian found the inexplicable urge to comfort her.

Which of course was ridiculous on many levels.

He moved away from her as if her very presence could burn him. If Marley saw his bizarre reaction, how-ever, she didn't mention it. She pushed herself onto her feet, staring around her in bewilderment.

"What am I doing here…" she began but then her eyes turned haunted. She gasped, trembling from the memory.

"What is it?" Christian demanded.

"That woman, the ghost I saw at the Hanging Elm, she was here," Marley said, her voice shook with fear at the mere mention of her.

"What woman, what ghost?" Christian asked, con-fused. "Explain!"

"I saw her before, when I was out with Tyler and Cassie, at the common. We were in a juice bar but then the air changed and I saw a figure materialize in the trees op-posite. She had a noose around her neck, and she was hanging from this big Elm tree," Marley replied. "She pointed at me and this horrible sound came out of her…"

She stopped, shuddering as the sound and image as-saulted her once again. "I did some research after that. I found out they used to hang witches there, on that very tree."

"Yeah. There's a lot of bad history around here," Christian supplied.

"After you guys had gone, I sat here for a while, but then I thought I could feel you behind me... except it wasn't you, it was her again. This time she got really close to me, she grabbed me by the shoulders," Marley made a move to shrug out of her shirt, when she became self-conscious under Christian's gaze. Still, needing to see if any damage had been caused, she examined her bare shoulders. There was nothing there.

"I was sure there would be marks, it felt like her fingers were burning into my skin," Marley said, shivering from the memory.

"She touched you? How? I tried and my hands went straight through you," Christian said.

"I don't know, but it wasn't pleasant. She tried to scream at me again but I saw that her lips had been sewn together. I must have blacked out after as the next thing I knew, you were here."

A sob caught in her throat that she tried to hide but Christian heard it anyway. A tear ran down her cheek that she wiped away. "What does she want? Why does she keep appearing to me?" Marley asked tearfully.

"She must have something to communicate to you," Christian replied.

"That's a pretty terrible way of trying to talk to me," Marley said bitterly.

"Maybe she's not trying to talk to you."

He trailed off, not wanting to finish.

If she can't talk, then what does she want?

Marley couldn't stop shaking at the thought.

THIRTY

What was Cassie's deal?

One minute they had been sharing their concern over Marley and Eve's silence, the next she was huddled on her bed looking upset.

Unsure what to do, Tyler left her alone. She went back to her own room. She sat down at her desk now, opening her laptop. While they waited to hear from Marley and Eve, she needed to take care of some important things.

Logging into her bank, she checked her balance, hoping that her Financial Aid had finally come through. The balance had changed since yesterday, unfortunately; it had gone down by another twenty or so bucks as her phone bill had come out. She tried to still the wave of panic that knotted her stomach whenever money matters were raised, but there was also anger behind it. Anger at her parents, who had lied to them about the state of their financial affairs. If she had known how stretched they were, how much they had borrowed to deal with Ally's healthcare, she would have sold the ponies to help out. Her parents had kept the truth from her, wanting to live the American Dream… leaving them with nothing.

Thinking of Ally, her last text message flashed into her mind.

She still had her birthday present to get. Logging into Amazon, Tyler found the bag Ally wanted, added it to the cart. She clicked the checkout button but needed her card details to pay for it. Looking around, Tyler realized her bag wasn't with her. More panic crept up inside until she remembered that she'd last had it just minutes before. Getting up, she walked across the hall, knocked on the door, opening it without waiting for an answer.

Cassie was inside Marley's wardrobe trying on her clothes, while some of Marley's things had obviously been rifled through in the minutes that she'd been gone. Cassie froze, taking off the shirt that she'd just been putting on.

"What are you doing?" Tyler asked.

Caught out, red with embarrassment, Cassie shrugged. "Nothing. Marley said I could borrow whatever I wanted, so I thought I'd try a few things on, just to see how they fit."

Tyler didn't want to dispute her claims, but if that were true, why was she looking so guilty? Wasn't it a weird time too, to be trying on your roommate's clothes when you were worried about them? As if she knew what was going through Tyler's mind, Cassie quickly changed the conversation.

"Did you hear back from them?"

"No, not yet," Tyler replied. "I just came to get my bag." She pointed to Cassie's bed, where her bag sat undisturbed, somewhat relieved to see that it was still closed. At least Cassie hadn't been going through *her* things. Picking it up, she made her way back to the door.

"You'll let me know if you hear anything?" Tyler asked.

"Sure," Cassie replied quickly, unable to shake that caught expression on her face. Tyler hesitated, wondering what to do. On the one hand, Cassie was obviously up to something. Then again, it looked harmless enough. Biting her lip, she shot Cassie a small smile before heading back to her room.

It really wasn't any of her business what Cassie did with Marley's clothes. She had her own problems to worry about without making new ones.

Taking out her card, she paid for Ally's bag then moved on to the next item on her mental to-do list.

Sighing, she pulled up Google, typing "part-time jobs" into the search bar.

THIRTY-ONE

The walk back to the dorm felt like forever.

Marley shivered, wrapping her arms around herself as she hurried down Main Street.

In the dim light of dusk, distorted shadows crawled along the sidewalk creeping ever closer to her. As if she were a child playing the floor is lava, she made sure they never quite reached her feet. Though she knew they couldn't harm her, she also knew unpleasant things liked to lurk in the dark, whether those things were supernatural serial killers or not. Her eyes darted every which way, watchful for another unwanted appearance from her ghostly visitor.

This time, it wasn't Christian she was worried about.

Marley felt more vulnerable than she'd ever been in her life. Even with all the episodes she'd experienced, she'd never been attacked by someone before, let alone a ghost. The experience left her shaken and very scared. There was a coldness inside now that no amount of heat or clothing would abate. There was the terrible realization too that the woman wanted something from her… which meant she would be back. She heard a strange chattering sound before she realized that it was her own teeth.

"We're almost there," Christian said, appraising her with his eyes.

His shoulders were tensed. He kept looking around them, watchful for anything out of the ordinary. Marley had expected Christian to berate her for being alone at the reservoir — it was a stupid thing to do after all — but he'd only tightened his lips into a straight line, urging her back to college. It was almost as if he were afraid. This frightened her more than anything else. He was dead after all, so if he was scared, then it didn't bear thinking about.

He walked quickly beside her, his shoes making a soft sound as he went. Marley found this detail strange as he wasn't a physical being anymore. His feet could not connect with the ground, even if they looked like they could, so how could he make walking sounds. She wondered if it was a figment of her mind, similar to how when people lost a leg they could still feel their toes moving.

Seeing how carefully he scouted the area for danger, for the first time since they'd met, she felt an immense gratitude towards him. Torn by having left her alone, he was determined to see her back safely, even though she had insisted she'd be fine on her own. They weren't in the remote reservoir now. It was early enough that couples and families walked the streets, contemplating which restaurant they wanted to dine in. Their chatter and excitement filled the air offering some small comfort. At least while they were around, she didn't feel so alone.

The familiar red-bricked buildings of BU finally appeared before them as they approached a signpost pointing to her dorm. On a whim, Marley changed directions, moving towards another building.

"It's this way?" Christian pointed, his brow furrowed in confusion.

"I'm not heading back to the dorm yet. I'm… going somewhere else."

"Where?" he asked, but Marley didn't tell him. She didn't want him to dissuade her from what she wanted to do.

"It's OK. I won't be long," was the only reply she would give. Christian followed, clearly concerned. He didn't say anything until they crossed into the history building. Marley swiped her student pass on the reader, waiting for the doors to swing open. Stepping inside, she found herself in an area with several glass offices. Two corridors flanked either end of the room. There were signs with names attached to each of the offices though none contained the name she wanted. Racking her brain, she tried to remember where he said his office would be. Was it in the East or West?

"What are we doing here?" Christian asked. When she didn't answer he swerved around her until he blocked her path. Marley just stepped through him.

"Oh, that's cold. You're just going to walk through me now?"

"Only when you get in my way," Marley responded, finally deciding that The West Wing sounded more familiar. She headed down the hall, past offices that were mainly closed now, until she saw one at the end that was still open. Welcoming light streamed out, illuminating the corridor. She moved towards it quickly, filled with the urge to see the one person in the world who would know what to do. Knocking on the door, she stepped inside.

"Hey, Dad."

Paul looked up from his computer, a wide smile on his face. He sat in front of an antique painting that Marley recognized immediately. An old family heirloom that had been passed down for hundreds of years, it showed a woman sunning herself along a river on a warm day. The familiar sight of it made her feel comforted somehow. Christian paid the painting no attention, however.

Having no idea that her father worked here, his face was shocked.

"Hey hon, so you decided to check up on your old man's first day after all?"

Shame wracked her body as Marley realized she hadn't even given her dad's new job a second thought. She wasn't the only one who was having first days and new experiences. Her dad was only really here so that she could live out her dream of studying here even though that was fast becoming a nightmare.

"Exactly," she lied. Plastering on an equally big smile, she hoped he wouldn't see straight through her.

"It went pretty much as expected. Students are the same everywhere during their first week, more concerned about where the best parties are than what's on their syllabus. Speaking of which, have you been to any?"

"Any what, parties?" Marley asked. Here it was. This was the opening she needed. She could spill out the whole sordid story right now and he would help her to make sense of it all, just like he'd made sense of all the other difficulties she'd endured. As long as he knew the truth, he would have her back. It was the two of them against the world.

"You can't tell him anything. If you do, you'll be putting him in terrible danger."

Christian's words came at her like a thunderbolt. He stood beside her dad looking deadly serious with no sign of his usual attitude.

"You have powers, Marley. He doesn't. If you reveal what's been happening, he'll either think you're crazy or he'll try to protect you, neither of which will help you in any way."

He paused, spreading out his hands beseechingly. There was a softness in his eyes she had never seen before like he knew how much he was asking of her. "I know this is hard, but you can't tell him."

"Marley?" Paul asked, his eyes crinkling with concern.

"Sorry, I was just thinking of something, but no. No parties or any other news to report. I've been super boring, not getting up to anything much at all. I *have* made three friends though," she added, relieved she could tell him something that was true. Lying to her father wasn't something she'd done very much in her life, and she wasn't feeling good about doing it now. It felt like she was betraying his trust.

"Well that's great news," Paul said, making her feel even worse about herself. He had always been her biggest cheerleader even when she didn't deserve it. Like now. Beside him, Christian gave her a small supportive smile then left the room to give them some privacy.

They shot the breeze after that as Paul talked about his new students and run-ins with other professors. All in all, it sounded like he was having a blast. At least one of them was. She gave a brief rundown of the other girls, omitting any of the stranger details.

When she eventually looked at her phone to check the time, she was shocked to see that it had run out of charge long ago. Bidding Paul goodbye, she feigned excitement for the days ahead, hurrying back to the dorm where she knew the girls would be worried sick by now.

As soon as Marley was gone, the smile left Paul's face. Marley had never been a good liar, and he had always known when she wasn't telling the truth.

Like now.

He stared at the empty space where she had been just moments before, worry clouding his features.

THIRTY-TWO

City lights blinked into the night.

The streets were filled with the kind of silence that only came with the lateness of the hour, though not everyone was tucked up in bed sleeping.

From his hiding place behind a bank of rose bushes, Fink stared across Copley Square towards the hulking Trinity Church. Michael had given him strict instructions to scope out the area. He was to let him know if the place was empty so he could continue with the task that he was so rudely interrupted from completing the night before.

Unfortunately, though the yellow tape that had been on the ground earlier that day had finally been removed, a pair of plainclothes cops patrolled the area.

He knew what they were the minute he saw them.

He saw it in the way they both walked as if they owned the place, with the kind of swagger that only those who wielded power had. Michael was the same. Fink had tried to move in the same way himself, but inevitably he would look as if he had pulled a muscle in an unfortunate region. This kind of swagger only came to some naturally. Even more telling than their walk, however, were the redhead's shoes, the men's shoes she wore for long days patrolling the city so her feet wouldn't hurt. Those were a dead giveaway.

And then there was the *smell*.

With one sniff, Fink could tell that before she had come to work, she had played with a long-haired dog with his favorite ball. He knew the dog was a male as they had a weaker scent. It was something to do with nature and female dogs needing to attract a mate. The ball was made of a strong rubber that had already lasted a good while which he knew from the many layers of dried dog saliva on it. Fink also knew that like any good cop cliché, the redhead had breakfasted on coffee and donuts. She had combated that later with a chicken salad for lunch.

It was because of Fink's incredible sense of smell and smarts that he had become Michael's right-hand man. After last night's mess, he had wanted to give Michael some good news. It didn't seem like that would be the case, however. He'd been watching the cops for over three hours now yet they showed no signs of retiring.

Steeling himself with the idea that he'd probably have to go back to let Michael know that their plan would have to wait and the rage that would inevitably follow such an announcement, Fink cracked his knuckles as he moved out from his hiding place. He studied the police who were oblivious to his scrutiny. Tonight was meant to be a recon mission... though maybe he could alter the plan, take the cops out of the picture?

The male cop might have a few pounds on him, but Fink was much stronger than he looked, and he was good at killing people, especially women. They were usually so frightened when they saw him that it rendered them almost helpless. He grinned to himself, feeling his mouth watering as he pictured the female cop turning on his specially made spit roaster at home. She was a little older than he usually liked them, but he was sure she would still taste good. She would go great with that honey glaze he had swiped from the market earlier. Almost dancing with the anticipation of his upcoming meal, Fink moved forward when two other figures approached the cops. Snarling with frustration, he darted back behind the bushes.

Who were these two now?

He knew the answer within moments when the redhead greeted the others warmly.

Wonderful. More cops.

Seething with resentment, Fink watched as the redhead and her partner were replaced by two other duty cops, both men this time. While he could do away with them easily enough, two dead cops was going to bring a lot of heat this way. Fink knew it would be the last thing Michael would want.

With his hand over his now rumbling stomach, Fink made his way back to the sewers. They would have to wait one more day to move on with their plan.

THIRTY-THREE

Thunder rumbled overhead, waking Tyler in her bed. Beads of rain littered the window like crystal drops. Usually, the sight and sound of them would relax her, but a flower of apprehension opened up inside her chest.

The last time there was rain, she had turned it into a weapon.

She fought to control the shiver that crept up her spine, drawing the sheets around her. The sky outside was a gloomy gray that matched her mood perfectly. Tyler kept her curtains opened as she couldn't sleep in the suffocating darkness. This was a new phobia she had developed after her parents had died. She knew she should see someone about it, but it had never seemed that important in the grand scheme of things.

She had hoped for an early night last night so she could catch up on sleep, prepare for what she knew had to happen today, but of course, they had been up well into the night again as Marley had had to relay her terrifying ordeal when she returned.

It was funny: if you had asked her only three days ago

if she believed in ghosts, she would have laughed and said no, but now…

Things could change so fast.

Rubbing the sleep from her eyes, Tyler looked at the calendar on her bedside table. One of the dates had been circled with stars and exclamation marks, courtesy of Ally. Although she would never forget her sister's birthday, Ally liked to make a game of marking the date on all of her calendars. It amused her to do it, so Tyler had never stopped her, even when her Gmail account had spammed her with a reminder every hour the day before the date last year. Ever the prankster, Ally had entered it into her online calendar multiple times. She'd been particularly proud of herself for that one.

Thinking about her took some edge off, and at least she didn't have any classes today. That brought a little relief too.

Climbing out of bed, Tyler slipped into her flip-flops, grabbed a towel, her wash bag, and ID card. Leaving her room, she went down the hall to the communal bathroom passing one or two other sleepy students on her way. She gave each a small smile of greeting but didn't speak to them. Stepping into the bathroom, fogged up mirrors and wet floors greeted her. Although it was pretty early, some of the dorm's early risers — probably the two she had just passed — had already washed up. Finding an empty cubicle in the corner, Tyler showered, allowing herself to gradually wake under the warm water.

A little later, she was dressed in a smart Bardot top and an A-line skirt, as ready as she'd ever be for the task ahead. She'd even forgone her usual Converses for these sensible-looking pumps. Armed with copies of her resumé — such as it was, as Tyler had never worked before — she hit the streets to look for a job.

Her online search yesterday had proved fruitless. Most of the jobs required that she either have experience or more hours to spare than she had. Figuring that her best chance was to make a face-to-face impression, Tyler headed to the main retail and food areas. There were a few signs on the door asking for help, but Tyler didn't rely on just those. Having found a Reddit thread yesterday that suggested she would have better luck enquiring in person rather than relying on For Hire signs as they tended to be inundated with job-hunters, she was determined to go the extra mile.

So she went into coffee bars, sandwich and salad shops, clothes and shoe shops, asking at every one, but all came back with nothing. It seemed that while they were busy killing Christian and learning about their freaky powers, other students had gotten there before her.

As luck would have it, the early morning rain had gone, leaving behind blue skies and bright sunshine. After hours of pounding the sidewalk, with sweat gathering at the base of her neck, Tyler arrived at the Star Market, a large grocery store popular among the students. Of all the places she had visited, this was the least glamorous. Sighing, not really expecting anything, Tyler stepped inside and asked to speak with the manager.

Moments later, she was greeted by a smarmy guy in his forties. He wore hipster glasses that seemed out of sorts with his too-long face and puffy lips. He wore the striped red shirt that was the uniform of the store, which strained over his protruding stomach. The name on his badge said WILLIAM, Store Manager. Taking matters into her own hands, Tyler introduced herself, explaining why she was there as William peered over the tops of his glasses, assessing her shrewdly.

"You have no experience?" he asked, making this sound as if it were a crime.

"No, but I'm a fast learner and I'm keen," Tyler intoned. This might've been the twentieth time she had said this exact same sentence today.

"So you really need this job?"

Did he want her to beg? How was she supposed to answer that?

"Yes, I really do. I'm happy to fit in more hours too as necessary, so long as I can still go to class and get my work done. Do you have a job going right now? I didn't see a sign but thought I'd ask any way…"

"Well, yes we do," William said, licking his lips in a way that made her skin crawl. "I actually take on many students like yourself, so we're very used to creating a schedule that works for us all."

"If you give me the chance, I promise you won't regret it," Tyler said, a flare of hope rising in her chest.

William smiled at her but for some reason, it left her feeling queasy. He reached out and took a resume out of her hand, his fingers brushing against hers as he did so. Uncomfortable at the contact, Tyler had to fight the urge to back away, not wanting to give him any reason to take offense. She stood there, bottling her unease as he read over her information.

"You went to Mayfield High School? That's an expensive private school, your parents must have had money to send you there. Why would you need a job if they can afford somewhere like that?"

Tyler thought the questioning had crossed over into private territory, but at least he was interested in her, which she was sure that was a good thing. "They passed away… earlier this year," was all she managed to reply. Gripping her hands into tight fists, Tyler willed herself not to feel the pain that always came with mentioning them.

"Oh, that is a terrible shame," he said as his pupils seemed to grow larger. Suddenly he clapped his hands together, startling her. "Well, I believe I have heard enough. I'm delighted to welcome you to the team Tyler. You'll be on minimum wage, to begin with, but you'll also get a twenty-five percent discount for the store, so it's not amazing, but it's better than a poke in the eye right?" He winked at her.

"I got the job?" Tyler asked, a little shell-shocked. "I haven't even filled in an application form?"

William shrugged. "That's just a formality. If you head over to the customer service desk and ask Catherine for one now, you can fill it out and leave it with her."

Tyler couldn't believe her good luck. "Thank you! I promise I won't let you down!"

He took her hand in his to shake it. "I'm looking forward to us working together," he said.

Tyler was so elated by the thought of having some money coming in that she pushed aside the uneasy feeling in the pit of her stomach that he caused. He was nice enough, so it made no sense why she felt so strange around him. More than that, she needed this job, so uncomfortable feeling or not, she was just going to have to deal with it.

THIRTY-FOUR

S un streamed in through the floor-to-ceiling windows of the classroom.

Sequestered in the back row of the large class, Cassie studied each of her fellow students walking into the room. As she had done with all her classes yesterday, she had arrived in advance so she could pick a seat at the back where she could see everyone. While it was important that she do well in this class, her grades weren't the reason she arrived ten minutes early to each lesson.

She needed to check out the competition.

She wasn't sure when this need first surfaced. Thinking back, it was possible that she had started this tradition way back in middle school. She had been a chubby girl who had needed to wear ugly silver braces on her teeth, the ones that wcrc impossible to clean and regularly caused canker sores in her mouth. Her parents had laughed off her fears, insisting that no one would even notice them, but on her first day of wearing them, cruel things were said, things that left Cassie crying into her pillow. She hadn't been able to confide in her mother. How could she? Her stunning mom would never know what it was like to be ugly. She couldn't go anywhere without people turning her way, their admiration clear for all to see. Cassie was nothing but a blight in her mother's bright light.

It was cold being in the shade her entire life.

After that day at school, Cassie really began to notice not just how people looked at her, but how they looked at her mother. No matter how anyone protested, she had seen the benefits that came with good looks. Her mom had never had to wait for a table at a restaurant and they were always seated at the best table — front and center of the action. She noticed too that men, in particular, were quick to offer any help they could. If her mom finished a drink, the waiter would be there to refill it before she could even turn to look for them.

Then there were the free things.

Although her mom had plenty of money, people kept giving her freebies, from clothes, to make-up that was passed on to her after her shoots, to household products — and even a car! A local dealership had given her mom a car in exchange for a picture of her driving it. The picture still hung now, suspended from the ceiling in his showroom, blown up to fifty times its original size.

Cassie wanted adulation like that. Craved it in fact. Which was why she had taken to studying good-looking people. She wanted to see how they acted, how they dressed, what they did that made them so special. As the students started to trickle in, Cassie waited. She knew it wouldn't take long.

Within a few moments, it happened.

A group of students came in, talking and joking together. There were three girls, the middle one she immediately noticed was the prettiest of the three. A group of guys had clearly noticed too as they were right behind her, jostling each other to get her attention. As they filed in, Cassie realized with a start that she knew one of the guys.

It was Trip. The guy from Tonic two nights ago.

The one who had blanked her so cruelly.

Despite his treatment of her, she still found herself admiring his glossy hair and muscular arms. He carried himself with such an air of confidence, who wouldn't be attracted to him? Those girls certainly were. They giggled at his every word, batting their eyelashes at him. He seemed most taken with the brunette, smiling down at her with so much charm Cassie wouldn't be surprised if his teeth started to glint.

The girl actually looked a lot like Marley. She had the same kind of curvy-but-slim figure Cassie could only dream of having. Long legs that went on forever that looked amazing even in jeggings, something Cassie and her dumpy legs could never get away with. She even dressed in a style similar to Marley, with the casual ease that spoke so much of how she took her appearance for granted. The orange top should not have worked with those bright blue pants, and why was she wearing ankle boots in the summer? Didn't her feet get hot? On an average person, the outfit would have been ridiculous, but on her, she could have stepped out of a catalog.

Cassie spent the rest of the class ignoring the syllabus talk, studying the two instead. Trip was as handsome in profile as he was face-on, maybe even better. She found herself daydreaming about the two of them dating. They'd go for a nice meal where Cassie would only have a salad, of course, followed by a romantic walk along the river. At the end of their date, he would lean in close and give her her first kiss…

When class finished, Cassie was jolted out of her daydream by the student next to her, struggling to get past. "Are you going to sit there all day or what?" he demanded.

Blushing, she grabbed her things, joining the rest of the exodus, bumping into someone next to her. She looked up to apologize only to find herself staring into Trip's face for the second time.

And he looked just as he had the last time he had seen her.

"Two times in three days. You sure you're not stalking me?"

"No," Cassie stammered as shyness took hold, flooding her body with awkwardness.

"You sure are brave, I'll give you that. I wouldn't be able to show my face so soon if I had embarrassed myself as badly as you had the other night. Good for you," he said, not actually meaning to be cruel, as he pushed past her to chase after the brunette.

Cassie didn't respond, rooted to the spot as a burning shame rose inside. All sounds blurred into one as she moved with the crowd without really seeing anything. She had hoped that the other night's travesty would be forgotten by all, but of course, that was too much to ask for.

Feeling the sting of tears, she pushed through the students until she came to the restroom. Bursting inside, she hurled her bag to the ground, grabbed the edge of a sink with each hand, glaring at herself in the mirror. Her rage was so great that she could almost see the steam coming out from her ears. Thankfully, the restroom was empty. Glaring at her reflection, she squeezed the sink until her knuckles turned white, she felt like her hands would break.

Did you hear what he said about you? He couldn't even look at you without flinching. Why do you have to be so ugly? Why can't you be pretty like… like that girl or Marley?

She has those amazing eyes and those lush lips that all the boys want to kiss. Even her nose is small and cute and perfect. And her hair, how does it look like she just stepped out of a salon, especially when you have to get yours done twice a month to not even look half as good? You're so hideous no guy is ever going to fall for you. Why can't you just look like Marley?

Closing her eyes, Cassie felt the thought consume her. If she looked like Marley, life would be so easy. All she really wanted was a break away from herself. She wanted to know how it would feel to be in her face and body. That wasn't a crime, was it?

Opening her eyes, black dots blurred her vision. She waited until they faded away leaving her with...

Marley's face.

Wait, what?

Blinking the fog away, Cassie moved closer to the mirror. Instead of her own face, she now wore Marley's. Startled, her eyes — Marley's eyes — grew wide with shock. Reaching up, Cassie examined her new face with her fingers only to find it wasn't her imagination. Her face had somehow turned into Marley's.

This must be what happened the other night! When I wore that other guy's face.

Was this her power?

Was she able to change her face into someone else's? As the thought took hold, Cassie found herself grinning from ear to ear. If that was the case, she could be whoever she wanted, whenever she wanted! Heck, maybe she wouldn't have to be her anymore! Thrilled with her discovery, Cassie reached for her phone to text the others her news when a couple of girls crashed into the restroom making her jump.

What if they knew Marley and started talking to her?

Other than a cursory glance her way, however, they didn't give her another look. Turning back to the mirror, Cassie saw that her natural face had returned. Picking up her bag from the floor, she hurried out of there, barely able to contain her excitement.

THIRTY-FIVE

Ten missed calls and just as many voicemails.

Eve stared down at her phone, swiping irritably away from her rapidly growing missed calls log. The others had been calling practically nonstop over the last twenty-four hours. She had refused to take any of their calls.

They knew she was safe; she wasn't a jerk after all. She had texted them to let them know as much, but then the flood of calls and messages had come, updating her on the latest events, begging her to get in touch with them. When would they get the hint that she didn't want any part of this?

As if Christian's death wasn't enough, or their dark powers, which none of them knew how to control yet, now Marley was being haunted by more than one ghost. Eve wasn't planning on hanging around long enough for when the ghost became bored and decided to go for her.

And what about the guy Christian kept warning them about? Now that Eve had some time on her own, she was able to regroup, to consider things. There wasn't any proof to what they were being told: who was to say Christian wasn't lying? Hell, what if Marley was? They only had her word. Why should Eve risk her life to trust a girl she had only known for a few days? Then there was the whole criminal investigation that was being conducted. Although they had yet to hear from the two cops, she knew it was coming. When they couldn't find a logical explanation for the hole in the church roof, they would come back to question them, even if it was just to finish off paperwork. She could not afford to have them sniffing around her, not after the *thing-that-happened.*

She had to stay as far away from the po-po as she could.

Music played in Shaken and Stirred, the bar Si managed. Not so loud that it would drown out any conversation, but loud enough that she could avoid speaking to people if she didn't want to. It was a low-key place, more like a British pub in design than an American bar. It came with oak-beamed ceilings, lead windows, and scratched wooden floors that hadn't seen a polish this side of the century. If people wanted cool, they went elsewhere.

Staring across the crowd, her eyes found her brother, chatting with a group of locals while picking up their empty glasses. The group laughed at something he was saying as Eve felt a deep flush of appreciation for him. She didn't know how she would have coped with any of the past year if it wasn't for him. He was her rock, though she knew that wouldn't be the case forever. Si was a catch, and one day girls would begin to notice. She dreaded the day when he would come home with a girlfriend when it wouldn't be just the two of them anymore. She knew it was selfish to feel that way, but when the world had shown her its true colors, the only constant in her life was him. It was hard to even consider letting him go.

A pair of unfamiliar faces walked up to the bar, gesturing at her, pulling her out of her thoughts. They wore cheap-looking black denim jackets and jeans with a white

T-shirt. They were so closely dressed they must shop in the same Walmart.

"Two beers, sunshine," one of them said as they both laughed at his wit.

Seriously? They were mocking her even though they wouldn't be winning any beauty competitions this lifetime. One of them was clearly hunched over having some kind of issue with his back.

Despite how often it happened, she still felt a small stab of pain when complete strangers felt the need to ridicule her appearance. It was her choice to look like this. She wasn't hurting anyone, so why did they feel the need to be cruel? They had no idea what she had gone through. That to hide under this many layers of makeup was the only way she felt safe enough to leave her house.

Shoving her emotions down, she grabbed two-pint glasses expertly filling them from the tap. Having turned twenty-one a few months back, she was finally old enough to help out in the bar, although she mostly came here for the company. The house could get too quiet at times, and with the silence came the bad memories.

She set the beer on the counter then waited for them to pay her. The taller of the two who had a seriously bad skin condition on his face, took out his wallet then stopped, leaning towards her.

"Tell me something, do you actually think that look is attractive?"

Eve was so taken aback by his comment that she didn't immediately reply. His friend laughed as if he'd just said the funniest thing in the world.

"I don't mind the makeup, it's not like I ever look at their faces," Hunchback said.

"You should take the poor girl out then, I'm sure she'd appreciate the charity," Bad-Skin laughed.

Rage overwhelmed her, making her tremble from head to toe. A million retorts ran through her mind but they crashed into one another until they were one big jumble. She wanted so badly to put them in their place, but it was like she'd lost the power of speech and her inability just made her all the madder.

Opening her mouth to say something clever, or really just anything at all, the moment was suddenly interrupted by the appearance of Si. Not noticing her reaction, he smiled at the men and told them the cost of the drinks. They paid, took their drinks, then left without another glance at Eve. She stood there, bristling with anger as with growing horror, she felt the sting of tears prick her eyes. Why, when she felt such rage, did she also want to cry? This wasn't something that happened to guys. When they got angry, they were strong, forceful, so why was she so pathetic and weak?

Completely oblivious to the turmoil going on inside her, Si shot her a confused look. "You OK? You look a little funny."

It was on the tip of her tongue to spill everything, but she stopped herself from explaining. What would it solve? He'd get angry and approach the two guys. There would be some kind of altercation. Worst case scenario, they'd gang up on him. Si could get hurt, and that she wouldn't allow to happen, not on her watch. She'd swallow the pain as she always did. She'd handle it on her own.

"Nothing… I'm not feeling well is all."

His forehead furrowed with concern as sympathy shone from his eyes. "It's not that busy tonight, why don't you go home and rest?"

Still numb from the guys' insults, she nodded, grateful that she could get out of there and not have to deal with those two again.

"You want to use the car? I can ask one of the others for a lift home," Si asked. When she worked here, she usually went home in the car with him, but since they only had the one car and he'd need to lock up, she shook her head.

"I'll be fine. I'll grab a taxi."

Nodding, Si turned away, already distracted by another customer waving a drinks menu at him. Walking to the staff room located in the back of the bar, Eve grabbed her purse, slipped on her jacket, then stepped out of the back door into the alley where staff came and went. The door clicked closed behind her as she took in the ominous black sky. The streets were slick from another bout of recent rain, the air heavy with tension. She knew without a doubt that more rain would be coming tonight, could almost taste the iron on her tongue. Pulling up the collar of her jacket, she started the short walk from the alleyway to the street where she could flag down a taxi when a bottle rolled past on the ground behind her.

Startled, she spun around.

The two guys from the bar stood behind her, their leers distorted by the heavy shadows cast down from a streetlamp until their mouths looked unnaturally wide.

"Oh look who we have here," Bad-Skin said.

"Seems like she couldn't get enough of us after all," said Hunchback.

Seeing them, Eve felt her stomach plummet and fear took hold. Despite all the girls' warnings, here she was alone in the alley with not one but two abusive jerks. While she knew they were probably just bullies out for a cheap thrill, she also realized they could be something much worse. Yearbook pictures of the recent student murders flashed across her mind as details of their deaths suddenly came at her. Although Christian had attributed the murders to Michael, he could be wrong... it could be the two standing before her who had committed the crimes.

And she could be next on their list.

She glanced back at the door to the bar, knowing safety lay within but the two blocked her path. She looked the other way, to the street which seemed much further away right now. She knew she wouldn't make it there before something happened. Swallowing her fear, she forced herself to stand taller.

"Leave me alone," she said, hating herself for the wobble at the end of the sentence.

"She speaks!" Hunchback said.

"Only just," Bad-Skin mocked. "Though it was hardly worth the effort."

"Go away or I'll scream for help," Eve said, fully prepared to make good on her threat.

"Who exactly do you think will hear you?" Hunchback said, advancing slowly.

"Who exactly do you think will care?" Bad-Skin taunted, echoing his buddy's words.

Suddenly, they launched themselves at her! Hunchback grabbed hold of her wrists, twisting until they were behind her back as Bad-Skin seized her shoulders and lunged towards her. Eve struggled desperately trying to reach the door, terror constricting her throat so that all that would come out was a cracked yelp. Flashbacks of another time and another attack assaulted her, its awful memory nearly crippling her completely.

No… this can't be happening.

Not again.

They forced her away from the door until they ended up directly beneath the streetlamp. Suddenly, she saw her attacker's faces *morph* until their mouths grew even wider as wicked fangs sprang out from behind their lips. Their eyes also changed, the pupils narrowing into reptilian-like slits. At that moment, she knew with crystal clarity that these guys weren't *human*.

Terrified beyond all reason, Eve bucked wildly, trying to shake them loose but they had a death grip on her, their hands cutting into her skin. She looked down to see that their fingers had elongated, the nails forming into wickedly sharp talons that were drawing blood. Her blood. At the sight of it, Bad-Skin licked his lips, his eyes turning bright with hunger…

And Eve knew that she would die.

As the sounds of her struggle dulled, she felt the air become electric and the rush of *others* in her mind. She didn't know what the "others" were exactly, she just suddenly knew she wasn't alone. Above the grunts of her inhuman attackers came a scuttling sound that echoed off the alley walls. They heard it too as they abruptly stopped, their heads tilted to the ground where the sounds were coming from. Suddenly, streams of rats burst out from behind trash cans and boxes, running out from the surrounding air vents, then the sewers. Swarming around the guys, they scurried up their legs, crawling all over their bodies until they were one heaving, pulsating mass of rodents. Stunned, they released Eve who backed away from them.

Then the rats started to bite.

First one, then all of them. They burrowed inside their clothing, up along their pant legs, clawing and snapping at their naked flesh, but they left Eve alone.

She, they protected.

Bloody gashes appeared as the rats attacked furiously, until the two ran screaming away, the rats chasing after them leaving Eve trembling in their wake. Bolting to the street, she watched as her attackers melted into the blackness, her rodent friends still pursuing them. Flagging a taxi, she jumped inside and gave her address. Once back home, she ran into her room, slamming the door closed behind her. There in the safety of her home, she took out her phone and made the call. When Marley's relieved voice answered, Eve spoke urgently.

"Tell Christian I'm ready. I'm ready to learn about what I am and what I have to do."

With Tweedle Dee and Tweedle Dumb out dealing with the one girl who didn't live in the college, Michael made his way to Trinity himself, to see if he could get past the police presence. Unlike last night, it had ended up being far easier than he had imaged as the Square was empty thanks to the return of this morning's storm.

Lightening streaked across the sky as an answering rumble tore through the heavens. Rain poured down, soaking him to the skin, but Michael welcomed the feeling. Where he was from, the heat was arid and never-ending, so the water soaking into him was a refreshing feeling that made him tingle to the core.

Then again, that could just be due to his nearing the search.

As the church had recently suffered from "inexplicable" damage, its doors were now locked, the public kept away in case of falling debris. Michael stood at the front door, tossing a quick glance around the square. Other than him, there was only one poor soul, sprinting through the square holding a plastic bag over his head to shelter from the rain. He was far enough away that he wouldn't hear what would happen next. Still, to be cautious, Michael waited until the next flash of light illuminated the scenery before smashing through the doors as easily as if they were paper.

One door flew across the room, torn from its hinges, while the other broke in half, crashing to the ground. No one would hear it, however, the sound of his destruction covered by another crack of thunder.

Leaves blew into the church, whipping past Michael's legs as he made his way through the pews to an arched doorway in the back. A steep set of stone stairs spiraled downward into the darkness. Turning on a flashlight, Michael shone the light ahead of him as he worked his way down well-trodden steps. They were an original feature and lead to the basement. He knew this as he had long studied the architecture of this place, as he had with all the historical buildings in the area.

Old buildings often held great secrets.

His foot landed on a cobbled stone floor. Shining the flashlight down, Michael saw that the floor of the room was covered in a giant mosaic made of hand-cut stone tiles that glinted in the light.

This was it! Excitement bubbled up, and he had to resist the urge to dance.

He moved across the floor, studying the mosaic, which depicted an impressive army of Angels hovering in the sky on their wings, their weapons aimed down in warning to any who might be foolish enough to incur their wrath.

He almost snorted with derision.

Like they would ever dirty their hands long enough to fly down from their high perches. He couldn't even think of the last time when an honest-to-God Angel had been spotted. If they had ever existed, they had long died out, which suited him just fine.

The beam of light stopped on a face he recognized. God's most powerful and trusted Archangel, coincidentally also named Michael. The irony did not escape him. Calling up his magic power, Michael channeled it between his hands. A swirl of energy crackled between them that he directed at the Archangel's face. As before with the door, a large hole appeared where the Archangel's face had been, revealing an endless pit below.

Magic surged from the mosaic now that it had been broken, gushing into him, filling him with more power than he had ever felt before. He was awash with so much power that he was almost thrust to the floor before he was able to take it all in. As he took the time to recover, he felt the presence in his mind.

"You have done well," it said in that low, rumbling voice that terrified even him.

"Thank you," Michael said, pride making his chest swell. "One of five."

"One of five," the voice in his mind repeated.

———

Christian watched helplessly as the girls Facetimed Eve, trying to comfort her as she relayed what had happened. By her description, he knew exactly who had attacked her.

Demons.

She had escaped this time. The next, maybe they wouldn't be so lucky. The girls were ready to listen now, to find out what they needed to do. Having finished relating her tale, they waited for her to have a moment to catch herself when the room was suddenly painted in an eerie red light.

They moved towards the window to see it wasn't just the room, but the entire city that now sat under a cloud of red. There in the sky, the full moon loomed before them, but under this strange light, the distant planetoid looked red.

"What's going on?" Marley asked nervously.

Seeing the Blood Moon, Christian had to swallow his fear. The time for guessing had passed. He knew what Michael was up to now.

And he was terrified.

"It's beginning…"

TWISTED MAGIC

3: SEE NO EVIL

JO HO

THIRTY-SIX

An unnatural light bathed the city in an eerie red wash.

As if the world was being viewed beneath a filter, everything had that crimson tone, from the full moon blazing down from the night sky, to the glistening sidewalks below, still wet from the recent rain. People stopped dead in the streets, their faces tilted upward to study the bizarre sight. Only Christian knew what the red light signified.

It was a dire warning.

Marley held her phone in her hand, Eve on the other end of the FaceTime video call. They could see her looking at the same light from inside her own bedroom, all the way across town. A lead weight settled in Christian's stomach, threatening to become an explosion. He finally knew what Michael was up to.

And it was far worse than he had ever thought it would be.

His already-pale face became even whiter as he fought to gain control of his fear. Whatever issues he had previously had with the girls were immediately set aside. It wasn't important. Nothing was important other than stopping Michael from continuing his mission.

"Marley, I need you to speak to the others for me," he began, voice tight with tension. Hearing his grave tone, she moved away from the window, her brow wrinkled in concern.

"What is it?" she asked.

Christian opened his mouth to explain the cause of the red light when, to his utter horror, he felt that familiar pull in his stomach that signaled he was about to be yanked back into his own world. The Spirit World. Eyes flaring open in alarm, he reached out to Marley but couldn't stop the inevitable from happening. He vanished.

Marley's mouth dropped open, not believing her eyes. "Are you kidding me?" She cried, her voice rising up an octave.

"What happened?" Tyler asked.

"Christian was about to say something then disappeared. It sounded important."

"Was he going to explain what the red light is?" Cassie gestured outside.

Marley shrugged. "Your guess is as good as mine. I can't believe he keeps disappearing like that, right when things get bad."

"Maybe we're not the only ones who need to learn about our powers maybe he needs to learn how to appear to you too," came Eve's sensible voice from inside the phone.

Still, Marley couldn't help the sunken feeling that made her body feel heavy and sluggish. What were they supposed to do without him when he was the only one who knew anything?

Tyler and Cassie started talking then, voicing their fears. Marley tuned them out, her own worries taking over. Her eyes drifted over to the window again as she stared out at that unnatural red sky when something about it caught her attention.

She blinked, letting her eyes readjust, staring harder. "Guys, does the red look like it's stronger above that building?"

The chatter died immediately as they gathered around her to look at the building she pointed to. From this distance, all they could see was a dark shape with some kind of spire attached to it.

"Yeah, it does," Tyler agreed.

"We should see if we can find out what building that is," Cassie said, suddenly pumped and excited. "Maybe we'll find some kind of clue there."

"That's actually a great idea. Well done, Cassie," Eve said. Marley was sure she didn't mean it to sound as patronizing as it did. Luckily Cassie didn't seem to have noticed, grinning as she was, pleased by the compliment.

"Do you mind if I don't come," Eve asked, her voice sounding quiet through the phone. "It's just, I'm on my own right now, and after the attack at the bar, I could do with a break..." She trailed off, letting the others fill in the rest of her thoughts in their heads.

"I'm sure we'll be fine," Marley answered for the group. "We'll keep you on the phone so you can see what we see."

"Thanks," Eve replied, shooting her a grateful look, relieved to stay home where she would be safe.

Outside, the streets were hushed, as if the red light had muffled all sound. Everywhere they went, people stood huddled in pairs or groups, staring up at the sky, wondering at the phenomenon. The eerie glow had sent the city into a watchful wariness, causing the usually-packed restaurants to be empty tonight.

The girls walked past the eateries, guided by the

strongest point of the red light. They weaved through quiets streets without chatting their senses honed for possible danger, until the roads turned into a pedestrianized zone. They crossed into an area that seemed familiar, where the ageless buildings of the past met the modern soaring skyscrapers of the future.

"Copley Square!" Tyler exclaimed suddenly breaking the silence, making Marley jump. "We're back here again?"

Marley stared at where the red light was concentrated the most. It shone like a beacon from a singular building. Her stomach clenched tighter when she recognized it.

"It's coming from Trinity Church." She barely managed to get the words out of her mouth. She took in a deep, slow breath, her heart thumping wildly in her chest. Even without Christian there, the guilt was overwhelming. They would have to go inside, to the scene of the crime.

She would be faced with her actions once again.

If the others knew how she felt, they didn't let on. Tyler led the way to the church, Cassie following closely behind. Willing her feet to move, Marley lagged behind them. She kept her eyes fixed on a point dead ahead, praying silently that nothing bad would happen.

Arriving at the church entrance, they stopped. The doors had been blown inward by something powerful. Marley would've known instinctively that no human hand could have caused it, even if she hadn't been able to see the traces of magic that had been left behind. It was like a cloud of black with blinking lights inside that hovered at the edge of the doors.

"Do you guys see that?" she asked.

"Yeah," Tyler confirmed as Cassie and Eve both nodded.

Not knowing whether it would harm them, they stepped around it, giving it a wide berth. They slowly entered the church, walking into the sanctuary. There on the floor lay the cross that had been destroyed, reminding them of their first experience here. This was where they had thought they were saving the good guy.

This was where Marley had killed Christian.

Even though his body wasn't there anymore, Marley could see it so vividly that her gut churned from the memory alone.

She could still see his awful expression, that realisation on his face for the split second he had known before she did, that she had killed him. Her fingers clenched reflexively, feeling his pulsating heart between them again. If Marley could rewind time, she would take them back to that moment. She wouldn't have killed Christian. She would have stopped to hear what he had been trying so desperately to tell her. They would have put an end to Michael. Then the only thing she would have to worry about was finishing school.

Unfortunately, that wasn't a power any of them had.

She moved past the spot where Christian had died in a daze, her feet seemingly having a mind of their own. The girls lead the way forward, Marley following blindly behind. She went down the stone steps, keeping her mind blank. It wasn't until she set foot in the basement that she was able to think again. The same black sparkling cloud she had seen upstairs hovered over a mosaic that covered the entire floor. A large chunk of the mosaic had been broken revealing a gaping hole below.

It was from out of this hole that the brilliant red light flared out.

Flinching from the brightness of it, moving closer, Marley felt a strange feeling, a magic pull of some kind coming from it.

"Can you feel that? It's like something's pulling me towards the hole, but only when I got close to it." she said. She knelt down by the edge of the hole, angling her phone so Eve could get a better look. Tyler walked the perimeter of the mosaic, treading carefully.

"Yes. There's some kind of force drawing me towards it."

"I feel it too," Cassie supplied.

"Well, now we know what's causing that red sky. If only we knew what it actually meant. The only other thing in here is this mosaic. Where it's been broken is where that magic cloud is most focused," Tyler observed.

"Get away from that!" Christian's voice yelled suddenly, straight into Marley's ear. She jumped, repeating his message as she searched the area for him, finding him at the foot of the stairs.

"Stop doing that!" she snapped, a hand flying to her chest. "You can't keep vanishing then reappearing without any notice! You're going to give me a heart attack!"

His face twisted into what passed as an apology. "It's not like I have any real control over when I appear and disappear. If it's any consolation, I get just as startled as you when it happens."

While they spoke, the others watched her, their expressions bemused, but it quickly sank in that Christian was back.

"Well, it's about time," Eve exclaimed. "Can he explain what's going on?"

"Yes, just tell them to back away from the magic," he warned. Marley repeated him then waited for an explanation. "That cloud is the physical trace that magic leaves behind. I mentioned this to you before, how magical beings can see it? Well, that black color means the magic that was used here was black magic."

"Black magic?" Cassie asked, her eyes shining with confusion.

"Yes. There are two types of magic, white and black. White is good magic: an extension of nature, it's typically used to heal, help, nurture or grow. Black magic is the opposite. It takes from nature and is used for evil purposes, to destroy."

Nervously, Tyler backed away from the black cloud. "OK, but why is it here? Why is that red light coming out of that hole? When you disappeared, we followed it all the way here…"

Christian hesitated, steeling himself for what he knew they weren't ready to hear. Yet, hear it they must. "Centuries ago, long before technology came into the world, magic was much more common than it is today. Demons, vampires, witches…. they weren't the stuff of folklore. They were real. And so was the threat of evil. Power has always been able to corrupt which is why, amongst other things, The Society of Guardians was created." He stopped, waiting as Marley relayed his words.

"In response to one of the greatest evils mankind has ever faced, supernatural seals were created to keep that kind of evil from ever crossing into our world again. They were strategically placed around the world in the areas where magic was strongest. This very city with its dark history has five seals of its own, but Michael has just broken one of them. That is why the red light is coming out of that hole, why it appeared to color the sky, painting the full moon red. A Blood Moon — which we now call an eclipse — has typically prophesied the end of days. It was even written in the Bible. The red light is a warning that the First Seal is broken. It is a warning of what might be to come."

Marley tried to understand, but his words whipped around in her head causing only confusion. "I don't understand, what we're seeing tonight is The Blood Moon that's mentioned in the Bible?" The passage he referred to ran through her mind.

The sun will turn into darkness, and the moon into blood, before the great and terrible day of the Lord comes.

She had her dad to thank for that and the Bible classes she attended every Sunday as a kid.

"No. It's not a real Blood Moon. That's not happening for another few weeks."

"How are you so sure that this isn't the real thing?" Cassie asked, wringing her hands nervously.

"Because I know the dates of all the future eclipses," Christian replied. "They were practically the first thing I memorized. Also, I have an app on my phone. Had," he finished. "This is just a warning that the real one is imminent."

"So what exactly does breaking this first seal mean?" Eve asked, voicing the thought on all their minds.

"It means something is coming. Something that could signify the end of the world."

Even as the words left her mouth, Marley felt the room spin. Was he for real?

"Hold up," Tyler said. "Are you saying literal end-of-the-world? This isn't like that Mayan Calendar scenario in 2012?"

"Unfortunately, no. The threat is very real."

Staring at the ground, Marley studied the angels depicted on the tiles, focusing on the area that was broken. "This mosaic, this was one of the seals?"

"It must be. No one actually knows what the seals are, they kept them secret so they couldn't be destroyed," Christian informed them. "Except, Michael found this one somehow."

"Can't we just put the mosaic back together again? I was pretty good at puzzles as a kid," Cassie asked hopefully. Christian shook his head, regret making his eyes bright.

"That's not how this works."

Marley paced back and forth, several thoughts racing through her mind. "Does this mean the other seals are also mosaics? If that's the case it shouldn't be too hard to find them?"

"I don't think it will be as easy as that. It's a pretty terrible hiding place if that's what they all are," came Eve's sensible voice from the phone.

Marley sighed, knowing that she was right. "I just wanted us to get a break."

Seeing their glum faces, Christian forced himself to sound optimistic, even though he felt anything but. The fragile group were hanging by a thread. While he wasn't completely convinced about them yet, he also knew there wasn't anything he could do on his own. "Don't forget you have your powers too. I'm sure there'll be a way for you to use them to locate the rest."

"If we have to use our powers, then we're pretty much screwed. I can barely figure out mine," Cassie said, unable to hide how hopeless this all seemed.

"If Michael found one of these already, doesn't that mean he can find them all?" Marley asked quietly, feeling an enormous weight on her shoulders that threatened to crush her.

Christian tried to keep his face stoic. He couldn't let them see his own fear.

"Tomorrow after your classes, we'll meet up. I will try to help you with your powers. Until then, we have to hope that Michael doesn't find out where the next seal is before you do."

THIRTY-SEVEN

S ALEM, 1693.
As the night drew close, another body was uncovered.

It was a young man this time, discovered floating amongst the river reeds. His bloated body bore signs of the struggle The Four had come to expect. This man had been strong, stronger than the previous female victims, though he had met the same fate. His face was twisted into a perpetual scream of agony.

The taint of black magic lingered over him too.

Mary pulled the sheet over his head, knowing she would never erase the look on his face from her mind. This made six. Six young people in about as many weeks all murdered in the same manner; their necks snapped with such force that it had caused a clean break. While they could see the touch of black magic that hovered over him, The Four kept that information to themselves. It would serve nothing to reveal its existence to the vil-lagers. This knowledge would only frighten them further. People were scared of what they didn't understand. It was this way throughout history and it would be the same in the future. There was plenty to be fearful of already without adding this extra layer.

A few nights ago, Esther had returned from a simple hunting trip to find a headless chicken lying across the doorway of their host's home. The next morning, they were awakened to screams from the children when they discovered archaic symbols smeared onto their walls with chicken blood. Tabitha had recognized some of the symbols from her studies. Traditionally, the symbols were used to heal, but as they were in their upside-down state, they could also be used to destroy. The discovery filled The Four with cold fingers of dread.

Frightened, not understanding what was happening, the villagers had asked them to leave. Though they knew the sisters would never cause them harm, they still wanted nothing more to do with their "kind". Understanding this, The Four journeyed to the next village, a journey that would take several days to make.

They traveled under the blistering sun with barely any food or water, until their feet hurt and Catherine's delicate skin burned. The new village, perched by the great river, didn't see many visitors and received even less outside news. They were welcomed with open arms.

The sisters administered their healing to the sick or elderly. They ate with the families and danced with them around the fire at night as they played their fiddles, singing harmoniously. After the night's entertainment, they retreated to the barn, making their beds amongst the cattle, and playful cats who kept the place free of mice.

One glorious day, a day filled with a breeze that eased some of the sun's heat, relieved to have a respite from the horror of the previous village, The Four decided to go fishing. Mary had rolled up her skirt, letting her feet dangle into the water as her sisters chatted around her when, out of the corner of her eye she caught a hint of that black magic cloud. Startled, she did not move, blinking into the sun in case she had made a mistake. As she wondered whether she should mention it, something brushed by the soles of her feet. Looking into the deep blue water, she was horrified when a bloated face stared back up at her.

She shot up to her feet, calling for her sisters. Someone was practicing black magic and it seemed they were doing it around them. Mary did not want to confront the thought that entered her mind. Though the facts were mounting up, though Mary did not want to believe it, she knew why the black magic had followed them.

The killer was trying to make it seem that they were the ones performing the crimes.

Mary looked at her sisters shaken to the core by this revelation.

"Who would want to harm us so?"

THIRTY-EIGHT

Her phone beeped on the bedside table, waking her from sleep.

Tyler woke instantly, the sharp claw of fear digging into her. The pre-dawn sky loomed pink and blue without any of last night's red lingering, but that wasn't what frightened her. It was too early for a message from anyone other than Ally, and she knew better than to text her this early unless there was a problem.

Sitting up in bed, Tyler picked up her phone to check her messages, instead of one from Ally, however, there was a text from an unknown number:

Tyler, it's William from Star Market. We are down a worker due to illness so we'll need you here today. Can you come at three pm?

Tyler blinked, rereading the message. Did managers usually text their employees? It seemed personal somehow like they were already friends. Still, she was thrilled: the sooner she started working, the sooner she'd be paid. With Ally's birthday looming, she needed to make it as special as possible under the circumstances. She sent a reply confirming that she could start and was in the shower before she remembered she'd be missing Christian's magic lesson. Her forehead creased into a frown, knowing he'd be upset with her but she couldn't go back on her word now, not before she'd made a good first impression on the manager. She'd have to get the cliff notes from the girls when she was done.

Classes went by without anything of interest happening which Tyler was thankful for. After her chemical explosions previously, she now approached each lab class with trepidation. There was talk of last night's strange light among the students though most reasoned it away with logic. Some blamed it on light pollution, others thought it was a phenomenon similar to the one Sydney had experienced recently, where hurricane winds had pulled up red dust from the Australian deserts casting the city in a bizarre red light.

Of course, no such desert existed on the East Coast, but no one seemed to want to consider that option. She wasn't really surprised by this, considering how many adamantly denied climate change, even when the proof was impossible to miss. People were bizarre creatures.

When the time came for her to be at work, Tyler arrived with as much enthusiasm as a girl could have for starting work in a grocery store. It was a nice place. A warehouse-sized space, with colorful displays that brightened every corner and giant hanging signs announcing the deals for the week. The sensible prices weren't just popular with students, they were also loved by local families who piled their shopping carts high with produce while pushing their toddlers around.

She was greeted by William, hovering by the cash registers. His plump lips spread into a wide smile on her arrival.

"There she is, our newest member of the team!" he announced to no one in particular. "Come with me, I have your uniform in the changing rooms." He walked to a door marked with an "Employees Only" sign and opened it. Tyler followed after him as he led her through to a staff area, a lounge with tables, chairs and a tea/coffee station that also contained a microwave. A few employees had their breaks now, looking at her over their snacks with barely concealed boredom. New staff were a regular fixture here and not exciting at all it seemed. William guided her through the place, giving what was obviously a much-rehearsed speech complete with well-used asides that she found cringe-worthy but which he laughed at. The guy just had no idea how to be cool.

He explained what her role entailed which mainly involved stocking the shelves. If she was deemed a good worker, she would graduate to add cashier work to her description. Tyler took in his tour, trying not to compare her life now to how it had been just a few months ago, knowing her parents would roll in their graves if they knew what she was doing.

Not that there was anything wrong with this work: Tyler didn't have a problem with it. It was just that all her life she had been wealthy — or at least, that's what her parents had led them all to believe. They wanted the American Dream, to keep up with the Joneses and whatever other clichés were popular. They were already deep into debt before Ally's health issues had even begun. Once that had kicked in, things had spiraled rapidly downhill.

Until she wasn't just an orphan, she was broke too.

A picture of her parents flashed up into her mind. Her dad had his arms wrapped around her mom; both of them were laughing as they danced around in the kitchen before dragging Tyler and Ally in too. Their lives had been filled with silly, happy moments like that. The sudden pain that flashed into Tyler's chest was so intense, she had to dig her nails into her palms. She wanted to curl into a ball, to let the world know exactly how she felt about all she had lost. Instead, she willed herself to focus on William's annoying voice.

Oblivious to what was going on inside her, William grabbed some new clothes from a pile in the staff room and presented them to her with a flourish. "Your new uniform! Wear it well and with pride," he said, not a hint of irony in his voice. Tyler took them from him and waited for further instructions.

"You can change into them right here," he said, looking at her with a gleam in his eyes.

Tyler hesitated. Did he really mean right there, in the middle of the staff room in front of him? A few uncomfortable moments passed. When she didn't speak he suddenly laughed.

"Of course, I'm joking. The female changing rooms are that way. When you're done, meet me back here and I'll start you on your first task."

Not knowing how to reply, Tyler nodded, going into the changing room, but she could feel his eyes on her back all the way there. He was a little strange that was for sure. She put it down to social awkwardness; he didn't seem like the kind of man who had many friends. She was pretty sure he didn't have a girlfriend either.

Shrugging out of her clothes, she changed into the uniform then checked her appearance in the mirror. The striped shirt felt stiff with newness, its collar uncomfortable against her neck. The knee-high beige skirt was a little tight around her hips, hugging her butt a bit too much, but as she wasn't here for the fashion, Tyler figured it would have to do. Folding up her own clothes, she put them in an empty locker but kept her phone on her. Thankfully, the skirt had pockets. At least whoever had designed them had thought to include those. She hated it when female pants or skirts didn't have pockets. There were some occasions, like now, when a girl couldn't carry a handbag but still needed to carry a few items on her person.

Making her way back to William, he appraised her appearance with another of those too-wide smiles that made her uneasy for a reason she couldn't explain.

"Well, that fits you perfectly! Be careful now, you don't want the other women to get jealous and catty!"

Not knowing how she should take his comment, Tyler chose to ignore it. Putting his hand on her shoulder, he steered her towards the canned meat aisle. Handing her a pricing gun, he demonstrated how to use it then set her to task. He watched over her as she priced her first few cans, stacking them onto a shelf. After what seemed like a really long time — though was probably only a few minutes — he finally left.

It wasn't until he was gone that Tyler relaxed into the job at hand.

Letting her mind drift, she tried not to feel overwhelmed by the ache in her heart that her parents' death had left. At least she had the girls now; that was something she could be grateful for. Despite all that had happened, and all that was to come, at least she wasn't alone any more.

She wondered how their magic class was going.

THIRTY-NINE

"She definitely said she isn't coming?" Christian asked Marley for what seemed like the fifth time.

The four of them were sitting inside Eve's battered car, a 2006 blue Toyota Corolla that she shared with her brother. Other than a faded air freshener in the shape of the Jamaican flag that had expired long ago that hung from the rearview mirror, there were no other items in the vehicle. Wind whistled through a gap in one of the back windows that someone had tried — and failed — to fix with liberal amounts of gaffer tape.

"She can't, she has to work," Marley replied, wondering when he would finally accept her answer.

"But... you know, the end of the world," Christian replied flippantly. "What's more important than that?"

"You've never had to pay bills have you?" Marley asked, a little tired of his spiel. She was rewarded by his look of shame that proved her point. Apparently Guardians had their rent and everything else taken care of. It was an amazing deal... until someone killed you. "Of course she wanted to be here, but it's her first day, she can't *not* go, can she?"

The rest of the drive took place in silence as Christian sulked in the corner. He barked out the odd driving instruction but other than that, he was blessedly quiet. Eve drove through downtown, taking short cuts to avoid the traffic that only a native Bostonian would know. She was a careful driver, sticking to the legal limits and lights until they arrived at the waterfront area known as the Long Wharf.

The historic pier served as a dock for passenger ferries and sightseeing boats though the girls weren't here for either. Eve parked the car and they piled out. Following Christian's lead, Marley lead them down weaving paths behind several rundown buildings. The area consisted of dilapidated warehouses that hadn't been used in a while it seemed. All in all, it was a bizarre place to base any headquarters much less the Guardians' yet this is where Christian had insisted they go.

They finally stopped outside one of the worst-looking buildings. The loft style windows were painted black and the roof looked in serious need of repair though it stood soundly enough. Rusting steel panels enclosed the outside walls making the place seem even less welcoming than it already was.

"You're sure this is where he wants us to go?" Cassie asked, eyeing the building dubiously.

Marley nodded. "This is it." Moving to one of the steel panels, she reached into a rusting hole causing Eve and Cassie to grimace.

"I hope you've had your tetanus shot," Eve warned.

"Relax, he says this is all for show," Marley replied as she turned to look at the air beside her. "Right?"

Christian nodded reassuringly. "Just reach in, you should feel the numbered panel in a second. The keycode is: 100214."

Blindly feeling around, Marley's fingers could find only eroded metal until they brushed against the smooth edge of a number pad. Unable to see it, she had to rely on her memory for the position of the keys. Biting the corner of her lip, she pressed the numbers one by one, listening to the corresponding key tone. At the last number, a beep sounded and the wall of steel slid sideways revealing a dark hallway beyond.

"Well, that was unexpected," Eve said arching a painted black brow.

Marley lead the way inside, the others following close behind. When they were all inside, the steel wall automatically shut behind them, locking them in. Eve spun around, not liking the closed quarters.

"How do we get out again if we need to?" she asked unable to hide the edge of panic in her voice. Marley was surprised she seemed so concerned and would have attributed her fear to claustrophobia if not for the warehouse being so huge. Its ceilings reached some three stories above them so that couldn't be it.

Christian explained as Marley repeated his instructions. "You just have to stand in front of the doors and they should open. In case of a problem, the override button is over there." She pointed at a small panel on the wall beside the door, half hidden by shadow.

Knowing she could leave if she wanted to, Eve felt herself relax, glad she wouldn't have to explain herself. If they knew what she had gone through, they would feel the same way about enclosed spaces themselves.

Moving down the hall, Marley opened a door at the end then stood back, awed by the sight before her. A giant, fully-kitted-up training area stood before her. An Olympic-sized boxing ring sat in the very center of the room. The latest exercise machines and riot gear filled the rest of the place, there was even a wall lined with weapons of every kind. Along with the standard guns and knives one would expect, there were also wooden stakes, silver bullets and blades, and vials of what was probably holy water. Some of the weapons seemed like they dated back to medieval times, weapons such as engraved swords and rune-studded shields. There was pretty much the ability to wage war from this one room alone.

"Whoa," Eve said, impressed beyond belief. "It's like the Batcave."

"This is where Eric and I trained," Christian explained. "It's where all the Guardians in the region trained."

Something in his voice made Marley turn away from the kettlebell rack she had been studying.

"There are more than the two of you?"

"There were," he corrected. "The rest are dotted around the country. I've heard a few work abroad, but there are none on the East Coast anymore. I'm the last of them."

As always, Marley felt the crushing guilt that came whenever she was reminded of her part in his death. Swallowing dryly, she went back to her study of the room, hoping one of the other girls would change the subject. She was rewarded by Cassie's question.

"Can we train in here now? Can we use this place?"

Christian nodded. "That's why I've brought you. You should be safe in here. No one but us know it exists. Let's get ready for your first lesson."

Moments later, the girls were lined up several feet apart as Christian paced up and down the line, Marley repeating him word for word. In front of Cassie, they had placed a mirror so she could see herself. Other than that, there was nothing else to prepare for the lesson.

"That we know, the first time all of you connected with your power was at the church. Can you remember what you felt then?" Christian asked.

Marley closed her eyes, trying not to see him in front of that altar, right before she killed him. She trained her focus on the room instead, on what she could remember of the night.

"Fear. I was afraid that you were going to kill Michael

because I didn't know he was the bad guy at that time," she said.

"What about you, Eve?" he asked, turning to her.

Eve's eyes were also closed, but instead of being fearful, she looked angry. She dug her fingers into her hands, speaking in a clipped tone. "Rage. Anger."

"Why?" Christian asked.

"I thought you were that serial killer we'd been hearing about. I was furious that you had hurt others, that you were about to do it again."

"Hold on to that emotion, that might be what you need to manifest your power," he instructed, making his way to Cassie.

"What about you, Cassie? Can you remember how you felt that moment, right before the attack?"

"I was scared and confused. I didn't know what was happening and it freaked me out," she answered in a small voice as if she were afraid she had the wrong answer.

Christian nodded encouragingly even though she couldn't see it.

"If that's how you felt, recall it now. Picture yourself that night. What you saw. What you could hear and smell. Use every one of your senses to put you in the same emotional state."

Channeling his words, Marley tried to feel the same as she had that night, but all she could see were her hands inside of Christian then his startled green eyes as they looked at her in betrayal. Guilt burst inside her chest, the only emotion she could raise.

With it came the sudden realization that she couldn't do what he was asking.

What if that ghost woman came again? What would she do to her this time? Frustrated, she opened her eyes to see the others struggling too.

As Marley watched, Cassie's lips suddenly blew up like they were injected by too much collagen. Her nose grew wider, then reverted back to its normal shape and size, as did her lips. She was breathing fast, her chest rising and falling quicker than usual at the strain this was all causing. She fought hard but she could not get her face to change completely or hold any of the changes for more than a second or two. Her eyes flashed open as she let out a frustrated sigh.

"I can't do it!" she cried, upset with herself.

Only Eve still had her eyes closed. They moved beneath the lids, darting left and right as she swayed on her feet, caught up in the memory of that fateful night. Her lips moved as if she were speaking, though no words came out of them. Marley felt a tingle of static electricity surge through her then suddenly the air changed around Eve. Marley could see it clear as day, like it had grown thicker, lifting Eve's curls so that they now swam through the air.

A cloud of black formed high up in the rafters of the building.

Marley squinted her eyes, staring up at the ceiling, wondering if her eyes were playing tricks on her... but no, there was definitely something moving up there. The cloud descended, slowly at first, then growing increasingly fast as it shot steadily down towards Eve. When the pulsating black mass was only a few feet away, it exploded outward, revealing bats that swooped down in every direction. They circled Eve, beating the air around her with their wings as the others looked on in fascinated horror.

Of Eve herself, she seemed not to notice what was happening, lost in her memories until Marley called out to her. At the sound of her voice, Eve's eyes snapped open. Seeing the swarm of bats flying around her, her eyes went wide as she lost all control.

The bats shot away, leaving her shaking.

"Moths, crabs, rats and now bats. On the plus side, at least I'm getting a real handle on my powers now," she smiled lightening up her whole face. "I'd love to see those girls try something on me now."

"What girls?" Marley asked, confused by the direction the conversation had gone to.

"Oh, nothing, forget about it," Eve replied shrugging her shoulders.

Though it should be a moment to celebrate, Marley couldn't help but feel uneasy by her power. Shooting a look at Christian and Cassie, she saw that they too seemed more creeped out than they wanted to be, though they did well to hide it.

Marley's eyes slid over to the last black shape as it disappeared into the rafters. She wondered if Eve's power would keep evolving... would it eventually extend to... people?

An icy shiver ran down her spine, that would still be there hours later.

FORTY

Tyler squeezed her aching neck.

Wanting nothing more than to sink into oblivion, she hadn't been able to sleep, however, try as she might. Exhausted from classes and then work, she had felt a weariness that she'd only experienced once before. Even more than the tiredness, however, was the knowledge that she had missed learning about her powers alongside the girls. While they had given her the rundown, it still wasn't the same. She was behind something which her A-grade self wasn't used to.

Which was why she was breaking into the science lab.

She gripped hold of the door handle, twisting it, but it stopped after only a quarter turn. Locked. She walked around the length of the classroom, hoping for another way in and found that one of the windows at the top of the wall was still open.

Studying the hall, her eyes swept over a display consisting of several chest-high units. Decorative bowls sat on top of the unit, which a small plaque helpfully explained were donated to the college from a previous student, Hank Wellington, who was now working for the Center for Disease Control and Prevention in a top capacity. *Thanks, Hank*, Tyler thought to herself as she carefully placed the bowls on the ground, then dragged a unit beneath the window. Grateful for the years of gymnastics that she had practiced since she was a child, Tyler climbed gracefully onto the unit, slipping through the window to land nimbly on her feet inside the lab. *Still got it*, she grinned to herself, throwing up her arms as if she were at the end of a floor routine that was being graded.

From what the others had described, Tyler knew the magic wasn't so much literal as the combination of channeling her mental and emotional energy then adding this to her already vast knowledge of science. Grabbing a glass beaker, Tyler headed to the nearest sink, turned on the tap then filled it with water. If what she suspected about herself was right, then it was the particles and molecules she could affect. All she required was a substance she could manipulate.

Thinking of the effect she wanted in her mind now, Tyler pictured the molecules in the water changing. She imagined the end result of her potion, felt how she would feel after taking it, then channeled it all into the beaker. Nothing happened. She frowned, fidgeting on her feet. This is how it had worked for the others so why wasn't it working for her? Trying to clear her mind, Tyler hunkered down until the sound dulled around her, and everything seemed much further away. There was nothing in the world, nothing but that beaker and the water that she willed to change.

As in the class before, the solution began to bubble though no flame sat beneath it. Wary of repeating what had happened in class the other day, Tyler kept a tight control on the solution this time. She wouldn't have enough lab partners or cardigans left to ruin if she kept that up. Maintaining her focus was proving much harder than she expected, however. It might have been a result of her long day or that she wasn't skilled in her powers as yet. She felt sweat gathering on her brows and her body began to shake from the exertion.

Hold it steady!

Just a little longer and the solution would be ready. Tyler wasn't sure how she knew this though there wasn't a doubt in her mind. She only had to keep it up a few moments longer. She held it there, her entire body trembling, until a small cloud puffed up from the solution and Tyler knew it was done.

She had brewed her first potion.

It all meant nothing, however, if she didn't test it. Without allowing herself a moment of hesitation, Tyler picked up the beaker and drank the solution down in one gulp. It was like she was drinking liquid silk. It slid down her throat tasting like a salty lemonade, causing a pleasant sensation. Wiping her sweat onto her sleeve, she suddenly felt her body grow strong. Gone was the exertion from just moments before, she was now filled with a sudden energy that was euphoric! It was as if she had just drank a gallon of the world's strongest coffee but without any of the side effects. Her heart was fine, there were no palpitations. She felt as if she could conquer the world.

Buzzing from excitement, she quickly made several more, pouring the solutions into the water bottle she had brought with her. Tidying away the beakers so there was no trace of her experiment, Tyler went to the exit and was relieved to find that the door could be unlocked from the inside. Leaving the room, she stepped back into the hall, closing the door behind her. Jogging over to the unit, she had tilted it, meaning to drag it back to its original setting, when she discovered that she could lift the heavy metal cabinet as easily as if it had been made out of cardboard.

Her potion hadn't just given her energy, it also made her physically stronger!

Grinning, Tyler set the unit down then jogged back to her room where, with energy to burn, she spent the rest of the night getting a head start on her coursework.

FORTY-ONE

The forest was dark and chilling.

She ran through it, branches whipping painfully against her skin, stones biting into her bare feet, but she couldn't stop.

Something was after her.

Tossing a look over her shoulder, she could see nothing except a gaping chasm of darkness, but the thing was there, its evilness reaching out towards her. She hurried forwards, desperate for a light to break the night. Instead, the blackness only grew deeper, swallowing the space around her until it was only her that remained. Of the forest, there was no sign, not even beneath her feet, which she now saw ran on that inky blackness.

Rising up from the blackness now were wispy tendrils of hair. Black hair. They shot up from below, curving around her ankles until she fell, headfirst, into the black void.

She screamed.

Marley woke with a start, hearing the sound of her own voice coming from her dry lips. Though it wasn't the scream of her dream, it was a pathetic croak. She wasn't in the forest. She was in her dorm room. Cassie lay across from her sleeping soundly, out to the world. The sight of her stilled Marley's thumping heart, providing some comfort, though she still had to fight the urge to flip on a light. She swallowed, memories of that nightmare still plaguing her mind. It had seemed so real that she could still see those awful black tendrils snaking towards her. She squeezed her eyes shut, willing them to go away. When she opened them again, the tendrils were still there. Blinking away the sleep, Marley peered into the blackness, trying to see if something was actually there or if it was just her eyes playing tricks on her.

A figure formed inside the darkness. Hazy at first, then growing rapidly clearer until a pair of eyes appeared inside the black void. Those terrifying eyes that Marley instantly recognized.

No God, please not again.

Fear shot through Marley as she scrambled away from the approaching figure until her back was up against the wall. Gripped by terror, she could do nothing as the ghost woman floated towards her, arms reaching out to her, those awful eyes burning into her soul. She screamed, louder than ever, hurting Marley's ears. For a moment, Marley was hopeful that Cassie would hear and wake up… then she remembered. Not only did Cassie sleep with ear plugs, but she could not see or hear this ghost.

Marley was on her own.

Tears streaming down her face, Marley found herself calling out for the only other person who might be able to help.

"Christian…"

Her voice was shaky, but she clung to his name like a lifeline.

"Christian! Christian!"

Over and over she called, as the ghost reached Marley's bed, covering it with that terrible darkness she had seen in her nightmare. As the ghost wrapped her hands around Marley's shoulders, Christian suddenly appeared behind her in a spark of bright light. The ghost screamed, a howl of utter frustration then vanished, leaving Christian standing there confused.

"What is it?" he asked. "Why did you call me?"

Marley pointed at the space the ghost had only just vacated. "You didn't see her? That ghost, the hanging woman, she was here again."

She couldn't stop herself from shivering. Christian looked though there was nothing he could see that shouldn't be there.

"She must be coming to you for a reason. You need to learn how to make contact with her," he began, only for Marley to cut in viciously.

"She's evil! How many times do I need to tell you that?! I'm not going to make conversation with her, even if I knew how!"

"But this is what you do, Marley! You see dead people! I know it's frightening…"

"Oh, do you?" Marley interrupted, unable to contain her growing fury. "How? Because from where I'm sitting, you've never seen her. You're not the one she comes after, screaming and hurting me where she touches me, waking me from my sleep, so keep your useless comments to yourself!"

Christian came forward, forehead furrowed with concern by her words.

"She hurt you? Where?" he demanded.

Marley stopped short, confused by the sudden change in his voice before she realized it was just part of his Guardian duty. Dropping the covers that she had pulled around her, she gestured at her shoulders. Christian moved closer to inspect them, so close that she could feel his breath on her, which she knew was stupid as Christian didn't breathe. He wasn't corporeal. So why could she still feel his breath on her?

His eyes slid down her bare shoulders though he couldn't see any sign of contact, any break on the smooth skin. Though the ghost's fingers had burned where they had touched her, once again, there was no sign of anything. He moved his eyes back up to her face, taking in how fragile she suddenly looked. He was getting used to her annoyed outbursts, so seeing her so scared was a shock to the system.

One he wasn't sure how to handle.

Uncomfortable with the effect she was having on him, Christian focused on the end goal.

"There's no sign of anything on you. I know this is difficult and I don't pretend to know how it feels to be haunted by a ghost, but this is your destiny, Marley. It's your fate. You can't run or hide from it. Neither can you ignore your powers or the ghosts who come to you. It's your responsibility to communicate with them."

He knew the minute he stopped talking that he had said all the wrong things. The vulnerability vanished from Marley's face to be replaced by a scathing hardness that she directed at him.

"I don't know why I bother to explain myself! You don't care about how I feel. You only care about avenging your precious Eric! You can't stop for even a second to understand how hard this is for me, for all of us. You were dead long before I killed you."

Jumping out of bed, she pulled out a shoebox from beneath it. Reeling from her words which had cut deeper than even she realized, Christian watched in stunned silence as Marley pulled out a vial of her meds. Snapping off the lid, she poured two pills into the palm of her hand then swallowed them.

"Luckily for me, I've got these. So long terrifying ghost woman. Goodbye Christian. You know what you can do with your responsibility?"

Christian opened his mouth to reply but he could already sense that he was fading from her view. *What had she done?*

By the time Marley settled herself back in bed, she couldn't see him anymore.

FORTY-TWO

His eyes ran over the ads section.

Supes Daily was a newspaper put together by the supernatural community for the community that contained interesting articles as well as recipes. A section called "Supes Soups" seemed very popular, as was a delicately worded section of ads where one could hire any kind of muscle that one desired… for a price.

A price that wasn't usually money.

Take Fink: he would do almost anything for human meat. Others desired blood or black magic. Almost everything was a currency that could be exchanged. Michael scanned through the ads, searching for a particular type of service.

Though supernatural beings had existed beside humans for thousands of years, it wasn't until the last few centuries that laws were put into place, laws that governed that they couldn't mess with humans. The laws had been created by those meddling Guardians, whose sole focus was to stop any enjoyment it seemed.

Fury burned inside him now as he thought of all they had endured while the humans carried on with their humdrum lives without any concern for how shackled the supernatural community was. Here they were, the ones with all the power, yet they had to hide away, to limit what they could do, just so the tiny humans could think they ruled the world.

Their time was fast approaching.

If Michael was successful — and he would be, make no mistake of that — he would usher in a new age, a new rule for all. The humans, these girls? All they cared about would be no longer.

Michael would have his revenge.

A revenge that had been over three centuries in the making. Michael circled an ad with a pen, smiling, though it never reached his eyes. His plan would start with this simple ad.

FORTY-THREE

The girls sat on the carpeted floor, a mound of books before them, sequestered between several shelves containing massive tomes with unappealing titles. Head tilted to one side, Eve ran her eyes over some of them.

"The complete volume of 8th century Eastern European existential poetry. Wait, that's actually a thing?"

Pulling the book off the shelf, she flipped it open. "Apparently nobody else thinks so either since this book has never been checked out."

"You're supposed to be looking for any buildings or artifacts that were around during the 17th century and are still here now!" Marley pointed out, not bothering to hide her annoyance anymore. She popped her neck, aching from being hunched over so many books for what seemed like an eternity.

"We've been at this through my sub and now halfway through my apple," Eve replied waving the last of her lunch around. "We've found nothing, just that mosaic, which we already knew about."

"That doesn't mean we should give up, does it? What do we know about the seals?" Marley said. They were missing something, she just knew it. After last night's horror, she had woken up determined not to feel helpless like that anymore. Fueled by this need, she corralled the others into joining her in the library, where they had decided to research Boston's history.

They settled on the 17th century, having pinpointed the rough era of the ghost woman's clothes with the stories of The Hanging Elm. The mosaic was proving harder to find information about. While they researched, Christian hovered close by though he had barely said a word to Marley. She knew she had hurt him yesterday, but she wasn't able to address it in front of the others even if she knew what she wanted to say. It wasn't as if she was sorry for any of it. She had meant every word. So if he was going to sulk all day, so be it.

"They were created to keep evil at bay, and they can be any object apparently," Cassie answered.

"Well that narrows things down considerably," Eve replied, snark flashing from her eyes.

"Maybe we're going about this wrong," Tyler began. "Maybe instead of the seals, we should be looking at something else." Her eyes gleamed brightly despite the dark shadows under them. Beside her sat a mountain of books, two or three times more than the others, which she had already gone through and discarded. She seemed to read at an incredible pace.

"Like what?" Eve asked, deciding she'd finally had enough of her apple, tossing it into a nearby bin.

Tyler tapped her fingers on the ground, drumming a beat. "Christian mentioned before that we aren't the only supernatural beings. Well, what if others know more about this than we do? Is there a place they're known to hang out?"

"Like a bar?" Eve said, laughing at the thought, when

Marley saw a strange expression flash over Christian's face. She knew they had hit on something he wasn't comfortable about discussing.

"What is it?" Marley asked, finally talking to him. He shook his head, folding his arms across his chest. Unable to see him, the others still managed to pick up on her thoughts.

"What's going on?" Cassie asked.

"Christian knows something, but he's not telling," Marley replied. Eve stopped laughing, her eyes growing suddenly wide.

"Wait, was I right? Is there an actual bar?"

Christian's eyes lowered to the floor, skirting the issue as Marley focused her own eyes on him, pinning him in place. He sighed.

"There's a place Eric used to go. He had a snitch there."

Cassie blinked, trying to take it in.

"Where is it?" Marley asked.

"Southie. In the factory district."

"That's still a decent-sized area…" Eve commented.

"I don't know the address, it's just next to that frozen meat place."

Eve grinned suddenly, excitement blazing in her eyes. "So we'll go there and see what leads we can dig up!"

At her words, Christian shot up to his feet. Before he could speak, however, he blinked out, leaving nothing but empty space behind him. Marley had to bottle her irritation. When she wanted to see him, he would disappear. When she didn't, he wouldn't leave her alone. Why were boys, whether they were dead or not, so infuriating?

"He's gone. I didn't hear what he wanted to say, but I think it sounds dangerous, especially since I've got classes in a minute."

"I don't," Cassie supplied in that small, shy voice of hers. "I can go with you Eve if you'd like?"

Eve nodded, trying to hide her surprise. "Sure. I wasn't planning on hitting the place on my own. It can't be bad though can it? Not if Eric used to go there. Other than being immune to being killed by black magic, he didn't have any powers to protect himself. We can just go see if we can find out who this snitch was. Maybe he'll be able to help us." She looked at Tyler. "Are you coming with us?"

"I can't," Tyler said, her regret clear for all to see. "I have a meeting then more work scheduled. Are you sure it's wise for just the two of you to go? Maybe you should wait until we can all make it."

"We're only going to scope it out. At the first sign of trouble, we'll get out of there. Besides, didn't Christian say supernaturals weren't supposed to mess with humans? In any case, I've got the best handle on my powers. If anything happens, I can deal with it. Plus I've got Cassie for backup."

Marley didn't want to rain on her parade. She had some deep misgivings about the plan, but Eve was right. She was the most in command of her powers; Marley was sure she could take care of herself. It was Cassie she should be more worried about, reeking of insecurity as she did. What if they could smell fear?

Seeing the concern, Eve rolled her eyes. "You know I'm the oldest here by several years, right? I'm not going to do anything stupid, so you can stop your worried looks. We'll be fine." Gesturing at Cassie, Eve headed off before Marley could reply. Moving her hair from her face, Marley shot Cassie another concerned look. Catching it, Cassie gave her a small smile.

"Don't worry. I'll call if anything happens."

With that, the two of them hurried out of the library. Tyler dumped the book that was in her lap onto her ever-growing pile then stood up, tapping her foot on the ground. "I should get going too," she said, sliding her bulging bag onto her shoulder, sagging visibly under the weight. Marley noticed two bottles of water inside.

"That must weigh a ton to carry around. Do you want me to take one of those off you?" she offered.

Tyler swung her shoulder away from Marley as if she didn't want her to get close to the bag. "No, no. That's fine. I just drink a lot," she answered, trying to pass it off but Marley caught some of her edginess. She took in Tyler's face, the too bright glare of her eyes, the dark circles ringing them.

And that foot that kept on tapping nervously, beating a rhythm into the carpet.

"Are you OK?" She finally asked. "You seem a little… wired."

Tyler waved off her comment with a hand. "You would be too after your third coffee of the day. I didn't sleep well so I'm caffeinated up to my eyeballs. I've got to get going or I'll be late for my meeting. See you later," she said quickly, hurrying away.

Marley watched her retreating back, trying to decide whether she bought her explanation or not. Finally, she decided it didn't matter whether Tyler was hiding something from her or not as she didn't have time for it. Grabbing her own bag, she started off before realizing that the books still lay in an untidy heap on the floor. Sighing, she picked them up and started putting them back onto the shelves, hoping she'd have enough time before her next class started.

The professor stood at the front of the room giving an uninteresting PowerPoint presentation that had already gone on for days it seemed. The room's blinds were drawn so that the presentation, which was being projected from the back wall, could be easily seen, though unfortunately, the darkness only caused

Marley to grow sleepy. She was a girl who liked a good eight hours of sleep at the best of times, so these recent sleep-deprived nights were playing havoc with her body. Blinking rapidly, she forced her eyes open, trying to ignore the sting of air that forced them to water.

"What the hell are you doing here, you need to go after them!" came the voice she so badly did not want to hear.

Christian stood on the chair next to her, hands on his hips, looking at her in disbelief. Sneaking a look around her, Marley lowered her voice into the tiniest of whispers.

"Go away…"

"How could you let them go on their own Marley? They have no idea what could be there!"

"I can't do anything about that right now," Marley hissed between clenched teeth, desperately hoping that no one would hear her. "Besides, Eve knows what she's doing."

"She absolutely does not know what she's doing! None of you do! My God, just when I think you're starting to get it, you go and do something even more stupid! You girls are worse than children!"

Glaring at him, Marley rubbed her forehead, wishing she could drown him out. Just one day. Could she get through one afternoon of classes without Christian bothering her? Suddenly, she sat up straighter, remembering her pills. Reaching into her bag, she popped open the vial, and broke a pill in half. She didn't need it for the rest of the day, just a few hours so she could have some quiet time. Taking out her bottle of water, she slid the pill into her mouth, washing it down. Christian was still ranting beside her, but his voice was starting to fade out. Marley grinned, thrilled to find a solution to one of her biggest problems.

Smiling at him, she shot him a tiny wave. He looked confused until he caught the edge of a pill bottle poking out from her bag.

"You haven't! Not again!" he demanded.

Marley didn't have to answer him. She watched as he became more translucent until he faded away completely. Leaning back into her seat, Marley grinned.

Alone again.

Finally.

FORTY-FOUR

Tyler arrived at the Financial Aid office with energy to burn.

A flower of unease opened in her stomach at the lie she had told. She had only known her for a few days, but Tyler considered Marley a friend, so the lie felt disloyal. She swatted the discomfort away with a mental wave of her hand. She didn't have the luxury of dealing with guilt on top of everything else. Reaching the office door, she rapped on it with her knuckles — much louder than she had intended. Inside, came a friendly female voice. "Come in."

Tyler turned the door handle, stepping inside. Behind a large wooden desk sat a woman in her fifties. Everything about her screamed order. From the immaculately pressed shirt to the hair pinned expertly into a bun and the papers stacked neatly in piles. A Newton's Cradle sat on the desk, its swinging metal balls colliding with one another providing a relaxing sound.

Plink, plink, plink…

The woman typed into her computer, reading whatever information had flashed up on the screen then smiled at Tyler from behind wire-rimmed glasses, gesturing to the chair in front of her desk. "Ms. Jones? Please take a seat."

Tyler closed the door behind her, sat down onto the chair holding her bag in her lap. Her hands clasped together instinctively, something she always did when waiting for important news. The woman smiled again.

"My name's Annabelle Bartlet, thank you for being on time for our meeting. You wouldn't believe how many students aren't." Her glasses slid down her nose, her hand reached up automatically to push them back into place.

"It's important to be punctual," Tyler said, silently urging the woman to give her the news. Her foot tapped on the carpeted floor as she found herself resisting the urge to pace the room.

"Exactly. It shows respect," Annabelle finished.

Though she had only been there a few seconds, she couldn't drag this out any longer. "So, has it come through?" Tyler blurted out, willing the woman to say yes. Annabelle typed into her computer, the keys clicking loudly as her eyes slid back to the screen. Tyler knew the answer the second her eyes turned sympathetic.

"I'm sorry, dear. It hasn't."

Tyler's heart started a dance inside her chest. *What was the hold-up?*

"Why? What's the problem?" she asked, hating how desperate her voice sounded.

"There might not be one necessarily, however, I see that you applied for your Financial Aid very close to the deadline," Annabelle replied, crosschecking her facts on the screen. "Sometimes, that does delay things. It's the admin work you see. It's why we always encourage students to apply for this as soon as they are accepted into a college."

"I didn't apply early because I... well, I was under the impression that my family had money so I wouldn't qualify for it but then, our circumstances changed..." She trailed off, eyes flicking down to the floor. Her family had been rich, at least that is what they had led her to believe. The truth was a much harder pill to swallow. She felt a tremor of resentment for how her parents had hidden the truth from her which immediately morphed into crushing guilt. They were doing the best they could, they couldn't have known this would happen. If only they were here. If only this was all just one big bad dream. She'd swap all the money in the world if she could be with them again.

"I'm sorry, dear. Can your parents help?" Annabelle asked innocently.

"No." Tyler didn't want to go into her whole sorry story for fear that she would become even more upset. "I just got a job though, I started yesterday."

Annabelle smiled again, pleased. "Well isn't that productive of you? I'm sure your parents must be very proud of the way you are handling things."

Tyler knew she didn't mean it. The woman wasn't to know they had died. If only she would stop bringing them up every damn second! Feeling her pain and anger grow, the air became charged with tension. The balls on the Newton's Cradle started speeding up even though no one had touched them.

Plink, plink, plink...

Annabelle frowned, training her focus on the metal balls as they flew faster and faster, gathering momentum.

"That's strange..." she uttered, watching as the balls swung harder, crashing into each other with such force that she winced. Knowing she was causing it, Tyler fought to regain her composure. Realizing that the balls had only started moving like that when she felt resentful, she tried to calm her emotions but she knew she didn't have a handle on them. The balls were crashing into each other now, so hard that Annabelle backed away from the desk.

Plink.

Plink.

PLINK!

Suddenly the metal balls EXPLODED sending steel shards every which way. Tyler ducked quickly as a shard whistled through the air where her face had been only moments before. Annabelle wasn't so lucky as a shard caught the edge of her brow, slicing into her face. She yelped, jumping back as blood welled in the corner of her eye. Horrified, Tyler reached into her bag, pulling out a tissue that she offered her.

"You've been cut," Tyler mumbled, hating herself for harming a woman who had only been trying to help. Annabelle took the tissue from her, dabbing at the wound. Blood seeped into the paper, staining it red.

"I'd better go and see the nurse," Annabelle stuttered, shock turning her eyes dull. She left, leaving Tyler staring at the wickedly sharp metal shards that were now embedded in the walls.

FORTY-FIVE

The walk to work went past in a blur.

Overwhelmed with guilt, Tyler had fought to keep her emotions as calm as possible, realizing that they were partly what caused her powers to materialize. Christian had been right when he'd said that Eve's animals came to protect her whenever she felt threatened. It seemed her own power came into play if she felt anything too strongly.

Annabelle's face flashed up in her mind. Her shock, the cut… and her blood. With it came the memory of the lab class, when she could have hurt the students too.

One thing was becoming crystal clear: their powers could do serious damage if they weren't careful.

Arriving at the market, Tyler changed into her staff uniform, glad that William wasn't there to see her. She wasn't sure she could take the weird vibes he gave off on top of what she was already feeling. The last thing she needed was for something unnatural to happen here. As she folded up her clothes, putting them away into a locker, a wave of tiredness came over her.

No! She couldn't afford to slack off now, not when she'd just gotten to work!

Reaching into her bag, Tyler pulled out her water bottle, quickly gulping down half of what remained of her solution. She was rewarded with an instant burst of energy that picked her right up. Straightening her back, she locked the locker and left for the shop floor to find her team manager, a skinny guy in his twenties called George.

George was one of those rigid types who had started work here in his teens, working his way up the chain. Though it had taken him eight years to get promoted, he lauded his position over the team, but only when William wasn't around. Tyler knew who he was within moments of meeting him during her induction. He had looked down his nose at her as if she wasn't worthy of his time. He stood at the end of the pet food aisle now, squinting at the paperwork in his hands. On her approach, his eyes slid up from the sheet.

"Finally. I wondered if you were bothering to show up today," he exclaimed. Though she'd shown up on time, Tyler didn't answer. Apparently, George liked to reprimand people even if they hadn't done anything wrong. He handed her a price gun and the sheet of paper he had been scrutinizing, gesturing at several crates of cat food stacked into a pile on the floor.

"We're having a sale on this brand of food this week. The prices are different for each type, whether dried, wet or bundles. Check the list on the sheet, price accordingly, then stack the food onto the shelves, making sure the labels are front-facing. I know you have only just started, but even you should be able to do this without any incident, what with being a student and all."

Tyler took items from him without comment. There wasn't really anything she could say to him really that wouldn't garner a warning or worse. On top of his general unpleasantness, it seemed George had an issue with students too. What joy. It looked like she wasn't going to like any of her superiors in this place. Then again, she wasn't here to make friends. Scanning the price list, she set the correct price into the gun. Grabbing a can of cat food, she stuck the label on, then set it on the shelf, front-facing like she had been warned. Fuelled by the second dose of her brew, she worked fast, pricing then stacking quickly. In no time at all it seemed, she had completed the top shelf. One of the floor assistants tossed an annoyed look her way.

"Slow your roll new girl. There's no point in showing the rest of us up. No one's impressed and you won't get paid any more for it," she hissed at her.

Startled by the comment, Tyler watched as the whip-thin girl crossing the shop floor to the household cleaners section where she was compiling her own discounted display. Deciding she had had enough of people telling her what she could and couldn't do today, Tyler narrowed her eyes, focusing back on the job at hand. She'd show this girl and George. She'd do her job faster than they could handle.

Burning with energy, she went at her job with a zest she hadn't felt in a long while.

FORTY-SIX

Gray clouds obscured the mid-afternoon sun as Eve and Cassie arrived outside their location.

It was a nondescript place, nestled between two factories including "REAL MEATS", the frozen meat place Christian had mentioned, and which they had Googled easily enough. Still, the place would have been easy to miss if not for the obvious security guard standing outside a steel door.

The girls stared at him, confused. By the sound of things, they had thought the snitch would be standing around, not hidden inside a mysterious building behind a big steel door and an even bigger bouncer.

He wasn't dressed like the usual bouncers found in the bars and clubs across the city. They wore pressed suits with polished shoes that shined. This guy was dressed in jeans and a jacket. It was only his rigid posture, the way his shrewd eyes cooly accessed the area that revealed his true purpose. No neon sign blazed above the door, and from where they were standing, they couldn't hear any music either.

If this was a club of some kind, it was pretty disappointing.

Still, Cassie practically reeked of excitement, asking questions a mile a minute the entire journey here until Eve had had to tell her to calm down, though she was clearly still filled with excitement.

Cassie was super excited at being Eve's wingman. Of all the girls, Eve was the one she had spent the least amount of time with. Though she didn't look like the girls Cassie usually admired, she knew that under the layers of makeup, Eve was as good-looking as Marley. More than that, she had a mysterious air about her that Cassie found intriguing. Eve was literally the coolest person she had ever met. She didn't care about being popular or looking like anyone else. She didn't seem to care about money. She did her own thing. In Cassie's world, she based so much of her self-worth on how others made her feel that Eve was like a goddess. One she wanted badly to impress.

Determined to show Eve how helpful she could be, she bounced up to the security guard, waving up at him.

"Hi," she said.

His eyes flicked down to her before moving elsewhere. If she was put off by his reaction, she didn't show it.

"We're… we're friends of Eric's," Cassie lied.

Eve tried not to show her shock at Cassie's outrageous lie. They'd have to run with it now. The bouncer stared back down at her, taking in Eve too this time.

"Eric only had one friend and you're not him," he replied.

Eve felt a shiver at his words. Was *he* Eric's snitch? He had obviously known Eric. She shot Cassie a look before turning her eyes back to him.

"You mean Christian?" Eve chimed in before Cassie could say something that incriminated them. "Tall, blond, good jawline, usually angry. Yeah, we're buddies too."

She hoped she remembered Marley's description of him correctly. They'd soon know.

The bouncer only grunted in response which they took as a good sign. At least he didn't send them away.

"We were hoping to speak to his person here about something," Cassie began, hoping he would fill in the rest of her sentence. Of course, he didn't.

"Yeah, we had some questions we thought he might be able to help us with," Eve said.

"Are you the friend?" Cassie asked, obviously coming to the same conclusion Eve had.

The bouncer glared down at them, not bothering to hide his irritation anymore. "What exactly is it the two of you want?"

Faced with the direct question, the two fell silent, neither of them knowing how much they should reveal. The thought crossed Eve's mind that maybe they should just get out of there, be better briefed so they didn't reveal something to the wrong person. Like she had swallowed a truth pill, however, Cassie started to babble.

"Well, a couple of things really. Have you heard of a guy called Michael? He's going around town causing trouble. We're hoping to locate him, or someone who knows him."

"Why? What do you think you can do about it, even if you found him?" The bouncer's expression didn't change.

"So you *do* know him..." Cassie said triumphantly, jumping wildly to conclusions.

"That's not what I said, is it?" he answered back, growing more annoyed by the second.

"You didn't deny it. In any case, why are you so interested in knowing what we can do, which is a lot, just so you know," Cassie said brazenly, making Eve squirm. Why was she being like this? Eve barely recognized her. Feeling uneasy about her revelations, she grabbed Cassie's arm, speaking quietly into her ear.

"I don't think you should be saying that much to him…"

In response, Cassie just shot her a look that clearly said 'don't worry, I've got this'. Then she continued. "If you won't tell us where Michael is, do you know anything about the Five Seals?"

At this, the bouncer's eyes narrowed. "Everyone knows about those, girl. It's one of the first things we're taught."

"Did you know he's broken the first one?" Cassie continued, smiling at Eve as if she really thought she knew what she was doing. Seeing the look on the bouncer's face, however, Eve knew Cassie had said the wrong thing.

"Stop talking," she hissed at Cassie.

"The first seal is broken?" The bouncer replied finally looking something other than irritated. He was too good at hiding his true feelings, however. Eve wasn't able to see whether he was interested or concerned. Alarm bells rang in her head as she knew they should get out of there. Gripping Cassie's shoulder, she dug her fingers in until Cassie yelped. She dragged her out of his earshot.

"What're you doing, he knows something," Cassie exclaimed, rubbing her shoulder. "I was just getting somewhere, why did you stop me?"

"Because you're telling him everything! How do you know he's not one of the bad guys?" Eve demanded, hands on either side of her hips.

"Because he's Eric's friend," Cassie mumbled back, hurt.

"We don't know that! Christian said Eric had a snitch here, not a friend. But you've been jumping to conclusions then blurting out everything that's happened! What if that guy's working for Michael? Now he'll know we're onto him! What if he comes after us? If he isn't friends with Michael, you've just told a complete stranger that the first seal is broken. Isn't that something any bad guy would love to hear? What if they're all out rejoicing now, as they go find the others to break? And why the hell would you be bragging about our powers when I'm the only one who has a real handle on them so far? How desperate for attention are you, that you would put us into such a terrible position just to make yourself sound better? How can you be so stupid?"

Eve stopped suddenly, her words seeming to echo loudly all around them. Seeing the look of horror that now appeared on Cassie's face, she felt awful. She hadn't meant to say all of that. She hadn't meant to hurt her with those last comments. It was her panic, her worry that had caused her to blurt it out. Looking stricken, Cassie's eyes turned bright with tears, the confidence immediately sapped out of her.

Eve reached out to her, desperate to take some of it back when Cassie spun on her heel, running away.

"Cassie, wait!" Eve called after her.

Cassie didn't wait, however. She ran blindly away, choking on her sobs.

Within seconds, she was gone.

Heart heavy with guilt, Eve made her way back to the car when her attention was caught by something flapping on the ground under her boot. Bending over, she stooped to pick it up.

It was a flyer with edges that were brown with dirt. It had obviously been out there for a little while and had taken quite a beating from the weather though the offers on display were still current. It wasn't the discount prices which interested her, however.

Staring at the name of the store, Eve folded the flyer, tucking it into her jacket pocket, mentally making a note to herself. She would bring this up to the girls when they were next together. Right now, her mind was on Cassie and she couldn't think about anything else, even something that might prove to be a lead.

She hoped Cassie was OK.

FORTY-SEVEN

Tyler stared down at the empty crates and empty packaging piled high around her, filled with a great sense of satisfaction.

Despite what her skinny colleague had said and George's prediction, she had finished pricing not just her end section but the entire pet food aisle. Pumped up from her potion, she'd had energy to burn and had spent the last few hours focused on the task at hand, determined to do a great job. Though he made her uneasy, she wanted William to see how indispensable she could be.

Her entire life would be riding on the job here if her aid didn't come through.

Bending down to scoop up the trash, Tyler looked up at a harassed-looking mom with two young kids. A cute toddler sat in the shopping cart, sucking her thumb. With her pigtails and big, curious eyes, she reminded her of Ally when she was little. God, she'd loved that kid so much. Baby Ally was almost as adorable as she was now as she fast approached her tenth birthday. The mom stopped in front of the cat food section that Tyler had just finished with giving a big smile when she saw the offer on display.

"Sweetie," she said to her oldest, a boy of around six. "Can you help mommy with those?" Together, the two of them began loading the cart with the food. They grabbed one box, then another, stacking them haphazardly into the cart as the baby watched giggling at this new game.

When she saw how many they were grabbing, Tyler wondered if she should offer to help, especially as she didn't want the kid to end up hurting himself by carrying those big boxes. She figured mom would know what was too much for him, however. Turning back to her job at hand, Tyler cleared away the rest of the remaining packaging when she heard a commotion behind her.

Glancing back at the pet aisle, she saw that the place was packed full of bargain shoppers now, stockpiling food like it was going out of fashion. A man practically shoved an old woman out of the way to snatch at the boxes before she could get to them. Leaning heavily on her walking stick, the old woman voiced her displeasure as she finally got her hands on a box. Tyler let out a slow whistle, taken aback by the ferociousness she was witnessing.

People sure loved a deal around here.

Feeling eyes on her, Tyler looked across from her to find the skinny girl from earlier watching her aisle and had to stop herself from grinning at the look on her face. It was obvious the other girl didn't like the competition which Tyler couldn't care less about. She wasn't here to be lazy, she was here to work, and if she showed everyone else up while she was at it, so be it. Snippy girl shot Tyler a look which she couldn't quite decipher then stalked off the shop floor.

Good riddance, Tyler thought.

Grinning, she carried the trash through to the dumpster in the back of the store, dropping a quick glance at the gold-encrusted watch on her wrist — a gift from her parents when she had turned sixteen and one of the few expensive items she still owned — three-thirty. Perfect timing. She was due a ten-minute break. Heading down the corridor towards the staff room, Tyler reached the drinks station where she studied the items on offer. Black coffee, hot chocolate, hot water and a box of individually packed tea bags, ranging from peppermint to green. Picking up a disposable cup — apparently, Star Market's staff weren't allowed real mugs — she slid it under the hot chocolate spout, watching it spew out some watery brown liquid. Giving it a tentative sniff, she wondered if she should actually drink it since it looked pretty unappetizing.

"Tyler, could you come into my office please?"

Setting the cup down, she looked in the direction of the voice. It was William, and he was standing beside Snippy Girl who wore a spiteful look on her face. Butterflies fluttered in her stomach as she nodded, following them out of the room, to his small office at the end of the corridor. What did he want to see her about that would involve that other girl? William took a seat behind his desk as the other girl stood beside him. They both stared unnervingly at her. Tyler swallowed, trying not to let her nerves show.

"We have a saying here, Tyler: we do things properly so that costly mistakes don't occur. Now, while I know you have only just started, speed isn't the only thing we value."

Tyler blinked, her eyes sliding from William to Snippy Girl, who stood opposite her, her arms folded over her chest. There was a satisfied smirk on her face that made Tyler want to slap her. She had literally just met her today, so it made no sense why the girl had such a problem with her.

"Have I done something wrong?" she finally asked.

William set down a sheet of paper onto the desk, turning it around so Tyler could see it. It was a copy of the price list she had been given. William tapped a stubby finger on one of the prices.

"You incorrectly priced up an entire aisle of goods, Tyler," William began as Snippy Girl jumped in, unable to control herself.

"Yeah, by several dollars a box!" she hissed. William shot her a warning look which had the effect of making her back down at least, but Tyler could feel the shock growing.

"No, I didn't… I did exactly what was written on the sheet…" Getting in close to the list, Tyler studied the prices only to see with growing horror, that they were right. She had made a mistake. A big one. "I'm sorry… I don't know how that happened."

"I warned you to slow down and check what you were doing, but you ignored me and carried on," the other girl said. Tyler wanted to correct her — they both knew that wasn't what happened — but she couldn't do it, not with William glaring at her as he was.

"Your actions have put me in a difficult position. That food has flown off the shelves, and though we have pulled the products off now, we can't make back the losses from what has already been sold."

A knot of anxiety grew in the pit of her stomach. "You don't expect me to pay it back do you?"

William stared down at her in silence, making her squirm. The thought of having the last of her money disappear for a genuine mistake made her heart thump so wildly, it was a miracle it didn't burst out of her chest. When William spoke again, his voice stern with a warning bite behind it.

"Not this time. Since it's only your second day, we'll chalk this down to lack of experience, but neither of us can afford a mistake like this again. Understand?"

Relief washed over her so great that she swayed on her feet. Snippy Girl looked at William, unhappy with his handling of the matter. She was obviously expecting a harsher punishment from him. Her eyes turned into slits as she shot daggers at Tyler.

William turned to address Snippy Girl. "Thank you for bringing the matter to me Stacey, you may go back to what you were doing," he said to the other girl. Knowing that she was being dismissed, Stacey issued a curt nod then left, tossing Tyler a look over her shoulder that all but screamed that she'd be watching her.

William suddenly smiled, crossing the room in several quick strides until he was standing beside her. He put a hand on the small of her back as he steered her towards the door. Although there was nothing strange about the movement, Tyler felt a chill race down her spine. It was all she could do not to spring away from him. He had just spared her from a grave mistake that could have really screwed her: she really had to learn when to bottle her stupid feelings away, especially when there wasn't any actual need for them.

"I don't want this to play on your mind. Mistakes do happen, even to the best of us. Go back outside and finish your shift."

She nodded, grateful that she would be getting away with only a warning. As she exited the room, William called out to her from inside.

"Remember Tyler, I'll be watching you."

She hurried away before he could see how his words had affected her.

***

On the way back to the shop floor, Tyler agonized over her gross mistake.

Her whole life she had been the type of person who prided themselves in everything they did. She was competitive, a strict A student. She'd never missed a deadline or failed a test, so this, this was a big deal. She looked down at her watch again, only to find that there was still several hours left of her shift. With that realization came another wave of exhaustion, so fierce that she had to put a hand against the wall to steady herself. The last time she had felt this kind of tiredness, she hadn't slept for days. It was right after her parents had died. Tormented by the guilt of not being there when Ally discovered their father had died, Tyler had gone the opposite way, trying to stay awake constantly in case Ally needed her.

Coming to the staff room, Tyler hesitated. There was no time for a pick-me-up coffee now since William's impromptu meeting had eaten up the only break she had. Opening the door, she stared across at her locker, knowing there was enough of her potion in there for another hit. There was a nagging voice in the back of her mind that wanted to warn her that maybe she was relying on her creation a little too much: however, Tyler didn't want to give that any thought. Shoving the voice firmly aside, she marched over to her locker, fishing the key from the pocket in her shirt and opened it. Grabbing her water bottle, she downed the last of her brew in two quick gulps.

As before, she was filled with an instant energy that made her feel as if she could do anything. Closing her locker, she went back onto the shop floor to finish out the rest of her shift as she mentally reminded herself to make more of her magic solution later on.

She needed to stockpile as much of it as possible.

FORTY-EIGHT

Marley approached her destination nervously, slowing down her walk as a large wrought iron sign arched overhead.

With classes over, Tyler at work, and the other two out on their recon mission, she'd found herself with some rare free time. She'd deliberated over her options and had thought about getting a head start on coursework before nixing the idea almost immediately. She couldn't focus on schoolwork knowing that so much was up in the air with them.

Before she'd forced him away, Christian's last words to her had been playing on her mind. Her guilty conscience couldn't reconcile itself with the idea that maybe he was right. It was beyond stupid to let Eve and Cassie go off on their own. If she were being honest with herself, Marley would admit that she didn't have a handle on Eve yet. Sometimes the older girl unnerved her so when Eve had insisted that she'd be fine without them to babysit her, Marley hadn't felt brave enough to challenge that. Now, in the cold light of the afternoon, she wondered if she should have insisted on the group going together at a later time, when they could all make it.

With the blessed silence that had come with the end of Christian yammering at her constantly, Marley realized that she was ready to learn more about her power. The meds she had taken should have worn off by now. Inspired by the others go-to attitudes, Marley decided to give her own powers a try by visiting the one place where spirits would naturally be.

Sunlight filtered down through green leaves, lighting a path along the grass. Rows of ancient headstones loomed around her, some majestic replicas of Angels perched on top of crypts, while others consisted of simple tombstones, decaying after centuries of neglect. She passed by one now, squinting her eyes at the faded writing that was almost impossible to make out. Weeds had long overtaken the gray stone, its words now covered over by wild ivy. Marley wondered if there was anyone left in the world who knew the person who was buried there. There was an ache in her heart when she realized the answer was no. If there was, the grave would have been taken care of. Soon it would be so overgrown that she wouldn't even be able to read the writing carved onto the stone.

She was thinking about what it must be like to die, to not have people miss you, when a stab of guilt made her gasp. Was that how it was for Christian now? She had killed him without the world knowing. He was alone, with only her for company… yet she had drowned him out by taking her pills, taking away the only person in his afterlife who could hear him.

She was his only connection to the world, yet she'd cut him out without giving him a second thought.

The guilt that flooded through her was almost more than she could bear. Marley had never pretended to be perfect, God knew she was far from it, but she had always considered herself a good person. Yet her actions of late didn't seem to match up to this. A dark thought entered her mind, one that caused her stomach to plummet.

What if there was some truth to what Christian had said the first time they had met? What if it wasn't only Michael? What if *they* were also the bad guys? It would make their twisted powers make sense at least.

Not liking where her thoughts were taking her, Marley shook her head to clear them away. She had to focus. The others were starting to get a handle on their powers. It seemed she was the only one who had no clue about how to use hers. If she didn't want another Christian-sized mistake, she needed to learn what it was she could do… so that if nothing else, she would never repeat it again.

Moving along the path, she studied the tombstones until she found the perfect one. Freshly-cut flowers sat in a vase in front of the grave. The water in the see-through vase was still clear, letting her know that it had not sat there long. While many of the graves surrounding it were overgrown, this one was neat. Someone was coming here on a regular basis to take good care of it. Her eyes flicked over to the words inscribed in the stone.

"Here lies Heather Forrest. Beloved wife, mother, and daughter, champion for the good."

The date on the inscription was only a few months old; Heather was only recently deceased, but it was the latter part of the sentence that drew her attention. Heather was an all-around great person it sounded like. It made sense then that she would also be a good ghost. Lowering herself onto her knees in front of the grave, Marley closed her eyes then pushed out her thoughts. She mentally called out to Heather, trying to picture a female figure in her head. Eve had mentioned the others before, how she could feel her mind connected to other beings around her when she used her power, yet Marley couldn't feel anything. Clenching her fists, she dug her fingers into her palms, forcing herself to try harder. The air changed, and Marley felt her hair lift away from her shoulders. It was working! Opening her eyes, she looked around her.

There was nothing there. No ghost. No feeling of any other minds touching her own.

She couldn't contain her frustration. Why couldn't she do this? Not bothering to stand, Marley, shuffled over to the next grave. This one wasn't as neatly kept as Heather's, but she rationalized that it probably wouldn't matter anyway as she wouldn't be able to summon any-one. Leaning forward, she brushed the ivy that covered the name on the headstone. Robert Sullivan. The rest of the inscription could not be made out, having long eroded away by time. Clasping her hands before her prayer-like, Marley closed her eyes. Pushing out her thoughts and energy, she called out to Robert, her brow furrowing with the effort.

Again, the air felt different, charged with electricity. Like it had felt in the church that first time. Her eyes flashed open expectantly.

Still, no ghost stood in front of her.

She felt the bitter sting of tears as she wondered why she couldn't command her powers to work.

FORTY-NINE

Shame overwhelmed the car, threatening to suffocate Eve.

She wove through the traffic, driving automatically, unable to wipe the image of Cassie's shocked face from her mind. She knew it was a low blow, that it was a terrible thing she had done. Cassie was the most insecure person Eve had ever known, even if Eve could have given her a run for the money in that department before. She should have never said those things.

Eve hoped she would give her the chance to apologize.

She'd called a bunch of times, left several messages, but Cassie hadn't returned any of her calls. Eve would have followed her in the car, but Cassie had seemingly disappeared into thin air. Eve bit the edge of a black painted lip. Unable to assuage her guilt, she pulled up Marley's number, hit call, then activated the speaker. Eve did not make it a habit of calling while driving; even if it wasn't a finable offense, she knew it wasn't a smart thing to do. But right now, the need to talk to someone else overtook that. Marley's dejected voice answered after a few rings. "Hey, what's up?"

"Are you OK?" Eve asked. "You don't sound very happy."

"I'm just trying to figure out how to use my powers, but nothing's happening," Marley answered with such despair, Eve could almost see the droop of her shoulders even without being there.

"It's a learning curve, I'm sure you'll figure it out eventually. We all will," she offered, hoping that she sounded optimistic even if she didn't feel that way right now.

"What happened to you guys? I'm guessing you didn't find out much since you haven't said anything about it?" Marley asked, surprising Eve with her question. Marley's intuition was sharper than even she seemed aware. She would make a great journalist if she were ever given the chance.

"We didn't get any leads, unfortunately, our questioning came up short." She would tell her the whole story, just not now, not while she was driving, Eve rationalized to herself.

"That's a shame," was Marley's short response. Despite only knowing her a short time, Eve knew this wasn't usual. The girl she was growing to know was sunny and bright, so she must be feeling really low.

"Where are you? I'll swing by," Eve offered, surprising herself. The thing with Cassie must have really thrown her as she wasn't usually so friendly.

"Mount Auburn Cemetery," Marley answered.

Eve didn't bother to hide the shock in her voice. "Are you sure that's a good idea? I mean, you couldn't even handle the one ghost before..." She stopped talking, wincing at the tactlessness she had just displayed. Luckily, Marley didn't seem to take offense.

"It only matters if I can summon them and since I can't..." She trailed off, drowning in a wave of failure.

"Just hold on, I'll be there as soon as I can," Eve said, stepping on the gas.

"OK," Marley answered before hanging up.

Eve gripped the wheel as an uncomfortable feeling crept up her spine. She couldn't put her finger on it, but something did not feel right.

T he rusty van had been stolen from a florist the night before.

Since then, they had driven across the city, searching for fun, draining the tank until it was almost empty. Once it was, they would replace it with another uninteresting vehicle, some other rust bucket that wouldn't draw any attention to them. Empty food wrappers and soda bottles littered the seats, all that remained of their earlier meals. They had been planning on hanging out at a bar, maybe shoot a game of pool or two, when the two girls had appeared.

They had known who they were the instant they had arrived, having fit the descriptions they had been given to a T.

The figures hunkered down in their van, several cars behind the oblivious girl. They wanted to go after the other girl at first, the one on foot, but she had taken a path where cars could not follow. Now they wove behind the Corolla with only one thing on their minds...

FIFTY

The streets blurred into one.

Cassie wandered the town aimlessly with no idea where to go; she just knew she couldn't go back to the dorm. She wasn't ready to face any of the girls right now, especially Eve. All she had wanted was to impress her, to be her friend.

But friends don't say the kind of things Eve had said to her.

Her put-downs ran through Cassie's mind again, a twisted replay that echoed on a loop. As if her own internal negative soundtrack wasn't bad enough, she'd have Eve's to cope with now too. The worst of it was, she knew Eve was right. She had behaved stupidly; she had put them all at risk just to make herself feel better in the moment. For what? Eve had seen straight through her. She felt hollow inside, like she wasn't a real person, just an empty shell that people saw through.

A group of girls walked past, discussing their latest boy band crush. The prettiest girl tossed her long blond hair over her shoulder, glossed pink lips curving into a grin at something one of her friends had just said. She wore a short flowing skirt that hit mid-thigh, showing off toned, tanned legs that narrowed into delicate feet. Cassie couldn't stop herself from staring at her perfect feet, immediately comparing them to her own wider-than-normal ones that often caused her to struggle with finding shoes that fit well. Just once, she'd like to try on an outfit — and shoes — and have them fit amazingly.

Looking up, she saw that she had arrived outside a clothing store. The window display showed a tall, slim mannequin wearing a cropped vest with a pair of denim hot pants and a pair of wedged sandals. The mannequin sat on a hay bale on top of a floor strewn with straw. Apparently farm chic was the in thing this season. Cassie stared at the mannequin, her eyes turning dark from her scrutiny. There literally wasn't anything on the mannequin that she could wear.

The cropped vest with the frayed hem was super low cut, so she'd need a decent pair of boobs for that to work. Then there was the length. Cassie for sure didn't have the kind of flat, toned stomach to pull that off. And the hot pants? They were almost indecently tight on even the rake-thin model. She had enough junk in her trunk that there was sure to be butt spillage, which wasn't a good look for anyone.

Her eyes lingered on the outrageous outfit, wondering what kind of girl would actually wear something like that, when her mind flicked over to Marley. From what she'd seen, Marley was the casual, dress-down type, so this getup would never be found in her wardrobe (and Cassie would know, having gone through it pretty thoroughly). She definitely had the figure to carry this off though. Eyes fixed on the clothes, she pictured Marley wearing them and tried to feel how it would feel to be her, wearing this get-up. In the back of her mind, she knew she wasn't dealing with the problems at hand, but she didn't care. She needed a break from all that pressure and the inevitable disappointment that would come from just being her. Closing her eyes, Cassie felt her energy begin to build like a hurricane inside her chest. When her eyes flicked open again, she saw her reflection in the shop window.

Except, she wasn't herself now. She was Marley — her face *and* body... and she was wearing the outfit in the window display.

A gasp escaped her lips — Marley's lips — as she looked down at herself. Yep, those weren't her boobs at all: these new ones were bigger. Running her hands over her new body, Cassie marveled at how amazing she felt. She had been right, Marley could pull the outfit off. She turned this way and that, admiring her new look, even if it was kinda slutty. It was the first time in her life that she could call herself sexy, so she would enjoy this moment for however long it would last.

Tossing her new hair over her shoulder, mimicking the girl she had seen moments before, Cassie started strutting down the street. She kept her shoulders back, chin up, boobs out, swinging her hips from side to side. It was a completely alien walk to her normal one, but she figured she was doing something right as she noticed a man throwing her an admiring glance.

The bolt of thrill his glance sent made her lift her head even higher, pointing her nose to the sky.

She walked to the edge of the curb then waited for the lights to change. Traffic flowed past, metallic finishes gleaming in the sunlight when a car slowed right down as its owner, a guy with a mohawk, wound down his window, sending her a low wolf whistle. Cassie froze, not knowing how to react to this new experience. A blush of pleasure spread from inside, rising to stain her cheeks. Lifting her arm, she waved shyly at the driver, causing him to stick his head out of the window.

"Hey, sexy! Where did you come from?"

Where indeed. Smiling happily to herself, she half crossed, half floated across the street to the other side, almost able to feel the admiration being sent her way. Cassie strolled past a coffee place with an outdoor terrace that spilled onto the sidewalk. Two girls looked up from their iced coffee drinks giving her the full once over, their eyes flat with envy. Cassie couldn't believe it! The girls were jealous of her, of how she looked! It was the cute guy in the corner that caught her attention, however. His brown hair was gelled up in that messy just-got-out-of-bed style that she knew actually took hours to do. He wore a stud earring in one ear and was dressed in a sleeveless black wife beater that showed off muscly arms. A heavy metal chain hung around his neck. At her arrival, his eyes honed in on her, raking up and down her body as his mouth spread into a lazy grin.

"I hope you didn't have any plans today," He said brazenly, his tongue darting out to lick his lips.

"Why?" Cassie asked, confused at where this was leading.

"Because you're going to be spending the rest of it with me," he replied coolly.

Cassie felt her cheeks blush. The guy was coming onto her! Her mind flittered across all the things she could say, the things she had watched her mom say whenever these things happened. Instead of her cool retorts, her mind went painfully blank. Seeing the blush only seemed to make him more confident, if that were possible. He stood up, revealing all six feet of himself as he towered over her. Stepping around the table, he offered his hand to her.

"Coming?" he asked simply.

Cassie froze, a dozen questions entering her head. What, just like that? Where was he asking her to go to? Who was he? She didn't even know his name, this was complete madness, wasn't it?

Unless this was how girls who looked like current-her behaved.

Eve's insults flashed into her mind again, cutting into her like a knife. She glanced behind the guy, into the window but instead of her new reflection, her mind saw her real state. Saw the downtrodden, ugly girl that nobody wanted to be around. The girl she never wanted to be again. Tossing her hair over her shoulder again, she reached out and took his hand.

"Why not?"

FIFTY-ONE

Gathering in his breath, such as it was, Christian yelled with as much force as he could manage. "MARLEY! YOU NEED TO STOP THIS RIGHT NOW!"

But the stupid girl still knelt there on the grass, dejected… completely oblivious to the chaos she was causing.

She had no idea he was there, had been there for the last half an hour. She couldn't see the elderly male ghost standing before her, growing more irate by the second by her not being able to see him. Dressed in a brown suit, the suit he had been buried in, he lowered his face until it was even with Marley's, but she looked right through him. Flanking either side of her were two more ghosts, one a woman, the other who must have been her child. They held hands, joined together for all eternity by the accident that must have killed them. Christian knew it was an accident as half of the woman's skull had caved in. The boy too showed signs of trauma, his small chest crushed by a great weight or collision. They hovered beside Marley, crying, desperate for her attention.

He was conflicted, feeling sympathy for all they had gone through, yet he also couldn't hide the finger of fear that slid up his spine. Could they be dangerous? Would they hurt Marley if she continued to ignore them? On top of her fear, there was his own confusion to contend with. His mind couldn't relate the fact that he too was a ghost, just like them. Most of the time he felt as he always had when he had been alive. It was only when he tried to touch something, or when he was pulled away, that the reality of his situation would hit him.

Watching the other ghosts, he noticed something different. They seemed… less human somehow, particularly the ones who had obviously been dead longer. He wondered if that was the natural process of the afterlife. That the longer a person had been dead, the more of their humanity they lost.

The thought made him cold.

He couldn't afford to turn feral. He needed to avenge Eric, to see this thing through. He was interrupted from his thoughts by Marley's voice as she sighed in frustration, moving to another grave, this time a large tomb with a crumbling statue on top. It was the most overgrown of all the graves in the current area, with several of the letters inscribed on the tombstone having long faded away. Like it was a crossword puzzle, Marley was able to fill in the gaps without much difficulty. Kneeling before the grave, she focused on the name.

A thunderbolt of fear shot through him as his eyes flicked over the ancient grave. With the ghosts moaning around them, Christian realized that if he was correct, this ghost would be the most feral of them all, having been dead the longest. He raced towards Marley, arms outstretched.

"NO! Don't Marley! Don't call him!"

The words had barely left his mouth before the ground shook beneath him. The air changed next as a metallic smell filled his nose. He knew what it was immediately, having long studied the strange scent a supernatural event or being often left behind.

Sulfur.

Then he heard a familiar clinking sound but couldn't think what it was until the towering black shadow appeared before Marley, his hands bound together by thick rusty chains.

Overgrown hair covered the ghost's face, hiding much of it away, except those piercing eyes that took in the sight of Marley and Christian as he tried to make sense of what was happening. He moved a step forward with his bare feet, stepping into the light. Christian could see his bare chest and the torn pants that were his only clothes. Vivid scars crisscrossed his back, a visual history of the many times the ghost had been whipped as a human though the punishment had clearly not deterred him judging by his unrepentant manner.

"Marley, back away from the grave." Hearing him, the ghost turned his eyes to Christian. Suddenly he half laughed, half growled as he understood the situation. The menace he exuded was palpable. A knot of fear blossomed in Christian's stomach, sending a cold chill inside as he became suddenly afraid for Marley's life.

"Marley," he tried again, hoping to finally break through to her. "Get up, you need to get up and get out of there!"

But it was hopeless. She couldn't hear him or see the ghosts she was unwittingly raising. The ghost roared suddenly, swinging his bound hands at the statue of his tomb. To Christian's shock, the head of the statue broke away as several pieces of rubble flew past Marley's head. Startled, she rose to her feet, staring blindly around her.

How did the ghost do that? How could he physically connect with anything when Christian couldn't?

Around them, the other ghosts became more agitated, as more of them emerged from their graves. They moved towards Marley, each of them desperate for her attention, desperate to be heard and seen after so long being kept in the dark. The chained ghost thundered towards her as he picked up the broken statue head. Cocking his arm back, he hurled it at her.

The stone head whistled through the air and would have hit Marley square in her face if not for another ghost appearing, standing directly in the line of fire. Her hand flew up at just the right time to catch the statue in the air, stopping it dead. Christian stared at the female ghost, awed. She wore a simple dress and no shoes on her feet. A long spill of black hair fell down her back, but it was the thick noose around her neck that caught his attention.

It was the ghost from the Hanging Elm… and she had just saved Marley.

She screamed, launching herself at the chained ghost. Instead of connecting with him, however, she disappeared inside him. He howled with rage as they both vanished.

***

The rock floated in the air, inches from Marley's stunned face.

One minute it had been launching towards her, the next it stopped dead, levitating harmlessly before her. Having just arrived to witness it, Eve could see from Marley's shock that it wasn't her own doing. At least, not consciously. Hurrying to her, she stopped beside Marley as they both stared wide-eyed at the suspended statue head.

"I don't know how that's happening," Marley admitted.

"That thing was flying right for you when it just suddenly stopped like that," Eve revealed, waving her hands above and below the rock to see if she could feel anything keeping it there, though of course, there was nothing. As they both studied it, the head suddenly dropped to the ground, whatever magic that had suspended it there, now gone.

"What does Christian say?"

Marley hesitated, her brow furrowing into a frown. "I don't know, I can't see him. I took half a pill earlier to drown him out..."

Eve stared at her, unable to believe what she was hearing. "You drugged up so you wouldn't be able to see him?" Her voice raised a notch or two at the end of the question.

Marley threw up her hands, caught yet exasperated. "What was I supposed to do? You don't know what it's like! He's at me, all the time! When I'm trying to sleep, when I'm in class. He's there yelling and bitching, I don't get a break. You three can't even see him so you have no idea what it's like to have people invading your space all the time!"

"No, but he's the only one who knows what's happening, he's a resource and you shouldn't treat him like that, especially after... you know." Eve trailed off though her meaning was clear. *After you killed him.*

As always, whenever that was mentioned, Marley felt a great wave of guilt. Eve was right. Drowning him out wasn't the way.

"Can you get him back?" Eve asked, stopping Marley dead. She'd been so preoccupied with making him go away, the thought that he wouldn't come back hadn't even entered her mind. Now Eve had raised that concern, the worrying thought lingered in her mind.

What if she'd made him go away forever?

"I don't know," she finally answered, hating how small and scared her voice sounded.

"Well, try Marley! We need him back," Eve demanded, surprising her with her forcefulness.

"Now?" Marley asked, feeling such pressure that her temple throbbed.

"No, two weeks from today… of course now!" Eve snapped, crossing her arms over her chest. Marley pushed her fear aside, closing her eyes as she conjured up an image of Christian's face into her mind. She let her thoughts still, focusing on the breath as it went in and out of her chest. Although she could feel Eve standing impatiently beside her, she blocked her presence out of her mind. It was only Christian she wanted to see.

Holding his face in her mind, she called out to him mentally feeling a surge of energy rush through her. She could feel the presence of others around her, wanting to connect, but she pushed them aside receiving howls of frustration for her efforts. *Not yet*, she told them. She had to find Christian first. The sound faded around her until Marley could hear only her own breathing tangled up with the others calling out to her. She flitted from one unfamiliar voice to the next, until she finally heard the one she was looking for.

"Marley, dammit! I'm here," Christian yelled at her.

Her eyes flew open as Christian emerged before her, but he wasn't alone. Standing all around her were ten or so gruesome spirits, each wailing in pain as they reached for her.

Letting out a yelp of shock, she stumbled away, straight into the path of two ghosts, a woman, and her child.

"What is it?" Eve asked urgently, unable to see the danger.

Marley tried to answer her, but her warning cry died in her throat as several shadowy figures emerged from behind the tombstones. These didn't have the misty air that seemed to surround the ghosts. They weren't distressed or crying. In fact, they made no noise except for the crunch of their footsteps as they approached them — fast. These figures were real. Something glowed red on each of their foreheads, a symbol of some kind that Marley could see but make no sense of.

"Who are they?" Eve said, pointing to the same figures coming towards them. Marley's head whipped round to her. So she could see them too?

"DEMONS!" Christian shouted suddenly.

"RUN!"

FIFTY-TWO

Christian's warning jolted Marley from the stupor she found herself in.

"Demons?" she repeated incredulously. Despite everything that had happened so far, this seemed a stretch too far for her brain to assimilate right now. Eve whirled around, moving away from them until her back was pressed up to Marley's. Her eyes raked their faces, searching for the tell-tale signs she had previously witnessed when she had been attacked by them before. *She* had no problem believing in their existence.

Clouds rolled past leaving the sun to burst forth. Its rays shone down, illuminating the three figures that moved towards them. From this distance, they could have been mistaken as human — if humans moved in a twitching, insect-like manner. Circling the girls, the demons advanced as one, seemingly communicating with each other via telepathic means as they didn't speak a word. This didn't mean they were silent, however. A bizarre clicking sound bounced back and forth between them.

"I told you to run!" Christian yelled furiously from across the way.

"We can't," Marley responded, eyeballing the one closest to her. "They've got us surrounded."

Eve shot a quick look at her. "Do the thing with the statue head, but throw it at them this time!"

But Marley knew the magic had not come from her. She hadn't felt a thing and if she had learned one thing by now, it was that, barring the side effect of her pills, magic left its trace in the air. You could feel it both inside and around you.

As if to emphasize her point, Christian spoke up. "That wasn't you!" Christian revealed, overhearing them. "That was your hanging woman. She stopped that rock from hitting you!"

Marley was so surprised by his comment that she took her eyes off the demon to flick them over to him.

Which is when they made their move.

Barreling towards them, Marley had only a moment to brace herself as her demon launched himself at her, knocking her to the ground. She fell on her right arm, feeling a sharp pain shooting up it. The demon's face lunged towards her, and she saw with horror that feelers reached out for her from his cheeks. Instinctively, she pulled back, as a sticky green substance leaked out of the end of them, filling her with disgust. Whatever that stuff was, it couldn't be good.

"Watch out for their feelers, don't let them touch you!" she warned Eve, locking her arms against her demon's shoulder, trying desperately to push him off of her. Turning her face away, she glanced over at Eve to see her struggling with the other two. One grabbed Eve by the shoulders as the other came at her from the front, but she was prepared for this. Her foot lashed out, kicking him in the groin, hard. The demon squealed as he fell to his knees, nursing the injured area.

As Marley watched, Eve's eyes went flat as she summoned up her power. Suddenly the area grew darker as the sun dipped behind a heavy cloud again. Except, as

Marley looked up to the sky, she realized that wasn't what had happened. A giant black mass of something else was approaching fast. Formed of what seemed like hundreds of things, the cloud surged towards them at a shocking speed until it abruptly broke away revealing hundreds of large black ravens.

Screeching so loudly that it made Marley wince, the birds dive-bombed the demons below, sinking their beaks and claws into the fleshy part of the demons' heads as they pecked at their eyes. Under attack, the demons let go of the girls, lashing out at the birds but their feathered friends simply skirted out of the way, reeling around to attack from a different angle. Again and again, they dived to attack, until howling in pain, the demon's retreated as the birds chased after them, leaving a mess of black feathers in their wake. Shell-shocked, Marley took the hand Eve offered to her, pulling herself back onto her feet.

"They came out of nowhere," she exclaimed, glancing around her for fear others would attack in their place.

"Not nowhere," Eve admitted, concerned. "I think they might have followed me from that place."

"I told you it was a stupid idea to go there!" Christian yelled at her, his fury making him forget for the moment that she couldn't hear him. Whirling around, he spun to face Marley, eyes shooting daggers.

"And you, I can't believe you did that to me! You see the damage your actions have caused?" He gestured around them, at the ghosts still hoping for an audience with Marley.

"I'm sorry, I didn't know this would happen. I wasn't thinking," Marley apologized. Seeing how restless the spirits were, she felt wretched by all the pain she had caused.

"You're damn right you weren't. Jesus, Marley, your powers are a *gift*. They were given to you for a reason, you can't take pills to switch them on and off, that's not how it works."

"I know," Marley answered quietly. "I realized something today." She waited for him to calm down, so he could actually take in her words. Eve nodded, encouraging her to continue. "I don't need pills to do that, I can do it with just my mind."

"I'm not sure I follow," Eve replied, confusion turning her eyes dark.

Marley tucked a strand of hair behind her ear as she tried to explain. "It wasn't my pills that stopped me from seeing Christian or the other ghosts. It was me, but I didn't know I could do that, so when I took my pill, it was like a placebo effect."

"You thought they would drown him out, so you somehow made it happen? How do you know?" Eve asked.

"Because my pills would have run out hours ago, but I was only able to call Christian when I opened myself up to doing it."

"At least you're finally learning something," Christian offered. Even in this small victory, he wasn't able to be gracious about his praise. Something from the fight still bothered her that she still needed an answer for.

"What you said before, during the fight. You said that ghost, the woman I keep seeing, you said she stopped that statue from hitting me? How do you know?"

"Because I saw her do it. One minute that piece of stone was flying straight for your head, the next she appeared from nowhere to catch it in her hand. Then she attacked the ghost who threw it at you! The effort it took for her to do that must have been monumental. They both vanished when she made contact with him."

Marley blinked, taking this information in. "So if she's not out to get me then what does she want?"

"Apparently, to help you," Eve finished.

"But why is she so freaky then?"

"I wouldn't knock it," Eve replied. "Especially when she just saved your life."

Marley stood, silent for the moment, trying to take it in. Had that ghost saved her? Staring across the cemetery, the face of the demon who attacked her flashed into her mind.

"Did you see the signs on their foreheads?" Marley asked them both.

Eve shook her head. "What signs?"

Christian frowned. "No?"

"Those demons, they had a glowing red sign on their heads." She unzipped her bag, taking out an exercise book and a pen. Opening the book to a blank page, she drew a symbol that consisted of three conjoined circles set inside a triangle. "Does this mean anything to you?"

Christian studied the image, but shook his head. "I've never seen it before."

"I'm guessing it must mean something," Marley continued. "If we can find out what, maybe we'll learn why they keep coming after us."

His tongue forced its way into her mouth, hot and slimy like a worm.

It wasn't the most pleasant thing she had ever experienced, but Cassie endured it for this, her first make-out session. His hands seemed like they were everywhere, touching, stroking, sliding across the bare skin of her legs. She had allowed the guy — whose name was Nick, she had since learned — to lead her to a park, where they sat now, under the large canopy of a cherry tree. White blossoms rained down around them, blown by a gentle wind. The whole thing should be so romantic, so exciting…

Yet she felt nothing inside.

So stunned by her first actual interest from a guy, Cassie had no real recollection of what they had discussed on the short walk here. Nick had boasted about himself, something about how he was the lead singer for a local band, but as he hadn't asked her any questions, she hadn't felt particularly engaged by the whole encounter. He had led her to this spot, then proceeded to kiss her.

Nick moaned into her mouth, making so many sounds that Cassie wondered if there was something else wrong with her. This was a super-hot guy, so why wasn't she feeling it? It wasn't like she hadn't dreamed of this moment her whole life, so it made no sense why she wasn't finding this as exciting as it should be.

"You have the nicest skin," Nick murmured into her ear. His hand slid up her arm until his fingers caught a lock of her hair. "And your hair smells amazing, like coconuts," he went on.

Suddenly Cassie realized why she was feeling a little out of it. Marley's hair smelled like coconuts because that was the shampoo she used. Nick wasn't into her at all. He was into Marley.

Maybe that wouldn't have bothered her too much if he'd at least tried to get to know her. As it was, they had barely exchanged two words together, so his immediate infatuation wasn't directed at her at all. If Nick could sense her reticence, he wasn't showing it, continuing to kiss her like his life depended on it. He let go of her hair and slid his hand down her shoulder, dragging his fingers along her collarbone with a light touch. He moved them lower, down to the tip of the V in her top. Cassie caught her breath as she realized he intended to feel a whole lot more… and that she didn't want him to.

This wasn't the special event she had pictured. She didn't know the guy, wasn't sure if she even liked him. Plus there was the fact that she wasn't even herself! She pulled away from him.

He lifted glazed eyes to hers, confused.

"Hey, come back," he said, but Cassie moved further away. Reaching for her bag, she rose to her feet as her bag vibrated then chimed. Relieved by the distraction, she fished out her phone to see an urgent message from Marley. Eyes growing wide by the words on the screen, she shot a distracted look at Nick.

"Sorry, I've got to go. It's an emergency," she said, already moving away.

Still on the ground, Nick gaped at her retreating back as she half ran out of the park. "Seriously?! You're gonna get me all worked up then leave just like that?!" he yelled after her.

But Cassie had already gone.

FIFTY-THREE

Water dripped down from the dank ceiling, pooling onto the filthy concrete floor.

The three figures huddled before Michael, their already unfortunate faces now covered by angry welts and scratches. Black feathers fell from them, floating into the water, proof of their unlikely tale. He had been told the group would finish off the girls no problem, yet here they were, their tails between their legs, returning his fee to him in the event of a catastrophic failure as was guaranteed in the newspaper.

Demons with a code of ethics. Whatever would come next?

A block of money sat on the table next to a large wooden bowl that was half filled with water. Together, they formed two of the few pieces of furniture that he kept in this section of the dead-end sewer. Though Michael liked to conduct his business deals here, several feet below the ground, away from cameras and prying eyes, this wasn't where he lived. Where he stayed, it smelled of freshly laundered Egyptian cotton sheets and vanilla candles. As much as Fink had tried to figure out where Michael lived, his base was a mystery, one he intentionally made sure was kept from them.

Fink moved forward, taking the money back from the mercenaries. Their feelers clicked at him unhappily, what remained of their eyes were glued to the money moving out of their sight. Fink tensed his shoulders, waiting to see if they would be stupid enough to attack him for it. The demons exchanged looks at each other but at a low click from one of them, they spun on their heels, scuttling away like crabs.

Despite being a demon himself, Fink shuddered. There were some things that affected even him. He handed the block of money to Michael, who shook his head: Fink could keep it. The money meant nothing to him. Behind him, he felt Pike bristle at the gift; he obviously wanted the extra cash. Smiling, Fink offered it to him.

"Here, you take it."

Pike's weary eyes slid over to him, trying to assess his intention, but Michael wasn't the only one who was good at keeping secrets around here; Fink had spent a lifetime perfecting his poker face. Pike's clawed hand shot out, snatching the money from him. Fink simply smiled, unnerving the other demon.

"Thanks," Pike finally hissed, his fangs emphasizing the 's' at the end of the word. Fink nodded magnanimously, letting Pike think they were buddies.

Keep your friends close…

"No problem," he replied, turning back to Michael, who was still by the table, his hands hovering palm down over the water in the bowl.

"What now?" Fink asked, wondering what the man was up to.

Michael's eyes grew dark as he focused on the water, summoning up his magic power.

"If today has shown me anything, it's that I can't underestimate these girls. They barely understand anything, yet they still managed to beat those thugs back."

"Since money doesn't seem an issue, we could just hire more of them. I'd like to see them go up against twenty or so demons," Fink offered, but Michael shook his head.

"No. I have a better idea. We need to be more clever than them. We need to go after their every weakness and exploit them. We need to keep them preoccupied so that I can locate the next seal." The surface of the water rippled as a fuzzy image appeared. Michael waved his hand over the bowl, making the ripples die down.

And there, in the water, a crystal clear picture formed of a young girl sitting in an armchair. Rolling her sleeve up, a woman with terrible hair slid a needle into her arm, hooking her up to a dialysis machine…

TWISTED MAGIC

4: THE BLOOD THAT BINDS

JO HO

FIFTY-FOUR

S hoppers strolled around on the streets outside, soaking up the last of the day's sun, not a care in the world. Inside the car, however, it was a different story. Its passengers sat shaken, their faces as pale as marble.

Overwhelming silence blanketed the car.

Christian sat in the backseat, his back ramrod straight, lips tightened into a thin line. While, gripping the steering wheel, staring dead ahead, Eve hadn't spoken at all the entire drive back. Marley was actually relieved, having no words left. She had used them all up apologizing for her reckless behavior which had nearly gotten the two of them killed.

The fight at the graveyard had taken everything out of them. Even before the demons had come, Marley had spent all of her energy summoning those ghosts, which she would have known were there if she hadn't taken that stupid pill, which had resulted in her somehow blocking them out. While she had now figured out that the pill only had a placebo effect on her, that she could willingly block out spirits using only the power of her mind, she hadn't been privy to that particular knowledge when had been most important. If Eve hadn't appeared at the right time, if she hadn't used her power to help, Marley would be in big trouble right now. At best, she would be captured by those demons.

At worst, she would be dead.

As shame flooded her body, red-hot anger also raised its head. What was the point of having a power if she couldn't save herself with it? The other girls had active powers. Even Cassie could escape any situation by 'becoming' somebody else. But what could she do? Talk to ghosts? How useful was that really? As she lamented her lack of abilities, her eyes flicked over to the rearview mirror… and there, despite all physical laws of nature, Christian's arresting face stared back at her, reflected in the glass.

The golden flecks in his eyes seemed even more prominent today, as if their brush with danger had caused them to shine with a brightness that made them almost glow. A memory popped into her mind then, of the first time she had seen his extraordinary eyes close-up… but with it came a darker thought that she couldn't stamp out quickly enough. Her powers weren't entirely useless.

Occasionally, she could stick her hands into someone's chest and stop their heart.

As always, the guilt she felt at killing Christian overwhelmed any other emotion, until she had to mentally shake herself from the pity party she was throwing. Though Christian was clearly upset, he wasn't whining about his lot in life — or lack thereof — not even when she knew he felt almost as helpless as she did.

Twice he had seen other ghosts interact with objects from the mortal world yet he had no idea how to do this himself. It hadn't really crossed her mind until now how terrible that must feel, to not be able to physically do *anything*. To have to just stand there, watching, while awful things happened around him. She could certainly relate.

It was how she had felt whenever that terrifying she-ghost appeared; however, even that wasn't as simple as it should be now. If Christian wasn't mistaken in what he saw earlier, it seemed she had saved Marley's life. The scary she-ghost was on her side.

Marley didn't know whether to be relieved about that or not.

The welcoming sight of the parking lot finally greeted them. Eve eased the car into a space, killing the engine. Getting out of the car, they had started the short walk to TJ Halls when a pain in Marley's side caused her to gasp out loud, resulting in Christian's concerned gaze. Gingerly, she reached down to investigate the area just above her waist when another sharp burst of pain exploded beneath the pressure of her fingers. The demon who had attacked her had knocked her to the ground. She must have landed harder than she remembered though it didn't seem like anything was broken — just bruised — though annoyingly, the pain worsened with movement. Gritting her teeth, Marley focused on putting one foot in front of the other. The sooner she got to her room, the sooner she could rest.

Arriving outside their dorm, Marley slid her ID into the card reader. The doors swung inward, revealing a few students in the hallway. A few of the doors were open. They passed by two girls heatedly debating the merits of a recently released television show, whilst another folded laundry as she sang along to the radio. Their chatter filled the air, which only served as a stark contrast to the silence between Eve and Marley.

After what seemed like an age, they reached Marley's room. She unlocked the door and they hurried inside. Marley felt along the wall until her fingers landed on the light switch. Four lamps blinked on simultaneously, bathing the room in a warm glow. Eve took a seat at the table. Although she couldn't see him, Christian joined her while Marley went into the bathroom. Pulling up her top, she turned, inspecting her injury in the mirror. As she had expected, an ugly purple bruise covered her side from the waist up to her rib cage. At least no bones protruded from her skin; that would have been really bad. A few bruises she could live with.

Rejoining the others, she went to the mini fridge by Cassie's side of the room. It was one of the pieces of furniture her parents had brought with them, even before Marley had set foot on campus. She took out two sodas, handing one to Eve. Sitting beside her, Marley popped open a can. "In all the crazy, I forgot to ask where Cassie went."

At the mention of her name, guilt flashed over Eve's face. She looked down, focusing on the drink in her hands. "We had a… disagreement. She went off on her own," was the mumbled reply.

Christian shot Marley a skeptical look over Eve's head. "Why do I get the feeling there's a lot more to the story than she's telling?"

Marley didn't know how she could respond to him without Eve hearing, so she said nothing, only issuing a small nod to let him know she agreed.

"I suppose we should be grateful that nothing else happened to them while they were gone. Of course, many of the problems we've faced so far could have been avoided had any of you just listened to me in the first place." Apparently, he just couldn't help himself from making the dig.

Whatever he was going to say next Marley would never know, as the door opened, revealing Cassie in the doorway. Seeing them, she froze as conflicting emotions flashed over her face. "Hey," Marley said finally, breaking the ice, since it seemed nobody else was going to say anything.

"Hi," Cassie replied back, though it was obvious the greeting was only directed at her. Eve put down the drink that she hadn't touched yet, licking her black-painted lips nervously.

Marley could cut the tension with a knife. "Eve was just telling me that you guys split up earlier because of a problem. What happened?" she asked, hoping that if she confronted the issue directly, she would get an answer.

Cassie looked at Eve as she went to her bed. She dumped her bag onto it and sat down, folding her arms over her chest. "It's nothing," she said. From the look on her face and the stiff body language, Marley knew she was lying. She glanced back at Eve, but Eve kept her eyes fixed on a spot on the carpet. Marley wasn't going to get anything out of these two.

"It's lucky we're not relying on their acting skills or we'd be screwed," Christian said.

Though Marley wanted to know what had happened between the two of them, she didn't have the energy to deal with it. What with the pain she was intermittently experiencing, her guilt of what she had done, and the flashes of that horrific demon face that kept reappearing in her mind, they would have to fix their relationship themselves. Marley was done refereeing their drama. She issued a long, impatient sigh.

Picking up on her irritation, Eve looked up from the floor at Cassie, summoning up her courage as she tucked a strand of curls behind an ear. "About before," she began. "I am sorry, Cass. I didn't mean for any of it to happen."

Cassie stared back at her, her eyes hurt and troubled, as if she were trying to accept the apology but struggling to do so. After a loaded pause, she nodded. "I told you it's fine, nothing happened." Her eyes slid cautiously to Marley. "Anyway, you haven't told me about the graveyard yet. Are you both OK?" Cassie asked, neatly changing the subject.

Relieved that they were talking again, Marley went over what happened, even though just speaking made the pain in her side ache again. When she was done, Cassie slumped back against the headboard.

"I'm kind of glad I wasn't there with you. I wouldn't have known what to do in your place."

Any response was drowned out by Tyler as she crashed through the door. Her eyes were a little wild, her hair disheveled. Dumping her bag onto the floor she moved to Marley's bed and flung herself over it face down. "I can't believe the messages I've been getting from you guys!"

"Yeah, we got lucky this time. Well, I did," Marley corrected herself. "If Eve hadn't been there things might have turned out differently." Her voice cracked as she thought about how close those demons' feelers had come to her.

"Probably would have helped if you hadn't drowned me out, huh? Hindsight," Christian said, not even pretending to be sympathetic. Marley kept herself calm, refusing to rise to the bait.

"Well, what we can do about this? We can't just keep sitting around waiting for the next demon attack. We need to do something, be on the offensive." Tyler said forcefully, popping her knuckles.

"Yeah. I'm tired of getting attacked," Eve agreed.

"I wondered how long it would take before you'd come to this conclusion yourselves," Christian said. "It's not like I've not been saying this since the minute I met you."

Marley had some choice words for him but thought better of it. "Then do we have any ideas?" Marley asked. "As far as I know we have no leads on the seals, and I'm not even sure that we're going to find any, not through our rather unhelpful school library."

A light came on in Eve's eyes. She reached into her jacket, speaking tentatively. "I found something earlier. I wasn't sure if it would be useful but…" She took out a wrinkled leaflet, unfolding it before setting it down on the table. Smoothing the paper back with her fingers she turned the leaflet face up.

They moved in for a closer look. The four of them were staring down at the table when Marley felt the presence of Christian peering over her shoulder. "Is that a discount leaflet?" came his incredulous voice. "You want to go shopping at a time like this?"

Marley repeated his comment resulting in an answering slit of Eve's eyes. "Of course not, stupid. Look at what the shop sells," Eve replied testily.

Marley took in the cursive silver font announcing the name of the store "Juju". She would have thought it was a new club or bar if not for the fact that a cauldron and a black cat formed part of the shop's logo. It was a magic shop that sold magical items and ingredients. Marley picked up the leaflet turning it over to find more bizarre things on discount. Things like powdered chicken feet, snake scales, and other mystical-sounding objects. "This can't be real…"

"I don't know, it looks legit, but we could check it out," Eve said.

"The place is obviously catering for idiots. No one needs a battery-operated broom," Christian said.

"To that, I raise you a Roomba," came Tyler's tired reply. "Have you not seen the cats riding Roomba's Reddit thread?" She seemed to be yo-yoing rapidly. Hyper one minute, crashing the next.

"It's not like we have any other leads to go on. Do you think it's a coincidence that this leaflet was right at the place where Eric's snitch is supposed to be? It couldn't hurt to see," Marley offered. "If it's a genuine magic place, maybe we'll find out what that symbol I saw on those demon's heads were."

"You could check that out at Guardian Base easily," Christian interrupted, clearly not happy for them to take this little side trip.

"But that doesn't have 15% off now does it," Eve suddenly grinned, pointing at the leaflet. "Plus it's all the way across town. This place is closer."

Tyler moved down to the floor. She bunched up her bag, resting her head on top of it. "Sounds like a plan, but it's late now and I'm wicked tired. We should figure out the details tomorrow." The words were barely out of her mouth before her eyes slid closed. Within seconds the rhythmic moving of her chest was the only clue that she was still alive. Marley marveled at how fast she had fallen asleep.

Eve glanced at her watch then jumped out of her chair, her eyes flashing with horror. "Is that the time? I've got to get the car to Si, he needs it to get to work." Without saying goodbye, she tore out of the room leaving Marley and Cassie staring down at the sleeping Tyler.

"Should we wake her so she can go to her own room?" Cassie asked.

"You saw how tired she was. Maybe we should just leave her," Marley said. Grabbing a blanket, she covered Tyler with it then started getting ready for bed.

E ve floored the gas all the way home.
She made it back in record time but she knew it wasn't good enough; Si stood outside the house, his arms crossed over his chest looking as mad as hell. She pulled in front of their house, hurried out of the car. "I'm so sorry. I didn't realize it had gotten so late."

"You're twenty minutes late! I would have called an Uber if I knew how long you were going to be. Instead, I just kept standing here thinking any second now..." He swerved around her, getting into the car, but he wasn't done laying into her yet. "You're usually so reliable, what is with you lately?" he asked, furious with her.

She wanted to explain herself, wanted to tell him every single thing that had happened to her so he could understand all that had been going on with her, but she knew she couldn't. She couldn't risk putting him in danger. All she could do was apologize and take the full brunt of his anger.

"I'm sorry," she tried again, but, disgusted with her, Si stamped on the pedal. Smoke spluttered out of the exhaust as he tore away, leaving Eve to face her guilt alone.

FIFTY-FIVE

A road sweeper swept past, yellow lights blinking, proximity alarm beeping.

Michael waited with barely concealed impatience until the vehicle passed by, taking with it the trash of the day. He moved with purpose, eager to implement the next part of his plan. Twilight had painted the area in a blue glow. A hint of pink sat just along the horizon though it would still be a while before the sun would rise. Michael had timed his arrival perfectly. What he intended to do wouldn't take long.

Crossing the road, he entered the college grounds.

His cold black eyes took in the immaculately tended grounds. The flower beds were in full bloom, the buildings picture perfect from their new coats of paint. To think this was only a place of education, yet it was grander than even the most prestigious of homes back where he was from. These pathetic people had no idea how good they had it. The thought had him burning with resentment.

He walked quickly until he came upon a two-story building. Only a few of the windows were lit up as a result of night-time cleaners, but Michael wasn't concerned. If he bumped into any of them he could dispatch them simply enough, although the undue attention a rising body count would bring, followed by the inevitable police presence, might prove a hindrance after all. Better they had no idea he had ever set foot in this place. It was why he had come alone. That and Fink was elsewhere, preparing for the next step, or his supernatural sense of smell would have come in handy.

His eyes scanned the area, searching for the best point of entry and settling on a side of the building that wasn't overlooked by any other. Walking towards the locked door, Michael held his hand over the handle and gestured. It immediately opened with a click. Normally, he would have preferred to make a much grander entrance, but as stealth was the name of the game, he would have to forgo his penchant for death and destruction tonight.

He moved down dark corridors, the soles of his shoes barely making a sound. As he passed by walls of framed photographs full of smiling student faces, he had to fight the urge to incinerate them all. They knew nothing of suffering, of the hell others endured just to stay alive.

But they would learn.

Finally, he came to the reception area. A large sign suspended from the ceiling said "WELCOME". Leading off from this area was a small office where several computers sat on tables. That must be where the administrative duties were handled.

He stopped by the most cluttered desk. Personalized items were *everywhere*. In addition to the compulsory pictures of an uninteresting looking middle-aged woman with her equally uninteresting children that were pinned to a board on the wall, there were also little mementos and hideous toylike things on springs. As Michael reached across to turn on the computer his arm brushed against one of those strange spring toys and the whole thing started moving in a way that made Michael itch to destroy it. Unable to help himself, he flicked his hand in the tiniest of gestures then watched as it melted into a pool of plastic.

The computer hummed to life as a greeting flashed onto the screen for Loretta, who Michael knew must be the woman in the pictures. Scrolling through folders — at least Loretta was well-organized where it mattered — he searched through each of the classes knowing this could take a while with a potential three-and-a-half-thousand freshmen files to go through. The computer beeped, processors churning until a face he recognised finally came onto the screen, the girl known as Marley.

He read her file with interest, absorbing the information. Like him, she was a recent transplant to the city. Unlike him, however, he could see that she already had quite the school record. Wherever she went, Marley seemed to get herself into trouble, alienating herself from the rest of the students until she became either a loner or a target for bullies. Michael was surprised by this as he would never have guessed by looking at her. She seemed the prom queen type, one of the popular girls. It filled him with cheer that she was neither.

The next file that came up was for the one they called Cassie. She came from a wealthy and well-known family; apparently, her parents were famous, which was something the secretary had noted down in the "other information" section. Records showed that Cassie was a quiet student who didn't participate in school activities very much. A few teachers were concerned that she seemed withdrawn, though none had done anything about it. There was nothing else of interest on her, so he moved on to Tyler with her pathetically sad history. What a wretched creature she was. Reading about her parents' death and subsequent upheaval, he almost would have felt sorry for her if he didn't know any better.

When he came to the last girl, the girl with the black lips and painted eyes, he could feel the excitement surge through his blood. Her file was filled with secrets so juicy, he could almost taste them. It was everything he had hoped for and more. He rubbed his hands together gleefully.

With what he had learned tonight, he would destroy her in no time.

FIFTY-SIX

Tyler woke with a start.

She felt like death; her back ached from the hard, unfamiliar mattress she was lying on. Shifting, she tried to get into a more comfortable position, but her weary body protested at the sudden movement.

Blinking, she opened her eyes, waiting for the black spots to recede. When they did, she realized that the room she was in was the same as hers, though everything was flipped in reverse. Hearing soft breathing in the bed above, she suddenly realized where she was and her confusion melted away. She was lying on the floor having crashed out the night before. Pushing up onto her elbows, she glanced over at Marley and Cassie's sleeping forms.

It wasn't quite light yet outside, but it was too early to be awake. Something must have woken her though. Clearly, it wasn't either of the two girls who were still fast asleep in their beds. Reaching up, Tyler was massaging her aching neck when her bag vibrated next to her. From her position on the floor, she could see the clock on Marley's bedside table. The display read 4:05 AM. Far too early for anyone to be contacting her.

Unless it was Ally.

The sudden terror this thought created forced her wide awake as she scrambled to retrieve her phone from her bag. Her fingers searched frantically until they felt the cold metal of the phone. She snatched it out. Hitting a button so that the home screen came on, she saw that she had one missed call, a new voicemail and text. The call had come last night around ten but Tyler had already crashed out by then. What if there was a problem with Ally? What if something had happened, and she had left it this long to find out?

Tyler activated the recording and waited anxiously for the voicemail to play. The surly voice of Cheryl Heep, Ally's foster mother came down the line. Rather than the terrible news she was steeling herself for, however, Tyler was relieved to receive good news. Cheryl had an appointment that day and couldn't find a babysitter for Ally, so could Tyler look after her sister for a few hours? Checking her text message, she saw that it was also from Cheryl asking essentially the same thing. Why the woman was up this early was anyone's guess.

Thrilled that she would be seeing Ally a few days ahead of her birthday, Tyler quickly messaged back that she would be happy to take her. Although it had only been two weeks since she had last seen her sister, it felt like forever. Then again, every day away from her was like that.

Pleased to have this sudden good fortune, Tyler grabbed her bag and got to her feet. Now that she was awake and excited about seeing Ally, she knew she wouldn't be able to sleep again. Might as well make the most of her early start.

Just as quickly as her excitement had appeared, a wave of exhaustion came, so great that it left her swaying on her feet. She knew it was a result of the punishing long days she had experienced lately, what with school and her new job, then all their extracurricular activity. It was beginning to take a real toll, but Tyler would not miss the opportunity to spend time with Ally. They were together little enough as it was.

Tiptoeing to the door, Tyler let herself out, but instead of heading back to her own room, she moved down the hallway. She would go to the lab, create more of her potion.

It was the only way she could guarantee enough energy for the day ahead.

FIFTY-SEVEN

The iron sign above read "Antique European Coins for Sale."

Marley looked down at the flyer then back up at the shop sign that was clearly nothing like the description of the magic shop in her hand.

"This is the right address? Corner of Main and Court Square?" Eve asked.

The four of them had decided on scoping out the place ahead of classes today and had followed Google Maps here. Marley looked down at the phone app. The pulsating circle clearly showed that they were in the right place, yet this shop looked about as unmagical as could be. It wasn't only the sign that was boring: everything in the dusty window display was unimpressive. An old sheet that might once have been a Merlot-red but was now bleached by years under the sun was draped across the bottom of the window. On it were the European coins, each of them sitting on an individual plinth.

All in all, the place was spectacularly unspectacular.

"We might as well go inside and give it the quick once

over," Tyler suggested a little impatiently. Her shirt, Marley noticed, was buttoned up wrong, as if she had gotten dressed so fast that she hadn't paid any attention to it. That booted foot of hers was still tapping a beat on the sidewalk. How could she have so much energy this early in the morning?

Eve made the first move. Marching to the glass door, she pushed it open and went inside as the rest of them piled in. Inside, tables stood around draped in more of that fabric. Covering almost every surface were those coins. From the back of the room, a beaded curtain was pushed aside as a rich female voice with a French accent called over to them. "Can you shut the door please, you're letting all the draft in."

Cassie, who had been the last one to enter the shop, jumped to do the voice's bidding despite the fact that it was such a warm day. Even if there had been any breeze today, it would have been a welcome relief in this stuffy shop. As soon as the door closed, however, the air shifted in the way the girls now knew only happened when magic was occurring.

Suddenly, everything changed.

Gone were the coins. In their place were all kind of fantastical items for sale. On just one table display, Marley could see what looked like different animal parts but these weren't the kind of thing you could find in a normal store. There were jars of what looked like eyeballs and claws and other disgusting things that she didn't want to examine in closer detail. A mountain made out of Tarot cards balanced precariously beside a glass bowl filled with runes. On yet another table, candles of every size, shape, and color were stacked into a pyramid.

This was definitely the magic shop though, though someone had gone to great trouble to disguise it. An exotic-looking woman with olive skin and smoky eyes approached them grandly. She wore a long purple skirt that swished across the wooden floors. Her feet were strapped in woven sandals and her hip-length black hair braided intricately, interwoven with strands of flowers that moved magically as if they were alive. Her arms were laced with bangles that jangled as she came towards them.

"I've not seen any of you before. My name's Helena and I'm the owner of the store. Welcome to Juju."

Stunned by the transition of the shop, none of the girls made a move to answer her. Only Eve managed a small grunt of response. Helena smiled, showing impossibly white teeth.

"I gather this is your first time here. Possibly a first time in a magic shop," Helena said.

"What gave it away?" Marley asked finally as the power of speech came back to her.

"Actually, my security system," Helena answered. "The hidden cameras around the store scanned your faces, cross-matching them against my database. It's important for me to know who my regulars are because the magic spell that disguises the shop only works on humans. Only those with a supernatural ability can see the real store. So tell me, are you just here to browse or were you wanting something specific?"

Faced with the direct question, the girls went silent, not knowing where to begin. It felt strange to even start the conversation.

"We were hoping we might be to get some help or advice from you," Cassie began before trailing off, embarrassed.

Helena studied their faces with open curiosity. "Well, speak child I don't have all day." As if to prove this, she went back behind the counter and waited, toying with a bracelet. The flowers in her hair swayed as if from an invisible breeze.

Cassie wanted to reply but she shot a look at Eve instead, remembering what had happened the last time she had let her mouth run off. She stayed silent, waiting for one of the others to pick up the slack.

Marley fished out an exercise book from her bag, opening it to the page where she had drawn the symbol revealed on the demon's foreheads, the ones who had attacked them in the graveyard. She showed Helena the drawing of the three overlapping circles sitting inside a triangle. "Does this sign look familiar to you?" Marley asked.

Helena's eyes flicked down to the page, then back up to Marley. "No," she answered. "I can't say it does."

"What about the Five Seals, have you heard of those?" Marley asked hesitantly. She didn't want to go in so heavily, but what with all that had happened, it seemed secrecy was the least of their problems now. Michael didn't seem to be acting very covertly. It was possible the supernatural community had information that they weren't privy to.

Helena arched a brow in question but nodded. "Yes, of course. Why are you asking me about them?"

Marley studied her, hoping to read into her body language. Helena's arms were down by her side; she stared unflinchingly back at them. It seemed unlikely that she was hiding anything, at least from what Marley could tell.

"Do you have any idea where they might be or how we could locate them?" Tyler asked.

Helena shook her head. "Unfortunately no. Many have tried and failed. If you ask me they're better off being hidden. Why would anyone want to find them? They've kept us safe for so many years."

"We think someone powerful is looking for them. He's already killed people to find them. We've had some dealings with him but we don't know much about him or how we can find him," Eve supplied.

Tyler stepped in a little closer. "We actually came into some powers of our own recently, but we don't know why we have them or what we are. Do you serve a lot of supernatural beings in here?"

"Yes. There's a strict policy with places like this. The community know not to cause trouble for us. In return, we can usually provide what they need. It's a little like Switzerland. We don't judge our customers. We don't really care what they do with our products so long as we make money from them."

Helena's honesty was incredibly blunt. Marley found herself a little in admiration of it. It must be nice to be able to say exactly what you thought with no concern about anybody else's expectations or response.

"Although I haven't a clue about the seals or the person searching for them, I might be able to help you with one of your issues," Helena offered. Bending down, she retrieved an ancient silver box engraved with a symbol of a star inside a circle that she set onto the counter.

"If you really want to know what you are or where you came from I just need a drop of your blood for a spell. I can probably find some information for you right now."

Marley felt tense. Could she really answer this question that nobody else had so far? Marley was interested but before she could respond Eve stopped her with a look. Stepping in front of the other girls Eve faced Helena head-on. "How do we know we can trust you?"

"You don't," Helena answered honestly. "But what would I gain from doing anything at this point? I don't know you. I have no history or bother with you. But what I do see are four girls looking for answers and this is an easy enough spell to do. Besides, you've intrigued me now. If you only came into your powers recently, I want to know why. Maybe the four of you will end up being my best customers."

"Do you really have to have our blood to do it?" Cassie asked. She looked a little green around the gills.

Marley figured she must be one of those people who were scared of needles or blood. Her complexion had gone several shades lighter in just the last few seconds alone.

"Yes, but only one drop from each of you. You won't feel more than a tiny sting."

Helena opened the box. Inside sat a container of needles, a small metal dish, and several pieces of fabric. Giving each of the girls a piece of fabric, she gestured for them to hold their fingers over the top of them as she took out four different needles. "You don't have to worry, I run a very sanitary business."

Setting the metal dish onto the counter, Helena drew a symbol into the air with her finger and a flame appeared in the dish. The girls gasped, witnessing this kind of magic for the first time. Helena smiled at their reactions as she held each needle over the flame, sterilizing it.

"How did you do that?" Cassie asked, impressed.

"I drew the spell for it while summoning the flame with my power," Helena replied.

"Does that mean anyone who knows the spell can do it?" Cassie asked, eager to learn more.

"No. One has to have the magic within them to cast spells. It is something you are either born with or not, which is why you four are particularly interesting."

As Marley wondered whether this was actually a good idea, Helena jabbed the needle into her finger. The sharp prick of pain made her flinch and she had to force herself not to snatch her hand back. A bead of blood pooled onto her finger.

"Press your blood onto the material," Helena instructed. Marley pressed her finger onto the piece of fabric, which wasn't any bigger than an inch square, watching as it blossomed over the beige. Taking a different needle, Helena did the same for Tyler then Cassie, though the latter had to close her eyes and look the opposite way. When Helena came to Eve, however, Eve shook her head. "No, give me the needle. I'll do it myself."

Shrugging, Helena gave Eve the needle then watched as Eve pricked her own finger. Gathering up the small squares of fabric, Helena put them into a black stone bowl. Reaching beneath the counter she pulled out a jar filled with a blue powder which she sprinkled into the bowl. A cloud of fog appeared over the bowl, sizzling as if it were meat on a grill. Channeling her energy, Helena stared into the cloud. Marley did the same but could see nothing inside that cloud. Helena could, however, as she grabbed a pencil and began writing into a notebook. The whole spell only took a minute or two. Helena stared into the fog, continuing to write into the pad until four words were written on it. Finally, with a snap of her fingers and a wave of her hand, the cloud dispersed. She looked over at the girls.

"Did that work?" Marley asked more anxious than she thought she would be.

Helena smiled, preening like a cat. "Yes, it did. I found the names of your ancestors, the ones you got your gifts from. Are you ready?" At their nods, she continued. "Marley you are related to a powerful woman named Mary," She looked at Cassie next as she spoke. "You are related to someone named Catherine. Your ancestor," she said to Tyler, "is Tabitha. And finally," she said to Eve, "yours was a woman called Esther."

After the tremendous build up, Marley couldn't help but feel greatly let down by the information. "Is that it? I was expecting something a little more… magical."

"Yeah," Eve chimed in. "And those are four pretty common first names. I'm not sure if that's actually that helpful."

Helena looked startled then a little peeved. "I go out of my way and *that's* the thank you I get?"

Marley felt like a heel, knowing she was right. She was behaving like an entitled brat, but it was because she felt so disappointed with the results. She had really be-lieved Helena would give them at least some kind of answer to their questions, not just four names that probably wouldn't amount to anything. "I'm sorry—" she started to apologize, but Helena stopped her with her hand.

"I think it's best if you all leave now," Helena said firmly. "I've got better things to do with my time than to help four ungrateful girls," she continued before disappearing back behind the beaded curtain.

FIFTY-EIGHT

Eve sped through the corridors, her mind awhirl.
The visit at Juju's hadn't done what they'd hoped, in fact, they probably had more questions now than ever before. Who were those women, their ancestors? How did they tie into things if at all? And then there was Helena herself… What they did know, was that more research was required, specifically those four names they had been given. But that wouldn't be happening until the end of the day.

After Juju, classes had taken over everyone's lives, except for Eve who was free until later in the day. She was glad of the time alone. While she mostly liked the others — time would tell if her opinion would change — Cassie had obviously not forgiven her, no matter how hard she was pretending. She was actually a pretty decent actress, as she seemed to fool the others, but whenever they weren't looking, Eve could feel Cassie's eyes boring into the back of her head. It seemed Eve would have to eat humble pie and make a concentrated effort to apologize to her.

Right now though, she was just happy for a little

downtime. Pushing open a door, Eve stepped out onto the green lawn. Bright sunlight spilled down from the sky as the welcoming sound of bubbling water washed over her. She was at the fountain in the little courtyard that was her favorite place in the college. The scent of roses from the hedge beside her wafted into her nose, filling them with their distinctive aroma. Sitting here amongst nature under the warmth of the sun seemed like a good way to kill time before her first class.

As Eve walked towards the fountain, leaves crunched underfoot. At this time of the morning, there was hardly anyone here. Just a small group of girls who sat behind the fountain opposite her. Paying them no attention, she found a nice spot and sat down, tilting her face to the sun. No sooner had her butt touched the grass then the four faces of the girls opposite turned to look at her, angered by the gall of this one student who would dare sit near them. With a sinking heart, Eve recognized the bitchy faces of her old crew. She should have known they might be here. It was while she was with them that they had discovered this place together.

Grace, who loved to dress in tacky clothes that revealed far too much of her, lowered the cup of coffee she was drinking. "I thought we got this place in the divorce," she remarked.

"Of course you would feel entitled to the place that *I* found," Eve managed to reply back even though she wanted to hide away. The last thing she wanted was to engage with the Meantastic Four, but she knew they would become ten times worse if they thought they were winning. She'd seen it happen, time and time again.

"I'm surprised you'd even show your face around here," said Carly who wore almost as much makeup as Eve, though she would deny it with her last dying breath.

"She knows everything that happened was her own fault. It's why she's gone for this dramatic change," Maxine, a tall blonde smothered in fake tan said.

"You know you could just do us all a favor and disappear again," another girl piped up airily. This was Yuna, an Asian girl who loved and thought far too much of herself. Eve had made the mistake of thinking they were real friends once until she realized that Yuna liked to put her down so she could feel better about herself. In fact, it had been Yuna who had spread the most lies about her last year, when Eve had been at her most vulnerable. Of all of them, she was the worst as she was the kind of girl who acted sweet and innocent when she was, in fact, the most deceitful. She had even tried to steal Eve's boyfriend at one point. She hadn't been interested in him, but she was jealous of Eve's happiness and had tried to destroy that for her own ego.

Eve hated her. Eve hated them all.

Despite what people thought of her, she didn't like confrontation, yet here they were all apparently eager for some kind of fight. She could feel herself rapidly losing confidence as she always had when she was around them. Feeling small, her shoulders started hunching over. Eve had to force herself not to stare at the ground.

Until she remembered she wasn't the helpless girl she once was. She had powers now, and they could be used on more than just demons…

Her head snapped up as she glared at their spiteful faces. Clenching her hands into fists, she sent her mind out probing for the *others* that she knew were all around her. Using her emotions, her fear and rage, Eve channeled her energy to send the call out.

It didn't take long.

The *others* heard her cry and came to do her bidding. Eve could feel them hurrying towards the four girls, who had no idea what was about to hit them. They sat on the grass in their miniskirts and tank tops, most of their flesh hanging out.

Flesh that could be hurt, Eve thought darkly to herself.

Yuna was saying something nasty when she suddenly

felt movement across the top of her hand. She stopped talking mid-flow to look down. A row of ants an inch wide were crawling over her right hand and running up her arm. Yuna yelped and swiped her other hand at them, trying to knock them off, when with horror she realized that they were also climbing up her left arm. The other girls started, confused by her behavior, but then they saw the ants swarming on their own naked flesh and recoiled in horror. Eve's eyes gleamed as she waited patiently, biding her time, enjoying the power this moment gave her. When enough of the ants had covered the girls, Eve gave the one-word silent command.

Bite.

Suddenly the air was filled with their cries as the ants bit into them. Screaming, tears mixing with the make-up that now ran down their faces, they darted towards the fountain, jumping inside. Huddling down, they tried to cover as much of their bodies with water as they could. Only when they were fully immersed did the drowning ants finally let go.

Grinning from ear to ear, Eve sauntered out of the area, listening to the sobs of the girls as they scratched at their bites.

FIFTY-NINE

The house was on the other side of town.

It took two buses and one Metro for Tyler to make it to the area known as Fortnite Gardens, but she was finally there. Already, she could feel the morning's energy beginning to seep away despite her excitement. Reaching into her bag, she fished out the water bottle containing her potion, gulping down half its contents without pausing for breath. The liquid barely made its way down her throat before she started feeling its magical effects.

The houses here were smaller than the ones they had grown up in. Although Cheryl fostered several children, she barely had enough bathrooms to cater for them all, so Ally had to share with one of the other girls. Luckily the two of them seemed to get along; at least that's what Ally always said when Tyler asked. Whether that was true was another matter entirely.

It wasn't that Ally was a liar. She was uncommonly sensitive to other people's feelings, had been even as a young kid. Knowing how much stress she was already under, Ally wouldn't tell Tyler anything that might have her worry, including whether she got on with her fellow foster siblings. This was just another reason why Tyler loved her so much: how many almost-ten-year-olds would be selfless like this?

Tyler walked down the sidewalk, passing by a couple of houses that had seen better days. Weeds and grass grew wild in the unattended front yards. The front fence belonging to another house was missing a few panels. Though this wasn't a horrible neighborhood exactly, it certainly wasn't anywhere close to what they had grown up in… and that was a problem.

Though Ally had tried to fit in, and God knows no sensible person could ever hate her, Cheryl seemed to have a problem with the fact that Ally had grown up with money. Tyler could see it in the little snipes she took at them. As if they could help how they were raised. It certainly wasn't that way now and Cheryl would never let them forget it. She had a habit of calling Ally "Princess" in a tone that implied everything but that always made Tyler rage when she heard it.

She approached the house now, trying to still her racing pulse. It wasn't just excitement, she knew, but one of the side-effects of her potion that made her so wired that she felt like she had drunk gallons of caffeine. She didn't need Cheryl to notice this about her today; although it was only a feeling, Tyler felt sure Cheryl was keeping a running log of her faults, and Tyler was nervous that they could be used against her when the time for her custody case eventually came.

Arriving at the front door Tyler rang the doorbell. Even before she could pull her finger away it flew open and Ally stood there beaming from cheek-to-cheek. Her kid sister was wearing her favorite denim skirt and a T-shirt with a lazy cat on it today. Her chestnut hair was pulled back into a neat ponytail and even the laces on her Converses were done up. She wrinkled her freckle-covered nose at her. "What took you so long?" she exclaimed as she threw herself at Tyler, wrapping her small arms around her as tightly as she could.

Tyler grinned, feeling the overwhelming love that she always felt whenever she was with Ally. Lowering her face, she spoke into the top of her head. "It's not like you live one block away. You know how many buses and trains I had to take just to get here?"

"At least you're here, that's what counts!" Ally said, bouncing up and down with excitement. Steps sounded behind her, pounding into the carpet that had faded from years of abuse. A shadow fell over Ally as her foster mom appeared in the hallway. She was dressed in an A-line skirt and a flowery shirt. Tyler had to blink twice to make sure this was the same woman that she had seen before. Cheryl lived in worn leggings, so this was the first time Tyler had seen her looking remotely presentable. There was even the faint dusting of blue shadow on the lids of her eyes and her lips shone with the recent application of gloss. Of course, she looked as pinched as she usually did, but at least she had made an effort for someone today.

"Going on a date?" Tyler asked trying not to smirk. The six months Ally had been with her, Cheryl had had a revolving door of men, hoping to turn one into her husband, but none of them had been stupid enough to fall for her charms (or lack thereof). Cheryl would go on endless internet dates, looking through lonely hearts columns. It was actually pretty sad.

"That's not where I'm going today," Cheryl responded, a little too quickly for Tyler to believe her.

Tyler shrugged, not really caring either way. All she cared about was this stroke of good fortune that would give her a few hours of her sister's time. Cheryl glanced at the clock on the wall then fussed with her hair which Tyler could see had been stiffly back-combed at the roots to give it more height.

"I'm running late. Have her back here in three hours,"

Cheryl instructed as she grabbed her car keys from where they hung from a peg on the wall.

"Will do," Tyler responded as she reached for Ally's hand. Ally picked up her battered pink bag with the fraying hems and broken zip as they started walking away. Remembering the cute bag Tyler had ordered for Ally's birthday, she couldn't wait until she could give her the present.

"Where are the rest of your foster clan?" Tyler asked, staring back at the now-silent house.

"A few of them went out. Alice is with her boyfriend."

"The one Cheryl doesn't know about?"

"Yep," Ally replied, then changed the subject. "Where are we going?"

"Since we don't have too long, I figured we'd keep it easy today. What do you say we go hang out at your local library?"

Ally bounced up and down with excitement. "That's like my favorite place!" she squeaked.

"I know, Bug," Tyler said laughing. "That's why we're going there."

Moments later they were ensconced in a comfortable corner of the library. It was an intimidating building with Baroque details and filled with stone gargoyles that perched on the walls, which Tyler found pretty creepy. In typical Ally fashion, however, she loved it.

She had always loved to read, though her tastes had grown to darker fairytales now. This was a new obsession. Before, when their parents had still been alive, Ally had been like any other little girl. She had loved fluffy tales of pretty princesses and the handsome knights who saved them. When their parents died, she lost her love for those happy tales: however, though her interests had taken a darker turn, she hadn't lost her love for the fantasy of fairytales. In recent weeks, Ally had developed a taste for stories with less happy endings; in particular, she loved Eastern European folktales.

Ally unzipped her bag and took out a pile of books that she gave to Tyler. Tyler gaped at them in surprise. "Are these books to be returned?"

"Yes. I knew we didn't have much time. I figured you'd be bringing me here and I packed my bag early, just in case," Ally replied.

Tyler stroked her hair. "You knew we would come here?"

"No," she corrected mischievously. "I hoped we would come here, that's different."

Rolling her eyes, Tyler took Ally's books to the front desk.

Alone, Ally turned to study the bookcase in front of her. Her head tilted sideways so she could read the titles of the books easier. As she started through the spines to see what took her fancy, she felt someone come up behind her. She didn't know how she knew, but it did not feel like Tyler. Shielding her eyes from the lamp shining above her, Ally looked up to see a man. He was also examining the books on the shelf. Seeing her looking at him, he gave her a smile. "This place is pretty neat isn't it?" he asked.

"Yes. I come here all the time. They have some cool books," Ally replied. She knew she wasn't supposed to talk to strangers, but Tyler was only a short distance away. She wasn't exactly hidden, so she figured it would be okay to respond, especially as she didn't want to seem rude.

"I see you like dark fairytales?" he asked, looking surprised.

"Yeah. They're better than the normal ones." Ali replied.

"My favorite is Baba Yaga. Have you read that story?" he asked as Ally's eyes flew open with excitement.

"Oh my gosh that's *my* favorite! I love her! She has those weird houses that are on chicken legs. And she eats children. It's super cool."

The guy, who seemed quite young, close to Tyler's age

actually, pulled a heavy book from the shelf, handing it to her. "Well, if you love Baba Yaga, you'll love these stories. I find them so amazing that I can't even sleep when I'm reading them."

Ally looked down at the book in her hands. The title of the book read 'Dark Tales' and was written in a raised font that stood up from the cover. There was a picture of a sinister forest on the cover with what looked like red flowers on the forest floor until Ally looked closer and saw that the flowers were actually drops of blood. It was a neat but eerie effect. Looking up, she went to thank him but there was only empty space in front of her. Surprised, she spun around in a circle looking for him but the guy had completely vanished. It was if it was as if he was never there.

"I leave you alone for two minutes and I see you've already found yourself another book," came Tyler's un-surprised voice. She studied Ally with barely concealed amusement.

"It wasn't me. This man gave me the book. He said I'd like it," Ally replied, still looking for him.

Frowning, Tyler turned around. "What man?"

"I don't know," Ally replied. "I don't see him any-more. He just disappeared."

Tyler felt a cold chill down her back.

Although this was a very public place, Tyler didn't like that a strange man had just spoken to her sister without her being present. She liked it even less that he had disappeared before she could see who it was. Taking the book out of Ally's hands, she shoved it back onto the shelf without even looking at it.

"You don't need his recommendation, Bug. You can find your own books to read," was all she said. As Ally shrugged off the incident, Tyler couldn't help but feel weirded out. Her eyes scanned the room, hoping to catch sight of this man, but he never materialized.

Hidden in the shadows of a particularly hideous griffin, a hard smile spread across Michael's face seeing how overprotective Tyler was with her sister. He watched as Tyler snatched the book from her sister's hands, putting it back onto the bookcase… as if that would do any good.

At least he knew he had been right.

He was right to delve deeper into these girls' lives. He now knew that in order to defeat them, he must go after their secrets.

He must go after all they hold dear.

SIXTY

As classes wrapped up for the day, the girls found themselves back at Guardian Base.

All but Tyler, who was spending some much-needed Ally time. As before, Marley had led them into the giant warehouse. Luckily — or not, depending on how she looked at it — Christian had made an appearance, critically watching over her as she typed in the passcode. His presence caused her to get it wrong the first few times. When the door finally hissed open, she breathed out a sigh of relief, not wanting to hear any more snarky comments from him.

Eve made her way towards the computers immediately. She'd been looking forward to researching the four names given to them all day. They were nearing some answers, she could feel it in every fiber of her being. Her enthusiasm wasn't shared by Marley though, who wasn't as eager to dive into it all, knowing that they were effectively looking for a needle in a haystack.

"Marley, can you come over here?" Christian asked from across the room. He was standing by a brick wall with an expression she couldn't quite place. Curious what he was up to, she joined him as requested.

"I need you to do exactly as I do," he said as he raised his hand over his head… and waved at no-one.

Marley didn't move. She stood, head tilted to one side, wondering if he was trolling her. "And why would I do that exactly?"

Sighing, his green eyes pinned her to the floor. "Will you just do it?"

Feeling ridiculous, Marley copied his exact movements.

Nothing happened.

Judging by the expression on Cassie's face, she was wondering whether Marley had finally lost it big time. She had half turned to Eve, her mouth open in a silent O, summoning up the courage to call her when Christian spoke again.

"Try again," he urged.

Rolling her eyes, Marley raised her arm into the air again, exaggerating her movements. This time they heard something click in the wall in front of them. Suddenly the entire wall of brick slid to one side, revealing an enormous library concealed behind it.

The library was octagonal, with several diamond-encrusted low-hanging chandeliers that were suspended from the dome-shaped ceiling. The walls were lined with shelves that spread so high up they could only be reached by the ladders set on casters that flanked each side of the room. The books themselves were not the usual paperbacks found in bookstores. These were ancient tomes bound in leather or crushed velvet with spines of gold lettering that glinted in the light.

"What the hell?" Eve exclaimed, awed.

"Did Christian just tell you that was there?" Cassie asked.

Marley nodded, shooting him a look. "These don't look like the sort of book you can check out in any old library," she commented, noting the flush of guilt that spread over his cheeks.

"These books hold all the knowledge that we have gathered from the supernatural community over the centuries."

"Why haven't you shown them to us before?" Cassie asked at the space where she thought Christian was standing.

"I wasn't really sure whose side you were on until now," he admitted.

Outrage flooded Marley's body making her shake. "Are you seriously telling me you thought we were working for Michael?"

"I didn't know who you were working for, that was the point," Christian replied, unwilling to shoulder the blame.

"But you've been with us for days now! You've seen us struggle to make sense of this, but all the while, you were hiding all this information from us?" Marley's voice raised several notches as she fought to stay calm. "Jesus, Christian, demons have been coming after us!" She couldn't believe he would keep something so big from them, especially when he had mocked their idea of going to Juju, when the information they had been searching for might have been here the whole time.

"I'm not going to apologize for this," Christian replied, shocking them all. "I had to be sure you were trustworthy. Look what happened when I met you. I tracked Michael down and was about to kill him when you turned up, used your powers against me and killed me. Can you say you'd be any less suspicious in my place?"

Any outrage Marley felt against him was instantly complicated by her feelings of guilt. She knew he wasn't using his death as a trump card, yet it didn't help with the way she felt. Was she always going to feel this wretched anytime it came up? Not wanting him to know the turmoil going on inside, she turned to focus on an ancient book with what seemed like an inch of dust sitting on top of it.

"Why are there more computers in here?" Eve asked, having come into the library to check it out.

"These are hooked into our private network and may contain information that isn't widely available on the other ones, the ones outside."

When Marley repeated his words, Eve's confusion was there for all to see. "You have two tiers of computers in the one building?"

Christian barely contained his irritation. "As I've already said, we can't always be sure who the good guys are. We found it best not to give away centuries of magical secrets to anyone who just asked."

As Eve wandered over to the new computers, having decided that the dust-covered book contained nothing of value, Marley moved closer to the nearest shelf. The books were organized by century, but other than that, the filing system left much to be desired. "Whoever categorized these needs to be fired."

"I'll make sure to index them to your satisfaction the next time I'm alive," Christian retorted, sparks flashing from his eyes. Realizing her blunder, Marley bit her lip and decided maybe it was best if she just didn't speak for the rest of her life. Standing in front of the section covering the 17th-century, Cassie turned to Marley, a questioning look on her face.

"That ghost that keeps haunting you, the one that's trying to help. You first saw her at the Common right? Where they hung all those people?"

"You think we should look at that Hanging Elm or the Common in general?"

"They do seem to keep cropping up," Cassie said, pursing her lips thoughtfully as she pulled a book off the shelf, opening it. Marley caught Christian studying them and had to resist the urge to ask what he thought. Clearly, he had no better idea on how to tackle this or he would have volunteered — scratch that — *forced* it upon them. Marley sat down on the plush carpet next to her as she found a book of her own.

Eve turned on a computer, pleasantly surprised when it booted up quickly with hardly any processor noise at all. A state-of-the-art wireless printer-scanner that had come off the line only last year sat off to one-side, a small distance from the bank of computers. The Guardians knew their tech it seemed and had spent a small fortune kitting up the base with fast-running hardware. She spun around in her chair, turning to face the others. "Hey, Marley. Toss over your exercise book a sec, the one with the symbol you drew."

Nodding, Marley fished it out of her bag, took aim, then threw the book to Eve who caught it easily. "Nice throw."

To Eve's surprise, Marley shot her a grin, flexing her arm. "Swim team, five years running."

Scanning the drawing into the computer, Eve waited, biting on the corner of her lip, hoping for results to appear. The computer went through the motions before it returned with zero hits. A wave of disappointment washed over her. The symbol was possibly their best lead yet it wasn't getting them anywhere.

"Anything?" Marley asked from across the room, looking hopeful.

Eve shook her head. "Nothing." Marley's face twisted with confusion.

Moving the cursor to search the hard drive, Eve typed in "Boston Common." The computer took a second to pull the information before what seemed like thousands of files flooded the screen. Stunned by the sheer number of them, Eve clicked on the first file.

She read through story after story about the innocent people — mostly women, though it wasn't always so — who had been murdered for the most ridiculous of crimes. In some cases, all it took was for a woman to be outspoken. If she dared speak out of turn, it was declared that the devil had possessed her. Eve read about one particular woman whose husband hadn't wanted to be with her anymore after she had put on quite a bit of weight following the birth of their eight children. He killed her himself by setting her on fire in the common, "to protect his children." A week after her death, he married a younger girl.

Eve read horror story after horror story, struck by how terrible history had been to people. Cassie and Marley too were overwhelmed with the stories they uncovered in the books.

They read until their eyes stung from dryness, yet still they hadn't made a dent in the search. Eve wasn't even close to getting through the files. Doing it this way would take an eternity. Since they didn't have that much time, she decided a different tack would serve them better. Clearing the menu, she thought back to their visit to Juju's, to what they had learned from Helena.

Despite knowing how common the names were and not having any other context to put them with, Eve typed in her ancestor's name "Esther." As expected, the results went several screens down. She scanned them quickly, hoping to find something of note, but there wasn't anything particularly interesting or relevant that she could see. Sighing, Eve typed in all four names into the search bar just for kicks, not expecting anything to come up. Drumming her fingers on the table, she waited as the screen froze, as if it were struggling to find the information.

Then the download of information came thick and fast.

Hundreds upon hundreds of hits flooded the screen, so fast that they blurred in front of her eyes. Eve shot up in her seat, clicking on the top headline article. Scanning it quickly, she gasped so loudly that Marley's head whipped up.

"Did you find something?" Marley asked hoping desperately that it was information they could use. They'd been at this for so long that she was losing the will to live. Eve spun around in her chair, eyes wide with amazement.

"Those four women, our ancestors? They were the last four people killed in the Salem witch trials. "

MASSACHUSETTS BAY COLONY, 1693.

Mary and her sisters flinched as another village slammed its door in their faces.

The last few months had taken a turn for the worse. With rumors spreading fear like wildfire, people had become scared of their own shadows. Strangers weren't to be trusted, particularly those who matched the description of witches. For the first time since The Four had dedicated their lives to helping others, they found themselves pariahs, cast out from those who had so readily accepted their help before. As they had never taken payment for their services, they had no food or money. Seeing how faint with hunger her sisters were, Mary worried for their lives.

They huddled around a weak fire, roasting the one small rabbit Esther had managed to catch. She felt awful for killing the little one: the sisters tended to eat only what they could harvest from the soil, but they were on their last dregs of food. What few crumbs of bread they had were stale, the cheese rotten. As Esther broke off pieces of meat, passing them around the fire, a great clap of thunder roared overhead, making them jump. All day the sky had been covered with gray clouds, but Mary had hoped they would pass over. Her hope died the second a fat drop of rain landed on the ground by her foot.

The heavens opened as a torrent of rain poured down onto them, soaking them to the skin, snuffing out their fire. Jumping to their feet, they hurried towards the edge of a forest that they could see on the horizon. They were too late to save their drenched clothes but maybe they could find somewhere to shelter until the storm passed.

The ground became slick with rain, their long skirts dragging through puddles of water, making it difficult to traverse. As they neared the forest, Catherine pointed to a lone building to the West. It wasn't much more than a shack, but there was a plume of smoke rising from the roof. It was a home.

The sisters shared a look of hope as they hurried towards it. When they arrived, Mary rapped on the rickety wooden door with her knuckles. A few moments later, it was opened by a young man who could not have been a day older than thirty if he was that. One of his feet was barefoot but the other leg ended at the knee. Several days of growth shadowed his face, and if the dark rings beneath his eyes were anything to go by, he had not slept in days. Seeing the women he couldn't hide his surprise.

"I am sorry to disturb you sir, but might we trouble you for some shelter from the storm? My sisters and I have been caught out in it. We have nowhere else to go," Mary beseeched.

The man looked uncertain, though not in the way they had grown accustomed to. His expression was not hostile, more concerned. Conflicted.

"It is not a good time," he began when an anguished cry came from the back of the house. Hearing it, he sprang into motion, hopping towards whoever had uttered it. "I am coming, dear," he cried, his worry apparent to all.

Left at the door, Mary shared a frown with her sisters before entering the home. She followed the man to the sleeping quarters, which wasn't more than several animal hides that had been sewn together on the floor. A heavily pregnant woman lay there with flushed cheeks, sweat beading on her forehead. Seeing them, she became alarmed. Mary spoke quickly, not wanting to cause her any more undue stress.

"We mean no harm. We just wanted shelter from the storm, though perhaps God has brought us here for a reason. We are healers and skilled with birthing. If you will let us, we can help you bear your child."

The man's shoulders slumped with relief. "Please. She has been this way for two days now. I do not know how to help her," he said, his voice cracking at the end. Tabitha took him gently by the shoulders.

"Come back into the other room and rest. We will see to it from here."

Mary had already rolled up her sleeves, feeling the woman's forehead for her temperature. She noticed that the woman had a large birthmark on one side of her face that caused her skin to look as if it had been burned. The other side that remained free of the mark was beautiful. She could see that even with her sweat-drenched locks. "We will need hot water and some clean rags."

The young man nodded, eager to perform this simple task. This he could do. He started making his way into the other room before Catherine stopped him. "What are your names?" she asked kindly.

He ran his hand through messy hair, his eyes dazed. "I am Ben. My wife's name is Sofia."

The birth was long and difficult.

It was Sofia's first. Had they not arrived when they had, it was likely that neither mother and child would have survived. Ben must have known this himself, as when Mary finally presented him with his daughter, he broke down in tears. Staring down at his child, he did not seem to notice that she bore the same facial disfigurement as her mother. He loved her from the second she was born.

Later, while Sofia rested with the babe in her arms, Mary and her sisters sat in the living area with Ben. Tabitha had made a stew out of what she could find and the five of them sat eating, celebrating the new life as Ben explained how, until he had met Sofia, he had not been whole.

As a young boy, his leg had been eaten away by disease. He had tried to live a normal life, but his village considered him lacking. Rather than focus on his abilities, his parents' were ashamed of what he could not do, while women refused to even speak to him. Ben knew that if he stayed there, he would live out the rest of his days alone. So he left, deciding to travel the world, doing whatever work he could. It was while he labored on a farm that he met Sofia. Like him, she had suffered from a physical ailment, though hers was but a simple birthmark. The villagers did not consider it harmless however, crying that it was the mark of the devil, that she was a witch. When they had cast her out Ben had already fallen in love with her. He could see her beauty even when no one else could.

They made a simple life here together and until that day, Ben had not wanted any interaction with the outside world. He thanked The Four, knowing that had they not appeared in so timely a manner, his family — his life — would be lost.

Hearing the babe cry, Ben went and fetched her from

her mother. Cradling the baby in the crook of his arm, he beamed down at her, his beautiful little girl, while Mary and her sisters smiled, bathing in the love around them.

Had they known what was to come, The Four would have not set foot in that shack. They would have let the storm do its will, coldness be damned.

They would have left that poor family alone…

SIXTY-TWO

Hunger made them call it a day.

As they went back to BU where Cassie had decided to treat them to takeout, Marley had been plagued with questions that had entered her mind ever since Eve had suggested that their ancestors were tried as witches.

Their research had shown just how many people had been accused of being witches and murdered. In a majority of the cases it simply hadn't been true. Which could mean that their ancestors had been innocent and weren't witches either. On the other hand, as they had personally experienced, magical powers weren't restricted only to witches. Demons had them as well…

A shudder went through her as she considered that maybe their powers descended from much darker beginnings.

Then there was the fact that her ancestor, Mary — if Helena's spell was correct — was likely to be White. She didn't know why she hadn't considered that before, though it was probably because she didn't really identify with her Asian side. Her mom had left when she was just a kid. Marley felt detached from her, the part of her that was Asian. She identified with being Caucasian, so it hadn't struck her until now that if her ancestor *was* one of the last witches who were killed in Salem, that would mean her powers came from her dad's side.

Which threw all sorts of problems into the mix.

Her dad hated talking about his family, to the point where Marley literally knew nothing about them. Whenever she asked, he always clammed up, changing the subject until she learned to leave that conversation alone. Well, she had no choice now. She'd have to find out about them, even if it made him uncomfortable.

And it would. It wasn't only his family issues that would be a barrier, Paul was also super religious. He attended church on the weekend — had done so all her life — and helped out with whatever they needed, be it Sunday classes or summer bakes. Any mention of witchy goings-on would be sacrilegious to him, even if she could raise that particular topic with him. He already thought she was crazy; she didn't need to add more fuel to that fire.

They had arrived back at the school a while ago, but Marley hadn't joined the others at the dorm, instead taking the short walk to the history block where her dad kept his office. Having been here once before, she knew her way around immediately. She'd always had a great sense of direction. If she'd been to a place once, she could usually find it again. It was an uncanny knack that she'd always had, but now Marley wondered if there was more to it than that. Maybe it was part of her powers?

A couple of students passed by, having finished with their professors. When Marley reached Paul's office, she saw with disappointment that the door was closed, the lights off. Still, on the off chance that he could be there, Marley wrapped her knuckles on the door. There was no response. She knew she could call, but what was she going to say to him? She had never been very good at lying to him, and not wanting to tip him off or give any reason to escape this conversation, it was probably best if she tried again another time.

Until then, her questions would just have to wait.

SIXTY-THREE

The rest of the library trip went as planned.
Ally grabbed several books from her favorite section. They read through a few stories together, while Tyler acted out the voices — though she knew she would never be an actress. The sad fact of the matter was, she wasn't particularly good at it, plus her voices tended to sound like a chipmunk from those Saturday morning cartoons. Ally didn't seem to care, however. Every time Tyler did one of her voices, she would send Ally into peals of laughter that had the librarians shooting stern looks their way.

With time almost up, they had made the walk back and were only a few houses away from Ally's current home. Her hand in Tyler's, Ally walked beside her though her happy jaunt had slowed down considerably. Tyler put it down to the fact that they would be saying goodbye to each other again soon. As if she read her mind, Ally looked up at her, smiling even as her face seemed a little wan. "I've got enough books to keep me going for at least five days," she said.

"Five days? Is that all it's going to take for you to read

all those? I should get you to do my coursework," Tyler said making Ally laugh.

"I'd probably be better at it too," Ally replied slowly, slightly out of breath.

Tyler looked down, grinning, trying to come up with a smart retort for her wise-cracking sister when Ally stopped suddenly, frowning, her face growing paler by the second. Her breathing came in shallow gasps and she seemed suddenly weak. The rapid change in her complexion stopped Tyler dead. "What's the matter?" she asked urgently.

"I don't know," Ally said softly. "I don't feel so great."

The words had barely left her lips when her entire body started shaking. As she started swaying on her feet, Tyler leapt forward, grabbing Ally before she fell backward as her eyes rolled into the back of her head. Her sudden deadweight would have had Tyler's arms screaming in protest if she wasn't still feeling the additional strength her energy potion gave her.

"Ally, what's wrong? Wake up!" Tyler screamed as she picked her up in her arms, carrying her towards Cheryl Heep's house. Carrying her as if she weighted nothing, she hurried down the overgrown path. Reaching the front door, she kicked at it with a foot.

"Open the door! I've got Ally, she needs help!" she yelled. She waited for what seemed like an eternity until the door was finally opened. Cheryl Heep stood there, her face distorted with annoyance.

"What the hell do you think you're doing…" she began, quickly trailing off when she saw Ally's condition. She pointed to a room. "In there. Put her on the sofa."

Tyler hurried inside, carefully setting her sister onto the faded floral couch. All she could do was stare at her little face as the blood pounded in her ears, causing a strange rushing sound. She felt disjointed from the world, as if she wasn't in her body anymore. She could barely hear Cheryl's voice as she dialed for help. All she could do was stand there staring down at her sister, one thought running through her mind.

Please don't die on me too.

Tyler was frozen in a black space. She didn't hear any of the chaos around her until Cheryl finally shook her. She turned her dazed eyes to the woman.

"The doctor's on his way. He said this is likely a side-effect from the dialysis and that it looks worse than it is. You need to go now," she said firmly, already pushing her towards the door.

"Go?" Tyler blurted out. "I can't go. I need to make sure she's okay."

Cheryl's lips tightened into a thin line that only emphasized her pinched features. "There's nothing you can do for her. You'll just be in the way. Go home and I will call you when we hear anything."

Tyler's feet were like rocks. She tried to force them into the floor but Cheryl was much stronger than she looked. With a few quick shoves, she had Tyler halfway out of the front door. Tyler gripped onto the doorframe, desperate to stay. "I need to be here for her. She needs me," Tyler said.

Cheryl shook her head. "This isn't the first time this has happened. I know how to deal with it. As her legal guardian, I'm telling you that you need to go and let me handle this. I can't look after her properly if you're here getting in the way so please just go."

With that Cheryl shoved Tyler out the house, slamming the door on her face. Tyler stood there frozen, unable to believe she had been pushed out when Ally needed her the most. Her shock quickly graduated to rage. She grabbed the door handle and twisted, but it was locked. She punched the door next, but all that resulted in was a hurt fist. The door stayed firmly closed. "Let me in, Cheryl! You can't keep ignoring me! She's my sister!"

Refusing to leave, Tyler paced the length of the house. She was still there when a black car pulled up a few minutes later, a medical logo painted on its side. A man jumped out carrying a large leather bag with him. The ID badge pinned to his chest revealed he was a doctor at Mercy General. As he hurried to the door, Tyler grabbed his arm.

"Ally needs help," she rambled.

His brown eyes scanned her quickly, assessing her as he spoke calmly. "You're Tyler, Ally's sister?"

Tyler, stopped, surprised that he would know who she was. "Yes."

"I've helped Ally before. She's spoken about you every time. Try not to worry, I'll do what I can," he said, his eyes exuding compassion. Relieved that she would get medical assistance now, Tyler stepped aside as the door opened and the doctor hurried inside. Tyler made a move to follow him, but the door was shut on her again.

Moving to the window, Tyler cupped a hand over her eyes so that she could see inside better. The doctor examined her briefly then gave her a shot of something. Then he sat down beside Ally, holding her hand until her color came back to her. He spoke with Cheryl for a while as Ally, who had noticed Tyler standing outside, gave Tyler a small wave and wobbly smile. Tears streaming down her face, Tyler gave her a thumbs up as Ally nodded.

When the doctor came out, he gave Tyler a reassuring smile. "She's fine. This will just happen every now and again. She actually wasn't feeling too well when she woke up."

Tyler felt her stomach clench. Had Ally been feeling sick all day? "But she never said anything to me."

His eyes turned understanding. "I gather that might have been so she could see you. She's fine, Tyler. She just needs to rest and have no excitement for a day or two. She'll bounce back in no time."

Giving Tyler a pat on the shoulder, he headed back to his car and left, having no idea how rocked to the core she was by his news. Ally hadn't been feeling well all day, but she had kept this from her, so they could still spend time together. Far from feeling angry at her, Tyler just felt responsible. She was the adult, she was the grown-up. She should have noticed something was wrong, but she was too selfish, wanting to spend time with Ally herself.

Tyler could kick herself.

Ally never complained, even when she needed to. She would never admit how much pain she was in, not if she thought it would inconvenience those she loved and what was the first thing Tyler had said to her? She had complained about how long it had taken for her to get there when she would have gone around the world if that's what it would have taken. The kid was a goddamn saint, but if Tyler had learned one lesson today, it was that she never wanted to feel this helpless again. She needed to help Ally. They were lucky that the doctor came quickly this time, but what if he couldn't the next time she fell ill? What if she wasn't home? What if, she took a turn for the worse and Tyler was all the way across the city from her?

Unwilling to accept that, Tyler realized a new option had recently opened up to her. What if she could use her powers to save Ally herself?

This new thought barreled into her mind like a rocket on jet fuel. Here she was, wasting her talent on essentially an energy drink when she could be putting it to much better use. Maybe there was something she could conjure up that would help Ally in a way that no doctor could. Determined to help her, Tyler started back across town to the lab. She would start working on a cure.

And she wouldn't stop until it was done.

SIXTY-FOUR

With hunger gnawing at her stomach, Marley hurried into TJ Halls, hoping that the others had found some decent dining options by now. Marley's mind drifted over to Tyler. They still needed to tell her what they had discovered today but had mutually agreed that it could wait until she was back from Ally's.

Moving up to the next floor, Marley was only a few rooms away from her own when she heard a familiar voice. She stopped, confused, craning her neck to locate the source of it. The friendly male laughed as he talked about one of those random facts that he loved so much. Rounding the corner, Marley found her dad talking with their RA Rhett and was struck by the coincidental timing. What the heck was he doing here?

Paul must have sensed her presence, as he turned in her direction, a big grin spreading across his face. "There you are. I swung by on the off chance of seeing you but got waylaid by Rhett here — as it turns out, has an interest in ancient religious artifacts."

Rhett greeted Marley with a nod as he gestured to

Paul. "Your dad's pretty cool. You never mentioned he was a professor here."

Rhett seemed like a nice guy, but Marley wasn't in the mood for him. She needed food, and now that her dad was here, it looked like she'd be having that talk with him after all. "It's not like we've had the chance to have any real conversation yet. Last time I saw you, you were surrounded by all those admiring female students."

A blush spread over Rhett's cheeks as he laughed, shaking his head.

"Anyway, we can talk more about what you think of my dad another time, but right now, I need to eat before I pass out."

Although he knew he was being dismissed, Rhett took it all in his stride. "Sure thing. Mr. Gray," he said to Paul. "Feel free to drop by anytime you want to discuss 12th century England. I'm obsessed with the medieval era. I'm actually writing a book about it now."

"Absolutely," Paul replied. "If you have any questions just shoot me an email." Rhett nodded then headed into his room. As soon as he was gone, Paul grabbed Marley in a bear hug. Marley felt instantly comforted. He looked the same as ever, neatly shaven, wearing those brown corduroy pants he seemed to live in. No matter where they were in the country, her dad would always be the same. She hadn't known until this very moment how important that was for her.

"You'll never believe this, but I actually just went to your office to find you."

Paul's eyebrows went up a notch. "Really? See that? Still have our psychic connection," he grinned. "Well, let's go grab some food."

Marley nodded as he tucked her arm into his. "Thank God, I'm starving."

They headed off together as Marley chatted away to him, even as she felt the anxiety over their upcoming conversation preying on her.

SIXTY-FIVE

E ve perched on the edge of Marley's bed as she watched Cassie fixing her make-up in the mirror.

Spending time on her appearance seemed almost like a comfort blanket for her. Of all people, Eve knew what that was like. They both hid under their layers of make-up… but for very different reasons.

Today Cassie was wearing a pink silk camisole with a matching knee-high skirt. The V-necked top hung a little low, as Cassie wasn't well enough endowed in that department to hold it up, but she tried to hide this with a thin scarf made out of a delicate fabric printed with flowers. It hung down the middle of her chest, distracting the eye from what Cassie didn't want people to notice. It was a neat trick that Eve filed away for future use. There were always body parts a girl wanted to disguise.

Swiping her finger across her phone screen, she was scrolling through some options for food when the phone buzzed, vibrating in her hand with a message from Marley that she read out to Cassie: "Bumped into my dad. He decided to take me out to dinner so I won't be joining you. See you guys later. M."

With Tyler still a no-show, and Marley now busy with her dad, Eve was stuck with Cassie. From the slope of her shoulders, she realized Cassie wasn't too pleased about this either. She still harbored a grudge against her that didn't look like it would be going any time soon. Eve could go home, avoid any attitude from her, but she was also big enough to know that she was at fault here. Their current estrangement was due to her own big mouth and it was up to her to fix it, especially if she didn't want this nonsense to keep happening every time they were alone. Forcing a smile onto her lips, she looked at Cassie. "Since everyone else has dinner plans, should we go out too?"

While Eve had watched, Cassie had been trying — and failing — to smooth out the frizz in her ginger hair and was now attempting to reapply the eyeliner around her brown eyes when Eve's question caused her hand to still. "You mean just the two of us?"

Eve shrugged. "Why not? Everybody else is out. We need to eat."

Cassie studied her through the mirror, holding her gaze as her eyes became distant. Eve could almost see the internal battle raging inside. "Yeah," she said suddenly. "That sounds nice. There's a place I like that's not too far."

Eve let out the breath she hadn't known she was holding. Relieved that she was finally getting somewhere, Eve stood up, heading towards the door. "Great. You lead."

Cassie had been right, the restaurant wasn't far at all. Only two short blocks away.

Seeing it, Eve wished it was on the other side of town.

Approaching the glittering glass windows of the restaurant Eve slowed her walk to a crawl, trying not look as incredulous as she felt. "This? This is your favorite restaurant?"

Diamond chandeliers hung over every table, their jewels polished to a gleam. A giant tank full of tropical fish took up an entire wall and separated the dining area from the kitchen where busy chefs in white uniforms hustled, creating lavish dishes that looked too good to eat. A model-like Maître d' stood by the door in what had to be a designer evening gown. Inside, the lighting was low, intimate. Jazz music played, the kind that had no words and seemed just a jumble of random notes.

It was everything Eve hated.

But that wasn't even the worst of it. The worst was the clientele. Like the Maître d', the women paired designer dresses with high heels, the men tailored suits. Whether it was a real rule or not, the place had a dress code. Eve looked down at her outfit, a black and purple corset that she teamed with leggings and biker boots, chosen when she had been half awake. Then there was the small matter of her face… she would not be allowed inside a place like this. "I can't go in there," Eve said.

Cassie stopped a few yards from the Maître d', staring back at her in consternation. There was no sign that showed she understood what the problem might be. "Why? I come here all the time."

She couldn't be this clueless, could she? Eve gestured down herself. "Not looking like me you don't," she said finally. Whatever privileged filter Cassie had been wearing suddenly fell away as she took in Eve's appearance.

"You don't look like the regular customers, that's true, but I'm sure they won't mind." Apparently not accepting that the restaurant would have an issue with Eve, Cassie marched up to the woman at the door. To her surprise, the Maître d' greeted Cassie with a warm hug. She really hadn't been exaggerating when she said she came here all the time. Cassie spoke animatedly with the woman then pointed at Eve. The Maître d' looked her over. Though the woman's eyes did widen, she kept her cool before nodding, gesturing for Eve to approach. A flower of appre-hension opened in her chest. Were they seriously letting her into this restaurant looking like this? Was this going to turn into a cruel joke? Was this how Cassie was going to get back at her, by humiliating her?

Despite any misgivings she felt, she couldn't just walk away. Steeling herself for whatever was going to happen, Eve moved forward. The Maître d' smiled at her with sultry lips. "Any friend of Cassie's is a friend of ours. Wel-come to Sherbrooke restaurant. One of our waiters will show you to a table."

Blinking, slightly shellshocked, Eve followed Cassie silently as their smartly-dressed waiter bowed his head at them. "If you ladies would follow me I have your table right here."

Cassie went with him, but Eve trailed behind, con-scious of the looks being shot her way. Some startled diners looked down their noses at her, but most seemed to have better manners, keeping their reactions to them-selves. The place was surrounded by glass and mirrors; she couldn't move a step without seeing her reflection and their responses. It wasn't even that she was dressed so differently to the other clientele that had her sticking out: she was also one of the few Black people in the room. Every inch of her wanted to run back outside, but she needed to make things up to Cassie. If she wanted to eat here then Eve would have to stomach her discomfort and deal with it.

They wove through the maze of tables as their waiter led them to a table right next to the fish tank. Pulling out a chair, he helped them settle in as he handed them the menus, then left to give them time to look at them.

"I can't believe they let me in," Eve said, still waiting for the other shoe to drop.

"I've been coming here almost every week for years with my folks. I practically grew up here. Whenever my parents have an event or party, they usually do it here, so

I figured they wouldn't have a problem with you, because otherwise, they would have to have a problem with me." There was no hint of guile or malicious intent in Cassie's eyes.

Eve was hit by a wave of gratitude. Yes, they had their differences, but Cassie was proving to be a loyal friend. They were worlds apart in just about every way, yet here they were, about to have dinner. Feeling her tension fade, she opened her menu when her eyes widened in horror. How could she be so stupid? Just one of the mains would cost her a week of wages at the bar. As if Cassie could sense her discomfort, she looked over the top of the menu at her.

"I forgot to say when I suggested this restaurant, but don't worry about anything. Order what you want. It's my treat."

"I'd love to say that's not necessary, except it actually is," Eve said, sighing with relief. "I could never afford this place."

"I know it's not cheap. I should have mentioned it earlier actually, but it kind of slipped my mind."

Eve wandered just how much money Cassie's family had that the price of a meal in this place wasn't something she even entertained. *It must be so nice to have unlimited funds.*

Scanning through the delicious-sounding dishes, Eve eventually settled on the seafood pasta with a side salad while Cassie went for a lobster risotto and grilled shrimp starter. They made small-talk while they waited, steering clear of any hot-button topics. When the food came Eve could have died from just the aromas alone.

Growing up, when her parents had owned a catering truck, Eve had developed a taste for seafood, but they couldn't afford it much now, especially as it was just the two of them, so this meal was a special event to be cherished.

On top of the pasta sat mussels still in their shells,

fried calamari rings, king-sized shrimp and crab claws — all the things she loved but couldn't afford. A grin spread across her face. Grabbing her fork, she speared a calamari ring, taking a bite. Her taste buds exploded; it was like heaven in her mouth. She dug in, eating enthusiastically, savoring each and every mouthful. Across from her, Cassie smiled happily, seeing how Eve enjoyed the food. "It's good isn't it?"

"It's *amazing*. I can see why this is your favorite place. I'd live here if I could."

They dove into their food, laughing and talking about random things as they ate, discovering their mutual appreciation for old 90s movies. Eve was surprised by how much fun she was having with Cassie. It seemed that in this place that she was familiar with, she loosened up until she was actually pleasant to be around. In no time, they had finished their mains and were waiting for their desserts.

"Cassie? I can't believe it's you!" said a stunning woman who had been walking past their table when she stopped, doubling back.

Cassie's reaction was extreme. She froze, a look of horror momentarily spreading over her face before it was quickly replaced with a welcoming smile that she directed at the woman. "Mom? What are you doing here?" Cassie asked as her mother bent down, giving Eve an eyeful of her cleavage from the low-fronted dress she wore. She dropped a kiss on Cassie's cheek, leaving a shiny pink stain on her skin. Behind her stood a group of people all dressed entirely in black with elaborate hairstyles — clearly fashionistas. There was even a man wearing a dress, though somehow, he managed to look cool doing it. They were all quite terrifying to Eve's eyes. Cassie didn't seem pleased to see them either as she ducked her face, trying to hide it behind a curtain of ginger hair.

"I just got done with a shoot and the gang and I decided to grab a late dinner. It's so lucky that we bumped into you! How are you, sweetheart? It feels like so long since we dropped you off at school. You promised to call, but I noticed you haven't yet," she chided in mock anger.

"I've just been busy," Cassie mumbled.

"I'll bet," her mother replied. "All those parties you must be going to! I'm sure you're having a wonderful time."

Cassie exchanged a loaded look with Eve. "Wonderful," wasn't quite how they would describe their experience to date. Turning to Eve, Cassie's mother gave her a smile that didn't waver even when she took in her appearance. "I'm Angie, Cassie's mom. And you must be one of her new friends. It's so nice to meet you."

Eve had to hand it to her, she didn't show even a hint of reservation and seemed genuinely nice. She was also quite possibly the most stunning woman she had ever seen in real life.

"I'm Eve." Behind her, Angie's entourage, who had been talking amongst themselves, had fallen very quiet. While they were still smiling, their expressions changed as they looked first at Eve, then at Cassie. While this was a common occurrence for Eve, it wasn't something she expected Cassie to experience. It suddenly dawned on Eve that they were judging her unfavorably against her ridiculously good-looking mom. They didn't say anything to her, nothing that could be taken as rude or obvious, but Eve could sense it in their demeanor, in the sidelong looks they directed at her. It was obvious what they were thinking…

And it made her livid.

Cassie, who literally just seconds before had been happy, suddenly had her head ducked so low that Eve couldn't even see her face. Is this how people treated her when they realized who her mom was? No wonder the girl had issues! Angie herself seemed completely oblivious to the situation. She couldn't see their shady behavior or read how uncomfortable her daughter was. Despite being a model, she was oblivious to Cassie's body language, which seemed ironic. Laughing at her friends, Angie gave Cassie a hug as she made her promise that they would have more contact in the future, then she swanned away with her adoring fans just as their desserts finally arrived.

Cassie had ordered a chocolate soufflé while Eve had gone for the ice cream sundae mostly because it was the only thing on the menu that she had recognized. Though her soufflé looked amazing, Cassie didn't touch it. "I'm kind of full. I don't really feel like any more food," she said quietly.

Eve knew immediately why she suddenly didn't want to eat. She had lost her appetite herself, but she picked up her spoon.

"We came here to eat a really nice meal, and it *has* been a really nice meal so far, so don't let those idiots get to you. It doesn't matter what people say or think about you. What matters is how you feel about yourself. Do not give your power away. Pick up your fork and eat your dessert."

Cassie's eyes suddenly started to water as she gave Eve a grateful, if wobbly smile. Wiping away a tear, she picked up her fork and took a bite of her soufflé. Smiling supportively, Eve dove into her own dessert, determined to end the meal as well as it had began.

SIXTY-SIX

Across town, in a lower key neighborhood, Marley sat in a booth across from Paul.

The diner was a small but bustling joint filled with junk food-seeking patrons. Burger patties sizzled on the grill in the nearby kitchen, their juices causing smoke to billow into the restaurant, though no one seemed to mind; it all added to the atmosphere.

Diving into a towering burger that contained two patties, cheese, pickles, *and* onion rings, Paul took an enormous bite while Marley watched on in amazement. Somehow, he was able to eat without half of the burger's contents sliding out of it. Marley's own burger was a smaller version of his, but wanting to talk to him, she left it alone, picking up a French fry instead. Dipping it into a pool of ketchup, she chewed on the end of it as she thought about how she could broach the subject on her mind, weary of upsetting him. Swallowing the fry, which seemed to have lodged itself in her throat, Marley reached for her water and took a sip.

"Hey Dad?" she began, psyching herself up.

"Mm-hmm?" he responded, still working his way through the mouthful of burger he had taken.

"You never talk about your family much…"

Paul's eyes turned curious as he swallowed, clearing his mouth so he could speak. "There's not really much to say. You know my mom died when I was a kid, and I never really got along with my dad. He wasn't exactly what you'd call a nice person. Our relationship took a turn for the worse after she died."

"What happened to her exactly? I know you must have mentioned it before, but I can't remember you ever telling me," Marley asked hoping she was being gentle enough.

Paul set down his burger, picked up a napkin and wiped his mouth. "There was an accident. A fire. She died of smoke inhalation."

Marley reeled, her whole body turning rigid with shock. "A fire? That's awful. I'm so sorry dad, I didn't know that."

Paul gave her a small smile, fighting to shield the terrible memories. "I never really mentioned it before because you were too young and I didn't want to upset you, but you're an adult now. I suppose it's time you heard the truth."

He picked up his burger again, taking another big bite. At least the conversation wasn't having an effect on his appetite, though Marley found hers rapidly dwindling.

"What about any other family? Where are they all?" she pushed on.

Paul swallowed again before speaking. "My dad's somewhere in the South, but I don't have any details on where. I cut ties with him a while ago. I have a brother somewhere, but we're not close either. Last I heard, he was living in New York trying to make a living as an artist." Setting down his burger, Paul's eyes turned serious. "What's with your sudden interest in all this anyway? What brought this on?"

Marley fidgeted with the napkin in her lap, hoping her dad couldn't see. "It's for school. I'm doing a project on our family tree but I'm not really getting anywhere as I don't know much about it."

Paul's face turned sympathetic. "I'm sorry hon, I'm not sure how much help I can be with that."

"Do you know if we've ever had any family live around here?" Marley asked.

"Not that I know of," Paul responded.

"Is there anything you can tell me that might be of interest? Anything special about our family line?"

There. Marley had asked the one question she had been leading up to this whole time, though what she really wanted to ask was if he knew of any *witches* in their family. Instead of responding to her question, Paul's eyes slid down to his plate where he suddenly focused on his food.

"I honestly can't think of anything," he replied without looking at her. While Marley had always been a terrible liar, she had clearly inherited this from her dad, who could never make eye contact with her if he wasn't telling the truth.

Like now.

Marley knew he was hiding something from her, but what? What didn't he want her to know?

SIXTY-SEVEN

The soufflé stuck to her throat, thick and cloying.

Not wanting to let Eve down, Cassie diligently ate her dessert, though she didn't enjoy a moment of it. All she wanted was to rush back to the dorm so she could hide away, pretend this never happened. She was so sick of their stares, so tired of their judgment.

It wasn't her fault she looked like this. She wasn't even ugly! Not really. She just couldn't match up to her fabulous mom. Then again, who could? She was one in a million — and unfortunately for Cassie, the DNA jackpot hadn't been as kind. It wasn't like she didn't have to face this cruel fact every day.

Setting her fork down, Cassie knew she had to admit defeat. If she tried to swallow another mouthful, she might just throw up. Setting her napkin on the table, Cassie slid her chair out. "I'll be right back. Restroom break."

Eve nodded, though she wasn't quite able to hide her concern. She hoped Cassie wasn't going to cry in the restroom. She'd done so well at ignoring their rudeness. All the way through dessert, Eve had been wondering about

Angie; how could the woman not see that her colleagues were being rude to her daughter? Was she that self-involved? She did seem to love Cassie though, so the whole thing just taxed Eve's brain. Steeling herself for another spoonful of the never-ending ice-cream, Eve watched Cassie's small figure as she wove through the restaurant.

L ights flashed on above as Cassie walked into the marble restroom.

A sigh of relief left her lips when she saw she had the place to herself. Moving into a cubicle, she sat down on the toilet, locking herself inside. She'd managed to keep her composure until now, but the tears simmered just under the surface, threatening to let loose.

Every time this happened, it shook her to the core, though contrary to popular belief, it wasn't just what people thought about her that unraveled her — it was how their judgment made her resent her own mother. She resented being anywhere near her, fearing the comparisons that she knew would come... invariably, that would make her feel even worse about herself.

Breathing deeply, Cassie fought to control her emotions. She didn't want to let Eve down, not after she had shown her such kindness. She was going to sit here until she was composed. She wasn't going out there again until she could face the world with a smile.

Her thoughts were interrupted by the sound of the restroom door swinging open, followed by the patter of several pairs of high-heeled feet, the owners of whom hovered outside Cassie's stall, chattering a mile a minute.

"This place is so gorgeous, I could just hang out in this restroom," said a perky female voice.

"Forget the decor, what about our waiter? Did you see how cute he is? Of course, he only had eyes for Angie, but I can dream," came a more wistful voice. At her mom's name, Cassie froze, hoping to God that they were referring to a different Angie.

"Angie's married to that hunky anchor, so he's got no chance. Maybe if you try a little harder though, you might get lucky tonight," said yet another person.

Cassie's heart dropped to her stomach. These *were* her mom's friends; her dad was the "hunky anchor" they mentioned. She was trapped in here with the very people who had made her feel so terrible about herself.

"Did you see her daughter though? I'd never have guessed they were related, not in a million years," one of them said, sending Cassie deeper into shock.

"I know. If she was my daughter, I'd fix that face with surgery, pronto!"

"Be cheaper just to use a brown paper bag wouldn't it? After all, there's only so much surgery one can do."

They laughed bitchily as if they'd said the funniest thing in the world while Cassie could feel herself wanting to die.

"Imagine being Angie then having an unfortunate-looking daughter like that. I'd be surprised if the poor thing ever found a guy who'd want to date her."

"Well, maybe Angie can help incentivize some poor soul. Failing that, they could just buy her a boyfriend."

More laughter came, cutting like a knife. Two of the women went into the stalls on either side of her as Cassie shoved her fist into her mouth to keep from making any sound. The women did their business, then one of them spoke again.

"Christ, there's no paper in here," she exclaimed. She tapped on Cassie's stall, her nails clicking against the metal. "Excuse me, could whoever is in the middle stall please pass me some toilet paper under the door? I'd really appreciate it."

Cassie couldn't believe this was happening. After what they had said about her, now they needed her help. She had half a mind to ignore her. Adrenaline kicked in, causing her blood to pound. What she really wanted was to leave her stall now and face these women directly, letting them know exactly what she thought of them. Then she'd march up to her mom and let her know too. Her mom would *ruin* them. All she had to do was open that door and let them have it.

But she couldn't do it.

Even though she hated herself for it, Cassie pulled several squares of paper from her toilet roll, handing it to the woman on the other side.

"Thanks, sweetie, you're a doll," the woman called out to her. Cassie didn't reply. She couldn't trust herself to say anything. She continued to sit there while the women spent forever tidying up their makeup before finally leaving.

As soon as they had gone, Cassie left the stall as the tears started to fall. Unable to hold them in any longer, she sobbed. She had to get out of there but she was afraid to bump into those women again. What if they came back? What if her mom was with them this time? She couldn't do it. Not as herself…

Turning to the mirror, Cassie started picturing Marley's face. Calling up her power, she began changing her features into Marley's. First the eyes, then the nose. The air hummed with energy as she worked through each of her features until Marley's face stared back at her. Then she changed her outfit, morphing into the first thing that came to mind, which just happened to be the tight-fitting dress her mom had been wearing. Eyes still blurry with tears, Cassie fled the restroom. Back in the main dining area, she glanced at Eve, who sat across the room from her, still working away at that ice-cream. She knew she should go back to her, but people were beginning to notice her distress. She couldn't face making a scene: she had to get out of there.

Though she knew it was a horrible thing to do, Cassie hurried out of the restaurant.

E ve's spoon froze halfway up to her face.
She watched, astonished, as Marley — dressed in an identical dress to Angie's — rushed out of the restaurant. Except, she knew it wasn't Marley. It was Cassie, and she was wearing their friend's face. Eve didn't know what had happened in the restroom, though clearly, she had no intention of coming back.

Stunned, Eve set her spoon down as the ramifications of this suddenly hit her. Cassie was supposed to be paying for this meal! There was no way she could afford this. As if by some great streak of bad luck, their waiter chose that exact moment to appear with the bill. He smiled at Eve, having no idea what had just transpired. As far as they knew, Cassie was still in the restroom.

Eve blinked, unable to believe what was happening. Cassie had stiffed her for the bill! She had come here to make up with her, to be her friend, yet this was the kind of stunt she pulled in return. Uncontrollable rage started building inside of her. Eve let herself feel it at first, until she remembered what would happen if she didn't put a lid on her negative emotions. She forced herself to focus, trying desperately to bottle the rage... then her eyes slid over to the bill. Seeing the ridiculous figure written on it, Eve lost any last vestiges of control she had left.

She felt the air hum with electricity as everything stilled. Then the screams came. First one, then more, as a sea of mice surged over the floor towards her. Panicked customers shot to their feet. Some jumped onto the tables while others ran for the exit. Everywhere she looked, mice and people converged. It was complete and utter chaos.

Shooting up to her feet, Eve realized this was the break she needed. Joining the mass exodus, she hurried out of the restaurant.

SIXTY-EIGHT

Cassie walked blindly, not knowing where she was going or even what she wanted.

Shops and restaurants blurred past. She walked without direction until her shoes were starting to pinch at the toes. She took them off. Holding the shoes in her hands, she suddenly noticed a pair of guys looking at her. They had slicked back hair and reeked of cologne. Both had brown eyes and the unnaturally tanned skin that spoke of too much time under a tanning bed. The taller of the two winked at her.

"Hey pretty baby, shoes hurting you?" he asked.

"Yeah," Cassie replied, not sure how else to answer.

He flexed his hands. "I'm pretty good at foot massage if you wanted to give me a try?"

Cassie could feel her cheeks reddening but she forced herself to keep looking at him. She wasn't herself now after all. She was Marley… and this was exactly the kind of distraction she needed.

"Out here, in the street?" she retorted bravely, thrusting out her now Marley-sized chest so they could get a better look at it.

He looked at his friend, not able to believe his luck. "Of course not. Where would you like to go?"

She knew she was playing with fire but somehow she didn't care. She'd had enough of the world treating her like she was nothing. To hell with it. It was time for her to grow up. "How about my place? I live in a dorm. I'm not sure if my roommate is back yet though." Even as she said the words, Cassie suddenly panicked at the thought of Marley arriving back while she was wearing her face. How was this going to work? She didn't have time to think of an excuse, however, as the taller guy came over, took her hand and kissed it.

"It's no problem if she is. The more the merrier. I'm Miles, and this is my cousin Jason."

If Miles's kiss hadn't charmed her, then Jason's bow definitely did. All concerns of the real Marley flew out of her mind, especially as she knew she was out with her dad.

"After you," Miles said to Cassie.

T he walk back to school had been filled with laughter.

Cassie found herself easily charmed by Miles and Jason; it wasn't only their hair that was slick, but their personalities too. They talked about recent movies they had liked, though Cassie didn't know much about them as they weren't really her deal. She walked between them as Miles casually slung an arm around her shoulders while Jason curled his around her waist. She felt special, having the attention of both of these guys, both of whom were also older than her.

Miles was talking about his job, which had something to do with IT. She didn't really understand what he was saying, but she nodded and made the right noises so that he would think she did. Jason also had a job. He worked for a local car dealership. They both found it endearing that Cassie was still at college, as neither had pursued a higher education. Cassie let herself forget her problems, enjoying the attention they gave her.

Anything to make herself feel better.

When they arrived at BU, Miles gave a low whistle. "Impressive," he said.

"Yeah. It's pretty nice," Cassie agreed as she led them towards the residential quarters. They were a few feet from the entrance when a voice greeted her.

"Hey Marley, how was dinner?"

Cassie stopped dead, recognizing the voice. Turning slowly around, she found their Resident Advisor, standing behind her, a takeout pizza box in his hands. He was just as good-looking as he had been the first time they had met when Cassie had barely been able to string two words together.

"Oh, hey Rhett," she replied in Marley's voice. Three words... that was an improvement already.

"I was just out grabbing some late food..." Rhett took in her dress and the two guys hanging off of her. While he didn't frown exactly, some of his welcoming manner turned to confusion. "You look... different."

Not understanding what he meant, Cassie tilted her head at him. "What do you mean?"

"When I saw you and your dad earlier, you weren't dressed like that."

Her head started throbbing as she realized Rhett had seen the real Marley. "Oh, you know us girls, any excuse to dress up," she mumbled, hoping he'd buy her excuse.

Rhett slid his eyes over her two companions, cooly assessing the situation. "Haven't seen you two around here."

Miles stepped forward, smiling. "We're new," he lied.

"You're both students?" Rhett asked, clearly not buying it.

"Yeah," Jason replied. "We live over there." He waved

his hand in the general vicinity of the place. Cassie's heart raced, knowing she was about to be busted. Terrified of what the others would think if they knew about her new habit, Cassie turned to Miles and Jason.

"Maybe we should call it a night," she began.

Miles scowled, his earlier good nature disappearing immediately. "But we just got here…"

"I'm not feeling too well suddenly," Cassie said lamely, knowing that no one would believe her. She felt bad at leading them on, but she also knew it wasn't a good idea to continue. Rhett stepped in gallantly to save the day.

"In that case, you should get some rest," he said to her before turning to the two guys. "I can take it from here fellas. I live in the same dorm. I'll make sure she gets back safely."

Miles and Jason shot an annoyed look at each other, but with Rhett refusing to budge, they wouldn't get anywhere without a scene. Finally, Miles shot Cassie an irritated look. "Maybe next time, you should figure out whether you're sick or not before you make us walk all the way here."

He spun around, Jason at his heels as they left leaving Rhett standing beside Cassie.

"They seemed nice," Rhett commented sarcastically. Cassie couldn't help smiling back at him. She'd only really met him the one time before, but Rhett seemed like he was one of the good guys. It certainly didn't hurt that he was super-hot too. Pushing the door open, he held it open for her as Cassie moved inside. They walked up the flight of stairs together as Cassie checked him out from the corner of her eyes. He really was a hunk. He was exactly the kind of guy she'd love to have as a boyfriend.

"So how have you been finding college life?" Rhett asked, interrupting Cassie's study of him.

"It's not exactly how I thought it would be," she answered honestly.

Rhett touched her shoulder, his fingers hot on her skin. "It'll get better, I promise. Just give it a chance. It's rough for everyone in the beginning."

Cassie smiled gratefully at him even though she knew he had no clue about her unique problem.

"Well, this is me. If you have any problems, give me a shout. I'm only down the hall," he said, unlocking the door to his room.

Cassie wished more than anything that she could take him up on his offer. She had already messed things up so much, she didn't know how she'd fix any of it. Giving him a small smile, she hung her head and went on her way.

SIXTY-NINE

Arow of beakers sat before her.

Channeling her inner energy, Tyler focused on the liquid in the glass jars. All she had to do was think of Ally, specifically her damaged kidneys. She pictured the organ in her head, familiar with the look and shape of it from her many attempts before at trying to understand why it wasn't doing its job in Ally's body. Holding the image in her head, she tried to think of Ally with healthy kidneys but the second Ally's face flashed up in her mind, all she could see was Ally collapsing in her arms, making her feel as helpless now as she had felt earlier.

Tyler fought to stay calm. If she could create a potion that gave her instant energy, she sure as hell could make one to save her sister. Fixing her eyes on the first beaker, she focused her energy on its contents, but something didn't feel right. The air didn't tingle as it normally did when she used her power. Her hair didn't become static. A small bubble appearing on the surface of the water was the only sign that something was happening.

Why couldn't she make this work?

Sweat pooled at the base of her neck. Irritably, she brushed it away and tried again. Gathering her inner strength, she let the power loose, but the water stayed stubbornly still.

A sigh of frustration left her lips as the room swayed suddenly, a wave of exhaustion overcoming her. It had been some time since she'd eaten, even longer since she'd had some of her own potion. Maybe she needed more energy to do this? Reaching into her bag, she took out her brew, downing the rest of it in two quick gulps. As before, a rush of energy flooded her body and Tyler felt immediately rejuvenated, though something else was happening. Feeling an unusual tremor, Tyler looked down to see that both hands were shaking. Not giving it another thought, she went back to her task. Completely wired, she tried again.

Again, the result was nothing.

Growing increasingly angry, yet determined to make a cure for Ally, Tyler readied herself until she could go at it again.

She would do this all night... even if it killed her.

The rest of the dinner was uneventful.

Marley ate her food without tasting a thing. She kept up appearances, not wanting her dad to know that something was wrong even though deep in the pit of her stomach, all was not well.

Through the trauma of her mom leaving when she was so little to the diagnosis of her mental illness, the one constant in her life was her dad. She could trust him with anything; he always had her back. So the fact that he was keeping things from her did not sit well at all. What was in their family history that he didn't want her to know?

Marley thought about the only living relative she remembered ever meeting. Her grandfather, Paul's dad. Although the two of them didn't speak now, there was a time when a much younger Marley had spent time with her grandfather. She remembered the leather loafers he always wore and the exotic spicy smell of the pipe he liked to smoke. Trying to picture when they had last been together, Marley realized that it must have been on her fifth birthday, as an image of her mom holding the cake set with five candles entered her mind. A year later, she would disappear out of Marley's life entirely.

She had been obsessed with bouncy castles then, frequently requesting one for her bedroom. Her parents had explained how that wasn't possible but had surprised her with a giant one for her birthday. She could see herself playing on the thing now, bouncing as high as she could while her parents and grandfather joined in. There were smiles all around so how could things have changed so dramatically just one short year later?

After they left the diner, Paul mentioned that a local theater was showcasing some arty European movie he wanted to see. Unable to sense Marley's turmoil, Paul revealed that he had already bought two tickets to the next showing. Marley didn't care to see the movie and actually wanted to go home to figure out her thoughts. She wanted to be with the girls so they could find out more about their ancestors. She also wanted to delve more into her own family mystery. Whatever her dad was keeping from her, Marley was more determined than ever to find out. Having offered her a ticket, Paul was still waiting for Marley's response.

"Sorry, Dad, I can't. I've got some things I should go back and work on," she replied. His face fell with disappointment.

"I understand, though I do feel like a loser that I can't even get my own daughter to see a movie with me," he answered, eyes twinkling.

"If you didn't keep picking these obscure films, you

might have a better chance," Marley joked back. Though they bantered, she wished that it didn't feel so hollow.

Glancing at his watch, Paul suddenly started at the time. "I'd better go if I want to make this thing. Take care of yourself, hon. Call me if you need anything, OK? Don't be a stranger."

"I won't," Marley said, even as the words stuck to her throat. Giving him a quick hug, she started on the walk back to the dorm, trying desperately to ignore the growing ache in her heart.

SEVENTY

Eve sat on her bed fuming.

Though it had been over an hour since she'd gotten home from the restaurant, she hadn't been able to shake the incident. Of all the terrible things Cassie could have done… Eve had been trying so hard to make things up to her when she shouldn't have bothered. Cassie was selfish and strange and it looked like that wouldn't be changing anytime soon.

Moving to her vanity table, Eve began to remove her makeup. As the heavy layers disappeared, revealing her real face, Eve stared at herself, at the girl that hid underneath. Her brown skin looked pale, the eyes haunted. Unable to handle the emotions that surfaced whenever she saw her real face, Eve turned away, keen to focus on something else.

The local evening news was currently on in the background when the footage suddenly cut to a shaky recording of the restaurant as floods of mice and diners ran screaming out of the place. Judging by the terrible camera work, it had been taken on someone's phone. The news anchor mentioned that the restaurant was currently being investigated by health officials and would be closed until further notice.

Hearing this, Eve felt a pang of guilt in her chest. The restaurant didn't have a problem with vermin… only her. Knowing that her actions had caused the place to close down until who knew when, Eve felt terrible, particularly as her own parents' livelihoods had depended on a catering business. Just imagining how the same 'outbreak' would have shut them down had Eve's stomach in knots. If there was a way to make it right, she would. The owners of the restaurant shouldn't have to pay for her actions.

Unable to listen to any more of the news, Eve turned her television off then flipped on one of her laptops. Usually, this would be when she would play World of Warcraft to mindlessly while away the time. Tonight she didn't want to do that. She needed to do something productive. Typing into her search bar, Eve continued her earlier research. Nothing jumped out at her, however, not until she went back to looking up the mural inside Trinity Church, which they now knew had been the First Seal.

Something came up in her findings, something that filled her with excitement, though she wasn't sure if what she was seeing was correct. Pulling out her notebook, Eve jotted down the date the mural had been created in the church, then cross-checked it against another event.

Eve gasped, knowing it couldn't be a coincidence.

The mural was created at the exact time when the Salem Witch Trials ended. Her head swam as she contemplated her findings.

Were their ancestors linked to the seals in some way?

Mulling those thoughts over, Eve got ready for bed where she fell asleep still mulling those thoughts over.

Ally stared up at the ceiling, hoping that her head had finally stopped spinning.

It was just her luck that something like this would happen on the day she finally got to spend some time with her sister. She knew Tyler must be feeling awful about her collapse, but Heepie Jeebie wouldn't let her call her. She said Ally needed to rest and talking to Tyler worked her up too much. She must have known that Ally wouldn't have listened to her, however, as her phone was gone now. A yellow post-it note sat in its usual place:

You can have your phone back tomorrow after you've had some rest!

Ally hated that woman.

She had been resting for hours now but couldn't sleep. Until her collapse, she'd had such a great time with Tyler. She knew she shouldn't have lied. She should have told Heepie Jeebie how she was feeling when she woke up, but people didn't understand how much she missed her sister. She missed her parents too, of course, but she and Tyler had always hung out together, so to only get to see her on such rare occasions now…

Ally sighed and tried not to think about things. It made her too sad. What she needed was something to do. Opening her bag, Ally pulled out her library books. Setting them on her bed, she went to toss her bag to the floor, but it was still heavy: there was something else in it. Surprised, she rummaged around until she came up with an extra book.

It was the one Tyler had put back onto the shelf. The one the man had recommended to her.

She stared the book, wondering how it could have gotten into her bag; she was sure she hadn't checked it out. The book was heavy, and Ally had to use both hands to maneuver it. She studied the title on the cover, its polished letters gleaming under the light. Feeling intrigued, she moved the other books onto the floor, then settled back into bed. Switching on a flashlight, she switched off the main light, then dove under the covers with the book.

And she began to read…

———

Sometime later, Ally had fallen asleep with the book lying open next to her. Her flashlight had rolled to the floor, its light still on. Her small chest rose up and down as she breathed, sleeping the sleep of the dead.

Something moved inside the pages of the book.

Something small, thin, and black.

It was one of the black printed letters — a capital "I". It pulled itself off of the page, as other letters began to do the same. The letters crawled together, converging until a shape began to take form… a spider-like creature that scuttled out of the book, across the bed and onto Ally's head.

Completely oblivious, Ally didn't wake. She didn't stir. Not even when the creature crawled into her ear and *into* her head…

SEVENTY-ONE

Everything was black.

A sharp pain stabbed at her head as she felt the world spinning. Forcing her eyes to open, she blinked, trying to get them to focus. When the blurriness finally receded, Eve saw that she was lying on the cold ground. The scent of crushed grass met her nose and she almost sneezed. She'd been allergic to grass since she was a young girl and knew well enough to stay away from it, so why was she lying with her cheek pressed so tightly against it?

Pushing herself into a sitting position, she looked down at the pretty yellow dress she wore. It had a brown trim and the whole thing had made her think of a sunflower, which is why she had bought it.

She had thought it would impress.

There was something flittering at the edge of her memory. A flashing red light of warning, but she couldn't think what it was. Had she hit her head? Is that why she didn't know where she was or what she was doing here?

The ground was cold and hard beneath her. She shifted her position, trying to get more comfortable when her body screamed out in protest. It seemed that she hurt everywhere. Her arms shook and her legs throbbed with a terrible ache. Even her ribs felt as if they had gone through a battle. Looking down at herself, she pulled up the knee-high fabric of her dress to see that her legs were riddled with ugly, purple, finger-shaped bruises. What was this? Twisting to examine the tops of her arms, Eve saw the same finger-shaped welts denting her skin.

What the hell had happened to her?

Suddenly, she heard a sound crashing through the trees behind her. Her blood turned cold. Whoever had caused those marks was still here. They were still coming after her. Stumbling to her feet, Eve started forward. She had no idea where she was going. All she could see was trees for miles. She caught the occasional glimpse of blue sky, but that seemed so far out of reach that it might as well have been another planet. It was just her in these woods.

Her and whoever was coming for her.

She ran through the pain, ignoring how much sound she made, desperate to put as much distance between herself and her pursuer as possible. She ran until her lungs were on fire and her heart threatened to burst out of her chest. When she could run no more, she braced herself against a tree, greedily gulping down air.

A sharp stabbing pain lanced her side.

Eve looked down to see red blossoming over the yellow dress.

Her blood.

Someone had just cut her with a knife. Before she could do anything else, she was tackled from behind. She flew forwards, landing on the hard ground with a painful thud. She could feel her attacker's body on top of her, crushing her with his weight. Her face was pushed into the ground until she tasted dirt.

Then suddenly everything went black again…

B ack in the safety of her room, as Eve tossed and turned from her nightmare, a moth landed on her window, quickly followed by another. Then several more. Swooping in, their patterned wings beat at the glass as they tried to get inside.

But Eve was oblivious, trapped in her nightmare.

E ve woke to the happy trill of a bird eagerly greeting the dawn of a new day.

Grimacing, she wished the stupid thing would shut up.

She felt like the dead despite knowing she had slept for a decent amount of time. Her mouth was dry like she hadn't drunk in years. Her body ached as if she had spent all night on the hard ground instead of her orthopedic mattress. She reached for the bottle of water she always kept next to her bed and sat up, twisting the cap off. As she raised the bottle to her lips, she saw something hanging off the end of the bed that gave her pause.

Something that was so battered, so covered with dirt and stains that it was almost impossible to see its original yellow color.

The bottle slipped from Eve's fingers, spilling water everywhere, but she didn't give it another glance, her attention fixed completely on the impossible thing in front of her. Sliding out of bed in a complete daze, Eve moved towards the piece of clothing, her heart thumping wildly in her chest.

Lying on the end of the bed was the yellow dress with brown trim that Eve had worn in her nightmare. As well as the dirt, it was covered with bloodstains and cuts. Her blood, Eve knew.

She remembered it well.

Although she wanted nothing more than to run away, she had to see if this was real. There was no way it could be, yet she had to know. Reaching out, she lowered her hand until it brushed against the dress. The dirty yellow material crinkled under the weight of her fingers.

Eve flinched as if it had burned her.

The dress was real. But how was that possible?

Feeling the edge of hysteria bubble up inside, Eve snatched up the dress, then ran out of her room and down the hall. Reaching Si's room, she didn't bother to knock. Gripping the handle, she flung the door open, racing inside. The door crashed against the wall from the sheer force of her actions, startling Si, who woke immediately in his bed.

"What the hell, Eve..." he managed to mumble. Eve didn't speak. She didn't have to. She held the dress out in front of her and didn't have to wait long. Si blinked several times, staring at it before his face mirrored her own shock.

"That's not possible," he finally uttered.

"I know. But here it is," Eve replied, feeling sick to her stomach.

ONE YEAR AGO.

Eve watched as the hole was dug in front of her.

She waited, trying to control her trembling, gingerly feeling her arms which were riddled with those finger-shaped bruises. Leaves were tangled up in her curls, slick with dirt. As if in a trance, she stripped out of her blood-soaked yellow dress, hurriedly pulling on the sweatshirt Si passed to her. Holding the soiled dress over the hole, she dropped it inside as Si buried the evidence where it would never be seen again.

Only then did Eve let out her breath.

Si enveloped her in his arms. There, in the safety of them, Eve finally let loose all the emotion she had kept repressed for so long. She sobbed, wailing her fear, her rage, until there were no tears left.

PRESENT DAY.
Eve stood in front Si, the dress in her hands. Only one other person could know where that dress had been buried.

And he was dead.

Unless… could it be possible?

Was he *back*?

TWISTED MAGIC

5: WHEN TROUBLE COMES

JO HO

SEVENTY-TWO

Orange flames burned as brightly as the mid-afternoon sun as the yellow dress inside the metal trashcan withered to a blackened husk.

In stark contrast to the riot of color before her, Eve's face was pale. She stared through the billowing smoke, her green eyes fixed on the dress as if there was nothing else in the world. She would not look away, not until the very last piece of it was destroyed.

Though the smoke stung her eyes making them water, she stared through the discomfort, watching with her hands gripped tightly by her sides until the battered material turned to ash. With nothing to feed on, the fire soon died out, but still, Eve couldn't move. She couldn't resign herself to what had happened.

A strong hand found its way to her shoulder, holding it in a firm grasp. It was her brother Si. While the dress had burned, he had stood in solidarity beside her, but now that there was nothing left of it, she could feel his unspoken need to move on. There were things they needed to discuss, things he didn't feel safe talking about, despite being in their own backyard where they couldn't be overheard by others. When she didn't respond, he shook her slightly to get her attention. Only then did she turn to him — though she didn't really see him, her eyes glazed over with shock as they were.

"Come inside," he said.

Eve blinked. She had heard the words that came out of his mouth but they reverberated in her head, echoing along with that crazy buzzing that sounded like hornets.

"What?" she asked.

He gestured towards the house. "Inside Eve. Come on. I'll get us some coffee."

He started inside, tossing a look over his shoulder to make sure she was following. Her feet moved obediently, though she didn't feel connected to them. It was as if she wasn't in her body, like she was floating all the way back. She followed him blindly inside "for coffee," because that is what people did apparently when their whole world came crashing down around them.

By the time she was inside their kitchen, Si had already set two mugs on the central island and was pouring their drinks. Black liquid swirled into the mugs as their familiar aroma brought Eve back into her body, little by little. With every inhale, she could almost imagine that it was just another Saturday morning. With no school, she could have a leisurely breakfast with her brother. Maybe he'd whip up those pancakes she loved.

She wrapped her hands around her favorite mug, a handmade ceramic cup with a blue lighthouse printed on it that she had bought on a family day-trip to Cape Cod. Though the lighthouse had faded from years of use and there was a chip on the rim, Eve hadn't been able to throw the cup away. Like most first-generation immigrants — her parents were originally from Jamaica — they had always struggled for money and had instilled in their children the need to be thrifty. Subsequently, Eve had a habit of hoarding things until they were on their last legs.

Well, some things. She hadn't given a thought to destroying that dress. Couldn't wait to get rid of it, actually.

Again.

Picturing that dress made unwanted memories surge to the forefront of her mind. She felt so cold inside that she wanted the heat from the cup to burn her fingers, anything to take that numbing chill away. Setting down the coffee pot, Si took a seat on a stool opposite her, concern oozing from his very being.

"We need to talk about what just happened," he began, his voice gentle, as if he were speaking to a scared child.

Eve's eyes slid from the table up to his face. "I know."

"We were the only people there, I know we were," Si continued. "It was a forest in the middle of nowhere!"

"I know," Eve repeated. "I don't think anyone else saw what happened."

"Then who could it be? It can't be him, it's not possible…" Si trailed off, desperately trying to wrap his head around it all.

"A lot of things happening lately that shouldn't be possible," Eve replied darkly before realizing what she had said. She hoped Si wouldn't pick up on it.

"There are? Like what?" he demanded immediately.

Of course he would. Just my luck.

More than anything, she wanted to tell him. If Si knew the truth, she wouldn't have this additional burden to bear on her own. Yes, she had the other girls, but they were still new to her. She didn't have the trust, the loyalty, the absolute faith that they would never hurt her that she had with her brother. If life had shown her one thing, it was that given the chance, people always disappointed you. Except for Si. He waited, watching her with that familiar concern of his that Eve had grown to know.

"Nothing. I'm talking nonsense," she mumbled hoping that he would accept her answer and move on.

"Has something else happened?" he pushed, apparently unwilling to let it lie.

"It's nothing, really. Just some stuff happening at school."

Si set his untouched coffee on the table, running his hand through his thick curls. "Until we can get to the bottom of this, I think it's best if you aren't alone. We'll spend the day together, go watch a movie or something before you come with me to work."

Ordinarily, a day hanging out with him wouldn't have sounded bad, but Eve could see the dark rings beneath his eyes, caused by a particularly late shift at work followed by her impromptu wake-up call. Her brother was the kind of person who needed at least eight hours to function. He would be next to useless without more rest. She didn't need that on her conscience along with everything else.

"I'll be fine. The girls are coming over today," she answered.

It wasn't strictly a lie. They *would* be coming over, once she messaged them all, although she couldn't tell them about the dress… That would lead to a conversation on *the-thing-that-happened* which she wouldn't, *couldn't* allow to ever happen. It just wasn't something she'd be able to discuss without someone, not even with these girls.

Her discovery last night had given her an idea that she needed to discuss with them, but there was an added bonus to see them — she knew she'd never be able to handle an entire day with Si without blurting everything out. He had a way of getting things out of her whether she wanted him to know or not.

"I'm glad you've made some friends again. It's been too long," he said.

"Look who's talking," Eve replied, to Si's astonishment.

"I've got friends. What do you think Gavin, Lee, and Stuart are?"

"Staff. They're not friends when you pay them to hang around you," Eve said.

Si dismissed her comment with a careless wave of his hand. "I'm fine. Besides, it's not like there aren't other things to worry about," he said, his brows knitting together. "What time will the girls get here?"

"I don't need a babysitter. I'm just down the hall from you until they arrive. You can go back to sleep."

He didn't want to concede her argument, but his eyelids were already beginning to droop. "Wake me if you need me to make you all some snacks or something," he said, half asleep already.

"And now you're back to thinking we're five again," Eve replied. It felt nice to joke with him, almost as if things were normal. He reached the edge of the room but stopped, turning back to face her.

"I'm leaving the door open. If anything happens, I'm right here."

Her throat choked up. Eve found she couldn't reply. If she answered, she knew she would start crying, so she gave him a small nod instead as he went out of the kitchen. She could hear his footsteps starting up the creaky wooden stairs, down the upstairs hall, all the way to his room.

When he got to his room, she took out her phone and messaged the girls.

A strange hissing sound woke Marley.

Forcing her eyes open, she blinked the sleep away until Cassie's back came into view. She was sitting in front of her make-up mirror applying foundation to her face with a gadget that looked like a chrome spray gun. It was a serious-looking piece of kit, but one Marley was beginning to get used to when it came to Cassie.

She stirred, stretching her arms over her head as she yawned. Cassie looked at her through the mirror.

"Eve wants us to meet her at her house this morning. She's got a lead or idea or something," she said.

Marley didn't take offense that Cassie hadn't bothered to greet her. It was just another of her quirks. She had found that it was easier to label Cassie's oddities as such, rather than to think they were anything personal. It certainly made life easier this way.

"Did she say what?" Marley croaked, her voice still not having woken up yet.

Cassie sprayed the tip of her nose delicately. "Nope, just that we should all meet there. She can't reach Tyler though. You haven't heard from her have you?"

Marley pushed herself up until she was sitting in bed, covering up another big yawn before answering. "No. Come to think of it, I don't think I've back from her since she went off with her sister."

Cassie put the spray gun down. She looked concerned, but she also looked like she was trying not to frown — not until her foundation dried, anyway. "We should check on her."

Marley nodded, already moving out of bed. "Can you do it? I need to pee and shower quick. I've got to see my dad before we head off to Eve's."

"But you were with him yesterday..." Cassie said, seemingly unable to understand why Marley would want to see her dad two days in a row.

"We've got some unfinished business," was Marley's only response as she headed into the bathroom with a towel.

With Marley busy in the bathroom, Cassie pushed her chair back and stood up. The rest of her make-up would have to wait until she'd spoken to Tyler. She wasn't used to the world seeing her without her made-up face, so this was by no means a simple feat. Sighing, feeling apprehensive, she left the room.

SEVENTY-THREE

Someone was trying to pound their way into her head.

Bang… bang… BANG! Tyler tried to drown them out with her pillow, but still, the noise continued unabated. Frustrated, she hurled the pillow across the room wondering who could be at her door at this time of the day.

The knocking came again.

Cursing under her breath, Tyler jumped out of bed but her feet got tangled in the sheets, almost tripping her up. Kicking them off, she staggered to the door, all as her head felt like it would explode from the pressure. Grabbing the door handle, she yanked it opened. It was Cassie. She stood there, looking apologetic, curious, and relieved. It was quite the combination of emotions.

"What?" Tyler managed to growl.

Cassie didn't answer. She stared past Tyler, her eyes growing wider by the second. It wasn't until Tyler took in her room that she felt her own shock.

The place looked like a hurricane had hit it.

Cups and glasses sat everywhere with varying

amounts of water inside. Papers scribbled with untidy notes and drawings littered the carpet floor, along with the wrappers of the countless candy bars that Tyler had eaten in place of an actual meal. In the harsh light of day, Tyler remembered how desperate she had been last night to create a potion that would heal Ally. She was so consumed with the thought that she had drunk her own energy potion and eaten the candy bars while she worked until her body had crashed. Seeing the wreckage from her long night, Tyler lunged for the papers, gathering them into an untidy pile that she dumped into her school bag. Picking up a trash can, she quickly threw the candy wrappers into the bin as Cassie entered the room gingerly, obviously wondering whether the CDC should be notified.

"What happened in here?" Cassie asked, moving towards the table that was also covered by glasses half-filled with water. "Did you have a party and forget to tell us?"

Tyler choked out a laugh. *As if.*

"Eve's been calling but you haven't answered your phone," Cassie supplied. This startled Tyler.

"She has? I haven't heard it ring," she said, looking for her phone and finding it half hidden beneath her bed, where it must have fallen. She picked it up, looking at the home screen, where it showed she had several missed calls. Luckily they were all from Eve, which meant no other horror had happened to Ally since yesterday. She never slept through calls like this, especially several in a row. What was happening to her?

Grabbing a pair of drinking glasses beside her, Tyler moved to one of the twin sinks, pouring the contents away. Cassie followed suit, grabbing the glasses from the table, helping her to tidy things up. A wave of gratitude came over her. Cassie could be a strange little thing, but at least she wasn't leaving Tyler to clean up by herself. She was still feeling this gratitude when she saw Cassie reach for the glass on her bedside, taking it towards the sink, where she went to pour its contents away.

"No!" Tyler cried, lunging towards her as she snatched the glass away from her. A few drops of the clear liquid splashed onto the brown carpet, leaving a wet stain, though luckily, most of the water stayed in the glass. Cassie watched her, wide-eyed, trying to make sense of her behavior. "This one has a drink I really like."

Cassie's eyes slid down to the glass in Tyler's hand. The liquid inside looked like normal water, and she clearly had a hard time trying to believe her, but Tyler needed her to, as the glass contained her energy potion. Feeling shaken and wanting to get rid of that terrible pressure inside her head, she gulped down a few mouthfuls now, desperate for it to do its work. She needed to feel rejuvenated, like she was ready to take on the world. As always, it wasn't long before she could feel its magic running through her body, healing the tiredness she felt and taking away the throbbing headache with it. She sat the rest of the glass back down on the table.

"How did it go with your sister yesterday?" Cassie asked, finally deciding that it was best if she just ignored Tyler's strange behavior.

"Great, until Ally took ill," Tyler replied, trying not to feel the helpless fear she had felt yesterday at seeing Ally's eyes roll into the back of her head and her sinking to the ground.

"Is she OK?" Cassie asked, unaware of Ally's health issues. Tyler didn't have the strength to explain it all to her now, so she simply nodded.

"What did Eve want?" she asked, changing the subject.

"She wants us to come over. She has something she wants to talk over with us."

Tyler nodded. "OK. But I'm on call with work. If anyone drops out, I'm first to go in."

"I'm sure that's fine," Cassie replied. "Marley's taking

a shower now, then she needs to see her dad before we go. She said she wouldn't be long though. You should probably clean yourself up. You're a bit of a mess."

Tyler knew she was right even without checking a mirror. Her hair was greasy and flat against her head. She felt dirty in general with the kind of grubbiness that could only be washed away. Sliding her feet into her flip flops and grabbing her wash bag, she started heading out when she noticed that Cassie was still there.

"I'll tidy up around here, you obviously need the help," Cassie said matter-of-factly.

Tyler was too relieved by her offer to refuse. "Knock yourself out," she said, leaving the room, taking her phone with her. She would give a quick call to Ally to make sure she was feeling better today, but she didn't want to do it in front of Cassie. She didn't feel close enough to her yet for her to hear a personal conversation between the two of them. Reaching the bathroom, she hung out in the corridor as she dialed Ally's number. Her heart swelled with relief and love when her little sister's chirpy voice answered. "Hey Bug…"

***

Cassie grabbed several mugs, taking them to the sink as she started cleaning up. She had meant what she said. Tyler didn't look too hot, and judging by the state of her room, she wasn't feeling it either. Not until she had taken a drink from that glass of her "special" water. Cassie wasn't born yesterday.

She knew there was something different about it, having seen Tyler perk up immediately after having only a few mouthfuls. She waited until all the mugs were clean. It had to look legitimate after all. She didn't want Tyler to realize that she had ulterior motives for staying in here.

Shooting a look at the door, she hurried to Tyler's bedside and picked up the glass. Raising it to her nose, she gave it an experimental sniff. Instead of the alcoholic smell she expected, there was a fruity sweetness to the scent the drink gave off. It wasn't like anything else she had encountered before but it seemed pleasant enough. Shrugging, she took a sip of the drink.

She was immediately hit by a wave of energy so intense that she gasped.

She took another sip, bigger this time, just to check and felt even more energized than before. Lowering the glass, Cassie stared at it hard.

What the heck was this stuff?

arley arrived outside Paul's office full of trepidation.

Since waking, all Marley could think of was coming to see her dad. Last night's questioning had left her feeling weirded out, like something was wrong but she couldn't put a finger on it.

Although it was the weekend, she knew he would be there. Being only the second week of his job, he had mentioned wanting to get a head start on work last night.

Balancing the two coffees and bag of donuts she had brought with her, Marley walked into the office. Her dad sat behind his desk, several journals spread open before him. He looked up at her arrival, a smile spreading over his face, though Marley couldn't help but notice the dark circles ringing his eyes.

"Two days in a row? Aren't you breaking the law of cool kids?" he said.

"You're the only one who has ever thought I was cool, Dad."

"Nonsense. Don't you remember that toy panda you

had? What was his name, Bam Bam? He thought you were the coolest," Paul grinned.

Marley carefully set the coffees down on the desk and unrolled the top of the paper bag, giving him his choice of the half dozen or so donuts inside. Ignoring his question, she gestured to his face. "What happened, you didn't sleep well?"

"New bed, new apartment. I'm sure I'll break it in soon," he answered, reaching for one of the coffees.

"How was the movie last night?" Marley asked, remembering that he had watched one of those random art-house numbers he loved so much after she had left him.

"Lots of existential angst and scenes without any dialog at all, just how I like them. You don't know what you missed."

"Except I do," Marley replied with a shudder. "You say you love me yet look at what you try to put me through."

Giving her a wink, he chose a chocolate-covered donut, picking it up with a napkin. She waited until he took a bite, chewing and nodding happily.

"So, about last night..." Marley began. "I just wanted to make sure things were OK with us."

Paul swallowed, looking surprised. "What would make you think they weren't?"

"I don't know. It just seemed like you didn't like my questions about the family."

Paul lowered the donut, wiping his mouth with the back of his hand. "They came out of the blue is all. I don't really think about my family all that often."

Marley picked up a napkin, fidgeting with it. "So you don't have a problem talking about them?"

He shrugged his thick shoulders as his brow furrowed with lines. "Like I said, I don't have much contact with my dad."

"What about his parents though, or my other grandparents? Not mom's… but your mom's parents? I've never even met them."

"That's because they passed away," Paul answered as if she already knew this fact.

"Did she have siblings? Where are they? I'd like to get in touch with them. Not to visit, maybe email or Facebook if they use it."

Paul's hand raised up. "Whoa. Where is all this sudden interest coming from? It can't just be for this school project."

It was Marley's turn to frown. "Why can't it? I know nothing about anyone else in our family. How have I managed to get to this point in my life without knowing anything? Don't you find that strange?"

Paul's head shook from side to side. "No. We just never really talked about them since we didn't have contact with them. We're not the only ones who have fallen out of contact with their family."

"No, but at least other people know why that's happened. I don't even know who they are," Marley's voice went up a notch as the stress started getting to her. Until this moment, she hadn't realized how not knowing any of this was a problem, but it was. Without this knowledge, she felt groundless, like she didn't belong.

Paul's mouth tightened into a thin line, a sure sign that he was becoming annoyed. "All you ever had to do was ask, Marley."

"I am, right now!" Marley cried, having to resist the childish urge to stamp her foot.

"Now is not a good time for me, unfortunately. I've got things to do, and while your visit was welcome, I need to be getting on with them," he replied with an edge to his voice that she had never heard before. As if to prove how 'busy' he had suddenly become, Paul got to his feet, leading her towards the door.

Stunned by his curt and sudden dismissal, Marley

didn't react until she was standing outside. As Paul went to close his door, she stopped it.

"Why do I get the feeling that it's never going to be a good time to talk about them?" she asked, unable to keep the bitterness from her voice.

"I can't help how you feel, Marley. You of all people know that," Paul answered as the door closed gently but firmly on her.

Feeling the sting of tears in her eyes, Marley left, wondering what on earth had just happened.

M arley sat cross-legged on Eve's bed as she took the glass of water Eve offered her.

She, Cassie, and Tyler had arrived a few minutes ago to find Eve more stressed out than usual. She tried to hide it, but Marley had noticed that her eyes seemed haunted. She kept glancing every which way as if she was afraid that something would jump out at them — which, if recent events had shown, was a complete possibility.

Eve finished handing drinks around the group. Everyone took one but Tyler, who sipped from her own bottle of water. Kicking off her flip-flops, Eve took a seat beside Marley, who was itching to ask what they were all doing here. She had better manners than to just blurt the question out, however, even when her thoughts were only half there, focused on her recent fight with her dad as they were. Eve turned to Tyler.

"How was your day with your sister?" she asked.

Tyler's eyes darkened in response. She paused, biting on the corner of her lip before she answered. "It started well, but then she almost collapsed in my arms."

Marley gasped, horrified, this being the first she had heard of this. "Is she OK?"

Eve and Cassie had similar responses though Marley

didn't hear them. Tyler played with the cap of her water bottle as she spoke. "Ally has a kidney problem. Marley knows, but I haven't mentioned it to the rest of you yet, mostly because it's not something I like to think about." Marley knew she must be thinking of her parents at that moment as her face turned stark and pained. "She has to have dialysis nearly every day. Sometimes it exhausts her. I guess yesterday was one of those days, except she didn't tell anyone how she was feeling because she wanted to see me."

Even though it wasn't her fault, her guilt was palpable. "You can't blame yourself for that: you didn't know," Eve said surprising Marley by the firmness in her voice.

"Yeah," Marley echoed her sentiments. "Is she OK?"

"As far as I know. I spoke to her doctor after he saw her. He said it's normal, though frightening. I just wish I wasn't so far away. I feel so helpless." Her shoulders sagged as she physically slumped.

Marley wanted to offer her some small comfort, but the reality was she couldn't. Tyler had already been through the horror of losing her parents, and now there was this to deal with. It made Marley's problems seem petty by comparison.

"If you ever need help with anything for her, let me know," Cassie offered, her face earnest. It wasn't just a platitude for her, she really meant it. Realizing this, Tyler smiled at her. She wasn't in a position to turn her down, and pride didn't factor when it was for the health of a loved one.

"Thanks," Tyler said simply, feeling a little better about things. It was a weight off her shoulders to know she could ask Cassie for financial help if Ally needed it, which, with the way things currently were with healthcare, was a real possibility. "What did you want to talk to us about?" Tyler asked Eve, done with the personal subject for now.

Opening her laptop, Eve pulled up a website of Trinity

Church. She clicked through to a page with the mural on it. "While you all were busy last night, I did some digging around… look what I found." She pulled up another window, minimizing it so that it sat beside the information of the mural. "The mural was created at almost the exact same time as when the Salem Witch Trials ended. I think that's too big a coincidence."

She raised her eyes to each of them.

"I think it's possible that our ancestors might be connected to the Seals."

SEVENTY-FIVE

MASSACHUSETTS BAY COLONY, 1693

The Four stood side-by-side as the angry mob advanced.

Though they were born of different mothers and fathers with bloodlines that stretched across many continents, they considered each other sisters.

Together, they had traveled the country healing the needy for more than a decade, going wherever they were needed using their magic only to help. In return, they only ever asked for room and board, or supplies. Never money, for they would not benefit from others' misfortunes. They lived as a family, sharing their lives and magic.

And they would die together if that was what was required of them.

Behind them, Ben, the new father whose baby they had recently delivered, snatched an ancient ax into his hands. A large crack ran the length of the wooden handle though the blade was as sharp as the day it had been made. He and his wife did not own much, but what they had they took care of, and at a moment's notice, it was the best he could do.

Having lost one of his legs to a childhood disease, he knew he was unfairly matched against the forty-strong mob who were coming towards the edge of the forest now, though he had no other choice in the matter. He was determined to fight for his beloved wife Sofia, and their new daughter who they had named Isabella. He would also fight for the four women who had saved his wife and child from a labor that would have gone terribly wrong without their help.

Mary and her sisters had been staying with the young couple for several days now. They had helped the over-whelmed father with household chores while the ex-hausted new mother recovered from the birth. Had they known that this would happen, they would have left the poor family alone. Now it was too late to get away from the rapidly approaching mob, whose insults and jeers peppered the night air, filling it with their hate.

The witch hunts had begun a few months ago. From out of nowhere, a council had sprung up, created by a handful of "concerned citizens" who had suddenly de-creed that witches and their powers were a threat to the world. They riled up the locals, scaremongering with their exaggerated and often completely fabricated stories until the uneducated villagers ran scared.

Of the instigators, there was never any sign.

They would appear mysteriously to make their accu-sations, pointing their fingers at innocent people in cases more often than not, but seemed to always disappear whenever The Four had tried to find them to explain themselves, to make them see that there was nothing to fear from them.

But now it had come to this.

After weeks of chasing them, the council had finally discovered where they were. Torches lit up both the night and the angry faces of the mob, which consisted of not just men, but also women and even children. They scurried across the ground, swarming around them, armed with daggers and farm tools, whatever they could get their hands on to use as weapons.

Mary, the unspoken leader of The Four, looked at her sisters, conflicted with feeling.

"If we defend ourselves, we risk hurting the children."

"But if we do nothing, they will kill us *all*," said Catherine, the youngest of the group and the most impetuous. Her eyes slid pointedly towards Ben, who huddled protectively with his wife and child.

"Not immediately," Esther said quietly. "They will have to trial us first." Esther had always been the wisest, although her quietness, brown skin, and freedom made people uncomfortable, often mistaking her for a slave.

Tabitha stared at her, instinctively knowing where her thoughts lay. It wasn't one of her powers, but Tabitha had always been an empathetic person, able to know how a person or animal felt. "You are thinking we should let them capture us?"

"It might be the only way to flush out whoever is behind all of this. If we do not do this, think how many more people will be killed?" Mary said.

"She is right. Hundreds have been murdered already, we cannot stand by and let them harm more innocents," Esther agreed, looking at Sofia cradling her babe.

"But to just hand ourselves over to our enemies… Look how they hate us!" Catherine cried, unable to fathom the thought. Catherine loved her sisters more than anything else in the world and every one of her instincts screamed at her now to protect them.

Mary knew how anguished she was, how they all felt. She felt it was her responsibility to keep them safe, but with this decision, she wasn't certain how things would play out. However, she also knew they didn't have any other choice. The flames from the torches grew ever brighter, casting their flickering black shadows onto the ground.

Reaching out, she stretched out her hand, palm upwards, and waited as each of her sisters laid their hands on top of hers.

"This will not be the end, my sisters. Our work is not done. There is still time for us."

She looked at them and smiled, her love shining through to them. Resigned with what they must do, the Four were preparing to leave the small shack when Sofia's horrified gasp stopped them dead.

"No, Ben! Come back!" came her anguished cry.

Mary's head snapped towards the door but it was already open, swinging on its hinges from the force of Ben's exit. She heard him roar a desperate yet determined cry as he ran towards the crowd using his ax as a crutch.

He was raised as a useless cripple, abhorred by his own family, his parents, but he would be damned if he was going to die as one. With his very last breath, he would fight these hateful people who wished his loved ones' harm.

He would die a hero.

Plowing into the crowd, he swung the ax in a wide arc. They were not ready for it, not expecting a cripple such as him to reach them so soon. The blade whistled through the air, ripping through the stomachs of the two men directly in front of him. Blood sprayed the area, splattering his face and the only shirt he owned, but Ben roared through it all, his fear driving him on. Readying the ax, he went to swing it again when a man twice his size blocked his swing, wrestling the ax from him as easily as if he were taking a toy from a child. Blind hate blazed from his eyes as he swung the ax at Ben.

The blade kept sharp by his own hands, tore into his neck.

Ben screamed out in pain as blood poured out of the wound, spilling down his chest. Raising stunned eyes to his attacker, Ben had a moment to take in his murderer as the faces of his beloved wife and child entered his mind when the killing blow landed on the side of his head.

He was dead in an instant.

Mary's hand flew to her mouth in horror. Even with their powers, there was nothing they could do to reverse death. Sofia had come to the door beside her, but she sagged against her now and would have fallen if not for Ester and Tabitha, holding her up.

"Ben, no…" she wailed, broken as Isabella also started to cry, disturbed by the pain she could feel but not understand. Mary gripped Sofia's shoulders, knowing she only had a few moments to stop another tragedy.

"I am sorry, Sofia, but you must save yourself and your child now. Stay here until they have taken us away. Do not leave this house!"

Sofia heard her words but could not tear her eyes away from the still figure of her husband lying on the ground. Far from being satiated with the death they had already caused, the mob bayed for more blood. Refusing to allow that to happen, Mary took a forceful step outside as her sisters flanked her side.

At their appearance, the mob hesitated as the horror stories they had heard of these demonic women filled their minds. Holding hands, the Four walked towards them, their faces grim. Tabitha could not stop herself from gazing down at Ben's fallen figure and the blood that now seeped into the ground around him. A sob caught in her throat as she felt Mary squeeze her hand, offering her the strength she needed to continue. She tore her eyes away from Ben, letting them settle on the face of her sister. Mary smiled at her, as she smiled back, echoing that love and trust as the mob swarmed around and captured them.

As they were forced away, Mary gazed over her shoulder to find Sofia, still cradling her babe, bent over Ben, her tears mingling with his blood.

SEVENTY-SIX

"It makes sense if you think about it," Christian said from behind Marley's shoulder, scaring the crap out of her, as she hadn't seen his arrival.

"Can't you wear a bell or something?" she griped, trying to still the thudding in her chest. At the others perplexed looks, she offered a single word as an explanation, "Christian," to nods of understanding from the girls.

Their arrangement might be unorthodox, but they were beginning to get used to it.

"It might go some way to explaining why your powers came into play when they did, just as Michael was at the church to destroy the First Seal. If your ancestor's created them before they were killed, maybe they also put a spell in place so that you would come into your own powers if the world ever needed you again," Christian continued as if there hadn't been any interruption.

Marley repeated his comment before making one of her own. "So, by that line of thought, you think our ancestors were witches?"

Christian's brow raised in surprise as the golden flecks

in his eyes seemed to grow brighter. "I didn't realize you didn't think that already."

Marley's shoulders lifted in a shrug. "We hadn't committed to it either way, seeing as we don't ever seem to have any real answers."

Eve closed her laptop, tucking a stray curl behind her ear as she got their attention.

"Well, this is actually why I asked you all to come here. I figured this is a safe place where we can contain any issues in case this goes wrong."

Christian's eyes grew a little wider. "In case *what* goes wrong?"

Eve turned to Marley. "Remember in that cemetery, when you were able to find Christian in the Spirit World by focusing on him in your mind? I was thinking that maybe you could do the same with our ancestors now that we know their first names. Do you think you can do it?"

Questions flooded Marley's body as she swallowed drily. "I don't know. It was different with Christian: I already knew him. I knew his voice, so I knew what to look out for."

"Wouldn't this be the same raising those ghosts from the graves? All you had there were their names too," came Christian's balanced reply.

"I can't believe we didn't think of this earlier," Cassie said, looking more excited by the prospect of some spirit raising than she had any right to.

The girl was just a little *off*.

Marley shook the thought away, focusing back on the subject at hand. "I guess. I don't know…" she trailed off, unable to voice the apprehension she felt.

Christian watched the emotions dance across her face. While he knew that this move could be dangerous — their ancestors had been dead for over three hundred years, which could make them quite feral if their experience at the cemetery was any indication — Christian was loath to talk them out of this. It had been over a week now since Michael had broken the First Seal and they were still no closer to finding the next one before he did. If Marley were able to raise one of their ancestors, she could answer one of their most pressing questions. If nothing else, they would learn more about what they were dealing with. Nothing else mattered more than stopping Michael, not even the possibility of the girls getting hurt.

Even as a wave of guilt hit him at the thought, he knew he was right. Though the girls were relying on him as their advisor, and as much as he wanted to keep them safe, that really wasn't what his job was. So, despite feeling like a jerk, Christian kept his concerns to himself. *With great power, comes great responsibility,* he thought to himself. Spider-man had it right. He knew what the deal was.

He hoped one day they would understand.

"Just try, Marley. Even if it doesn't work, it's worth a shot," he said, hoping he wouldn't be struck down by lightning.

Nodding, she agreed to try, though fear was quickly beginning to build like a tornado inside her. Her palms were sweaty and everything around her felt heightened as her senses became charged. Closing her eyes, she focused on the one thing she knew about her ancestor… her name.

Mary… she called out in her mind. *Can you hear me?* Without a face to place, all Marley could do was focus on the name as flashes of other things came to her. Marley saw herself at Juju's, the magic store, as Helena stabbed the needle into her finger. She watched again as her blood blossomed onto the square piece of fabric. Her blood that was also of Mary's blood. Now she found herself in a black void with stars that blinked around her. She glided forwards in this new space, searching for the spirit she wanted.

The air began to hum as Marley felt herself connecting to Mary. It was working, she was on the right track!

Focusing with every fiber of her being, Marley called out to her ancestor as she swam through more of that black space.

Mary… are you there?

There was a thin cloud of fog covering everything so that it seemed that Marley was looking at this world through a sheet of muslin.

Mary… come to me…

Now the fog started to fade away as a hazy black shape appeared in front of her.

MARY, I SUMMON THEE!

A jolt shot through Marley's body, not sure where the archaic language had come from, nor the sudden command that had blasted out from her mind. Abruptly the fog, the black void, and the hazy figure all vanished. Marley frowned, whirling around in the white space that followed.

"Marley," came Christian's voice, pulling her back. "Open your eyes."

She opened her eyes, letting the blurriness fade away until she saw the figure standing before her. A gasp escaped her lips as she recognized that terrifying face that had haunted her dreams.

It was the hanging woman who had been haunting her.

She was Marley's ancestor.

She was Mary.

SEVENTY-SEVEN

The ghost stood in front of her, dark hair floating in the air.

Her black eyes were as frightening as they always were, her lips still sewn gruesomely together. Marley had to resist the urge to run away. She had summoned her, this ghost, her ancestor. Clearly, Mary had something she had wanted to tell Marley all this time, but it wasn't only her sewn lips that stopped her. Mary had a feral energy that was impossible to miss. It was as if she was more animal than human. Marley wasn't sure that Mary would be able to speak even if her lips were free from their bonds.

Moving slowly around so that he could get a better look at her, Christian watched Mary carefully as the others looked on in bewilderment. Lost in the moment, Marley had forgotten that only she and Christian could see the ghost. She had no time to explain what was happening, however, not wanting to break the spell. Swallowing the lump of fear that had wedged its way into her throat, Marley spoke.

"What is it you've been trying to tell me?" she asked the ghost.

Mary's hair seemed to move faster in response. She didn't speak, didn't make a sound this time as she turned to look around the room. Suddenly she blinked away, only to reappear by the corner of Eve's table. Then, very deliberately, she knocked a pot of loose black eyeshadow onto the cream carpet.

Tyler and Cassie both jumped while Eve's face turned annoyed. "What the hell?" she asked, not realizing that it was Mary who had knocked it onto the floor. Grabbing a box of tissues that sat on the bedside table, she started for the pot when Marley stopped her.

"Wait… It's Mary. She's trying to tell me something."

Mary bent down until she was close to the floor. Using her finger, she dragged it through the black eyeshadow as she drew a shape onto the carpet, followed by another, then another. Finally, she enclosed the shapes into an uneven circle, but she must have run out of whatever energy it took for her to do that, as she suddenly shot Marley a look before she disappeared.

They crowded closer to the sign on the carpet. It was three conjoined triangles, but they overlapped in such a way as to form seven triangles. Marley couldn't stop the gasp that escaped her lips when she saw it.

"That's the symbol I saw on those demons' heads, the ones who attacked us in the cemetery."

Tyler frowned, looking down at the carpet then back at Marley. "But we didn't get anywhere looking for it before?"

Marley's face became animated. "That's because I remembered it wrong! My diagram only had the three triangles in it, this one has seven!"

Excitement bubbled up as she realized that she had successfully raised a specific spirit and communicated with her. Her ancestor had been trying to help this whole time, which meant that Christian had been right before when he had insisted she find a way to communicate with the ghost which they now knew was Mary. Knowing this, the guilt hit next. She needed to apologize to him, but when she saw the frustration in his face, worry nagged at her. "What is it?" she asked him.

"She made it look so easy, connecting with physical items, but I still don't know how to do that."

"Maybe we can find out from her another time," Marley answered hoping that was true.

He ran a hand through his mussed blond hair. "I've seen her do that twice now. If I can learn how to do that, I won't be as ineffectual as I am now."

His jaw tensed. Marley hadn't known until now how much this had bothered him. She promised herself that they would figure this out together.

"So now that we have the actual symbol, we should check it against the database at Guardian HQ, shouldn't we?" Eve said.

Christian nodded, trying to ignore his own frustration. "We should go now."

The girls got ready to leave when Tyler wrapped her arms around herself and shivered. There were goose pimples up and down her arm though it wasn't the least bit cold. Rubbing her arms, she approached Eve.

"Hey, have you got something I can borrow? I didn't bring anything with me today since it's been pretty warm out, but I'm feeling kind of cold now, and if we're heading off to the HQ for the rest of the day..." she trailed off, not needing to finish her sentence as Eve was already nodding, making her way to her closet.

Opening it, Eve's hand reached in for a cardigan when it froze as something caught her attention. It was her yellow dress, the one with the rips and bloodstains, the one she had destroyed in the fire this morning. It was now hanging up inside her closet like nothing had happened.

Ice daggers raced down her spine as she slammed the

door closed so fast that it made Tyler jump. Backing away from the closet, she grabbed a hoodie that was slung over a chair. "Here, take this," she offered Tyler, steering her out of the room as she tossed a terrified look over her shoulder at her innocuous closet.

She knew she had burnt it this morning, so how was it *back*?

SEVENTY-EIGHT

Within the hour, they were settled at what was quickly becoming their second home — the Guardian base.

As Eve was the most proficient with computers, she had become their de facto research guru, with the others deferring to her skills. Not that they had had much of a chance to try. As soon as they had left Eve's house, she had been super quiet while the others talked about Mary and what might be going on. Eve hadn't engaged with any of the conversation, choosing to focus on the drive instead. If Marley didn't know any better, she'd have thought something was seriously eating away at her. She wasn't close enough with Eve to ask though. The girl could still be quite intimidating at times so Marley left her observations alone, figuring that Eve would explain herself when she was ready.

She sat in front of the banks of computers now, within the hidden room containing the Guardian's secret database, scanning in a diagram of the new symbol. Processors spun as the computer struggled to cope with the amount of information it was pulling up.

Eve drummed black painted nails on the tabletop, waiting impatiently for the results to appear. When they did, they flooded the screen.

"Holy…" she exclaimed. "This symbol goes waaaaay back." The others crowded around her, craning their necks for a better look at the screen.

"There are so many hits," Cassie said, shocked by what she found. And there was. Seemingly, hundreds and hundreds of pages of it.

"Well, here comes the bad news. The system isn't sophisticated enough to pick out what any relevant information might be so we're going to have to manually read through all of them."

"But that will take all day," Cassie gasped, intimidated by the sheer scale of it all.

"Do you have someplace else to be?" came Christian's cutting response, though Marley decided not to repeat it, to his annoyance. "Your job is to repeat everything I say, not pick and choose," he said.

Marley didn't reply, however, something else on her mind. She turned to him, her eyes troubled. See her expression, his own softened. "What is it?"

Marley stared at him, torn by whatever it was she wanted to say. She swallowed, taking a breath before speaking. "I've been thinking… I'm basically the most useless member of this gang."

Having overheard her, Tyler whirled around, shocked. "That's not true! What are you talking about?"

Marley gave her a smile of thanks though her eyes remained firm. "It is true. I can basically summon ghosts, possibly talk to them, but that's all. In a physical sense, I'm practically useless. I can't do anything. Think about the times we've been attacked, I've only been able to do something once…" She paused momentarily as Christian's shocked green-gold eyes flashed into her mind as her hands squeezed his heart until it stopped. She had to wait until the image disappeared before she could speak again. "And I've no idea how to do that again, even if I wanted to. I can't be a liability, I need to be able to help defend us."

Christian wasn't sure what she was getting at. "Continue."

She looked at him directly. "I want you to teach me self-defense. I want to learn how to fight so that if we are attacked again, I won't be so useless."

"That's not a bad idea," Tyler said, nodding in agreement.

"Um… how is that going to work though?" Cassie raised, a tentative lilt to her voice. "When Christian can't actually touch anything?"

"No, but my voice works fine," he said before realizing his error. "Well, for one of you, anyway."

"You guys can start training now if you want, while the rest of us go through this stuff," Eve offered. "We're probably not going to make much of a dent in it anyway, so you might as well."

Each of the girls nodded, letting Marley know that they were in agreement.

"You're sure you don't mind?" she asked, just to make sure.

"Knock yourself out," Tyler said.

Surprised by how fast this was happening, Marley felt a shiver of excitement. She wasn't going to be defenseless anymore! She was going to learn how to protect herself and the others. Smiling at Christian, she gestured.

"After you, Sensei."

<hr>

Marley padded barefoot onto the mat-covered floor.

She stood in the enormous workout space on the other side of the warehouse, taking in the display of weapons that lined one wall. There were guns, old-timer rifles, crossbows, and bladed weapons of every kind. She even saw a pair of nunchucks, which she immediately knew she would never use. Gathering up her hair, she tied it up into a ponytail so it wouldn't get in her face. Christian stood in front of her, pacing back and forth.

"The first thing you need to learn—" he began only for Marley to interrupt.

"About fight club?" she asked, earning a *look* from him in response. "Sorry, couldn't help myself."

"Try," he replied. "Anyway, as I was *saying*," he continued, drawing out the word 'saying'. "The first thing you should learn about self-defense is that, if you are in danger and you have an opportunity to, you should RUN."

Marley shot him a perturbed look. "Surely that's the last thing?"

"Absolutely not. Your goal is to stay alive so if something happens and you can get away, do it."

"Run... got it," she replied.

"Next lesson: staying alive isn't like what's it's like in the movies. It's not all martial arts and pretty kicks. It's ugly. It's messy. You need to learn that everything is a potential weapon — it's all about how you use it."

He gestured to her handbag. "Bring that over here."

Wondering what he was getting at, Marley did as he commanded. "Tip the contents onto the floor."

She hesitated, shooting him a look. "Are you sure?"

He nodded, barely able to hide his impatience. "This would go so much faster if you just did as I said without questioning me every step of the way."

Shrugging, thinking 'so be it', Marley tipped out the contents of her bag. Out spilled a few cosmetic items — the leather purse she had used since high school, a pack of limited-time Tic-Tacs, her vial of meds, a pen and notebook that she always carried with her... and a couple of tampons. Seeing them, she arched a look at Christian. Either he didn't know what they were, which seemed un-likely, or he was just ignoring them.

"How many weapons do you see in those contents?"

Marley looked down at her items, her features twisting with confusion. "Er, none, unless you count the Tic-Tacs, which are probably only useful for fighting bad breath."

Christian pointed. "Your pen. You can use that to stab someone in their eye…" he began as Marley recoiled with horror.

"That's horrible," she said.

"Trying to stay alive isn't pretty, Marley. Get used to that. Now, what else can you use?"

Her eyes ran over the items on the floor, but she couldn't think of a way to use any of them. "I don't know."

"Your credit card," Christian commented. "If push came to shove, you could snap that card in half. The edge of the card would be sharp enough for you to slice some-one's neck with it."

An image of herself doing just that popped into her mind as did the answering spray of blood such a cut would cause. She felt the blood draining from her face but Christian didn't seem to notice, warming up to his subject.

"OK, you've got the gist. Lets move on to common holds and how to break them, or we can jump straight to how to behead a demon using only household furniture."

"Could we maybe save that for the next lesson?" Marley asked a little desperately, hoping that he was joking.

So far, this wasn't going as anticipated.

She hoped it would get better from here on out.

SEVENTY-NINE

The words blurred together on the screen.

Eve rubbed her eyes, trying to blink away the haziness. They'd been at this for hours now and any initial excitement had long worn away. Tyler's nose almost touched her printouts as her chin rested again her chest. Her eyes were closed. It wasn't clear whether she was just resting them or had fallen fast asleep.

While Eve had been keen to focus on the research, she found her mind flicking back to the yellow dress, despite how she fought against it. It had returned from being buried, but now it had survived being burned to a crisp as well. How could that be possible? Was the dress enchanted in some way? Or was Eve beginning to lose her mind? Her eyes slid over to Marley, who now lay on the mats, exhausted from the punishing workout Christian had put her through. She'd been called many things before in the past, and as a Goth, she took her fair share of hits, though she was beginning to understand what hell Marley must have gone through to believe that she had a mental illness her whole life… And Eve had been experiencing her own issues for less than a day.

Shaking herself from the direction her thoughts had gone in, Eve gathered together a list of things they had found, mostly places that were aligned to that symbol somehow. Places they would have to investigate on foot. Stretching, she rubbed the back of an aching neck, hoping they could call it day soon.

Across from her, Cassie had diligently poured through the research, all the while noticing how every time Tyler sagged from a lack of energy, she would take a sip from her water bottle and immediately perk back up again. She kept her suspicions to herself, however. She would wait until the right moment to bring them up…

As if she could read Cassie's thoughts, Tyler jerked suddenly awake, staring around in confusion until she remembered where they were. She was exhausted, her nap not having brought her any relief whatsoever. Automatically, she reached for the bottle of "water" that was beside her, only to discover that it was out. A moment of utter panic flashed over her face before she quickly covered it but Cassie had caught it and knew without a doubt that she was onto something.

Tyler stood up. "Guys, I think we need to stop. I've run out of water and I need to get some food.

From the mats, Marley raised her weary head. "You've got my vote. I'm sticky with sweat, I can't do any more today."

"Is Christian cool with that?" Cassie asked, just to play devil's advocate. She was immediately rewarded with a flicker of annoyance on Tyler's face.

Yep. Definitely onto something.

"I don't know," Marley replied. "He disappeared a while ago. He's getting better at staying but it's still taking him a lot of focus to do it."

"I've put everything we've highlighted so far into a list. We can go over it back in your dorm while we eat," Eve said.

"You don't want to go back to your place?" Cassie asked, surprised, as that is where they had been earlier.

"No, Marley said needs to shower. We can do it all back at the dorm," Eve spoke quickly, hoping she didn't sound as desperate as she thought she did. There was no way she could risk going home and that dress appearing again in front of them. She was not ready to have that conversation with anyone.

"So let's go already," Tyler said, unable to contain her need to go.

Cassie stepped in line behind her, studying her quietly all the way back.

A plan forming in her mind.

A cross town, Ally's head dipped low as she fought off another wave of tiredness. However, she knew this wasn't a side effect of her dialysis.

This tiredness was caused by the nightmares.

Ever since she had started to read the book that the man had recommended to her, Ally had found herself dreaming about monsters every night. Terrifying, shadowy things with creepy black legs who scuttled back and forth in her mind, their pincers reaching out, hoping to catch her in their grasp. She always managed to just evade them, though she would still wake, dripping with sweat, her heart pounding like it was trying to beat its way out of her chest.

But Ally was almost ten and knew they didn't exist, which was why she felt so frustrated with herself. The worst thing that could have happened to her already had. Her parents were dead, and she and Tyler were separated; what were monsters going to do to her that would be worse than how life already was?

She trudged along the sidewalk, watching the cracks

blur into one. Her foster mom, Cheryl, walked beside her, talking a mile a minute into her cell. The woman loved to talk and was always on the phone with one of her friends. Currently, she was going through the details of her recent internet date in excruciating detail. Ally had heard enough about his trendy clothes, polished leather shoes, and immaculate hair to last a lifetime. Luckily, the local bank of shops was just appearing ahead of her. Cheryl said goodbye to her friend, promising to catch her up on the other details, as they stopped outside Ally's library, one of the buildings that formed this small cluster of businesses.

"I'm not going to be long. I just need to grab a pair of shoes that doesn't pinch my feet. You've got fifteen minutes, twenty max before you meet me back here," Cheryl said, looking down at her.

Ally nodded, holding her bag to her chest as she went inside the library, glad for this time alone. The sudden stillness was a relief for Ally, who found it difficult to cope in the noisy house that Cheryl ran. Though she kept to herself, she could often hear her foster siblings through the thin walls of the house as they fought over everything. A few of the older ones actually scared her, but she hadn't told Tyler any of this. She didn't want her to worry any more than she already was. She hated that her sister had so many problems to shoulder now. She was determined not to add to her burden.

The line for returns was small as it wasn't very busy this time of the day with most people out having fun on their weekend. A young mom walked past holding the hand of a girl not much younger than her. The girl was having some sort of tantrum, not wanting to be there, while her harassed mom tried her best to placate her. Bitterness flooded Ally's mouth as she thought how lucky the girl was to have her mom in her life, yet she didn't even know it. She wanted so badly to tell her not to take these moments for granted.

"Hello again, sweetie," a female voice called out to her. It was the old librarian who worked there. Ally recognized her from her previous visits. She had platinum hair that she wore in an elaborate up-do that seemingly stayed there of its own accord. Her clothes were always impeccably neat, and she smelled of roses. Ally had liked her on sight.

"Hi," she answered as she took out the big book she had been reading every night. Although the stories were exciting, the nightmares she had been having due to them were less fun. Having decided that sleep was more important than entertainment, Ally had decided to return the book. Hoisting it onto the returns desk, she slid the book over to the librarian who peered over the tops of her glasses at the title.

"Hmmm, I've never seen this book before. Is it any good?" she asked.

Ally nodded. "Yeah, but it might be a bit too exciting for me. I keep having nightmares when I read it."

The librarian took out a scanner, opening the book to the inside page. She flipped through several pages of the book looking confused. Finally, she put the scanner down.

"I'm afraid I can't take this book from you. It doesn't appear to be one of ours."

Ally's nose wrinkled in confusion. "It's not?"

The old woman shook her head as Ally marveled at how her hair didn't move at all. "Nope. You must have picked it up somewhere else." She helped Ally put the book into her bag.

"If you're having trouble sleeping though, I suggest you just put the book somewhere out of sight and forget about it. I find that helps," she smiled, kindness crinkling her eyes.

"I guess I will," Ally said, turning away. The book felt heavy in her bag, weighing her down. She knew she could just leave it on a table or something, but somehow that felt wasteful. It wasn't the book's fault that she found the stories a little too vivid. Shrugging her thin shoulders, she walked back outside to wait for Heepie Jeebie's return.

EIGHTY

Water poured off Marley's back as she washed away the hard work of the day.

The others were in Tyler's room, debating on a pizza delivery or a trip to the food court. As bad as it seemed, it was leaning towards the pizza. Everyone was exhausted from the work they had put in on their first 'rest day,' yet as they still had papers to go through, and vegging out with a pizza didn't seem a terrible way to go.

Thinking of the food, Marley's stomach rumbled as she hurriedly finished rinsing her long, dark brown hair. Wrapping herself in a towel, she padded into the next room, where her sweat-encrusted clothes lay on the floor in a messy heap. Rifling through her wardrobe, Marley realized suddenly that she was running low on outfits. She sighed inwardly. Great, she'd have to do laundry today too. A meme that she had seen recently flashed into her mind. It was of a cat sleeping in a funny position, its paws draped over its eyes dramatically with the words "Adulting is hard work" stamped across the bottom of it. That meme was her life now.

Grabbing a pair of jeans from her chest of drawers,

Marley gave them a cautious sniff before stepping into them, then threw on a faded T-shirt that had been a constant when she was on her old swim team. While it wasn't glamorous, it was one of the most comforting shirts she owned, and she felt almost as if she were back home on the West Coast wearing it.

Taking the dirty clothes that had somehow spread over her side of the room into an untidy mess — Cassie's side was frustratingly neat — she shoved them into her laundry bag, heaving the bag over her shoulder. Leaving her room, she stuck her head in through Tyler's door to find the others poring over a pile of menus like they were the latest Pulitzer winner. "Just make sure to get me ham and pineapple," she requested to a shudder from Tyler.

"*Pineapple?* What kind of sick person are you?" Tyler's brows raised in mock horror at the thought. Apparently, the girl took her pizza *very* seriously. Eve shot Tyler a grin, playing along.

"Forgive the uncultured swine, she does not know of what she speaks."

Marley swapped shoulders with the heavy bag, rolling her eyes. "Yeah, yeah. Just make sure it's here by the time I get back. I'm *starving*."

T he laundry block was only a short distance away, though by the time Marley stepped into the building, she could already feel herself breaking out into a new sweat.

Fantastic. At this rate, she'd need another shower.

Rows of washing machines lined the perimeter, with a small square of machines in the middle of the room. There was only one other student there, a girl listening to music on her phone who she thought she recognized. It was possible she was in one of Marley's classes, or maybe she had just seen her around campus before. Whatever it was, the girl didn't have the same recollection, as she paid her no mind. Though many of the machines were empty, Marley chose the one farthest away from her, aware of that unspoken rule for personal space.

Bending down, she had started to load it up with her clothes when, from the corners of her eyes, she saw the other girl pick up her basket full of fresh clothes, making her way towards the exit. She passed two figures who stood waiting outside; one held open the door for her. Marley heard her says "thanks" as she moved past and left. Opening her box of detergent, Marley fished out a pod as a hit of lavender filled her nostrils. Tossing the pod inside, she sniffed as another strong aroma filled the air. It was some kind of cheap cologne that had been sprayed so liberally that she wanted to sneeze. Her eyes began to water from the overpowering smell as she felt a tickle in the back of her throat. God, she wasn't allergic to it was she? She wondered why anyone in their right mind would ever wear so much aftershave.

"Hey, I recognize that view," a male voice said, breaking the silence.

Still bent over her machine, Marley froze. Was he referring to her?

"Surprise, we're back." This was from a different male voice. Though she had yet to see who was speaking, Marley could feel her body tense. Adrenaline kicked in as she realized that she was alone in this stone block with these two guys, whoever they were. Her fingers gripped onto the detergent box — the only thing she had to hand — as she started to turn slowly around until she faced the speakers.

The two guys were older than the usual student. Both had the sickly glow of too much fake tan and slicked back hair. More alarming than their too-slick appearance was the hostility they exuded towards her.

"I guess you thought you'd seen the last of us last night. I gotta say, it wasn't very friendly of you to lead us on like that then send us away," the taller of the two spoke.

Marley's eyes whipped around the room just to make sure that they weren't speaking to someone else before landing on them again. "I think you've got me confused with someone else," she began.

Taller Guy, laughed though there wasn't a hint of humor in his eyes, which were growing more hostile by the second. "Are you calling me stupid?"

"No," Marley said quietly as an icy finger of fear ran up her spine. She looked over their shoulders, at the exit beyond, hoping desperately for another student to arrive, but the path outside was empty. Somewhere in the back of her mind, Marley remembered it was dinner time on a weekend. If anything, the students would be far away in the food court if they were even on campus at all.

Shorter Guy sidled closer, invading that personal space Marley held so dearly. "So where's my hug? Aren't you glad to see me?" he asked, stretching out his arms.

Marley didn't know why these guys thought she knew them, but it was clear that they weren't going any-where. She stood up straighter, pulling her shoulders down hoping her more confident stance would deter them.

"Look, this isn't funny. I don't know either of you and you're coming across very aggressively. Please back away so I can leave." Marley felt proud of the way her voice never wavered at the end. She might feel vulnerable, stuck here with these two, but she was damned if she was going to show it. If experience had taught her anything about bullies, it was that they tended to leave you alone if you stood your ground and showed no fear.

The two guys swapped a look at each other. "Ooo, she's getting feisty now," Taller Guy said.

"Way more fun than when they're just lying there," Shorter Guy finished for him. Suddenly he launched for-ward grabbing her by the arms. Marley yelped as she tried to wrench herself free but he was a lot stronger than he looked. Taller Guy side-stepped behind her, wrapping one arm around her shoulder while the other one forced her face to his friend's.

"We only came to finish what you started last night, sweetie, so open up," he commanded coming in with his disgustingly thick lips to kiss her. Marley opened her mouth alright, but not to kiss him. Sucking in as much air as she could, she let out a scream of rage.

"NO! Let me go!" she yelled, twisting every which way to get free.

Annoyed with her struggles, Taller Guy seized her chin in his hand, his fingers digging into her until they hurt, while his buddy readied himself to come in again. Abruptly Christian's early self-defense lessons came into her mind. Thinking of the holds he had demonstrated to her, Marley desperately tried to remember what he had taught her when her stomach sank like lead. As it was only her first lesson, they had only tackled how to escape from a single attacker's hold, not two.

She didn't know how to get out of this.

As Shorter Guy's face came in, Marley felt herself calling out with her mind for the only person who might be able to help.

CHRISTIAN! CHRISTIAN! Please help!

She felt herself leaving her body almost as her spirit searched through that black space for him, she was rewarded by his appearance just moments later, just as the Shorter Guy landed a sloppy wet kiss on Marley's lips.

Christian couldn't hide his distaste. "Of all the… why on Earth would you summon me now?" he asked, misreading the situation entirely until Marley twisted her face away.

"Help me!" she called out desperately, staring him dead in the face. Her words had the effect of making the two guys pause as they looked around the empty room before deciding she was full of it.

"More games, huh?" Taller Guy said. "Well, I like to play too." Sliding his hands down, he gripped them around Marley's wrist, forcing her arms behind her back.

Any bravado Marley might have felt earlier faded away into nothing as she realized that these two would not stop until they got what they wanted. Christian's already pale face grew even paler as he summarized the situation.

"The others," Marley managed to get out before she found those fat wet lips on hers again. Nodding, Christian choked out, "I'll be right back, hang on."

Then he vanished.

<hr>

Christian reappeared almost instantly in Tyler's room where the girls were now huddled over several boxes of pizzas. Choosing a large slice of pepperoni, Eve picked it up as Christian ran in front of them, yelling as loudly as he could.

"Marley's in trouble, you've got to help her!"

But like every other time, they couldn't see or hear him.

Knowing that Marley didn't have much time, desperation flooded him. He had to get through to them, but how? The more the girls talked inanely, enjoying their food, the more Christian felt like his head would implode, until Eve raised the pizza slice to her mouth to take a large bite and he went to slap it away from her.

Instead of his hand flying through the pizza as expected, it connected to it. The slice flew out of her hand, landing on the carpet topping side down. Eve started, shocked.

"What the hell? My pizza just flew out of my hand."

The others stopped eating, all having seen the same thing. "It was like someone knocked it away."

Eve blinked, looking around the room, suddenly creeped out. "You think it was Mary?"

"But why would she do that?" Cassie asked, eyes troubled.

"Maybe it was Christian," Tyler suggested as Christian jumped up and down in the background.

"YES!" he said even as he knew they couldn't hear him.

"Well, if Marley would hurry up we could ask her," Eve said as she went to pick up the pizza to clean up the mess. Tyler didn't move, her mind working through several thoughts.

"Shouldn't Marley be back by now? I mean, it doesn't take long to dump in a load of washing?" she said, a nervous feeling forming in the pit of her stomach.

Eve and Cassie stared at her, then the pizza as the three of them grew suddenly cold.

"No, it doesn't take long at all," Eve finally finished.

EIGHTY-ONE

The acrid smell of cigarettes and alcohol flew into her nose as Marley braced her hands against Shorter Guy's chest.

He lunged in for another disgusting, horrific kiss but she was better prepared for it this time. Wrenching her chin out of the other guy's grip, she stamped her foot down onto Shorter Guy's toes and was instantly rewarded with his shriek of pain. Hopping on the one foot, he hissed out another reeking breath.

"You little…" he uttered between gasps as his friend's grip loosened a bit, seemingly amused by what she had done.

"Man up, Jason," the one behind her said. Like a flaming rod of fire, his name burned into her mind, even as she wondered whether it was a good thing that she knew what one of them was called. Having watched enough episodes of CSI as a kid with her dad, Marley knew that perpetrators typically hid their identity… unless they weren't worried about Marley staying alive long enough to ID them. The terrifying thought tore into her brain until Marley struggled more fiercely than ever. With

Jason preoccupied, she knew this might be her only chance to get away.

Though Taller Guy had his arms around her, Marley didn't try to pry them apart as was her natural instinct. Instead, she used the laws of gravity in her favor and simply ducked down. She slipped right through his arms as Christian had taught her she would. Free, feeling suddenly hopeful, she took one step forward only for her attacker to snag hold of her shirt. She felt a powerful pull as he yanked back but Marley threw all of her weight forward. Time slowed to a crawl as her father's face flashed into her head, followed a little later by that of her mom, the latter of which made some of her fear recede to be replaced by rage.

How dare they do this to her?

She hadn't gone through everything she had just for these two to have their way with her now. Balling up her fists, she pushed forward with all her might as her battered shirt began to give way, tearing from the collar and along one arm. Refusing to give way, she let out a blood-curdling scream…

Suddenly, the door flew open as Eve, Tyler, Cassie, and Christian raced inside.

"Marley!" Eve shouted, understanding the situation immediately.

Taller Guy immediately let go of Marley. Not expecting this, she fell forward, carried along by her own momentum until she hit the ground, hard. She was dazed but so relieved by the other's appearance that a sob caught in her throat. She reached out for them as Eve and Tyler dashed forward, helping her up as Christian hovered around them, feeling helpless as usual. Only Cassie didn't move. She stood stock still, horror turning her face slack.

She recognized these guys.

It was Miles and Jason, the two cousins she had led on then so callously tossed away the night before. They had come back, but they had attacked the wrong girl. She looked at Marley, at her ripped shirt where she was holding it up, trying to cover her bra strap.

This was all her fault.

Jason stopped hopping, putting his foot down as he shot a look at his buddy then over to Marley. Holding out his hand, his face took on a bashful look as he addressed the group. "This isn't what it looks like," he began, to their utter disbelief.

"It never is," Eve spat out, her eyes haunted yet flashing with fury.

Miles took a step backward, away from Marley as if it would absolve him of any crime. "You don't understand. It's her fault. She led us on, this would never have happened if she hadn't been such a tease yesterday."

Feeling the fear leaving her now that she was safe with her friends, Marley shook her head adamantly. "I've never met them before. I kept telling them, but they wouldn't listen."

Miles throw up his hands. "Oh, come on, it was last night! You think we'd forget what you look like?" His voice had turned ugly again, unable to hide what he was really like.

It was enough for Tyler.

After having such a tragic loss recently, what with her fears of Ally's health still unresolved and her own exhaustion coupled with her financial worries, seeing her friend being attacked like that was just too much. She couldn't stop the familiar swell of magic rising up inside her, and to be honest, she didn't want to.

These two had it coming.

She let herself feel the rage and fear that seeing Marley in their grip had caused, letting it bubble and simmer inside. A rush of sound flooded the room suddenly as water coursed through the metal pipes and the temperature rocketed up. Sweat glistened on her brow, but Tyler ignored everyTHING but the pain she felt. Miles' eyes grew wide as he realized that something unnatural was happening. He stared at the surrounding pipes, alarmed, wondering what was going on with them when boiling hot water BURST out of the pipes, scorching the two of them. Tyler and the others were safe from the burning water; only the area where the two stood was attacked.

Throwing up their arms to protect their faces, Miles and Jason backed into the corner of the room to escape the water. They huddled in shock, peeling their wet shirts aside to reveal the skin starting to blister beneath. Unable to get past the water raining down around them, they were trapped.

The others stared at Tyler, knowing she had caused this to happen.

Taking out her phone, Marley tried to dial the listing she had saved into her phone during that first meeting with their RA, but her hands were shaking too much. Reaching across, Eve gently took the phone from her and dialed the number. When the call was answered, she reported the incident while Marley tried to regroup. Seeing that Tyler was still lost in herself, Marley touched her on the shoulder. Only then did Tyler's emotions recede.

Marley gave her a wobbly smile of thanks, touched that Tyler had done this for her. Needing to relay her gratitude, Marley didn't notice Cassie hovering behind her, trying desperately to keep her guilt from showing.

Marley could never know the truth.

News of the attack had spread like wildfire.

Within minutes of Eve's call, two security patrol cars full of campus police had arrived, sirens blaring, lights flashing red and blue into the night. They had leapt out of their vehicles, weapons raised, charging into the laundromat as they quickly handcuffed Miles and Jason, noting down the group's statements before hauling the men away.

Students stood gossiping in the corridors of TJ Halls, openly watching the group as they passed by, wondering if the girl who had been attacked was among them. Marley kept her eyes on the floor, not wanting to make contact with anyone. She didn't want people to guess it was her. She didn't want to be known as "that girl." Showing surprising empathy for what she was going through, and knowing that being outed was the last thing she needed, Eve had given Marley her shirt to wear, hoping that it would hide her torn one underneath. She clung to the opening of the shirt now, as if by drawing it closed she could erase the fear and pain.

Eve's eyes were flat as she walked beside Marley. In

her mind, she kept seeing Marley being attacked, over and over again. The image brought other horrors to surface that she had to suppress a shudder. A different thought broke through the unwelcome trip down memory lane. If she shared her own experiences with Marley, maybe it would help her through this horrific experience… except she knew she'd never do that.

She'd never tell.

She shot a look at Marley through the corner of her eyes, feeling shame turn her cheeks red. Some things were better left dead and buried in order for a person to move on. Even as the thought came, a voice sounded in her head. It was the voice of her younger self, the girl she had been before *the-thing-that-happened*. She whispered, her voice as fragile as the wind. *Some things can never be forgotten.*

Someone must have warned Rhett, their RA, what had happened, as he was waiting for them when they arrived warily at their rooms. He hurried towards Marley, concern radiating from him.

"Marley… are you OK?" he said, feeling stupid for even asking — but what else was he supposed to say? His eyes raked her pale face, his lips curving downward into a frown.

She gave him a small nod, grateful for his concern, yet wanting to be alone with the girls.

"It was those two guys, wasn't it? The ones I saw you with yesterday. I knew I should have done something more," he said, almost talking to himself.

Having reached the door, Marley stopped dead as his words sank in through the fog. "You saw me with them? Yesterday?" she asked, astonished.

Rhett ran a hand through his hair, wishing he could have done things differently. "Yeah, you don't remember? I noticed you had changed after your dinner with your dad. You were wearing that designer-looking dress with two guys hanging onto you. They left when I turned up though, after you changed your mind about entertaining them."

He managed to make the word "entertaining" not sound terrible or remotely shaming but Marley caught his drift immediately. She had opened her mouth to ask for more detail when she suddenly saw Cassie trying to hide behind Tyler. Eve must have figured something out at that exact moment, as she couldn't stop a gasp from escaping. She turned to eyeball Cassie, shooting what could only be accusatory looks at her.

Marley felt sick to her stomach.

Christian had been quiet since the attack but he now looked at each of the three girls, trying to understand the sudden electrifying undercurrent in the air. "What is it?" he asked Marley.

She didn't answer. She couldn't, not with Rhett still standing there. She touched her head, flinching as if it hurt, which wasn't far from the truth.

"I'm really exhausted. Can we talk about this another time?" she pleaded weakly to Rhett.

He bought the excuse, hook, line, and sinker. "Yeah, of course. I'm so sorry, Marley. If there's anything you need, even if it's just to talk, you can call me anytime OK? I mean it." He looked at each of the girls. "That invitation extends to all of you. What happened tonight was awful. I'm here if you need me."

Marley nodded gratefully as he shot her one last concerned look before leaving. Marley opened her dorm room, stepping inside as the others followed. As soon as they were all in the room, Marley slammed the door shut, whirling on Cassie. She jabbed her finger at the other girl's chest so hard that Cassie stumbled back.

"It was you wasn't it? You were going around with those creeps pretending to be me!" she demanded.

Having not figured out the truth, Tyler and Christian looked at Marley in shock. "No... that's so messed up," Tyler finally managed.

Guilt turned Cassie's eyes wide as she started stammering a reply. "I'm… sorry. I didn't mean for any of that to happen. I can explain…"

But Marley wasn't ready to listen to reason. The terror she had felt earlier washed over her, making her feel violated all over again. "What were you thinking? They were disgusting! How could you even let them touch you? How could you be that desperate?"

With every question, Cassie visibly flinched more, but she took it all willingly, never even trying to defend herself.

"Have you done this before, Cassie? Do you go cruising for guys wearing my face?"

All eyes were pinned on Cassie. Blinding panic threatened to crush her chest. She felt her blood racing through her veins and the beginnings of what might be a migraine. They looked at her like she was worse than trash, like something stuck to the bottom of their shoes.

It was all she could do not to bolt outside.

Three knocks sounded on their door, brisk, businesslike. Relieved for the interruption, Cassie grabbed the door handle, yanking it open without thinking.

A familiar redhead stood outside, her partner next to her.

It was the two cops from Trinity Church.

They were here.

EIGHTY-THREE

The redheaded woman, Detective Saunders, raised a brow as she took in each of them.

"We meet again," she said. While her tone wasn't accusatory — it was more of an observation — Tyler still felt as if they were guilty of a heinous crime. She moved past Cassie with a confident swagger until she stood in the center of the room. Even though her partner stayed by the door, Saunders' very presence seemed to suck all the air out of the room. Marley forced herself to stand tall, to ignore her instinct to shrink back.

Saunders glanced down at her leather notebook then looked back up. "Which of you is Marley Gray?"

Marley's head nodded in the smallest of motions. She wasn't looking forward to the questions that she knew were coming. Neither was Cassie, she noticed. The other girl seemed even more nervous than Marley felt. A sheen of sweat glistened over her usually immaculate make-up.

Saunders turned to her. "I've read the statements you all gave to the campus security, but there are a few facts that aren't clear. I'm hoping you could help me out with them."

"OK," Marley answered, her voice thin and dry. She cleared her throat, hoping that would rid the anxiety that suddenly lurked inside. Although they now knew it was Cassie who had been with those guys, it wasn't something they could reveal to these cops, so how was Marley going to dig their way out of this hole they now found themselves in? She went and sat down at the table where Eve and Tyler were already seated. Cassie still stood by the door, looking like she was going to bolt at any second if not for Detective Brooks, standing in the doorway, blocking her way.

"I'm a little confused. It says in your statement that you have never met Miles and Jason Martin, yet they both insisted you have. They were able to describe how you were with them yesterday, each corroborating the other," she said, tapping her pen on the side of her chin.

"I can't help what they said, I just know that I haven't met them before. I couldn't have been with them anyway as I was already out at that time," Marley replied.

"And what time might that be?" Saunders asked, keeping her tone neutral.

"Around seven. I didn't get back until quite late, maybe ten."

Saunders leveled her piercing blue eyes on Marley. "What were you out doing?"

Marley had to resist the urge to snap at the cop. "I was having dinner, as you no doubt already know."

"On your own?" Saunders' voice had a challenge to it, a little note at the end that made Marley bristle.

"I was with my dad. At a burger place across town. He's a professor here," Marley finished.

At her answer, Saunders nodded, not in the least surprised by the connection. Apparently, this wasn't new information.

"What were you wearing when you were out with your dad Ms. Gray?" Saunders asked.

"How is that relevant?" Marley asked, her eyes confused.

"If you could just answer the question," Saunders continued.

Marley thought back to last night which seemed so very long ago. "Jeans, and a shirt over a tank top. My usual get-up."

Saunders noted this all down, her pen skimming quickly across the page.

"Do you own a black strapless, low-fronted dress?" she said, waiting for Marley's response.

Marley shook her head. "No, I don't have many dresses, definitely not one that would be strapless and low-fronted."

By the door, Cassie suddenly tensed, giving herself away completely. Butterflies flitted in Marley's stomach. If the cop asked to look through Cassie's wardrobe, she knew instantly that they would find the dress she wore when she was with those two guys.

Eve and Tyler had stayed quiet during the interrogation, but Eve spoke up now. "Why are you asking her what she was wearing? Even if she had been naked, it wouldn't justify what they did!"

Saunders' eyes slid over to Eve, accessing her. "I'm trying to clear up some conflicting facts, Ms...?" she waited for Eve to offer her name.

"Richards," Eve said, even as Marley thought she blanched a little. Despite how brave she came across, how together, Eve really didn't like cops.

"Sounds like slut-shaming to me, when you blame the woman for being attacked," Eve said, as Tyler's eyes grew wide. "You've already arrested the guys, and four witnesses have given you their statements. Anything else can wait, can't it? Marley has had a terrible ordeal and we just want her to get through tonight."

Saunders' mouth tightened. She did not like having her authority challenged but Eve had a point, which she must have known. Slipping her notebook into a pocket, Saunders nodded at her partner. An unspoken agreement that spoke of their familiarity with each other, Brooks stepped aside so Saunders could walk through as Marley followed her to the door, eager for them both to leave.

"I am sorry for what happened to you Ms. Gray. It's my job to uncover the facts is all." She handed over her card. "If you think of anything that might be pertinent, this is where you can reach me."

Marley took the card, giving her a stiff nod. Then they were gone. Marley shut the door on them with relief.

Almost immediately, Cassie tried talking to her again. She inched forward, wringing her hands as she tried to find the words to convey just how sorry she was. Marley could see it coming, however, and she wasn't interested. Turning away, she went to speak to Tyler when there came another knock on the door.

Sighing, Marley opened it expecting to see the two cops again, only to be met with Paul's panicked eyes.

"Dad?" she said, shocked.

Paul gave her a quick once-over before he grabbed her in a bear hug. "Your RA told me what happened. Why didn't you call me, Marley? I've been worried sick!"

"It all happened so fast. I haven't really had time to," Marley replied.

"But you're OK? They didn't hurt you?" Paul couldn't stop looking her over as if he might have missed an injury.

"No. The others got there just in time," Marley replied causing Paul to finally look at the other girls.

"I'm so grateful to you girls for turning up when you did. Thank you," he said simply, eyes shining bright with unshed tears.

"We're just relieved we got there in time," Eve replied earning another grateful look from him.

"I want you to stay with me tonight," Paul said to Marley, his tone implying that he thought she would disagree. "I know you're an adult, and I'm happy you have friends who care about you, but you are my only child and I need to know that you are safe tonight."

Marley didn't even look at Cassie when she responded. "Actually, I'd like that, Dad. I can't stay here tonight." Though she left out the words "with her", Marley's intent was clear for the other girls to see.

Cassie looked stricken as Marley gathered together some items. When she had everything she needed for the night, she put her hand on Eve's shoulder. "Thanks for everything tonight," she said simply, then turned and gave Tyler a smile too.

"No problem," Eve replied.

Then, deliberately blanking Cassie, Marley left with Paul as Tyler went back to her own room.

Silence hung over the room like a dark cloud.

Eve looked at Cassie, though it wasn't with all the disgust she thought would be directed at her. In fact, Cassie thought she could see a hint of sympathy behind her black-rimmed eyes.

"Aren't you going to ignore me too?" Cassie asked, steeling herself for Eve's response.

"No. I think you've already gone through enough," Eve said to Cassie's surprise. She went to Marley's bed, took a seat on it and started to remove her shoes.

"You're staying?" Cassie asked, not prepared for that at all.

"Someone has to keep an eye on you since you can't seem to stop getting yourself in trouble," came Eve's level reply. She kept herself focused on the job at hand, but there was another reason that she didn't want to go home.

She didn't want to be faced with that yellow dress again.

Si would be leaving for work soon. Suddenly, Eve realized that she had the car again even though it was Si's shift with it now. Taking out her phone, she sent Si a message to let him know what had happened with Marley, explaining that she'd be staying with the girls tonight. She ended with an apology for still having the car, promising that she'd cover him for his Uber rides.

As she suspected, Si messaged back immediately, letting her know that she wouldn't have to do that. He just wanted to make sure they were all OK — in particular, that she was OK after what had transpired that morning. She promised that she was and that she'd be home the next day. Texts done, she looked over at Cassie, who sat at her vanity desk, not knowing what to do with herself.

Eve felt a pang of sympathy for her. The girl was awkward and kind of messed up, but she knew instinctively that Cassie hadn't meant for any harm to come to Marley.

"You want some pizza?" Eve asked her as she moved to the table and opened one of the boxes. "We never got to eat earlier."

Cassie was so grateful at the question you'd think Eve had just suggested so much more. She joined Eve at the table as they ate together in silence.

EIGHTY-FOUR

Marley lay on the bed in the room that Paul had kept for her, her eyes glued to the ceiling.

Several boxes were stacked onto a table. A box marked with "Marley's Room" in a neat cursive black pen had been started on but had never been finished, clothes spilling down one side. A full-sized mirror sat propped up against a wall, while a blanket had been flung over the window until curtains could be bought. Having only recently moved to the city, Paul hadn't had time to do much to the place, but the decor was the least of Marley's concerns.

It hadn't been more than an hour since she'd left her dorm. Marley had taken a long shower in a desperate bid to wash the stain of her attackers away. Standing under the pulsating water would normally have calmed her, but she felt vulnerable, even in her dad's new apartment, away from the college.

Of all the stupid, risky things Cassie could have done… not to mention the creepiest. Marley did not consider her actions flattering in the least, especially when she combined it with that whole-body scrutiny she had caught Cassie doing on many occasions. The entire thing creeped her out.

Which was just great considering how they were indelibly tied together now.

The sound of Paul watching a sports game on the TV in his room came from across the hall. He had always kept his door open at night so that he could listen out for Marley and the night terrors she had experienced ever since she was a child. It was a habit that he stuck with even now. She found it reassuring, even if things were a little strange between them.

On the drive there, they had talked a little. Well, Paul had talked, Marley had mostly listened. Understanding that she wanted to put the attack behind her, Paul had chatted about work, and movies — just about everything other than what had happened today.

He also avoided any mention of their last conversation and how that had ended.

While she knew he would always have her back, that he was her person, there was now a small cloud of doubt that hung in the air, making unease flood her body.

She lay on her back, an arm flung over her eyes to block out the stray beams of light that came through the gaps in the blanket on the window. Exhausted, she had lain there hoping for blissful oblivion... but sleep would not come.

She wasn't sure exactly how she knew she had company. There was no noise, no change that she could pinpoint or explain. The air just suddenly *felt* different. She froze, half in fear that her visitor would be Mary. Although she knew that the ghost had not only saved her life but was also her ancestor, she was still a feral spirit who terrified the crap out of her every time she appeared. If she was back, Marley needed to prepare herself for it.

"Are you asleep?" Christian's voice softly from the darkness.

She turned to face him, found him standing by the window, his face hidden by shadows. "No."

He was silent for a moment until Marley began to wonder what he was doing there if he didn't have anything to say. When he finally spoke again, there was a strain in his voice that she didn't expect.

"I'm sorry," he apologized.

Marley waited, expecting him to expand further but he didn't say anything else. Propping herself up onto her elbow, she peered into the room, where she could just make out his silhouette.

"Why?"

"I'm a Guardian. I'm meant to protect people like you, but the only thing I could do today was to slap at a slice of pizza." There was no humor in his voice, only anguish.

"Wasn't it precisely that action that got the girls to come and find me? You saved the day, Christian. That's no mean feat."

"But I should've done more. I'm supposed to do more," he said. Marley didn't need to see his face to know how tortured he was by his perceived failure.

She softened her voice. "I don't know what more you can do, Christian. You are dead, after all."

He didn't reply. She didn't think he would. She knew her words might have sounded a little harsh, but she couldn't have him blaming himself, especially when there was a prime suspect for that. As far as she was concerned, his actions helped to stop something even more terrible from happening. She needed him to know that she was grateful, but she also needed him to realize his very real limitations.

Christian stepped forward into a ray of moonlight. No hint of his usual sardonic manner remained. This Christian was humble, worried… Marley wasn't sure but she thought she also caught the hint of fear in his eyes. Was he worried about her because it was his duty or was there something else driving his concern? He was a mystery, as ever.

"You should rest," he said to her.

Marley was about to say that she wasn't tired when a wave of exhaustion hit so hard that she had to stifle a yawn. Even as she tried to resist, her eyelids lowered of their own accord. As she spiraled into the depths of sleep, her last thought was how strange it was that she found Christian's presence comforting.

Christian knew the second she had fallen asleep. Her shoulders relaxed and the tension she had been holding onto all day finally seeped away.

He wished he could get that same relief.

In his mind, he saw Miles and Jason coming at her and instantly felt that awful, petrifying fear consume him once again. Having trained his entire life to fight evil, he could handle himself against most physical threats, and those two scumbags? He could have dealt with them so easily if he were still alive. Instead, he'd had to leave Marley there to fight them off by herself, knowing that they wanted more than a kiss.

His stomach churned, round and round until he felt sick. His mind knew this was an impossible feat, yet his body hadn't come to turns with this new state — and might never come to terms with it. Feeling conflicting emotions well up inside, he watched as Marley slept.

EIGHTY-FIVE

Impatient knocking on the door woke Tyler.

She staggered to the door, opening it to reveal Eve and Cassie, both already fully dressed. While Eve had tried her best to Goth up, Cassie's box of tricks obviously didn't cover much black, which meant Eve was revealing much more of her actual face than normal. She held a sheet of paper in her hands, barely able to conceal her impatience.

"What on Earth are you two doing here so early?" Tyler asked hoarsely as she cleared her throat.

Eve waved the sheet of paper at her. "With all the stuff that happened yesterday, we completely forgot about the research we were doing. Well, last night, I couldn't sleep, so I started going through it all, and then something happened!"

At the excitement in her voice, Tyler stood straighter, eager for some good news for a change. Eve went to the table, setting the sheet onto it as the others crowded around her. "I was going through the list when I suddenly felt this magic *pull* is the only way I can explain it. It happened when my hand was over this particular page of the list and it grew stronger and stronger until I put my finger on this entry.

Tyler tried to blink the rest of her sleep away. "Saugus Iron Works? Is that supposed to mean something to me?"

Eve shrugged. "I guess not, but it's a historical site, known as the birthplace of America's iron and steel industry. It's a National Park now, only ten miles or so outside the city. I think we should investigate."

Tyler gaped at her, her mouth open. "What, now?"

Finally taking in her glazed eyes, Eve softened her approach, taking pity on her. "Tyler, why don't you grab a quick shower to wake up. Cassie can go pick up some breakfast for us all while I call Marley and update her…"

Eve had already started steering Tyler away, neither of them paying Cassie any mind.

"I'll go get us some food then," Cassie said to no one in particular before moving off down the hall, cutting a lonely figure.

A little later, they pulled into the communal parking lot for Paul's building.

What the apartment block lacked in interest, it made up for in newness. Neutral paint coated the walls with the only pop of color coming from the young plants spilling down from a handful of hanging baskets. This was one of those newly-built blocks that seemed to be popping up everywhere lately.

Marley had agreed to come with them today — much to Eve's surprise — but she'd needed a ride. Paul had offered, but the girls hadn't wanted to clue him in on their plans. The fewer people they had to explain their actions to, the better. Having decided that they didn't need to all go storming into Paul's apartment, Tyler and Cassie had decided to wait in the car, leaving Eve to climb the two flights of stairs to his new home.

He'd let her in with a warm smile and an offer of coffee, which she declined, and she sat now in Marley's new room.

"Are you sure you don't want to sit this one out? We'd totally understand if you wanted to spend the day with your dad or something," she offered understandingly.

Marley shook her head. "No. I want to come. It'll be good for me to get out of here, get some air."

Eve's eyes turned bright with approval. "I was hoping you'd say that."

"I just need a few minutes to wash up, then I'll be ready to go."

She seemed to be coping well. Eve watched as Marley opened her overnight bag, taking out clean underwear and tying her hair up into a knot, but Eve knew she was struggling inside. She saw it in the way Marley's hands occasionally trembled, or how she stared at her own reflection in the mirror as if she were haunted by what she saw there. Eve wanted to comfort her, but truth was, there was nothing anyone could do. Marley would have to deal with this on her own and in her own time.

Walking to the door, Marley suddenly stopped. "Oh hey, can you toss me over a towel? There should be a bunch of them inside that opened box on the table."

Since Eve was standing right next to the box, it made no difference to her. She reached inside for the towels when her hand froze mid-search.

There, folded neatly on top of Marley's clothes was her bloody, yellow dress.

Fear constricted her throat even as her mind tried to reconcile what she was seeing. It was all in her head, she knew that, yet it didn't make it any easier to accept. The dress had been destroyed, so there was no way it was there now, much less in this box, in Marley's dad's new apartment. All she had to do, was still her beating heart and carry on as usual.

"What's that?" Marley's voice carried across the room

cutting into the fog in her head. "I don't own anything in yellow… it clashes with my skin tone."

The heart that had been beating now threatened to burst its way out of her chest. Marley could see it! But that would mean, it wasn't in her head at all…

It was real.

Snatching a towel out of the box, Eve threw it across the room at Marley, then while her head was turned away, she shoved the dress into her bag, thankful she had thought to bring it with her.

"Oh, it must be your dad's then. Probably got put in with your things by mistake."

The lie rolled easily off her tongue. Thinking nothing of it, Marley left to go to the bathroom, closing the door behind her leaving Eve to stare at the dress so hard that her eyes began to water.

What is happening around here?

Two hours later the girls found themselves pulling up to the historic park.

On the banks of the Saugus River, acres of rolling green surrounded them. The park was big. Very big. Imposingly so. Climbing out of Eve's car, Tyler made her way to a map, trying not to feel overwhelmed by the scope of what she saw there.

"This place is nine acres, how on Earth are we going to cover all of that on foot — and in one day?" she asked, barely able to keep the incredulity from her voice. She reached into her bag almost as a reflex, taking out her trusty "water" bottle, quickly gulping down several big mouthfuls as Cassie quietly but noticeably watched her actions.

Marley and Eve flanked her side, each of them studying the map.

"We probably won't have to cover the whole park,"

Eve began, her eyes narrowing in on places of interest. She pointed to a row of buildings. "There are some forges here, with mills and a house. Then over here…" her finger moved across the map, "are the waterwheels. I think we should try these first, considering the first seal was inside a building. It seems unlikely that it would be a tree or something."

"Sounds like a plan," Marley replied, if a little distantly. The entire car ride over, Eve had noticed that Marley hadn't said much. She also hadn't made any eye contact with Cassie, though as Cassie had sat on the back-seat with Tyler, it hadn't been too obvious that she was avoiding her. As if she knew Eve was thinking about her, Cassie flittered towards Marley hesitantly.

"How are you feeling this morning?" she asked nervously.

Marley looked at her but kept her voice and face neutral. "I've been better."

"Right," Cassie replied, feeling terrible all over again. Marley noticed that Cassie's eyes, which were usually made-up perfectly, were smudged today. There was a splotch of shadow on her cheek that had obviously dropped from her eyelids, but she hadn't caught it. Even her lips seemed hastily dabbed in gloss that went over her lip line. All in all, if Marley didn't know better she'd think that Cassie truly felt remorse over her actions.

Yet just seeing her made Marley feel sick again.

She wasn't ready to deal with her just yet, couldn't quite look her in the eyes. Turning away, she moved passed her, missing the compassionate look Eve shot Cassie.

"Let's head across to the other side of the park and work our way back to the car lot," Tyler suggested, sounding suddenly energized. One minute she was falling asleep in the car, the next she was hopping around like the Energizer bunny. Eve couldn't keep up with the girl. "What do you think, Cassie?" Eve asked, hoping to draw her out of that shell that she had retreated back into again. Cassie turned startled brown eyes at her, shocked that she would be asking for her opinion. She mumbled an answer back that Eve was just able to make out as her consent though it seemed actual words would take a little longer to surface.

Locking the car, she quickly checked her phone — Si had already messaged to see what she was up to today… and to gently remind her that he would need the car back by tonight if possible. She sent back a quick reply so he would know she was still with the girls and safe when a flash of that yellow dress appeared in her mind. It was still in her bag, waiting for her to deal with it again.

As the other's led the way, Eve hurried towards a trashcan. Making sure the girls had their back to her, she took out the yellow dress, throwing it into the bin before quickening her steps to join them.

The walk to the other side of the park felt long and arduous. The hot and humid sun beat down and there was barely any breeze to speak of. Added to the punishing weather, the place was packed with visitors who, as luck would have it, had come due to a recent new radio ad. Everywhere they went, they had to navigate past groups of sightseers and rowdy children with sticky fingers that they wanted to place everywhere.

Eve found herself wishing that she could just hide away at home with her computers and fantasy games, except she knew that her safe place wasn't quite as safe now. It had been violated. Looking at Marley, Eve saw that her eyes didn't have that same spark she had come to expect of her. Despite thinking that she had had a mental illness all her life, Marley was still one of the sunniest people she had ever met, so to see her subdued and quiet like this… to see that new awareness in her eyes… Eve felt for her.

As the sun rose into the midday sky, they finally arrived at the furthest building, the Blacksmith Shop. A large stone anvil took up one wall of the simple wood structure that wasn't much bigger than Marley's old living room. It was here where half-finished products from the forge would be turned into completed items. Eager to focus her mind on anything other than her attack yesterday, Marley examined the breadth of the room as the others did the same, hoping for that magic pull Eve had mentioned. Whatever it was they expected, however, a quick search found nothing of note.

From here, they worked their way back towards the parking lot to the Slitting Mill, then the forge, reading up on the odd bits of history dotted around the place, but still, there was nothing that jumped out at any of them, magic or otherwise. Growing increasingly more frustrated, they were making their way to the Blast Furnace when Tyler stopped, reading from a leaflet that formed the park guide. She looked at them, excitement blazing from her.

"Guys, I think I know where the seal is! These buildings we've been looking at, they're all reconstructions! There's actually only one building in here that's an original property that dates back to the 17th century…"

She pointed at a building in the guide.

EIGHTY-SIX

The black painted timber-framed Colonial house loomed above them.

Only the faded red of the front door provided a hint of color to what was otherwise an oppressive looking house.

"This is it," Tyler said. "This is the Iron Works House. It's where the workers and owners lived."

A tour guide opened the door just then, leading a group of visitors as he talked about the history of the house. The girls waited until the group moved away before heading inside. Gloominess pervaded. The small diamond-paned windows barely let any light in and what light came through, was quickly swallowed up by the dark furnishings inside.

Referencing the guide, Tyler led the way forward as they examined each room, but the tight confines proved quickly claustrophobic. Eve could feel her forehead turn clammy.

"We'll cover more ground if we split up," she advised. "I'll go with Marley, Tyler, maybe you and Cassie can search the other end of the house."

If Cassie noticed the deliberate pairings, she didn't say anything. She nodded silently, her eyes seemingly overly large in the dimness. As they took off to the other side of the house, Eve followed Marley up a steep, winding staircase that had Eve clutching at the banister. She knew her fears were unfounded. The house was entirely stable, she just wasn't used to the rickety steps or narrow hallways and low ceilings.

She knew too that it wasn't only the structure of this place that had the sweat dripping down the back of her neck.

But those things shouldn't be thought of right now. She had already experienced enough shocks today without her own mind torturing her with what had passed.

Marley entered a reconstructed bedroom. A single bed was shoved against the wall while a writing desk and chair sat beside it. She approached the desk, snuck a quick glance at the empty hallway outside, then started opening the draws on the desk as quietly and carefully as possible.

"When I was a kid, I used to like to hide things behind the drawers in my desk," she offered as an explanation to Eve when she caught her curious stare.

"Smart kid," Eve replied as she made her way to the only other piece of furniture in the room, a free-standing mahogany wardrobe. She reached for the door handle but froze, remembering what had happened this morning. Marley wasn't busy with her own investigation by the desk, however, so Eve was safe for the moment. She pulled open the wardrobe door quickly.

There was nothing inside.

Not even pretend clothes or shoes to make up a display. It seemed the park's visitors weren't supposed to be quite this thorough. "I can't find anything here," she said, turning back to Marley, when her eyes shot to the bed.

Where it had been empty a second ago, her bloody yellow dress now lay across it. A half-strangled cry of fear left her mouth before she could stop it. Marley's head swung to her, concerned, but Eve quickly glanced at her hand.

"What's wrong?" Marley asked.

"Nothing," Eve said, desperate to keep Marley's eyes on her. "I caught a sliver in my finger is all." Then she strategically placed her body in front of the bed, blocking the dress from Marley's view. "Have you found anything?"

Marley stood up shaking her head, having replaced each of the drawers. "I've got nothing."

"Let's try another room," Eve suggested, trying not to sound too desperate lest Marley pick up on it. Nodding, Marley left as Eve called out after her.

"I'll join you in a sec, my phone's ringing."

It wasn't, but Marley wasn't to know that. Lunging towards the bed, Eve snatched up the dress for the third time that day and shoved it into the wardrobe. She knew it wouldn't stay there for long, but it was all she could think to do.

How did you get rid of a dress that was haunting you?

She hoped she'd be able to find an answer before she completely lost her mind.

The living room housed only a few pieces of furniture.

Other than a simple wooden table and chairs, there was only a painting of the surrounding area on the wall and a fireplace where several plates hung over it as decoration. A plaque embossed with information but which was too small to make out sat on the wall opposite the fireplace. Cassie and Tyler were already exploring in-side when Marley and Eve stepped in. At their appear-ance, Cassie, who had been speaking to Tyler, fell immediately silent, as shame flickered over her face.

"Have you found anything?" Marley asked though she directed her question at Tyler, still unable to face Cassie. Tyler picked up on the slight immediately, shooting an awkward look at Cassie.

"No."

Marley opened her mouth to answer when the air changed. It was subtle, not perceivable by most, but she was beginning to understand that it meant a spirit was here.

Luckily, it was one they knew.

She wasn't sure how she knew that exactly — call it intuition or maybe an extension of her power — but she knew without looking that Christian had joined them. She turned to face the side of the room where she could sense him standing and was rewarded by the sight of him, although he looked as confused as he could be.

"What is this, some kind of day trip?" His voice rose at the end of the sentence, not even trying to hide his in-credulity.

Marley had to stifle the urge to snap at him. "We got a lead to this park, but we can't find anything that could be the seal," she replied as she gestured to the others that he was there.

"What lead? How?" he asked.

Although she felt irritated, she brought him up to speed knowing that he wouldn't be much help to them until she did. He stood watching them now, a hand scratching at his chin as he stared around the room.

"The seal is magic so there should be something that makes it stand out. Like that cloud you saw or Eve's magic pull. You need to look closer, and at everything."

Marley hadn't slept well the night before, and she

hadn't been particularly happy at having to deal with Cassie in any capacity today, so to have Christian making his usual disapproving comments was the last straw. She felt the anger flood her body but did nothing to stop it.

"What do you think we've been doing all day? I can't believe you turn up like this — several hours after we've already spent our day off searching — and after what happened yesterday…" Her voice broke, but she pushed on, needing to finish. "Do you really have no idea how hard this is for us?"

Christian managed to look ashamed though not enough to back down. "Of course I do, but I also know how much is riding on this. What happened to you yesterday was terrible… but we can't turn back the clock. We can't change it, just like you can't bring me back. All we can do is move forward and hope that we can stop Michael before he finishes whatever he is up to."

Marley hated how reasonable he sounded. He was so much easier to deal with when he was annoying and un-realistic. She repeated his words miserably, so the others could understand what he was saying.

"I think he's right," came Cassie's hesitant voice, sur-prising them all. She moved towards Marley, eyes looking beseechingly at her. "We can't fix what's already happened…"

Instantly, red-hot rage flared up in her chest. "Of course *you* would say that!" Marley snapped. "You're the one who constantly messes up! First, you try to stiff Eve with the bill after making her go to that restaurant that she would obviously never feel comfortable in, then you go and do this to me! You'd love for us all to forget the stupid, horrible, things you've done, but maybe, instead of our forgetting, you should just stop being so horrible!"

Cassie flinched from the vitriol in Marley's voice, wringing her hands.

"I'm sorry, Marley. I really am," she tried again.

But Marley wasn't sure she believed her. Ever since the moment they had met, Cassie had been scrutinizing her appearance, always watching her and generally being creepy. Marley had tried with her, but now everything was too much. Christian's death, her part in it, and Cassie's weird behavior. Marley couldn't stop the eruption even if she wanted to.

"Are you though? Or are you just sorry we found out? If we hadn't caught you, how much longer would you have carried on doing that?" Her voice rose in volume with every word as she gripped her hands by her sides.

Cassie looked utterly wretched and turned to Eve and Tyler for help but she could see they were torn. There was just no way she could justify her actions — she could barely make sense of them as it was. Biting her lip, she decided to let Marley take out her anger on her.

After all, she deserved it.

As Cassie's inner voice started its vicious tirade, Marley mistakenly took her silence for something else… and her fury grew until the room began to hum from her anger.

Tyler felt it first. That telling thickening of the air, the static in her hair that caused her bob to start moving as if she were swimming in water.

"Marley…" she called out in warning, but Marley was too far gone to rein it all back in now. She felt a bolt of magic as Marley's power blew outwards in a ring around them.

Then suddenly, the room began to vibrate.

First the plates on the wall, then the tables and chairs.

Anything that wasn't nailed down in the room started to move.

Eve backed away from the phantom furniture. "What's happening?" she cried.

Christian understood it first. "Marley! I think you're summoning up the spirits from the past!"

Through the mist of fury in her head, his voice called out to her. Her head snapped round to him.

"What?"

"Your anger is causing you to use your magic. You're summoning up the spirits that are attached to this place and these objects!"

"Maybe, they can help us?" Eve said hopefully when a plate tore off the wall and flew across the room at her! Eve ducked just in time for the plate to smash the wall just behind the space where her head had been.

Stunned, Marley could only watch as more plates lifted from the wall. Anticipating what was going to happen next, she raced for the table and turned it onto its side.

"Get behind the table!" she yelled just as the plates launched themselves off of the wall and flew at them. Nearest to the door, Tyler ran out of the room as Eve dove behind the table with Marley, just in time. The plates sailed over their heads to land behind them, smashing onto the floor, but Cassie — who was the furthest away from them — had more area to travel. She froze, standing there as an iron poker from the fireplace lifted into the air…

Aiming it's wickedly pointed end straight for her.

"CASSIE!" Marley cried out. "LOOK OUT!"

Unable to make her feet react in time, Cassie stood there, eyes wide with terror as the poker flew straight for her face.

A cry came from Tyler from the doorway. "NO!" she screamed, her hand outstretched as if she could somehow stop the weapon from reaching its intended target.

Abruptly, the air around the poker changed, thickening around the metal and diverting its path. The poker curved away from Cassie at the last minute, missing her face by a whisker to impale itself onto the plaque in the wall. The plaque broke into two, falling to the floor.

Before any of them could react, a bright beacon of red

light flared out from the broken plaque, covering the sky outside in that same eerie light they had seen before.

"Oh no. It was the sign," Eve gasped. "The sign was the second seal…

"And I just broke it myself," Tyler replied, sickened to the core.

EIGHTY-SEVEN

Marley had bent down to pick up the broken pieces of the plaque when she suddenly felt that magic pull Eve had described. It seemed that they could trace where and what the seals were, but only if they were very close to them. She didn't know if there was anything they could do with the seal, but leaving it there for anyone to find didn't seem like the right thing to do. They fled the park before anyone could spot the damage left in the Iron Works house.

The ride back was a somber affair as each girl contemplated their own part of the destruction of the seal. Even Christian didn't seem himself, choosing to keep his thoughts to himself, which somehow made the whole thing more devastating. Marley was getting used to his outbursts now, so the fact that he wasn't saying anything... well, that was more frightening than anything else he could have done.

At least one good thing had come out of this whole event, however.

Marley was back to talking to Cassie again, though it was still strained. Marley would need more time before she would fully warm up to Cassie again, but Cassie was happy that she was at least speaking to her without biting her head off.

She'd take whatever progress they made.

Eve had dropped them back at the dorm and taken off to the bar to help her brother at work. Marley unlocked the door to their room, but Cassie didn't go inside after her.

"I'll be there in a minute," she said to Marley, who simply nodded, too exhausted and down to care about where Cassie was going.

Cassie waited until Tyler had let herself into her own room before stepping inside. Tyler looked up, surprised to find her in her room. "I'm sure Marley won't object to you sleeping back in your own room again," she began. Cassie didn't answer until she had closed the door behind her.

"I'm not here because of that."

Removing her shoes, Tyler rubbed her tired feet. "So, what is it?"

Cassie gestured to Tyler's bag. "I want you to make me a potion."

Tyler's fingers froze around her foot. Her shoulders tensed as she raised her eyes to Cassie. "What potion? I don't know what you're talking about..." She kept her voice even, hoping Cassie wouldn't be able to tell she was lying.

Having expected this, Cassie lunged for Tyler's bag, snatching it up before she could grab at it. Opening it, she took out Tyler's water bottle, which still had some solution left inside. "This is what I'm talking about! You've been using your powers to make this energy drink, haven't you?"

Tyler snatched it out of Cassie's hands. "Give me that back!"

"Fine, but you can't deny it. I already drank some of it

earlier. I know what it is," Cassie retorted, eyes flashing at her.

Tyler suddenly felt the room spin. She didn't want the others to know what she had been doing, even though it wasn't really that terrible. She had always prided herself on doing the right thing, on being a nice girl. Well, nice girls didn't use their powers to make their own drugs, did they? All the fight left her. She sagged down onto the bed, deflated, but before she could speak, Cassie spoke again, wringing her hands.

"Please, Tyler. I need you to do this for me," Cassie said desperately. "You have no idea what it's like to be me. How could you when you look the way you do? I've had it my whole life, even when I was a little kid. People would say horrible things to me just because I wasn't pretty like my parents. It was as if they didn't consider me human as if I didn't have feelings like everyone else. But now that I have this power, it's too tempting to look like someone else — anyone else, but me. Please help me by making a potion, something that will help me to look better."

Tyler gaped at her, reeling. "I… I don't know how to do that…"

"Well, figure it out," Cassie snapped back, looking increasingly more desperate. "I can't put Marley or any of you in that position again. I don't want any of you to ever get hurt because of me, but I know myself. And the temptation is too strong to look like one of you. I don't trust myself not to do that again, so please do this for me, Tyler," she pleaded, sinking down onto the carpet in front of her.

"Help me make a potion so I can stomach being myself."

Ally brushed her teeth the way Mom had taught her.

She had been obsessed with cleanliness, something which had rubbed off onto Ally so that even at almost ten, she was way tidier than most adults. She was certainly tidier than Tyler.

Rinsing her mouth, Ally put her toothbrush into the plastic tumbler that sat on the sink when she frowned, noticing that her foster-siblings' toothpaste cap was off and oozing the white paste. Unable to help herself, Ally closed the cap, setting the tube into her foster-sibling's own tumbler before she headed back into her own room.

Moving towards the bed, her eyes slid over to her bag, which still sat on the carpet where she had left it after her trip to the library today. The top of the mysterious book that did not belong anywhere peeked over the edge of her bag, taunting her with its existence.

She didn't understand where the book had come from if it didn't belong to the library. She remembered so clearly how that man had pulled it off the bookshelf as he had recommended it to her.

None of this made any sense, but what Ally did know was that there was something about the book that made her wary of it. Maybe it was the stories inside or the way it seemed to have come out of nowhere. She was too old for monsters to scare her now, but she knew she couldn't sleep with it there right in front of her. Grabbing the book, she slid it under the bed, shoving it right into a back corner where it had to compete with all the dust and pens that always seemed to find their way there.

With it out of sight, she climbed into bed, pulling the covers over her head.

She hoped she would finally get a good night's sleep and not wake up feeling like something was crawling around inside her head...

The sky was already dark when Eve pulled up outside Shaken & Stirred.

The alley where the staff entrance sat seemed more ominous than usual — not that Eve was going to chance it. Since the night she was attacked by those two demons, she had taken to only using the front entrance.

She walked inside the place now, letting the warm lights and soft music soothe her soul. Until this moment, she hadn't realized just how much tension she had been carrying, and this place, with its familiar sounds and smells instantly relaxed her.

Spying her from across the room, Si shot her a big, relieved smile. She had kept him up to date on her whereabouts, though she knew him well enough to know that he wouldn't actually relax until he could see her.

The-thing-that-happened had really brought out the protector in him.

She crossed the room to him, stepping neatly around drinking patrons until she came to the bar. His eyes scanned her from head-to-toe as if to make sure she was OK, as he followed her into the staff room.

"So, how was your day with the girls?" he asked.

"Oh, you know, uninteresting. We just hung out," she finished, not entirely sure which parts of their day she could discuss without revealing the whole sordid story. Removing her handbag, she opened her locker to hang it up inside when the blood drained from her face.

Inside the locker hung her bloody yellow dress.

Her insides turned to ice. Terror constricted her throat so that she couldn't speak even if she had wanted to. She knew now that this was only the beginning. He was back…

And he wanted revenge.

Eve went to slam the locker door closed, but Si was too quick for her. He grabbed hold of the door, staring into the locker. When he took in the dress, his face went slack.

"But we burnt that this morning. I watched it turn to dust," he said, unable to believe his eyes.

Eve could feel her whole world imploding. She couldn't hide what was happening anymore. She had to tell him what was going on. What she *thought* was going on.

She spoke, her voice so strained that she could barely recognized it. "I don't know how this is possible, but somehow… he's back."

Si tore his eyes away from the dress to look at her. "But he can't be, Eve. You know that." Those kind eyes of his that she loved and knew so well stared deep into her soul, firm in their own belief.

"You know he can't be back… I killed him."

TWISTED MAGIC

6: BAD HABITS

JO HO

EIGHTY-EIGHT

Shadows danced around the room, created by the naked bulb that hung over their heads, suspended from the ceiling. Since the time he had taken over as manager, Si had always meant to put a shade around the bulb, but with one thing or another, it was always shoved to the bottom of the To-Do List.

Eve stared at it now, wishing she could have smashed it into a million pieces.

Without any light, Si wouldn't have seen the thing hanging in front of them, and maybe, just maybe, Eve would have been able to talk herself out of this. But now, her world had imploded, and the one person she was trying to protect would be drawn into the madness.

They stood frozen in front of the locker, staring at that impossible sight. Never had a simple yellow dress struck such fear in two people. Eve hoped desperately that it would all be a figment of her imagination, but with every blink, every new breath she took, the dress seemed to become more and more real.

Si's soulful eyes looked uncertain even as his taxed brain tried to understand the sight.

"Since people don't come back from the dead, and as I've always adhered to the logic that the same rule extended to things including dresses that were destroyed in a fire, that only leaves me to one conclusion: someone knows what happened last summer and they are using it against us."

Eve found herself unable to voice what was really happening. Her tongue felt dry but worse was the chill that raced inside. She was cold, like the icy fingers of death were tracing a wicked pattern down her spine.

Mistaking her silence for agreement, Si continued. "I don't know what they want, but until we find out, you can't ever be alone. You're going to be with the girls or with me, that's the deal we're making right now — understand?"

"I don't think that's feasible, I'm not in any of the same classes as the girls..." Eve began, immediately hating herself for how weak she sounded. A braver person would have disagreed or tried to reassure him otherwise, but right now, Eve had to admit that it wasn't her own life she was afraid for, but his.

After all, she wasn't the helpless victim she had once been.

"We'll figure that out later. Give me a minute to brief the staff. I'll tell them we have an emergency. Then we'll go home."

He waited for Eve to nod before heading back outside, but he didn't go far. He stood in the entrance where he had a clear line of sight to her. She turned away from the dress, unable to look at it anymore, wrapping her arms around herself. Though she couldn't see it, she could almost feel the malicious energy coming from it.

It was all she could do not to bolt from the room.

Her eyes flew open.

Blackness greeted her, and the eerie silence that only came from the early hours of the night.

Though Eve had just been sleeping, she knew that something was *wrong*.

After they had come home, Si had kept her company the whole night. He'd cooked spaghetti, then they'd watched a Netflix comedy, though neither of them had laughed once, their minds on other, more sober matters. They talked a little about their situation, as Si tried to compile a list of all the people who might use something like this against them. The only names on that list though were the girls Eve had previously called friends before she had known any better.

They'd each had a mint tea which was supposed to relax but Eve hadn't noticed a discernible difference. After the tea, Eve had taken a bath and shortly after, fell asleep, exhausted from the stress and tension.

The sleep hadn't been restful.

Eve knew she must have experienced a nightmare as her hair was dripping with sweat and plastered to her forehead and neck. But that wasn't what felt wrong.

Something covered her from the neck to her feet.

Something that seemed to *move*.

Sliding her arm out from the sheet, she clicked on the lamp on the bedside table. The lamp sparked to light, illuminating the blanket of *ants* that lay on top of her.

Screaming with fright, Eve shot up as the ants quickly scampered off in different directions, disappearing in the cracks between the floorboards, and under the window. They moved so fast that they were gone in several blinks of her eyes.

The door burst open as Si — wide-eyed with fear yet determined to protect her — charged in waving a *gun* around.

"What happened?!" he demanded urgently, scanning into every corner of the room. "Is someone here?!"

Eve got out of bed, stretching out her hands in front of her in a bid to calm him.

"I just had a nightmare, that's all," she replied, unable to take her eyes off of the gun clutched in his hands. She was totally thrown. Until that eventful night in the forest, Si had always been a peaceful soul, so where had this gun come from?

"Where did you get that gun, Si?"

He tore his glazed eyes from the closet which he had yanked open and was currently investigating to make sure no one was hiding in there to focus on her. Reading her concern, and confident that there was no imminent danger, his shoulders relaxed some. "It's legal, don't worry."

"But, when did you get that? I had no idea we had one."

Si shrugged, running a hand through his hair. "I got it after last summer. I didn't tell you because I know how you feel about them."

"Only because more gun owners end up harming a loved one, than a criminal," Eve replied.

"I bought it so we would have protection, and after tonight, I was obviously right to do so," Si said, a tone coming into his voice. "Nothing else is going to happen to you, not on my watch, and if that means having a gun to protect you, then you'll just have to deal with it."

Eve knew she should have been reassured by his confident tone, but staring at the gun in his hands, at the cold gleam of black metal, all she felt were the goosebumps along her arms and a terrible foreboding that refused to go away.

Exhaustion clung to Tyler like a cloud.

Although she wanted nothing more than to collapse in bed, she forced herself to stay awake. She needed to make that potion for Cassie, that much had been made clear to her. The girl was hanging by a thread.

An image of Marley struggling against those two slime-balls flashed into her mind, and she had to suppress a shudder. All night, she would get a random flash of the attack that would leave her feeling terrified one moment, and rageful the next. When she had finally used her magic to hurt them, she had felt power like she had never felt before.

And truthfully, it had been quite the rush.

It hit Tyler then, that kind of powerful feeling she had experienced might be in some way how Cassie felt when she wore Marley's face and body. If she was right about that, then she could start to understand just how difficult it might be for Cassie not to give in to what was rapidly becoming her addiction.

When Cassie had initially broached the subject, Tyler had felt mad at her for allowing her vanity to get in the way of their friendship. But she had seen the desperation in her eyes, the pitiful way she had begged for something that would make her, how had she phrased it? *Be able to stomach herself.*

Still, wanting to help Cassie was one thing, being able to stay awake long enough to do it, was another thing entirely.

Realizing that she just didn't have the energy to troop all the way to the lab, Tyler decided that she would set up her own in her dorm room. She'd already made a potion in here before, how hard could it be to do another?

Rising from her bed where she was currently sitting, Tyler collected the glasses and mugs she had previously used and set them up in a row onto the roundtable that divided the room. Without a roommate, Tyler had full run of the place which came in handy at moments like these.

Half-filling the drinking utensils with water, she sat on a chair, elbows propped onto the table, pulling in her focus as she called up her magic. Picturing Cassie in her mind, Tyler tried to imagine her but as the best possible version of herself. Like she was using photoshop, Tyler smoothed away Cassie's rough edges, tweaking her features here and there as the water in the containers began to bubble.

She flamed out on the first few attempts, but by the fifth, things were firing. Tyler could feel her magic working until that telling puff of smoke appeared over the solution signifying that her potion was done, although she wouldn't really know if it worked until Cassie tried it.

Completely drained, she fell onto her bed and was asleep within seconds.

EIGHTY-NINE

Black coffee swirled into a paper cup as Marley poured herself a large drink from one of the many drinks stations in the Food Court. Beside her, Christian stood, head tilted to one side as he considered the options before him.

"Is it necessary to have so many variations of what equates to the exact same thing? Can you tell me the difference between a Mocha and a Chocolate-infused beverage?"

Marley tried not to look too conspicuous as she stared at him. "What are you, an alien — how do you not know coffee?"

"I'm a tea drinker."

"That answers so many things about you," Marley replied, earning a frown from him. "How long have you been standing there, anyway?"

"Long enough to know that $3.99 is an extortionate amount to pay for hot water mixed with a few java beans."

Marley's lips opened as she restrained a sigh. "It's like you're twenty-going-on-sixty." Spotting a familiar face across the room, Marley took her drink and made her way over to a table where Eve sat, nursing a drink of her own.

"Can you believe Christian is a tea drinker?" She said by way of greeting.

Eve rolled her eyes, but she wasn't able to hide her tension over last night's shock. "Next you'll be saying he likes pineapple on pizzas too," Eve replied.

A look of consternation came over Marley's features. "Sweet and savory is a typical, well-loved combination. I don't know why so many people have an issue with it," she said, genuinely confused.

Eve was saved from answering by the appearance of Tyler, looking frazzled. Her usually chic bob had kinks in the hair as if it hadn't been brushed, and there was a small stain on the collar of her shirt. She flopped into a chair tiredly, holding her bag in her lap.

"Trouble sleeping?" Eve asked, staring at the rings under Tyler's eyes.

"Oh no, I had no trouble sleeping. My problem was getting to sleep," Tyler answered without thinking as she yawned loudly.

"Catching up on coursework?" said Marley, sympathy turning her eyes soft. "I don't know how you're managing to hold down a job, study, and do all this "magic" stuff."

Tyler sat up in her chair in an attempt to wake herself up. She had almost blurted out that she had been up all night working on Cassie's potion. Somehow, she knew this bit of news wouldn't have gone down well, that it was best left hidden. Thinking about Cassie, Tyler looked around the area, wondering where she was when she caught sight of Si, a few tables away, eating a muffin while reading something on a laptop.

"That's your brother, isn't it? What's he doing here?" she asked Eve. As if he had heard her, Si looked up from the laptop. Seeing her, he waved and shot her a smile.

Tyler was struck by how *nice* he was. The guy was always friendly, always in a good mood.

It was hard to believe that he and Eve were related.

Eve chewed on a painted black lip as she tried to come up with a believable explanation. "He's meeting a friend who studies here," she said in what she hoped was a nonchalant fashion. Maybe they would drop the conversation, move on to something else.

"This early in the morning? That's keen," Marley commented, now focusing on her brother too. This was not going to plan. Eve needed a distraction… just as she was beginning to lose hope, she finally saw her opportunity.

"Hey, look, it's Cassie," she said enthusiastically, and completely unlike her normal self. Hearing the welcome, Cassie approached cautiously, looking around her as if she was expecting some kind of prank.

"Ah, yeah. Hi," she said, then turned to look at Tyler a second longer than was comfortable. Marley thought she saw something pass between them, but the moment was fleeting and was gone in a second. Taking a seat opposite Tyler, Rhett, their RA appeared, holding a bunch of flyers in his hands.

"Oh good, I'm glad I caught you girls," he smiled, flashing that cute smile of his.

A chorus of lukewarm hi's greeted him back, not because they didn't like him — they all thought he was a cool guy — but because there was business that needed to be attended to, which they couldn't get at with him being there.

"I thought you might be interested in this event that's happening next week." He handed passed them all a flyer, ending lastly with Marley.

"What's about?" Marley asked, glancing down at the information in her hand.

"We have this amazing TED speaker coming who's an expert on self-empowerment. I thought you might really get something out of it," Rhett said, looking directly at Marley.

Confusion swept over her. *Why would Rhett think she would need help in that department?* While it was true that she had some things to work through — then again, who didn't? — being empowered wasn't one of them. The question still ran through her mind when she suddenly realized that he was under the impression that it was *her* and not Cassie who had been so desperate as to hang out with those low lives. Cassie must have come to the same conclusion at that moment as she suddenly flushed bright red, dropping her eyes to the floor.

"Thanks," Marley said through gritted teeth. "I might go check it out, I'm sure Cassie would like to go too, right?"

Barely peeping at her, Cassie nodded. Eve read the unspoken communication between them and the reason for it, though Tyler seemed a bit oblivious, clearly needing something to pick her up this morning.

"Great, so I'll probably see the two of you there?" Rhett asked. From the corner of her eye, Marley saw Christian cross his arms, frowning at the other guy.

"Possibly," Marley answered as Cassie mumbled a response. Apparently happy with her answer, Rhett headed to the next table to continue his recruitment drive. As soon as he was out of eyeline, however, Eve snatched the flyer from Marley's hands.

"I think we've got more empowerment than we can handle right now," she said. Crunching the flyer into a ball, she tossed it into a nearby trashcan.

Still glaring at Rhett, Christian said, "I hate that guy."

Marley blinked, surprised. "How can you hate Rhett when he's so nice?"

"*Exactly!*" Christian replied, not bothering to explain himself.

Realizing that she wasn't going to get anything more out of him, Marley focused on her drink. Despite the noise of the food hall, silence fell on the group, as each of the girls focused on their own pressing concerns.

Christian finally noticed the strange tension. He stared at four solemn faces, taking in Eve's nervous energy, Tyler's tiredness, and Cassie who seemed to be fidgeting more than usual. Only Marley seemed normal, the thought of which made him snort out loud.

"Jesus. Look at you. What has happened to you all?"

Marley repeated his question, but the others only looked more shame-faced until Christian couldn't hold himself back any further.

"You're all feeling down-hearted because of the seals aren't you?"

Again, Marley repeated him. When she was done, the others looked at her surprised. While the broken seal was a problem that they felt ashamed by, there were so many other things going wrong in their lives, that it was hard to function. Not knowing any of their inner turmoil, however, Christian continued his pep talk.

"OK. Breaking the last seal isn't good, but learn from it. There are still three more seals that we might find before Michael. All is not lost until you're dead and apparently, not even then. Look at me for proof of that. The four of you just have to focus and continue on. Success isn't about whether you fail or not, but about picking yourself up when you do."

He stopped, waiting for Marley to pass on his words. Instead, Marley looked at him, one brow raised.

"We know what we've done but you're making it all so much worse. This being nice thing doesn't suit you, and it's making me uneasy. Please stop."

The forced smile he had on his face immediately disappeared to be replaced by relief.

"Oh, thank God. That took a LOT of effort. I could almost feel myself fading…"

"I wish," Marley mumbled to a sudden grin from Tyler who had overheard her.

"Listen, you're still learning. As long you ask for help when you need it, as long as the four of you stick together, you'll be able to pull each other through anything. Trust yourselves and each other, work together and I think we might have a chance of winning this thing."

The girls nodded, agreeing to his sentiments.

"Absolutely," Tyler said.

"Agreed," Eve echoed.

"Ah huh," Cassie mumbled.

"One hundred percent," said Marley.

Pleased, Christian rubbed his hands together as Tyler stood up, slinging her bag over her shoulder. "Classes are starting…"

"Yeah, I need to jet," Eve replied, sliding her chair back.

"Same here," Cassie said as she shot Tyler another loaded look before heading away.

Christian frowned as each of the four girls took a separate direction and left without another backward glance at each other.

His words having clearly fallen on deaf ears.

***

It seemed ridiculous that they were in class, considering all that had happened over the last few days, yet here Cassie was, sitting in the back of her Creative Writing, watching students trickling in as if nothing was wrong.

Christian's pep talk was kind of sweet though he really didn't have a clue what was going on. Of course, she couldn't talk about her problems with the others, not all of them, especially not Marley. It was hard enough having to confide in Tyler, and having seen the looks Eve had shot her when she realized her part in the attack on Marley — even though she had been nice to her after — she felt as if their budding friendship might have stalled.

And Marley? She knew she'd never be able to speak to her about these matters. They were on talking terms again but there was a definite strained air around them. Cassie knew it would take some time for Marley to get over everything if she ever could.

Tension gnawed against her stomach. Since the attack in the laundry block, Cassie kept reliving Marley's anger, but then her face would morph into disgust: disgust at both her actions and the men she had willingly led on only for such disastrous results.

Flicking a pencil between her fingers, Cassie felt the shame flood her body once more as her cheeks flamed red. Seeing those guys from Marley's eyes, she knew she had been right — they had been disgusting, so why had she not seen that at the time? Was she really as desperate for attention as Marley said she was? Was she really that lame?

Didn't she know better than that?

Her inner diatribe was interrupted by a coy giggle, a few rows from the front. Standing with one foot on the bench, elbow resting on top of his knee, Trip openly flirted with yet another pretty girl, this one, a flame-haired red-head. Cassie tried not to flinch with envy. This girl had the kind of sultry red hair that guys found alluring, the kind Cassie had always wished her own ginger frizz would be. Maybe if she looked more like this girl, Trip would pay attention to her.

Thinking of this, Cassie took out her phone and shot off a quick text to Tyler asking if she had finished with the "thing." She'd wanted to ask her that morning when the group had met for coffee, but there hadn't been a way for her to do that without the others noticing. Rather than to text her the minute they separated, Cassie had waited until now to contact her — just in case. She didn't think Tyler would be with the other girls right now, but it was best to be safe, she didn't want to take any chances. She used the word "thing" as typing the word "potion" might raise a few eyebrows if the message was seen by someone else.

Tyler's reply came almost instantly.

It's done.

A flicker of excitement coursed through her. She had to force herself not to grin as she sent back a reply.

Great. Meet me outside my English class at eleven.

Putting her phone away, Cassie's eyes slid back over to Trip. Tyler's potion would work — it had to. And when it did, Cassie would be so much prettier that maybe even someone like Trip would finally notice her but for a *good* reason. Smiling to herself, imagining what it would be like for Trip to flirt with her, she erased the redhead from the scene in front of her, replacing the student with how she imagined Cassie 2.0 would be.

Having waited her entire life for a miracle like this, she couldn't wait to get the potion from Tyler.

NINETY

Marley was halfway to her class when her phone chimed. It was a text from the college: her professor had fallen ill and since they were unable to provide a substitute at such short notice, her class for the morning was canceled.

Not knowing what else to do, she went back to the dorm, kicking off her shoes as she flicked the large flatscreen television — another addition courtesy of Cassie — on to her favorite quiz show and went to the wardrobe. The list of results Eve had printed out from Guardian HQ was still here as was the broken seal, both of which sat in a box on the top shelf. Reaching up, she took it down then went to sit on her bed as the game show host supplied the answer to a Jeopardy question: "The 224-mile-long Shannon River flows through this country…"

Without even thinking much about it, Marley answered, "Ireland," at the same time Christian's voice sounded close by as he too answered the same.

Marley jumped, not having felt his presence on this occasion. "Would announcing your arrival be so hard?"

"Sorry, I was distracted by the Jeopardy question." He nodded to the television.

"I'm surprised you actually got it," Marley replied without thinking.

Christian frowned at her. "Why?"

Marley shrugged, not sure how she should answer. "I guess… with all your Guardian duties, I didn't expect you to have traveled out of the country much."

"You don't have to have traveled to a place to know about it," he replied, looking somewhat peeved. "There is such a thing called the Internet… and besides, I happen to love watching Jeopardy."

Marley couldn't keep the surprise off her face at having something in common with him. "Me too, I watched it a lot with my dad growing up."

"Same. Though I watched it with Eric."

Marley felt a burning curiosity in her stomach. Christian had not explained too much about his history other than the fact that Eric was like a father to him, but for the first time since she had known him, she found herself wanting to really know what his past was. Where *were* his parents, and how had he gotten involved with the Guardians? But Christian seemed as enigmatic as usual, and something about him always made her feel that she couldn't reach out to him: he would tell her when he was good and ready to.

"Anyway… how are you?" he asked.

Marley froze, staring at him in with something akin to suspicion. She had grown so used to his tactless and demanding personality that the simple question threw her completely. "First the pep talk, now this. Who are you and what have you done with Christian?" she finally managed.

Frown lines furrowed his brow as he stared at her, not understanding the joke. "You're usually so bossy and demanding, no time for pleasantries… What happened?"

The frown turned quickly into annoyance but it was

tinged with something else — embarrassment maybe? Marley couldn't tell as Christian moved away from her as if she had burned him.

"Nothing happened, I was just being considerate," he replied, somewhat surly.

Marley tilted her head at him, trying to figure out why he looked so uncomfortable today. Though she didn't think ghosts slept, he somehow managed to look tired: dark circles ringed his gold-flecked eyes, and his hair wasn't perfectly sculpted — he usually looked like he'd just stepped out of a boyband — instead, this morning, tufts of his blond hair stood up on end giving him a somewhat startled look. Marley couldn't help thinking that it made him seem more human.

Cute even.

Realizing she hadn't answered him yet, she said, "I'm OK. Trying to focus on moving forward, but… thanks for asking."

He mumbled something that may or may not have been a reply then left it at that. It was awkwardville to be sure. Finally deciding that it was too early for all this emo-talk, she lowered her eyes to the box, opening it.

"I thought you'd be in class by now," he said, walking around her to get a better look at the list.

"Class was canceled so I thought I'd do some research," she replied, gingerly taking out the two pieces of the broken plaque that had been the second seal. In the cold light of morning, it didn't look very special. The aged metal was dull, no fuzzy cloud or blinking stars surrounded it. Whatever magic it had was long gone.

"I'm getting nothing from this," she revealed.

"Try the list," Christian suggested at the same time she was already reaching for the papers. She had to stifle a flicker of annoyance. Maybe it was the way he always turned up just to boss them around, but he could do with working on his personal skills, especially as it seemed that they were stuck with each other.

Her phone buzzed in her pocket, making her jump. Somehow she had missed a call from her dad, but he had left a voicemail. She pressed the voicemail icon and waited for his familiar voice to come over the line. "Hi Hon, just wanted to check on you today, see how you are doing. I'm stepping into class in a bit and won't be out until noon, but I'll call you back then. Love you, Dad."

Anyone looking in from the outside would think that was a normal message between a father and daughter but Marley knew different. Paul's voice had held a note of strain and seemed far more formal than their usual banter. While it could be that he was just concerned over her recent attack, Marley knew there was more to it than that.

Things were somehow *different* with them now.

Unable and unwilling to focus on that difficult subject, Marley went back to studying the list though the words seemed to blur on the page. It was a moment before she realized that her eyes were filling with tears. Mortified that Christian might see her lose it like this, she turned to the television. Jeopardy had finished by now, having been replaced by a local news item. A news anchor stood outside a house, speaking with a member of the public. When he turned to face the camera, Marley recognized him immediately.

It was Cassie's dad, the man who could double for Hugh Jackman if he wanted to. She was struck by the thought that she could find no similarities in his features with Cassie — it was hard to believe they were related really. Shame knotted her stomach as she wondered where that thought had come from. It was thinking like that which had made Cassie the mess that she was today.

Cassie's Dad was trying not to laugh at the person he was interviewing, a man in his fifties with wide-set eyes that looked too big for his face — especially with the bug-eyed expression he currently wore — who was talking animatedly about recent things happening at the house. A lot of unusual activity that he had previously attributed to a hoaxer, but was growing increasingly convinced that something more otherworldly was going on. It wasn't until he mentioned that the house had recently turned into a hotbed of paranormal activity that Marley truly paid attention.

Moving around the bed so that he could get a better view of the television, Christian started to watch the news item too.

"Can you explain what kind of things have been happening that has caused so much alarm?" Cassie's dad asked.

The man — whose name was Philip Glass and the next-door neighbor a helpful headline said — licked dry, cracked lips, looking nervous. "I know how this is going to make me sound, but we hear strange things happening every night. Lights go on and off, taps that turn on by themselves. Just the other day, the bathroom was flooded because a tap had come on."

"Couldn't these just be the everyday occurrences of a forgetful person?" Cassie's dad said.

"Well, no," Philip answered nervously. "The family was out when that happened. When I saw the water coming out, I rushed in to turn the taps off. I honestly think the place is haunted, it is freaky as all hell. And I wish someone would do something about it! It's driving down the price of my place and I only got it the last year. Wait, can I say "hell"?" he asked suddenly, staring straight into the camera. Cassie's dad laughed about how he had used the word twice now, live on air, so it was a bit late if it wasn't.

Christian's demeanor had changed while he'd been watching the report. His shoulders were pushed back, his eyes filled with a quiet frustration.

"What is it?" she asked him.

His eyes flicked over from the TV to rest on her. Whatever he saw seemed to trouble him. "Nothing."

Marley could feel the frown spreading over her face.

"If there's something on your mind just spit it out already, it's too early for guessing games."

Christian hesitated, battling with whatever it was he had on his mind. When he finally spoke, it was with regret. "This is the sort of thing I would investigate. These kinds of reports and anything with a supernatural slant. It's what I do. It's what Eric and I *did*," Christian corrected himself.

Suddenly, it all became clear.

Hearing this kind of news would normally spur him into action… but he was dead now. He wouldn't be able to solve the mystery, his days of helping people were over. His shoulder's slumped and he exuded defeat. While the last thing Marley had wanted was to do anything — truthfully, a day vegging out in the safety of her room did not seem like a bad idea at all — one look at Christian and she knew she couldn't just leave this. Though he would never say it, his death was on her, and if she could do this to help him then she would, comfort be damned.

"Let's go investigate the house," she suggested.

His green-gold eyes flashed opened with surprise.

"You can just rest today, take the day off—" he began, only for Marley to cut him off with a hand.

She knew the out he was offering was legitimate. She could stay in her dorm room and no one would blame her for wanting to take it easy, but she didn't want to be the girl who hid away after something bad happened to her. If she gave in to that temptation, she might never leave this room again. It was better than she went out and faced her demons so to speak — though any *real* demons would have to wait until the gang was back together where they had a chance of fighting them off with their magic powers. Right now, however, with Christian's help, she could investigate that house. And if there were any spooks, she'd be the best person to communicate with them.

"The sooner I get back on the saddle, the better it is.

Besides, if I hide away in my room then those slime balls would have won. I won't give them that. I won't let them intimidate me or turn me into a victim."

Her eyes flashed fire as Christian found himself mightily impressed by her attitude. This was a new side of her that he had not seen before, and it was one he admired greatly. Seeing her determination, Christian felt something stir in his chest. Absently, he reached up to rub at it, even though it would do no physical good.

Setting the broken seal carefully back into the box, Marley set the list on top of it, and put the box back into the closet. Since it was already broken, there wasn't too much she could with it anyway, not without the others help. It didn't seem likely that the seal had a spirit attached to it... unlike the house on the news item.

Softly, she sang to herself: "If there's something strange, in your neighborhood..."

NINETY-ONE

Eve sat fully upright, with her back pressed against the chair, hoping that — despite her outward appearance — today would be the one day that no one would notice her. She had wanted to stay home, had wanted to hide away playing Warcraft all day, pretending that her world wasn't one giant mess of fear and confusion. She hadn't bargained on her brother though, or that stubborn streak of his that rarely raised its head, but when it did, it couldn't be moved, not even with a tow-truck.

Despite how she'd said it was a bad idea, despite how she thought this would be a one-way ticket out of school, Si sat in the class next to her right now, looking for all the world as if he belonged there.

After their fraught morning, Si had stuck firmly to his decision not to let her be alone not even for a minute. Hearing that the other girls all had their own school commitments, Si had grabbed his laptop and snuck his way into class beside her.

All it had taken was a simple distraction at the entrance and he'd been with her ever since. His laptop was open on his seat's connected laptop tray, and he was making tweaks to the bar's website on it now. Though he seemed completely relaxed, Eve was worried that her professor or one of the other students might notice a new face, even if the reality was he was unlikely to be recognized — Eve's class was *huge*, with maybe some one hundred-dred students sitting inside the lecture hall.

Her professor was a stern-looking woman in her forties, though when she got into her lessons, her face lit up and it was hard not to be caught up in her enthusiasm. Listening to her now, Eve caught Si flashing a grin at her. It was his way of letting her know that he was just fine beside her, that she shouldn't concern herself with anything other than her class.

That he was there for her and always would be.

A lump formed in her throat that she cleared away with a cough.

As long as she had Si, she could face anything. As long as they were together, he would be her strength.

Cassie's class ended uneventfully but she was so excited, she felt like she could almost burst!

Pushing past the wave of other students, she found her way to the nearest restroom, relieved to find Tyler waiting outside for her as agreed. Tyler looked nervous, clutching her bag close to her chest. A light sheen of sweat glistened on her forehead even though it wasn't very warm that morning. Seeing it and Tyler's general demeanor, Cassie felt a moment of guilt: it was her fault Tyler was so uncomfortable. But she pushed the thought away as she nodded a greeting at Tyler and opened the restroom door.

"Is anyone in here?" Cassie quietly asked only for Tyler to shake her head.

"I've been here for ten minutes, there's no one but us," she confirmed. Even so, Cassie crouched down, giving the stalls a quick sweep with her eyes to make sure they were empty before standing up again. She watched eagerly as Tyler opened her bag, taking out a small water bottle containing a liquid that had a purple-pink tone to it. Tyler barely offered it to Cassie when she felt herself reaching out for it and snatching it out of her hands.

She couldn't help it, she was that desperate and she didn't care if Tyler saw it. In fact, maybe it was better that she *did*, maybe then she would understand. Twisting open the cap, Cassie took a cautious sniff. This potion had a fruity smell mixed with something spicy.

"Look, you need to know that I haven't tested this potion. I think it will work but there could be side effects which we won't know about until—"

She stopped, eyes wide open in shock as Cassie raised the spout to her lips and quickly downed the whole bottle in seconds.

"I was going to say that maybe you should take it slowly, just in case..." Tyler finally managed. "I can't believe you did that."

Cassie ignored her comment and span to face the mirror, inspecting her face anxiously. "How long before I can expect to see some changes?" She tried but failed to keep the impatience from her voice.

Tyler shrugged her thin shoulders. "I don't know. You'll just have to wait and see, but since you drank the whole thing... I'd think the answer was pretty soon." Her voice was flat, she had none of the excitement Cassie felt.

"I'm sorry you had to do this for me Tyler, but it really is necessary. It's just too tempting for me to use my powers otherwise. I was already becoming addicted to being Marley... this is the only solution. You'll see. Your potion will fix everything. I just don't want to be a freak anymore."

Tyler heard everything Cassie said, but the doubt

churned in her stomach. If not being a freak was Cassie's end goal, she wasn't sure her potion would be the answer…

NINETY-TWO

Ally pushed the mop back and forth across the linoleum floor.

The black and white diamonds had been caked with grease — as a result of Heepie Jeebie's love of deep-frying everything — and hadn't seen a clean in at least several months, but after a solid hour of washing the floor, the dirt had finally been removed. A gleam of pride burst in Ally's chest as she stared at the now sparkling floor.

All the foster kids had chores to do in the house, from cleaning their rooms to doing their own laundry, but this was being done voluntarily. After seemingly waiting for forever, her birthday was finally coming and Ally was making sure to score points ahead of time so nothing would get in the way of whatever it was that Tyler had planned for them.

Birthdays had always been her favorite time of year, those and Christmas of course, but Ally wasn't sure how it would feel now that there would only be two of them to celebrate. She wouldn't count the cheap cake and snacks Heepie Jeebie would have for the day. They were always the same, regardless of whose birthday it was — or even if they liked what she gave them. Cheryl would grab the cheapest big cake that Walmart had, plus these little sausages she liked to pair with a block of cheese that she would be the only one to eat. There would also be one of those buckets of candy that she'd have bought post-Halloween the year before on a massive discount which she would dump into a bowl. And that would be pretty much it.

None of the kids liked the cake, though the candy would be eaten quickly enough since there were a lot of sweet-tooths in the house. Ally hated both, so she usually gave them a wide berth, and her own birthday wasn't going to be different.

Rinsing out the mop, Ally supressed a tired yawn. She was still having trouble sleeping, suffering from those monster nightmares as she was. If anything, the nightmares seemed to have ramped up. She was so confused. As soon as they had begun, she had stopped reading that book so why the monsters still came for her at night, she had no idea.

Rubbing her eyes, Ally poured the dirty water away then went to wash her hands, passing by Cheryl as she made her way to the bathroom. Cheryl caught a glimpse of the glistening kitchen floor and did a double take.

"Nice work," she said to her begrudgingly. Cheryl didn't like to dish out compliments at the best of times, but Ally didn't care what she thought. She only cared about her sister and being with her again.

Sunlight filtered in through the trees above as Ally collected the trash that always seemed to blow into the backyard.

It wasn't much of a yard — just a square of patchy grass bordered by a ring of oaks that had recently been stricken with some kind of disease that was killing off some of the branches, leaving the stems bare and naked-looking, but Ally liked it out here. She had always felt more at home outside than stuck within four walls.

Back when things had been better, when her parents had still been alive, Ally had loved nothing more than to go riding on their ponies, Tyler by her side. They'd fill their pockets with carrots and apples, surprising their ponies with the treats whenever they reached their favorite spot, a lake that overlooked rolling green hills for miles around. Standing there, Ally had been struck by how large the world was, brilliant and filled by a riot of color.

Now the only green Ally saw came from the dried-out weeds beneath her feet.

The others barely came out here, preferring to spend their time on their mobile devices or gaming. Ally didn't mind that though; in fact, she preferred the quiet time this allowed her. The noise from the house was too much. At least out here, she could listen to the birds instead of whatever lame boyband the others were currently into.

Stooping down, Ally picked up an empty juice box, throwing it into the trash bag she had brought with her. Several chip bags followed, then a couple of candy wrappers. She pursed her lips thinking of how her mom — and by extension, her — had hated people who left their trash everywhere. They only had one world, she had often said.

As she worked her way through the yard, a strange feeling came over her. It started with the tingle that went up the back of her spine. Then came the absolute certainty that *someone* was watching her. She glanced back towards the house thinking that one of the foster kids was probably about to hurl a water balloon at her or something equally terrible, but the windows were all closed. She was alone.

Why then did she have this feeling? The sun chose

that exact moment to dip behind the clouds, leaving the area with an eerie dim filter. She spun around quickly, unexpectedly, hoping to catch the person before they could hide…

She saw a shadow *move* within the trees.

Startled, the bag slipped out of her hands. She didn't give it another thought, however, her eyes glued to the figure before her. Despite the human-like form, there was something weird about the head. It seemed almost monster-like.

It seemed like one of the monsters she had been having nightmares about!

A cold chill spread over her as Ally froze with fear. She couldn't look away, couldn't move an inch. She knew without hesitation that if she moved, that *thing* would come after her. And the horrible thing was, she couldn't even call for anyone. They were all inside and wouldn't hear her above the racket they were making, and, she had, of course, left her cell upstairs on her bed so calling Tyler was out of the question. There was nothing she could do but to stand there, waiting for whatever would come next.

She was still expecting the thing to come for her when the sun burst suddenly out from behind the clouds, showering the area in its yellow light, causing black spots to appear in front of her eyes from its sheer brilliance.

When the spots receded, Ally saw that the human-shaped monster she had been so scared of, was just the shadow of a gnarly, dead tree. Feeling ridiculous, she picked up the bag, leaving the trash that had spilled out of it on the ground. She'd pick it up another day, but right now, she needed to hear from her sister who, had still not messaged her today. Ally tried not to bother too often — she knew Tyler had a lot on her plate now, what with college and working in that grocery store — but unable to shake that weird feeling despite seeing the cause of it, she needed to be comforted and there was only Tyler now who could do that.

She hurried inside.

***

The girl half-ran back into the house leaving Fink bereft.

While she had been tidying up the yard, she had been giving off all kinds of mouth-watering aromas. As much as he loved eating humans, Fink had yet to try eating a child, but now it was all he could think of.

Would her flesh be tender like a lamb's?

It was all he could do not to go after her from behind the tree he now hid behind. That had been a close call. The girl had seen him for a moment with his true face, and the sight had sent her into shock. If Michael hadn't sent him on this research mission, if he hadn't given strict instructions not to hurt — or eat — the girl, well, let's just say the world would have become less populated by one.

The phone in his pant leg buzzed, interrupting his daydream. Fishing it out, he saw the caller number with annoyance. Why in all that was unholy, was he calling him *again*? Pressing 'answer', he forced his voice to sound normal so the caller wouldn't hear his irritation.

"Hello, Pike. I'm on a bit of a stakeout right now…"

Seeming to not pick up on the fact that now was not a convenient time, Pike's nasally voice came over the line. "Well so am I! Boss asked me to tail those girls, but they're so boring! One of them just goes to school, then works, the other three don't do anything else that's different. I don't know why we don't just end them right now."

"Because the last time we tried, the girl retaliated and hurt us," Fink replied evenly.

"Yes, but that's because we went after the strongest one! What if we went for a different one, like the ugly one, we could take them out one by one until we've wiped them out?"

"Michael has a plan, Pike. You know that. He has his own reasons for not explaining it to us just yet, but you must know he has carefully planned every step of this. You know how long he has waited for revenge. I propose that we stick to his instructions... unless you would like to inform him that you are not happy with your job?"

Fink left the threat hanging, knowing how Pike would react. He didn't disappoint. Fink heard the other demon swallow loudly as he stammered back a reply. "No, that's OK. I'm just shooting the breeze, killing time, you know?"

"Well, if it's nothing important, I must get back to my own task at hand..." Fink said.

"Course, sure," Pike responded, suddenly uber accommodating. "I'll leave you to it."

Fink hung up without saying goodbye. He sighed wearily, staring at the phone. Since he had given Pike the money that had been returned to Michael after those demons that he had hired from Supes Daily had failed their contract, Pike had made the mistake of thinking that they were friends. The fool had been calling him regularly, first just to chat, but now he had apparently moved onto complaining about Michael. While it served Fink to let him believe that, it still grated to have to deal with him on a regular basis. Fink knew it wouldn't last though. Pike would obviously make a mistake in the near future, and when that happened, when Michael decided he had also had enough of the low-level idiot, Fink would be more than happy to lend his services and dispatch of him.

Putting his phone away, Fink turned back to face the house where he could see the girl was now in her room.

Thinking of what was to come, he smiled.

NINETY-THREE

The Cape-Cod style clapboard house seemed, at first glance, like every other in this nice neighborhood.

All white, picturesque flower boxes hung beneath the large windows though the flowers in them — which must have flourished at one time — were now dried to withered brown stems. A pile of sealed removal boxes sat on the porch by the front door. As Marley and Christian neared the property, the steel chains of a swing suspended from the roof of the porch creaked. A soft toy bear sat on the swing, the sight of which brought a pang of sadness into Marley's chest though she couldn't say why that was its effect on her.

"So, what's the plan?" she asked, having no clue what they should do now that they were here. In fact, the more she thought about it, the more this seemed like a fruitless idea. How had they even decided on this?

"Well, you've got to get us inside."

"OK. Thanks for the tip," Marley replied, her eyes flashing sarcasm.

"What else do you want from me? Isn't it obvious?" he replied seemingly genuinely baffled.

"I just thought, with all your experience… never mind." She stopped herself from continuing this particular line of conversation, feeling a little stupid.

He must have picked up on her feelings, however, his voice taking on a contrite tone. "Sorry. It's your first time at this… I should show a little more patience and understanding."

Marley's mouth dropped open in an exaggerated motion. "Wait one second, I have to record that so I can play it back to you the next time you become insufferable."

"When have I ever been insufferable?" he retorted, instantly on the defensive.

"How about every time you've demanded that we save the world and risk our lives to go after Michael when we didn't even know what we were or how to use our magic?"

He crossed his arms over his chest. "Well, there was some urgency behind that. Also, I hadn't really had any time to get over Eric's death before I was killed myself, and it's not like I was given a heads-up that I'd be back as a ghost. That's a lot to process, so yeah, maybe I didn't always come across as well as I should, but it's not like there weren't any extenuating circumstances."

There wasn't any of the usual snark in his voice now, only sadness and pain that made Marley's heart do a flip-flop. Pain and loss she understood only too well.

"I'm sorry if I haven't given that enough consideration. It's just… all of this? It's a lot," she replied.

His eyes seemed to sparkle in the light. "You don't need to apologize, I was just trying to explain why I might sometimes come across a little… intense. I'm new at this too. Besides, after what you went through the other night… I should be the one to apologize."

This was news to Marley. She stopped, tilting her head up at him. "Why? You didn't attack me? And you weren't the one who led them on while you pretended to be me. Why would you feel responsible?"

Christian's eyes turned bright with the intenseness of feeling. "I should know better, that's all."

She felt surprisingly connected to him at this moment. They had been thrown into so much madness so fast, that she never really thought about how all of this must affect him. He always came across so sensible, that she often forgot that he was only a few years older.

News crews were still dotted about the area. Whatever was happening in this place was really exciting the media — that, or it was a slow news day. Either way, their presence only served as a hindrance, one Marley didn't want to encounter. Staring at the front entrance, Marley watched as a smartly-dressed reporter — who wasn't Cassie's dad she was relieved to see — rapped on the front door with his knuckles. He was being filmed by a cameraman carrying a large camera on his shoulder. The door stayed firmly closed though a man's face appeared in the window beside it. Even from her position fifty or so feet away from them, the man exuded a bone-weariness that was palpable.

"I thought the house was empty. Are you telling me that someone lives inside it, and these news crews are just out here hounding the man?" Marley exclaimed. It wasn't really a question, more a statement of her shock.

"You'd be surprised what reporters are allowed to get away with." Something in his voice made Marley think he might have had experience of this but she was stopped from asking as the reporter and his cameraman had left the house and was nearing them.

"Good luck getting anywhere with him," the reporter said, nodding to the house, mistaking her for one of his own.

Not sure what to say, she mumbled "thanks," then started up the stairs to the front door. Wooden boards creaked loudly underfoot, as the same man appeared again in the window. Rather than knock on the door, Marley made her way to the window.

"I'm sorry to disturb you, I just need a moment of your time," she said.

The man inside, shook his head at her, clearly mouthing "go away." Marley hesitated then, not entirely sure what to do.

"I would never have gotten anywhere if I gave up at the first hurdle. You've got to get his interest. Right now, he just thinks you're one of the vultures."

Steeling herself, Marley squared her shoulders and pointed to the door. "I'm not a reporter. I just need a word with you. Please?"

The man didn't even bother to look at her again, clearly fed up with the constant interruptions that all led to the same place.

"You're losing him, Marley," Christian warned. "Tell him why you're here! Grab his attention!"

The man was moving away from the window. Marley only had a second to speak before he would be gone. "Have you been feeling cold all the time, even though it's a warm day?" she blurted out.

The man stopped, just behind the edge of the window. He looked over at Marley though he didn't say a word. Encouraged by this, Marley continued.

"Do you feel like you're being watched all the time, but there's no one there?"

Now the man took a step toward her. Christian's voice sounded clearly in her ear.

"Now, Marley… tell him now…"

"I know you might find this difficult to believe, but I can see and communicate with ghosts. If one is haunting you, I might be able to talk to it and find out why."

Just saying the words made Marley feel ridiculous, even though she knew it was true. The man stared at her — hard. Marley didn't move, not wanting to break the moment. "I've got nothing to gain from doing this. I don't want your money, I just want to see if I can help. What have you got to lose but a few minutes of your time?" she pleaded.

Abruptly, he moved away and Marley felt her shoulders slump. "It didn't work…" she said to Christian.

The handle on the door turned and the door suddenly swung open.

"Come in," the man said in a gruff voice.

Marley stepped past him inside, almost stumbling on the several packed suitcases that were leaning by the door. Though it was the middle of the day, many of the curtains had been drawn throwing the place into an eerie twilight. A woman sat huddled with a small boy in front of the television watching a kids channel, its cheerful music a stark contrast to the purveying sense of gloom that clung inside. Looking as exhausted as her husband, the woman glanced over at Marley before turning back to the television in apparent disinterest.

The man gestured into the house. "Come through here." With Christian watching her back, she followed as he led her into a kitchen, taking the seat he offered her.

"I'm Chris Smithington," he said, extending his hand.

"Marley," she replied, shaking it.

"I wouldn't normally invite a stranger into my home…" he began, trailing off as if he didn't know how else to continue.

"But what's been happening can't be explained away, can it?" Marley offered. Christian nodded with approval, liking that she was taking control of the situation.

"No. And I don't even know how to try at this point. All I know is that we're desperate. So if you really can help…" Again he never finished his sentence. Marley sympathized with him, knowing how difficult this conversation must be. It wasn't so long ago when she had to deal with the fact that ghosts were real herself.

As Marley started to talk, Christian examined the kitchen — for what she wasn't sure. Tuning him out, she pulled her focus back to the conversation at hand. "I saw the news report this morning and that's why I'm here. I promise, if there's something I can do to help, I will."

Chris squeezed his eyes closed as some of the tension he had been holding visibly left. "God, I hope so. We're mortgaged up to our eyeballs because of this place. If we can't make it stop, then we'll have to sell it, but we'll be stuck here until we can. We won't be able to move and I am not having my boy grow up like this, not with all the things that keep happening."

"Can you tell me what exactly?" Marley asked gently.

"We only moved in a few months ago. It was such a great deal, in this nice neighborhood that we snatched it up without thinking. We should have known that there was a problem with it but nothing started happening until a few weeks after we were settled. One night, the lights started flickering, flashing on and off. I put it down to faulty wiring, but it started happening more and more, and only in the rooms that we were in."

Marley nodded, encouraging him to continue.

"Then we started hearing footsteps in the house, like someone thundering up the stairs. The footsteps would get to the top and the bedroom door would slam shut. But nothing would ever be there. The windows would be closed so we knew it wasn't the wind that had caused it. But that wasn't the worst of it. We started hearing mumbling which turned into actual shouting, but we would never be able to make out what they were saying or where the voices were coming from."

"That's not true. We know where the voices came from. They came from inside the walls," this had come from the doorway, where the woman Marley had seen in the living room now stood, her arms folded over her chest. She was alone, so the little boy must still be watching television which Marley was thankful for. He shouldn't be hearing this conversation.

"This is Gloria, my wife," Chris said, making the introductions. "Marley is a medium. She thinks she can help us with our problem."

Gloria didn't even bat an eye, letting Marley know just how bad things had gotten. "We don't have any money left—" Gloria began only for Marley to interrupt her.

"I don't want your money. I really just want to help you get down to the bottom of this."

Some of Gloria's defensiveness dropped away to replaced by a tiredness Marley could feel. "I really hope you can. We're at our wits end. It's not safe for Junior. He's only four and he's already started to see and hear things too."

Marley had heard enough. She knew she had to help this poor family. She had to find out what exactly was going on. Pushing her chair back, she stood up.

"Leave it with me. I'll figure out what's happening."

NINETY-FOUR

The chatter of hungry students filled the air, but Cassie blocked the sound out. She had one thing on her mind and one thing only.

Standing by one of the numerous vending machines, she took out her compact to inspect her face for what had to have been the millionth time today. The face that stared back at her was her own — except it wasn't.

Ever since she had been young, she had had a problem with zits. They weren't the kind that appeared overnight only to disappear of their own accord, these were the kind that left ugly scars which no amount of expensive oils and creams could erase — and she would know, having tried everything that money could buy — except, she had been watching the scars vanish all morning. Even as she stared now, she could swear that the gap between her two front teeth was closing, not all the way, but enough that it looked cool now, instead of goofy. And the frizz in her hair that she had never been able to control had begun smoothing itself out, leaving only glossy red hair be-hind. Though she was still herself, she was becoming the best version of herself that she could be: Tyler's potion was working and Cassie couldn't be more thrilled about it!

Dropping the compact into her bag, Cassie made her way to her usual sushi place. She was going to celebrate this piece of good news with some delicious sashimi. Smiling, feeling her whole face light up, Cassie reached for a box of pre-packed sushi when she saw Trip standing just in front of her. As usual, he had his entourage of five or six adoring male and female students with him. His hair was flicked up at the ends in that messy-but-actually-styled manner she thought was super cute, and he wore another of those sleeveless sports shirts he seemed to favor — and why wouldn't he? He looked so good in them — with cargo pants beneath which, she could see his ripped muscles. Cassie had crushes on many guys throughout her life, but Trip… he just did something to her that no one else did.

She was about to move away when she caught a glimpse of Cassie 2.0 in the reflection of the refrigerated unit. She stopped, staring at herself again, at how she now looked *almost pretty.*

Maybe even good enough for Trip to talk to and not make fun of.

He still hadn't noticed her yet, joking around with one of his guys about a football game that had been on television the night before. Fuelled with a newfound confidence, Cassie thrust her chest out and deliberately bumped into Trip as she reached for her lunch. He stopped talking, glancing at her but then he stopped, doing a double take.

"Wait, is that you, Tonic Girl?" He stared, so startled that Cassie didn't even mind the nickname, much as she'd like to forget that first night. "Have you changed something, you're looking *good.*"

Heat spread through Cassie, filling her with warmth and delight. He liked how she looked now! She smiled, shrugging thin shoulders carelessly. "Oh, nothing much. Just watching my diet. I've started juicing too."

He nodded, suddenly interested. "Oh yeah? I'm more of a smoothie guy myself. I just pop a scoop of protein powder into my morning shake and that's one of my meals done for the day."

"Well, I do that too," Cassie replied quickly. "I love my NutriBullet but that isn't as good for detoxing. Fasting then juicing helps clear away the toxins in the body." It was easier to channel her mom than expected, this being a conversation the two had had many a time.

He nodded appreciatively. "Well, keep doing it. It's working for you."

Cassie couldn't stop the beam from bursting out. She was so happy, there was even a lightness in her step. Turning, she moved towards the line waiting for the cashier when she felt a hand on her arm, stopping her.

It was Trip.

Her brows rose in an unspoken question, wondering what he wanted. She didn't have to wait long.

"We're about to have lunch too. Why don't you join us, you can tell me some more about this fasting and juicing thing you've got going on," he asked, gesturing at the group with him.

Cassie didn't respond, momentarily frozen. *Had he just invited her to eat with him?* She blinked, wondering if this was another one of those cruel pranks she had grown up with, but Trip just grinned back at her expectantly, waiting for her response.

This was the moment she had been waiting for all her life.

Not trusting herself to speak, she simply nodded. Trip grinned then, turning back to his friends, started heading away.

Floating on air, Cassie followed, smiling from ear-to-ear. Moments later, Cassie found herself sitting beside Trip at a table as he regaled them with one funny story after another. Other students kept stopping, just to say hi as they passed, each of them seeming to want to bask in Trip's light as much as Cassie did.

For the first time in her life, she felt like a rock star.

She felt, *like her mom*.

And it was a heady feeling. Thrilled to be with the cool kids for the first time in her life, Cassie ate her sushi as she laughed to one of Trip's punch lines, even though she hadn't actually heard the joke herself.

NINETY-FIVE

The long hand of the clock inched closer to one.

Eve stared down at her watch, willing it to move faster. The day had crept by so slowly that Eve had felt as if it would never end. Barely able to focus on her classwork, the pencil between her fingers flicked back-and-forth as she watched Si still working on Shaken & Stir's website. She found herself wishing for the kind of concentration he seemed to take for granted.

He had always been this way, ever since they were little. While Eve found it easy to get started on any task but would lose interest just as fast, Si took much longer to get going but would be next to impossible to stop if he wasn't ready to either. They were opposites in so many ways yet he was her rock, her best friend. Especially since their parents had moved back to Jamaica. They had always been close, but their relationship had gone to another level once they had been left to their own devices.

Guess that's what a little murder can do for two people.

Movement beside her woke her from her thoughts. Class was over and students were racing to get out of there, apparently each more desperate to leave than the next. Si closed his laptop, stretched then turned away to gather up his things. As Eve went to do the same, as she grabbed the cardigan she had slung over the arm of her chair, something yellow flashed up from beneath it and her breath caught in her throat.

Without even checking, she knew it was *that* dress again.

She felt ill at the sight of it. And fear. And rage. Like a person going through the several stages of shock, Eve wanted to howl out her frustration, but she couldn't. Not in here. Not in front of the class who already thought she was weird. And definitely not in front of her brother.

Opening her bag, she shoved them both inside, relieved to see that Si hadn't noticed. While he had already witnessed the dress that morning, she didn't need him to see it again. There would be questions that she wasn't ready to answer yet, and Si was like a dog with a bone when he wanted to know something: she knew that from experience. More than the fear of his questions, however, was the fear that his actions would inevitably be outed. She wished she could spill her sorry tale to the girls, but doing so would incriminate Si, and that, she would not do.

However, that didn't mean there was nothing she could do.

Thinking about the dress, an idea began to form in her mind. The more thought she gave to it, the more wings it seemed to have.

She wasn't going to sit idly by while this thing, whatever it was, kept happening to her. She would take charge of this herself.

She wasn't anyone's victim.

Not anymore.

Two walls of empty shelves as high as the eye could see flanked Tyler, the sight of which almost caused her to turn around. She wanted to run out of the store, through the city, and back to her dorm room where she could curl up in bed until tomorrow came.

But no. She didn't have a choice in the matter. She had to work to pay her bills, to save money so that she'd have a better chance of fighting for legal custody of her sister when the time came.

Exhaustion coursed through her body until she found herself swaying unsteadily on her feet. This was a newly refurbished section of the store which would be opening in day's time. Her manager William — the one who always made her uneasy and seemed a little bit *off* — rounded the corner and came up to her, his beady eye's raking her body from head to toe. Tyler had to stop the urge to cover herself. She was fully dressed and the store uniform wasn't at all revealing in any way though by the way he was looking at her, she felt as if she were naked.

Giving herself a mental shake, Tyler shoved the thought out of her mind. All he had done was look at her. He was probably just making sure her uniform was up to code. Why was she making a mountain out of a molehill? William finally took his eyes off of her to glance at the mound of products by her side.

"Big day for us tomorrow, Tyler. Now, I know you asked to have it off for personal reasons, which I have agreed to, but you must finish loading these shelves before I can let you go. We're short-staffed again or I would find someone to assist you."

Tyler was scheduled for a four-hour shift today, but looking at the empty shelves, she wasn't sure she would be able to handle the task on her own. And that was even if she wasn't feeling ready to drop. Not wanting William to pick up on this, however, she gave him a wan smile. "I'll be fine. I'll get it done."

William slapped his hands together, making her jump. "That's what I like to hear. If you do find you can't manage, however, do let me know. I'll be just around the corner in my office."

Tyler couldn't imagine having to spend time working beside him, jumpy as she was around him. And she was not going to miss Ally's birthday tomorrow, so rolling up her sleeves, she summoned up the strength to start.

"Thanks, but that won't be necessary," she replied, sounding strong even to her own ears.

William gestured to the boxes which had been separated into two piles. "Now remember, the liquid detergent goes on this "M" aisle." He pointed to a small sticker stuck to the shelf with the letter "M" on it. "The powders are to be presented on the "N" aisle."

"Liquid, M. Powders, N," Tyler repeated. "Got it."

Itching to get started, Tyler opened the first of the many boxes and began loading the shelves with products. William watched silently behind her. He said nothing, barely moved at all in fact, but his mere close proximity had Tyler feeling strange.

Finally, after what seemed like hours had past, he turned and left her alone.

Only then did the tension — that Tyler hadn't even known she was experiencing — leave.

NINETY-SIX

The sun shone, bathing Cassie with its warm rays.
They had moved from the food court to the gardens outside, Trip's group of friends. Cassie didn't know how exactly, but she was still with them. Still with him. And Trip didn't seem like he was tiring of her. She glanced at her watch to see it was almost two'o'clock and gave an inward sigh. She'd have to leave soon if she wanted to make her psychology class. Gathering her bag onto her shoulder, Cassie made a move to stand up from the ground she was sitting on when Trip's voice stopped her.

"Where are you going?" he asked.

She stopped, self-conscious as the rest of the gang looked at her, waiting for her reply.

"I've got class in a bit…" she finished shyly. Although she had been with them for a few hours now, Cassie had mostly enjoyed listening to the discussions around her; her confidence not quite matching her newfound better-looking appearance yet.

"But it's such a nice day. Why don't you blow it off, come hang with us?"

"And do what?" Cassie asked, unable to hide her surprise and delight at being asked.

Trip grinned. "I'm sure I can find us something fun to do."

Laughter sounded around her, but it wasn't the kind that she was used to. It wasn't the laughter that proceeded a cruel joke, like that time she had gone to a girl's fancy dress party as a Disney princess only to find that she was the only one in fancy dress. This sounded genuine, and the realization of that brought tears to her eyes.

Was she finally becoming accepted?

Was she finally not a freak?

Joy filled her heart, but she forced herself not to let it show. She wanted to seem cool and confident like this was something that happened to her all the time. Class put firmly out of her mind, she nodded.

"Sounds good," she said, keeping her voice natural.

Shooting her a heart-stopping smile that practically melted her, Cassie happily followed Trip as he led the group off campus.

The green tiled Paifang gate marking the entrance to Chinatown loomed above her.

Cassie stared up in awe at the elegant structure that was flanked by two Imperial Foo Dog statues. Although Cassie had lived in Boston for quite a bit of her life (when they weren't traveling to New York or the West Coast for her parents' work), this was her first time in Chinatown.

Eateries with colorful signs flashed blinking lights at her. In their window displays, she could see cakes, dumplings, and all kinds of meat hung on hooks from the ceiling, some which looked kind of terrifying if truth be told. Catching sight of a tray of what had to be chicken feet, she had to suppress a shudder when she suddenly thought of how she had eaten snails at some of the city's top restaurants throughout her life, and the thought of them wasn't exactly appetizing either, so who was she to judge?

Following the others, she walked past stalls selling gold and jade trinkets, good luck charms, and a chef making something called Dragon Beard Candy which looked like strands of cotton candy that was being hand-pulled. The sights and exotic smells made Cassie's mouth water, and she decided right then that she would come back with the girls. Who knew, maybe they'd be able to persuade Marley to try some of her culture's food!

"You coming, Cass?" Trip called out to her.

She'd been so engrossed in the food being prepared before her that she hadn't noticed that the others had walked into a restaurant with a grand red phoenix embossed on the velvet black door. This establishment was much more exclusive than the other places they had passed by so far. In fact, it felt like one of the restaurants her own parents would frequent. Trip held open the door, waiting for her. Cassie found herself hurrying to meet him even though she wasn't sure what they were doing there as they had all eaten not too long ago.

Not wanting to be the only one to question their visit though, Cassie followed as Trip led her through the busy room full of diners — many of them dressed in suits. It seemed this was a favorite of the businessmen in the area. She wove through the sea of red covered tables until she arrived at a round one where the others already sat.

A Chinese girl as thin as a blade of grass whose delicate features made Cassie feel clumsy and giant by comparison arrived with two pots of steaming tea that she placed onto the rotating glass turntable that sat on their table. Smiling at the group, she handed out several menus.

"I give you minute for menu," she said with a heavy accent to her voice.

Trip cupped his ear as if he couldn't hear her. "What's that? I didn't understand?"

Cassie grew momentarily confused as it was very clear to her what their waitress had said. Unperturbed, however, their waitress bowed her head in apology and tried again.

"Sorry. I say I give you minute for menu."

"Just one minute, that's all we get?" Trip asked, frowning as if he were actually not understanding her. A niggling doubt of unease fluttered at the pit of Cassie's stomach as she watched the poor girl try to explain herself.

"No, you have more minutes," she finally spluttered, a flush spreading over her neck.

"Trip, stop being mean," a girl with curly brown hair and hipster glasses said. "She probably only just got into the country."

Though her words seemed innocent enough, Cassie caught the snide edge in which she had said them and it made her want to sink lower into her seat. Their waitress blinked, turning away to give them more time to decide when Trip stopped her from leaving.

"Where are you going? We know what we'd like to have."

"Oh," was all their waitress managed. She opened a small white notepad and waited, a pen gripped in her hand.

"We're just here for Dim Sum. We'll take two of each thing on the menu," he instructed in a lazy tone.

The waitress blinked, not sure that she heard him correctly.

"Two each?" she asked, needing to clarify.

Trip nodded, even as Cassie felt her eyes grow round. There must have been forty items on the menu - how on Earth were they going to eat all of that straight after lunch?

"Correct," Trip replied, seemingly confident in their ability to finish off the order.

Nodding, their waitress left leaving Cassie to face Trip. "I don't understand. We just ate lunch back at school, how can you all be hungry again?"

Trip winked at her, grinning from ear to ear. "Don't worry about it. We do this all the time."

He hadn't really answered her question, yet Cassie didn't want to be a heel, especially as this was apparently normal behavior for them. Leaning back into her seat, she poured some of the tea into a china cup and sipped from it, letting the hot liquid soothe her mind.

Trip regaled the group with story after story of his sporting feats. Being the college quarterback was a big deal for him, and it was something that afforded him a celebrity-like status. Cassie could see it in the adoring faces around him — it was much like this for her mom and dad too. Finding herself blocking out the noise, Cassie took in the plush red interior of the restaurant. Calming music played from speakers set discreetly in every corner of the oval room. The place was so packed that there was only one man who sat alone, and he was half-hidden behind a tall Cheese plant. Cassie marveled at how popular this place was and made a note to bring her parents here when she next saw them, knowing they would get a kick out of discovering somewhere new. She sat there, taking in the ambiance just enjoying this moment of inclusiveness and hoping that there would be much more to come.

Laughter sounded, jolting her from her reverie. One of Trip's friends was scrolling through Tinder. "This one… maybe… if she wore a bag over her head," he said, as Trip grinned at him. He continued perusing the offerings. "Jesus, I'd be buried alive under this one, no thank you." He swiped again. "OK, we've clearly got to the retard section. This chick is cross-eyed."

Trip laughed, finding the whole thing hilarious while

Cassie sat uncomfortably, her hands in her lap. Of all people, she knew what it was like to be physically challenged, and this was not a conversation she felt comfortable listening to.

Luckily, their waitress returned at that moment with two helpers, each carrying several trays of steaming bamboo bowls filled with small dumplings of seemingly every kind. There were ones in a translucent wrapper of some kind, others that were deep fried and served with tiny dishes of savory sauces. Then there were the individual steamed buns with barbecue meat filling inside. Everything smelled so good that Cassie found her mouth watering despite not being in the least hungry.

The food was set onto the turntable and they were left alone to feast. Cassie reached for her pair of chopsticks, slipping them out of their paper sheath; she'd had enough practice eating sushi that she was an expert with them. Trip though, not so much. Not bothering to use the forks their waitress had thoughtfully left out for them, he grabbed several dumplings with his fingers, dumping them onto his plate. Then, picking them up one-by-one, he tore open the dumplings spilling their fillings onto the plate.

Frowning, not understanding what was happening, Cassie's chopsticks froze halfway to one of those glossy steamed buns as she watched the others imitate Trip.

"What are you doing?" she finally asked.

Grinning, one of Trip's friends, a fellow teammate whose name was Louis, spread a napkin over his lap, then reached below it. Moments later he tossed something onto his plate of food. It was so small, so thin and hard to distinguish under the food that she almost missed it. Shocked, she said nothing as Trip suddenly started retching, pointing to the plate.

"Is that what I think it is?" he asked no one in particular, his brows raised almost comically high in his fake outrage. "I can't believe what I'm seeing."

"That's disgusting," one of the other girls, a curvy blonde with neat bangs and blue polished nails said, right on cue.

"How can they sell food when it's clearly unsanitary in here?" piped up another.

By now, it was growing increasingly clear what they were trying to do, and Cassie felt a little sickened by it. She wanted to say something, to stop what she knew would happen, but the words stuck in her throat. All she could do was watch as their concerned waitress hurried over.

"You have problem?" she asked, clasping her hands before her.

Trip pointed down at his plate. "What does that look like to you?"

Their waitress leaned in closer for a better look. Unable to see what he referred to, she wrung her hands in confusion until Trip picked up his still-wrapped chopsticks and pointed to a short, fat piece of black hair.

"That is a pubic hair if I've ever seen one! Look at it. It could only have come from one of you."

The waitress's eyes were almost as wide as Cassie's as she took in the group to see that none of them had dark hair so it couldn't possibly be theirs. Horrified, yet lacking the language to convey her thoughts, she bowed several times in apology. "One minute," she pleaded, hurrying away to speak with a smart Chinese man in a gray suit. She gestured frantically to their table, speaking fast. Within moments, he was at their table.

"My waitress has explained what the issue is here, but I am certain that this is not of our doing. We run a very hygienic establishment," the man who must have been the manager said quietly but firmly.

Trip looked at him, affronted. "So you're saying we did this?"

"Of course not," the manager immediately replied. "I

am merely stating that it was not of our doing. I don't have any staff who would do such a thing."

It didn't seem like he was backing down. His intelligent brown eyes took in the group. When his gaze found Cassie's, she had to look away, worried that he would be able to read the truth in her eyes.

"Well, I take offense at your accusation. I have plenty of money and don't need to do such a cheap trick to get a free meal, which, as you can see, we have barely touched." Trip threw down his napkin to emphasize his point. As if he had given the others a silent command, they pushed back their chairs and stood up. "Saying that, however, I am not going to pay for a meal that is clearly unsanitary and I'm sure the rest of your customers wouldn't want to either." His voice rose, drawing the attention of nearby diners, who frowned their way.

The manager raised both palms, lowering his voice. "You have very clearly stated your opinion. Since I obviously cannot change it, can you please leave my restaurant? I will take care of the bill so there is nothing to pay. I would just like you to leave quietly so you don't disturb any more of my customers."

Cassie shot up to her feet, mortified for him. Why was Trip doing this?

"Oh, I can't get out of here fast enough," Trip said, already heading towards the exit. The rest of the group followed, leaving Cassie at the end of the line. She took a step towards them, but stopped, quickly shooting the manager an apologetic look.

"I'm sorry," she mumbled before taking after the others.

Hurrying outside, she found the others doubled up in a heap, laughing until tears ran down their faces, Trip the loudest of them all. "No matter how many times, it never gets old."

Hearing his comment, Cassie felt cold. They did this to these poor restaurants all the time? Before she could say anything, Trip slung his arm her shoulder and squeezed it.

"You're alright, Cassie, you know. Some girls are stupid and freak out, but you, you're cool. You rolled with the punches. I dig that."

Cassie smiled back at him, shoving the uncomfortable feeling in her stomach away, allowing herself to just bask in his glory.

It was only a joke after all. It wasn't like there was any damage done to the place and they could obviously afford it. Thrilled by the sensation of his arm around her, Cassie allowed Trip to steer her to their next entertainment, whatever that might be.

***

Sipping from his own cup of tea, Michael watched Cassie from his table behind the plant, having purposely asked to be seated there so he would be out of sight.

He watched as the doubt that had been on Cassie's face was suddenly washed away, erased by the stupid boy's arm. This girl was so desperate for his attention that she ignored how she really felt. He found it funny how people always ignored the truth before their eyes if it was something they do not want to see.

Luckily for him, he now knew a way into her life.

And it wouldn't be any bother at all.

Drumming his fingers on the table, he smiled to himself. Unlike these youngsters, patience was a virtue of his. As long as the end game was in sight, Michael would bide his time.

And when he finally struck, these girls wouldn't know what had hit them.

NINETY-SEVEN

Marley moved around the house, trying to see what she could pick up.

She was actually hoping that she might just come across the ghost if there was one here — and it certainly sounded like there was. Normally, she would know the name of the person at least, but the couple here had no idea who their predecessor had been.

She stood in what was being used as Junior's room. His tiny bed sat next to the window, still fully made-up despite those suitcases outside. A row of soft toys was propped up neatly by the pillow, arranged in such a way that it seemed their heads were resting on it. The wall was a calming green and the silhouette of birds had been painstakingly hand-stenciled as a border at waist height.

Whatever was going on, it was clear that Junior was loved.

With the parents watching her from the hallway outside, Marley walked around, trying to get a sense of something, anything. Though she felt a cold that had nothing to do with the temperature pierce her bones, she could not feel anything. Casting a sidelong glance at

Christian, who was also examining the room, she spoke under her breath. "I'm not getting anything."

He frowned at her. "OK. Try researching this house to see if anything violent ever happened here. There's usually a direct link to violence and poltergeist activity."

Taking out her phone — in full view of Chris and Gloria, she Googled the address of the house. Hits flooded the screen, mostly other houses that were currently being offered on the market. She scrolled almost all the way to the bottom of the page before a headline jumped out at her.

Lonely, elderly man commits suicide in his house.

The house in the picture beneath the headline was this very house. Beside it, there was a headshot of the smiling man, before he became the recluse this article described. His bald head was littered with age spots, and though he was dressed impeccably in a smart brown suit, there was a sadness that came off of him in waves. She showed her phone to the others. "I've found something."

They came into the room, peering over her shoulder, both looking disappointed when they saw what it was.

"We know about that of course. Looked it up on the internet ourselves, but he can't be our ghost."

"Why not?" Marley asked, confusion making her brow crease.

"He did kill himself, but it was relatively peacefully, with pills. We just figured he was lonely like the article says. Our ghost doesn't match with the man mentioned in there. Our ghost is furious. He hates us," Gloria blurted out. Seeing his wife's distress, Chris put his arm around her shoulders offering what small comfort he could.

"Well, this the only lead I have right now. So, I guess I'll have to try to summon his spirit to see if it is him," Marley said.

"At least I have a name now… Daniel Leonard."

oments later, Marley was alone in the room. Well, alone with the exclusion of Christian who no one else could see. He stood beside her, waiting, hands clasped tightly down by his sides. Marley could see he was nervous about what might happen.

If she was honest, so was she.

Chris and Gloria waited outside in the corridor, a safe distance away. Marley hadn't been able to convince them to move into another room. She hoped they would be safe where they were. Closing her eyes, she felt herself sinking into the black veil, that world where spirits resided. Holding his face firmly in her mind, Marley called out.

"Daniel… Daniel Leonard… come forward please."

Shapes flitted past the edges of her vision, other spirits perhaps, moving out of her way as she traveled through the black mist of this world. She knew her real body was still standing in Junior's room, but her, her own spirit maybe was flying past in its search for Daniel.

Soaring past a group of hazy figures, Marley suddenly felt herself inexplicable drawn backward. Retracing her path, she stopped by the figures as they moved away to reveal the elderly man behind them. He looked as he had in the picture in the news article, though his suit seemed to move around him as if it had a life of its own.

"Daniel?" She asked.

"Who the hell are you and what do you want?" he demanded in a voice that was nothing at all how she imagined. There was that fury, that rage that the new owners of the house had warned against.

Despite knowing that her body was safe in the mortal plain, Marley found herself backing up. "I came to help you. I came to find out what it is that is causing you so much distress."

"And why would you care?" he snarled, spittle flying out of his mouth.

"That's a nice family you're scaring, Daniel, and it isn't fair. They haven't done anything wrong," Marley replied, hoping that by taking a stronger tone, he wouldn't see how scared she really was. There wasn't a handbook for these things, as such, she was completely winging it.

"Life isn't always fair though, is it?" Daniel snapped back, not giving an inch at all.

"Please, Daniel. Let me know what happened. I can't help unless you tell me what's wrong," Marley pleaded.

Suddenly, Daniel glitched away only to appear right in front of her.

"I'll do better than to tell you," he said, brown eyes hard with contempt. Lifting his arms, he grabbed Marley on each side of her head. She felt an intense pressure where his fingers pressed.

And then everything changed.

NINETY-EIGHT

MASSACHUSETTS BAY COLONY, 1693

The dark, dank cell reeked of human waste while despair clung to the air like a blanket.

Rainwater dripped in from a hole in the rotten roof which no one had bothered to take care of. It was much the same for the rest of the building. Straw was strewn carelessly across the dirt floor, its thin yellow strands the only barrier from the bitter cold of the ground where The Four huddled together now to stay warm.

After the mob had taken them, after they had beaten them with sticks, they had been tossed into this cell without any food, water, or explanation where they had been now for two days.

And they weren't the only ones.

There were a dozen or so other cells in the room, each containing several people: a few were men, but the majority were women. Mary had studied the faces of all the prisoners but other than their expressions of utter despair, there were no similarities between any of them that she could find. Their ages ranged from seventy to… twelve. Since their arrival, a young girl had been curled into a ball in the next cell, sobbing, not speaking a word. Even now, Tabitha tried to connect with her. She knelt on the other side of the bars, speaking quietly to the girl, but it seemed as if nothing was getting through to her. More than anything, Tabitha wished she could read her mind and know what was ailing her.

"We have all tried to comfort her, but I fear something inside her mind might be broken," came a voice beside them. It was one of the men. A thick gray beard covered much of his face but could not hide his brilliant blue eyes. He was barefoot, his breeches caked with dirt. When he moved he grimaced as if it pained him.

Catherine's eyes slid over from the girl to meet him. "What happened to her?" she asked quietly.

Sadness came over him. "After being tortured by her father for so long, she and her mother had tried to leave, but he found them, forced them back home with him. Then, to punish them, he claimed they were witches."

He paused a moment, as the memory of what happened next filled his mind, sending a fresh wave of sympathy over him. "Her mother was tried yesterday. The girl had to watch as they tied heavy rocks around her mother's ankles then threw her into a lake. If she drowned, then they knew that she was innocent of the charges, but if she floated, then that would be a clear indication of her guilt."

Esther's eyes flashed with fury. "That is ridiculous! There isn't a way to survive a trial such as that — sink or float, you would lose either way."

"Her mother, what happened after they did that to her?" Mary asked, worry twisting her stomach into knots as she steeled herself for his answer.

"She drowned. And her daughter had to watch it all."

Tabitha gasped as her eyes turned bright with tears.

"She hasn't spoken a word since," the man said, finishing his tale.

"But why is she still in here?" Esther demanded,

forcing herself to stay calm even though she wanted to tear through the place with her magic.

"She is to be tried in the same manner in the morning," came another voice from across the room.

The girl shuddered and began to sob more earnestly. Unwilling to let her suffer a moment longer, Tabitha reached through the bars of the cell laying her hand gently on the girl's shoulder. Muttering under her breath, she summoned her magic, feeling it flow through her fingers and pass into the girl. Within seconds her sobbing abated. Closing her eyes, she fell into an instant deep sleep.

Pacing the small cell, Esther looked across at the other prisoners. "That's why you're in here? You're all waiting to be tried?"

Their nods confirmed her worst fears.

Any who were thrown into these cells were awaiting a death sentence.

The Four gathered together as one, outrage causing their faces to pale. Mary's hands were like claws gripped by her sides. "How can this council do this? It's madness, cruel and absolute madness!"

"We must put a stop to this," Esther urged, pacing back and forth, her long skirt swishing as she moved. "I of all people know what it is liked to be condemned to a lifetime of misery based on my appearance alone."

Esther was referring to the color of her dark skin. She was one of a handful of dark-skinned people who could freely walk amongst the land, who wasn't a slave, though that was more due to their nomadic lifestyle which kept them free from the usual bonds that kept others bound.

"Agreed," Mary replied, her mouth grim. "We need to gain an audience with this so-called Council if we're to put a stop to these barbaric acts."

Hearing their conversation, the bearded man spoke up. "How will you do that? They never come into these cells and you won't be able to break out. We have all tried and failed."

Catherine peered at him through the dim light. "But you are not us."

Snapping her fingers, the gas lights dotting the room suddenly blazed to life, lighting the room.

"And we will not stand idly by any longer," Mary finished firmly.

NINETY-NINE

Tyler dug down into the box, pulling out the final bottle of detergent.

She wasn't sure how she had done it, but the shelves surrounding her were almost done. After William had left, she'd gotten a second wind — that, or the copious amounts of her potion she had drunk earlier had finally kicked in — and she'd become like a small hurricane, whirling through the aisles, unpacking the boxes and loading the shelves without any pauses until her heart raced and sweat dripped down between her shoulder blades.

Feeling a huge sense of achievement, she smiled to herself as a buzz sounded in her skirt. It was a message from Ally. A growing horror came over her when she realized that she had forgotten to call her sister that morning, and in fact, hadn't contacted her at all today.

The message was short and to the point which only made Tyler feel worse about herself:

Where are you? I'm getting worried. Please call me! Bug
xoxoxoxo

Sneaking a quick look around, she saw a few of her co-workers across the way, but no one within earshot, hopefully, not if she spoke quietly. Dialing Ally's number, Tyler put her back to her co-workers, ducking her head so they couldn't see what she was doing: making calls from the shop floor was one thing they had been warned from doing.

The call barely rang before it was answered by Ally's breathless voice.

"Tyler! I was so worried!"

There was actual fear in Ally's voice, the kind of utter panic that normally would not be caused by a missed phone call by a regular person, but for the two of them, who had lost their parents and only had each other… A terrible weight fell on her shoulders as she heard Ally's worry. "I'm sorry, Bug. Things just got on top of me, are you OK? You sound breathless?"

Tyler lowered her voice into a whisper, hoping no one would hear her.

"That's because I heard the phone from the bathroom and ran all the way back to make sure I didn't miss you." She paused a moment before continuing. "Why do you sound so weird?"

Tyler's eyes slid around the room. "I'm at work and we're not allowed to take calls on the shop floor."

"Oooh. I'm sorry. I'll go then!" Ally immediately apologized.

"OK. We'll see each other tomorrow, make sure you get enough rest for the big B-Day celebrations!"

"I can't wait! It's going to be awesome!" Ally replied. Tyler could almost hear her bouncing up and down on the carpet back at Cheryl's house.

"See you then," Tyler whispered, hanging up just as William appeared by her co-workers, making his hourly rounds. She slipped her phone back into her pocket, turning back to the empty boxes ready to flatten them.

Giving the shelves a final once over, Tyler suddenly froze. She blinked, unable to believe her eyes.

The shelves were wrong.

She'd stacked the liquid detergent in the aisle labeled 'N', and the powders in 'M'. A cold sheen of sweat burst out on her brow. She'd heard William's instructions very clearly, could, in fact, picture him right now in her head, telling her how the shelves were to be filled.

But somehow, in her heightened work state, she'd done it completely wrong.

William said something to the co-workers that had them all awkwardly laughing then his eyes looked over their heads at her, and she knew without a moment's doubt that he would be heading her way next.

His earlier warning sounded like klaxons in her head. He would not let her have tomorrow off if she didn't get this fixed! There was no way that she would miss Ally's birthday, yet she couldn't risk her job either.

Digging her nails into her hands, Tyler did the only thing she could. Focusing on the shelves, she began to channel her magic. She had no idea if what she was about to attempt would even work, but she had to try. A strange noise sounded in her head as pressure built up inside. Turning to one of the shelves, she began to mentally picture the products as she wanted them: liquids on the left, powders on the right. In her mind's eye, she saw the molecules of the products changing, morphing into what she wanted.

As the pressure of the magic built up, she felt herself become detached. All sound from the shop floor receded until there was just the rushing, pulsating sound of the magic.

Holding up her hand, she made a gesture as if she were wiping from left to right. As her hand went past the products on the shelves, they morphed into what they were supposed to be.

Tyler felt a jolt of electricity from the shock of seeing it work, but there was no time to celebrate. William was fast approaching, and she needed to finish. Pushing herself to continue even as an all encompassing weariness started in on her, Tyler reached the last shelf just as William appeared by her side.

He stared at her work, wide-eyed and silent. Taking in the sight. Finally, he turned to her. "Well, this is very good work, Tyler. I didn't expect you to get this all done."

She tilted her head up at him, frowning. "If you didn't think I could do it, then why did you say it had to be done in time?"

William looked like a rabbit caught in the headlights, but he quickly recovered. "I only meant that you — new to the store — might have some difficulty. Of course, any of the others could have finished this too, and probably much sooner."

Tyler knew he was lying, she could recognize the bluster, but she didn't really care. She was exhausted and all she could think about was getting enough rest so that she'd be sufficiently energetic for Ally's birthday.

"Well, I'll be off now. Good luck on the opening of this section tomorrow," Tyler said. Without waiting for a reply, she hurried away leaving William to frown at her retreating back.

ONE HUNDRED

It had taken some doing, but Eve had finally managed to persuade Si to leave her alone for a few minutes.

She stood outside Juju, the magic store, pretending to stare at the glamorized "coin display" as she surreptitiously watched Si cross the street to the Starbucks opposite. He'd only agreed to leave her when she said that it was Tyler's birthday tomorrow and she needed to grab her a present. Si had seemed surprised that Tyler would like antique coins while Eve had been surprised that Si had thought about Tyler at all.

At least, he was gone now for the moment. Just long enough for her to do what she needed to.

Pushing open the door, she went inside, and just as in the first time they had come here, she marveled at the change in the place once the door was closed to the public. Where once the coins were, they now reverted to their real appearance. Magic items of all kinds were on sale to any buyer.

Moving towards the front counter, Eve saw the store's exotic owner, Helena, frowning into her laptop. Hearing

Eve's approach, she glanced up. Seeing who it was, how-ever, she pulled a face.

"Oh. It's you," she said without any hint of welcome.

If Eve was taken aback by the greeting, she tried not to show it. She needed the woman's help after all.

"I'm sorry if we came across as ungrateful last time," she began by way of an apology.

"You didn't come across as ungrateful, you were un-grateful," Helena said, arching a perfectly plucked brow at her. For the second time since meeting her, Eve was taken aback by her directness.

"We've had a lot to deal with lately," Eve replied. "It's not an excuse, but an explanation. It's not easy to sud-denly learn that you can do magic."

"I wouldn't know about that. I've known what I can do since I was a little girl," Helena said, not quite bending just yet.

"Did you come into it by accident?" Eve asked, partly from genuine curiosity, and partly as she wanted to warm the other woman up.

"No. My mother was a witch, and my grandmother too. I grew up studying the craft; magic has been a part of me since I knew how to speak."

Eve felt such a flash of resentment that shocked her. She wished someone had taught her all she needed to know about her powers. Life wouldn't be quite as fright-ening, without that prevailing sense of unease she could always feel hanging over her now. As if she had read her mind, Helena shot her a look.

"Simple magic such as elemental spells, truth and lo-cation spells can be taught to some if they have the innate ability but others, like you and your friends, come into your power all on your own. The most powerful of witches don't require spells that use ingredients or words, they can just do things using only the power of their mind."

Helena snapped her laptop closed, drumming her

painted blue nails on the glass counter in irritation as Eve's eyes grew round, realizing what she was saying.

"You mean us? The Four of us are more powerful than you?"

The question slipped out without any thought. Helena's face turned hard, her lips pursed into a thin white line.

"Is there a reason for your visit today, or did you just want to rub my face in it?"

Embarrassed, Eve got quickly down to business before Helena threw her out again. Opening her bag, she took out the yellow dress. Even though she had seen it several times over the last few days, the sight of it still caused terror to strike. Flashes of her time wearing it, of the attack… and the subsequent event made the blood drain from her face.

None of which Helena seemed to pick up on.

She stared down at the dress as her face ran a gamut of emotions: confused, irritated, and dismissive all in one.

"Why are you showing me that?"

"I wanted to know if there was a spell or test you could do on it," Eve answered slowly.

"A test for what, exactly?" There was that arched brow again. Apparently, it was Helena's default expression.

Eve felt her mouth turn dry as her throat closed up. There was an uncomfortable scratch at the back of it that she wished she could get rid of even though she knew it was all in her mind. Her nerves were shot. Adrenaline spiked through her body so that she felt everything tenfold, but she couldn't stop now. She had come this far already, there was no turning back.

"To see why it's haunting me."

Helena's expression finally changed as her eyes grew dark with interest. She stared down at the dress as if she would be able to answer Eve's question just by looking at it. Slowly, her gaze raised back up to Eve.

"And what would make you think such a thing?"

"Because no matter what I do to it, no matter how many times I throw it away or burn it, it keeps coming back," Eve admitted. A wave of relief washed over her as she was finally able to tell the truth, to voice the words that she hadn't been able to say to anyone until now. Having been in this voiceless position before, she hadn't realized just how much pressure she had been under. Somehow, the very act of speaking the truth out loud now released some of the terrible stress she had been keeping in.

Helena's lips pursed as she ran her fingers through her hair absently. "You can't be haunted by an object, only spirits. If only you can see it than someone must be doing that to you, but since I can also see it, it seems more likely that this dress has been cursed so that it will keep returning to you. The question is why? What does this dress mean to you?"

Eve fought to keep her face stoic. Helena didn't need to know the details after all even if Eve *could* tell her. "That's not important. I just needed to know that I wasn't imagining things or going crazy."

"Well, no you're not. But this isn't the kind of magic that regular magic users can do. Something like this requires advanced knowledge and a lot of magical power."

A lightning bolt flashed through her mind.

"The kind of power that could be granted by destroying powerful magic objects?" she asked.

"Yes, of course," Helena replied. "Magical objects often act as conduits or they can be used as batteries essentially. The user can drain the object of its magic and channel it into their own spell or some such thing."

As soon as the dress had reappeared in her life, all the fear she had buried away had risen to the surface. Thrown into a pool of terror, she had jumped to the natural conclusion that although impossible, somehow *he* was back. And if he wasn't then even worse than that, it

meant someone out there knew what they had done —
what Si had done.

But with Helena's answer, everything had changed.

Eve had to stop herself from physically gasping, not
wanting to give too much away to the woman. *Of course!*
It wasn't who or what she had been scared of all at.

It was Michael!

He knew what had happened and was now using it
against her!

One minute Marley had been inside that black veil looking at the ghost, Daniel, with the mortal plain in sight behind him, as if she were seeing both through a thin piece of material.

The next, both were gone, replaced by a *new* dimension.

She was still in the same house, at least, it seemed to be the same, though it was different in many ways. Where the current house was decorated in a simplistic design, this house was full of clutter. Every inch of wall space was covered by framed photographs, certificates, and metal signage. The edges of her vision flickered black and white, the only hint she received that what she was seeing wasn't real.

She had asked and he had answered.

Daniel was showing her what she needed to know.

Marley moved toward a wall now, inspecting the sea of signs. From pub signs to street signs, to hand-painted depictions of women, there seemed nothing that linked them other than they were part of an extensive collection. As she continued searching the wall for a clue as to what she was supposed to find here, her eyes alighted on a picture of Daniel.

It was the same picture they had used in the article she had read earlier.

A sound from next door caught her attention, the sound of angry, raised voices. At least, that's what she initially assumed, but on further listening she realized only one of the voices was shouting — a man. Of the other person, she couldn't hear a thing.

Moving to the window, she stared out at the neighbor's house, at their window which this house overlooked, as a couple appeared in the window. They were both dressed in light, summer clothes: he in a shirt and she, in a pretty white dress but which now had a crimson stain over it as if someone had thrown a glass of wine at her. The man screamed at his wife as she sobbed quietly, trying to calm him down. Marley couldn't understand what they were saying, then again, she didn't really need to. Their body language told a very clear story.

More surprising than the scene unfolding before her, however, was how she felt inside. Looking at the woman, there was what could only be described as a deep longing, but that longing turned into fury when her gaze shifted to her husband.

As she continued watching, wondering if she was supposed to act, the scene before her changed. The man stood at the window with his wife again though this time, he wore a wool sweater and she, a thick cardigan. Again, he screamed at his wife as she simply stood there taking his anger as if this was something she regularly experienced, which, Marley was beginning to suspect, it was. Again, she felt that yearning in her chest when she looked at the woman. More than anything in the world, she wished she could comfort the woman, take all her hurt away.

The scene changed again, but this time, the couple were out in their front yard. He was shovelling snow to make a path when she arrived home with a bag of groceries. But something about what she had bought displeased him as he yelled at her, hitting the groceries out of her arms. Fruit and bread spilled onto the glistening snow.

Over and over, the scene changed as frequently as the weather, as Marley saw the man screaming at his wife. She never argued back, never seemed to do anything to deserve his vitriol. With every appearance of the woman, the yearning inside Marley grew, until it almost overwhelmed her.

Finally, she realized with a start that the feeling in her chest was unrequited love.

It was the hopeless love that Daniel must have been feeling for his neighbor's wife, but which he could do nothing about except to watch her be abused by him, day after day.

She felt herself moving to the neighbor's house carrying a bowl of tomatoes, though Marley knew she was still seeing and feeling this event from Daniel's point-of-view. It was as is she was living inside Daniel's body.

She knocked on the door, offering the bowl up to the woman whose name was Sarah. Sarah quietly accepted the gift, all while Marley eyes ran over her body, checking for bruises or wounds, but as always, she was covered up. There was never any proof of what Daniel suspected.

Watching the story unfold, Marley felt breathless from the cruel torture they both had to endure.

The scene changed again. Now Marley sat in Daniel's lazy-boy chair in his bathrobe and pajama's when there came pounding on the front door.

It was Sarah, and she was frightened for her life having just endured her most terrifying fight with Alfred.

Marley welcomed her inside as she sobbed in her arms. Though Alfred had taken off somewhere, Sarah didn't feel safe going home alone, could she stay there, just for the one night?

Marley felt herself agreeing. She tried to persuade Sarah to call the police but she was exhausted. She was overwhelmed. She just wanted to sleep. Could they go in the morning? Unable to say no to her, Marley agreed.

That night, Jane slept in Daniel's bed while Marley took the couch downstairs. All night, Marley could feel herself wanting to declare her — Daniel's love — for Sarah, but now wasn't the time. This situation had to be resolved first.

Marley woke in the middle of night as the front door burst open, kicked down by a drunken Alfred. Turns out, he hadn't gone far. Having seen Sarah go into Daniel's house, he had jumped to conclusions. Marley rose up, ready to defend Sarah when Alfred flew at her, throwing her to the floor. Unaccustomed to fighting, Marley hit the floor awkwardly, cracking something in her side. In agony, she could do nothing but watch as Alfred ran up the stairs and fought with his wife. A violent crash sounded, followed by Sarah's scream. Then all was quiet.

Marley knew from the silence that followed, Sarah was dead.

The scene changed quickly as the pain that had debilitated her suddenly subsided.

Police arrived, taking Alfred away. In the weeks that followed, he was eventually convicted and jailed for killing his wife, but that wasn't enough. Not only had he lost Sarah, but Marley could feel Daniel's guilt weighing down on him, heavy as stone. He believed that her death was his doing, that he could have helped Sarah so many times before. He had left things too late and this was the devastating result.

She could do nothing but watch as she swallowed a bottle of sleeping pills and the world faded to black.

But as Marley already knew, that wasn't the end of his story.

With unresolved issues, Daniel came back as a spirit, hoping he would see Sarah in the past life, where he could finally tell her how he had loved her. But, unlike him, Sarah wasn't a ghost. Trapped in the house where she died, Marley could feel Daniel reliving those moments over and over again. When the new owners moved in, they unconsciously picked up on his unhappiness and began to argue, sending Daniel spiraling until he took out all of his pain on the new owners.

Abruptly, Daniel released his hold on her and Marley was jerked back to the present.

Reeling, Marley turned to Christian who had been waiting there anxiously for her return.

"What happened?! Are you OK?" he asked, concern flashing from his eyes.

Quickly, she explained everything that had happened.

"You can end his agony in a way I would never have been able to do had this been my case," Christian said quietly... and with something akin to awe.

Marley nodded, having already made up her mind to try.

Overhearing them, Daniel, who now hovered close by, stared at them both, wide-eyed. "Can you really help me?" he asked, his earlier hostility having vanished.

In answer, Marley went back into the black veil, confident she could find Sarah. Holding an image of her in her mind, she called out to her.

A hazy shape appeared before them in a ball of white light as Sarah's outline began to form. When she finally stepped forward, Marley could see her as clearly as if she were Christian.

Sarah's eyes were wide, her mouth spread into a delighted smile. Seeing her, tears ran down Daniel's face as he bounded toward her, engulfing her in his arms. The two held each other as if they would never let go.

In that moment, it was clear that they had both felt the same way about each other. No words even needed to be spoken. Taking Sarah's hand, Daniel turned to Marley and Christian, happiness turning his eyes bright with gratitude. Nodding his thanks to them, he and Sarah stepped into the white light together.

Moments later, they were both gone.

I t took a while to explain all to Chris and Gloria, but when Marley finished her tale, the relief that poured out of them was palpable. Thrilled that they wouldn't have to move homes, they couldn't wait to thank her.

"You shouldn't have any more problems with ghosts now," Marley reassured them.

Gloria looked so relieved, tears filled her eyes. "Thank you so much. I don't know what we would have done without you."

"Yes, if there's anything we can ever do to help you back, you only have to let us know," Chris replied.

"Can you just promise not to tell anyone what I did here? I don't want my life to become a circus with camera crews following me around. I want to be able to continue helping others like you, but I can only do that if no one knows," Marley asked as they escorted her to the front door. While she meant every word, Marley was actually more concerned that their fight against Michael would be hindered should the public know about them. They had to keep their powers secret to have any chance of beating him.

"Of course," Chris agreed.

"We won't breathe a word to anyone," Gloria nodded.

Chris opened the door as Marley stepped outside. The news crews were still around, though not in as great a number as before. Hopefully, they would soon disappear altogether. Turning, she gave them both a smile.

"Take care of each other," Marley said.

"Oh, we will," Chris responded. "If this has taught me anything, it's that we should never take another person

— or our lives for that matter — for granted as at any point, it can be taken away from us."

Marley nodded, descending the few stairs on the porch.

And as Chris's parting words went through her mind, she found herself sneaking a sidelong glance at Christian.

ONE HUNDRED TWO

The urgent message requesting that they meet had come from Eve.

Having rushed back to the dorm, Marley sat with Tyler and Cassie now, as they waited for Eve who was outside parking the car. Having finished another punishing shift at work, Tyler was looking the worst for wear. There was a coffee stain on her shirt which was also missing a button, though luckily, it was nowhere indecent or Marley would have said something. Hair crisscrossed haphazardly over her usually neat middle parting and not in that hipster I-actually-spent-hours-to-make-it-look-this-messy-way. Her hands were jittery and her eyes kept moving around the room as if trying to keep up with her racing thoughts.

All in all, Marley was beginning to seriously worry about her new friend.

By comparison, Cassie almost glowed. Marley had noticed that her skin was clearing up rapidly, and whatever new makeup regime she had going on was really working for her as she looked better than ever, which reflected in the way she carried herself. Marley was glad to see that

Cassie stood taller now, her shoulders weren't hunched forward like they used to be. Even with their difficulties, Marley was pleased for her. Maybe, with this newfound confidence, Cassie wouldn't get into any more trouble.

One could hope

Meanwhile, Christian paced back and forth, burning a hole in the carpet. Apparently, he wasn't a fan of surprises, and in the time since they had arrived back, his imagination had run riot, to the point where Marley had had to calm him down.

The door opened suddenly as Eve walked in…

"Thank God!" Christian exclaimed right as Si followed Eve into the room causing a vein to throb on his forehead that Marley noticed with some amusement.

Eve was so ready for business, that she hadn't even knocked, drawing a look of consternation from her brother. He smiled apologetically at them all.

"Hi girls, sorry for barging in. Eve seems to have forgotten her manners today," he said pointedly though without bite.

Tyler immediately sat up straighter in her chair, fussing with her shirt as if she had only that moment cared about her appearance. Marley wasn't the only one to notice her reaction, however, as her actions also drew a look from Eve, though Marley could not read her expression, much of it hidden under her make-up as it was.

"Hi," Tyler said to Si, trying to look normal though there was a slight pink tinge to her cheeks that hadn't been there a moment ago.

"Hey Tyler," Si replied. "How are you doing?"

"Oh, you know. It's all work, work, work," she answered lamely, wishing immediately that she had said something more interesting, or at least, something that didn't make her sound as if she wasn't interested in carrying on a conversation with him, especially when that was so far from the truth.

Although she had only met him a few short times,

there was something about his easy smile and manner that she liked. She also liked how close he and Eve were, something which she obviously had with Ally.

"I hope not, after all, tomorrow is your birthday, right? You should relax, enjoy yourself," Si answered, flashing another of those sweet smiles of his. Tyler went to correct him when she saw Eve nodding her head wildly behind him. Confused, yet taking her cue, Tyler nodded.

"Right. Except for tomorrow, when it's my birthday," she said as Eve let out a silent, relieved breath.

"Well, whatever you do, I hope you'll be having a good time," Si replied. "I've gotta head to work so I'll leave you all to it." He turned to Eve, leaning forward so that only she could see the sudden seriousness in his eyes. "Do you need me to come and pick you up after my shift? It'll be late."

"No, I'll bunk in Tyler's room," she said, knowing that it would be fine without even asking her — particularly after she would be done telling them what she had discovered.

"I'll see you tomorrow for breakfast then. I'll call in the morning to arrange," he said, giving her a quick hug. Spinning around, he waved at the other girls then left.

"Good! I thought he'd never go," came Christian's impatient voice. Marley didn't bother to repeat him. Eve watched until he disappeared around the corner before shutting the door.

"What was all that about?" Tyler asked immediately, wondering what stories Eve had been spinning to her brother — and why.

"I needed an alibi for something, so I might have embellished on the truth. Anyway, it doesn't matter, what matters is what I found out," Eve replied a little breathlessly as she took a seat by the table with them.

"I went to Juju's today," she said to surprised gasps from the others.

"Why?" Marley asked.

"I don't think she likes us very much," Cassie finished for her.

"She was fine," Eve continued, needing to move on. "Thing is, I found out that Michael isn't just going after the Seals… he's also coming after us."

"What, were you attacked again?" Marley asked quickly.

"No, not directly. He's doing it in a more subtle way. Let me just ask you this: is there anything strange happening to you? Anything new or weird that you haven't mentioned before?"

She stared at each of them, waiting for their answers. Marley was the first to speak up. "I went with Christian to investigate a haunting today. Turns out it was real, and the spirit just needed some help. It was very moving actually. He refused to leave this plain until his relationship issues were resolved."

Cassie looked a little horrified by the confession. "You just went with Christian? But he can't help you if something happens?"

"Hello, I'm standing right here!" Christian glowered, though of course, only Marley could see him.

"I was fine, and Christian was a huge help," she said drawing a look of gratitude from him.

"But when did this happen? I thought you were in class?" Tyler asked.

"They were canceled. I can explain all after," Marley said, eager to hear the rest of the story from Eve.

"Well, I just worked at the store. And nothing happened," Tyler added quickly, unable to admit the truth. It wasn't like what she had done made any kind of difference to anyone other than herself and Ally, what was the point in bringing it up?

"I sort of had something new happen today," Cassie spoke up quietly, her cheeks flushing red. She squirmed under all their attention. "I kind of hung out all day with this guy from school…"

Barely had the words left her mouth than four faces stared at her, incredulous.

"Have you not learned anything?" Christian began as Eve spoke at the same time.

"I don't think that's a good idea…"

But Cassie held up her hand, begging them for a moment to explain. "I know what you're all thinking — and you have every right to — but this time it's different. I already know him. Plus, I'm not going into this with blinders on. He actually didn't behave so great today, so I'm just going to wait to see if anything, happens. I've learned my lesson, trust me. Whatever happens, I'm taking it slow."

Tyler blinked at her, not even bothering to hide her surprise at Cassie's new, mature and smarter attitude.

"As long as you're going into it with your eyes open…" Eve finally said.

"And as *yourself*," Marley interjected pointedly.

"Yeah. Just be careful," Tyler warned.

Cassie turned to Marley, her hands clasped in her lap. Marley's opinion was the one she wanted the most. Despite the gnawing unease she could feel in her stomach, she forced herself to smile.

"I'm with Tyler," she finally said. At her response, Cassie's shoulders suddenly relaxed.

"Why are you asking this anyway? What does it have to do with Michael?" Tyler asked Eve.

"I just need you all to watch out. Michael knows things about me that he shouldn't, and he is using them against me."

Her words sent a chill into the room.

"But what does he know?" Cassie asked without thinking.

Eve knew the question would come up. She had been dreading it all the way here. But having realized what they were up against, she knew she had to tell her story.

At least some of it.

"I was in a relationship last year, but he wasn't a good guy. He hurt me." Her voice had lowered to a whisper as her own screams of pain echoed inside her head. "He's gone now, but somehow, Michael found out and is using that against me. He's making me see things that aren't there and making me relive what happened last summer. I just don't understand what he gains from doing that, but if he's trying to exploit my weaknesses, maybe he's going to try to do the same to all of us."

Silence fell over the room as each girl considered what that might mean for them.

ONE HUNDRED THREE

The blond student, the jock, the one they called Trip sauntered into a bar without a care in the world.

Michael knew he was underage, but it wasn't a concern of either of the two security men by the door apparently, though the hundred bucks he brazenly slipped each of them might have had something to do with that.

He had been studying the boy for several hours now, watching with seething resentment — resentment that life could have been so easy for such a lowly specimen whose only real claim to his ridiculous popularity was a not-so-hideous-face and his ability to run with a ball tucked under his arm.

Despite his afternoon spent flashing his charm at the girl, Cassie, here he was now, attempting to get the number of another one. It made his blood boil, not out of any care for the witch girl — she would get what was coming to her — but that he felt no responsibility or pressure and was simply able to flit around doing whatever he pleased.

Michael had never experienced that kind of freedom.

For all of his life, it was made very clear what was expected of Michael, what part he had to play in the world. There were those who had suffered because of him, and who relied on him now.

And he would not fail them.

Hearing his thoughts, the presence in his mind reappeared.

"No, you will not," it said with the greatest certainty and only a hint of malice in its rumbling voice. Michael could feel himself tremble as he always did from its power.

The streets were beginning to fill with night-time revelers looking for a good time. Crossing over, Michael walked past the two guards and into the noisy bar. A flashing disco globe was suspended from the ceiling, casting irregular patterns over the room. Music played, of the thumping, headache-inducing type that made Michael think of childhood tortures that he had been forced to endure back home. It was strange that humans would willing listen to noise such as this.

He moved past a group of girls wearing next to nothing. Their faces were plastered with paint and fake lashes, as they studiously checked out every male who danced near them, desperate for their attention.

Humans were the same. Every one of them. Wretched, pathetic creatures who didn't deserve to call this world home.

Michael found a spot in a dark corner where he leaned against the wall, arms folded across his chest in the hope that he would seem unfriendly enough that no one would bother him. He stood, waiting, biding his time, his eyes pinned on the hapless boy.

He watched as the insufferable boy danced with the girl and bought her drink after drink, clearly hoping that she would become drunk enough to go home with him. They laughed, swaying to the ridiculous music, becoming more and more intoxicated, but just as Trip thought the girl would be going home with him, her friends detached the two, letting him know that they were taking her home.

Alone, left to his own devices he was easy prey.

Michael waited as Trip relieved himself in the bathroom. When he came out, Michael stepped out from the shadows.

"Hey, are you Trip?" he asked in a friendly voice.

Trip stopped, turning around, a confused look on his face. "Yeah. Do I know you?" he slurred.

"No, but Lisa said you should meet her out back," he gestured to the exit behind him.

"She's gone already…" Trip replied, eyes clouded over with puzzlement.

"She got away from her friends. She's waiting out there for you. I'd hurry though, she doesn't look like the kind of girl who would wait too long if you know what I mean," Michael grinned, winking in the way he had seen Trip do.

"Thanks, man," Trip said, shuffling past him. Opening the door, he stepped into a dead-end. The scent of rotting food and alcohol blew in from the dumpsters outside, assaulting Michael's nostrils. Trip, however, didn't seem to notice, craning his head every which way to look for the elusive Lisa. Slipping out behind him, Michael shut the door. Without the thumping music, the alleyway seemed suddenly dead. Unable to find the girl, Trip span clumsily around, almost tripping over his own feet — a play on his name that made Michael smile as he reached out with both hands…

And easily snapped Trip's neck.

His body hit the ground with a thud. Casting a quick look around the area to make sure the coast was clear, Michael summoned up his magic. What he would do next would require every ounce of skill to maintain… and even then, the cost of using this magic would be dear.

Slipping his hands under the dead boy's armpits, he hauled him into a standing position. Drawing in the boy's life-force, he channeled it into his own magic, letting it bend and twist until he felt them combine into one…

And then he stepped *into* Trip's body.

Opening his eyes — Trip's eyes — he examined his strong, new, and young body. His own physical body was gone now. This body was where his soul now lived.

A wave of exhaustion came over him, so great that he stumbled and would have fallen if he hadn't thrown out his hands to catch the edge of the wall. Like a depleted battery, his magic had nearly been used up by the takeover — he would need to find a magical artifact and power up.

Not that he was unduly concerned.

He knew where he could get one.

Straightening up, he started out of the alleyway his excitement growing, when he found himself suddenly stumbling again. It was as if his legs had turned to jelly and they were refusing to cooperate. The world swam as a crushing pressure built inside his head.

What great hell was this?

Confused and concerned, he forced himself to continue, the act of keeping this body alive taking a much larger toll than he had expected. He could not afford for whatever this was to happen. He had to be strong enough to proceed with the next part of his plan.

Or there would be severe consequences.

Tomorrow, he would acquaint himself with the weakest of the witches.

Tomorrow, he would be going after the one they call Cassie.

TWISTED MAGIC

7: LEFT BEHIND

JO HO

ONE HUNDRED FOUR

The walk to the Common was excruciating.

Each step forward was an effort of seemingly epic proportions. The world swam as every sound that erupted in the night boomed like the hammer of God itself was pounding into his head. There was a constant pressure that grew increasingly.

He felt like his head would explode.

To the outside world, Michael was now the jock formerly known as Trip. The truth was a little more difficult to explain, however. Like the ghosts who could sometimes possess its host, he squatted inside Trip's body while in full command of his own, although it didn't quite feel that way currently. Try as he might, this new body moved sluggishly, his knees buckling alarmingly every few steps as both arms hung limply by his side. It was almost as if he wasn't quite used to walking — which, in a way he wasn't. Not in this body.

Still, the takeover shouldn't be affecting him this way. It had certainly never troubled him so much before.

Although only a few hours had passed since Michael had killed Trip and possessed him, the toll it had taken seemed to have drained him to the point where simply moving required his every concentration. He had never experienced anything like it at all, not in the countless times he had performed this very same task so why it affected him like this now… that was a very real concern. He could almost feel the magic seeping from him, rendering him more and more powerless.

Pike and Fink walked on either side of him as they approached the peaceful green park. A thin cloud of mist danced close to the ground basking in the glow of the full moon. At this time of night, the city was fast asleep with only the odd person — who was most likely up to mischief, as they were — still walking around.

Forcing one foot in front of the other, Michael couldn't suppress a moan when an animal screeched into the night sounding almost like a screaming child.

Hell on Earth, what was that unholy racket?

It was gone in a moment but the damage had already been done. The moan burst out of him, embarrassingly loud in the now silent night. Startled, Pike turned to face him.

"Are you OK, Boss?" he asked.

"Whatttt doessthh it loook like?" Michael slurred when a look of horror came over his new face. "Why am-mmaa talkin like thisthh?"

Pike and Fink stared, each as surprised as each other. Fink's brow knotted in consternation as he studied Michael, wondering if the takeover spell had gone awry. It wasn't until he registered whose body Michael had possessed that a sudden understanding fell over him.

"Can you touch the tip of your finger to your nose?" he asked.

Michael swung his head around to give him a look but the motion caused his already unstable body to lurch to the side. Throwing out both arms he managed to stop himself from falling. He stood, wobbling unsteadily until he finally regained his balance.

"What kindddd offf ridicu… ridicule…" he started to ask but trailed off, unable to think of the word he wanted. Blinking, he tried again only for a disgusting belch to explode out of him. His mouth snapped shut, unable to bear hearing himself sound so much like an imbecile.

By now, Fink had stopped walking. When he spoke it was with an amused tone that made Michael want to snap his neck in half.

"Just try, Michael," the demon urged looking expectant. If Michael didn't know any better, it would seem that he was actually enjoying this moment.

Straightening up — or as straight as he could currently manage — Michael pointed a finger and, despite feeling ludicrous that he was even entertaining the suggestion, moved his finger to the tip of his nose… where he missed completely, stabbing himself in the eye.

"Whatttt sorcery isth thisthh?!" He demanded, concern weighing down his stomach like lead.

Pike's reptilian eyes focused on him as he suddenly burst out laughing.

"Wait a minute, are you *drunk*?"

A grin came over Fink's features revealing his fangs as they caught the moonlight, glinting wickedly into the night. Michael felt a surge of irritation flow through him. Fink, the smarter of the two, must have read the murderous look in his eyes as his smile instantly disappeared. Coughing, his voice took on a more respectful tone.

"It's the body you possessed. He must have had too much to drink. What you are feeling are the effects of too much alcohol and not enough sense."

Michael's new eyes peered at him in the dark. "So thisthh isthh normal?" he asked.

Pike nodded. "Oh yeah. Humans can't hold their liquor like demons can."

At their explanation, Michael felt a surge of relief. He wasn't losing control. He wasn't growing too weak, and the magic wasn't leaving him as he had feared. This was just a passing condition brought on by the stupid boy's drinking.

Had he known how it would have affected him, he would have killed him much earlier.

Gazing ahead, Michael looked across at the city skyline. Lights blinked in the distance almost as if they were mirroring the stars. This world was so different to the one he had been raised in. No stars shone in the sky there, no sun or moon. All they had was that God-awful eternal heat.

The memory of that place caused an unpleasant shiver to take hold. He forced his thoughts back to the present as his eyes took in the surrounding area.

There was so much history here.

So many acts of murder that had been committed in this one place that he could almost feel the darkness calling out to him.

"Anything we should be aware offf?" Michael asked.

Lifting his nose, Fink sniffed in every direction, closing his eyes to get a better sense of things. "There were a few homeless men here a while ago, but they moved on when they ran out of beer. Further in that direction," he said, his nose pointing East, "a man with expensive aftershave is letting out his dog but they should be far enough away not to bother us."

A flash of jealousy shot through Pike. Fink was so impressive with his nose that Pike wished he had such a skill. Something that would make Michael think more of him, after all, he wasn't only in this for the money although that was nice; like everyone else, Pike had bills to pay even though he tended to live down in the sewers. Above the financial security, Pike wanted respect. From Michael, from Fink, from the rest of the supernatural community who had never thought much of him, and in particular... from his own parents.

Like most of his kind, Pike had been born into a large litter. At last count, there was still some thirty of his brothers and sisters in existence. The youngest of the brood, Mother Nature hadn't been kind to him, giving him not only a frail body but a back so hunched over that he looked like an old man when he was only a child. Expecting his lifespan to be short, his parents hadn't cared for him, focusing on the rest of their clan instead. But Pike had shown more resilience than anyone expected; he not only survived, he left the safety of their nest to strike off on his own.

Though life hadn't been easy.

Pike had to fight for everything; every meal and dime he had ever earned until Michael had come along. Contrary to what most would think, it was Pike who found him, dazed and confused, when he had appeared before him in the alley in the blink of an eye and a flash of fiery red light. One minute, Pike had been contemplating what store he would rob for food, when the next, Michael had quite literally walked into his life.

When Pike had crossed over to him, he had felt a blast of heat so strong that he thought his hair had caught on fire. It seemed unbelievable that such heat emanated from the male figure huddled on the ground who stared around him as if he had never seen the world before.

Curious about his story, Pike had helped Michael with clothes, food, and shelter for the night. When he woke the morning after, that terrified, vulnerable Michael he had met had long gone. In his place was the Michael he knew now.

They had never spoken of that first night.

Even Fink had no idea how Michael had come to be here. Pike knew that most mistook his bluntness for stupidity, but even he was smart enough to know that Michael would not appreciate the truth getting around. Despite how they had started, Michael was fully in charge, and Pike had seen enough to know he needed to stay along for the ride. Having spent a lifetime striking out on his own it was a relief to finally be a part of something bigger than himself even if deep down, he knew that neither Michael or Fink thought that much of him.

Finally, after what had seemed like the longest walk in history, they arrived at their target and stood before it in its centuries-old glory. The majestic tree towered over them seemingly as tall as a skyscraper. Michael could feel his senses firing as the tree's magic began to energize the very air he breathed. Electricity crackled as the alcoholic daze he had been suffering under abruptly went away, unable to compete against the strength of the magic. For so many years, this tree had sat waiting for someone to utilize its power.

And that time was now.

Channeling the last of the magic inside him, Michael pushed out his mind, searching for the dead parts of the tree, knowing that his powers relied on its host being dead — or at least partially dead — in order for him to take any kind of control over it.

Sending forth a crashing bolt of energy, he seized hold of the tree as he began to magically *unearth* it from the ground...

ONE HUNDRED FIVE

Pans clanged in the kitchen as Eve walked in half-asleep, having just woken from another night filled with flashbacks of past horrors.

Though she was pretty certain that it was Michael who was behind her recent woes — and not someone who had witnessed what had been done to her ex-boyfriend as Si believed — it still didn't help with the feeling of foreboding that clung to the air. It was everywhere she went, seeping into her pores like it wanted to suffocate her. She could feel it every second that she was awake.

It almost made her want to take something to drown it away.

Seeing her climb onto a stool by the island, Si dished up a stack of pancakes and set it down in front of her. "I heard you get up a couple of times last night. You couldn't sleep?" he asked, studying her with an intensity that made his green eyes almost glow.

"Not really," she answered. While she didn't want to worry him, there was no point lying about the obvious.

"You can't keep getting up on my schedule, Si, you'll

exhaust yourself," she started, but he cut her off by pouring her a large cup of coffee. Smelling its nutty aroma, her mouth instantly started salivating. The last thing she wanted was some heavy pancakes, but coffee? Now that she could do.

"I don't know if you've noticed but I'm the older one around here. I'm a big boy. I can certainly handle a few hours of less sleep," he retorted. "Besides, by hanging out with you in class, I'm getting to finish all those long-running items I can never usually find the time for."

Taking a sip of her drink, Eve let the hot liquid soothe her soul while she studied him. Despite how affable her brother looked, he had quite the stubborn streak. It was pointless to argue with him: once his mind was made up, that would be it.

"Are you meeting with the girls today?" he asked, turning his back on her, making his way to the sink with the pan.

"Why?" Eve asked. She didn't know why but the question seemed a little loaded. She found herself bristling, waiting for the other shoe to drop.

"No reason, I was just wondering. Didn't you say it was Tyler's birthday today?" he said, still with his back turned. A flower of apprehension opened in her chest.

"Yeah," Eve replied, remembering the lie she had told him to buy herself some "present shopping" time when really, she had been asking Helena for help with that yellow dress.

"I thought you might be doing something fun for that."

"Why are you so interested in Tyler's birthday?" Eve snapped unable to hide her growing — and irrational — irritation.

Si stopped scrubbing the pan and set it down in the sink, turning to face her, surprised by her reaction. "It's her first birthday since her parents died. I just thought you might want to make it a little special to help her get through it."

A wave of shame crashed over her.

Eve couldn't believe she hadn't realized this herself, hadn't given it any consideration — although Si wasn't right about one thing: it wasn't Tyler's birthday, it was Ally's — but he wasn't to know that. This *would* be a difficult time for the sisters so what did it say about her, that as little as he knew her, Si was showing more compassion for her friend than she was.

Eve felt like a selfish jerk.

"We've got something special planned for her," she lied. Straightening up, she took a large gulp of coffee, resolving to be the friend that Tyler deserved. Taking her coffee and the plate of pancakes, she started out of the room. "I'm heading upstairs to get ready. I'll be done in around an hour."

Si nodded as he started loading the dishwasher. "I'll meet you out front then."

A few moments later, he heard Eve's footsteps disappearing into the bathroom upstairs. Only then did he move the hand towel that lay on the stone counter, revealing the gun underneath. Checking that the safety was on, he slipped the gun into the holster he wore around his ankle before continuing about his day.

***

Someone coughed nearby.

Through a daze of foggy sleep, the sound woke Marley. Her eyes fluttered opened but snapped shut at a bright beam of light seeping in through a crack in the curtain. She flung an arm over her eyes, hoping to keep the light away but when it was clear that the morning was here to stay, she lowered it, glancing across the room to see Cassie's sleeping form as she snored quietly.

Curious. The cough hadn't come from her.

As she puzzled over this, the cough came again, louder and muffled, as though it came from outside the room. Pushing herself up, brushing the hair from her eyes, Marley frowned at the door.

"Christian, is that you?" she called out.

"Of course it's me. Who else would it be so early in the morning?" his voice shot back.

"Why are you standing outside?" she finally asked when it seemed no explanation for his bizarre behavior was forthcoming.

"It came to my attention that it just appearing in your room might not be the thing to do."

Though he couldn't see her, she rolled her eyes.

"Oh, now it's come to your attention? What's changed?" she asked, getting out of bed. Walking to the door, she opened it to find Christian looking like he couldn't decide whether it was too late or not to flee.

"Nothing's changed. Why do you always have to…" he started to say then stopped, distracted by her appearance. "Can you please put some clothes on?"

Startled by his comment, Marley looked down at herself, but she was wearing her normal sleepwear of a tank top and shorts. Nothing unusual or too revealing there. Still, hoping to wipe the bug-eyed look from his face, she grabbed the cardigan that was slung over the back of a chair and slipped it on.

"So, to what do I owe this morning's appearance?" she asked, sitting down onto a chair, tucking one leg beneath her.

"Something's going on, but I don't know what. There seem to be a lot of harassed looking students running around campus."

"You didn't check it out?" she asked.

"My first instinct was to check up on you… On you all," he finished quickly though Marley didn't get a chance to respond, distracted by a song that had started playing on her phone.

"Is that the music from The Fifth Element? From the cab ride scene?" Christian asked.

"Yeah! Wow. I can't believe you got that. It's the ringtone I gave my dad. We love that movie," Marley replied as she went to retrieve the phone.

"It's probably the most underrated movie of the 90s. I watch it once a year. At least, I did," Christian corrected himself.

As she answered the call, Marley felt that familiar knot in her gut whenever any mention of his death was mentioned. She wondered if it would ever fade. "Hey, Dad, what's up?"

Paul's voice came over the line against a cacophony of blaring horns and raised voices.

"Hey Hon, hope I didn't wake you?"

"No, that prize goes to someone else," Marley answered, looking at Christian who turned away to give her some privacy. "Where are you, it sounds crazy loud?"

"I'm in my car. Listen, no one can get across town, the streets are grid-locked. I've been stuck in traffic for an hour now and no one can get to school so I think it's probably off." He stopped as another horn screeched so loudly that Marley had to move her ear away from the phone. When it died down, she tried to listen to him again.

"I just wanted to let you know," he said.

"Thanks. I appreciate the heads-up," Marley replied, then fell silent as she didn't know what else to say which left her feeling awful. Never in their life together had she ever had trouble speaking to her dad. This new development didn't sit well.

"How are you?" he asked carefully. "We haven't really spoken again since that night."

He meant the attack in the laundry block. Marley had been able to keep her thoughts from lingering in that dark place, but whenever it was mentioned, she would feel the cold in her blood like ice water flowed in her veins.

She shivered, unable to stop the sudden chill.

"I've just been getting on with things, trying not to focus on it." A quick flame of anger flared inside her chest, surprising her. She hadn't realized until now that she had been mad at her dad. A big part of her had expected that he would show more concern, yet he hadn't even called.

As if he could read her mind, he spoke again. "I wanted to call and check up on you but I was trying to respect your space. That was why you chose to move into the dorms instead of living with me after all."

He sounded so reasonable that Marley felt ridiculous and found herself tripping over her words in a bid to reassure him. "It's OK. I'm just trying to deal. It happened, it was handled. We don't have to keep talking about it."

Paul's sudden silence filled the space leaving Marley questioning what he was thinking. When he finally spoke again, he sounded remarkably cheerful.

"Good philosophy. So, in other news, what have you been up to lately? Anything fun or new to report other than how hard you've been hitting the books?"

Marley almost snorted at his comment, not remembering when she even last *looked* at her books.

"It's way too early to do a blow-by-blow of my studies," she answered blithely.

"But if I call at night, you'll say it's too late," he replied.

"Exactly," Marley said.

Paul laughed. "I see what's happening here. Fine, I'll leave you to it. Call me though, OK? I don't want to be that dad who has to keep harassing his daughter to stay in touch."

"I will," Marley promised, even as she wondered what — if anything — she could ever tell him.

Paul came off the call filled with concern.

He knew his daughter better than she even knew herself… and he had no idea why she was lying to him so much.

His gripped the wheel, his knuckles turning white from the pressure. He watched the driver in the car in front of him get out of his vehicle and gather with a group of other drivers in the middle of the road. No one understood what the delay was, and news was slow to come down the line. It was chaos everywhere he looked.

Cars were rammed up against each other as the lights changed from green then flashed back to red without any cars having gone through.

Pressing the home button on his phone, he activated an app he was frequently using more and more often. It was a tracker app that he had installed before they had moved out here… and it was synced — secretly — to another phone.

He waited until the familiar map displaying Marley's college came onto the screen, and within it, a pulsing blue icon flashed up that marked her as being inside her dorm room.

He felt a great rush of relief that at least she hadn't been lying about where she was.

Setting his phone on the passenger seat, he switched the radio onto a local channel as he waited for the traffic report to come on.

ONE HUNDRED SIX

By the time Cassie woke, Marley had already been up for a while. Cassie gave her a baleful stare, seeing how she looked like she had just stepped out of a commercial for deodorant or something similar.

Turning on the bathroom tap, Cassie watched the water gush out as she loaded toothpaste onto her electric toothbrush. Staring into the mirror she started brushing her teeth when she caught sight of her own reflection and stopped.

Though she had only just gotten up — and this normally meant her ginger frizz would resemble a bird's nest — her hair was perfectly straight, as if she'd just spent an hour using the straightening iron. She noticed the silk top she wore next, how it hung in a more flattering manner. In particular, she noticed the deep valley between her boobs, a valley which had not been there before.

The brush fell out of her hand, clattering into the sink, splattering toothpaste everywhere but Cassie didn't give it a second thought.

It wasn't her imagination… her boobs were bigger!

Grinning from ear to ear, Cassie examined her new assets, admiring how much weightier and rounder they now seemed. Tyler's potion was working just as she had hoped it would! Moving closer to the mirror to inspect her face, she saw that her skin was now clear of acne and glowed.

Giggling, Cassie danced around the small bathroom, thrilled that she was finally turning into that swan her mom always said she would become. She was still dancing when a message arrived on her phone. When she saw that it was from Trip, she stopped, her eyes widening as she read the short message.

Morning Cassie! I had a great time with you yesterday.
Sorry, I was a bit of a jerk at the restaurant, I got carried away.
The others have that effect on me.

She stared down at the phone as if it had sprouted legs and was about to take off from the counter.

After what had happened in Chinatown, she had written him off. Despite crushing on him, she knew she couldn't hang around with someone who behaved that way to anyone who didn't speak American properly. It had made her especially uncomfortable as Marley was Asian even if she didn't identify with it too much.

But here Trip was, apologizing to her now.

Feeling happier, a million possible responses ran through her mind, but she scrapped them all, thinking that they sounded too keen, too much like the old Cassie. If Trip was actually interested in her, she had to play it cool. She couldn't do what she usually did only to make another big mistake. Pausing, she thought about what Marley would do in her place.

Then you should pick better people to hang around with.

She typed the message and hit send before she could

second-guess herself. As soon as the message left her phone, regret flooded over her. That was so stupid! Why, when he was being nice to her would that be her reply? What a way to end that budding whatever-it-was.

Cassie pushed the phone against her temple, lamenting her stupidity when the phone buzzed in her hand again with another message from Trip.

Right? That brings me neatly to my next question: would you like to hang with me again today?

Cassie stopped dead, frozen in her tracks. Was he asking her out on a date? Or was this just a hang out as he said? How was she going to find out without sounding too eager? Channeling Marley again, and maybe now with shades of her mom who she had seen in action many times before, Cassie replied.

That depends. Hang, as in a literal gathering with no plan for anything where anyone can join, or hang as in, go someplace nice, just the two of us?

The message went off. The ball was in his court. Cassie chewed on the end of a nail, holding her breath until she felt like she would burst. Only when the telltale buzz came, did her breath come hissing out.

Just the two of us. Like a date. What do you say, would you like to go out with me today?

Cassie squealed, clapping her hands together, delighted by this, her first actual pre-arranged date. She didn't count the disgusting make-out session with that guy from the coffee place since she hadn't really liked or knew who he was… plus she hadn't even been herself at the time! This was a real date, and she would be going as herself. Thrilled, she sent back another message.

In that case, I'll be free after class from four.

Trip confirmed the time and meeting point a moment later. On cloud nine, Cassie hurried through her morning routine, marveling at how much less she had to do to make herself presentable today. Not only did she look so much better, but it was taking far less time to do so. As she washed, then dried her hair, her thoughts flitted over to the shoes her mom had given her the day she had moved into the dorm.

An image of the cream-colored peep-toed heels came into her mind. They were a custom the women in her family had started: first, her grandmother who had worn the shoes on her first date with the man who later became her loving husband. They had been together for over forty years and were still happily married now. Her grandmother had passed the shoes to Cassie's own mother, who wore them on her first date with Cassie's dad. And she knew from experience that the two loved each other just about as much as any two people could.

Now the shoes belonged to Cassie.

Today would be her first date with Trip. Though she would love to continue with tradition, she could feel a slight gnawing of doubt. Trip had said all the right things to her just now, but that wasn't how it had been yesterday, and she had promised herself that she had learned from her earlier mistakes with guys. She knew she couldn't rush things.

Despite how she wanted to, she made the decision not to be wearing those shoes today. They would have to wait until she was sure about the guy she was seeing whether that would be Trip or not.

ONE HUNDRED SEVEN

Tyler's heart was going to explode out of her chest.

She woke, hands pressed against her chest as her heart thumped wildly, sounding a beat so loud that she wouldn't be surprised if the girls across the hall could hear.

The fear struck next, sending ice down her spine.

What was happening to her? Had the stress of the last six months proved too much — was her body failing against her now on top of everything else?

Terrified that she might be experiencing a heart attack, she commanded Siri to look up her symptoms. When Siri's calm voice relayed what he had discovered, she was relieved to hear that she had only one symptom in common with the condition which could just as easily be attributed to a caffeine overload — or, in her case, an energy potion one.

As soon as the realization came, the palpitations seemed to die down. More and more, she was beginning to think that her magic might come with some unwanted side effects, like the jitteriness she had been feeling for days now that no amount of potion or coffee would abate.

But today was an important day so she would have to ignore any discomfort. Whatever this was, it had to wait.

Today was Ally's birthday.

Her eyes slid across the room to the table where Ally's main present, the ladybug bag sat waiting to be wrapped. It wasn't the only gift Ally would be getting, however. Tyler had thought long and hard about how she could incorporate her parents today. With money being as tight as it was, her choices were limited, but she had finally settled upon two things that felt right.

Setting down her phone, she made her way to the table where squares of colored paper were spread messily around. Many were crushed into balls, a reminder of each time she had failed in her task to make a set of origami bookmarks in the shape of animals. It had taken most of the night but sitting in a neat row, weighed down by a textbook so they wouldn't be blown away, were the lions, elephants, giraffes, and penguins she had already folded after countless failed attempts. All she had left to make were the pair of pandas. She had wanted to finish them last night but when her eyes started blurring from tiredness, she'd had to stop.

She opened the origami book that had been her mom's favorite. The original had been lost amongst the rest of the things they had owned when their home had been repossessed; this was a used copy she had bought from eBay. Following the instructions carefully, Tyler folded and twisting the piece of paper until it finally started to resemble the animal it was supposed to be. With only a few folds left to go, however, Tyler got stuck. Without thinking, and as she had done a million times before when in the same predicament, she opened her mouth to call out for her mom who had been the origami expert in their family. It was a moment before she came crashing back to Earth.

And along with that, came the pain that always followed the sudden realization that she was gone and would never be able to help her with anything, origami or otherwise.

Tears pricked the back of her eyes as her chest tightened, the ache of missing her parents so much that she almost couldn't breathe. Lowering her hands, Tyler mentally chided herself.

Get it together!

Across town, there was a young girl who was relying on her, who was stuck in a house with troubled kids and a mean foster mom.

And she would die rather than let her down.

Blinking, she ran her eyes slowly over the instructions again, taking it slow. Over and over, she studied the diagrams, reading the words until they finally began to make sense. Folding the last crease, she turned the shape over to find a happy little panda face smiling up at her.

I did it, Mom.

She could almost feel her mom's approval. Quickly, before she could forget how to do it, Tyler made a matching panda — Ally was such a sensitive thing that she hated when things were alone. Carefully, she slotted them neatly into a cute box she had made out of a leftover cereal box and some wrapping paper printed with an image of rolling hills, sweeping valleys, and rivers. These animals were not going into a zoo. More than being solitary, Ally hated cages of any kind. She believed all creatures should be free to roam, living their lives as they saw fit.

Finished with the origami, Tyler reached for the final present. It was a little music box engraved with flowers in glorious full bloom. When Tyler flipped the box open, a tiny ballerina popped up as music from the Nutcracker played. When Ally had been little, their dad had given her a similar though much more expensive one. The original box had been made out of silver and not the cheap nickel that encased this one. Ally had loved it, but like everything else they seemed to have cared about, it had disappeared after their parents' deaths. Though these material things would never replace them, Tyler knew Ally would love this small reminder of them even if it would be bittersweet. It was important that Tyler keep their memory alive for her, no matter how painful that might be.

Her phone buzzed from across the room, jolting her from her thoughts, and she felt an instant flash of concern. If this was Cheryl telling her that she couldn't see Ally… so help her God…

She crossed the room in three quick strides, snatching up the phone only to find that it was a text message letting her know that her student loan had finally come through. Thrilled, Tyler punched the air.

Now she could actually treat Ally to that cool diner she had always wanted to go to, but that was always out of their budget. Scrapping her plan for a low-key picnic, Tyler found the number of the diner and dialed, hoping that they would be able to accommodate her last-minute birthday plans.

Tyler was heading to Marley and Cassie's room when they came out of it.

Marley had one ear pressed to her phone. Seeing Tyler, she started talking to her. "There's something happening downtown. Eve is stuck in traffic, she can't get here. My dad, too, mentioned that the place is gridlocked. No one can get anywhere."

"Do you think classes are canceled today?" Tyler asked, hoping for more time to prepare for Ally's birthday.

"I think a better question would be to see exactly what's causing all those problems downtown," came Christian's voice behind Marley.

"Christian wants us to check it out," Marley explained.

Cassie's first instinct was to ditch the girls, after all, she had a big date — her first — coming up. She'd need time to get ready, even if her new appearance wouldn't be as labor intensive. As soon as she realized what she was thinking, however, Cassie pushed the thoughts firmly aside.

Wasn't this her old self talking? The one who was so desperate she put a guy's attention above everything else? If she really was going to change, she would have to start by resisting her natural instinct — and that meant, not ditching her friends at the first opportunity.

"Why don't we go meet Eve?" Cassie suggested. "If it's nothing we can head back here or hang around campus since it's not much of a walk."

If she could have patted herself on the back, she would have.

Marley and Tyler looked at her, a little surprised by her sensible suggestion.

"Sounds good," said Marley.

"Sure," Tyler replied.

"Let's go," Christian said joining in, though Marley was the only one who heard him.

Feeling proud of herself, Cassie smiled, pleased by this new improved version of herself.

ONE HUNDRED EIGHT

After wading through crowds of the confused public, Marley, Cassie, and Tyler finally arrived by Eve's car where she sat beside Si, who was fast asleep in the passenger seat. Seeing them, she put a finger up to her lips as she got out of the car quietly, trying not to wake him. Marley was about to ask how they were when she looked ahead and saw the cause for the city-wide disruption.

The infamous Great Elm tree which had previously had its home in the Common had been uprooted.

All one-hundred and thirty foot of the tree now lay across Washington Street and on top of the entrance to DTX, the Downtown Crossing subway station. Whatever sat beneath the tree had been crushed by the very weight of it. Cars, motorbikes, telephone poles, even the corner of a building now lay in ruins. Thankfully, the building only housed a bank. A chill rose sending goose pimples along her arms when Marley thought how it could just as easily have been a residential home.

People stopped by snapping pictures of the tree, mar-veling at the bizarre sight. It wasn't only that the tree had been uprooted which had the city abuzz, but the fact that it was now some distance away from the site of its original home. While everyone else wondered how this could possibly have happened, the girls came to the same conclusion straight away.

This was the work of magic.

"Do you think it was Michael?" Marley asked no one in particular.

"This would have taken a great amount of power to do… added with the brazen showmanship of it all, I'd say that was a pretty good assumption," Christian replied.

"But I thought… isn't it normal to hide the use of magic from people?" Cassie asked, her eyes big and round as she studied the damage the tree had caused.

"There are no hard and fast rules about it all, but generally, yes. It's frowned upon to display any magical skills, especially to the public like this," Christian finished, his eyes dark with concern.

"So this is bad?" Tyler asked.

"Well, it's not good," Christian answered.

Eve studied the tree, her eyes dark with concern. "He must know we'd investigate something as impossible to miss like this. Do you think this is to draw us out?"

Silence fell over the girls as a cold chill rose through the ranks. They searched the faces of the crowd until Eve felt an uncomfortable feeling at the back of her neck, as if someone was watching them but she couldn't locate the source of it. Putting it down to general nerves, she turned back to the girls, but the feeling refused to fade.

"Maybe? I don't think he knows we're students at BU," Tyler replied.

"Or maybe, he just did it to let you know how strong he is becoming, and how he isn't afraid to show it," Christian supplied.

Marley had been taking in the area but she now turned to Christian, chewing on the corner of her lip. "What would you do if you were us?" she asked.

"I'd investigate. Try to find evidence or proof of what may have happened. That's what I would do, but then I didn't have any magical powers," he said, gesturing with his hand.

Marley repeated what he said as Eve stared at a point over Marley's shoulder. "Ever since my visit with Helena, I've been thinking a lot about everything that's happened. The thing is, it's looking more and more likely that we're witches, right?"

Cassie and Tyler nodded at her while Marley just shrugged her shoulders.

"If that's the case, shouldn't we be able to do spells?" Eve finished quickly, hoping that the suggestion didn't sound ridiculous. The thought had wormed its way into her mind though voicing it now she worried that it would be shut down and mocked.

"Maybe," Christian replied. "Some basic spells can be taught to anyone who has the ingredients and incantation, but other spells can be created if one were to have the power."

"I want to try," Cassie piped up suddenly. "We've been given these powers for a reason — at least, that's what I believe — so we should learn everything that we can do."

"So what are we saying? We're going to try to create a spell to find out who did this and why?" Marley asked.

"I'm game," Tyler replied, nodding. If they could add spell-casting to their skills, maybe that would aid in her quest to heal Ally. It was worth trying at least.

Eve nodded her agreement which left only Marley.

Though she was as excited by the possibility as they were, there was also a part of her that secretly wondered if more power would be a good thing. The way things were spiraling downhill so fast though, it didn't look like they had much choice. "OK," she finally answered. "How do we do this?"

"Traditionally, a spell would require something tangible, like an object or ingredients," Christian supplied.

Tyler stared beyond her to the tree that was causing so much havoc to the city. Her eyes zeroed in on the tree. "Like maybe a piece of the tree? Would that work?" she asked.

"It's as good a place as any to start," Christian said.

ONE HUNDRED NINE

MASSACHUSETTS BAY COLONY, 1693

On Mary's magic command, the gas lights blazed to life lighting the previously dark room, illuminating the shocked faces of the prisoners.

"Witchcraft!" came a cry from the back of the room.

Mary did not answer. Firmly, but calmly, she gestured. "Stand away from the doors," she commanded as Esther and Catherine moved to the front of their cell, their hands outstretched. Esther muttered under her breath, chanting an incantation as her eyes fixed on the locked door holding them inside. At her sudden gesture, the door flew open as if it had been kicked open by a terrific force.

Gasps rose into the night air as the prisoners watched on. A few wore expressions of terror at this blatant display of power, though more of them seemed amazed, pleased by this unexpected outcome.

The crash woke the young girl who had only moments before been sent into a deep slumber. Staring around her, dazed and confused, it took a few moments to recall where she was. The moment the recollection came, her face turned stricken.

But Tabitha had been prepared for this.

Hurrying out of their cell, she made a gesture in the air and suddenly, the door to the girl's prison also burst open. The girl's eye's grew wide with apprehension as Tabitha reached out a hand to her.

"Come with me, little one. I will keep you safe."

The girl stared at her with eyes the color of the sea but did not move. Long past feeling any fear, she had settled into a mindless numbness, which Tabitha knew was largely caused by having to watch her mother being tortured to death.

"We will stop the people who killed your mother. Her life will not have ended in vain," Tabitha promised.

"Promise?" the girl spoke up suddenly and clearly, with surprising determination in her voice.

"I promise," Tabitha replied with all the sincerity she could muster. She meant every word of it and the girl must have sensed that as she got to her feet and slid her hand into Tabitha's.

Across the way, Mary and the others corralled the prisoners into a corner of the room. When all were gathered they turned their focus to the gas lights… and, as if each were being seized by an invisible hand, every one of the lamps tipped over.

Flames leapt across the ground, eating everything in its path. The straw bales which had been used in place of furniture imploded, sending plumes of fire into the ceiling.

Yet strangely, the fire was confined to the area furthest away from the prisoners.

The fire blazed and acrid smoke began filling the air. The temperature rose, though no smoke or flame reached the prisoners. They watched, huddled together in awe as the wall where the fire was concentrated began to buckle under the immense heat.

Tabitha turned the girl's head to face her, not wanting her to be afraid. "What is your name, dear?"

"Bridget," her answer came.

"This will be over in just a moment," Tabitha explained. "Do not be afraid."

"I am not," Bridget replied, tilting her face up to Tabitha.

As Tabitha smiled down at her, the burning wall finally gave way leaving a gaping hole in its place. Fresh night air spilled into the room, yet still, the fire burned in that controlled manner.

Eve led the way forward, gesturing towards the exit. "Follow me."

Despite how they wanted to flee this prison, the prisoners hesitated, fearful of that fire that was only contained by the invisible magic The Four had cast.

"We cannot hold this much longer," Mary warned from the back of the crowd. "Hurry!"

Right then, a chunk of the ceiling fell down, crashing to the floor, sending up a cloud of dust and rubble. Coughing, the bearded man who had caught the most of it, sprinted towards the opening.

"Come!" he shouted, signaling for the rest to join him. Seeing that he now stood safely outside, the rest of the group quickly followed suit. One by one, they ran through the opening to freedom until Mary — who was the last — finally joined them.

With a wave of her hand, the invisible walls that had held the fire in check abruptly disappeared. Unconstrained, the fire exploded outward and upward, burning not only the prison level but the floors that sat above it.

The Four did not bother to watch.

With the burning building ablaze behind them, they started for the town center to find the ones responsible for these heinous crimes.

They would not allow any more people to be harmed. The time for standing silently by was over.

This time, they would take matters into their own hands.

ONE HUNDRED TEN

"Um, we might have a problem with that though," Cassie volunteered, nodding surreptitiously to the tree.

Police had arrived on the scene and were cordoning off the area with yellow tape, forcing the sightseers back for safety.

"How are we going to get past the police?"

The question had barely left Cassie's mouth when a familiar red-head stalked onto the crime scene — Detective Saunders, the cop they'd had the misfortune to run into twice already.

Patrolling the area, her eyes quickly assessed the scene. Marley could almost see her mind ticking over as she made a mental catalog of whatever evidence she found. But that wasn't what worried her; if she looked over their way, she would see them all immediately.

And maybe coming across them three times in just as many weeks would be one time too many.

Not wanting to risk being discovered, Marley darted out of sight behind Eve's car, dragging the others with her. Eve stole a look at her brother, but he was still fast asleep, his head propped up against the window, apparently far more tired than he had been letting on.

"We're definitely going to have trouble getting through her," Marley raised the concern they all felt.

"Not if Cassie uses her powers," Tyler said. "She just needs to look like one of the cops and they'll wave her right through."

Peeking out from behind the car, they stared back at the crime scene where Saunders marched back and forth behind the yellow tape.

"I think maybe there's only one cop who's allowed back there…" Marley said, her forehead creasing into a frown. The others looked at Cassie expectantly.

"You want me to be her?" Cassie asked, her voice rising in pitch with every word. "Are you crazy? What if I make a mistake?"

"You've managed it fine all the other times," Tyler answered encouragingly.

"True. You would've fooled me too, that time we were at the restaurant. I only knew it was you because of the circumstances," Eve agreed.

Cassie couldn't stop her worry from showing. "But she's right there…"

"You'll have to wait until she goes off," Christian joined in, warming to the idea. "If it looks like she's coming back, we'll get one of the others to cause a distraction, buy you enough time to get back here."

Marley repeated his words, but when Cassie still looked unsure, Marley finally voiced her own thoughts. "Isn't this what your power is for? To do things like this?"

She made sure there was no reprimand in her tone. More than anything else, Cassie needed encouragement. Staring at them, her eyes wide with apprehension, Cassie finally nodded.

"OK, but if it goes wrong…" she started only for Marley to cut her off.

"It won't. You'll be great," she replied.

Decision made, they casually observed Saunders as she continued working the crime scene until her phone rang and she crossed the barrier moving towards an unmarked sedan car where another familiar face already sat — her partner, Brooks. He opened the door for her as she slipped inside, then still on the phone, she pulled out a laptop and began typing into it as Brooks sipped from a coffee, listening in to the conversation.

"Now, Cass," Tyler urged. "Go now."

Completely unsure yet committed to the plan now, Cassie summoned her magic, letting it wash over her as she took in Saunders' face and body. Her eyes changed first, her glasses vanishing as her features began to morph into those of the other woman. Her hair grew longer and redder, her body fuller and her clothes changed until in just a few seconds Cassie was gone leaving only the spitting image of Saunders.

Christian whistled under his breath. "That is so impressive yet also really bizarre."

Cassie ducked down to check her reflection in the mirror of Eve's car.

"I think you'd better hurry up," Marley urged, watching the real Saunders. "We don't know how long she's going to stay there."

Steeling herself, Cassie threw back her shoulders and moved out from behind the safety of the car.

***

Keeping her eyes peeled for signs of the real Saunders, Cassie moved forward though it soon became clear there was a problem when she caught sight of her new reflection in the glass of a nearby shop front, where she saw herself walking in her normal, dainty, and distinctly unSaunders-like manner.

If she kept that up, her cover would be blown.

She knew she needed to *be* Saunders, not just in appearance, but in mannerisms too. Frowning, she tried to hold herself in the confident manner with which Saunders navigated her way through life. Squaring her shoulders, she took her hands out from the jacket pocket they rested in, letting them go slack by her sides. She worked on her footing next, forcing herself to hit the ground with purpose as she had seen Saunders do.

Stalking purposely towards the tree, Cassie reached the yellow tape when one of the guarding cops, a young guy not much older than she was, shot a glance her way. Cassie froze, a deer in the headlights. Should she say something? Maybe she was supposed to flash a badge at him?

Oh God, why didn't I pay more attention to Saunders before agreeing to this stupid plan!

"Back so soon?" he said, cutting into her panicked thoughts. There wasn't any urgency to his tone, no hint that he had seen straight through her charade. If anything, he sounded bored, like he needed a distraction.

Which meant, he didn't suspect a thing.

Suppressing the smile she could feel wanting to burst out of her, she nodded but stayed silent, not wanting to engage in the chat that she could see he hoped for. Turning away from him, she picked up the corner of the yellow tape, lifting it over her head as she ducked inside. If the cop was disappointed in her response, she couldn't see it. She moved quickly to the tree.

Bending down as if she were examining it, her fingers closed around a shriveled root and quick as a flash, she snapped it off. Letting Saunders' long hair curtain around her face, she tucked the broken piece of root into her pocket, straightening up. Not wanting to face the bored cop again, she walked round to the back of the tree, exiting the crime scene from a different direction.

Resisting the urge to run back to the girls, she forced herself to walk at a normal speed when the real Saunders appeared, having gotten out of the car. Cassie stopped dead. Though Saunders had her back to her, Cassie knew that if she ran, she would draw the cop's attention for sure, but if she didn't do something quickly Saunders would see her!

Her heart racing, Cassie conjured up an image of the first person she could think of, which happened to be Marley, but Cassie knew that morphing into her wouldn't help matters. Quickly, she ran through their faces desperately until she came to one who maybe wouldn't draw any attention. Holding her breath, she ducked behind a family of tourists standing nearby. When she emerged on the other side of them, she had turned into Christian.

Which is the exact moment that Saunders' eyes slid over to her.

Cassie didn't know what instinct it was that forced her to keep going at a normal pace when every nerve in her body was shrieking at her to run, but she continued calmly as if she had all the time in the world.

She didn't let out her breath again, didn't breathe at all until she made it back to the girls.

Marley felt a bolt of shock when Christian came strolling over to them and had to check the real thing — his ghost — was still standing beside her. When he looked like his eyes would pop out of his face, she knew she wasn't seeing things.

"You changed into Christian?" Marley asked, wondering exactly what had happened.

"I had to! Saunders almost saw me pretending to be her! What happened to my distraction?" Cassie admonished, glaring at them.

They reeled at her accusation. "I'm so sorry, Cass. We couldn't see for a moment because this group of people passed in front of us. It must have been right when it happened."

"Yeah. We're really sorry," Marley apologized, hoping that Cassie would understand. They had to get better at this kind of thing.

"How's Christian taking this?" Cassie asked curiously, gesturing at herself.

Marley glanced over at him — he still wore that same expression, like he didn't know what to think. He walked around Cassie, studying himself from every angle.

"He seems to be checking out the size of his butt, so I think, about as well as can be expected."

"She's got me all wrong — my butt is way perter than that! Do you have any idea how many lunges I did a day?" Christian said. "And my hair is blond, not strawberry blond.

In response, Marley gave Cassie a thumbs up. "He said you did a great job!"

"Did you get it?" Tyler asked.

"Yeah," Cassie nodded.

"We should go somewhere a little less crowded," Christian suggested even as he continued to study Cassie's version of him.

"Give me a sec," Eve asked. While she didn't want to wake him, she knew Si would have a meltdown if she disappeared without a word; besides the traffic had to move — eventually. As she got back into the car, she caught a streak of yellow in the rearview mirror. Her blood ran cold as she saw the yellow dress now lying in the middle of the backseat.

Twisting around in her seat, she snatched up the dress but jostled Si awake with her movements. He blinked sleepily at her, taking in his surroundings.

"I must have dozed off…" he trailed off, seeing the dress in her hands. "What are you doing with that?"

Caught, Eve couldn't think of any excuse. "It was on the back seat," she admitted.

Si shot up in his seat, scanning the crowds surrounding the car. "Someone put that there? How?"

Out of Eve's eyeline, his hand reached down to feel the gun in its holster. Reassured by the weight of it, he kept his hand on the weapon.

"I don't know," Eve replied. "I was here the whole time. So were the girls," she gestured out at the others a few feet away. Seeing them, Si's shoulders relaxed a little knowing that they weren't alone.

Still groggy from his nap, Si didn't know what to say. It seemed unlikely that someone had snuck up to the car and placed that dress inside without any of the girls noticing, and somehow — call it intuition — he knew it wouldn't have come from one of the girls.

"We'll have to talk later. I've got to go right now," Eve said, hoping he wouldn't disagree. "The girls are waiting for me." When he didn't reply Eve spoke again. "I don't want to keep Tyler waiting when it's her day." The lie rolled out as smooth as silk.

Having looked as if he might argue, Si suddenly caved. "When the traffic clears, I can come to find you?" He offered, unhappy with the return of the yellow dress and all it might signify.

"I'll be OK with the others. Whoever is doing this is only trying to scare us. If they wanted money or to expose us, they would have let us know by now," Eve replied logically and in a manner that almost had her believing the sentiment too.

Si looked unconvinced but by now, the girls were all beginning to wonder what the hold up was. Tyler shifted her weight, unable to hide her desire to get going. He gave her a wave, winding down his window to call out of it as Eve rejoined them.

"Happy Birthday, Tyler. Hope this traffic hasn't messed with your plans."

Catching a warning look from Eve, Tyler shook her head. "It hasn't. Thanks."

"Well, have fun whatever it is you're doing. I'll see

you later, Eve," Si said, watching as the group walked away.

"What was all that about?" Tyler asked. "Why does he think it's my birthday?"

"Don't worry about it." Eve's response was curt — she clearly didn't want to expand on that conversation. Puzzled, yet respecting her space, Tyler kept any further questions to herself.

Moments later they crossed into the park known as the Common, searching until they settled under a dense crop of trees that all but shielded them from sight. Cassie took out the piece of the root she had broken off and held it in her hand, palm facing upward when Tyler shrank back from it, immediately alarmed. *"What is that?"*

"The root?" Cassie asked confused, not understanding her intense reaction.

"No... That horrible sensation. You guys don't feel it? It's like someone just walked over my grave. My stomach's churning. It started the second you took that thing out."

Christian studied Tyler with open interest. "I think she's picking up on the energy from the tree. It was used to murder a lot of people; maybe she can sense that?"

Suddenly, Marley sensed a shadow falling over them as a hazy figure appeared in a flickering black mist. She knew immediately that it was a ghost but before she could warn the others, another appeared, this one behind Eve, then another and another.

"Guys... there are ghosts appearing all around us," Marley warned softly, wary of alerting the spirits in case any were malevolent.

"How many?" Eve asked, her green eyes darting about nervously even though she couldn't see them.

"Eight, maybe?"

Their faces — or what remained of them — were beginning to form out of that flickering black smoke. She saw several female faces, though there was one man stood, all looking desperately unhappy. Marley gasped, feeling sick when she also spotted a young girl of five or six. They wore the style of clothing that Marley had seen her ancestor wear. Around each of their necks hung… a heavy noose.

"I don't think they're going to hurt us, they're just standing there looking really unhappy. I think they were hung on that tree," she revealed. "They're dressed the same as Mary and they all have a rope around their necks." Her mouth went dry finding it difficult to continue. "One of them's a little girl…"

The others gasped as the horror of her words began to sink in.

"Can we help them?" Cassie asked.

Marley studied each of the ghost's faces. They weren't like Daniel and Sarah, the two ghosts at the house she had recently helped to cross over. Marley wasn't sure exactly how she knew that, but she felt it, clear as the ground beneath her feet.

"They just want us to know what happened to them so that their deaths weren't in vain," Marley explained, becoming overwhelmed by a feeling of gratefulness which she knew came from the ghosts. One by one, the ghosts vanished as quickly as they had appeared.

"They're gone now," Marley said, wishing she could have done something to right the wrong that had ended their lives so horrifically.

"Are you ready to try a spell or do you need a moment?" Tyler asked.

Nodding, Marley looked to Christian. "Any advice on what we're supposed to do?"

"I'm no expert. Maybe try connecting with it, focus on what you want it to do. If it works for your other powers, maybe it'll work for this too."

Relaying his advice, Marley reached out and set her hand on top of the root. Eve followed suit. They waited for Tyler who was much more reluctant to touch it. When she finally laid her hand on top of theirs, a bolt of electricity rose through them. Marley could feel it pulsating both above and below her hand. Seeing the awed looks on the other girl's faces, they must be experiencing the same. By simply joining their hands, it was as if they could feel each other's magic.

Pulling in her focus, Marley began to think only of the root and what she hoped the spell would find. The air throbbed with energy as the others each thought something similar. Though they hadn't said anything, Marley instinctively knew what they were thinking.

Feeling a warm sensation beneath their hands, they moved them away to see that the root now hovered an inch above Cassie's hand.

A small distance away, a thin trail of glistening light appeared, leading out of the park.

Marley was as shocked as anyone.

"The spell worked!"

ONE HUNDRED ELEVEN

The magic trail led from the Common and onto the streets beyond.

Trying to act natural, the girls followed the blinking light that only they — much to Christian's consternation as he had been hoping to be privy to it — could see.

They walked through the crowds, acting as naturally as possible until they got past downtown. When they saw that the trail continued much further than they could walk, they jumped into an Uber heading East. Their driver, a British man in his fifties who had driven cars for most of his life as he was quick to explain wasn't happy when the girls revealed that they didn't know the exact location of where they were headed.

It wasn't until Eve came up with the story that they were pledging to a sorority house and this was a treasure hunt of sorts, that he agreed to take them, but only after mumbling something about the stupidity of students.

They rode in silence watching the streets blur past. While she had been initially thrilled that they had managed to cast a spell, with every passing second Marley could feel her unease growing. They had no idea what waited at the end of the trail.

Their driver took them through the city, listening to their ad-hoc directions until they heard the sound of gulls screeching overhead. Marley wrinkled her nose, picking up the unmistakable scent of salt water as the tightly packed buildings slid away to reveal the crystal blue expanse of the ocean beyond.

The trail didn't here however, flying over the edge of the harbor to continue across the water.

"Guess this is where we get out," Eve said, nodding at their driver.

"Thanks, this is good right here," Cassie told him. Their driver tipped an invisible cap, staring at them through the mirror.

"Girls, can I offer some advice? If you feel like you're on a wild goose chase then chances are, you are. Maybe you should stop before this thing ends up costing far more than you are willing to pay."

Although he had been referring to the price of their ride, his words hung like a black cloud. Giving them a two-finger wave, he pulled away.

"How far do you think this goes?" Tyler asked.

"I was wondering the same since I've got to get back in a few hours," Cassie said only to draw Christian's ire.

"Oh, that's right. I had forgotten how you had more important things to deal with. We should tell the upcoming apocalypse to wait until a more convenient time," came his cutting voice.

Marley didn't want to repeat him, but Cassie picked up on her expression. "Is Christian saying something?"

"He might have commented about your lack of commitment," she reluctantly revealed.

Cassie's lips parted into an O as she looked suddenly stricken. "I guess I deserved that," she answered, her cheeks hot with shame.

"No you didn't," Tyler said, her eyes flashing danger-ously. "We can't all be a virtuous monk like him."

Folding his arms across his chest, Christian shot Marley a look. "A monk? What have you been telling them?"

"Just that you had no life and didn't like to do any-thing that didn't involve violence," Marley quipped, hoping to lessen some of the tension that seemed to have risen.

It seemed to work as looking around, Eve spotted something that made her perk up. "Hold up, I have an idea."

She headed towards one of five telescopes that faced the water, placed there for tourists who might be inter-ested in the area. Pushing her eye against the telescope, she followed the magic trail across the water until it came to an abrupt stop on an island in the distance.

"It ends over there, at Fort Warren!"

"What is that?" Marley asked.

"It's a tourist site now. During the Civil War, it was used for captured Confederate soldiers. The fort has these holes called Murder Holes that were created in the en-trance tunnel to kill invaders, it's very cool," Christian said, warming up to his subject as Marley fixed him with a triumphant look.

"Aaaaand we're back to the violence."

"So I know my history," he said. "There are worst things in the world than knowledge."

"Did you ever have fun when you were alive? Did you go out, date, have a girlfriend?" Marley asked.

"That's none of your business," he replied, a little surly.

"So we were right on the money with the monk thing," Marley finished for him.

"Well, the good news is that we know where to go, but how are we supposed to get there since Uber's out?" Tyler asked, ignoring Marley's one-sided banter since she couldn't hear Christian. She cupped a hand over the top of her eyes to see the island in the distance better.

"We get on that," Cassie suggested helpfully, already heading to a boat that was moored nearby. A painted sign on the side of the boat read Harbor Tours.

A guy of around twenty waved when he saw them coming towards him. Dressed in cargo pants and a T-shirt with a matching Harbor Tours logo printed on it, muscles rippled beneath the shirt as he flashed a big smile at them. "Hi guys, can I interest you in a tour around the harbor? I'm due to take off in the next twenty minutes or so," he called out to them.

"You don't just go when you have customers?" Cassie asked, looking up at him from the ground.

"Well, if I have enough customers I could, but there are only four of you right now. I don't know what's happening but it's been a really slow day. All the other tour boats have gone home." he answered.

Eve arrived by Cassie's side just then, giving him a knowing look. "I think he's trying to say that four of us aren't worth his time."

He mimed being stabbed in the heart though his eyes sparkled at Eve. "The lady cuts me with her words! Although, she's kind of right. Though not from a mercenary point of view, this boat just costs a lot to run so I need to make sure I'm not out of pocket after a trip."

Cassie took in the schedule that was pinned onto a bulletin board staked to the ground. "But this says you only get to Fort Warren after making all these other stops along the way? Won't that take forever?"

Their potential guide shook his head as the sun shone down on his skin, tanned from long sessions working beneath it. "It's the sixth stop, so we'll get there around forty minutes into the tour."

Cassie did the math inside her head. "So we wouldn't actually be getting there for almost an hour? That's too long. What if I just hire you and the boat for the whole day? Forget the tours, you just take us to the Fort and back when we're ready. How much would that cost?"

Tyler tried not to react at Cassie's lavish spending, while Eve smiled, impressed by this new, more assertive version of their friend that was coming through. Their guide tilted his head, studying her to weigh how serious she was being.

"I guess two hundred would cover it," he replied.

"Done. Do you take credit card?" Cassie asked.

"Heck, yeah," he smiled reaching out to help her onto the boat. She took it, climbing onboard only to realize that the others hadn't moved an inch. She turned, frowning down at them.

"What's the matter? Are you coming or not?" she asked.

Tyler jumped to attention. "Yes, of course," she replied as she climbed into the boat. Eve followed, an amused, approving smile on her lips. Marley gave Christian a quick look, wondering if he was thinking the same thing: where had *this* Cassie come from? Catching her look, his only response was a quick shrug of his shoulders. Throwing caution to the wind, Marley followed them onboard.

If nothing else, they would get a nice ride out of this.

***

Their guide for the day was called Darren. After welcoming them onboard, he had introduced himself with a clearly rehearsed yet no-less charming speech. He came from a big family, who all worked on the water. His parents were fisherman while several siblings operated seasonal watersports across Boston. Marley liked his easy manner though she was kept busy with Tyler who, it turned out, had a problem with sea sickness. Almost as soon as the boat had lurched forward, Tyler's face had turned a queer shade of green and

Marley was kept busy trying to keep her from throwing up.

Pumped by taking charge for the first time in her life, and liking the respect she could feel exuding from the others, Cassie sat quietly by herself, admiring the smells and sounds of the ocean. She allowed her thoughts to drift between curiosity at what they might find waiting for them at the Fort and excitement at her upcoming date. Having narrowed her outfit down to one of two, she ran an image of herself wearing them in her mind in an attempt to make a final decision. Having waited her entire life for this first date, she was surprised at how little prepared for it she actually was.

With the others preoccupied with their own thoughts, Eve found herself standing beside Darren as he steered the boat with the kind of easy confidence that belied his history with them. She stared at the horizon, watchful apprehensively for anything unnatural.

"So, what's your deal?" Darren asked suddenly, cutting into her thoughts. Eve looked at him but found only open curiosity on his sun-beaten face.

"What do you mean?" she asked.

He gestured at her. "I'm just wondering why you're hiding under all of that getup?"

Eve's lips parted with annoyance. "I'm obviously a Goth."

Darren made a sound that was part snort and part laugh. "Oh yeah? What bands do you like?"

Eve blinked, frowning at him. "What does that matter?"

"Quite a bit. I mean, are you old school, do you like The Cure or Siouxsie & The Banshees. What about Sisters of Mercy, Faith and the Muse, The Damned?"

Eve's eyes turned dark with confusion. "I don't know, I'm not into the music. What do you know about it, anyway?"

"A lot. I have a sister, Ellie, who's a Goth and I know

all of her friends… and you don't strike me as a real Goth, so what gives?"

He still spoke in that easy-going tone though the questions were personal and making her uneasy. Yet, there was something about him, the way he seemed to look straight past her makeup to see into her soul that she found strangely appealing. Still, she didn't like talking about herself. That was off bounds. She turned away from him.

"Nothing gives. Maybe you don't know as much about this as you obviously think you do," she replied pointedly.

Darren shrugged. "I've obviously crossed the line. Sorry about that, I have this problem where I speak without thinking."

Eve knew that he was just being nice, something which she hadn't experienced much of in the past year. "No, don't apologize. I've gotten a little too used to being closed off lately. Has your sister always been a Goth?" She asked, hoping that by making an effort he could see that she hadn't meant to insult him.

"Ellie? No. She got into the music around two years ago. She changed her appearance quite a bit, but she's not the tortured, emo Goth that's normally depicted. She's a sunny girl who just happens to love The Cure."

"I'm not familiar with their music," Eve revealed, feeling a little silly that her cover was being blown like this.

"I just hear what she plays in her room. Her favorite track, Charlotte Sometimes is not one of their big hits but she listens to it all the time."

"I'll have to check it out sometime," Eve said.

"Do. They are a cool band. Anyway, I was just asking you the question because I wanted to know why you hide when it's clear that you're very beautiful underneath."

The compliment came out of left field and Eve found herself reeling by it. No one ever noticed what she looked like under the make-up — no one ever cared to find out. She snuck a sidelong glance at him, to see if he was serious but the sincerity shone from him.

"So you don't know the usual Goth bands, you're only a recent convert, and you've been closing yourself off to people... I hope whoever it was that hurt you, that you kicked him to the curb," he finished quietly.

She felt a jolt of shock. This guy had known her all of five minutes but already, he knew things about her that she had kept buried away. She could feel a growing attraction between them that she couldn't explain. It had been so long now since she had felt that spark between her and someone else that it came now from this complete stranger shocked her to the core.

But, she had to admit... she also kind of liked it.

Afraid of killing the moment, she remained silent, but she stole another look at him to find him smiling back at her.

Unable to stop herself, the sides of her mouth rose up to meet his.

A little way away, Marley also smiled having overheard their conversation over the sound of Tyler's moans. She looked discreetly away, hoping that they wouldn't feel embarrassed at her overhearing them.

***

They reached Fort Warren and docked at the end of a wooden pier.

Nestled on a wash of green, the Fort was surrounded by raised banks that made it impossible to access it from anywhere but the dock. Stone walls ringed the perimeter of the island, further lessening the chances of an invasion: the Fort was both aptly named and designed.

As soon as the boat was moored, Tyler jumped off of it, eager to be on solid ground. She held a hand against her stomach, managing to keep its contents intact but the effort had cost her greatly; she could feel herself sagging with that fast-rising exhaustion. Eve was the last girl to leave the boat. As Darren helped her off, he squeezed her hand, holding it a moment longer than was necessary.

"Don't be gone too long now, I'll get lonely," he said.

Overhearing him, Tyler's eyebrows almost shot off her face. Marley couldn't hide her smile, while Cassie just looked wide-eyed, wondering what she had missed. Feeling her cheeks redden, Eve didn't reply as she snatched her hand back, but Darren took no offense at the gesture, smiling at her instead.

"I'll be waiting right here when you need me," he called out.

Hurrying to join them, Cassie and Marley fell into step by her side.

"Did you have a nice chat with him then?" Marley grinned at her.

Eve choose not to ignore the question.

ONE HUNDRED TWELVE

Waves crashed below, but other than the sound of their own nervous chatter, the fort was dead.

The only other soul they had seen since stepping foot onto the island was the bored-looking ticket seller who sat beside the entrance — and he had seemed more interested in the graphic novel he was reading than what the girls might be doing here.

He had straight hair that was almost shoulder length which kept falling in front of his eyes while he read. He wore a shirt with a futuristic soldier emblazoned across the chest that Eve had commented on, drawing a sudden interest from him. All Eve had mentioned was that it was a Spartan soldier from the Halo games series and it was like a light had come on as he engaged her in conversation about the merits of Xboxes against PCs. Tyler had to step in and cut their talk short when it became clear that they weren't all enjoying the conversation as much as she had been.

After leaving his booth, they crossed a wooden bridge suspended over the crashing water into the internal area of the fort as Marley opened up a map that came with their tickets.

"I'm getting flashbacks of our time at the Iron Works. I guess we look around until we find something?"

"I think it's going to be easier than that," Tyler said, pointing at where the white trail danced in front of her.

"The spell's still working!" Cassie exclaimed, surprised yet relieved to see it again.

"Let's see where it's taking us," Eve said. Marley found herself looking for Christian but was surprised when he wasn't there, having long over-used whatever energy it took for him to appear. Even more surprising than his disappearance was the disappointment she felt at his absence. Troubled by her feelings she pushed the thought aside, bringing her mind back to the task at hand.

They followed through dark corridors, the light twisting around bends and doorways as shadows danced around them, their elongated limbs ducking in and out of cover.

Feeling a sudden wave of exhaustion, yet knowing that she couldn't afford to be tired — not for whatever they would find here, and certainly not for Ally's big night — Tyler took out her trusty "water" bottle. She unscrewed the cap then hesitated, thinking of the heart palpitations she had experienced only that morning. She wondered if she should lay off the potion, but even as the thought came she could feel herself sagging, dragging her feet. A fog clung to her head making it hard to think.

She knew she couldn't function this way.

Lifting the bottle to her lips she drank until her energy reappeared. Wired, the mental fog vanished though she could still feel that jitteriness that just wouldn't go away. Tyler wondered if she just needed to get better at making these potions though it also crossed her mind that this could just be the cost of doing business…

"What do you think we'll find at the end of this?" Eve asked a nervous note to her voice.

"Do we think it's Michael you mean?" Marley translated. Eve's black curls tipped with red bobbed up and down as she nodded.

"I hope not. We're so not ready to deal with him," Tyler added. They turned into a central courtyard when Marley stopped moving. Her dark eyes wide and uncomprehending.

"Look," she said quietly, gazing ahead of them.

A bright red flare of light shone from an old statue of an eagle into the mottled sky. Where the head of the bird should be, there was only empty space. Dust swirled around the base of the statue, mingling with that same black glittering mist they had first found in the basement of Trinity Church. It was at this statue that their trail ended.

"No," Tyler gasped.

"The statue's the Third Seal," Cassie gasped.

" And now it's broken," Eve confirmed.

"But how? We would have seen that red light from the boat," Marley said, unwilling to believe her eyes.

"Unless it only just happened," came Eve's frightening thought.

They pressed together, staring at the black shadows that seemed present in every corner of the courtyard. They watched, huddled close, senses honed for danger. When several moments passed and nothing jumped out at them, they inched closer to the statue.

Beside the seal lay a pile of still smoking ashes inside a ring of stones. The black light that they knew signified the presence of black magic was the most concentrated here. Tyler crouched down. There was something knotted and spindly that hadn't been burnt away. "That's a tree root, isn't it?"

"I think so," Eve confirmed when something within the pile caught her eye at the same time that Tyler spotted it. Picking up a stick, Tyler pushed the ashes aside to reveal a piece of burnt fabric. Although the edges were black and scorched, Eve recognized it straight away.

It was a piece of her yellow dress.

"What's this?" Tyler asked, not making the connection herself.

"Just some fabric it looks like, probably blew in when the roots were being burned," Eve replied, trying to keep her voice stoic so as not to reveal the panic that simmered just under the surface.

"I think we were right. Michael unearthed the Elm tree so that he could use its roots somehow to find the Third Seal." Cassie said.

"Maybe," came Christian's voice behind Marley's ear as he reappeared again. "Or maybe, he needs more magic to break the seals and this is how he's doing it."

"You're saying the tree was magical?" Marley asked him.

"I'm saying that it's possible for things to be considered sources of black magic if many terrible acts were committed with them."

Marley repeated him, drawing apprehensive stares from the others.

"So he's not only breaking the seals, but he's using black magic artifacts and getting more and more powerful while he's doing it?" Marley asked, hoping to mask the great sense of doom that she was starting to feel.

"I think so. Yes," came Christian's unhappy answer.

ONE HUNDRED THIRTEEN

Failure weighed heavily on them.

With no need to remain on the island, they made they way back to the exit, but as they crossed the bridge, Marley slowed.

"Where's your friend, the ticket guy?" she directed the question at Eve though it was meant for them all. Where the ticket seller had been, his cubicle was now empty.

"Restroom break?" Cassie offered up nodding at a square block with a restroom sign that sat adjacent to the exit. But something stopped her too, something *red* seeping out from the doorway of the restroom block.

Seeing it, Christian immediately warned, "That's blood!"

Marley froze. "It's what?" she turned to look at him when the wooden boards beneath her feet began to vibrate from the weight of something rushing towards them. Swinging her eyes back to the front, she caught a glimpse of a sinister figure hurrying over the bridge.

"Look out!" she cried as whatever it was, was joined by two others flanking its side. They moved on all fours with an eerie loping run, their heads low to the ground.

Almost like dogs, but if the dogs were deformed with twisted limbs and fangs. The most awful stench arose from them, the foul odor of sewage mixed with rotten food. They growled, displaying brutally sharp teeth but didn't attack. It was as if they were waiting for something.

"What are those things?" Eve asked, backing up, pulling Cassie — who seemed rooted to the ground — with her.

"It doesn't matter what they are, just get out of there," Christian commanded.

Marley starting back towards the fort, keeping her eyes glued to the terrifying figures in front of her.

"We need to go back inside," she said when she felt a knot of fear in her stomach as the hairs raised on the backs of her arms.

Spinning around, she saw that five more of the dog-things had blocked the path behind them. A glowing red symbol appeared on their foreheads — the same symbol she had seen on the demons at the cemetery — but she didn't have time to think about it right now.

"We're trapped," she said desperately.

The words had barely left her mouth when all eight of the creatures launched themselves at them.

Cassie screamed as she was knocked to the ground, her arms locked against the hound snapping its jaws at her. Hot, putrid saliva shot out of its mouth as Cassie twisted her head, trying to avoid its spray.

Eve grabbed her bag and started hitting the back of the hound's head, trying to get it off Cassie while Tyler's leg lashed out at the beast that was racing toward her. It was a lucky hit as she managed to catch it on its hind side. The thing whined and skidded to a halt, not pre-pared for her sudden attack.

Tyler saw her opportunity and kicked at it again, harder this time, knocking it towards the edge of the bridge. The hound's paws scrambled for purchase but the momentum of Tyler's kick was too much. It toppled off the edge, it's screams echoing around the rocks as it fell onto the crashing waves below.

"What the hell…" came a stunned male voice in the middle of the chaos.

Eve shot a sideways look to see Darren barreling across the bridge to them, drawn by Cassie's scream. The hound's jaws were getting closer and closer to Cassie's face as her arms grew weak from the fight.

Seeing this, Darren leaped into action jumping into the fray as he started pummelling the back of the hound's head. His years of working on the boats had made him wickedly strong and the beast quickly found itself switching targets to face this new attacker that was causing it so much hurt.

Darren's fist came at the thing, one, two, three times. Eve shoved her curls out of her face as she watched him rain blows on the beast until it backed down, shaking its head warily. Darren pulled Cassie to her feet, then turned to Eve, taking his eyes off the creature for only a second.

"Are you OK?" he asked her.

But a second was all that it needed.

Suddenly, it flew towards them again, but this time, it went for the back of Darren's neck. Unaware, with his back to it, Darren had no chance of defending himself.

Eve realized this a split second too late.

"Behind you!" she screamed, but the beast had already locked its jaws around his neck.

Darren's eyes flew open with shock. Then the pain must have registered as a dull glaze went over his eyes. He reached up one hand, trying to grab onto the hound, while the other stretched out to Eve.

Suddenly, his whole body jolted. There was a sharp, uncomprehending look on his face as he fell to the ground in a heap.

Then he was still.

Eve's heart caught in her throat, unable to reconcile

the sight before her. Cassie covered her mouth with a hand, equally horrified.

Two hounds came for Marley then, but she managed to dodge the first as it overshot her, skidding behind her to crash into several of its friends. The other lunged for her while she wasn't looking, sinking its teeth into her arm.

Searing hot pain lanced through her.

Marley screamed and tried to shake it off, but her movement only caused more agonizing pain to shoot up her arm as the beast hung there, anchored by its crazy sharp teeth.

"The eyes! Go for the eyes!" came Christian's command from somewhere beside her.

Remembering their first self-defense lesson, Marley locked two fingers together and started jabbing blindly at the hound's face. Her fingers hit the hard bone of its nose at first before they found the soft, vulnerable part of its eyes.

She plunged her fingers in — hard — and was rewarded by its own howl of pain. The jaws suddenly released around her arm as Marley stumbled away. Moving towards the others, she suddenly felt the air change and knew immediately that Eve and Tyler were both calling forth their power.

Black specks gathered into a cloud above. The air was abruptly filled with the cries of the ravens as they swooped down with pointed beaks and claws. Like Marley, they were going for the eyes, forcing the hounds to back away from the girls. It seemed almost to work, but though the birds were many in number, there was only so much they could do.

And the hounds knew it.

Already, they were rounding up for another attack.

Tyler's hair swam in a sea of static as she stretched out her hand, her eyes flashing with anger. Below them, the crashing waves stilled. Glancing down, Marley saw that the water immediately beneath them had been frozen solid with jagged edges as sharp as razor blades. Seeing them, the idea came to her immediately.

"Knock them off the bridge!" she yelled.

Eve's eyes darted towards her taking a moment for her words to sink in. Looking out towards her flock of feathered attackers, Eve sent them a mental command as she channeled every ounce of the pain and fury she felt at Darren's death.

Down.

It was only a single command, but the birds veered round, altering the course of their attack. The air became littered by the sight of wings and feathers.

With the hounds now preoccupied with the onslaught of birds, the girls found their chance to attack.

Screaming, they lashed out, swinging their bags at the beasts as one by one, they plunged to their deaths below until the air became still with only the sound of the girls' thumping hearts to break it.

They gathered around Darren, staring down at his lifeless body.

Tears streamed down Eve's face as her makeup ran in rivulets leaving her with ghoulish black eyes. Sobbing, she bent down, trying to grab him by his armpits.

"What are you doing?" Tyler asked, still shaking from their attack.

Eve's eyes were glazed. Marley knew she was in shock and reacting only from instinct. "We've got to get him on the boat. We'll get him to a hospital, they'll be able to help him there."

From experience, Tyler knew the only way to cut through shock like this was to gently approach the truth. Pretending otherwise only delayed the pain.

"He's gone, Eve. There's nothing anyone can do to help him," she said gently but firmly.

Eve snapped her head round to her, eyes flashing daggers. "You're not a doctor! That's not your call! If we just get him back, it might not be too late!"

Cassie looked away, unable to take the raw pain in Eve's voice as Marley looked to Christian for help.

Christian looked towards the water, to where the boat bobbed up and down. "If you take him with you, there are going to be questions," he said quietly.

Marley blinked at him uncomprehendingly. "Are you saying we'll have to leave him here?"

"No!" Eve cried, not even waiting to hear what the question had been. "This happened because he was trying to help us. We can't just leave him here! That's barbaric!"

Christian didn't respond, but he blinked away only to return seconds later. "The ticket guy is dead too. They must have killed him while we were looking around." He waited, knowing how his next suggestion was not going to be popular, yet it had to be said.

"You all need to get out of here, Marley. Two people have been killed. There just isn't a way for you to explain this in a believable manner. The last thing we need is for the four of you to get locked up, with Michael running around, free to find the other seals. Make her leave," he instructed even as a great weight settled into the bottom of his stomach. After what they had just gone through, if he could shoulder this burden, he would gladly have done so. But as usual, no one but Marley could see or hear him.

Hating herself, but knowing that he was right, Marley touched Eve on the shoulder. "We can't head back to the city with two dead bodies in the boat with us, Eve. That just isn't going to work."

"Two?" Cassie gasped, her eyes round with horror.

Marley nodded toward the restroom block. "Christian

said the ticket guy is in there. They must have killed him after we got onto the island."

Cassie's hand flew to her mouth as Tyler went white.

Two people were dead.

"Come on, we've got to go before the authorities get notified," Marley began steering Eve away but she was rooted to the spot, looking down at Darren's blank face.

"His family," Eve mumbled. "They won't know that he died a hero. They won't know anything." Her voice caught at the end of the sentence.

"We'll find a way to let them know," Marley suggested gently. "Let's go, but I promise we'll find a way to tell them."

Eve nodded stiffly, allowing herself to be steered away. As they walked back to the boat, Marley looked down to see that the waves had unfrozen and all signs of the hounds had vanished. They had likely sunk to the bottom of the ocean.

Blood poured from her wound but luckily, it didn't seem like the bite had hit any major arteries. Examining her injury, she saw a few holes where the hound had punctured her skin, but it was mostly in one piece. Slipping off her shirt, she tied it around her arm trying not to wince from the pain.

"You should get that seen to," Christian said, eyes dark with concern.

"Maybe. Let's just get back to the city and go from there," she replied, wanting to get off the island.

"OK, but look out for anything… weird," Christian said, causing Marley to take pause.

"Weird?" she asked.

"Yeah. I don't think they had venom in their bite, but best to be sure," he replied only to be rewarded by a startled look from her. Quickly, he tried to reassure her, "I'm sure you're fine. If there was a problem, you would probably be dead already."

Marley fixed him with a stare. "You really need to work on your bedside manner."

Reaching the boat, Tyler suddenly stopped. "Wait. How are we going to get back without Darren? Are we stuck on this island?!"

Realizing that she had a point, Marley felt a surge of renewed panic when Cassie stepped forward. "I can drive the boat. I've grown up on them."

"Really?" Tyler asked, somehow surprised that she would be able to do such a thing.

"Yeah," Cassie said, as she climbed onto it easily. "I've spent a lot of summers vacationing on them."

Moving to the boat's wheel, she performed a few checks. Within moments, the purr of the engine kicked in.

The ride back to the city was heavy with silence.

Numb with shock, unable to feel a thing, Eve stared down by her feet. Marley sat beside her, offering what small comfort she could. Even then, she was acutely aware that Eve was shouldering more blame than she should, thinking that her earlier flirtation with Darren had ultimately led his death. Grief poured out of her so intensely, Marley could almost taste it.

She shifted position, wincing as pain shot through her arm, though thankfully, it didn't seem that it was infected — at least it wasn't yet. Beside her, Christian stared off into the distance. He hadn't said a word since they had got onto the boat. He only stood there, his hands gripped into fists, his face unreadable.

Tyler clung to the side rail, desperately fighting her sea sickness again though the boat sliced cleanly through the water. Cassie, it turned out, was a very good driver. In no time they arrived back on the shores of Boston Harbor.

Cassie steered the boat into a quiet spot where there hopefully wouldn't be spotted. As soon as they touched the ground, they moved a safe distance away and were now standing outside a coffee shop, its cheerful music in an eerie parallel to the dark cloud that they stood under.

Glancing at her watch, Tyler blanched. "Guys, it's Ally's birthday. I can't not go…" she began but trailed off, feeling terrible for even bringing it up. Marley gave her a smile that was echoed by Cassie though Eve couldn't bring herself to do the same.

"We understand," Marley said.

Still Tyler hesitated, feeling terrible and shaken. "It doesn't feel right to leave you, not after what just happened."

"It wasn't your fault. None of it," came Eve's voice, raw with grief. Though she was standing right there with them her voice sounded far away.

"It's probably best that she does go," Christian suddenly interjected. "In fact, if any of you made plans for today, you should stick to them. If any of this does come back to you, it will look less suspicious if you didn't cancel your plans last minute."

Marley repeated him, word for word.

"I guess he's right," Tyler replied, wrapping her arms around herself in an attempt to lessen the chill that had settled on her since the moment they were attacked.

"Go to Ally," Marley said.

"Say hi from us," Cassie added.

Tyler gave them all one last look. "We'll talk about our next steps when I get back. I'll see you all later. Stay safe."

Shooting Eve one last concerned look, she headed away. Cassie stood awkwardly wringing her hands, clearly something on her mind. Picking up on it, Eve spoke, "I'm OK, Cass. Honestly. You should go too."

Marley smiled at Cassie. "Go on your date. Just don't do anything I wouldn't do," she warned gently but with meaning.

Cassie darted forward suddenly, grabbing Eve in a hug. Not prepared for the physical contact, Eve tensed up, but if Cassie noticed it she didn't react. She squeezed the older girl as hard as she could before finally letting go. Giving Marley a quick nod, she darted out of the harbor. Christian watched her figure growing smaller until she disappeared around a corner though he was starting to turn a little translucent having clearly pushed himself to stay with them a bit too long. Marley could see the coffee store sign right through him.

Marley turned to Eve. "What now?"

Eve dragged her feet, something preying on her mind. "I can't just leave like that. I know we couldn't bring him with us, but we can't just leave him there either."

"I agree," Marley replied much to her surprise.

"I want to call the cops to leave them an anonymous tip," Eve spoke quickly, afraid that Marley would stop her.

However, Marley didn't, having half suspected Eve would say this already. She waited for Christian's objection, knowing that it would come, but when it didn't, her eyes slid over to the spot he had been a moment before. There was no sign of him now; he had gone.

And maybe, that was fortunate for them.

"OK. We need to do the call quickly and from a public phone, one where there aren't any surveillance cameras in the vicinity," she replied.

Eve looked a little startled. "Anyone would think you've done this before…"

"Nope, but I have watched a lot of CSI reruns," Marley said.

They scoped out the area, looking for public phones until they eventually found a few of them beside a convenience store. Before Eve made the call, however, she gestured to Marley's arm.

"That's a little conspicuous."

Having been focused on what they were doing, Marley had completely forgotten about her injury, which must have been a good thing. If it didn't hurt too much then it *probably* wasn't infected with demon poison.

"Stay out here a sec," Eve instructed then she went into the store returning a few moments later with some bandages, antiseptic spray, a couple of baseball hats, and a checked long-sleeved shirt. Moving to the restroom that was attached to the store — though thankfully, the entrance to it was on the outside — Eve helped Marley clean up the wound the best she could though when the antiseptic was used, Marley's face drained of all color. She sucked in a sharp intake of breath.

"Wow, that stings."

They bandaged her arm and Marley slipped into the new shirt which hid her wound nicely. She kept the old, blood-soaked shirt in her bag, however, knowing to dispose of it somewhere else.

"Ready?" Eve asked Marley as they went back to the phones. On Marley's nod, Eve picked up the phone with a napkin so that she wouldn't leave any fingerprints and dialed 911.

Within two rings, the call was answered and a male voice came on the line. "911, what's your emergency?"

Lowering her voice so that it was almost unrecognizable, Eve spoke into the phone. "Fort Warren, two dead."

As soon as the words left her mouth, she slammed the handset down. Disconnecting the call, they hurried back to the coffee shop. The place wasn't close enough to the edge of the water for them to be seen but they would have a clear view of the harbor.

Marley bought them coffees as they sat, nursing their drinks, more to keep up appearances than anything else. They were still watching when several police cars screeched into the area, followed by the harbor patrol arriving on the water.

Like a Hollywood movie unfolding before them, the patrol shot off towards the island while the land cops waited, pretty relaxed. There wasn't much they could do for now. The minute they received confirmation of Eve's tip, however, everything changed. The cops flew into action, sectioning off the area, moving tourists and members of the public aside.

Against the afternoon sun, the harbor patrol finally returned with two black coroner bags.

Marley reached across to take Eve's hand as the two body bags were loaded into a van marked with the Boston General logo, watching in silence until the van drove away.

Still, Marley could feel that Eve wasn't satisfied.

"They've taken his body, but his family won't know that he died to save us. It doesn't feel like enough," Eve said, her eyes dark with pain. Marley knew she was right.

"Let's go to the hospital. His family will probably be there. Maybe there's something we can do," she offered. It was all she could think of in a pinch.

"You know it'll be risky?" Eve warned, even though every fiber of her being wanted to do what she had just suggested.

"Couldn't that be said of everything we do lately?" Marley flashed her a smile.

And as a wave of gratefulness washed over her, Eve finally smiled back.

ONE HUNDRED FIFTEEN

Cassie reached the dorm in double quick time.

It seemed that after the gridlock of the morning most of the city had decided to stay home, subsequently, the streets were clearer than they had ever been.

Cassie had thought that she would feel relieved by this, but having witnessed Darren's death and the death of the ticket seller, a date with Trip was the last thing on her mind. If it wasn't for Christian's instructions, she would have canceled on him altogether.

Now that she was back and getting ready for her date, she found she couldn't concentrate on her make-up. The silence in the room was like a tomb, smothering her with its cloying heaviness. She missed the girls and wondered how they were all doing but especially Eve. She was always so strong, so decisive that seeing her like that had thrown Cassie for a loop.

Not having the energy to shower, she ignored the several outfit choices that hung in her wardrobe. Having agonized over them for so long, Cassie now found them too frivolous and fussy. If she must go on this date then she wanted to be comfortable, to feel grounded. Instead of the designer dresses, she grabbed a pair of jeans, a light-woven Bardot top and a pair of Converse sneakers that she had bought a while ago on a whim but had never worn (her mom abhorred sneakers and had encouraged Cassie to wear heels almost as soon as she could walk).

Running a brush through her hair, she added a little gloss and mascara but left it at that. It wasn't like Trip hadn't already seen her at her old-self worst and she honestly couldn't be bothered. It all seemed like too much effort particularly when all she wanted was to crawl into bed.

A little later she strolled out of the dorm to find Trip waiting outside the Creative Language block as arranged. The sun hit his sandy blond hair in all the right places and Cassie found herself suddenly taken aback by his angular face and broad shoulders. Despite how she had been dragging her feet she felt a small flutter of excitement inside her chest.

"There you are. You look great," Trip exclaimed as he whipped out the hand he had been hiding behind his back to reveal a bouquet of red roses.

Cassie's eyes widened. "Are those for me?"

"I don't see any other pretty girls around here," Trip answered smiling.

She took them from him, stunned at this romantic gesture particularly as he hadn't seemed the type.

She had obviously gotten him all wrong.

"Thank you," she said, taking in their spicy floral scent. "They're lovely."

"Of course," he shrugged nonchalantly as if he did this all the time. And maybe he did. Cassie had to still the sudden stab of jealousy that reared its ugly head.

"I thought you'd like to grab a drink then maybe a movie or some food, whatever we feel like?"

"Sure," Cassie agreed, relieved that he was taking charge. "Sounds good."

They walked off campus towards a strip of shops that students often frequented. Trip smiled at her often, but he otherwise kept his respectful distance. Cassie found herself charmed by the restraint he was showing, having seen him practically hanging off girls before.

Unless of course, he didn't really find her attractive.

The sneaky thought slid into her mind before she could stop it. Her lips tightened, but she shoved the thought aside. That was her old-self talking. If Trip wasn't interested why would he have asked her out in the first place? It wasn't as if he was lacking in attention.

"So, that was crazy, huh? All that commotion downtown. Did you get caught up in it?" Trip asked, cutting into her inner dialog.

"Oh, not really. I just hung out with the girls since school didn't look like it was happening," she replied and it wasn't really a lie.

"The girls?" Trip asked.

"You don't remember? The ones who were at Tonic with me," she replied before thinking. Suddenly, the horrors of the night came flooding back, along with it, all the embarrassment she had felt when she had been shoved to the floor. And God, Trip had been there to witness it all. What was wrong with her that she couldn't think before blurting things out?

But Trip looked at her as if he had no recollection of that night at all.

At that moment, Cassie knew he was being kind by pretending to have forgotten. She felt a happy little flutter inside, knowing that he was going out of his way to make her feel comfortable.

"Sorry, I don't recall. Are these your best friends?" he asked. "Why don't you tell me about them?"

Buoyed now by how he was making her feel, Cassie started talking.

S he felt like the worst person alive leaving the girls like that, especially Eve, who was clearly in shock, but Tyler knew Christian had been right about continuing with their plans; besides, she couldn't disappoint Ally. Torn as she was, she arrived to pick up her sister, a giant grin plastered onto her face.

She couldn't let Ally pick up on any of her unhappiness.

Today was her day, and she deserved to have the best time that Tyler could give her. The air was heavy with the smell of cinnamon pretzels and cotton candy as stalls covered with colorful handmade goods blazed in the last of the day's sun. They had arrived at a park that was hosting a traveling fair. Within moments of setting her eyes on it, Ally had fallen in love with a classic style carousel. Tyler laughed watching as Ally rode on a unicorn, waving her arms in the air.

"Look, no hands!" she giggled as Tyler snapped a picture on her phone. Ally's cheeks were flushed with excitement and her eyes sparkled with the kind of happiness that was all too fleeting these days. Tyler framed her shots taking more pictures wanting to record as much of this as possible.

God knew when they would next have a carefree day like this again.

After the carousel came a tour of the food stalls as Ally considered what sweet treats she wanted, only to settle on one of those freshly baked sugary pretzels. Tearing off a chunk, Ally took a tentative nibble and sighed. "This is so good!"

"Make sure there's some left for me," Tyler laughed, as Ally took another giant bite.

Conscious of her kidney issue, Tyler was careful how much of it Ally actually consumed. Her parents had always kept Ally on an organic diet, low on sugar, salt, trans fats, and anything else that could prove too much of a strain on her stressed system. The daily dialysis was a Godsend, however, so Tyler was watchful but she intended to let Ally enjoy herself.

They were walking around, searching for their next ride when the unmistakable sight of bumper cars appeared. Tyler slowed, conflicted emotions racing through her mind. Before their parents had died, this ride had been a firm favorite, but now, considering the manner of their death… Tyler wasn't sure how Ally would feel about them.

As if she had no idea of the turmoil going through her sister's mind, Ally tugged on her hand, leading her towards the ride.

"Come on, I'm driving!" she yelled as she skipped up to the attendant who helped her into a car. Apparently, she didn't associate these vehicles with the ones that had ended their parents' lives.

It made Tyler wish that she could also go through life without spotting every little association with their deaths, no matter how slight.

It sure would make life easier.

Ally shrieked, yanking the wheel furiously as they flew headlong into a collision with a neighboring pair: a young mother and her son, around the same age as Ally. They laughed, waving their fists at them, swearing to get their revenge as Ally and the boy drove their car around the ring, chasing the girls.

When she bored of the cars, they tried their hand at the games. They fished for rubber ducks, shot tin figures that scrolled past, and bobbed for apples until water ran down their necks. All the while, Ally's chatter and laughter began to erase the horrors of the day.

All too soon, the sun set in a blaze of glory leaving streaks of orange and red across the rapidly darkening sky.

"That was super fun! Thank you so much, Tyler!" Ally

exclaimed throwing her thin arms around Tyler as they headed out of the park.

"What, you think we're done?" she asked Ally, looking down at her.

"There's more?" Ally's eyes went round.

"Oh yeah, there's more. Now, we really celebrate."

A few short blocks away, they arrived at a food joint — but this was no ordinary diner.

Monster Mash was a themed diner popular with kids where the servers dressed up as monsters, from Frankenstein to vampires. Any manner of monsters could be found here (though the owners had steered away from clowns, knowing how frightening they were to most people, even the adults). Buckets of glowing green goo greeted them, challenging the bravest among them to stick their hands inside to see what treasures might lie beneath.

"Wait, this is where we're eating?" Ally asked.

There was a slight hesitation in her voice, but Tyler knew it was probably to do with the cost. They stood next to a menu that was tacked to the window where they couldn't avoid seeing the prices.

"Don't worry, Bug. My loan came through today, so we can finally do this," Tyler revealed.

Ally had heard about this diner from her foster-siblings and had told Tyler about it a while ago. She'd seemed so excited by the prospect of going that Tyler had kept it in the back of her mind for months. She felt a buzz of excitement of her own knowing that she could finally spoil Ally here.

Ally smiled up at her but her eyes still looked a little hesitant. Tyler felt a burst of love for her; what other ten-year-old would be this compassionate?

A woman with a blue wig wearing a long black dress

that dragged along the floor came up to them. "Can I get you girls a booth?" she asked.

"I have a booking under the name Tyler," Tyler responded. Their witch, whose name badge said she was "Ursula" smiled at them.

"Ah yes, so this must be our birthday girl, Ally?" Ursula beamed at her as she took out a crown made of black card that had the silhouette of the moon and some bats cut out of it, and fastened it around Ally's head.

"That's pretty cool," Tyler commented as Ally nodded carefully so as not to shake off her crown.

"Do I get to keep it?" Ally asked looking hopeful.

"Of course," Ursula grinned. "Follow me, I'll take you to your special booth."

They exchanged a curious look, wondering what would be so special about it as they wove through the busy diner after Ursula. Everywhere they looked kids were eating with their parents though Ally was the only one wearing a crown that night; for most of them this was just a regular night out. Tyler tried to quell the bitterness inside as she thought of the many places like this they would have gone to with their parents had they been alive.

When they arrived at their booth, they found it covered with fake webbing and plastic spiders. Bottles of soda sat inside a cauldron filled with ice. Tyler admired the little touches, grateful to the restaurant for providing them — they were going out of their way to accommodate. Ally slid in beside a giant spider, careful not to touch it even though it wasn't real.

"It won't bite," Tyler laughed.

"I know, but it just looks so real," Ally replied, giving it a sidelong glance.

A figure leapt out at them, making Ally jump. It was their server, a guy dressed in an old-fashioned suit that had been made to look as if it had been eaten by moths.

He wore a monster mask over his face and plastic fangs in his mouth as he flashed them a gruesome grin.

"Hello, Girls! Whatever your ghoulish demands might be, I am here to provide them!"

He passed them both a menu then leaned in to Ally. "I hear it's a special day for you. I have lots of fun things planned for you so you will not be bored tonight!"

"Thanks," Ally responded. Looking over at Tyler, she saw that she watched everything eagerly. She wanted so badly for Ally to enjoy herself and was trying so hard that Ally knew she had to fake it.

But the truth was, the minute they had turned up outside the diner she had been dreading it.

And she felt terrible about that.

If this was a month ago, if this was even a week ago, Ally knew she would love this place, but ever since that creepy book and the nightmares that plagued her every night, the last thing she wanted was more monsters.

Even if she knew they weren't real.

But seeing Tyler's expectant face, Ally knew her sister couldn't know the truth. She couldn't know that she hated every minute of this, that their server made her skin crawl even though he was only doing his job.

Keeping a smile plastered on her lips, Ally soldiered on.

ONE HUNDRED SIXTEEN

A terse bus ride later, Marley and Eve arrived at Boston General.

Both now wore the baseball caps Eve had bought from the convenience store, shielding their faces from any cameras that might be installed in the hospital which brought some relief though neither could stop feeling exposed.

Marley had to keep fighting the urge to look behind her, wondering if a cop or security guard would be watching her suspiciously.

They sat in the main waiting area where they had a full view of the front entrance and reception.

Eve knew the second Darren's family arrived.

There was at least eight of them. All had his tanned skin and blond locks. His father was the spitting image of Darren though he was older. Darren's mom was small — not much taller than her two daughters, one of which was dressed in that familiar Goth style Eve had chosen to emulate.

She carried the youngest of their clan, a boy of around six who was too old to still be sucking on his thumb. He obviously knew something was terrible wrong as he wailed into his mother's arms. The family wore identical expressions of grief and shock that was hard to witness.

"That poor family," Marley said, fighting to stop her own tears.

A hospital representative arrived and spoke to the family. Although they were too far away to hear what was being said, they understood his grave body language only too well. Shell-shocked, the family followed him inside.

Eve shot to her feet. "Come on," she said to Marley.

They stood beside a water cooler, some distance away but still with the family in sight as the parents went into the morgue.

When they came out, Darren's mom could barely stand. Her legs were buckling and she had to be held up by her husband though he wasn't faring much better himself. Tears ran down his face as he tried to gather his remaining children into his arms.

Marley felt Eve sag against her. There was nothing to say. All they could do was feel the pain. Eve was still leaning up against her when Darren's sister — the Goth, Ellie — headed towards them holding her youngest brother's hand.

"They're coming over," Eve hissed, unsure what to do.

"Act natural," Marley warned before they both fell silent as the two arrived by the water cooler.

"Sorry," Eve said, moving aside so the other girl could reach it. Ellie gave her a wan smile and grabbed a paper cup from the dispenser. Filling it with water, she handed it to her brother.

"Drink slowly," she instructed.

Eve looked at Marley over the top of Ellie's head, knowing that she couldn't stand there and say nothing.

"I'm sorry for your loss," Eve suddenly blurted.

Ellie straightened, raising startled eyes to her. "You knew Darren?"

"No," Eve lied. "We just saw your parents come out of the morgue and put two and two together." It wasn't the best excuse, but it was all she could come up with at a moment's notice. Luckily, Ellie accepted it.

"I don't even know what happened. It looks like he was bitten by an animal, and there was another guy who was dead too. But they said someone had called it in. They found him on the ground," she caught herself as a sob escaped.

"An animal killed him?" her brother asked, tugging on her arm as his eyes flooded with tears again. Instantly, the girl looked aghast.

"No, I'm not sure what happened, Lucas, they haven't really told us," she backtracked quickly. "Why don't you go back to Mom and Dad, see if anyone else wants a drink?"

Lucas nodded his big eyes at her then ran back to the others.

"I hope whatever did this is going to meet with a world of pain!" Ellie, suddenly said.

Eve flinched at her words though when Ellie caught it, she mistook her reaction for something else.

"I'm sorry… I don't know what I'm saying. I'd better go."

She fled back to her family.

* * *

Tyler dug into her ribs and fries watching as Ally inhaled her own Mac and Burger combo. She was obviously loving the food as Tyler had never seen Ally eat so fast before in her life. It almost made her wonder if Cheryl wasn't feeding her enough, but she knew her kid sister and starvation wasn't something Ally would ever keep from her.

In no time at all, Ally threw down her napkin, burping loudly before covering her mouth with embarrassment. "Sorry," she apologized.

"In some cultures, it's a sign of respect to burp after eating. Shows you liked the food enough to eat a lot of it," Tyler explained.

"I'll remember that the next time I burp and someone tells me off," Ally replied.

"Are we all done here?" Their waiter sprang up again. He was certainly observant, having come to their table a handful of times already without being summoned. Ally nodded though she didn't look at him as the plates were being cleared away.

"Do you want dessert now?"

He seemed almost as eager as Tyler for the next surprise but seeing how antsy Ally was, she made a snap decision. "No. Give us a few minutes."

He nodded but Tyler couldn't help but pick up a sense of disappointment from him even if she couldn't see his real face beneath the mask.

Reaching into her bag, she took out the gift-wrapped boxes.

Ally's eyes brightened. "Three presents?!" she exclaimed, practically bouncing in her seat.

Tyler passed over the biggest gift. "Open this first."

Tearing off the paper, Ally squealed when she saw the black spots on the red background beneath. "It's the bug bag I wanted! Oh, I love it!" she cried, holding it up so Tyler could see it.

"Well, it is what you asked for," Tyler answered wryly.

"I know, I just wasn't sure I'd actually get it," Ally said. Ally beamed as she tackled her next gift. When the music box appeared, her eyes brightened with tears. "It's just like the one Dad got me."

Through the tears, Ally smiled as she opened her final

gift. As first one pair of origami animals appeared, then another, and another, she gasped.

"You made these? Without Mom's help?"

"It took a while and several paper cuts but I finally got there," Tyler said. "I wanted to make sure that you knew they were here with us in spirit. Even though they can't be here, they're never going to stop loving you, and neither will I."

Overwhelmed with feeling, Ally leapt off of her seat, ran around the table and threw herself at Tyler.

"You're the most important thing in my life, Bug and I promise we'll be together, soon OK? Just hang on in there," Tyler said into the top of Ally's head as she squeezed her tight.

ONE HUNDRED SEVENTEEN

Marley and Eve stood around for another hour after Ellie had spoken to them, but neither were ready to leave, each rocked by guilt.

They had come to help the family through their grief but couldn't think of anything that wouldn't implicate them. When the family looked as if they might be leaving, Eve grabbed Marley's arm.

"They're going! If we're going to do something, it has to be now!"

But what could they do?

What could Marley do to help?

Suddenly, the idea came to her like a lightning bolt. She cringed inwardly, reprimanding herself for not thinking of it earlier.

"I've got it. Quick, we need to get Darren's sister's attention."

Thinking fast, Eve took out a twenty-dollar bill from her purse and went after the girl. "Excuse me, I think you dropped this when you were at the water cooler," she said.

Ellie stopped while the rest of the family continued

on. "No… I'm pretty sure I didn't. But thank you," she said, turning away again when Marley placed a hand on her shoulder and stopped her.

"Hey…" she began nervously. "I just need a moment. I don't know if you believe this kind of thing but I have to try."

Ellie's face turned confused.

"The thing is… the thing is I'm a psychic. I can see and communicate with spirits that have unfinished business… and your brother has something he really needs me to tell you."

Ellie's expression went from confused to angry, as she tossed a look between the two of them. "What is this, some kind of sick joke?"

"No," Eve jumped in quickly. "She really can do this." Getting the gist of Marley's plan, she hoped that it wouldn't backfire on them.

"Really…" Ellie demanded, crossing her arms over her chest as she waited for proof.

Marley had to think fast since she couldn't actually see Darren's ghost. "He says the two of you are really close," she began only to receive a snort of derision.

"That's patently obvious from how upset I've been."

"He says he worked on a boat and that it's a family tradition to work on the water."

Ellie looked surprised but suspicion clouded her face. "You could have overheard one of us talking today."

"True," Marley said going in for the clincher. "But how would I know that your favorite band is The Cure… and your favorite track of theirs is Charlotte Sometimes," Marley said, hoping frantically that she had remembered Darren and Eve's conversation correctly.

"How could you know that?" Ellie paled as the incredulous expression on her face turned to shock. She gasped suddenly, her knees knocking together. Eve rushed forward as Ellie's legs gave way completely. She half pulled, half lifted her onto a metal seat that was welded to the wall.

"There's no way you could know any of that," Ellie whispered, staring around her wide-eyed as if she might be able to see Darren's spirit herself.

"He doesn't have long with us," Marley spoke quickly, hoping that she would be able to relay "his" message before Ellie asked any question she wouldn't be able to answer.

"He wants you to know that it had only hurt for a moment. He was trying to help someone when he died. He wants you to know that he didn't suffer, that it was over quickly."

Ellie gaped at Marley as a ragged breath escaped her lips.

"Can you ask him who did this to him?" Ellie requested.

"Who? What do you mean, I thought you said it was an animal attack?" Eve asked, shocked.

"The police contacted my dad asking if there was anyone he could think of that would to hurt Darren because the first caller said he'd seen a group of girls on the island, just prior to his death," Ellie replied.

Marley shot Eve an alarmed look over the top of Ellie's head as a sick feeling started to gnaw at her stomach. Keeping her voice as neutral as possible despite how desperate she was to get out of there now, Marley replied, "I'm sorry. I've lost him now, but he didn't say anything about someone hurting him."

Ellie blinked, trying to take it all in. By the hospital exit, Ellie's Mom had suddenly noticed that she wasn't with them. She searched until her eyes found her. Saying something to her husband, she started heading towards them.

Marley knew she had to finish this before her mom got there.

"I'm sorry if we upset you, I just thought you should know your brother died a hero."

Before Ellie could say anything else, Eve and Marley hurried away, disappearing around the corner, each thinking the same thing.

Two callers?

Someone had deliberately implicated them in those deaths and it didn't take a genius to figure who that could be.

Michael.

They felt the icy knife of fear on their spine, knowing that they had quite possibly just fallen into Michael's trap. Somehow, he knew they would be going to that island. He had set a trap there for them that they had walked right into.

"How could he have known we would go there though?" Marley asked. "He couldn't have known we were going to do a spell?"

"Maybe he had someone watch us downtown. All they had to do was follow us from the tree to the island," Eve answered, working through the steps logically. "Maybe that's why he made the grand gesture of dumping that tree on the city in the first place, to draw us out."

"And the dogs were supposed to either kill us..."

"Or the cops would arrest us," Eve finished the thought for her. "Either way, the result is we would be taken out of the picture."

They left the hospital chilled, each considering the implications of what they had just learned.

The table had been cleared and wiped down, the presents put away. There was only one thing left to finish what had turned out to be a nice birthday despite the two parent-sized holes in the picture.

Having signaled their waiter, he now appeared with a chocolate cake shaped like a ladybug. It wasn't one of the designs the diner usually offered but Tyler had slipped them an extra fifty bucks for the honor.

Seeing Ally's smile she knew it was money well spent, although — she noticed with a frown — none of the ten candles that were stuck into the cake had been lit.

Their waiter hadn't noticed, however, as he began to sing Happy Birthday in a loud and awkward baritone. Setting the cake before her, Ally beamed when she saw it. "There's cake too?"

Tyler gestured to their waiter. "The candles aren't lit?"

He did an exaggerated double-take. "Yikes, I'm so sorry for this oversight. One second, I have a lighter in my pocket."

Taking it out, he lit the candles but when all ten were burning they suddenly exploded, sending ten plumes of fire upward.

Ally screamed shrinking back as Tyler froze, not knowing how to react. The fire alarm sounded then, shrieking overhead.

Suddenly, the sprinklers turned on flooding the place with water and jolting Tyler from her shock. Smoke cloaked the air, choking her as she jumped out of her seat to grab at Ally, but somehow she was knocked down. She went flying sideways, hitting the chequered floor heavily, her breath knocked out of her.

"Ally!" Tyler called out, but she wasn't sure her sister could hear her above the mayhem. People shrieked loudly holding menus over their heads stampeding outside to safety, dragging their family members with them.

"Stay in your seat!" Tyler warned, not wanting Ally to get carried along in the sudden exodus. "I'm coming for you!"

Tyler tried to get back up only for a pair of steel-capped boots to land right by her fingers. She snatched them away just in time to save them from being crushed and got to her feet.

The heavy black smoke covered everything now making it difficult to see, which through her shocked daze struck Tyler as strange. Even as she got up, her scientific mind wondered how those ten small candles could have caused this much smoke, this quickly.

Finally back on her feet, Tyler saw that the candles had fizzled out — they had gone out almost the instant that the sprinklers had touched them. With the cause of the "fire" eradicated, the sprinklers turned off.

Through the smoke that was clearing in front of her, Tyler found herself staring at the empty seat where her sister should be.

But Ally wasn't there.

Thinking that maybe she had been scared by the commotion, Tyler ducked under the table in case she was hiding there.

No Ally. No sign of her anywhere.

Her heart beginning to race in her chest, Tyler shot back up, her eyes desperately skimming over the glistening wet surfaces searching for a glimpse of that impish little face she loved so much.

But there was nothing.

Ally was gone.

Tyler's gaze finally flicked over to the floor. There, lying on the chequered black-and-white tiles, sodden and trampled to death — it was Ally's cardboard crown.

ONE HUNDRED EIGHTEEN

Detective Saunders sat in the manager's office which had luckily escaped the watery shower that the rest of the joint had recently endured.

Staring into a TV monitor that contained a live feed of the place, she could see the BU student, Tyler Jones, huddle in her seat clutching that battered cardboard crown while her partner conducted a standard missing person's interview.

She cricked her neck, rubbing the back of it — it had been a very long day what with the mystery of that tree that had decided to uproot itself and land in the center of town, then the two mysterious deaths on Fort Warren — and it was looking like it would be an even longer night now.

Jones exhibited the classic signs of shock. She shook uncontrollably, her face was white as a sheet. She could see the girl's teeth were chattering so much that she half expected to be able to hear them from even here, several rooms away. She would have to be a monster not to feel for her, but she couldn't ignore the many questions that hung over her head. The group of girls Jones spent her time with seemed to get involved in an awful lot of mysterious crimes.

And if she knew one thing in this line of work it was that coincidences didn't much exist.

Despite this, however, Jones's story had so far checked out. Saunders knew this having carefully studied the security footage from the moment the girls had arrived.

"Detective?" a nervous voice called over.

Saunders hit pause on the security footage and flicked her eyes over to the figure who stood in the doorway, holding a clipboard. It was the diner's manager, a man whose eyes looked almost as wide as Jones.

"Yeah?" Saunders replied.

"Here's that information you asked for," the manager, whose name was Colin, handed the clipboard to her.

"Thanks," Saunders replied, already scanning the list of names to see if any sounded familiar. They didn't, of course. It was never that easy. She looked up at him again. "These were all the staff who worked tonight?"

"Yes," Colin nodded, eager to assist.

Then again, a missing child was everyone's priority.

She nodded that she was done with him. Colin stood for a moment longer before he realized he had been dismissed. Giving her a half nod he left leaving Saunders free to continue with her work.

Pressing the play button, she watched as the girls ate their meal, then took in Ally's delight with her presents. Having been briefed on Tyler's unfortunate background, she felt a sudden lump in her throat when the origami animals were produced. They didn't seem like much, but judging by both girl's reactions they had meant a great deal to them.

Saunders would bet the house that they had something to do with the memory of their deceased parents.

Which made what had happened next even more painful to watch.

She continued watching as the cake came out.

Knowing that the moment was fast approaching, Saunders body tensed. She stared at the screen determined not to miss a second of the action.

The candles were lit and as many had already reported, they flamed crazily, setting off the sprinklers. Then came the smoke that had made it difficult to see everything on the ground, but Saunders could still make out enough as the camera was suspended from the ceiling where the smoke hadn't yet reached.

Saunders blinked suddenly as her finger darted forward to hit rewind. She studied the video again to make sure of what she had seen.

There was Jones trying to reach out for her sister when their waiter — whose face was hidden beneath that mask — had deliberately knocked her to the ground.

Chills racing down her spine, she watched as the waiter grabbed Ally's things then snatched her up. Ally immediately opened her mouth to scream, but the waiter slapped a cloth over it. Within seconds, Ally went limp as he raced out of the diner with her in his arms.

Saunders shot up to her feet.

"COLIN!" she barked and was rewarded by the man reappearing by the door.

"Yes?" he asked, clenching his hands into balls.

Jabbing her finger on the video, she rewound the tape then paused it on a clear shot of the waiter before he had kidnapped the girl.

"Who is this?" she demanded, pointing at the screen.

Colin studied the screen then frowned. When he finally spoke several seconds later, it came out as a stammer. "I don't know… we don't have a mask like that."

"Are you sure?" Saunders asked, needing the clarification.

"Yes. We have specific costumes for our servers… and that isn't one of them."

Saunders turned back to the monitor staring at the screen.

"Well, if he isn't one of your waiters, then who is he?"

H er head felt funny like it was made of cotton candy and wasn't fixed to her body. She felt like it would float away at any moment.

Her eyes seemed glued together though she knew they couldn't be. All she had to do was to force them to open, but that seemed almost as difficult as getting up.

What was she lying on? Why could she feel biting cold metal against her skin instead of the rough but familiar warmth of her carpet? And where was Tyler? The last thing Ally remembered was the cake and then… there was a blank void.

An icy chill coursed through her veins.

Something was very, very wrong.

"Are you sure you didn't give her too much?" A male voice asked, sounding peeved and concerned.

"I gave her exactly what you told me to," came the answering response from another man, this one spoke with a bit of a lisp as if he had teeth that were too big for his mouth.

"Then why isn't she awake?"

"I think she's pretending," said the man with the lisp. Ally knew she had guessed right when something clanged loudly next to her, rattling her to the core. She could feel the vibration of it everywhere like the entire room was made out of metal.

Her eyes flew open despite the fear that was beginning to cut into her strange daze.

What she saw made her gasp out loud.

She was somewhere underground. Curved concrete walls surrounded her. The unmistakable drip of a leaking pipe echoed from beyond. The place was cold, not that well lit, and it had a horrible smell like something had died in this place but had been left there to rot.

But that wasn't the worst of it.

Ally could see now where the sound of that metal had come from. Walls made up of thin steel bars circled her, keeping her trapped. They went around her in a three-foot radius, stretching overhead to form a raised dome.

It was, as Ally started to realize, a giant birdcage but where the door handle would be, there was nothing.

The only way in and out of this cage was from the outside.

A sound came out of her, a whimper of fear that the two figures huddled close by seemed to enjoy. One of them came towards her, towards a lamp which hung by the cage.

Ally recognized him immediately.

It was the waiter from the diner, and for some reason, he was still wearing the monster mask on his head. The mask had seemed pretty horrible in the diner, but it looked so much scarier in here — wherever here was.

"Where's Tyler?" Ally asked, hoping that she didn't sound as frightened as she was fast becoming.

Their waiter pushed his masked face against the bars of the cage. Up close like this, Ally could see what looked like the pointed ends of fangs peeking out from the hole in the mask where his mouth was. He laughed without any mirth.

"Freaking out in the diner, the last I saw," he said, seemingly enjoying her fear.

"Well, she's going to come for me," Ally said, full of confidence in her declaration. "And you're both going to get in trouble for kidnapping me."

She was hoping that by not letting them know how scared she was, maybe they would just leave her alone so she could try to figure out how she could escape or call for help. Where, oh where was Tyler?

"But that's the plan little girl," their waiter said. "Big sister will come for you, and when she does…"

He reached up to remove his mask and as the

shadows fell away, Ally saw that the actual monster that lay beneath was far more frightening than the one on the mask.

"We will be ready for her," Pike said. Laughing, he struck the edge of the giant birdcage with a knife, as Ally flinched back in terror.

TWISTED MAGIC

8: HELL HATH NO FURY

JO HO

ONE HUNDRED NINETEEN

Over and over the questions had come yet Tyler could barely hear them anymore, much less answer them.

For close to an hour the cop called Brooks had interrogated her, asking such seemingly unrelated questions that Tyler had wanted to scream. What did their parent's death have to do with Ally's disappearance, or for that matter the state of her finances?

Though his tone didn't imply that he held her in any way responsible, the fact that he was with her at all and not out policing the streets for Ally made Tyler want to take matters into her own hands.

It was all she could do to stop herself from tearing the world apart to find Ally herself.

When the immediate shock had dialed down to a nine, and the smoke cleared enough that she could see a path through the gray haze, she had scanned the faces of the families outside, hoping desperately that one of those parents had mistakenly dragged Ally out to safety. But she could see them all from where she sat now, shivering in their damp clothes as they hugged their kids, watching the diner burn from a safe distance away.

Nowhere in that crowd was that impish little face that she loved more than life itself.

Not wanting to face the immediate crushing fear that loomed in the corners of her mind, she had still been considering where Ally could have possibly gotten to when her eyes had landed on that trampled cardboard crown lying on the tiles like roadkill. And just like that, she knew something terrible had happened to her.

Call it gut instinct, intuition, or an extension of her powers — whatever it was, Tyler knew without a doubt that Ally was in grave, grave danger.

"Ms. Jones?"

Tyler looked up from the booth she sat at to find Saunders staring down at her. The detective's eyes bore none of the usual suspicion that seemed to be her default expression whenever they had met before. Instead, concern flooded out of them.

Which made Tyler feel sick to her stomach. If even Saunders was worried, this would not be good.

"Can you come with me? I have something you need to see."

Tyler got up, wordlessly following Saunders past a pair of uniformed cops who stared at her gravely, and into a small, cramped office in the back. A TV monitor took up most of one wall. On it, there was a frozen image of the diner. Tyler gasped when she recognized herself. The footage was paused right at the moment when the cake was just arriving. Ally's delighted little face took up most of the frame.

"Bug," Tyler gasped, drinking in the sight of her.

"What you're about to see is going to be disturbing, I need you to steel yourself," Saunders instructed in an authoritative yet calm voice. Almost, Tyler noted, as if she were on her side.

Confusion and fear waged a war inside as Tyler

clenched her fists, preparing herself for whatever was going to be shown. Leaning towards a control panel, Saunders pressed a button, and the image unfroze.

There was no sound, but Tyler didn't need it: in her mind, she could hear what she and Ally had been saying as if she were hearing it from a distorted replay. Ally beamed, clapping her hands with delight as the cake was placed onto the table by their waiter. Tyler watched herself pointing toward the cake to let their waiter know about the candles. Looking aghast, he quickly lit them all.

And then the mayhem began.

Tyler's heart thumped wildly in her chest as the crushing memory of it fell upon her again. As if she was back in that moment, she could feel it all, but this time it was much, much worse as she knew what was to come. The blaze plumed toward the ceiling as water started to rain down from the sprinklers. There was the smoke now which had obscured so much of Tyler's view at the time, but which now, she could clearly see over from this low-angled security camera.

As on-screen Tyler screamed for Ally, their waiter deliberately tackled her to the floor.

Tyler gasped, her eyes wide and unbelieving. Beside her, Saunders wasn't watching the tape — she had already seen it multiple times and could recite every detail if needed. Instead, her eyes were pinned to Tyler's face, scrutinizing her every expression.

While on-screen Tyler scrambled on the floor, trying to pick herself up, the waiter knocked Ally unconscious, tossed her over his shoulder like she was nothing more than a sack of potatoes, then *left* with her.

"As you can see, it was your waiter who took your sister. We are obviously searching to see who it was but my initial investigation has revealed that he isn't one of the diner's usual members of staff. In fact, nobody has seen him before today..."

Saunders' voice carried on, explaining what she

would do to find the waiter but Tyler couldn't hear her through the rush of blood in her ears. There was a strange high-pitched keening sound that may or may not have been coming from her. Through the dark place that her thoughts were rapidly spiraling to, Tyler could feel the air begin to hum with her magic.

Called forth by her fear and the white-hot fury that had begun to burn inside her from the second she saw their waiter touch Ally, Tyler let loose all of her emotions now, channeling it into her power.

A spark flashed to her left, then one to her right. Then two more around the small office. Electricity crackled seemingly from within the very walls themselves as more sparks burst out. Saunders reacted first, frowning at the strange phenomena when a cloud of sparks rained down from the ceiling above her head. Saunders ducked, shielding her head with her hands as her eyes grew progressively rounder.

"What's going on?" Someone cried from outside but Tyler made no move to look where. Inside the thick wave of panic that pounded against her chest, she knew she was causing this — whatever it was. And that she was doing it in full view of the police.

She had to stop it before it got worse.

Desperate to dial it down, she focused on her breathing as she had so many times before when the world had become too much. Stilling her head, she pulled her focus inside. Forcing herself to breathe slowly, she counted… One… two… three…

But the rage, fear, and confusion would not go away. If anything, her attempt to control it only made it grow stronger. Her stomach began to churn as all she could see in her mind's eye was the moment their waiter had grabbed Ally then knocked her out with a substance that was most likely chloroform.

The light exploded above her shattering glass everywhere as the room plunged into a near darkness. The only light now came from the TV monitor. Someone grabbed her arm — Saunders.

"We need to get out of here," the detective warned leaving no room for argument.

Blindly, Tyler let herself be drawn outside into the hallway that led to the diner, but even in here, those same electric sparks spat out of the light fixtures and sockets. A few landed on Tyler's ankle, burning into her skin as a shock of pain cut through the black hole she had fallen into.

Though it seemed whatever magic Tyler had called forward, it was too late to send it back.

Another light exploded above them.

"DUCK!" Saunders yelled as she shoved Tyler along until they reached Brooks who had been talking to the uniformed cops in the dining area when this had started.

"What the hell…?" he asked when he saw an electric cable come to life, a giant black snake dancing across the chequered floor tiles that were still slick from their recent drenching.

His eyes burned bright with sudden clarity. Snapping his head to Saunders, he pointed at the cable and yelled. "Get her out of here!"

Seeing the danger, Saunders' lips tightened into a thin, white line as she grabbed Tyler's shoulder and began sprinting to the exit.

"Move Jones!" she barked into Tyler's ear, steering her outside.

Hearing the warning in her voice, Tyler didn't bother to look around for the problem. Adrenaline pumping through her veins, she bolted for safety, instinctively knowing that if she didn't… it would all be over.

She burst out of the exit, Saunders so close on her heels that she could feel the woman's breath burning into the back of her neck when the diner *exploded*.

Saunders crashed into Tyler. She went down onto the cold hard ground, pain shooting up her side. As the thought flew into her mind that this was the second time that night that someone had tackled her, she felt the weight of Saunders on top of her, pushing her so close to the ground that she could taste the dirt.

Behind them came an almighty roar and a blast of heat as the diner burst into flames casting a fiery orange glow over everything. Those alarms Tyler had heard earlier came back on, shrieking into the night.

Saunders rolled off of her, staggering to her feet. Grabbing Tyler by the collar of her denim jacket, she hauled her a safe distance away from the burning site… then she started back toward the diner, her eyes flashing with shock.

"Brooks," Tyler heard the detective say.

A wave of horror crashed over her as Tyler stared at the burning building with the knowledge that Brooks was still inside. Saunders stumbled towards the entrance way, favoring her left leg which she must have hurt while trying to protect Tyler. Tyler saw that the door to the diner wasn't there anymore. Having blown clear off of its hinges, it now sat some distance away, rocking in the streets.

Tyler held her breath, watching as Saunders reached the entrance but she couldn't get inside. A thick steel beam blocked her way. Still, this didn't deter Saunders who dropped to the ground, meaning to crawl beneath, only to find her way forward blocked by a pile of rubble.

Inside, a man's scream of pain rose, seemingly amplified by the otherwise silent night.

Hearing it, Tyler recoiled, feeling sick to her stomach.

Brooks was dying in there, burning alive… and she was the one who had caused it.

ONE HUNDRED TWENTY

The next few moments were absolute agony.

Brooks' screaming cries pierced into her head, cutting a path through to her heart where the shame and guilt of what she had caused, festered.

Saunders called out to him from her position by the blocked entrance, trying her best to offer what small comfort she could. Though she couldn't get to him, Saunders refused to leave her partner behind. She lay on her stomach, face pressed as close to the entrance as she could get it without the smoke and flames overpowering her.

Not even when the fire trucks finally pulled up and a crowd of firefighters fought their way inside did Saunders move from where she was. Saunders called out to Brooks, speaking in that reassuring manner she had adopted even though he had long fallen silent.

Tyler was lost in a dark place. Combined with the echoes of Brooks earlier screams, she kept hearing her own voice promising Ally only moments before that they would be together again properly, soon…

Who could have known what a lie that would be?

After what seemed like the entire night but was not

even an hour, the firefighters finally emerged from the building black with soot and smoke carrying Brooks' prone body between them.

Tyler shot to her feet as Saunders raced around them, firing questions that Tyler couldn't hear from where she stood but understood all the same.

Will he make it?

How badly is he hurt?

Catching a glimpse of Brooks' injuries, Tyler stifled a sob, left reeling. His short brown hair had burned away leaving only a red, raw mess behind. What wasn't charred black on the rest of him were lanced with open flesh wounds. Tyler swallowed the dry lump in her throat. It seemed impossible that he could still be alive after having endured so much.

Brooks was laid gently onto a gurney then wheeled into a waiting ambulance when she heard the familiar voices call out to her.

"Tyler! Oh my gosh! What happened here?"

She turned to see Cassie, followed closely by Eve and Marley rushing up to her. Seeing their faces, Tyler felt a wave of emotion as she realized that she wasn't alone in the world as she had felt these past few hours. Their concern radiated from them, letting Tyler know that they genuinely cared about her, and the realization of that caused fresh tears to fall from her eyes. Marley acted first, grabbing her in a tight hug.

"We got your message. Have you found out what happened to Ally?" Marley asked.

"Someone took her. Our waiter," Tyler managed to say.

"What?" Eve gasped, her horror making her makeup look more gruesome than usual.

"The cops have no leads," Tyler went on to explain even as she felt her throat closing up. Just saying the words made the whole thing feel so much worse. More than anything, she wished her parents were alive to take over. They would know what to do.

"It only just happened, I'm sure they'll find her," Marley said trying desperately to remain optimistic knowing that it was what Tyler needed though a seed of doubt gnawed inside her stomach.

"Right," Eve agreed. "There are so many people here, someone must have seen something that will lead them to him."

"Unless it was Michael," Tyler responded. Her voice sounded strange. There was no emotion remaining, no tone. No life in it whatsoever. Any life that she'd had left had been taken with Ally.

"What happened to this place?" Cassie asked, reeling at the devastation all around them. Emergency crew littered the scene trying their best to help all those affected by the explosion.

"This only just happened..." Tyler replied as a strange numbness started taking over her body. "I did it."

Her words were thick with grief.

Ah, there it was, Tyler thought as she constrained a hysterical laugh. *There's my emotion.*

Marley had been studying the blaze, but she snapped her head back to Tyler. "What do you mean?"

"Saunders showed me the security footage of the moment that Al..." The name stuck in her throat and she found she wasn't able to complete it. "That she'd been taken," she continued. "I got so overwhelmed that my power just started building up. I didn't even know what I was doing. It just happened."

"That's how it is with me," Eve spoke gently as if she were dealing with a child. "Whenever I get scared, even if it's just a nightmare, I wake up to find a blanket of insects over me."

Cassie visibly recoiled while Marley shuddered.

"It's not your fault, Tyler. You didn't know this would

happen," Eve said firmly hoping that her words would cut through her guilt.

Seeing Saunders wandering around so close to them made Marley feel a nervous kick in her gut. Maybe it was the memory of that last time she had spoken to her, right after the attack in the laundry block, but she didn't want to be questioned by her again and she could almost feel it coming.

"Do they still need you here?" Eve asked, nodding toward Saunders. She must have been feeling the same unease as Marley as she couldn't quite suppress her shudder when she looked over at the cop.

"I don't know," Tyler spoke to no one in particular, her eyes having taken on a glazed look.

Eve took the initiative. Walking over to the cop, she spoke to her for only a few seconds before returning.

"She said we can take you home but she'll be in touch," Eve said. "Come on."

Eve put an arm around her shoulder while Marley picked up Tyler's bag which had sat on the ground in a damp heap this whole time. Silently, they headed back to BU.

B y some unknown miracle, Brooks was hanging on by a thread.

Though Saunders wanted nothing more than to be by his side at the hospital, she was needed here.

The two had been partners for more than a decade now. They had saved each other for more than double of that, so to see him like this killed her, particularly as he was the one who warned her to get Jones to safety. He had put their lives above his own, yet this horrific outcome was the reward for his sacrifice.

Brooks had a family, two young sons and a wife that he adored who was constantly trying to match Saunders up with one available bachelor or another. They were as much her family as the one she had been born into.

Feeling the heavy weight of grief beginning to overwhelm her, Saunders shook herself. There was time for that later when she was home with the pup and a bottle of scotch. Right now she still had work to do.

She needed to find who had taken that girl — the first twenty-four hours following a kidnap were always the most crucial. After that, the chances of finding the victims alive began to dwindle… She would do what she could to find the girl, then she would investigate the cause of this explosion.

Brooks would be expecting nothing less of her.

Drawn by a movement, Saunders tore her eyes away from the back of the ambulance that rushed her partner to help and turned to see that Jones' friends were taking her away.

Her dark eyes alighted on each of the girls as she wondered about the curious timing of the blaze — a blaze which had started seconds after Tyler had been shown the footage of Ally's kidnapping.

Feeling her spidey senses tinglingly as they always did when these girls were around, Saunders resolved to look into the matter further.

There was something strange going on with those girls and she was determined to find out what.

ONE HUNDRED TWENTY-ONE

Long white curtains swayed in the night breeze as Michael stood silhouetted against the full moon, gazing down at the city beneath.

Up here some twelve stories from the ground, all Michael could hear was the odd car in the distance or the ruffle of wings close by. From his terrace in the penthouse apartment of the hotel, Michael had a clear view of the city for miles. The twinkling lights blinked at him, as pockets of color — highlighted by a streetlight or a shop front window — reminded him once again, just how different this world was from his own.

And how different it would become once his plan came into fruition.

The rustle of moving wings caught his attention again. His eyes slid from the view to the corner of the terrace where the one luxury he allowed himself sat in an ornately gilded cage.

The large bird was smoky gray with an impressive crest, but it was its prominent red cheeks that changed color depending on its mood that had drawn Michael to it. That and its ability to mimic the human voice.

When Michael had first heard the bird calling out to him as if he were human, Michael had been floored and wondered what kind of enchantment the bird was under. He'd been searching for a place to call home when he'd first seen the bird as its owner — an obnoxiously wealthy businessman from the West — had been checking out of the hotel.

Michael had only meant to inquire about his bird, but after the man had sneered at him only to dismiss him by revealing that the bird was *very* expensive and way out of his league... Michael was obviously forced to teach the fool a lesson he would never forget.

Michael not only took the bird, but he also took the man's life and all of his wealth. It was the reason why money was not an issue for Michael as technically he was a millionaire several times over. If his funds ever ran out, it would be a simple case to replace it.

Moving to the bird, he took out some sunflowers seeds that he knew was a favorite snack. The bird, whose beak had been tucked into its wings suddenly swung its head around to face him.

"Hello!" It greeted him in that human voice. Smiling, Michael fed it a few seeds, marveling at how though this world liked to pretend that magic didn't exist, it could still be found in some of nature's most unlikely creations.

He ran a finger across the bird's head as he had seen its previous owner do, watching as it preened under it and gave a happy little squawk. Michael allowed himself a small smile before forcing it away.

It was time to update *Him* on their progress.

Though they were bonded in ways that came from only the harshest of histories, Michael was still afraid of Him.

And with good reason too.

Michael had seen Him do things that had made even him shudder. It was one of the reasons he had taken to only contacting him when there was good news to relay. Tonight, Michael had very good news.

Standing beneath the open expanse of the night sky, Michael summoned the presence into his mind. He knew the second it was there when he felt the flickering, probing entity leech inside. Despite the many times he had done this, he still felt the icy chill that now ran through his veins. Apparently, he would never get used to having his soul invaded.

You have taken up the body of another. Have you become so tainted with the views of this world already? The voice inside his head sounded amused though Michael knew not to trust that.

One of the witches is partial to this body, Michael answered, sending out his reply as a psychic thought that he knew would reach even into this other realm.

What news have you brought me? The presence demanded, moving to the task at hand, impatient as ever.

Then again, centuries of enduring that kind of hell would do that to a person.

I have the young girl, the sister of one of the witches.

The innocent? The voice came again, pleased this time. *This will unravel her for sure. Good work, Michael.*

A burst of pride erupted inside his chest. Praise of any kind from Him was as rare as a demon with a conscience.

Thank you. Micheal replied.

And the seals — what of those? Have you found them all?

Michael felt his heart flutter in a panic, knowing that *He* would be less pleased about the progress there.

Three are broken, but there is still two more to be found.

The silence that came was as nerve-wracking as any explosive outburst *He* could have made. From experience, Michael knew it was the quiet displeasure that was the most deceiving. Those were the moments He would lash out unexpectantly.

Michael flinched inwardly, steeling himself, waiting for the blow he was sure would come. If he was lucky, maybe he would only hurt for a few days this time, after all, it would be difficult to continue his mission with his insides lit on fire.

He waited, the seconds ticking away into minutes, but still, no pain came. Letting out the breath he hadn't known he had been holding, Michael felt the tension leave his shoulders when a terrified squawk sounded from beside him.

He turned to see gray feathers floating around as the bird flapped its wings in great desperation when it suddenly stiffened and fell headlong to the bottom of the cage.

Now you share my disappointment, the voice growled into his mind. *You know what will happen if you fail me again,* it warned.

And then it was gone.

Michael stared down at the dead body of the bird wondering why he could be feeling so much grief for something so inconsequential.

He should have known better than to become attached — however slight — for anything else.

He would never allow it.

Hardening his heart, Michael affirmed never to let himself care for another creature again, after all — as in all the times in his past — it would only be taken away from him.

Better to not care for anything at all.

ONE HUNDRED TWENTY-TWO

Tyler sat on Marley's bed staring blankly into space.

They had been back at the dorm a while now. Marley wrapped a blanket around her, as Cassie sat beside her, holding her hands in her two small ones while Eve busied herself at the drinks station making hot chocolate.

Through the numbness that had first started settling in on the ride back, Tyler wondered how Cassie's hands could feel so sturdy and strong when they were as tiny as the rest of her.

Stirring a cup of the hot chocolate, Eve pressed it into her hands. "Drink," she commanded.

Tyler shook her head, but Eve's expression became firm. "You're not going to be any help to your sister if you collapse from exhaustion or dehydration. Drink," she said again, even more sternly.

Tyler knew it would be a waste of energy she didn't have to argue with her. Besides, there was something about her manner that comforted. It reminded her of her own mom. Given the chance, she was sure her mom would be doing the same thing.

Raising the cup to her lips, Tyler sipped the hot drink, surprised when the warmness of it cut into her shock. It was nice to finally feel something other than that freezing, numbness that had settled in since Ally's disappearance… or the rage that had caused Brooks to possibly die.

The girls shot each other concerned looks, none of them knowing what they should be doing to help her.

"You don't have to babysit me," Tyler began only to stop at how unfamiliar her own voice sounded. There was a rawness to it, an overwhelming pain and stress that she had only heard one other time in her life…

"It's not babysitting. It's solidarity," Eve answered.

"You've had a terrible shock, Ty. It's awful what you're going through, but you need to know that you are not going through this on your own," Marley supplied with feeling.

"We're here with you," Cassie said quietly, giving the hand that wasn't holding the drink a squeeze.

Tyler shot them all a grateful look, feeling tears prick the backs of her eyes. "Is Christian here too?" she asked, looking around the room even though she knew she wouldn't be able to see him.

"No. I didn't want to call him yet. I thought… I just thought you might prefer it if it was only the four of us here," Marley answered, care and concern shining from her eyes.

"Where are your keys?" Eve asked suddenly.

Tyler gestured towards her bag which now sat on the floor beside her feet though she had no recollection of how it had gotten there. One of the girls must have brought it with them.

Eve opened up Tyler's bag, fishing them out. "I'll be right back," she said as she left the room. Tyler barely had time to think about what she might be doing when Eve came back under a mountain of pillows and blankets.

"Thought we'd need these since we're all staying here tonight," Eve smiled.

"You guys don't have to do that," Tyler began, only for Cassie to stop her.

"You're not going anywhere and neither are we so you should get used to that," Cassie replied.

Despite the fear that lanced her heart, Tyler could also feel the beginnings of a deep gratitude knowing that she wasn't alone in this nightmare. She wanted to reply, to say thank you but she could feel herself choking up.

And if she started sobbing, she might never stop.

As if they knew she was at the point of losing all self-control, the others discreetly turned away and started setting up their beds for the night. Marley offered Tyler her own, choosing to sleep on a makeshift one on the floor instead since the beds weren't big enough for two girls to comfortably share.

When they were done, Tyler joined them in a circle on the carpet. While they had been preparing the room, she had become fixated with a thought that ordinarily, she would act on alone, but seeing the girls now and all that they were willing to do for her… Tyler knew it was time to ask for their help.

"Guys," Tyler began nervously. "I can't just sit here hoping for those cops to find Ally when you know we could do something about this. I want to cast a spell to find her, and I want your help to do it."

The others stopped what they were doing but none wore any expression of surprise. If anything, they each looked as if they knew this request was coming.

"I was going to raise this myself actually," Eve began. "If this was my brother, I probably would have done it already."

"Of course I'll help," Cassie responded.

"Yes," Marley agreed. "If there's something we can do to get her back, you know for sure we will."

The tears Tyler had been holding back finally spilled

down her cheeks. Cassie leaned her head on Tyler's shoulder, giving her moral support as they sat in a tight circle.

Reaching out her hand palm facing up as they had done when they had cast their first spell, Tyler laid the paper crown that she had kept from the restaurant across her hand. It still had a strand of Ally's long chestnut hair on it. Tyler found herself fixated on the sight of it as she waited for the others to lay their hands on top of hers.

The second the four were in physical contact, Tyler could feel the magic current traveling through them all. She could sense what the girls were feeling though any were yet to speak a word. Not only were they were joined magically, but they were also able to understand each other in a way that no one else ever could.

They felt like family, like a sisterhood.

Pulling in her focus, Tyler cleared her mind from the fearful clutter that churned inside until only one thought remained.

Ally.

The magic swelled up, lifting her hair until the strands swam in the air. All around them the magic hummed and crackled like electricity, though this felt different from the diner when Tyler's pain had been the driving force which had then unleashed a catastrophic event of its own. The magic here was under command, it was being controlled.

Even without looking, Tyler could feel the crown levitate from her hand. Sending out her thoughts, Tyler commanded the spell to find her sister, to let her know where she was.

The magic built around them as a white ball of light began to shine inside their joined hands. The ball pulsated and grew as the white light intensified until Tyler found herself squinting from the brightness of it. Abruptly, it exploded as the air returned to normal and Tyler felt her hair floating back down.

The spell had been cast.
All they had to do was wait.

ONE HUNDRED TWENTY-THREE

It was a little after two am but there was no sign of the spell working.

One by one, despite their every intention to do otherwise, the girls had fallen asleep until only Tyler remained awake. More than anything, she would have loved to have that same blessed break from her terrible thoughts and that mind-numbing fear that Ally could be hurt. If she was awake now, she would definitely be scared out of her wits. Tyler refused to allow that other dark thought that flittered at the edge of her mind, the one that wanted to say that she could be dead already. She refused to give thought to it knowing that that way lay madness.

Instead, she had to think. Their spell must not have worked or she would have experienced something by now. The next step was simple.

She had to create another spell.

She didn't care how many spells she had to do until she found one that actually worked, Tyler was determined to work all night at it. There was only one problem.

Tyler tried to stifle a yawn, but it burst out of her, anyway.

Her neck ached with weariness and she could feel her eyes wanting to close. Exhaustion overwhelmed her — she knew she was only moments away from giving in to its call, but every second that Ally was gone, was another where she could be drawing closer to her death. Tyler couldn't afford to rest, much less sleep. She had to keep going to find her sister.

Ally was relying on her.

Getting up quietly so as not to wake the others, Tyler crossed over to the sink and poured herself a big glass of water. She'd made her energy potion so many times before that it was second nature by now. Focusing on the water in the glass, she let her magic do its thing. The water bubbled as a mist appeared over it.

As easily as brewing up a pot of coffee — and maybe even faster than that — Tyler had made another energy potion. Lifting the glass to her lips, she drank it all down, hoping that she wouldn't experience the heart palpitations that had recently become a side effect.

When she felt her body near buzzing with energy, she got down to work. She would spend the night working on the right spell.

Even if it killed her.

Marley woke to feel the sun on her face and a massive crick in her neck.

Yawning, she stretched only for her back to ache. Immediately, the shocking events of the previous night flooded into her brain. Abruptly awake, she forced herself up to see Cassie across from her, already up — though she was still in yesterday's clothes — nursing a cup of coffee. Eve sat beside her on the table, also drinking a cup like her life depended on it. It seemed Eve wasn't a morning person.

Her eyes moved across the room to her bed, expecting Tyler to be in it, but the bed was still made; Tyler hadn't slept in it at all. Frowning, Marley wondered where she could be when Tyler came out of the bathroom, surprisingly wired though dark circles ringed her eyes.

"Good, you're up," Tyler began briskly. She went to the table and unfolded a brochure that sat on the wooden surface. "While you were all sleeping last night, I spent some time going over this map. I've marked all the areas known to have a high crime rate. If we split up, we can cover more ground."

Marley blinked at her, barely able to comprehend the words coming out of her mouth. She was saved from answering by Eve, who pretty much summed up what she was thinking.

"While I'm sure that you have given this much thought, I have some concerns with what you are suggesting," Eve said gently with kid gloves.

"Oh, I know what you're thinking. Believe me, I've gone through every objection that you might have myself, but I've been working on this the whole night and I know it will work," Tyler answered without missing a beat.

"How do you know?" Cassie asked, hoping that she didn't sound unsupportive at all. It just seemed a little unlikely particularly when she considered all that Tyler had gone through in the last twenty-four hours.

"Because after our first spell didn't work, I cast several others," Tyler answered as if it was the most natural thing in the world for her to have done.

Marley's eyes flared open in alarm as Cassie tried to stifle her gasp. Eve opened her mouth to speak, but it wasn't her voice that Marley heard first…

"You did what?! On your own?"

Marley sighed inwardly, knowing that Christian now stood somewhere behind her as he so typically liked to do. She turned to see him looking every inch as incredulous as she expected.

"What happened to coughing in lieu of knocking?" she asked, hoping that by lightening up the mood, what followed wouldn't be as bad as she anticipated it being.

"I was coughing! In fact, I almost coughed up a lung but apparently, you couldn't hear me." He looked as outraged as he sounded. To Tyler, he said, "What on Earth would possess you to try spell casting on your own?"

Marley repeated him as Tyler stared at her, concerned.

"Is he saying that casting spells is dangerous?"

"Of course it is!" Christian answered. "It requires so much mental concentration and that's even when you're skilled. With the four of you together, the magic grounds you, but on your own if your head is in the wrong place, the spell can go really wrong."

"It was a long night," Marley began by way of explanation.

"Then you'd better explain to me why that was," Christian replied, not bothering to hide his aggrieved tone.

Marley inclined her head at the bathroom, not wanting to repeat everything with Tyler there. "Can you girls hold the conversation until I get back? I need to brief Christian."

She went into the bathroom, Christian storming in behind her. Closing the door behind her, she quickly gave him the low-down. By the time they emerged from the bathroom, Christian was as wretched as the rest of them. Moving to Tyler, he looked as if he wanted to say something to her, but even though his mouth opened, then closed several times, nothing came out of it.

Taking pity on him, Marley spoke in his stead. "Christian says he's really sorry, and that if there's anything he can do, he will."

They both nodded their thanks to her and for a moment at least, Marley was glad to have been able to do something right.

"Although this doesn't detract from the fact that you did a dangerous thing," Christian couldn't seem to resist admonishing.

He waited for Marley to repeat his words, but when she wouldn't, he shot her a withering look. "You know I'm right."

"So are you ready or do you need a minute to get dressed?" Tyler asked, as if the conversation had never stopped.

"But have any of the spells worked?" Cassie asked, hating herself for even volunteering what would sound like an objection but the whole idea seemed far-fetched, even to her.

"Not yet, but they could kick in at any moment," Tyler replied, a manic gleam in her eyes.

Marley swapped a concerned look with Eve: Tyler was on the brink of a meltdown. It wasn't only her eyes that looked wild, but her hair was a mess of tangles. There was a hot chocolate stain on her top which was already marked by the fire in the diner. She spoke way too fast, like she'd had a dozen coffees.

The crash was coming, and they had to do something about it.

They couldn't let her roam the streets like this; God knew what would happen if they did, or if she received bad news from the cops. The imaged of the wrecked diner came into her mind, reminding her of what could happen when Tyler lost control. Marley knew it was up to them to handle this.

"Give me a few moments to wake up and grab a drink. You should freshen up and grab a new change of clothes before we head out," Marley said calmly even as Eve and Cassie shot her a startled look. She gave only the smallest shake of her head in warning, but they both picked up on it. Whatever objection they were about to voice, they both held back on. Not so, Christian, however, who hadn't picked up on her subtle gesture.

"Are you seriously agreeing to this? Look at her! The girl's about to have a breakdown."

Marley heard his objections — she couldn't not hear them with him yelling into her face as he was — but kept her expression natural even as he stormed around the room, muttering about her stupidity.

A relieved smile appeared on Tyler's lips. "OK. I suppose I should change out of these. I want to make sure I don't scare Ally off when we find her."

When she left, the others huddled around her. "What

is going on?" Eve asked. Christian stopped ranting, realizing that something was up.

"Quick," Marley said. "Pour me a cup of that coffee."

Without waiting to see if they were doing as she'd instructed, Marley darted to her bed, pulling out the shoebox that contained her meds inside. She'd researched them all enough times to know what each of them was used for, and in a double dose as in the one she intended to use, it wouldn't have any harmful effects.

Wising up to her plan, Eve handed her a fresh cup of coffee as Marley crushed the two pills inside, stirring it with a spoon. "At this dosage it will just knock her out. She's exhausted and needs to sleep. It's the only thing I could think of," she explained.

"Good idea," Eve agreed.

"Thank God, I thought for a moment that we were really going to humor her suggestion," Cassie said.

Only Christian had the decency to look embarrassed at having gotten Marley so wrong.

"Oh," Christian mumbled.

"I'll take that as an apology," Marley shot *him* a look this time, as she set the cup onto the table and went about her business until Tyler returned, looking much the same although she had changed into a new top and jeans, though she clearly hadn't bothered to run a brush through her hair.

"Here," Eve motioned to the drink they had prepared for her.

Tyler shrugged it off with a wave of her hand. "I don't need it. I feel wired enough."

But Eve picked it up and offered the cup to her. "I know how keen you are to get out there, but you still need sustenance, Tyler. You're not a robot. Drink this, and we'll grab some pastries or something while we're out."

Eve fought to sound natural, nervous at sounding too forceful in case Tyler picked up on it. Tyler didn't move, and for a moment, it wasn't clear what she was thinking.

Cassie found herself wringing her hands when Tyler suddenly snatched the cup from her.

"You're obviously not letting me out of here until I drink this. Fine. But like I said, I am good to go."

She gulped down the coffee which had grown lukewarm in the wait for her return. It didn't take long for the drugs to kick in. Just moments later, Tyler was curled up on Marley's bed, out cold to the world.

"I actually did not think that would work. She must be more frazzled than even I realised," Christian commented, staring down at her prone body.

"You and me, both," Marley replied.

Looking at their tired faces, Christian felt like a jerk for what he was about to say. It seemed that all he did was make demands of them, all while he stood around, unable to do a thing to help while they risked their lives trying to stop whatever it was Michael had planned.

"I know it's been a rough night, and you all want to be here for Tyler, but we don't have that kind of luxury. Michael is growing closer to breaking all the seals, and with Tyler out of commission, I can't have the rest of you just waiting around. You've got to find a way to stop him," Christian said, his eyes almost flashing with regret at even asking this of them.

"But what are we supposed to do?" Eve asked, after Marley had reiterated his words. "Our spells don't seem to be working very well, and we've gone over that list we printed out at Guardian HQ several times now but nothing more has come of it."

"Isn't there anyone else who can help us?" Cassie asked as a thought came to Marley.

"We can go back to Juju to speak with Helena. She seems to know a lot, and she's right in the middle of the whole supernatural community. Maybe there's more we can get out of her if we ask the right questions," Marley said giving them a meaningful look.

"OK," Eve agreed, "but what about Tyler? We can't leave her alone."

Marley stared down at her, thinking fast. "Christian can stay with her. If she wakes up, he can let me know and we'll come right back."

"Wait, I'm being benched?" Christian asked, looking unhappy.

"It's not like there's anything else you can do," Marley answered without thinking.

Christian felt like she'd kicked him in the nuts. Although he knew she hadn't meant anything by it, it hurt to know that was what she thought of him — even if it was true.

He watched the girls troop out of the room, then sat down, folding his arms across his chest as he stared longingly at the large plasma television.

"God, what I wouldn't do for a way to work the television right now."

ONE HUNDRED TWENTY-FIVE

Helena looked up from her tablet as the girls filed into the magic shop, a curious gleam in her eyes.

"If it isn't the Fantastic Four… minus the one with the good haircut. Back with more demands?" she asked, arching one perfectly painted black brow.

"I know we came off badly the first time we met," Marley by way of an opening, choosing to ignore the slight. "But Eve said you helped her recently. We were hoping you'd give us a bit more of your time."

"Especially as it's not actually for us exactly, we're trying to help someone else," Cassie interjected quickly. It was hard not to hear how genuine she was not with her voice being as earnest as it was, but it seemed Helena wouldn't be swayed.

"And what, you want a prize for that?" Helena asked, not at all impressed.

Eve stepped forward, hoping that Helena would give them a break. "We've had a bit of a rough time lately so it would be great if you could just hear us out without the cutting remarks."

Rather than be insulted by Eve's direct approach, Helena's eyes filled with admiration. "A girl who doesn't beat about the bush — I knew there was a reason I liked you."

She waved her hand grandly, apparently granting her consent. "You may continue," she said.

"Do you know who might have uprooted that Elm tree the other day?" Eve asked.

"No idea," Helena replied unhelpfully though her expression had taken on a sudden interest at the turn of the conversation. "I suspect they did it so they could leech the black magic from it though."

She said it so easily that it had obviously been a hot topic of conversation around here for days. Marley looked at her, surprised by the revelation. "You knew about that?"

"Honey, most supernaturals know about it. We just don't have the kind of skill it would take to do such a thing or that magic juju would have been long taken, believe me, I've tried."

Her eyes darkened with something akin to respect. "That tree has sat for centuries with all that power that no one could touch. Whoever has taken it now, must have skills beyond the norm to have sucked every ounce of magic out of that tree."

"How do you know it's all gone? Maybe there's some left..." Cassie began hopefully only for Helena to cut her off with a look.

"That tree is fried. By the time I got there — and I got there fast, let me tell you — there wasn't anything left of its magic. The only thing that tree is good for now is firewood."

Listening to Helena, an uncomfortable thought occurred to Marley. "But if the tree is a source of black magic why would you want it?"

Helena's eyes slid over from Eve pinning her with their ire. "White, black, I don't discriminate. It's how I've stayed in business so long."

Marley shared a look with the others, not sure how she felt about this bit of information.

"So the only source of great magic is gone," Cassie said, chewing on the corner of her lip.

"That's not what I said, is it, Red? I said all the power from the tree is gone..." Helena replied.

"There are other sources of black magic?" Eve gasped.

"Magic is everywhere if you know where to look," Helena said unhelpfully.

It was Cassie who finally understood what the woman was hinting at. Opening her bag, she looked her in the eyes. "How's one hundred for the information we want?"

Marley snapped her head round to her. "You don't have to pay her, Cass..." she began.

"She's not going to give us anything unless she can benefit from it, right?" she asked Helena as the witch's lips turned up into a satisfied smile.

"At least Red's getting how it works around here," Helena answered, staring at her intensely until Cassie felt uncomfortable.

What was the woman looking at?

"I've already helped you out twice before, time to reward Helena with a little thanks."

Eyeing up the brand of Cassie's purse, Helena's smile grew wider. "But if you can afford Gucci — and at that big size of a bag — you can afford to pay more. Three hundred."

"That's ridiculous," Eve burst out, outraged but Cassie was already forking over the bills.

"Just tell us what you know," she said to the older woman in a resigned voice.

Folding the notes, Helena slid them into the cash register beside her. "In addition to the tree, there are two other sources of black magic that I'm aware of. You might have heard of the highway robber, James Allen? His exploits are detailed in a memoir of all the people he robbed and killed throughout his thirty-plus year crime span...

but the thing that makes the book special is that it is bound in his own skin."

The girls recoiled from this information as Helena enjoyed watching their reactions.

"The other source is the actual stocking The Boston Strangler used to kill his thirteen female victims," she finished.

"Where are they?" Marley asked.

"Oh, that's next level kind of information," Helena replied archly.

"Three hundred bucks doesn't even buy us the locations?" Eve asked not bothering to hide how incredulous she was.

"Careful child," Helena warned, her voice deceptively soft though it carried a definite edge to it. "You are at risk of sounding ungrateful again..."

Taking out her phone, Eve typed into it then read the information she had found there. "Look, Google says where they are! They're both in private collections, held under lock and key. If we search a little harder I bet we can find them ourselves." She flashed a triumphant smile at Helena, but the older woman sighed as if she were dealing with a young, ignorant child.

"You really think it would be that easy to find them? Those are fakes. The real ones are hidden away." She trailed off, letting her meaning sink in.

Sighing, Cassie took out the rest of the bills from her purse and gave them to her. "Here, that's all I've got. Where are they?"

Taking the money, Helena smiled. "The memoir is in the Athenaeum, locked in a private room somewhere, but the stocking is hidden in The Castle downtown."

"The Castle?" Cassie asked, her brow knotted in confusion.

"It's a lowly hole-in-the-wall bar. God knows, who put it there."

"But why a bar where anyone can just walk in and get it?" Marley wanted to know. It didn't seem very logical.

Helena shrugged her shoulders. "Who knows, but you're mistaken about one thing. If it were both easy to find and retrieve, it would have been done so already."

Questions ran through Marley's mind but she didn't want to air them in front of Helena. "I think that's all for now."

"Wait, I have one last question," Cassie piped up. "Do you know any spells that we can use to locate a missing person?" The question brought Helena up short.

"Someone is missing? Who?" Helena asked.

"Someone close to us," Cassie added. It seemed likely that they couldn't really trust her.

"The one with the good hair?" Helena asked again, hoping for more information.

"No… someone else," Marley answered cagily.

"Unfortunately, I don't have anything like that in my arsenal, c'est la vie," Helena responded in her native French.

Knowing that they weren't going to get any more from her, Marley nodded. "Thanks for your help."

As they made they way to the exit, Helena called out to Cassie. "By the way, I like what you've done to yourself, Red." She winked at Cassie, gesturing at Cassie's face causing Cassie to look like a deer caught in the headlights.

"What is she talking about?" Eve asked.

"Nothing, probably my new makeup regime, I'm using some new mineral-based cosmetics," Cassie mumbled, hurrying out of the store.

Moments later they filed out of the shop watching as the glamor that covered the shop reverted it back to its non-supernatural disguise of an antique coin shop.

"How long will those pills knock Tyler out for?" Eve asked Marley, her mind ticking over with a plan.

"At least four hours, if not half the day. Maybe even longer given that she hasn't slept since the day before, why?" Marley asked, feeling apprehensive.

"If Michael has Ally, God knows what he's doing to her. If we're lucky, he's just using her to get to Tyler, in which case, it's working. But we can't afford to let him have those two items too, he's already so far ahead of us in the search for the seals," Eve said.

"He's more than ahead of us, we don't actually have any clue right now where the last two are," Cassie clarified somewhat unhelpfully.

"I think we need to get those artifacts before he can," Eve finished.

"Now?" Cassie asked, her eyes wide. "Without Tyler?"

Eve took out her phone, typing quickly into it. "We're not far from The Castle. We should at least try. If we don't get it, we can come back later with Tyler."

"I don't know…" Marley responded hesitantly.

"Look, I didn't want to say this earlier, but it needs to be said. It seems likely that Michael has taken Ally and if he has, who's to say that our loved ones are safe? I'm not willing to stand around waiting for him to go after Si. Do you want him to go after your dad? What about you, Cass? What if he goes after your parents?"

Eve paused to take a breath before continuing. "So if we can get these black magic artifacts before he does and stop him from growing even more powerful, then isn't that what we need to do?" Fire flashed from her eyes.

Cassie answered before Marley had a chance to. "I think Eve's right."

"But we have no idea of how to actually find it since it's hidden. We don't know what it might do to us if we touch it. There are too many variables," Marley protested, hoping they would see sense.

"So ask Christian," Eve said. "See what he knows." Cassie nodded in agreement. Backed into a corner, seeing no way out, Marley focused on summoning Christian who appeared in a burst of light, looking suddenly panicked.

"What happened? Has something gone wrong? It's only been a little while," he demanded, feeling that sick nervous feeling that had come to be all too frequent whenever he was abruptly summoned by Marley like this.

"No, no, we just had a question for you," she said.

Marley filled him in with what they had learned from Helena, then translated for him. "Artifacts and objects containing black magic or evil energy won't hurt you just by being close it. You'd have to be trying to use its magic for it to have an actual affect on you. Most likely you'll just end up feeling sick if you come into proximity with it as you might be able to pick up any negative energy that has leeched into it."

Cassie gasped as a memory crossed her mind. "Like that time with the tree root? Remember how Tyler could feel all those bad things from it?"

"So Tyler could probably sense them… but she's out cold…" Eve hated to bring up the obvious.

"Should we cast another spell, one to make us as sensitive to black magic as she is?" Cassie put the thought out there.

"While I'm not comfortable with the idea of you doing this, I also don't have anything better to suggest," Christian supplied, wishing as always that he could be more useful.

"What part are you not happy with, the casting the spell part or the going to find the artifact part?" Marley didn't know why she was asking since she probably wasn't going to like his answer.

"Both," Christian said, cementing her suspicions. "But maybe Michael won't be expecting this. It'd be great if we were one step ahead of him for once."

"So we're doing this?" Eve asked for clarification.

They looked at Marley, waiting for her reply. "I guess. But just so you know, I think this is a bad idea."

ONE HUNDRED TWENTY-SIX

The darkness was all around, swallowing her in its sea of blackness.

She tried to move forward, but it felt as if she was swimming in mud with heavy weights strapped to her ankles. Every movement required a Herculean strength that she just didn't have. In the black space that span above her like a whirlwind, lights blinked on and off spotlighting the way ahead while a voice sobbed eerily from the outer reaches of her mind.

A female voice.

A young and vulnerable voice whose fear and misery was palpable.

It was a voice that Tyler instinctively knew she should recognize, but in this muddled, dark world which she was desperate to escape, it was next to impossible to place.

She waded forward, fighting against the thick air that pushed her back, wondering how nothingness could do that to her when the sobs came again.

Closer this time, from behind her shoulder.

Tyler whirled around to see a faint white outline of a

figure, but where the person should be, there was only more of that wispy nothingness. Tentatively, she reached out to touch the figure but as soon as her fingers made contact with the cool mist it vanished only to reappear some distance away from her.

Tyler pushed toward the figure needing to stop its misery, but when she finally got close to it, the figure turned into a bright ball of light before vanishing completely.

A scream of frustration burst out of her lips.

Turning, she continued wading through this dark nightmare, searching desperately for that bodiless voice.

Tyler tossed and turned in her sleep.

Having answered the girl's questions, Christian returned to Tyler's side only to find her whimpering from whatever nightmare was bothering her.

Before Marley had suddenly summoned him, Christian had been trying to touch the remote control. He'd tried to remember exactly what it was that he had been thinking, how he had been feeling when he had made contact with that pizza box the night of Marley's attack, but try as he might, his fingers kept going through it.

While being able to watch the television to pass the time was something he'd like to achieve at some point in this afterlife, it wasn't actually his true goal. With everything that was happening, it was becoming more and more apparent to him that he needed to do more than be a mentor to the girls.

Hearing that Ally had been kidnapped on his watch had damn near killed him (again). Of all the girls, Christian had considered Tyler the most stable. Despite the recent trauma of losing her parents and being torn from her sister, *and then* discovering that she was broke, Tyler had started college, gotten herself a job, and slowly worked at bettering herself so that she could be with her sister.

Though Christian wasn't that expressive a person, he had been deeply impressed by all that she had taken on.

So seeing her destroyed like this… it hurt.

And now, he had just sent the girls off on another potentially dangerous mission. He was a blind man leading a flock of even blinder sheep.

He wasn't sure why it was now that he was beginning to see how fragile life truly was, but all those life-affirming messages he had seen Eric pin around his workstation flashed into his mind, Eric's favorite in particular:

Courage is not the absence of fear, but the ability to act in the face of fear.

Eric had quoted it so much that Christian had threatened to have it printed on a T-shirt that he'd force him to wear, except Eric had seemed thrilled by the prospect which kind of took all the fun out of it.

Thinking of Eric, a sharp pain rose in his chest.

Eric would know what to do. He was the wise one, not me.

Refusing to wallow in that space, knowing that the girls needed him now more than ever, Christian forced himself to snap out of it.

Staring down at her troubled face, his own concerns fought for space in his mind. There was Michael, the Seals, Ally's kidnapping, and his own physical challenges…

And then there was Marley.

He wasn't sure what was happening, but she had gotten under his skin in a most irritating way. Initially, he had thought it was just the way she always seemed to have a smart comment to shoot back at him that he found annoying. But lately, no matter if she were just commenting about the weather, everything that came out of her mouth got a rise out of him.

She bothered him almost to distraction.

He found her unpredictable and that worried him even more, particularly when they had to work as a tight team. More than how she affected him, though, he was beginning to think that his unnatural reactions might actually be a symptom of his being a ghost for too long. Hadn't they already seen how the longer a spirit had been away from his body, the more feral it became?

Was this what Christian had to look forward to?

Was it already happening?

He hoped to God it wasn't.

ONE HUNDRED TWENTY-SEVEN

The gray-bricked building seemed like any other in this part of town.

The girls arrived at a bar that seemed like it had seen better days. Nestled against its newer and flashier neighbors with their floor-to-ceiling windows, contrarily, the grime on the glass at The Castle made it difficult to see inside from the sidewalk.

Then again, maybe that was part of its charm.

After summoning Christian, they had worked together on casting a spell. Much like the two times they had attempted one previously, they found something tangible to base the spell on — they used a strand of Tyler's hair that Cassie had found on her hairbrush from the night they had gotten ready for the party at Tonic. It felt so incredibly long ago now — like months had passed — though the reality was this was only their third weekend together. Holding hands, they'd focused on the outcome they wanted until something had sparked between them, a fire inside their hearts.

Pushing open the door, they walked inside.

They were hit by the darkness first.

Light struggled to come in through the windows but it was a losing affair and the decor didn't help. Everywhere they looked, dark furniture was paired with even darker curtains.

It was enough to make a girl's skin crawl.

Laughter sounded from across the room where a group of guys sat nursing mugs of beer — and not their first by the looks of things. Empty glasses formed a small mountain on the table before them.

There were six of them, all looked to be in their mid-twenties. One guy wore a shirt with the old BU logo on it. Marley knew the college had revamped their branding in the last few years so he must have gotten it before the new facelift.

There was a scattering of other tables but most were empty that they could see. There was one solitary figure, half-hidden in one of the shadowed covered corners. He sat, still as a statue and could have been asleep for all they could see of him.

Cassie stepped closer to Eve until her shoulder touched hers but Eve didn't move away. Though she would never admit it, the physical contact provided comfort that she welcomed.

They moved to the end of bar away from the lone female bartender who worked with a bored expression. She wiped down the counter with a cloth, staring into her phone, not paying them one iota of attention — yet. Marley whispered to Eve and Cassie. "You know we're going to get thrown out of here in a minute for being underage?"

"Relax," Eve shot back. "I have a fake ID."

"You do?" Cassie gasped, trying but failing to keep the shock off her face.

"I got it when I used to hang out with those other girls. They gave them out to anyone who joined their crew along with a gym membership."

Marley couldn't stop the hint of jealousy that came

over her. "I want a free gym membership."

"What'll you girls wanna drink?" The bartender asked in a bored drawl having finally come their way.

"Just three cokes, thanks. Too early for anything heavy," Eve replied smoothly.

"Ha," their bartender said. "Try telling them that," she gestured at the group of guys.

"This doesn't look like their first time," Marley commented.

"It's not. They're in here every day like clockwork. Same with that guy," she nodded in the direction of the lone drinker who was now talking quietly into his cell.

"Wow, must be nice not to have a job," Eve said.

"Yeah, wish I knew how that felt," their bartender said, disappearing off to get their drinks. They fell silent as they casually scanned the room, looking for anywhere the stocking might be. When their drinks were set down before them, and the bartender went back to her corner of the room, Marley thought it safe to talk again. "I've got nothing."

"Me neither," Cassie replied.

"We need to search the place, but we've got to look natural while doing it. I'll start," Marley suggested, as she headed in the direction of the restroom walking as slowly as she could without drawing attention to herself. She returned moments later, shaking her head.

Sitting with the girls, they sipped their drinks as Cassie went next, moving in the opposite direction as she pretended to study a wall of black and white photographs that had been displayed so long the edges were turning yellow with age.

Taking a creative route back to them, Cassie managed to cover most of the room that Marley hadn't been able to reach, only she too returned empty-handed, passing their bartender on her way back as the other girl disappeared to the restroom.

"It's right here, we just have to find it," Marley said,

so frustrated that she wasn't paying attention to her drink which slipped out of her hand, spilling over the bartop.

"Wow, what is it with you and throwing drinks around?" Cassie commented as Marley immediately searched for something to mop up the mess. Seeing the dish towel behind the bar, Marley leaned over to grab it…

When a wave of nausea turned her stomach.

She froze. "Guys, I feel it! It's somewhere behind the bar!"

Eve nudged Cassie with her elbow. "Do your thing, go!"

"What?" Cassie asked, startled.

"Become the bartender, search the bar! Do it quickly before she comes back. I'll buy you some time," Eve said, her eyes turning dark with concentration. "Get ready, Cass," she warned as the air became heavy with the weight of magic and the sound of scratching came from the direction of the restroom.

"What did you do?" Cassie asked.

"I asked a few of my four-legged friends for help. They'll keep her entertained for a little while but you need to hurry."

Calling up the bartenders face, Cassie morphed her features into the other girl. Moving to the back of the bar, Cassie walked along it, but somewhere around the middle, her stomach did a flip flop. Scanning the area quickly, she took in the bottles, cash register and mountain of glasses, leaning toward each thing, but it was when she came within inches of a painting that Cassie could feel her stomach churn.

The oil painting was small, around 8x10 inches and depicted a Civil Rights rally. Testing her reaction to it, Cassie brushed her fingers along the edge of the painting and immediately felt a wave of evil so strong that it made her gasp.

The stocking was in this painting, she knew it without a doubt.

Gritting her teeth, she took hold of it, lifting it off of its hook. Half-expecting to see something stuck to the back of it, Cassie felt a surge of disappointment when she couldn't see anything even as the waves of negative energy ran up her arm and into her body. She hurried to the exit wanting to get out of there as quickly as she could so she could set the painting down and not have to touch it anymore, but a few steps from freedom, her way was blocked.

It was the lone drinker they had noticed earlier.

Now that he was much closer to her, Cassie could see the sharp fangs and reptilian eyes that made up part of his face.

"*Demon,*" she gasped, shaken to the core.

He blinked at her, eyes flicking to Eve and Marley coming up behind Cassie quickly.

"I can't let you leave," he warned them, his voice sounding strangely alien.

"You're not going to stop us," Eve shot back dangerously when the door opened behind him…

As Fink and Pike entered.

Recognizing them from the night they attacked her in the alley behind Shaken & Stirred, Eve stopped dead. "More demons!" she hissed, grabbing at Marley and Cassie's shirt, pulling them back. "Those are the two who attacked me before!"

"Well, this is awkward," Pike finally said.

Fink had turned his gaze to the painting in Cassie's hands, who in the shock of the moment, had reverted back to her normal face.

"So the stocking's in the painting?" he said. "What a clever little girl you are for finding it when so many have looked but failed." His eyes pierced into her with their blackness. Cassie turned away from them only to see the other demon's reptilian eyes blink at her. She took a step back, fear racing down her spine.

"I don't know what you're talking about," she managed to stammer as she clutched the painting to her chest.

"If it's nothing then I'm sure you won't mind showing it to us," Fink said deceptively softly. Though he wasn't that much bigger than them, he moved in a manner that belied his physical prowess.

"Get away from us," Eve warned, her eyes flashing daggers at them.

"What are you going to do? Your rats cannot get in, and it looks to me like the most powerful of you isn't even here. So who's going to stop us?" Fink replied looking like he couldn't wait to tango.

"Hey, are these guys bothering you?" a voice called over to them.

It was the six guys who had been drinking in the corner. They lurched onto their feet and approached. Even from where she stood Marley could smell the alcohol on them. Knowing they had no idea what they were getting into, she felt a flash of fear. She didn't want these guys to get hurt.

"It's OK," she said at the same time when the smaller of the two demons, the one with the hunchback turned his focus to the group of guys.

"Why? It's not like you punks are gonna do anything about it?" Pike leered at them.

The guys looked at each other in disbelief. Were they really challenging them? The guy with the BU shirt stepped forward, a grim smile on his lips.

"Just let the girls leave and we'll pretend this never happened."

Pike looked at Fink then back at them, both bursting into laughter.

It was the wrong thing to do.

Fueled by round after round of alcohol, the BU guy swung a fist at Pike, catching him on the side of his head. Fink gave an almost imperceptive nod at Pike and the demon behind them.

And then all hell broke loose.

ONE HUNDRED TWENTY-EIGHT

The hunchback guy flew at the group of guys. Fists went flying, chairs and tables hurling past as they grabbed whatever they could as weapons.

The girls backed up quickly. Marley searched frantically for another way out as her eyes alighted on a green exit sign past the restrooms. "Over there," she pointed. They rushed towards it only for the demon who seemed to be in charge, the one who had spoken to them, blocked their way.

He sneered, flashing teeth with jagged edges on them as he plowed toward them.

Cassie screamed, ducking behind a table with the painting as Eve tried frantically to summon the rats that she knew were in the restroom to help out here. She could feel her mind reaching out to them when two arms tightened around her in an iron embrace.

And immediately the memory of another time when she had been restrained like this sent her body shaking with fear.

Although Eve knew logically that this wasn't that time, her mind shut down, and it was all she could do not to freak out. Her breath came out in short, sharp bursts as her heart raced. Crippled by the panic attack that she knew was coming, it was all Eve could do to stay upright.

Marley glanced her way, wondering what the hold up was. She had felt the magic current that always came when one of them were summoning their powers, so why wasn't the help coming? When she took in Eve's reaction, though, Marley could feel her own stomach plummet. Eve was in no position to help and with Cassie doing her best to hold on to the painting, her hands were tied even if she could help.

She was on her own.

The remaining demon's eyes narrowed into slits as he flew for her, but Marley had anticipated the move, having read his body language and side-stepped out of his way. He went charging into a table instead. Quickly, before she could talk herself out of it, Marley rushed up behind him, hooking her right arm around his neck. Stepping in close, using her body for leverage, she linked her hands together, squeezing her arm as tight as she could. The demon's head snapped back as he felt the pressure against his throat. Surprised by her attack, he hadn't been prepared for it and now he was paying the price of that.

His hands reached up to grab Marley's head, but she twisted out of his way each time. Struggling to breathe, he suddenly used all of his weight to force them back. They staggered back across the wooden floor until Marley felt her back slamming into a wall. The breath was knocked out of her and she could feel the shock wave of pain rattle through her bones as she dropped.

Thinking that she was down for the count, the demon turned his attention to Cassie. Cassie's eyes were still on Eve and the demon who had her locked in his steel embrace — she had no idea that Marley's guy was coming for her.

"Cassie, look out!" she screamed, jumping to rush him with her arms outstretched. Marley wasn't sure what she intended to do, she only knew she had to stop him from hurting Cassie.

Suddenly, she felt her hands sink *into* his back.

His organs slid into her hands as she found herself instinctively squeezing them.

The demon froze in his tracks, the blood draining from his face. There was nothing he could do but stand there as Marley squeezed the life out of him.

When the demon's body went slack, falling to the floor in a heap, Marley knew his life was gone.

She had killed him.

She had killed again using the same power she had used to kill Christian.

Suddenly, his body began to steam and bubble as it started to *melt* until all that was left of him was a puddle of green goo.

Reeling, she staggered onto her feet in time to see the ex-BU guy's beating the hunchback demon back, though it took all six of them to fight him. The demon might have been small, but he was cleverly several times stronger than the average man.

"I've called the cops," a female voice yelled out from across the room. "They're on their way right now."

Suddenly, everyone stopped. It was the bartender who had returned from the restroom to see the chaos in the room. She held her phone in her hand to show that she had made good on her promise.

Knowing they couldn't risk getting more witnesses involved — especially the police — Fink who had been keeping Eve restrained released her. She stumbled into Cassie almost knocking them both over..

"Go. Now," Fink commanded Pike as the two suddenly bolted for the door.

The six ex-college guys hesitated for only a second. "Oh no, you don't!" One yelled, tearing after them.

"You're going to face the cops," another promised as all six charged out of the bar for them.

With the danger gone, the girls shot each other a look. Eve and Marley gave Cassie cover as she slid the painting into her bag and slipped out of there. Once she was outside, they quickly followed suit leaving the bartender staring at the green slime on the floor.

"What is this now? I don't get paid enough for this crap," they heard her say as they ran away.

Jumping at every noise and shadow, the girls ran until they were out of breath.

"I can't," Cassie gasped, the most unfit of the trio. "I need to stop."

Marley had already taken her bag from her, but the sick feeling it caused was almost too much to bear. Seeing her reaction, Eve took it from her. Marley shot her a grateful look.

"What if those demons are coming back for us?" Cassie asked the thought that was on all their minds.

"Let's hope those boys chased them far away," Marley answered, hoping that she was right.

"Still, we should get that painting to a safe place, once we've checked to see if the stocking is actually there," Eve suggested.

"Well, I for one don't feel safe standing out here," Cassie said, wrapping her thin arms around herself.

They had arrived on a street full of shops. Marley stared around them, trying to find something of use when her eyes alighted on a busy dessert place. "The place is packed, I doubt they would follow us in there with all those people around."

Moments later, they sat in a booth, with their orders of cheesecakes. As soon as their waitress left, Eve opened the bag and held the painting in her lap beneath the table, out of sight from anyone who might be looking their way.

Marley reached over and ran her fingers along the surface of the oil painting to see if she could find anything special about it, but it wasn't until Eve turned it over that her fingers felt a bump beneath the surface.

"There's something here, under the backing," she said feeling a surge of excitement. Reaching into the pocket of her jeans, she took out a folding knife. At Eve's questioning look, Marley explained, "I've taken to carrying one around. Seems sensible to…"

Running the knife under the canvas backing, she peeled it away to reveal a hardback envelope, inside which… was a single tan stocking. Even if she couldn't see the black cloud of magic hovering above it, the waves of evil coming off of it would be impossible to miss.

"So that's it," Cassie said, eyeing the stocking, putting as much distance as she could between them.

"I guess," Marley answered, wishing she could also put the thing as far away from her as possible. Now that they actually had it, she found she didn't want it at all.

"Where are we going to keep it?" Eve asked. "If Michael's demons are looking for this, the dorm is the first place they'll go to next, followed by my house if they have any sense."

"I don't think either of those are viable," Marley agreed. "We need somewhere we can get to but isn't linked to us."

"Like Guardian HQ?" suggested Cassie.

"But it's all the way across town and pretty far from us. I think I'd feel better if it was closer, though obviously not too close," Marley mused out loud.

"What about your dad's office?" Eve asked. "Not many people know he's your dad right? And it's still on campus so about as close to us as it can get."

"I guess," Marley answered, not particularly thrilled with the idea of leaving a black magic artifact in such proximity to him. "He's probably there now though, he works there on the weekend."

"You'll need to get him out, so we can sneak it in," Eve suggested.

"Any ideas how?" Cassie asked.

"Yeah," Marley answered glumly wishing that she didn't. "The man can't resist a good burger."

ONE HUNDRED TWENTY-NINE

Getting Paul out of his office was a relatively easy matter.

As Marley had anticipated, all it had taken was a quick fly-by visit to his office where he had been marking his class's assignments and a bribe of a hot new burger joint that Marley knew he'd been wanting to try. When they had left, Marley tried her best to distract him, hoping that he would forget to lock the door, but unfortunately — and as she should have known — that wasn't the kind of luck she had.

How were the girls going to get inside without actually breaking in?

A little later they had arrived outside the burger place only to find it packed to the brim. Feeling panicked at the thought that her dad might just head back to his office, Marley pointed at the next nearest restaurant without even looking at it.

"Let's go there," she said.

Paul stared at her, surprised. "Really? Since when have I ever been able to get you into a Chinese place without dragging you into it?"

Marley stared at the restaurant trying to contain her dismay. Chinese? Why hadn't she paid more attention to it? Still, it would look weird if she changed her mind now. She just needed to get him inside and eating.

"It's fine," she said.

Sat inside the restaurant with her dad now, Marley fidgeted with her phone, jumpy as all hell, worried that they would send her some kind of S.O.S text that he would see.

The place though not as packed as its neighbor, was doing decent business. An Aretha Franklin classic played from hidden speakers which Marley found a blessed relief from the usual orientalized music she usually found in such restaurants. Marley's eyes slid over to Paul, who sat, looking relaxed in his chair, taking in the day's specials.

Though she wanted to enjoy this downtime, she couldn't stop picturing her hands inside that demon. She had killed again using her own bare hands.

What was this terrifying power of hers?

She had no idea how to activate it which meant she could just as easily kill someone else with it by mistake. What if next time, it wasn't a demon she killed?

A shiver went down her spine, an ice-cold dagger that pierced her to the core. Moving her hands into her lap, she hoped the numbness would go away. Her hands did not feel like they were her own.

Their waitress arrived, a woman with black hair wearing a traditional looking dress. She smiled as she waited to take their order.

"Are you ready to order?" she asked, running her eyes up and down on Paul. Apparently, she liked what she saw as she adjusted her stance to throw more of her small chest out.

"Let's see, how about the Ma Bo Tofu, Steamed Gai Lan, Salt and Pepper Squid, oh and half a roast duck,"

Paul said. Turning to Marley, he grinned. "That's me, what about you?"

She rolled her eyes knowing it was important to keep up appearances. "Tofu and squid? Can't you just get chicken like normal people?"

"I could have gone for the chicken feet, but I decided to give you a break…" he responded coyly.

"Chicken feet," Marley shuddered then felt bad for doing so in front of their waitress. "Sorry," she apologized, a blush spreading over her cheeks.

Their waitress smiled. "Don't worry, I get that all the time. Would you like some sweet and sour chicken, maybe? That's usually very popular with our customers, in case your father's dishes aren't to your taste?"

Marley gave her a grateful smile. "Yes. Thanks."

She highly doubted that she'd be able to get through the meal, but she knew that the longer it took for her to eat it, the longer the girls had, though the duplicity of the situation had her feeling even worse about herself. Knowing that her dad would know something was up from her silence, Marley searched for a conversation opener.

"So how're things? What's the latest with you?" She asked in as engaged a voice as she could muster.

Paul grinned, happy to chat about his life and work. He talked about new friends he had made on the faculty, bragged about some of his students who were already getting straight A's, and moaned about a neighbor in his apartment block who loved to play video games late into the night with his surround sound blaring. Paul complained that he had woken up a time or two thinking that he was in the middle of a war.

Listening to him talk, it almost felt like old times. Back before she had committed murder. Twice.

When their food came, Marley was forced to admit that it all looked and smelt pretty good. Paul expertly picked up a piece of the glistening roast duck with his chopsticks waving it under her nose.

"Are you sure you don't want to try this, Hon? It is so good."

But, ridiculously as stubborn as she always was in this matter, Marley shook her head. "Nope. I'll just stick to the chicken."

The mischievous look left his face and was now replaced by a sadness that she could feel. He set down his chopsticks.

"It's just food you know. And part of your culture. It wouldn't kill you to try to get to know some of it," he said, his eyes gentle despite his words.

"It's not my culture, Dad. It's Mom's and since she couldn't be bothered to have anything to do with us, I can't be bothered to deal with any of that, even if it is just food."

If her words bothered him, Paul tried to hide it. "Well, you don't know what you're missing."

They ate in silence for a while as Paul searched for a safer topic of conversation.

"Have you and girls managed to explore the city much?" Paul asked, munching on a large piece of Chinese broccoli.

Marley looked up from her bowl, setting it down onto the table. "School's been keeping me pretty busy but I've seen a few hotspots. There's a juice bar I like, but it's probably too hipster for you."

"Sounds like it. Give me fries and a shake any day, or chicken feet," he grinned. "I've been too busy to take in much of the area myself, would've liked to have seen the harbor too though. One day, when I get on top of things," he continued, scooping up a heaping spoon of the tofu dish.

Reaching for a piece of pineapple that came in her dish, Marley's hand froze, a flower of apprehension opening in her chest. "Too?" She asked, fighting to keep her voice natural. Paul hadn't noticed her reaction, however, enjoying his food.

"Just jealous you got to see the harbor already when I've been stuck to my desk. You know I love the ocean."

The flower turned into a lead weight that plummeted to the bottom of her stomach. Marley's eyes shot to Paul's face.

"I never told you I went there," Marley said quietly.

Paul slowed his chewing as his eyes rose to meet hers. Though he spoke normally, there was a wariness now in his eyes that Marley picked up on.

"Yeah, you did," Paul answered quickly. "When we spoke last."

But Marley knew that was a lie. The last time they had spoken on the phone was the morning the Elm tree had caused a city-wide gridlock. And Marley knew she hadn't gone to the harbor until the early afternoon.

So how could her dad know she had been there?

"Or maybe I've got it wrong, and it was someone else who went there. Who knows? Wait until you're my age, you'll be as confused as I am," Paul continued in his normal tone as if nothing was wrong, but inside, Marley felt the alarms shrieking inside her head.

Not only was her dad lying, but he had been spying on her.

The question was why?

Marley escaped to the restroom to clear her head and still her nerves.

In her mind, her questions competed for space. Though her dad had done a good job of pretending nothing was wrong, this latest revelation on top of everything else was one thing too many.

Staring at her pale reflection in the mirror, she tried to quell the chill in her heart. Nothing was turning out the way it was. She almost laughed out loud, thinking of how just a few weeks ago, her only concern was that she get through college without anyone learning of her mental illness — an illness, she now knew wasn't an illness at all but her magic power. Feeling the air growing cooler around her, Marley wrapped her arms around herself, noticing that there was a faint pulse of magic in the room.

Suddenly another figure appeared beside her. She gasped, jumping back before she saw those green-gold eyes she was beginning to know so well.

"Jesus! You scared me half to death!" Christian gasped, looking almost as startled as she did.

"I scared you? You're the one who just appeared!" Marley shot back.

Christian looked around, noticing his surroundings for the first time. "Wait, what the hell am I doing here, is this the ladies restroom?"

Marley's brow knotted in confusion. "You didn't want to come here?"

"No. I was with Tyler — she's still sleeping, don't worry — and then I was thinking about you and now I'm suddenly here. Hold up, is that *hand lotion*? We don't get that."

Ignoring his comment, Marley probed further. "Well, what were you thinking about me?"

Christian froze as if she had just asked a loaded question. "Nothing. Why would I have to be thinking anything about you?"

Marley stared at him as if he was losing his mind. "Because you said you were when you… just forget it," she suddenly replied, giving up. It had been too long a day already.

Christian tried to recover. "Did you get the stocking?"

"Yes. There was a small problem, but we handled it," Marley said even as the dead demon's body flashed into her mind again. She couldn't talk about it now though, not while she was in the middle of this thing with her dad. "The girls are hiding it in my dad's office."

"Smart thinking," Christian replied. "Is that why you're here?"

Marley nodded. "I'm the distraction while they do it. I should get back actually, I've been in here a while."

"Yes. Good work, glad to see it's all working. Well done," Christian said lamely looking immediately like he regretted it before he vanished, leaving Marley wondering what on earth that was all about.

Eve kept her eyes fixed firmly on her phone, pretending to be fixated with whatever it was that she found there.

She'd been waiting for Cassie's return for a while now. With every second that passed the anxiety in her stomach grew until she was at the point where she would jump at every shadow or sound that came.

And in this breezy open-ended corridor, there had been a lot.

While Marley had been talking to her dad, Cassie had discarded the painting in some nearby dumpsters. On her return, however, after Marley and Paul had taken off, giving them the distraction they needed, they had met with their first problem — Paul's office was locked. How none of them had predicted this issue? Well, that was a discussion for later.

Since neither of them had breaking-and-entering as a skill yet, Eve sent some of her insects inside to scout for a key. They had watched, fascinated yet with some unease as a row of ants had crawled beneath the door to explore inside.

Somehow, Eve's mind had connected to theirs in such a way that she could almost see what they were seeing. It was as if she had developed a hundred more pairs of eyes. While she found the sensation thrilling, Cassie had to suppress a shudder, privately thinking that the whole thing was just a bit too creepy despite how useful this new skill of Eve's might prove to be.

Unfortunately, Paul was a pretty tidy person and not the kind who left spare keys lying around. The ants had come back with nothing, so it was on to Plan B.

Glancing at the time on her phone for maybe the hundredth time, Eve chewed on the end of a black polished nail that was already bitten down so much that it was starting to hurt. Where was the girl? Surely she should be back by now?

Something moved down one end of the corridor. A black shadow of a tall figure, but as Eve's eyes shifted over to it, the shadow darted away.

A finger of unease slid down her back.

That end of the corridor had been empty only moments before so it seemed strange that someone would be skulking around only to move away at the exact moment she chose to look over. Then again, she'd been here for so long now that her eyes were likely to be playing tricks on her.

She was still wondering whether she should take a break and wait elsewhere when Paul rounded the corner.

Seeing her leaning against his office wall, he started approaching. Eve straightened up immediately, every instinct screaming at her to get out of there. She wasn't in any of his classes and he had seen her with Marley before. He would recognize her immediately, she knew.

This was bad…

Except Paul flashed Eve a cheesy Cassie-sized grin. As Eve took in the very unmanly walk that Paul seemed to have adopted, the truth sank in. That wasn't Paul at all but Cassie!

"You took your own sweet time," Eve said, relieved despite her words.

"Getting the spare key from them wasn't that hard. I just had to ask nicely, and they checked me — well, Paul — against their files, but I needed to make sure that only a few people saw me there. Can you imagine if one of them knows the real Paul? That's what took the longest time but I'm here now and I've got the key!"

Eve stepped aside giving Cassie cover while she slipped the key into the door and turned. A click sounded letting them know they were successful. Eve cast one last look down the long corridor, but seeing nothing, she followed Cassie inside.

Books and papers were neatly stacked on the desk. A selection of neutrally toned jackets hung on a metal coat-stand in the corner. Other than a few framed photographs of Marley that sat on his desk by his laptop, the only decoration came from an antique painting of a woman washing her long hair by a river.

Eve shut the door behind them as Cassie took the envelope containing the stocking out of her bag, holding it at arm's length.

"Where's a good place to hide this that he won't see?" she asked, staring around the room.

"Taped under the desk, maybe?" Eve suggested though she dismissed the idea almost immediately. "But all he has to do is drop something then when he crouches down to get it, he'll see it straight away."

"Maybe inside a vent, that's what they always do in the movies," Cassie said, looking behind a row of filing cabinets before shaking her head. "That's a bust, there are no vents in here, none that I can see, anyway."

Searching for any possible hiding place, Eve's eyes finally landed back on the painting. "Maybe we should just tape it to that painting. I mean, it sat for years undiscovered behind that other painting in the bar, seems as good a place as any?"

Not having a better suggestion, Cassie approached the painting with the envelope.

Passing her the tape dispenser off Paul's desk, Eve took a few steps back. "Tape it to the back, I'll stand over here to make sure it can't be seen from the front."

As Cassie worked at getting the envelope in the right position, Eve found herself studying the painting. She wasn't an art expert by any means but there seemed something different about this painting. The river had been recreated so well that the water seemed to glide over the smooth rocks which glinted under the sunlight. Where the light bounced off the water, Eve could almost see a shape… No, make that a symbol of some kind. Squinting her eyes, she tilted her head.

There *was* something camouflaged inside the water.

She had to force herself not to make a sound for fear of alerting Cassie. There was a symbol hidden within the painting, and it was a symbol she had seen before on the carpet of her very own room.

It was the symbol which Mary, the ghost of Marley's ancestor had painted on her floor using her eyeshadow.

While Cassie fidgeted with the painting, Eve thought back to the times Marley had seen that symbol before… it was on the first group of demons who had attacked them at the cemetery when Marley had been trying to learn how to use her power, and again on the heads of those demon hounds at the Fort.

Whenever they had seen this symbol before, it had been in relation to the demons… or as a warning from Marley's own ancestor which she had felt so strongly about, that she had come back from the dead to warn her of it.

Her heart thumped wildly in her chest but Cassie couldn't hear it, focused on securing the stocking to the painting. It was on the tip of her tongue to mention her discovery to Cassie, but something stopped her. Paul was Marley's only relative. He had single-handedly raised her, and up until recently, she had relied on him for everything.

He was in a word, her Si.

If Eve was going to mention this to anyone it had to be to Marley herself, and yet, she knew from the churning in her stomach that it might not be something she was willing to do just yet.

"I'm done," Cassie's voice cut into her thoughts. "Can you see anything?"

Eve shook her head, looking away from that symbol which now that she had seen it, seemed so clear.

"Let's get out of here then. I've got to get this key back," Cassie urged, already heading towards the door.

Giving the painting one last look, Eve followed her outside.

ONE HUNDRED THIRTY-ONE

By the time Marley got back to the dorm, Cassie was already waiting for her outside their room. She had been busy volleying a round of texts on her phone but she jumped to attention at Marley's arrival.

"You didn't go inside?" Marley asked, surprised to find her standing in the corridor.

"I didn't want to wake Tyler without you," Cassie replied as a flush came over her cheeks. "I… I don't know what to say to her," she finished looking ashamed. "I'm not really any good at this sort of thing."

Marley took pity on her. "I don't think anyone ever is. How could they be?"

After their reverse heist, Si had arrived and taken Eve to the bar for his shift, which for some reason, left Marley feeling a little peeved. She had thought Eve would have wanted to know how her meal with her dad had gone, and they still had to check up on Tyler so her disappearance seemed out of character.

"It all went as planned?" Marley asked, trying to shove her annoyance aside.

"Only once we figured out how to actually get into his

office," Cassie revealed. "I managed to get the spare key from the main office. It's back with them now so hopefully, no one will be any wiser."

"Nice work," Marley replied catching some of Cassie's excitement. Of them all, she seemed to be blossoming the most. It was hard to reconcile her with that awkward girl who could barely speak to her only a few weeks ago.

Amazing what a few murders and some magic could do for a girl.

Sliding in the keycard, Marley let them into their room only to find Tyler still asleep. The bedding was twisted around her legs as if she'd been tossing in her sleep, and Marley's pillow lay on the floor a few feet away apparently having been knocked there. Even now Tyler mumbled in her sleep, twisting with agitation.

There was no sign of Christian. Thinking that he must have used up whatever magic he needed to be here, Marley shook Tyler gently awake. Tyler's eyes flicked open immediately, her senses on high alert.

"Has there been any news?" she asked, sitting up so fast that the room begin to swim.

"We haven't heard anything," Marley answered.

Staring around her, taking in the room, Tyler frowned. "Why am I in your room?"

Cassie shot Marley a look that Marley tried to ignore. "You fell asleep here. You must have been exhausted," she replied keeping her voice as neutral as possible, hoping Tyler would buy the lie.

Confusion flicked over her face before it turned into alarm. Looking at the clock and seeing the time, she gasped. "I've been out for most of the day? What if Ally needed me?"

Sensing her hysteria beginning to rise, Marley laid a hand on her arm. "Tyler, if anything urgent happened with Ally, you know we would have woken you. You were exhausted from being up all night, stressing and casting spells which, God knows how much that must have taken from you. It's OK that you needed a few hours of rest. Ally would understand."

She stared at Marley, eyes reeking of desperation. She needed to believe her, needed to know that she hadn't messed up or let her sister down in any way.

"Well, it wasn't very restful. I kept dreaming of her. I'd hear her crying or calling out my name but there was nothing I could do..." She stopped as her voice cracked and she felt the pain threatening to overwhelm again.

A buzz sounded from Cassie's bag. She jumped, shooting Tyler a look of apology as she grabbed it and read the message that landed on the home screen.

"What is it?" Tyler asked.

"Oh, nothing. Just Trip," she answered already putting the phone away.

"What does he want?" Tyler asked.

"He just said he's free if I want to do anything," Cassie finished guiltily almost wishing that she could lie about it. It didn't seem right that life was going on as normal for the rest of them when Tyler's world had stopped to a crashing halt.

Tyler managed a smile through the pain. "You and he are getting on well?"

Cassie's thin shoulders came up into a shrug even as a small, wondrous smile played on her lips. "I don't what's happening really, but yeah, we seem to like each other's company."

Climbing off Marley's bed, Tyler mentally shook herself. When she spoke again, her voice was firmer, more decisive. "You both have things to do. You should go and do them."

"I don't, actually. I'm happy to stay with you..." Marley began only for Tyler to cut her off.

"And I appreciate that I really do, but I need to stop wallowing. I'm no good to Ally that way. I need to sit and think and come up with ways to find her."

"I can help you with that," Marley tried again. She

couldn't imagine what a dark place Tyler must be in right now, and if there was anything she could do to help her, she would.

"No… I just want to be alone," Tyler said, walking to the door. "I'll be fine, I promise." Seeing the look that passed between the girls, Tyler said, "I'm not doing any more spells, but I've got a list of other things I could be doing. I'll see you both later."

Before the girls could respond, Tyler left.

M arley and Cassie stared at each other, at a loss what to do.

"Do you think she's really OK?" Cassie asked, her eyes wide with concern.

"Of course not. But maybe she needs some alone time. At least she seems better than she was this morning," Marley noted.

Another buzz sounded from inside Cassie's bag causing Marley to smile. "Go and have fun with Trip. He's obviously keen to hang out with you."

Cassie hesitated, one foot already moving to the door while the other pointed back to Marley. "Are you sure? What will you do?"

"Oh, I'll think of something. There's always course-work to catch up on," she smiled looking anything but thrilled.

"If you're sure," Cassie said, still unsure whether she should go.

Marley waved a hand at her. "If you stay, I'll only force you to help me on my assignments."

Giving her a smile, Cassie left the room closing the door behind her, but it didn't quite latch leaving the door swinging open again. Moving to over to it, Marley had her hand on the handle when Rhett, their RA suddenly passed by. Seeing her, a welcome smile spread over his face.

Not for the first time, Marley was taken aback by his smile and kind eyes that seemed to sparkle with warmth. There was a hint of stubble on his cheeks which only caused him to look even hotter than usual. And was that a *dimple*?

"Hey Marley, what're you up to?" he asked, cutting into her thoughts. Marley could feel herself blushing and dug her nails into her hands in a bid to stop being stupid.

"Oh, nothing much. I was just thinking I should probably make a dent in my work," she answered before immediately wishing that she could have sounded a little cooler. What was so wrong with washing her hair?

"Tonight?" he asked, sounding disappointed.

"Yeah… Why, what's tonight?"

"That talk I mentioned to you the other day, the TED speaker who's an expert at self-empowerment. Should be really good. I'm actually about to head there right now. You want to come with?"

He asked so naturally and so easily that Marley knew this wasn't in any way a date, in which case, there would be no expectations. Just two people going to an empowering talk together.

"Oh, I don't know…" She probably should hit the books. Then again, the thought of studying after all they had been through these last few days made her want to give up all hope. Taking a few hours to do something productive didn't seem like a bad thing.

"It's only two hours. You can still work after," Rhett said, smiling that sexy smile of his.

Which kind of cemented the deal for her.

Grabbing her bag, Marley shut the door behind her.

"What the hell. Let's go."

ONE HUNDRED THIRTY-TWO

Some twenty tabs were opened on her laptop as Tyler jumped from one internet search to another.

In one tab she had called up all the reports of missing children in the state of Massachusetts in the past year. Seeing how many there were, and what percentage of the kids were never found alive, Tyler felt her stomach twisting with anxiety.

Another tab listed the top twenty things someone should do if a child went missing. Seeing that she had only done one of them — talk to the police — Tyler felt a surge of guilt on top of her mounting concern. Other tabs contained information that she had randomly Googled, stats and figures as well as real-life reports.

The more she read, the more she felt her heart pound until she was almost suffering from those same palpitations that had sent her asking Siri for his advice.

Realizing that she hadn't checked in with Saunders or any of the cops for a while, Tyler rummaged in her bag until she found her phone but when she hit the home button, it didn't come on.

For some unfathomable reason her phone was off.

Thinking of all the possible people who might have been trying to contact her while she had lain there sleeping with her phone off, Tyler plugged it in even as she repeatedly hit her forehead, furious with herself.

What if the cops had been trying to call?

What if Ally had?

It was a few moments before the phone had enough juice to come on, but when the Apple symbol came onto the screen, Tyler saw that there *were* a bunch of missed calls and text messages. Accessing the call log, they were all from the same number.

Unfortunately, it wasn't Saunders or any of the cops as she had hoped.

The messages were all from William, her boss at Star Market grocery store.

Hitting play, William's voice came over the line. Even though she couldn't see him, just the sound of his voice was enough to make her feel a shiver of apprehension. What was it about that guy that made her feel like this?

The first message revealed that Tyler was late for her shift that day and William was not impressed. He was expecting to receive a very good reason for her tardiness when she finally decided to grace them with her presence.

The second message came another twenty minutes later as William sounded more peeved than before. Tyler was now over half an hour late though apparently, she did not feel her lateness worthy of a phone call to explain herself. He hung up after wondering about her commitment to the job.

By the third message, William had taken to texting too. She was now over an hour late and with no contact from her, William was forced to reconsider ever having taken a chance on her.

Baffled by his calls and messages, Tyler pulled up her calendar only to discover that she was scheduled to work today, but in all the madness her shift had completely slipped her mind. Knowing that she was in the wrong —

although William's messages had seemed off-kilter and he seemed to have taken her absence as strangely personal — Tyler called him back.

"Star Market, William speaking?" came his weaselly voice over the line.

Clearing her throat, Tyler spoke. "William, it's Tyler. I'm sorry for missing my shift today but I had a family emergency. I've only just picked up your seven messages." She stressed the word "seven", hoping he would pick up on it.

"Oh really," William said, not buying a word of her excuse. "What kind of emergency would necessitate a complete radio silence from your end?"

While Tyler didn't think it was any of his business, she also knew she was in the wrong. As she struggled to find the words to apologize, she heard a strange sound, a sound that was like... crying... Thinking it might be coming down the phone line, she asked, "Did you hear that?"

"Hear what?" came his annoyed voice.

"I thought I heard someone crying," Tyler finished awkwardly, knowing how strange she must sound.

"I don't know what you can and can't hear, although I am most interested in learning about this family emergency that has taken you away for all the day."

Thinking that her mind was playing tricks on her, Tyler tried to explain. "My little sister disappeared yesterday. She was... taken," even as she said the words her heart seized with pain.

Silence came down the phone.

"What do you mean, taken?" William asked, sounding not quite as weaselly now.

"She was kidnapped. Someone took her from the diner we were in yesterday. It was her birthday," Tyler added, not sure why she had revealed that information.

"I am sorry to hear that, Tyler. It seems I was mistaken about you. Why don't you take a leave of absence so you can deal with all of this, say one week? I'd love to grant more but we're short-staffed right now and if you don't return by then, I might have to find a more permanent replacement."

Finding his comment a little insensitive yet not really able to think about something like work, Tyler took what was given. "Thanks."

"I hope you find her soon. Best wishes to you both," William said. It was only when she heard the dead dial tone that Tyler realized he had hung up on her. Relieved that at least she wouldn't have to deal with him or her job, Tyler turned back to the laptop when the sound of crying came again.

This time, a small voice whispered with it.

"Tyler… where are you?"

Tyler reacted as if someone had slapped her.

It was Ally's voice!

"Keep calm… she's coming for you… she promised we'd be together…"

Came Ally's voice again sounding all around her. "Ally?!" Tyler cried out, spinning around desperate to contact her. "Can you hear me?"

But there was no response.

Only the soft sobs of her kid sister as she tried to comfort herself.

Suddenly, a strange light flittered in the middle of the room. Tyler's eyes snapped over to it as the light grew until it formed a live picture of Ally. There she sat, in the same clothes as Tyler had seen her last, huddled on the floor of a giant birdcage. Tears streaked down her face as Ally rocked herself in that way Tyler had seen her do when she had tried to comfort herself after she had received the news of their parents' passing.

And now Ally was feeling that same fear and terror again.

"Ally!" Tyler called out to her, reaching her fingers towards the vision. When her fingers touched the vision, however, it vanished. Ally was gone and so were her cries.

"No! Come back!" Tyler screamed, spinning around the room, hoping desperately that she would come back.

But she was alone.

With the absence of the vision, something had become clear. Tyler realized that one of her spells *had* worked. While she had been sleeping, she had heard Ally cry out to her…

Only she had been too stupid to piece it together.

The whole time, Tyler could have been trying to locate her sister. Instead, she had been sleeping. She felt a furious anger at herself that was only dampened by the fury she felt at that terrible knowledge the vision had granted her.

Seeing that birdcage, Tyler knew that Ally hadn't been taken by a normal person.

Ally had been taken by Michael.

ONE HUNDRED THIRTY-THREE

Saunders aimed her arm and tossed the disgusting salvia-covered rubber ball that her dog Milo loved, watching as he bolted down her fenced-in backyard to retrieve it.

Despite having a trunkful of more expensive toys, whenever she came home from a shift at work, he would greet her at the door with that ball in his mouth, tail wagging from side-to-side as his body shook with the happy anticipation of what was to come.

Rushing back to her, Milo dropped the ball by her feet, prancing back, getting ready for the next toss. Trying to ignore the feeling of her fingers slipping around the ball from its wetness, Saunders pulled back her arm only to fake the throw.

But her pooch was too used to her ways.

He barked at her, as if to say, "you can't fool me" and waited, stomach lowered close to the ground. When the ball flew out of her hand again, he took off like a rocket.

These calm little moments were what Saunders lived for.

It was only at home with Milo that they could shut out

the rest of the world and the horrors it contained. It was during these times that she could almost ignore the evil that people did.

But not today.

She sipped from a glass of red wine — nothing fancy, just something she picked up at the gas station — a pile of paperwork on the table in front of her. The sun wouldn't be setting for two more hours so she still had a bit of light to work with out here, and after being cooped up with the smell of that burning diner for the entire night and most of the day, she needed the fresh air as much as she needed the downtime with Milo.

Opening the file, she tossed the ball again a few more times before stooping down to scratch Milo's face.

"Hey Bud, I've gotta do a bit of work now, but I promise we'll play some more later, OK?" She said to him as his intelligent brown eyes looked up at her. He barked once which Saunders took as a yes, then settled by her feet to chew at a large marrow bone he had been tackling all day now. As she always did, she marveled that he seemed to understand her so well. Animals were filled with such love and the simple enjoyment of life, she wondered what it was that made man so different.

Different enough to kidnap a little girl on her own birthday.

All night she had gone through what files they could retrieve from the diner. They were lucky enough that the owner had regularly backed up their data onto an online drive though it wasn't much use in the end: the waiter who had taken the Jones' girl wasn't even an employee it seemed.

Saunders was still trying to find out how that could have happened, but it seemed that the place had a high turnover of staff, and added with the costumes and masks their servers wore, no one had thought anything more of the new waiter.

He'd kept to himself, coming in to start his "shift" several hours before the girls had arrived. He'd served other tables without issue, so Saunders wasn't clear whether this kidnapping was pre-planned or just an opportunist at work; however, those exploding candles might suggest otherwise.

She flicked through to the early results of the lab report which had proved inconclusive. As far as the experts were concerned, the candles that had set the sprinklers on didn't exist. Sure, they had conducted their tests and watched the footage, but there wasn't anything they could think of that would cause such a strange reaction.

Then there was that explosion in the diner itself which Saunders had witnessed. What could have possibly caused the place to react as it had done? There was no gas leak that they had found, nothing that would cause an explosion so big. Saunders had spent the night thinking back, but it always came back to the one thing.

Tyler Jones.

Nothing had happened until the moment she had been shown that footage after which all literal hell had blown up.

Her phone buzzed with a message about Brooks. He was still unstable. The docs were working on him as best they could, but he had sustained a terrific amount of injury. Seeing his body with those horrific wounds brought tears to her eyes.

Sensing her pain, Milo dropped his bone and padded over to her. Lifting one of his big paws, he set it onto her knee and whined. Saunders reached across to stroke him.

"Thanks, Buddy. He'll be fine, I know he will. Mom just needs to find that little girl and get her home safe."

But there was another thought on her mind, one no amount of wine would shake.

She also needed to find out why those four girls kept cropping up in her investigations…

The last few hours had passed by like a dream.

After leaving Marley, Cassie had been picked up by Trip who, it turned out, had his own driver! Cassie was surprised as she was sure she'd seen him driving around campus before until Trip revealed that he just wanted to focus on her. She couldn't actually see his driver though, as a dark partition separated them, which Cassie liked. It gave Trip and her more privacy in the car.

They went to a little Italian place for food but Cassie couldn't eat, too troubled by Ally's disappearance and her concern for Tyler. Though Trip had ordered a table full of lovely food, Cassie couldn't do more than push it around her plate. As soon as Trip picked up on her mood, he had persuaded her to talk to him. He wanted to know all of her, even her worries no matter how small they were.

With that bit of gentle persuasion, she knew she was lost.

She told about the night's events leading up to how they'd had to drug Tyler to get her to rest. It was shocking really, how Cassie found herself spilling so much information to him, but he seemed genuinely interested and such easy company. She shared her concerns, her guilt at not being able to help Tyler more. All the while, Trip listened, fully focused, seeming to almost share her pain.

They rounded the corner to EJ Halls as the familiar lights of her dorm came into view. The night had grown chillier and Cassie found herself suddenly shivering. Seeing her reaction, Trip slid out of his jacket and set it over her shoulders. Although he only touched her through the denim fabric of his jacket, his touch was electric, sending a different kind of shiver down Cassie's spine.

Opening the door Cassie stepped inside but Trip hesitated.

"I should probably go," he said looking torn.

"You don't want to come in?" Cassie asked, hating how disappointed she already felt.

"Of course I do, but you've had a bad time of it and Tyler is upstairs. The last thing she needs is another face to contend with."

He was so understanding that Cassie almost threw herself at him. That guy she'd had to witness harassing that poor Chinese waitress had long disappeared. This Trip was just perfect. Perfect in how he was, perfect right down to those long lashes that she wanted to feel against her skin.

"You're probably right," Cassie replied though every instinct of hers wanted him to change his mind. After all, she had her own Tyler-free room that they could hang out in…

"Maybe I'll see you tomorrow?" he asked, clearly having made up his mind to go.

"That would be nice," Cassie answered softly.

The air felt charged between them though this was a different sort of magic. Cassie's body practically hummed with anticipation as Trip came closer to her. Taking her by the hands, he leaned in close until she could feel his breath on her face.

Softly, gently, he lowered his soft lips to hers.

The sensation was both delicate and as hot as a fire. Reeling from being kissed by a boy she actually liked for the first time, Cassie felt like she would explode.

When Trip finally pulled away, Cassie thought she could see stars. The world swam, and she had to force herself not to crash into a wall. Smiling happily, she went into the building as giving her a quick wave, Trip disappeared into the night.

Michael had listened to the girl's boring twittering as she'd gone on and on about her friend's problems when all he'd wanted to do was snap her neck in half. Instead, he'd had to force his new face to look interested, while offering her small words of comfort as he hoped for juicy information that he could use against them.

But Cassie had a one-track mind and seemed to have nothing inside that little head of hers other than the crush she had for the boy-jock.

When it was blessedly time to say goodbye he knew he had to ramp things up. Either the witch was holding things closer to her chest, or he had to ask more leading questions, but it was clear that she wouldn't reveal more to him unless she trusted him fully.

And to do that, he would have to do the unthinkable.

When he had gone in for the kiss, he had pictured all the things that made him rage with anger knowing that it was the only way to get through it. Where he was from, affection wasn't something that was much on display if at all, and any who tended to show it was considered weak, marking the recipient of their affection with a death sentence.

He had gone in with the kiss expecting it to be as disgusting as it looked.

Except, the girl's lips were not unpleasantly soft. And she had smelled of sweetness and roses which had proved quite the heady mix. All in all, it wasn't the horrible experience he had expected it to be.

In fact, if he were being honest, he'd actually enjoyed it.

Which was clearly unacceptable on so many levels.

Michael had never felt any sensation close to this before, but the fact that it was happening now... well, it could only mean one thing.

It was the stupid jock's body that was doing this.

Like the drunkenness and hangover — as he now understood it to be — that he had suffered from when he had taken over Trip's body, these new and complicated feelings must also be as a result of human weakness.

But it was a weakness that he knew he could not feel again.

Weakness meant that you were powerless. Weakness held you prisoner, and he intended on never being a prisoner ever again.

ONE HUNDRED THIRTY-FOUR

MASSACHUSETT'S BAY COLONY, 1693
The Four burst into the house above.

Though the fire raged below, and the upper floors were soon to be consumed, they knew they had enough time to do what they needed to.

Shaking out two pillows and keeping their cases as bags, Tabitha urged the young girl that they had saved, Bridget, to take whatever they could find of value though Bridget hadn't moved at first, confused by the instruction.

"Trust me, Child," Tabitha urged. "All will become clear."

And so Bridget followed behind her, grabbing what she could, lugging the heavy bag over her shoulder.

Across the way, Mary, Esther, and Catherine searched the house for any signs of the Council that had trapped them. They went through the desk and files but all they could find of note was a symbol that kept reappearing through the paperwork. Folding a letter with the symbol inked onto it, Esther tucked the evidence into her skirt as the smoke from below began to blacken the air.

"We must go," she cried, sensing that their time was nearly over.

Mary threw one last look at the house before nodding. Together, they went back down the staircase they had used before but the way ahead now was thick with smoke. "We need another way out," Mary called out.

Catherine's eyes alighted on a window off to the side that was away from the smoke. "Here!" she said, as she went to pick up a chair. But the mahogany wood that the chair was made from was too heavy for her to manage alone. Esther moved past the others to help her with it.

Together, they picked up the chair and threw it at the window. It smashed through the thin glass, leaving several wickedly sharp pieces still attached to the frame. Mary picked up a heavy bound book from a table, using it to clear the remaining shards of glass. Then she searched for something to cushion their fall. Finding a mattress in the bedroom next door, they shoved it through the window. Throwing a rug over the frame, she gestured to her sisters, "Follow me," and disappeared over the side.

One by one, the sisters followed as the mattress cushioned their fall, helping Bridget down until all five were safe on the solid ground outside.

"Where are we going now?" Bridget asked Tabitha, her small voice ringing clear into the night.

Mary thought for a moment, looking down at her little face before the solution came to her. "I know the perfect place."

As if she could read her mind, Esther put her hand on Mary's shoulder, silently asking her to wait. Her eyes turned cloudy as Esther used her gift to send out a call. Moments later it was answered by a horse still attached to a wagon.

Mary smiled at Esther. "You think of everything."

Getting into the wagon, they took off into the night. They remembered the way clearly, having traveled that same path not so long ago. When they arrived outside the tiny shack by the edge of the forest again, Mary hesitated at the door, knowing what grief must still lay inside.

Raising her hand to knock, the door was abruptly pulled open as Sofia, the grieving wife of Ben, the one-legged man who had risked his life for them, stood glaring at them.

"How dare you return to interrupt my grief," she said, her voice icy in its coldness.

"My heart goes out to you at this time," Mary replied. "But we have urgent need of your assistance."

Sofia's hands went to either side of her hips as she looked at her incredulously. "What possible assistance would I want to give you?"

Nodding toward Bridget, she urged the girl forward. When she stood in the doorway, Sofia's eyes looked her up and down, turning confused.

"Just like you, Bridget has gone through unbearable loss. Condemned as a witch, she was forced to watch her mother be killed right in front of her, and was awaiting her own death when we saved her. We cannot take her where we are going, for what we do will be filled with danger not suitable for an innocent as she. We are hoping that you will take her in as your own."

The birthmark that covered half of Sofia's face and which was the cause of her own banishment seemed most prominent tonight. Bridget looked up at Sofia, her eyes wide with sadness and a knowingness that shouldn't be in one so young. Seeing it, Sofia's anger instantly melted away.

"But I barely have enough for one baby, how will I care for another child?" Her fingers reached out to Bridget's shoulder, softening the blow of her words.

Tabitha and Esther set down the pillowcases filled to the brim with valuables.

"These are for you to do as you wish," Tabitha said.

Seeing the riches inside, the likes of which she had never seen before, Sofia's eyes widened with shock.

"There should be enough here to take care of the three of you for the rest of your lives," Esther finished quietly. "Take the horse and wagon, go far from here. Put as much distance between the town and yourselves as you can and begin a new life elsewhere."

"Will you accept the care of this child?" Mary asked formally.

Nodding, her eyes filling up with tears, Sofia nodded as she crouched down to Bridget. "You and I have gone through some terrible things, but perhaps together we can get through the days ahead."

Reaching out her hand, Sofia offered it to Bridget.

Bridget looked up at Tabitha as if seeking her approval. When Tabitha nodded, Bridget took Sofia's hand.

Seeing them together, Mary knew that they had righted one wrong in the world… but there was still one other, much greater wrong that needed their help.

Thanking Sofia, they bid goodbye to them both as they prepared for the battle that they knew would be coming.

ONE HUNDRED THIRTY-FIVE

Shaken & Stirred was dead tonight.

Though Saturday night was usually one of the bar's busiest times, only a handful of customers were present. Eve sat behind the bar as Si finished stacking up the latest batch of glasses to have come out of the dishwasher.

"Wonder where everyone is tonight?" he said, looking around.

"Who knows," Eve replied, not really paying attention to the conversation. Since they'd arrived back, she'd struggled to focus, her mind kept drifting to Tyler and Ally.

"OK. You need to tell me what's bothering you or I'm just going to make things up and you know I have quite the imagination," Si demanded, straightening up and folding his arms across his chest.

Eve hesitated, wondering if Tyler would mind if Si knew her business, but she knew she wouldn't. Quickly, she filled him in on events. When she was done, he gaped at her, in total incomprehension.

"Someone kidnapped her?" he asked, needing confirmation that he was hearing right.

"Yeah."

"Poor Ally… Poor Tyler," he said, mind thinking things over a mile a minute. "Why can't they get a break?"

"Makes you wonder if there really is a God right?" Eve asked bitterly. She had never been the religious type before but Ally's disappearance really made her question everything she thought knew. She believed everything happened for a reason, but what possible reason could there be for this?

"You're safe here with the others, right?" Si asked suddenly, gesturing to the staff who seemed equally bored by the lack of things to do.

"Yeah, why?" Eve asked, wondering what he was up to. He had that expression on his face that she'd seen many times before when he'd made his mind up about something but wouldn't be telling anyone about it until he was good and ready to.

"I've got to run an errand, but I'll be back soon," he said, untying the half apron he'd been wearing around his waist. Grabbing the car keys from the hook on the wall, he took off leaving Eve staring after him.

Tyler pressed the buzzer that opened the door to the dorm with puzzlement.

What was he doing there?

Realizing that she had slept most of the day and hadn't checked her appearance once, Tyler ran to the mirror to see her hair in tangles and a stain on her shirt. Grabbing her brush, she ran it quickly through her hair as she wet her fingers with saliva and worked at the stain.

A half laugh, half sob spilled out of her.

Ally was gone, yet here she was, worried about how

someone might think of her wild appearance. What idiocy was this? She was still wondering this when the
knock sounded on the door.

Burning with curiosity despite herself, Tyler opened it
to reveal Si, Eve's brother, standing there with a bag of
groceries. He ran a hand through his own mess of black
curls as he spoke.

"This didn't seem as weird when I thought of it a
minute ago," he began.

"What're you doing here?" Tyler asked.

"Eve just told me about Ally. I'm so sorry, Tyler. I can't
believe this has happened. How're you holding up?" He
asked, looking immediately like he wanted to kick himself. "Sorry, that's a dumb question."

"It's not dumb. And the answer is, about as expected."

"I don't want to intrude as you must have stuff going
on…" As he said this, he looked past her into the room to
find that papers littered every surface. Each had a picture
of Ally with the words "MISSING: Have you seen her?"
Even now, as he read the one closest to him which lay on
a pile of the same, more of the notices were coming off of
the printer that was attached to Tyler's laptop.

"I just thought with everything that's happened… I…
here," he said, shoving the bag of groceries at her. "It's
nothing special, just a bunch of ready meals that can go
into any microwave. I figured you won't be thinking
about food at this time, but you need to keep your
strength up." He spoke fast, his words coming out in a
blur.

Stunned by his care and thoughtfulness, Tyler felt her
face crumple as all the composure she'd been holding
back today suddenly disappeared. Exhausted, frightened,
and feeling desperately alone, the tears came flooding
out. Si reacted immediately. Dropping the food, he
jumped forward, enveloping her in his arms.

"It'll be OK, I promise," he said into the top of her

head as she held onto him, sobbing for all that she had lost.

A warm and welcome vibe exuded from the packed crowd.

Their TED host it turned out, a woman with a rich voice and a seemingly endless portfolio of stories who was also an incredibly moving speaker. Despite only initially coming to blow off steam, Marley found herself taking in the life lessons she imparted.

Even more surprising than that, however, was the way she felt so carefree with Rhett. He had such an easy-going manner that it was impossible not to like him, especially when he kept tossing her those sexy grins that lit up his face like the one he wore now.

Grins that made her feel warm inside.

As if he could feel the heat himself, Rhett rolled up the sleeves of his shirt. Toned muscles rippled, the sight of which only caused Marley to feel even warmer. She returned his smile as they both turned back to the stage.

ONE HUNDRED THIRTY-SIX

Drumming her nails on the bar top, Eve's eyes slid over to the clock hanging on the wall.

Si had only been gone a half hour or so, but already it had felt like forever. She wished desperately that she had one of her laptops with her; business was so slow tonight, no one would mind or even notice if she whiled away the time on Warcraft.

Some people drank, while others stuffed themselves with food, but Eve's comfort of choice was losing herself in a video game. There was something so cathartic about becoming a character so much stronger than you were in real life, not to mention all the killing you could do in a game yet not feel the slightest bit of guilt or shame.

People who didn't play video games never understood the value they held. They were great for stress relief, and if you played online with friends, there was the social aspect of it too. Online, no one cared who you were in real life, what you looked like, what grades you made, or who you dated. She missed being able to switch her brain off and go to that safe world for a few hours, particularly as she was still torn up inside from seeing that symbol in the painting. She had hoped that she would have come to a decision by now, but her brain stubbornly refused to cooperate.

Needing to use the restroom, Eve headed there. When she was done, and as she was as she was washing her hands she saw something moving behind her. Glancing up, she looked into the mirror…

The person standing behind her had the kind of model good looks that made it seem like he had just stepped out of a bad boy biker catalog.

One look at him and just like many other girls had before her, Eve had fallen for him so hard… but how was she to know that such a pretty face harbored so much hate? Or that the square jawline that Eve had thought so manly would later become her point of focus during all those times when his fists would do the talking?

But it was the eyes… his eyes which would go from smoldering to cold and calculating in a single moment as they accused her of yet another crime she hadn't committed that had really crushed her.

They bore into her now burning a path into her soul.

Eve froze, unable to move as ice water flooded her veins. Her heart thumped so loudly that it threatened to burst out of her chest. Unable to believe what she was seeing, all she could do was stare at that ghastly reflection of the person who had caused her so much terror and pain.

And who should, by any stretch of logic, still be six feet under the ground.

He leered at her, his cold eyes seemingly turning even blacker than they already were. Eve couldn't move, couldn't even blink, so stark was the terror that flashed through her. Her emotions running riot, Eve could feel the air becoming static. She hadn't even known that she had sent out the call for help, but as always, the *others* came to answer it.

She heard the sound of something soft hitting the

glazed window that shielded any customers inside the restroom while still letting in the light. It was quickly followed by another bump, then another as a thousand moths descended onto the window, their wings beating at the glass as they tried to get in.

Eve tore her eyes away from him for a moment, just in time to see the moths rapidly covering the glass in black before darting back to him. His mouth curled into an evil sneer.

"Hi Honey, have you missed me?"

Then the room plunged into pitch black. Struck suddenly blind, Eve yelped as she stumbled in the direction of what she hoped was the door. Her senses were on fire, listening for any sign of him. Her breath came out in panicked bursts and her body felt like it was on fire as every nerve went into overdrive. She didn't know how any of this could be happening. All she could focus on was being able to see again and getting out of there.

Scrambling around, her arms stretched in front of her, Eve's fingers found the cool hard ceramic edge of a sink. Letting her fingers run along the edge of it, she worked her way towards the door even as a burst of warm air landed on her cheek.

His breath! My God his breath was on her!

Shaking now, with a weird soft mewling sound coming out of her, Eve finally felt the cold metal of the door handle. Seizing it into her clawed hands, she yanked the door open.

Blessed bright light flooded the room, blinding her for a moment.

She darted out of there, spinning around, ready to call for help, but as the black spots faded from her eyes, she saw that the restroom was empty.

He was gone.

But lying on the floor tiles mocking her with its very existence…

It was her yellow dress.

The cold metal was everywhere, burning into her skin.

Ally shivered, wrapping her arms around herself as she wiped yet another tear from her eyes.

All day she had tried to be brave while she waited for Tyler to find her, but with every passing hour and as the sky grew darker, she found her hope fading with the light.

That monster had left a plate of sandwiches and a bottle of water for her, but Ally hadn't wanted to touch it, worried about what it might contain inside. Her parents had always warned her not to eat or drink anything that wasn't prepared by someone she knew and trusted, but after hours of crying, her throat hurt from the dryness. She knew she had to have at least a drink.

Reaching through the bars, she picked up the bottle of water, twisted the cap off and drank until she coughed. The monsters had left her alone today, and for that she was grateful. It was when they were around that she found herself the most scared, especially from the quiet one. He always looked at her as if she were a piece of meat, something he could eat. She had caught him looking at her with a hungry look in his eyes that had scared her more than the other monster who liked to rattle her cage to make her scream.

Whenever that happened, Ally had taken to closing her eyes, willing herself to picture one of her happier moments. She kept coming to the same safe place, to those weekend pony rides with Tyler.

Every time she felt scared, she would see them both in her mind's eye. She would hold on to that moment for as long as she could. She would not panic.

She knew that come what may, Tyler would find her.

Michael stalked through the streets of Boston, angered beyond all reason.

The stupid, insufferable demons had failed him.

It was supposed to be an easy mission, retrieving the stocking from the bar. With a little misdirection and timing, no one even needed to get hurt, which would at least keep the cops off of them. But no, the fools had run into a group of ex-students who just happened to call The Castle their watering hole, and who had chased them off! Two demons!

Well, Michael had a bone to pick with anyone who muscled in on his plans, even if they didn't know it themselves.

Storming into the bar, he found it much as Fink had described it, except there were two bartenders now, a woman and a man sharing a shift. The group of ex-students were back in the same corner as when they had been there earlier.

Michael knew it was them by Pike's description, even if he couldn't see the cuts and bruises they had sustained in their earlier battle. A few other drinkers were dotted around the place but this really was a hole in the wall that didn't make the "must-visit" list on any publication.

Marching to the bar, Michael leaned across it, grabbed the startled male bartender by the neck then hurled him across the bar. He crashed into a display of bottles, shattering them on impact. Glass rained down as alcohol spilled onto the floor. The girl took one look at the murderous expression on his face and sprinted for the back door. Elsewhere, the few solitary drinkers were also backing out, not wanting any of this trouble. Only the group of boys were left.

Exactly how he wanted it.

Crossing over to them, eyes spewing hate, he made a

gesture with his hand as the tables in front of him flew away as if they had been thrown by giant invisible hands.

"Those who get in my way, get punished," he threatened in a low growl as he advanced toward them. The boys looked at each other without any of their earlier bravado. The air crackled with magic as Michael tossed aside every bit of furniture until there was nothing between them.

And nowhere they could hide.

Moments later splashed with their blood, Michael left the bar unaware that his face — Trip's face — had been captured on a streetcam...

TWISTED MAGIC

9: IN HER SKIN

JO HO

ONE HUNDRED THIRTY-SEVEN

Black coffee swirled in the styrofoam cup, its hot steam soothing her dry, tired eyes.

The harsh overhead lighting, the stark sterile corridors… none of them did anything for the looming migraine that Saunders could already feel pressing into her head.

Rubbing the tight muscles on the back of her neck, she stared down at her partner Brooks, taking in his grave injuries.

Since he had been freed from the rubble of the diner, he had yet to regain consciousness. Machines beeped by his side attached to him by a network of wires. His limbs were covered in bandages and casts; what part of his face she could see was a vivid black and blue. That thick mane of hair that he'd been so proud of had been burnt clear off of his scalp. Though his chest rose and fell at regular intervals, it looked as if the very effort was costing him.

He looked so weak, so vulnerable, so different from the gladiator she knew that she barely recognized him.

The doctors hoped he would eventually wake when his body had recovered from the trauma. She had overheard them discussing the possibility that he had suffered a blow to the head though, in the explosion, which could have rendered him comatose.

She hoped for all their sakes that it wasn't the case.

Her eyes slid from his face to the cards and gift baskets that took up every spare inch of space on the cabinets on either side of the bed. Most were of the highest quality with Hallmark messages printed on thick paper — as befitted someone of his rank and service — but the one she noticed the most had a crudely drawn picture in crayon.

The words "Daddy, get better soon. We love and miss you," had her bottom lip trembling.

Saunders wasn't the type who showed much weakness or emotion — it was one of the reasons she was such a good detective. Her unflappable manner and nerves of steel made even the most hardened criminal think twice before messing with her, yet here she was, getting upset over a hand-drawn card.

Thinking of Brooks' kids, another child's face flooded into her mind. That of the recently-turned ten-year-old, Ally Jones.

She'd hit a dead-end.

Every lead she had found had dried up. The waiter was a ghost; having appeared out of nowhere he'd disappeared just as fast. No one knew who he was, or what his motive was for taking Ally, least of all her.

Their hopes were now pinned on the results of the forensics team who were on the last leg of their examinations.

She hoped that when the results came, there would be something tangible for her to follow up. Every second that flew past without a lead was another toward the unthinkable.

Pouring her untouched coffee into the sink, Saunders tossed the cup into the trash and started for home.

The night blurred past outside her window, dark with mystery as a heavy blanket of silence enveloped the car.

Eve rode shotgun beside her brother, her eyes glued to the blackness for any sign of that figure which would signal the return of her worst nightmare.

Her hands were gripped together in her lap, her breath coming in short little bursts. Though she desperately wanted to reveal what had happened earlier, Eve couldn't find the words to tell him. Her tongue felt glued to the roof of her mouth.

Despite what he had said, it had taken a lot longer for Si to return to the bar from wherever it was he had disappeared to. After they had arrived there, after she had told him what she could about her day, he had taken off with barely a word. He was always good at his word — reliable to a fault actually — so it was unusual for Eve to find herself irrationally mad at him... yet here she was.

It was an hour or so after the incident in the restroom, and in that time, Eve had almost convinced herself that it had just been a trick of Michael's — horrible though it had been. Though that hadn't helped with the feeling of dread that had overtaken her since the moment she had seen Jason's ghastly face leering at her in the mirror.

Fingers numb with fear, Eve had tried calling Si immediately after escaping the restroom. He hadn't picked up, and she hadn't found any more traces of Jason other than that yellow dress which now lay in the bottom of a trash can, like so many others that had come before it.

While Eve struggled to find the words, Si was distracted too: though he drove with the careful consideration he always did, it was clear his mind was elsewhere. He hadn't once tried to initiate a conversation with her.

They sat in silence until they turned into their street and saw the familiar features of their road.

There was that flamingo-toned house on the corner

which Eve had loved as a kid during her pink phase, but which now looked lurid next to its more conservative neighbors.

The Bauers' pretty front yard — which had the best floral display year-after-year — passed by. Then Mrs. Jackson's giant RV came into view, bought after her husband had passed away. Determined to begin a new chapter of her life, the vehicle had sat parked in her driveway for two years now with no sign of it ever moving.

As their headlights flashed onto their home, Si parked the car, killing the engine. In the stillness that followed, Eve knew she had to speak but as she opened her mouth, Si went first.

"So, I went to see Tyler," he began.

His words were so unexpected that Eve's own revelation flew straight out of her mind.

"Why would you do that?" she asked, wondering what could have possessed him.

"I didn't actually think too hard about it, but when you told me about Ally, all I could think was how she must be feeling right now. She only just lost her parents, now her sister is gone too. I could only think about what a mess I would be in her place..." he paused, turning his eyes on her. To Eve's shock, she saw they were glistening with unshed tears.

"What a mess I was when you had disappeared last year," he continued.

Hearing the rawness in his voice, Eve felt the shame that she always felt whenever this was raised. Not only had she allowed herself to be demeaned by a guy — and then *stayed with him* — she had put her brother through hell too.

"I needed to do something to help, let her know she wasn't alone. So I picked up some microwave meals and took them over. That was all I did, really. Nothing special."

Eve began to smile through her guilt. "That was pretty

special, actually. Not many people would think to do that, especially for someone they barely know."

Her compliment threw him. He shrugged it off, reaching for the car keys so she wouldn't see how affected he was.

"Like I said, it was nothing. No need to make a deal out of it."

Knowing he didn't want to pursue that line of conversation, Eve flipped it back to Tyler. "How did she take it?"

Getting out of the car, Si waited for Eve to emerge before he locked it. "My visit? She was… emotional. It's why the whole thing took longer than I thought it would. She needed a shoulder to cry on and I couldn't leave until she was calm again."

They walked up the few steps toward their front door. As Eve waited for Si to let them in, she felt her stomach begin to churn nervously but wasn't sure what the cause of it was. Her eyes darted behind them, but the way was clear: there were no demons or Jasons in sight; so what was this feeling she had?

Following Si inside, she found herself staring at him with something akin to anger. With a jolt and a mixture of guilt and shame, she realized what it was that she was feeling.

It was jealousy.

Picturing Tyler crying on his shoulder had brought the green-eyed monster to the surface, though she knew that was ridiculous. Tyler was her friend and a good person. If she and Si got together even as friends, surely that would be a good thing.

What with chaperoning her whenever he could, Si didn't have much of a life outside work — wasn't she always saying he needed more friends?

Yet why did it have to be *her* friend?

They stood in the hall as Si locked the front door. "I'm going to take a quick shower then hit the sack. I'm exhausted," he said, already heading up the stairs.

He was gone before Eve even remembered she had wanted to tell him about Jason.

E ve stood outside the bathroom her knuckles paused an inch away from the door, wrestling with her emotions.

Si had only been inside for a few moments, she had time to stop him, to tell him what had happened, yet... with every second that passed, she could feel common sense taking over.

Jason was dead, and she already knew that Michael was messing with her by making that dress appear; so it wouldn't be an unnatural leap for him to add Jason's image to the mix.

The sound of the shower turning on woke her from her thoughts. She couldn't tell Si, not without delving into that giant black hole. Lowering her hand, she headed into her room.

Removing her makeup, she toned then creamed her face. Although she didn't like to show her true face to the world, she still kept with her usual beauty regime, knowing how important it was to keep the skin healthy.

While the act of getting ready for bed would normally relax her, Eve found she couldn't shake that nervous feeling that had started when she had first stood on their doorstep.

Something felt *off*.

Moving to her window she checked the locks, making sure they were latched tight as she stared outside...

There was a man standing at the bottom of their porch!

Eve's heart leapt into her mouth as her pulse raced. Even from here she could see that he had rippling muscles that could only have come from regular sessions in the gym. He looked so familiar, so much like Jason that she felt her mouth go dry. Much of the man's face was hidden in shadow but the eyes… the eyes she could see.

And they were staring right up at *her*.

Blood pounded in her ears, her eyes locked on the nightmare figure below. Neither of them moved, not even when a car approached from the end of the street. As the car's headlights crept closer to the figure, Eve's breath caught as she waited for his full face to be revealed. When they finally drew close enough to land on him, however, the figure vanished.

Eve's eyes scanned the area, darting every which way, but there was nowhere he could have hidden; nowhere that he could have gotten to without her seeing.

Either it had been a figment of her imagination or it was another of Michael's tricks.

Shivering, she pulled the curtains closed but the coldness inside stayed with her long throughout the night.

ONE HUNDRED THIRTY-EIGHT

The dark, dank sewer resounded with Michael's footsteps as he stormed through the twisting network of corridors.

The blood of his victims was still fresh on his skin yet he hadn't bothered to wipe them away. He wanted the world to see how unhappy he was.

With the black magic artifact gone, stolen by the stupid witches, Michael would need to find another source to power up from. The life force from those drunken ex-students at the bar would suffice for now, but he would need another injection fairly quickly or his new body would start to reveal its true state. And as the jock had been dead for days, it would definitely be noticeable.

Rounding a corner, he finally came upon the area where the innocent was being held.

He saw immediately that all was not well.

The girl lay asleep shivering on the floor of the birdcage, looking pale while Pike, who had grown bored with babysitting an unconscious girl, jumped to attention when he saw him.

"Boss! To what do we owe this honor?" the pathetic demon asked, sucking up to him in his usual fashion.

Though he found him annoying, Michael tolerated the demon because he was loyal and could be trusted. He knew Pike had never spoken of that day when he had first arrived in this world, naked and cowering much like the child before him now.

At the end of the day, loyalty like that was priceless.

"Have we any news from Fink?" Michael wanted to know. The demon was on a reconnaissance mission but had yet to report back.

"Nothing yet," Pike answered. "Then again, he doesn't exactly keep me in the loop," he couldn't help complaining. He'd tried so hard to befriend him but Fink kept keeping him at arm's length.

Michael choose not to respond, knowing that he had nothing nice to say. Studying the girl, Michael took in her shivering state though her face perspired at the same time.

"Why is she like that?" Michael asked softly. "I told you to take care of her."

Pike blinked at him, his ugly brow with its zit-like depressions furrowing into a frown. "She gets food and water. I drugged her up too to knock her out since she wouldn't stop crying. It was driving me nuts."

"But she's cold. I can't have her falling ill. I need her alive and healthy," Michael responded.

"Well, we have her in the sewer, Boss, not sure how much warmer I can make her."

"Would a blanket have been too much to ask?" Michael asked though his tone implied it wasn't an answer he was expecting, but action.

"Sorry, Boss. I'll get right on it," Pike said but Michael waved him off.

"No, you clearly can't be trusted with this task. We're moving her. Call Fink and get him back here."

S ome clever timing and a few disguises later — courtesy of the two decorators they had found and killed, taking their overalls — Fink and Pike had both Ally and her giant cage parked in the West-facing corner of Michael's penthouse suite where, like the bird he had owned before, she would get the best of the sun.

Pulling a thick wool throw off the corner sofa and a couple of its many cushions, he shoved them through the bars of the cage. They fell onto the girl who finally woke from her sleep.

She blinked up at him now, her green eyes confused and groggy as she took in the gifts he had just bestowed upon her. Staring at her new location, the girl grabbed the throw, covering her thin shoulders with it then spoke to him in a wobbly voice.

"Thank you."

Her comment confused him. He had taken her from her sister, trapped her in this cage, yet she was thanking him for this simple thing?

There was a small twinge in his chest, a knot of something uncomfortable that pricked at his heart. Subconsciously, he found himself rubbing at it as if he could erase the feeling away, but there it sat like a brick, refusing to budge.

Was he feeling *sorry* for her?

Horrified that it must be it, Michael backed away from the girl like she was poison. Turning his back to her, he resolved to move forward with the next part of his plan more quickly.

Before this jock's body — which was obviously the cause of these ridiculous feelings — made him lose his mind completely.

A loud crack woke Eve from sleep.

Her eyes flew open as a bolt of lightning streaked across the sky so bright that it lit up her room through the thin curtains.

In that flash, she could see movement across her body where a blanket of ants covered her.

Far from the disgust they had initially caused three weeks ago when this sort of thing had first started happening, Eve was now bizarrely comforted by their presence. The creatures were only there to protect her. They came only when she felt threatened whether real or perceived or even if it dredged up in a nightmare.

Fat droplets of rain pelted the window as thunder rumbled in the distance. Dismissing the ants with a mental command, Eve got out of bed and pulled back the curtain.

The gray world looked to be drowning as the storm raged overhead. Across the rooftops as far as the eye could see the heavens performed a wicked display of its might. Eve stared at it, awed until, almost of their own accord, she found her eyes sliding down to the spot where she had seen the Jason-like figure last night.

There was nothing there now, only the rain.

Hearing a knock on the front door, she glanced at the alarm clock that sat beside her bed. The digital display revealed that it was early still, only six twenty in the morning.

Far too early for the mailman or any visitors to be calling.

She rubbed at the goosebumps that had suddenly sprung up along her arms. Slipping into a thin sweater she padded downstairs.

As she drew closer to the front door, she felt a flash of confusion — she couldn't see anyone through the glass-paneled door.

Jason's leering face flashed into her mind suddenly,

making her jump. The fear she had felt then, and the fear she had felt last night when she had thought he was standing outside their house, rose up like a wave overwhelming her with its intensity.

She froze stock-still, a hand resting on the door handle.

Yet even through the fear, there was a rising rebellion inside. A small part of her whose screams cut through, telling her that she couldn't be this much of an idiot.

She couldn't stay scared forever — the guy was dead after all!

And Michael's tricks, frightening as they were, were only tricks or he would have done some real damage to her — to any of them — by now.

Clamping down on her worries, Eve pursed her lips and flung open the door.

There was no one there.

Only that rain that came down continuously at an angle, but instead of landing on the wooden floor of the porch, they sank into the soft fabric of a familiar item that lay right outside the front door.

Her yellow dress.

White-hot fury burned inside as Eve's curls began to whip around her head. She was sick of seeing the thing, sick of being taunted by it every single day. She grew so angry that she could feel the sting of tears in the backs of her eyes which only caused her to grow more furious.

Bending down, she snatched up the dress only to notice the rain settling into a pattern in the flowerbed opposite her.

Straightening back up, Eve realized that the pattern wasn't a pattern at all — but a pair of footprints. They had been created by a man's boots... biker boots.

They were the kind of boots that Jason had lived in.

A crack of thunder made her jump. Clutching the dress to her chest, Eve stared at the footprints in the ground as the rain continued to pour into them.

"Eve…. What're you doing?"

She spun around to find Si on the stairs looking at her in bewilderment. When he caught the dress in her hands, however, his eyes took on a hooded look.

"Is that what I think it is?"

There was nothing Eve could do to deny it.

"I found it on the doorstep. Someone knocked on the door. It woke me up, so I came downstairs…"

"I didn't hear anything," he said, his expression not changing.

This was all too much now. While she might have passed off the Jason incident in the bar as a figment of her imagination or one of Michael's attempts to unravel her, those footsteps outside, they were another matter entirely.

She had to say something. She had to warn Si though she knew enough to stick only to the facts.

"I thought I saw someone last night, standing right there, but they disappeared," she pointed at the foot-prints. "But just now, someone knocked on the door, left this dress, and there are footprints in the mud right where I saw the figure."

Si's eyes went to the spot she pointed to. Instead of the alarm she expected him to express, however, he showed only concern — concern that he turned on her.

"I don't see any footprints," he said quietly.

Stepping out into the rain, she pointed to the spot when she saw that the footprints had gone.

She lowered her arm, startled. "They were right there!"

"They can't have disappeared, Eve, there's not enough rain to wipe out footprints in the mud," he replied keeping his tone calm yet certain.

Laying a hand on her shoulder he pulled her back in-side. "It's early, it's cold. Come inside and we can talk about it."

By the gentle tone in his voice, Eve knew that he

didn't believe her… which meant he thought she was either lying or seeing things. Her brother who had always been her rock, who had killed to protect her… *did not believe her*.

She shrugged his hand off angrily. "I'm not making this up!"

Then stormed back upstairs to her room.

She couldn't rely on him on this particular matter. Whatever the hell was going on, she would have to find out herself.

And she would.

She had powers now. She could do this. She could handle whatever was coming her way.

She wasn't anyone's victim anymore.

ONE HUNDRED THIRTY-NINE

The smell of frying bacon and brewing coffee filled the air.

The food court was riddled with hungry students, all who seemed to get right in Marley's way as she stumbled to the nearest coffee machine.

Filling her cup as high as it could go, she grabbed a blueberry muffin from a towering display, paid then wove through the crowd until she found an empty table where a seat was promptly taken up by Christian.

"What, do you just lurk around until the moment I want some peace then bam… there you are," she growled at him.

Taking in her red-rimmed eyes he read the situation. "Bad night?"

"Yeah," she said, slumping into a chair. Taking out her phone, she attached the hands-free earphones and put one of the buds into her ear.

"That's a little rude don't you think? I mean, I'm sitting right here," Christian said, affronted.

She rolled tired eyes at him. "This is for them, dumb-ass," she explained, gesturing at the world at large. "So they don't think I'm talking to myself."

"Right. You're pretending to be on a call," Christian answered, finally getting it.

"Someone give the boy a prize."

She took a large gulp of coffee and broke off a piece of the muffin.

"So what's troubling you? Anything you want to talk about?" He asked those green-gold eyes of his studying her intensely.

"No," Marley started to reply only to change her mind. If anyone were to understand, it would be Christian.

"Actually, yes… Have you… killed anyone before?" She kept her voice low so that only he could hear her question.

"A few," Christian finally nodded. "But they were always demons.

Marley put her muffin down, unable to stomach eating. "Did it bother you?"

"The first time, yeah. I don't think you ever forget your first. The taking of a life isn't a simple matter even if they are the bad guys. It's not something I ever enjoyed, but it was a necessity in my line of work."

"I couldn't stop thinking about it all last night," Marley started, lowering her muffin. "I killed a demon the same way that I killed you. My hands just somehow sank into his back like it was nothing. I found myself squeezing… and then he was dead. What kind of witch does that?"

She stared into his eyes, her own haunted by the memory of the act.

"The other girls all seem to have one specific power. Cassie can morph herself, Eve has her creepy animal army, and Tyler, well, I think she can alter things. I just assumed that my power was being able to communicate with ghosts, but how does this other thing fit in?"

Her eyes were so troubled that Christian had to look away. "I don't think you're just a witch, Marley. I think you might have some other skills."

There was something in his tone that implied he knew more than he had been saying.

"Please tell me what you know," she pleaded. "This is freaking me out."

"I've actually been thinking about this… The fact that you don't just see and talk to ghosts, but you can actually cross over into the Spirit World and back… I think you might have shamanic skills."

"Shamanic… like a shaman?"

He nodded. "Typically they are able to access good and evil spirits though shamans usually have to enter a trance to communicate with spirits. If you can cross dimensions into the Spirit World, you must be very powerful, Marley… and that kind of power only comes from having it in your bloodline for generations."

The room began to swim as Marley felt herself reeling. "Bloodline? Like the one my dad won't tell me about?"

Christian shot a look at her. "Is it possible that your dad knows things that he's keeping from you?"

Marley couldn't speak. She couldn't answer as all the weird conversations she had ever had with her dad about their family flooded her mind.

Even as a kid whenever Marley had asked about them it seemed her dad had side-stepped the subject until she just gave up. It wasn't important he'd always said, his dad wasn't a nice guy and the rest of them were gone. No point digging up the past.

Except now the past was rushing up to meet her.

"There you are!" Cassie's panicked voice interrupted her thoughts as she rushed over, Tyler following close behind. Marley picked up on their alarm immediately.

"What is it?" she asked.

"We just saw the news… you know those guys who helped us yesterday… at that *place*…" Deliberating omitting the name, Cassie cast a nervous look around her as if she was expecting someone to be listening to their conversation.

"The Ca…" Marley almost finished the word 'Castle' but Cassie shook her head, cutting her off. "Yes, I know the place you mean."

"They were murdered last night. It's all over the news. Someone went in there yesterday and killed them all," Marley gasped, horrified while Christian sat up straighter, his eyes hard.

"Ask her how? How were they killed?" He demanded.

Marley didn't want to, thinking it a gruesome question, but he insisted. "Do it, Marley."

"Christian wants to know how they died," she reluctantly asked.

If Cassie thought the question weird, she didn't show it. "They said the guys were torn apart."

The blood drained from Marley's face. It was their fault the guys were killed. They had no idea what they were walking into.

"Michael must have gone after them…" Christian trailed off, not wanting to finish his thought for fear of upsetting them more, but Marley picked up on it.

"As retribution for what we did."

"So we should stop?" Tyler asked the first thing she had said since she'd arrived. She looked even worse than she had yesterday if that were possible. Her hair hung in a greasy streak, her skin ghostly pale. She looked weak as if she could be knocked down with a feather.

"No, actually," Christian replied. "You must keep on."

"What?" Marley gasped at him, not understanding why he would say such a thing. "Didn't you hear what she just said?"

"Loud and clear," Christian replied. "If Michael's doing that, it's because you're getting in his way."

"Yes, but he's killing innocent people while we do."

She could feel a sob rising up in her throat and had to swallow it back down.

"This is a war, Marley. There will be casualties, but you can't let your fear of that stop you from stopping him. If Michael manages to break those seals, he'll open up a gate across other worlds and dimensions letting in any and all supernatural creatures. It won't just be bad for you then; it will be catastrophic for everyone."

ONE HUNDRED FORTY

"This is too much," Marley said suddenly.

"Let's call Eve and check in with her," Cassie suggested sensibly. "Though we should probably lower the volume so the entire world doesn't hear we're discussing.

Moments later Eve's face — bare of makeup — stared back at them from the phone. Without her heavy layers, she looked so much prettier, but the tiredness that dogged Marley and Tyler had also struck Eve. Cassie was the only one of the group who looked fresh-faced and rested.

"Christian thinks we should carry on with our plan to get the second artifact?" Eve asked.

"Yeah, but I'm not so sure I agree," Marley answered, earning a frown from Christian.

"I'm not sure when would be the time to raise this, so here's nothing: I think Michael has Ally," Tyler blurted out suddenly. "One of my spells did work yesterday only I was too stupid to realize it, but he has her trapped in a giant birdcage."

"A birdcage?" Cassie asked, looking so shocked that her eyes seemed even bigger than normal.

"Yeah. For a moment, I could see and hear her. And then she disappeared. I've been hoping to get the visions back but I've had nothing since last night," Tyler revealed.

"How do you know it's not just Michael messing with you as he has been with Eve?" Marley asked.

"Because Ally really has been taken, and it's a bit of a coincidence to think someone else would have done it at the exact time with all of this going on," Tyler replied as calm as she could under the circumstances.

"But how are we supposed to steal this other artifact? Helena said it was under lock and key at that private library, plus we know Michael had someone waiting for us at the Ca... *place*..." Cassie quickly corrected herself. "Isn't he likely to have the same at the Athenaeum?"

"Maybe," Eve replied. "But we know to expect that this time so they won't have the element of surprise, plus we'll have Tyler with us. Only Cassie can't be any help if we get into a fight."

"Hey!" Cassie protested. "I can do things! I'm not useless!"

Eve winced at her lack of tack. "Sorry, you know what I mean."

"I can't," Tyler cut in, shaking her head. "I've got to speak to Ally's foster mom. I need to see if she's heard anything that I haven't.

"I've got classes and a paper for my Journalism is due," Marley said earning a look from them all. "I know you might not care that much about school, but I was looking forward to this. I just wanted to be normal. I'm not saying I won't do it; I'm just asking if we could do it after my school obligations. We've only got this one life — as far as I know — so shouldn't we be able to live it while we deal with this other stuff?"

"*Other stuff*? That's what you're calling the fate of the world?" Christian didn't bother to hide his disgust.

"Even Superman had a day job, that's all I'm saying," Marley said.

A knowing look fell on Cassie's face. "You got that from your Ted talk yesterday didn't you and… ooh, I just realized you haven't dished on Rhett??! How was it?"

"Wait, RA Rhett? What have I missed?" Eve asked, confused.

"You went on a date with him?" Tyler chimed in, also looking confused.

Christian stared at them as if they'd all grown an extra head. "Are you kidding me right now?" Shaking his head, disgusted with them, he vanished.

Glancing at her watch, Marley shot up to her feet. "We can talk about that later. I've got to get to class now. I'll meet you all after."

She hurried off as Cassie faced Tyler. "I should probably get going too… are you going to be OK?" she asked with a voice full of trepidation. She had no idea how to comfort her, but she wanted Tyler to know that she was there if she needed her.

"Yeah. I'll be calling Cheryl, then depending on what she tells me, maybe I'll check in with the cops, and then hand out some more flyers."

"Have you been granted an exemption from classes?" Eve asked from inside Cassie's phone.

"Yeah. The Dean knows what's happened. I'm OK for now."

Cassie looked as if she wanted to say something important; instead, she gestured to Tyler. "Oh, can you wait a sec? I'll be right back."

She hurried away leaving Tyler with her phone.

"Where's she gone?" Eve asked.

"Who knows?" Tyler replied, wondering how much longer she would have to be here now that she had to wait for Cassie's return — she couldn't just leave her phone here unattended.

Eve asked how things went last night and if she'd received any news. Tyler filled her in until Cassie came rushing back some five or so minutes later carrying a tray of food which she set onto the table.

There was a full cooked breakfast with bacon, eggs, and hash browns. A glass of what looked to be freshly squeezed OJ, a large mug of coffee, a bowl of cereal and another one of fruit. There was also a plate of fluffy pancakes that had glistening syrup dripping down the sides.

Despite how she was feeling, smelling the food, Tyler felt her stomach growl.

"I want you to eat as much as you can," Cassie commanded suddenly.

"This is all for me?" Tyler asked, shocked.

"Yeah. You've barely eaten since… well, you know. You look like you might pass out at any second so, eat please," she said handing Tyler a fork.

Tyler took it from her as Eve smiled up at them from the phone. "Cass, I am liking this new, caring side to you."

"Well, it's that or be useless, right?" Cassie shot back, wiping the smile from Eve's face.

"I totally deserved that."

"I don't see you eating," Cassie said to Tyler suddenly, sliding her eyes back to her.

Rather than argue with this new, confident — and kind of bossy — Cassie, Tyler scooped up a forkful of scrambled eggs and ate it.

"There," she said. "Happy?"

"Much," Cassie smiled suddenly, lighting up her whole face. Swinging her bag, she picked up her phone. "I'll see you both later," she said, as she too left, taking Eve with her.

Alone, Tyler sank back into her chair.

She ate fast, surprised by how, now that she had started, how hungry she was. She gobbled up the cooked breakfast, then the pancakes, and was halfway through the cereal before she stopped to take a breath.

The food sat lodged in her stomach suddenly, making her feel sick.

She had eaten too much, way too fast and the resulting uncomfortable bloating of her stomach was the result of that. Still, setting down her fork, she sent a grateful thought Cassie's way.

Even if she could still be a little strange at times.

Pushing the tray away, Tyler took out her own phone, called Cheryl Heep's number. With everything that had happened, it had slipped her mind entirely to call her... but why hadn't Ally's foster mom called her? The police must be in touch with her, but what news had she been given, if anything?

Tyler waited impatiently for the call to be put through, but after seven rings it went to her voicemail. Leaving a message for Cheryl to call, Tyler hung up the phone.

ONE HUNDRED FORTY-ONE

MASSACHUSETT'S BAY COLONY, 1693
Faces dark with soot and ash, Mary and her sisters stood outside the noisy tavern.

Amber light glowed from the lamps inside, battling with the encroaching night, yet darkness wasn't all that the men inside should fear.

After bidding farewell to Sofia and Bridget who had taken off to start their lives anew, The Four had returned to the town where the bloodshed had begun. What villagers they had come across were so terrified by their frightening visage that they were willing to answer what questions they had.

It had not taken long for them to find the tavern, filled to the brim with patrons that their drunken singing could be heard from even outside.

That they could be feeling so much joviality only made Tabitha's blood boil.

Try as she might, she could not erase the sight of Bridget, curled into a tight ball on the straw-covered ground, traumatized by the actions of the mob inside this very tavern.

She knew it was they who had led the council to Bridget's family home.

It was this very same mob who had rushed poor Ben and Sofia's rundown shack after the birth of their child only days before.

The men who, cheering and chanting without a care in the world right now, had so much to answer for.

The Four knew that the key to identifying — and stopping — the council lay inside.

"Prepare yourselves, sisters," Mary warned softly, her dark eyes glowing with an apprehensive light. "Our presence will not be welcomed."

Though Esther abhorred fighting of any kind, even she seemed prepared to deal with whatever might await them inside. Her lips pursed into a thin, tight line. She nodded grimly. "No, but as long as they do not lay a finger on us, all will be well."

Catherine nodded her head, steeling her thin shoulders for what lay ahead. "I am ready."

Taking a big breath, Mary pushed opened the heavy oak door as the four went inside.

The tavern reeked of alcohol, sweat, and dirt, personal cleanliness not being high on the list of its rowdy clientele's minds. Lamps glowed on crowded tables and in the corners of the room though shadows still loomed here and there, shielding entangled couples with more than drinking on their minds.

The Four's silent, obvious stance was a stark contrast to the noise and chaos that surrounded them. They stood, cooly accessing the room until the tavern crowd finally noticed their arrival.

All sound faded as they became first curious then growing increasingly more concerned as they recognized the four women.

"It's them! The witches!" A man cried out.

"But they were captured, we did it ourselves!" Another baffled — and frightened — voice said.

"They are to be tried tomorrow," came yet another.

A hulking large man with cheeks that were flushed with beer, pinned his cold eyes on them. "Then they must have broken out of their cells."

A rumble of unease rose through the ranks at the far side of the room, gathering momentum as it carried to the front. Hoping to calm the situation somewhat, Mary spoke.

"We are not here for any trouble. We only want to know where we can find the Council in charge of these witch hunts. We have no quarrel with you." Her voice rang clear and pure as a bell, cutting through the growing fog of hostility that emanated from the crowd.

"Do not listen to her! She lies like the Devil!" A woman cried. Catherine recognized her as one-half of one of the amorous couples and felt a sinking feeling in the pit of her stomach. The woman had gone from love to hate in the blink of an eye.

"Witch!"

"Whore of Satan!"

More rumbles came, louder this time. The edge of the crowd drew closer to them. Mary attempted to stand her ground only for Esther to pull her back.

"They are not listening!" She hissed at Mary when a pitcher flew across the room at them. The Four ducked, and the pitcher went soaring over their heads, but like a starter's pistol had gone off, the place suddenly erupted.

Mugs of beer and plates of half-eaten food came their way. They evaded the first few, but then a chipped mug caught Catherine on the side of her face. With a cry, she stumbled back into the wall, a vivid red cut appearing on her cheek.

Furious that one of their own had been hurt, Esther suddenly called upon her magic as the others did the same. Joining their powers and their will together, they formed an invisible barrier around them that stretched out several feet. Chairs, plates, and bottles bounced harmlessly off of the barrier.

The mob was stunned into silence, this being their first display of such power, but then a man climbed up onto a table — the towering man who had first spoken and who Tabitha now recognized.

It was the hateful man who had killed Ben so cruelly.

"Kill the witches!" He yelled, rousing the crowd once more.

At his cry, the crowd surged forward.

Under attack by so many of them, their barrier began to fade, unable to sustain such force. Their magic become strained, the barrier blinking a few times before vanishing completely, leaving them vulnerable.

Realizing that it was gone, the man threw up his arm and commanded, "Now!"

Tabitha did not think twice.

Focusing her magic on the instigator, she let the memory of Ben's face at the moment that his own ax had been ripped from his hands to slice into his own neck, flood her mind. Her magic surged anew, powered by the rage she could suddenly feel.

Charging forward, Tabitha broke rank as one of the mob ran for her, his arm raised overhead, armed with a dagger that he had removed from his belt. The dagger slashed down at her chest but when it came within inches of her, the metal of the blade melted into a pool of molten lava that dripped onto the floorboards below where it burned away at the wood.

The hilt of the dagger must have grown as hot as its blade as the man suddenly screamed, his hand beginning to smoke. Dropping what remained of the dagger, he opened his hand to reveal that where the weapon had touched it, the skin had melted away leaving behind a raw, bloody mess of burns.

Fuled by the alcohol and mob mentality, and not quite seeing what had happened to Dagger-Man, another villager rushed Tabitha, this one armed with a bottle. He swung the bottle at her head only for it to explode in his hand before it got anywhere near enough to do any kind of damage. Ale rained over him, soaking his dirt-encrusted tunic as glass shards sliced into his hand. Blood sprayed the air in an arc, staining it pink as he screamed with horror, cupping his bloody hand while watching his life force pooling onto the floor below.

The mob had stopped their braying now, frightened by what they were seeing. They stopped rushing the others, were backing away from them in fact. Only one man refused to retreat.

The man on the table.

The instigator who Tabitha made a bee-line for now.

Arriving at the table he stood on, she slammed her hand down onto it. The entire three-inch oak table top turned into a storm of wind and splinters that hurled him across the room, slamming him into the back wall and shattering his spine. What splinters that didn't spear him were impaled into the wall behind forming a gruesome frame around his body.

He dropped like lead, a stunned, dazed look in his eyes.

The rest of the crowd had frozen in abject terror. Tabitha walked to him through the remains of the ruined table that magically slid out of her way. Crouching down, she could see that his legs were useless now: he would never walk again.

Feeling a grim satisfaction, Tabitha leaned in close to whisper into his ear.

"Remember Ben? The "cripple" you murdered in cold blood? He sends his regards."

Eyes flashing with barely suppressed hate of her own, Tabitha rejoined her sisters.

ONE HUNDRED FORTY-TWO

Time seemed to lag, so it was with a huge sigh of relief when Marley finally found herself finished with the day's classes. Yes, she wanted to study, she just hadn't expected for the day to have taken as long as it had.

Hurrying towards her dorm room, eager to dump her course books before they moved onto their next task, she saw that Tyler's door was wide open. Inside, she paced back and forth, yelling into her phone while Cassie and Eve, who had finished before her, watched from the sidelines.

At her appearance, Cassie gave her a troubled look. "Ally's foster mom still hasn't called Tyler back," she said by way of explanation.

Dropping her bag by the door, Marley walked over to them as Tyler finished what was obviously the last of many calls.

"I don't know why you're not calling me back, Cheryl but this is outrageous. Ally is my family! You can't keep ignoring me! Call me back!"

Disconnecting the call, she ran a hand through her

messy hair, looking at the silent phone in a daze. "Why won't she call me?"

"I don't know, but this isn't doing you any favors. Let's go get that artifact and then we'll figure out a plan of attack for the foster mom," Eve suggested in what she hoped was an understanding yet firm voice.

"I'm sorry," Tyler said, apologetic even through her anxiousness. "I can't really focus on that. I need to go to Cheryl's in person, find out what she knows…"

While Marley understood how she must be feeling, she also knew that it was up to them to remind her of all that was at stake — even if it meant tough love was in order.

"Ty, I know this is hard — and we can go with you to Cheryl's after — but we need to do this now before it gets too late and harder for us to see if there's going to be an ambush like last time. Plus we need you… look what almost happened when you weren't there."

Marley felt like a jerk for saying that last part even if it was the truth. Emotional blackmail wasn't something she would ever resort to normally.

Then again, everything was far from normal.

Eve must have known what she was doing as she joined in. "It was hard going there, Tyler. Especially since I kinda froze. I messed up leaving Marley and Cassie to fight by themselves. If it wasn't for those guys, God knows what the outcome would have been."

Tyler raised tortured eyes at them, battling with her inner demons.

"Please, Tyler. We can't do it without you," Cassie pleaded softly.

The enormous three-story mansion loomed, a hulking monster covered with gothic features. Ugly gargoyles perched on twisting spires that glared down at the girls as they stood outside the six-foot-tall steel fence that surrounded the property. Beyond the fence, a thick hedge made it impossible to see anything other than the second floor of the building. A gate that formed part of the fence stood before them, locked and impenetrable.

The place was like Fort Knox.

"On the plus side, it doesn't look like any demons would be able to get over that fence, so we're about as safe as can be once we get inside," Cassie said optimistically, looking for the silver lining.

"I'm instantly regretting my decision to come with you," Tyler said, staring up at the impenetrable-looking fence.

"In fairness, you didn't decide so much as we guilt you into coming," Marley responded, trying to add some cheer into what was fast looking like a dead end. "Yay, for peer pressure."

"Hey, look at this," Eve called over from where she was standing in front of a noticeboard of sorts, on which there was written a few paragraphs about the building. "It talks about the architecture, mentions that the library holds some of the country's oldest privately held books, but it is not open to the public."

"Does it mention who owns the place?" Cassie asked.

Eve's eyes looked over the writing again. "Yeah, Mitchell Smithingtonson."

"Smithingtonson, that's an actual name?" Marley said, her tone implying anything but.

Cassie didn't answer, busy typing into her phone. Within seconds she had pulled up several hits on the elusive multi-millionaire.

"He doesn't seem to like being in the public much. No

reports of him out and about even though he regularly purchases some of the most expensive antiques in the world. Books are just one of the things he collects. It's weird — he seems to have more money than God, but no one knows where it came from." She swiped quickly on the screen, chewing on the corner of her lip. "I can't seem to find… no wait, here's a picture… oh," she said suddenly disappointed.

"What's wrong?" Marley asked, wondering what she was up to.

"It's only of his face. I can only find a few images of him but they're all the same — which means I only have an idea of what his face looks like, not the rest of him."

"Right… which means it'll be difficult for you to become him," Marley realized where she was going with all this.

"Exactly. I figured I could be him and then I'd just walk right on in, once we figure a way through this fence."

"The fence part is easy," Tyler said suddenly as if she wasn't giving it any consideration whatsoever. Moving to the locked gate, she moved her hand over the lock as her eyes took on a distant look. The air thickened for a moment as they felt her magic take hold, then the lock suddenly ripped apart, falling to the ground in two pieces.

"Remind me to bring Tyler to all our future break-ins," Eve commented wryly.

Cassie stared at the dead lock. "What did you do to it?"

"I heated it up on the inside until the fittings were fried," Tyler said without any kind of excitement as if she did this kind of thing all the time.

"What are you?" Cassie asked, her eyes flashing with admiration, but Tyler didn't seem to care, her mind very much on other matters.

"The sooner we do this, the sooner I can get to Cheryl's so can we speed this along?"

Quickly, Cassie morphed into Smithingtonson. No matter how many times they did this, Eve was always startled by Cassie's physical changes. She stared at the grey pinstripe suit Cassie had decided to wear. It was a similar suit to the kind that was in the photograph. She had made him an average height and build. A gold Rolex sat on his wrist, and the platinum cufflinks were inscribed with his initials. His shoes were polished until they shone.

All in all, it seemed a good interpretation of how Smithingtonson might look and Eve was impressed by the subtle details Cassie had put in.

"The cufflinks are genius," she congratulated her.

Cassie flashed her a grin. "Thanks. I thought of what my Grandad looks like and kind of went from there. He has money too."

"Is your entire family loaded?" Tyler wanted to know.

Cassie shrugged. "I guess. He owns a big shipping company."

Moving to the gate, Cassie pushed it open, stepping through, trying not to look self-conscious.

"Can you see what's up ahead? I can't see over this hedge," Marley asked, trying but failing to see over the top of the green border.

"There's a guard with a dog, he seems to be patrolling the place," Cassie's headless voice whispered back to them. "He hasn't seen me yet but he probably will when I get closer."

"So what's our plan?" Tyler asked. "Do we just walk in with her and hope that the guard's going to believe he has three nieces of three different races?"

"That depends if, by nieces, you mean lady-of-the-night?" Eve answered a brow arched airily on her face.

"Ew," Marley commented, her lips twisting into disgust.

"It's not like these things don't happen," Eve finished.

"I think I'm just going to go inside, then when I find a

back door, I'll let you in or Tyler can do her thing," Cassie interrupted their banter, her head clearly more in the game than theirs.

"Good idea," Marley said. "We'll keep an eye on the guard and sneak around when he's not looking."

Consenting to the plan, Cassie starting toward the mansion. Her eyes took in the landscaped gardens with flowers in full bloom and young trees that had been perfectly trimmed into geometrical shapes. It was amazing how much went into the upkeep of this place for only one man and his family to enjoy. Thinking of how they lived at home, with their own designer houses and gardens, Cassie resolved not to lock herself away in the same manner — life was better when you had people to share it with.

Thinking of that, an image of Trip appeared in her mind and she found herself smiling. She'd already received several sweet messages from him this morning immediately upon waking. She loved that she was the first thing he thought of when he woke up, it made her feel so special.

She was still thinking of him when the security guard came back upon his route only to freeze at the sight of her.

"Mr. Smithingtonson," he exclaimed, looking about as shocked as Cassie felt for having forgotten herself for a moment. "I didn't expect to see you here."

"Yes… hello," she said, before realizing that it wasn't the greeting of a man whose wealth surpassed many of those before him. "And why is that?" She asked, hoping by asking him the question, it would buy her time to collect her thoughts.

"You usually only come during the winter," the guard said nervously, wondering if he was speaking out of bounds. He shook the lead that was attached to the dog who bared his teeth at Cassie and growled.

"Stop it, Thunder," he commanded, but it just seemed

to make the dog more upset. He lowered his head at Cassie, straining at his leash as she tried not to shudder at the rows of wickedly sharp teeth.

"Times change young man. I like to be unpredictable," Cassie said.

The guard dug his heels into the ground, struggling against his dog. "I'm sorry, Sir, I don't know what's gotten into Thunder, he usually loves to see you."

Cassie knew exactly what was wrong with the dog: he knew she was an imposter and was trying to let his handler know the only way he knew how. Though she could feel a finger of apprehension sliding down her spine, Cassie forced herself to stand tall.

"I got a few cats a while ago, I think he can smell them on me," she said stepping around them so she could move ahead.

By now, Thunder was straining so hard against the leash that it was all the guard could do to stop him from flying at Cassie. "I think I need to get him to cool off, Sir. Sorry about this. I don't know what's gotten into him."

"The door's open?" Cassie asked in a neutral tone.

"Of course not, Sir," the guard responded quickly, mistaking her intention for asking. "I always keep it locked as per your instructions."

"Very good, though I seem to have forgotten my own key today," Cassie replied stretching her hand out so he could give his to her.

Thunder was whining now, upset that he couldn't get to Cassie to tear her apart.

Embarrassment and concerned for his dog's erratic behavior, the guard unclipped the set of keys from around his belt and handed them to her.

"You may go," Cassie waved her hand grandly at him, hoping he would get the hint and take the dog as far from her as was humanly possible. It wasn't in her plan to get eaten by an angry dog today.

"Of course, sir… Sorry again."

He hurried away with Thunder, scolding him the entire time.

Looking at the lock, she selected a key which seemed a match but it wouldn't even slip into the lock. Taking another, she tried again. This time, the key went in but wouldn't turn. Over and over, she tested more keys. With every one that she got wrong, Cassie grew more panicked in case the guard — or worse, his dog — would appear again.

When the lock finally clicked open with only two keys left remaining, Cassie was close to tears. Hurrying inside, she closed the door behind her and took a moment to center herself.

She was standing in a large hallway, a sweeping staircase directly in front of her that branched off in two directions.

Dark mahogany wood covered most surfaces, from the banisters on the staircase to the paneling on the walls. The only color came from a stained glassed window overlooking the staircase that left a rainbow on the steps below.

Ignoring the stairs, Cassie went right, hurrying down a long hallway that led into a grand room where a diamond chandelier hung, suspended from the ceiling. Oriental rugs and antique furniture littered the polished parquet flooring.

She crossed the first room which connected into another where a giant oval table sat. Here she was relieved to find a door that led outside though it was locked and the key was nowhere to be found.

Taking out her phone, she sent the girls a quick message, giving directing them to this door. Moments later, they arrived outside. Cassie showed the keys she had acquired but Tyler stepped forward, shooting her a look as if to say they wouldn't be necessary.

As before, Tyler placed her hand on the doorknob.

Cassie saw the brass knob glow red before a click sounded. Opening the door, Tyler came inside when…

Alarms started shrieking overhead.

Startled, Cassie turned around to see a sensor above her head.

They had tripped the alarms!

ONE HUNDRED FORTY-THREE

Marley froze as alarms screamed from every direction.

Close by, Thunder began barking, warning his handler of this new threat. They only had seconds before they would be spotted.

"I knew we should have used the keys!" Cassie cried, flinching at the surrounding noise.

"Well, it's too late now!" Tyler snapped back, unhappy with the shade being thrown her way. "Besides, you were plenty happy when I did the same thing to the gate outside, how was I supposed to know this door would be alarmed?"

"We don't have time for this!" Eve snapped at the two of them as if they were bickering kids.

"You three hide, I'll distract him," Cassie said, moving toward the door.

As the others ducked beneath the window, Cassie saw the shadow of the guard and his dog appearing on the path outside, their footsteps crunching into gravel. Cautiously, the guard slid his weapon out of its holster but kept the muzzle pointed to the ground.

"Sir? Mr. Smithingtonson?" he called out. "Are you alright?"

Putting on an embarrassed smile, Cassie planted herself in the doorway, physically blocking him from entering. "My absentmindedness strikes again. I can never seem to remember the alarms."

The guard eye's turned confused for the moment, this clearly not what he was used to from the real Smithingtonson. Seeing right through her disguise, his dog barked at Cassie still trying to get to her. He shot the dog an irritated look. "What is with you today, Thunder?"

A voice crackled over the radio the guard wore clipped to his belt. "What's the issue, Bishop?"

The guard, Bishop unclipped his radio, shooting a look of apology at Cassie. "Sorry Sir, but I'll have to call this in, even if it's only a false alarm." He spoke into the radio. "Sensor's been tripped on the West Side door, but it's a false alarm."

"Affirmative. We'll still have to send a car out. Protocol, over."

"Roger that," Bishop said.

Marley felt a jolt of unease. Like the others, her back was pressed up against the wall, but the guard and his dog were only on the other side of the wall to them.

If he managed to come in through the door, he would see them.

But they couldn't attack him. He wasn't a demon, he was one of the good guys. A man just doing his job.

What on Earth were they going to do?

Unable to think fast enough, Marley felt like her racing heart would explode out of her chest. Pressing a hand against it, hoping to still the pounding, she suddenly felt the air turn heavy with the weight of magic.

Turning, she saw Eve's eyes had taken on that distant look she had whenever she was communicating with her *others*.

Cautiously, Marley inched upward to look outside

where a cloud of black was forming in the sky. She couldn't see what it was made of exactly, only able to identify that there were lots of them, whatever they were. Only the top of her head showed above the window ledge, still, it was a risk to peek outside — if Bishop happened to glance her way, he would see her, but his attention was drawn to the strange sight of that moving cloud which rushed toward him.

Beside him, Thunder howled in absolute agitation. The alarm, the smell of intruders, Cassie wearing Smithingtonson's face, and now this cloud was all too much for him. Straining, he jerked his leash free from Bishop's grasp.

Finding himself suddenly free, the dog bolted toward the window Marley hid behind. Launching himself at it, his paws hit the glass his jaws coming within inches of her face. She reeled back even though the glass separated the two of them.

"What the hell is that?" Tyler, across from Marley on the other side of the door, heard Bishop say, as he stared up at the cloud that was only a few feet away from him now. He became conscious of a low hum next, like the soft buzz he would hear if he turned on his surround system too high while nothing was playing. It was the sound of electricity springing to life, but out here, it had to be something else altogether.

He blinked, wondering if he was seeing things as the cloud dispersed into millions of bugs that flew out of it toward him. He swung at them, trying to keep them from his face but there were so many that no matter how many he was able to swat, more than double remained. He heard a peculiar sound come out of Thunder who had returned to his side; it was a mixture of a snarl and a yowl. The poor guy was as freaked out as he was.

They had to get away from this swarm to safety — and that meant inside the building, where Smithingtonson still stood in the doorway, gaping at the scene outside.

"Inside sir!" Bishop managed to shout, spitting out the few bugs that had managed to fly into his mouth. Covering his head the best he could, he meant to rush inside when through the black haze several figures appeared.

Thunder spun instantly around, his snarls increasing by savagery tenfold.

Bishop had raised Thunder from a puppy. He had adopted him from the animal shelter, where they had found him, the smallest of his litter, cowering beneath a dumpster where some awful person had left them. Their mom was nowhere in sight. The entire litter had been close to death when they had been found.

Thunder had been the runt of the litter and the most unwanted. When his siblings had been adopted, he was still waiting in the shelter for someone to save him. Serendipitously, Bishop had been thinking of getting a dog to train to use with his security business. One look at the tiny pup so down at the world that he couldn't even wag his tail and Bishop had known he'd have to save him.

He knew everything about this dog. They'd trained together for two years, Thunder by his side through each of his jobs. He knew what every resonance, every growl signified.

This particular growl he had never heard from the dog.

Whatever this new threat was, he knew he should be very concerned.

Every one of Thunder's protective instincts kicked in. Not caring that they outnumbered him five to one, Thunder ran at the group of men. Bishop didn't stop to think, following to give his partner backup.

"Stop what you're doing! This is private property!" He called out, pointing his gun at them.

One of the shadowy black figures, a monstrous guy had proportions that didn't seem possible. His head seemed too small for the size of his body and though Bishop couldn't see too clearly, it seemed that he had elongated arms with pinchers for hands.

He was still looking at the pincher-hands when one of them went for Thunder sending him flying through the air. He hit the ground hard, whined, but got back onto his feet. Even from where he stood Bishop could see the glaze in his dog's eyes.

The world turned red as Bishop felt a rage like never before. No one messed with his dog. No one hurt Thunder. He ran at the group of men…

Back in the house, Tyler grabbed Eve's arm. "Those are demons! Can you get your birds or rats to do anything? They're going to kill that guy and his dog!"

Sweat broke across Eve's brow, as her brow furrowed with concentration. "I can't! I've already summoned the bugs…"

"But they're not going to hurt those demons!" Tyler began only for Eve to cut her off.

"I know! That's why I called them in the first place! We wanted something to distract the guard not hurt him that's why I sent for the bugs. But now I can't seem to call them off, and I can't summon anything else — they're here until the threat's gone."

Marley called over to them, worry clouding her eyes. "They don't know what they're up against. We can't just stay here."

She looked down at her hands thinking of what they had done before, and what they could do again. Her head snapped to Cassie. "Cassie! Go find the book now! We'll deal with this," she instructed.

Cassie shot her a startled look, swallowed the dry lump in her throat before hurrying into the building. Without pausing to think about her decision, Marley sprinted outside. Eve and Tyler shot each other a startled look before they too ran after her.

***

Bishop pointed his gun at the men but they didn't seem the least bit afraid of him. He shot a warning shot into the air, expecting them to back off but instead, they inched closer.

He pointed the gun at each figure as they approached. He could see them clearer now, could see that they looked to be wearing masks on their faces — which was a bad sign. Only people who meant to do real harm hid their faces. Through the swarm of insects, he could make out reptilian features: yellow eyes with thin oval pupils, and even what looked to be *gills* on the side of one guy's neck.

Thunder limped back to his side, pressing into his leg to let him know he was there, but his buddy was hurt.

Where the hell was back-up?

At an unspoken command, the group rushed him. Bishop fired his gun, but it was next to impossible to aim with the damn bugs flying everywhere. Still, he felt a moment's triumph having caught one of the thugs on the shin. Blood sprayed into the air but instead of being red like regular blood… his blood looked *green*.

He didn't have time to think about it as the rest of the group reached him. Hands flew out at him, pummelling him like he was a punchbag. The blows were crushing, winding blows that felt like weights were being hurled at his stomach. He fell to the ground unable to fight back. He could only lie there as blows rained down on him.

He heard Thunder's snarls turn into yelps as they hurt him again. He felt awful for not being able to protect him, for letting this be their end after all they had gone through together.

Curled into a tight ball, he waited for death to take him.

ONE HUNDRED FORTY-FOUR

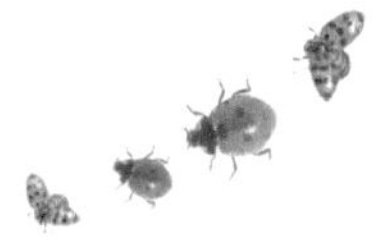

Hurrying through the house, Cassie scanned the spines of every book in every room that she went into. The further she got into the house, the more rooms she flew past as she searched for the actual library.

Shouts sounded outside.

There was some sort of commotion behind her where she had left the girls but she wouldn't allow herself to see what it was even though her nerves were shrieking at her to go back. Whatever it was, the girls would handle it.

At least, that's what she kept telling herself.

Holding onto that thought Cassie sped through the house searching the ground floor, but there was no sign of the library. Coming back to the main staircase, she sprinted up the stairs, two at a time until out of breath from her efforts, she reached the next landing.

Standing right before her was a set of double-height oak doors. The wood was intricately carved with the scene of a heavenly battle in progress. Angels fought, their wings spread magnificently around them as their foe fell one by one, plunging down to hell.

It was a stunning piece which any other day Cassie would have loved to examine further.

Grasping the brass door handle, Cassie tried to turn it only to find that it was locked. She hesitated, not sure what to do next when several symbols began flashing up on the carving.

They weren't in any language she recognized yet there was something ancient and powerful about them. The symbols glowed with a dazzling white light that almost blinded her. She felt the handle grow warm to the touch as it too began to glow with that same white light.

Suddenly the light vanished and Cassie found that she could turn the handle. Opening the door, she stepped through.

The domed room was lined with bookshelves on every wall. Though the height of the room seemed to soar into the sky — an optical illusion which was helped by the clear glass ceiling — the actual shelves weren't too tall, stretching maybe only six feet from the ground. There wasn't even a need for a ladder — if Cassie stood on her toes, she could reach the books on any of the top shelves, a fact which she found of huge relief.

Moving to the first bookcase, she glanced at the titles but they weren't alphabetized as she had hoped, organized instead by century. Googling James Allen, the highwayman, Cassie learned that he was active in the 1900s.

Her eyes took in each of the labels until they landed on the corresponding bookshelf. She worked quickly, but it wasn't until she reached the bottom shelf that her stomach flip-flopped when her hand passed over a book. She stopped, moving back to the volume which had caused the feeling.

It was a thin book — so thin that its spine only measured a few millimeters across. She would have missed it completely if it wasn't for the evilness that came off of it that sent her stomach lurching.

Cassie pulled the small book from the shelf trying to

ignore the fact that it was bound in human skin. Her skin crawled. It was all she could do not to drop it.

Hurrying out of the library, Cassie started back for the girls. She was at the top of the giant staircase when she found herself suddenly grabbed from behind. Thick arms tightened around her vice-like, pulling her back until the breath was squeezed out of her.

Her magic disguise vanished, unable to maintain her power and focus. She was vulnerable and helpless.

She was herself.

"Thanks for the book," a male voiced hissed into her ear. "We couldn't get past the wards so it's lucky you could," he revealed, snatching the book from her terrified hands. His breath was so close to her that she could smell the foul stench of it as he breathed into the side of her face. The arms released her next with such suddenness that she wasn't prepared for it. Her relief at being free lasted only a moment, however, as his hands shoved at her — hard.

She felt herself falling through space in slow motion.

Faces of loved ones flashed into her mind. She thought about her parents, how much she loved them; how she was glad to have finally found some real friends even though their friendship hadn't lasted long. Trip's face came into her mind too as she wondered what might have been if the two of them had been given a chance.

She was thinking all of these things when she started toppling over the stairs.

***

Bishop was down on the ground being beaten to a pulp. His dog wasn't faring much better.

Marley had to get there quickly if she was going to do anything to save him. A sound burst out of her, a rebellious yell that caught their attention and halted their actions. Marley charged at them her hands out-stretched like weapons.

The demon she got closest too, simply sidestepped out of the way, knocking her hands into the air where they met with nothing. She stumbled past, carried by the momentum of her charge. When she could stop, someone tackled her to the ground. Her hands, her potential — and only weapon — were pinned uselessly beneath her.

"Leave her alone!" Eve called out rushing the demon who had her on the ground. Twisting her face to one side, Marley could see the swarm had gathered around Bishop and his dog in a cloud so thick that she couldn't see through it.

The other demons were turning their attention to Tyler and Eve, though their movements were cautious — having been warned about them. Marley felt sick inside knowing that they should have expected this. Just because the demon's hadn't gone through the gate at the time, it hadn't meant that they *couldn't*.

A piece of the gravel that her face was pressed against suddenly lifted into the air. Marley blinked at it, wondering if it was just one of the black spots caused by the lack of air when another piece of gravel levitated, followed by another, then more.

The world fell silent as they all took in the bizarre sight of so many of the tiny stones hovering a few feet from the ground.

"Now." Tyler spoke so quietly that Marley wondered if she had heard her correctly.

Suddenly, the gravel flew at the demons, pelting them like millions of tiny bullets. One covered his eyes where the gravel had caught him, while another tried to shield his face as he ran for cover behind a tree. The remaining demons took cover as the gravel projectiles shot after them.

Marley felt the pressure from her back release as her restrainer left. One of the demons gave a signal then he also left. The remaining demons followed after him without a second glance at the girls. Marley felt confusion combine with relief.

Why were they leaving?

They hadn't killed them, and though Tyler's neat trick with the gravel had hurt them, it wouldn't have killed any of them. They were clearly winning the fight… so why were they leaving?

"Cassie!" Her name burst out of her as she realized that while they were fighting, they didn't know where she was or if she had found the memoir.

But if the demon's had retreated by themselves, it could only mean one thing.

They had the book.

Where then, was Cassie?

ONE HUNDRED FORTY-FIVE

Time seemed to have frozen for Cassie.

Even as she went over the stairs, she knew there was nothing she could do to brace her fall. Those majestic stairs she had noticed when she'd first stepped foot inside the building were going to be her downfall.

The world spun, sending her dizzy as she went down. Over and over she tumbled, hitting the first step with such impact that she felt a tooth bite into a lip. She tasted the metallic taste of blood, felt her body collide with every step but had the presence of mind to try to shield her head on the way down.

When she finally hit solid ground, and the world stopped spinning, she lay there wondering if she was dead.

She couldn't feel anything.

Her body was numb.

"Hell, Pike, what have you done?"

Hearing the peeved voice, Cassie closed her eyes and lay there, still as a mouse.

"It was an accident," came another male voice, this

one more weedy, subordinate.

And lying through his teeth.

"We need to get out of here so Michael doesn't lose his mind," the one who was obviously in command said.

A sound came out of the one called Pike that was half squeal, half whine as he fretted over the likelihood of his mortality.

"Leave the bag. Let's clear out before the cops or the other witches get here."

Cassie heard Pike thundering down the stairs toward her. Then something soft landed beside her before both demons hurried away.

When their footsteps faded, she tried to sit up but pain lashed at her body, seemingly from everywhere. She sucked in a shocked breath, never having felt anything like this in her life. Her initial numbness was just shock, and now that it was fading, the hurt was hitting her hard.

Tears sprang into her eyes. Gingerly, she moved each of her limbs, testing to see if anything was broken. When she tried to move her right leg, blinding pain that brought fresh tears to her eyes forced her to immediately stop. Gritting her teeth, she pushed into an upright position only to find that her leg was bent at an awkward angle.

Definitely broken.

She was trying to figure out how she could get up and walk when footsteps approached. She went deathly still, afraid to move even an inch in case she made a sound.

"Cassie, oh my God! Are you OK?"

It was Marley.

The girls raced toward her, their faces stricken by the sight of her.

"One of the demons, the one called Pike pushed me down the stairs. I… my leg's broken," she stammered, feeling both relieved yet wanting to cry at the same time.

Tyler examined her broken leg, her face looked grim. "Can you get up?"

"I tried, but it hurts too much," Cassie admitted.

Eve said, "The cops are on their way, we need to get out of here before they do."

But they all knew that it would be impossible for them to move Cassie with her leg like that. Marley stared at Tyler, something on her mind.

"What is it?" Tyler asked, picking up on her indecision.

"How did you get that gravel to do that outside?" Marley asked.

"I manipulated the surrounding air."

Marley's eyes grew darker. "Every time you've used your power, you've manipulated what was already there haven't you? When you turned the rain into those glass shards, or the sea beneath us into frozen spears..."

Tyler thought back, wondering where she was going with this. "I think so. Apart from the spells we've cast, I mean. Why are you asking me this?"

"I'm wondering if you can manipulate Cassie's leg to fix it?"

"Unbreak it?"

"In a word, yes," Marley replied.

Tyler blinked, startled by the question, having never considered such a thing before. "I don't know..." she began, worried at all the things that could go wrong.

"I'm sorry to rush you, but if we're going to do this, we'd better do it now," Eve urged, casting a nervous look through a window where she could see all the way back to the front gate. It was still clear now but it wouldn't be for long.

Tyler shot a nervous look at Cassie: she was in so much pain that Tyler was terrified she would be the cause of more if she tried this.

Understanding the doubts she had, Cassie forced herself to smile through the pain. "You can do this, Tyler. I believe in you."

Knowing that leaving Cassie wasn't an option, Tyler lowered onto her knees beside her. "Hold on to the other two," she instructed quietly, waiting as Marley and Eve took hold of her hands. When Cassie nodded that she was ready, Tyler focused on Cassie's leg. Placing her hands gently onto it, Tyler pictured Cassie's leg becoming whole again in her mind.

She saw the shattered pieces of bone as easily as if they were a detailed, three-dimensional picture in her mind. Willing the bone to heal, Tyler felt heat flowing out of her hands.

Suddenly Cassie tensed. Gripping onto Marley and Eve's hands, she went white as tears started spilling down her face. Tyler almost stopped but Cassie shook her head. "Keep going," she hissed at her, the pain so intense that it was all she could do not to scream.

Marley didn't know how but she suddenly started feeling Cassie's pain herself. As if it was happening to her own leg, she felt the pain of her leg being forced to knit itself back together. Across from her, Eve too had grown paler, and she knew she was going through the same. Even Tyler wasn't exempt, tears welling up in her eyes too.

Cassie's grip on their hands lessened as her breathing became more normal. Blinking in wonder, Cassie realized that the girls were taking on her pain so that she wouldn't feel as much of it.

They watched, awed as her leg began to heal in front of their very eyes. The shattered bones moved back into place beneath the skin until Cassie's leg finally straightened. "Is it OK?" Tyler asked her, helping her up.

Cassie tested her leg by shifting her weight to it gingerly at first, then more forcefully when no pain emerged. Beaming, she flashed a grin at Tyler.

"I told you you could do it."

The girls were staring at Tyler with such expressions of awe that she found herself feeling embarrassed. "Stop looking at me like that," she said, backing away from them when she almost tripped over something on the ground.

Managing to catch her balance, Tyler looked at the offending item only to gasp, startled. There, sitting on the floor, was Ally's ladybug bag.

"That's the bag! It was with her when she was taken. What's it doing there?"

"Pike, that demon left it there," Cassie suddenly remembered. "It didn't make sense to me at the time, but I heard them say to leave the bag here. They left it here for you to find."

"They left it here to taunt me, to let me know that Michael has Ally."

All the joy Tyler had felt only seconds ago at healing Cassie vanished in the blink of an eye. Before they could react, approaching sirens sounded.

"Go… We need to leave!" Eve urged, sprinting for the door.

They hurried to the back of the building, running through the gardens until they came upon the fence. Though she was drained from using her power twice already, Tyler held her hand out at the metal fence which grew hot enough that it became pliable. They pulled the bars wide apart enough to slip through.

As more security guards spilled onto the property, the girls hurried away.

R age coursed through her veins painting the world red.

The whole way back to their dorm, Tyler had sat quietly in Eve's car, Ally's bag gripped in her hands as the inferno of fury built into a tornado that threatened to burst.

She wanted nothing more than to cast a spell to find Michael and rip him to pieces.

"No, Tyler! You're not strong enough to do that," Marley said her voice heavy with concern as they walked down the hall that lead to their rooms. She had felt the magic Tyler had subconsciously started to channel.

"You admitted that you've used up all your magic juice for today, you don't know what forcing the issue will do," Eve admonished taking on her I'm-the-oldest-so-don't-mess-with-me voice.

"He wants you to get angry. Michael wants you to lose it. Why else would they leave that bag for you? Don't give in!" Cassie pleaded.

Whatever they were going to say next was stopped by the appearance of the student who lived in the room next to theirs. The few times Marley had seen her, she always had her head buried in a textbook. In fact, there was one clutched in her hands now. Seeing them, she shot them all a look of great disdain. "Hey," she said, her voice loaded with loathing. "Do you mind keeping the noise down? Some of us are actually here to study."

Spinning on her heel, she took off before any of them had a chance to understand her comment. Frowning, Marley neared her room when thumping music coming from inside the room caused the door to judder in its frame.

Unlocking the door, she opened it to find the place in utter disarray. Clothes were strewn all over the room, furniture upturned. Their books, DVDs, and things were *everywhere*. No inch of the place had been left unscathed.

Wind blew in from a window that had been pried wide open. A trail of dirt started from the window ledge, leaving footprints along the carpet.

Cassie gasped as she took in the damage. "They've been here."

"That window wasn't open when we left today," Marley pointed out the site of their entry.

Cassie crossed the room to her sound system jabbing

at the off button with her finger. Mercifully, the head-pounding music stopped.

"They were using the music to cover up what they were doing," Eve said.

Hurrying to her own room, Tyler flung open the door to find that it too had been given the same treatment. Locking the door behind her, she headed back to the girls, unable to deal with the mess now. "They must have been searching for the stocking while we were out."

Stepping over the mess, Marley went to her bed. "We should have known they'd come here. We're just lucky that they waited until we were gone."

"What the hell happened?" Christian asked suddenly, having appeared before Marley.

She filled him in quickly as the others tried to clear up. By the time she was done, Christian had grown uncustomary silent.

"Don't we need to find a way to stop this from happening again? We need to protect our homes and the stocking. If they got into the dorm, they're going to eventually figure out where else we go… Isn't there a spell we could cast to stop them from getting in?"

Cassie's eyes grew wide. "When I found the library, the doors were locked at first but then these symbols lit up and the door just opened on its own for me. Then that Pike guy, the demon? Before he threw me down the stairs, he thanked me. He thanked me for getting through the wards when they couldn't."

"Wards?" Marley asked. Something about that term rang a bell. "Didn't you mention something about the Guardian HQ being protected by wards the first time you took us there?" The question was directed at Christian.

"Yeah," Christian answered carelessly. "But wards are only good for protecting buildings and places, not people."

He stopped, seeing the astonished look Marley gave him.

"Don't you think that's important information for us to know?" she asked, her voice rising, incredulous. "How could you not have told us this? How could you not ward our homes?"

"Because I can't ward anything. Only witches can," Christian replied not realizing that he was just digging a bigger hole for himself.

The stress of the day coupled with seeing her home invaded like this was too much for Marley. She didn't feel safe here anymore. She felt violated. Shooting daggers at him, she stormed up to his face, so that she was only inches from him.

"But isn't that what we are? Seriously, Christian! How can you not have told us that? How can you call yourself a Guardian when you seem to know nothing? You're no help to us whatsoever!"

Flinching at her words, Christian looked stricken. Growing pale, he disappeared abruptly. Faced with his sudden absence, Marley felt a hint of guilt beneath her anger, even though she knew she was right.

Why then, did she feel so terrible about upsetting him?

ONE HUNDRED FORTY-SIX

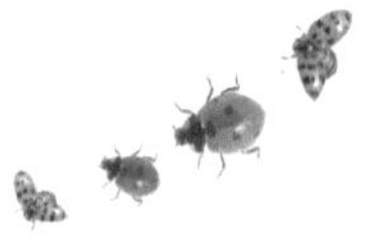

Marley reached into the hidden keypad, typing the code that would let them inside Guardian HQ.

They had agreed that they needed to learn more about warding — well, mostly agreed... Tyler wanted to go after Michael but since they didn't want him to find the stocking too, it was decided that this would be a better course of action.

"What's the code?" Tyler asked. "We should probably know it in case we ever need to come here separately."

"Sorry, I thought I'd already told you. It's 100214."

The girls stored the number into their phones as the wall of steel slid open. Overhead lights flashed on illuminating the large warehouse that the Guardians had used for years as their base camp.

Marley took in the prominent weapon display that covered every wall. Her eyes moved over the room to the Olympic-sized boxing ring that formed the center of the space. Seeing it, she couldn't help but remember her first training session with Christian...

How much things had changed since then.

Maybe it was the very thought of him that summoned him — he seemed to be more and more in tune with her lately — but Marley could sense the instant Christian was back.

He stood a way off from them. Expecting some form of his usual snarky greeting, his silence was therefore conspicuous. She had hurt him earlier, and it looked like he wasn't over it yet.

"You look for information on warding, I've got to speak to Christian," she said.

Clearing her throat, she wandered over to him.

"Hey," she began, keeping her voice low so the others couldn't hear the conversation. "I'm sorry about earlier. I didn't mean for it to sound quite that harsh. I was just taken aback, especially after what we'd just found."

His green-gold eyes shifted from the wall of weapons he'd been studying to settle on her face. "No, but you weren't wrong." There was no hint of sarcasm in his voice, only pain and something else that colored his words… Regret.

"I didn't lie to you when I said I'd had years of training. I really have." He gestured at the wall of weapons. "I can use most of these, kill with them if I have to. I spent years of my life perfecting my physicality to become a demon hunter. Though I would never have the strength they have or any of their powers, I could hold my own. But that was only the beginning of it."

His eyes shone with the intensity of his passion. "The thing is, to become a Guardian, you have to pass the final initiation. When you have proven yourself physically capable of the job, magic sigils are tattooed onto your body in a ceremony that marks you as a Guardian. The sigils protect you from being killed by supernatural evil, but the real Guardian training begins after that."

"So it's like becoming a cop and only being able to use a gun after it's official?" Marley asked, attempting to make sense of his words.

"Right. Except Eric was killed shortly after my initiation. And then I died right after that..." he admitted, his voice so soft that Marley could barely hear him. "I only know the physical side to it as I never had the chance to begin my real studies."

Marley could feel herself reeling. It all made so much more sense why Christian's help had always been so spotty: he hadn't finished his training! "Why didn't you say anything about this?"

"I was embarrassed, but then, as things became progressively more dangerous, I didn't want you to think me more useless than I already am. My job is to protect you, yet I'm stuck as a spirit who can't even pick up a remote control."

"Well, it's not like there's anything good on TV these days, anyway. It's all reality this and Kardashian, that," Marley grinned hoping to lighten up the mood but she couldn't get even a hint of a smile out of him. Her eyes grew serious.

"Those sigils you mentioned, they're different from the protection wards?"

"Yes."

"So if we had them tattooed onto us would they would protect us in the same way?" Marley grew excited at the thought. Imagine not having to worry about demons being able to hurt them!

"Technically, yes, though it's not so much the sigils as the very process of the tattooing. It's passed down through the Guardian line. It's a fine, delicate art." His voice turned miserable again leaving Marley to jump to the obvious conclusion.

"Let me guess, one that you haven't mastered yet?"

"It's the last thing we are taught so that it can't be misused," he answered.

"What about the protective wards? What do you know about those?"

"I know that they're around the place but not where

they are. They were cast way before my time by some local wizards and witches."

"Wizards? Like Harry Potter?" Marley didn't know why she had never thought of the possibility of a male witch before, not when she had grown up with the books after all. "So we really could ward places ourselves?"

"Yes, but I didn't mention it until now because I know what you're like."

"You might need to explain that comment," Marley suggested carefully, folding her arms across her chest.

"Warding spells mess with evil. The caster has to know exactly what they are doing, be unshakeable in their belief and concentration or the reverse of what you are trying to do can happen: instead of warding against evil, you can invite it in."

A shiver as cold as ice ran down her back at his words.

"Can you see now why I didn't tell you? I knew that if you knew, you would all rush headlong into it any way… God knows what could have happened. You weren't ready," he finished.

"Do you think we are now?"

"Let's see what we can find out about the warding spells and go from there," he evaded, but Marley didn't push the question.

They rejoined the others and got to work searching for information. Eve utilised her skill with computers to compile a list of quick references to warding but it was Tyler who hit pay dirt when she came across a series of leather-bound tomes with gold titles embossed on their spines in the hidden section of the library.

"I seem to have found a chapter in this book which explains how a person would go about warding a place," she said, keeping her voice steady. The others looked over her shoulder.

"How to ward buildings from evil," Marley read the entry out loud.

"Wow," Cassie exclaimed. "This is amazing, what is this book?"

Turning the book to its side, Tyler read the title out loud. "The Fundamental's of Magic. Volume 2 out of 8. Well, this would have come in real handy a while back."

"It's not like I've read every book in here," Christian defended himself though only Marley could hear him. "I just can't get a break."

The instructions in the short chapter flew past. It was a simple incantation they had to learn, the hard part would be channeling their magic to make sure that no evil would be let in. They poured over the spell until they had it committed to memory.

When they felt ready, they would try to cast their first protective ward.

———

Against the sinking red sun, the girls arrived at Eve's house knowing that the risk of discovery would be minimal here. With Si having already left for work, they had the place to themselves.

Standing in a ring in Eve's room, the four held hands, picturing the warding symbols they had studied in the book of magic. They chanted the incantation, its unfamiliar archaic words twisting around their tongues as each of the warding symbols appeared in a brilliant white light, floating in the air before each of their faces. When four symbols had appeared, they exploded outward in each direction of the compass.

The girls had successfully cast their first warding spell.

Moments later, they drove across town until they pulled up outside Shaken & Stirred, the bright blue neon sign, reflected on the windows of Eve's car.

Not wanting Si to know they were there and the in-evitable questions that would follow, they darted into the alley out back. As before, they chanted until the symbols appeared. Slipping back to campus, they protected Paul's office before finally arriving back at the dorm.

And as the color seeped out of the sky, replaced by a blanket of black, they set up their final warding spell.

ONE HUNDRED FORTY-SEVEN

As Eve left for the night, Tyler went back to her own room only to be immediately overcome by an overwhelming weariness seeing the cleanup she would have to do.

Before she had left, Eve had volunteered to help her with it. Much as she would have appreciated that, Tyler knew she needed some alone time.

Over the past year, she had grown accustomed to dealing with things on her own and it would likely be a while before she fully accepted these girls as her new family, much as she was growing to like them. Her family had been her world; they would not be easily replaced.

Grabbing a chair, she turned it upright when her phone buzzed. Scrambling for it, she expected the call to be from Cheryl, but it wasn't a number she recognized though it did start with the Boston area code. Answering it, an unfamiliar voice came over the line.

"Hi, I'm calling about the missing person poster," the woman began.

Tyler's heart leaped into her throat. "Yes! Have you seen her?"

"I think so. I caught a glimpse of a young girl who matched the description. Have you got a pen? I'll give you the address."

Tyler found a pen among the detritus on the floor, scribbling the address onto the back of her hand. "When did you see her there?"

"Ten, maybe fifteen minutes ago. I'm sorry, I would have called sooner if I hadn't been debating about it all. I didn't want to get your hopes up if I was wrong…"

"No, no… I'm really glad you called," Tyler thanked her, grateful beyond words.

Grabbing a jacket and her bag, she raced out of the room. The thought that she should tell the girls where she was going didn't cross her mind once. All she could think about was Ally.

Nothing else carried any importance, not even her own safety.

Stars blinked overhead breaking up the otherwise endless ocean of black.

Eve drove in a daze, her eyes barely able to take in the dark streets blurring past. It wasn't until she had gotten into her car that she had felt how exhausted she was. Wanting to feel cocooned in the safety of her room, she sped through the streets, watching as the needle flirted dangerously toward city limits.

With so much going on, she had found it easy to compartmentalize her own troubles, but now that she was alone, the silence was overwhelming as was the general sense of foreboding. It had been with her since that restroom incident, seeping into her very bones.

Part of her knew she should tell the girls everything even if it was just Michael toying with her sanity. The fact that he knew about the incident at all was terrifying though not only for her. It hadn't escaped her attention that Michael could be going after Si — he had already taken Ally after all. It was entirely possible that her brother would be next, which was why she had insisted upon the protective wards at the bar.

At least she knew that no demons would be able to get inside now. If only she were able to place them around the entire city, but they had learned that the wards were generalized and had their limits.

Turning, Eve was suddenly blinded by bright head-lights behind her. Flinching, she fought her instinct to slam on the brakes, knowing that it wouldn't help and might even put her in danger.

Twisting the rearview mirror so that the lights weren't directly in her eyes, she hit the horn angrily. "Stupid jerk, turn your lights down!"

But the lights stayed brightly on, blinding her with their brilliance. Unable and unwilling to drive with them behind her like that, she pulled up to the curb.

"What the hell is your problem?"

She waited, expecting the jerk to go past because ap-parently, he was in a greater rush than she was, but the headlights — which she could now see was only one light and not two — slowed to a stop behind her.

She became very very still.

Whoever it was was doing this deliberately.

Eve's fingers crawled across the passenger seat to where her phone sat. Snatching it into her hands, she felt instantly better for having it, even though if anything were to happen, there was no one she could call who would be able to do anything.

All she could do was wait as her breath came grew in-creasingly more strained.

After several moments, the light finally lowered to normal until Eve could see clearly see the outline of the vehicle behind her, silhouetted by a streetlight.

It was a motorbike. The rider's face was hidden beneath a helmet but Eve didn't need to see it under the visor to know who it belonged to.

In much happier days, before she had known any better, she had spent many summer nights holding onto its owner as they flew past the city sights.

It was Jason.

He had come back from the dead to finish what he had started.

Her body grew numb with cold as she slowly set her phone onto her lap knowing that there was nothing the police or Si could do.

She was the only one who could protect her.

Taking hold of the wheel, Eve slammed her foot on the gas. The engine roared to life as she took off like a demon on wheels. Behind her, the bike followed. Keeping her eyes front, she peeled past several blocks until she saw that flamingo-colored house. Never had a pink house filled her with such relief before. Yanking on the wheel hard, she swerved into her street, burning rubber until she screeched to a halt outside her home.

Jumping out of her car, keys in hand, Eve sprinted up the few steps to the front door just as Jason's bike reached her car. Panic had taken hold causing her fingers to fumble against the lock.

Filled with a stark terror, she found that she had no voice. All that came out of her was a weak squeak. She fought to get the key in the door as footsteps came rushing up behind her.

She got the door open just as she felt Jason's presence near. Throwing herself inside, she whirled around, a hand raised up to protect herself.

But there was nothing there.

Only the wind whistling an eerie tune as an empty soda bottle rattled in the gutter.

Of Jason and his bike, there was no sign.

Tyler checked the address on her hand against Google maps.

This was the right place, yet it wasn't what she had expected.

Cheap mobile homes sat neglected in this rundown trailer park, their rusting doors patched over and over with tape. Tyler moved through the park stepping over empty fried-chicken boxes, beer bottles, and the occasional syringe

She took in the numbered doors, walking briskly, senses honed for anything unusual. Despite rushing here so fast, she wasn't a complete fool. She knew this could be a trap, but the urge to find her sister safe was more than any fear or concern for her own well-being. If it meant dying to save her sister, Tyler was willing to do much worse.

Rounding the corner, she set eyes on the trailer the caller had given her. It was in better repair than the surrounding others. Short red curtains hung in the tiny windows in an effort to brighten up the place. Flanking the front door were two rows of potted plants.

But these weren't what caught her attention.

Lying on the ground in front of the door, was a pair of red wellington boots that were so small, they would only fit a young boy or girl. Her pulse began to pound as Tyler approached the door. She didn't know what she was going to say, or even what she would do if Ally was in there. She only knew that she had to act.

She grabbed the door handle but before she could twist it, the door was pulled open from the inside.

Standing before her was a young girl of Ally's age. She had the same slim build, but Ally's hair was the same chestnut shade as Tyler's while this girl's hair was more of a mahogany. She looked up at her with curious blue eyes — eyes that were not her sister's.

"Mom!" The girl called out. "Someone's here!"

"Who is it, Ally?" Came the girl's mom's voice as a woman appeared. Wiping her hands on her apron, a wooden spoon still in her hand, she looked at Tyler quizzically. "Yes?"

"Sorry, I think I'm at the wrong address," was all Tyler could think of saying.

The woman laughed. "Oh, no problem. You won't believe how much that happens around here. I keep telling them they should have a better system but you know, my comments always seem to fall on deaf ears."

Tyler couldn't stop staring at the little girl. She was so similar to Ally that she could feel her heartache. She had to fight off her irrational instinct to throw her arms around the girl. More than the physical similarity, however, was the name. That she was also called Ally was something Tyler found surprisingly painful.

This could be her kid sister.

It should be her Ally.

With growing horror, Tyler realised her eyes were beginning to fill with tears. Whirling around, she hurried away from the woman and her child as they stared after her at her strange behavior.

ONE HUNDRED FORTY-EIGHT

The annoying ringing sounded so close that it could have been in her head. Flinching at its loudness, Tyler felt something hard pressed against her face. Her entire body ached; she felt weary beyond belief. Opening her eyes, she was confused when she saw that the world was tilted at an angle.

Blinking the sleep from her eyes, she realized with a start that she was slumped over a table in a Starbucks and had fallen asleep there.

After she had stumbled out of the trailer park, her phone had gone off intermittently throughout the night. She had been on her way back to the dorm when another sighting had come through. After a few quick questions, however, it had become obvious that it wasn't Ally.

Before she could get very far, she received another call, then another. All from people who thought they had seen her sister. Most were busts, some were even crank calls which had sent Tyler into a rage, reaching for her magic to teach them a lesson. She had managed to rein her fury back in the end though only just.

On and on the calls came until Tyler found herself

seeking refuge at the Starbucks. It was the only thing that had been open in this part of town that early in the morning, and it had been blessedly quiet.

Between hot coffees, she had gulped down another of her energy drinks — made this time from a bottle of Evian she'd purchased. That drink had been drunk several hours ago now which might explain how she had passed out at the table.

Looking at her phone, Tyler could see that there was still no call from Cheryl. It seemed that if she wanted to speak to the woman, she would have to go there in person. As soon as the sun came up, Tyler would head over there.

For now, at least, she could make another potion to take the edge off.

A commotion sounded by the front counter. The night shift was leaving and being replaced by the day crew. Moments later a new barista appeared at Tyler's table.

"My colleague's told me you've been here a while. I saw you were empty so thought I'd give you a free refill," the girl who wasn't much older than Tyler smiled at her. "Don't tell anyone."

Bowled away by the kind gesture, Tyler looked for her name to thank her. The badge that was pinned to her chest revealed a four-letter name. Tyler had to look twice before she could believe what it said… The name on the badge was ALLY.

Through her shock, she was able to mumble, "Thanks."

When her barista moved away, Tyler stared after her.

The sun was just beginning its ascent into the mottled purple sky. It was early still, not even six yet when Cassie had snuck out of her room. It had been hard to contain her excitement, but Cassie made sure to keep as quiet as possible in order not to wake Marley.

Last night, after they had gotten back, she'd told Trip about her accident when he'd called to say goodnight. She'd left out details of where and why it had happened of course, revealing only that she had fallen down a flight of stairs. He had been so horrified that he'd wanted to see her straight away, but Cassie's weary body had screamed at her that she'd needed rest. Her newly healed leg had started to throb; so instead, they'd arranged to meet before classes today.

It was Trip's idea to watch the sun come up along the waterfront.

It was such a romantic notion and like nothing that she had ever done before that Cassie had jumped at it. She stood now, on a bridge overlooking The Charles Esplanade, watching the sky as she waited for Trip to join her. Water lapped gently beneath as a bird sang its joyful morning song from the trees.

Despite the danger that had dogged them since they had discovered their powers, Cassie found herself feeling at peace here.

"Good morning," Trip said, his voice sounding as rich and sexy as she always found it.

Cassie turned to find him with a box of chocolates wrapped with a pink bow. "I got you these, I've heard they help soften most sicknesses and pain."

Seeing how thoughtful he was, how much he cared for her, a warm glow spread in her stomach. Taking the chocolates from him (though they weren't actually ones she liked), she leaned in close, her face tilted up.

Trip seemed almost startled by the move at first, and she almost thought she saw a moment of panic in his eyes, but it was quickly gone, replaced by his usual attentive stare. Lowering his lips to hers, he kissed her so gently, as if she was a delicate flower that would be bruised from too much pressure, that she almost couldn't feel it.

"Thank you, I love them," she lied, putting the box into her Gucci bag.

They started walking, not saying much at first, both of them just admiring the morning quiet. "I've never seen a place like this," Trip admitted, staring around with an expression she couldn't quite fathom. It was as if he had never seen a river before.

"It's nice, isn't it? I love being by the water although I've never managed to learn how to swim, which is crazy right, considering how many summers I've spent on a boat," she revealed.

His dark eyes focused on her intensely. "You weren't scared of falling in?"

"Not really. We had so many people on the boat with us, staff and crew, and they all knew that I couldn't swim so they made sure I was always safe."

"Well, you don't have to worry. I'll protect you now," Trip said, as Cassie's stomach did a flip-flop. They passed by a series of large, colorful banners announcing an upcoming music festival. It was one of the city's fall highlights and revelers were known to come from several states away just to participate.

Seeing that she was looking at them, Trip smiled. "We should go to that together."

"That sounds nice," she replied calmly though inside, she wanted to dance and scream and pump her fist in the air. She had read enough Cosmopolitan magazines to know that making dates ahead of time was a sure sign of a guy's interest. "I've only been to it once before."

"What was it like?" he asked genuinely curious.

"I don't really remember too well; I was only five or six at the time. My mom was asked to do something there, to present some awards I think. I came with her. I mostly remember the noise and the crowds. It had scared me as a kid."

She stopped, thinking suddenly. "Wait, I bet there's a picture of it on her timeline. One second," she asked, taking out her phone and searching through her mom's Instagram account. It took a while as there were so many pictures posted but Cassie finally found the one she wanted.

"Here we are," she showed him the photograph. She was a tiny thing even then. Her hair had been expertly styled into two French braids, and she wore an identical dress to her mom though hers wasn't anywhere near as revealing. Staring at the phone, Trip's eyes grew wide.

"That's your mom?" he asked, sounding as impressed as every other guy she had ever met who saw Angie for the first time. Her heart plummeted, and she felt suddenly on edge. "Wow, she's beautiful."

"Yeah, she's something," Cassie responded moving the phone quickly away. Just once, she'd like a guy to respond in a way that didn't seem like he wanted to get with her mother.

Trip noticed her reaction with a great deal of interest, though Cassie didn't pick up on this, too busy battling her own inner demons.

"No, but she's like model beautiful. I can't believe she's your mom," Trip replied staring at her even more intensely than before seemingly not realizing how every compliment he gave to Angie was a knife in the heart for her.

"You and the rest of the world," Cassie said an edge coming into her voice.

Taking her phone from her, he started scrolling through her mom's timeline, studying the photographs so closely that it made her feel strange. "This thing… her entire life is here."

"The woman lives on Instagram," Cassie answered shortly, wondering if she should snatch her phone back though she worried it would be rude.

"Do you have one too? An Instagram?" he asked as Cassie felt the relief coming back to her. At least they weren't talking about her mom anymore. Usually, the conversations and questions about her went on much, much longer.

"Unfortunately, yes. My mom set it up. She loves to post things of us up on there together. She set up all my social network profiles, YouTube, Facebook. I don't really use them but she likes to be able to tag me."

Trip stared at her as if she was speaking another language. Her cheeks turned pink with embarrassment. "Sorry, I guess this isn't your thing."

"It hasn't been, no. Can I see your Instagram?" he asked.

Not finding any reason why he shouldn't, Cassie pulled it up and showed him. There weren't nearly as many pictures on her own account and what was there was from her mom tagging her on her own pictures. Cassie had no posts of her own, no personal information to share. Still, Trip seemed to look at it all with a great deal of interest.

"We should take a picture of us and put it up," Trip said, surprising her with his suggestion. Ordinarily, Cassie hated having her picture taken. Whenever a phone or camera turned her way, she would run the opposite way, but this was the best she had ever looked, *and* it would be her first picture with Trip. It would be so amazing to finally have something great to post about herself that she found herself caving to his suggestion.

"OK," she answered shyly. Giving him the phone, he reversed the camera so that they could see their own faces in its display. Angling it so that there was a clear view of the river behind them, they smiled into the camera as Trip took the shot. Posting the picture to her timeline, he suddenly tagged her mom on the picture so that it would show up on her timeline. Not expecting this at all — especially from someone who didn't even seem to know what Instagram was a moment before — Cassie snatched her phone back.

"Why did you do that? Why did you tag my mom?"

Trip gave her a reassuring smile though it didn't quite reach his eyes. "I thought it would be nice for you to show her that your life has meaning too. You've literally had no life until now, I thought you'd want the world to see that it's very different now."

He gave her that cute grin of his which took some of the sting from his words. Still, she felt a little weird, like the rug had been pulled out from beneath her feet.

No sooner had the picture appeared on her timeline then her phone began to ring. Cassie wondered who could be calling at this time in the morning — and a Face-Time call at that. Looking at the caller ID, she was shocked to see her mom's smiling face flashing up at her.

Angie was always awake early — she got up every day around five so she could work out with her trainer. Of course, she'd see the picture and then want to know all about it. She felt a flash of anger at Trip's action but shoved it quickly back down. He hadn't known what he was doing. He was just trying to show them off.

"Aren't you going to answer that?" Trip's voice interrupted her.

"I'll call her back later," Cassie began but Trip wouldn't hear of it.

"What if it's important?"

Stuck, not able to think of a reasonable excuse, Cassie reluctantly answered the video call. Her mom's face came on the screen, glowing with health and beauty, making Cassie want to scream.

"Cassie honey, I just saw your picture and… wait… is that him? Are you with this gorgeous guy right now?" Angie asked, looked surprised.

Trip waved at her. "Hi, I'm Trip. Cassie and I are dating." He volunteered the information so easily that Cassie was taken aback again. While she wasn't keeping their dating a secret, she had thought that *she* would be the one to break the news to her mom.

"That's wonderful!" Angie exclaimed, clapping perfectly manicured hands. "And how long has this been going on?"

"Not long," Cassie finally spoke up.

"Well, you two look as cute as can be. Cassie, Trip's obviously doing you the world of good — I've never seen you look better! You must be putting those seaweed mud packs to good use."

Embarrassed that she would bring up her skincare regime, Cassie shot Angie a look that her mom picked up on right away. Angie became instantly contrite. "Wait, what am I doing? Interrupting your early date time. I just wanted to say hi, and to let you know that you don't call me nearly enough. I don't think you've actually called me at all," Angie said looking hurt. "Wasn't that our deal? Once a week so you can update me on everything?"

Cassie squirmed under both of their gazes. How could she tell her mom that she hadn't called because there literally wasn't anything she could tell her?

Before she could reply, Angie looked offscreen as someone spoke to her. Suddenly, she looked shocked. "Sweetheart, I've got to go, I'm being interviewed for the Body For Life magazine and it had totally slipped my mind! You two have fun. We must arrange a dinner so I can meet your new beau in person. Kisses!"

Pursing her lips at the screen, Angie mimed kissing it before the screen went blank. In the sudden silence that followed, Cassie put her phone away.

"That sounds nice," Trip said finally, breaking the ice. "I'd love to meet your mom in person."

"Yay," Cassie responded, her voice devoid of enthusiasm. "I'll set something up," she lied even though she knew she had absolutely no intention of the two ever meeting.

ONE HUNDRED FORTY-NINE

Marley woke to find Cassie's side of the room empty.

Even from her bed, Marley could see the sky was still painted with hues of pink — it was way too early for her to have gone to classes. Might even be too early for the Food Court to be open. Wondering where she might have gotten to, Marley suddenly saw the note propped up against her clock.

Cassie's neat handwriting explained that she was spending a little pre-school time with Trip but she'd catch up with them later.

Yawning, Marley stretched when her eyes landed on a framed photograph that sat on the shelf opposite. It had been taken when she was around eight, a few years after her mom had left them. She and her dad had been at the zoo back in San Fran. They'd had a great day watching the animals, going to a Rainforest themed restaurant after Marley's apple pie had arrived, shaped like a red panda. It was one of the happiest days she could remember from her childhood so the sight of this picture usually made her smile.

Though not so today.

Alone, those troubling thoughts that she had bottled away came rushing up to the surface. There was her dad's increasingly strange behavior, coupled with the fact that she knew he was lying to her. Worse yet, she still didn't know how he had found out about their visit to the Harbor… Did he also know about the other places they were "visiting?"

These issues alone would have been enough to cause sleepless nights, but the thought of her terrifying fatal power overshadowed her questions about her dad.

Sitting up in bed, Marley tucked her hair away from her face as she stared at her hands, wondering about the two occasions she had inadvertently used them to kill. What was it that she did with them? How exactly did it all work?

A face came into her mind then, one with a wild, frightening visage and a noose around her neck. Realizing that her powers might come from Mary — or that at least, Mary might know more about them — Marley held in her breath and began to summon her.

The air went hazy as her hair lifted off her shoulders. In the blink of an eye, as if she had been waiting for Marley to summon her, Mary appeared looking as fearsome as always. Though Marley knew she meant her no harm, it didn't lessen her fear of the spirit. Mary had been dead for so long that her spirit was like a wild, feral animal that could attack her at any moment.

"Where do my powers come from, Mary? What are they? I don't know how to use them and I'm afraid that I'll kill someone by accident again… or that I can't use them when I need to. Can you help me?"

Mary watched silently, her black eyes burning a hole into her. She disappeared suddenly only to glitch forward, standing now beside Marley's shelf. Her arm shot out, deliberately knocking the framed photograph Marley had been looking at only seconds before to the floor.

The frame smashed, its glass crisscrossing with cracks. Confused by her actions, Marley went to ask why she had done that when a peculiar movement stopped her dead.

The glass wasn't just cracking in a random fashion — it was forming a symbol.

One that Marley had seen before that Mary had already tried to warn them about. It was the symbol that had been associated with two demon attacks…

And the symbol was now appearing on the glass but *only on Paul.*

Marley's side of the photograph was clear.

Chills ran down the length of her spine, filling her blood with ice-water. Having passed on her message, Mary vanished. Marley hugged herself, filled with more questions than when she had begun.

A fter several hours of following up more empty leads, Tyler was desperate to crash.

Forcing her aching feet to move, she wanted nothing more than to head back to BU to rest, maybe even grab a short nap, but she knew it wasn't possible. Since Cheryl refused to answer her calls, Tyler had no choice but to go there in person.

Traffic flew past on the streets, their owners going about their day as if it was like any other. Bitterness flooded her mouth when Tyler thought how they weren't having to worry about the life of their only surviving loved one. They weren't alone in this madness.

Knowing that she was feeling sorry for herself, and beginning to sink into a black, depressing hole that she might never claw her way out of, Tyler took a deep breath. She couldn't lose it now, not when Ally hadn't been found yet.

Reaching a crossing, she waited for the lights to

change. As the green light flashed to amber, a voice called out behind her.

"Ally! Hey Ally! Wait!"

Tyler turned around so fast that her foot almost slipped off the curb. Her eyes darted wildly, searching for the Ally in question. An irritated man pushed past her, annoyed that she was in his way, but Tyler ignored him, staring blindly behind as two figures came into view.

It was a girl, around five foot two and she was carrying a box. Hearing the shout, she had stopped and was now staring behind her, a quizzical expression on her face as a guy in a Kinko uniform ran up to her.

"You left these," Tyler heard him say as he handed her another box.

The girl smiled her thanks, rolling her eyes at her forgetfulness. "Thanks! Can't believe I left those."

"No problem, Ally," he said. "See you next week."

The two went their separate ways but Tyler found she couldn't move. All these Ally's appearing before her, it just couldn't be a coincidence. Why then was this happening? Was the universe playing a cruel trick on her? Or maybe… maybe this was the result of one of the spells she had cast the other night!

Her body practically hummed with the revelation. That must be what was going on! The spells that she had cast the night Ally had been taken when the girls had fallen asleep… they had all been variations of "Find Ally."

And they were working now, kind of.

They were finding all sorts of Ally's… just not hers.

A sudden sob choked her throat. Why wouldn't the damn spell find her sister?

ONE HUNDRED FIFTY

Tyler knocked impatiently on the faded door.

As always, Cheryl's house sounded manic inside, which was only to be expected as she fostered several children for the State — though who in their right minds would consider Heep a suitable guardian was anyone's guess. As far as Tyler was concerned, Ally should have been placed with a much better human.

Footsteps sounded inside, the door opening to reveal Cheryl seconds later. She looked startled to see Tyler, running a hand through her mess of tangled hair.

"What are you doing here?" She asked.

"I must have left you a million messages, why the hell haven't you called me back?" Tyler demanded. "What have you heard? Have the cops told you anything?"

"They've called several times a day, though they don't have any leads right now. No one knows who that waiter was so they're just trying to find him."

Though Tyler heard the words, she found it difficult to understand. "You're telling me the cops have been in touch with you?"

"As I said, they call several times a day," Cheryl answered impatiently.

"Then why haven't they called me? I haven't heard from them once? Why am I being kept out of the loop?" Tyler demanded, unable to hold back her emotions anymore.

"I'm Ally's guardian so they have to talk to me. If you have a problem with them, I suggest you take it up with them," Cheryl snapped back, unwilling to deal with Tyler's frustration.

"But this is insane! She's my sister! You're only looking after her for the money; we all know that. I can't believe they would tell you over me. I can't believe they would shut me out like this," Tyler said, almost to herself.

Cheryl's eyes turned a flinty gray.

"I know you don't think much of me, Tyler. You've always made that very clear, but I do actually care about Ally, and her disappearance has affected us all here. So if you're done yelling at me, I need to get back to the other kids."

Tyler didn't answer immediately, taking in the woman's appearance. There were coffee stains on her shirt and bags under her eyes. It seemed that while she never offered Ally the level of care Tyler thought her sister deserved, Cheryl did actually care about her.

This revelation sent her head spinning.

Taking her silence as consent that she was done, Cheryl slammed the door in Tyler's face.

S taggering blindly through the streets, fuelled by rage, fear, and exhaustion, Tyler wasn't sure how it was that she found herself inside the police station leading Ally's investigation.

Uniformed cops went about their day, not in the least bit concerned that her sister had been taken by a monster.

These cops stood around typing into computers, drinking coffee or worse, shooting the breeze with their co-workers.

Tyler actually heard a trio discussing last night's football match.

It was no wonder that they couldn't find Ally if this was what they did all day long. Clutching Ally's ladybug bag to her chest, she approached the front desk where an unsmiling female cop worked at a computer. Apparently, it was important stuff as she didn't bother to greet Tyler.

After an uncomfortable wait, Tyler cleared her throat — loudly. The cop's eyes finally flicked over to her, looking annoyed at the interruption.

"What can I help you with?" She asked.

"You can start by telling me why no around here seems to be concerned that my sister has been kidnapped!" Tyler snapped, much louder than she intended to. Her raised voice carried over the general sound of the office as several cops peered over their computer screens at her.

Tyler swallowed, mentally telling herself to get a hold of herself.

"Who is your sister?" The cop asked, staring at her without any hint of emotion as if she could be asking for her bank card.

"Alison Jones," Tyler replied, twisting the strap of Ally's bag round and round as she waited for her details to flash up.

"And what's your name?" The cop's eyes skimmed the screen, taking in whatever information was stored there.

"Tyler Jones."

"It says we've been keeping her legal guardian informed with regular updates, Cheryl Heep," she began but never got to finish as the emotion of the last few days coupled with all the exhaustion finally caught up with her.

"SHE IS MY SISTER!" Tyler suddenly yelled, slamming her hand onto the counter so hard that the papers and leaflets that sat on it jumped.

"Miss, you need to calm down," the cop had backed away a little now, her right hand hovering over her holstered weapon. Tyler felt a grim sense of satisfaction to see the cop finally showing some emotion on her face even if she was the one to have caused it.

"I don't need you to tell me what to do, I need you to find Ally!" Her senses were on fire, each of her nerves bristling with the beginnings of her magic. Belatedly, Tyler tried to rein it in knowing this would be the worst place in the world for her to display her power but as if the magic had a mind of its own, she could feel it leeching out of her.

"What is the world is going on here?" A commanding voice called out, cutting through the fast-emerging chaos.

Tyler turned to find Saunders standing in the station's entrance behind her. She had a takeout box in one hand while the other gestured for the other cops — who were now alert to a potential situation — to back down.

"Why isn't anyone doing anything to find Ally?" Tyler blurted out. "They're all just standing around acting as if everything is fine when her life is in danger! You know she has a kidney problem, right? She's already missed several days of dialysis. I don't know how much longer she can hold out for before she gets really sick."

Saunders approached calmly though her eyes never left Tyler. "Let's talk in my office, Jones."

Then she turned her back to Tyler, disappearing down a corridor. The act of making herself vulnerable seemed to diffuse the tense situation as the tension suddenly left the other cops. Tyler took after Saunders, hurrying until she arrived at a glass-walled office.

Inside, paperwork was stacked neatly into mounds. Numerous trophies and certificates of distinction were proudly displayed on a shelf. There were even news-paper clippings of Saunders being recognised by the mayor.

Seeing how decorated she was, Tyler felt herself grow calmer. It seemed she already had the best person on the job looking out for her sister.

Saunders gestured for her to sit, made a space for her food on the desk then sat behind it. Putting her elbows onto the desk, she clasped her hands together.

"Despite how it looks, we are doing everything we can, but turning up out of the blue and shouting at my colleagues isn't doing you any favors."

Sitting down across from her, Tyler gave her a dirty look. "It seems the only way that I'll actually get any an-swers from you. You've been keeping Cheryl informed but not me? She's my sister!" Tyler said, hating the weak crack that came at the end of her sentence.

"We're legally bound to report to your sister's guardian, but I can give you a break. How about I person-ally keep you in the loop from now on?"

Her voice sounded almost pleasant, but Tyler wasn't born yesterday. She knew the cop was up to something though this wasn't an offer she could refuse. Swallowing any abrasive comment she might have said otherwise, Tyler nodded. "I would appreciate that."

Saunder's studied Tyler, looking from her face to her hands in her lap. Here they grew darker as she noticed Ally's bag. Keeping her voice natural, Saunders asked, "Is that the bag that you gave Ally for her birthday?"

"Yes," Tyler said, setting it onto Saunder's desk. "That's why I came here, someone left this for me."

"Who?" Saunder's question shot out, quick as a flash.

"I don't know."

"Where did you find it?" She asked, picking up a pen to spin the bag around without touching it with her own hands.

"It was just left with me... outside the dorm," Tyler

finished lamely. There was no way she could reveal where she had really found it.

"Why didn't you call me?" Saunders asked. "This is crucial evidence, you should have reported it straight away." Her tone implied that Tyler was keeping things from her, which, though she knew it was true, was one thing too many for her taxed mind to bear.

"Are you seriously questioning me?" Tyler asked, her voice rising higher with every word. "You're going to treat me like *I'm* a culprit?"

Saunders stared at her as if she wasn't sure which tact to try first. When she spoke, it wasn't what Tyler expected to hear.

"You have to admit that strange things just keep on happening around you. First, from your own mouth, you and your friends called in a murder — except we never recovered a body and the only crime we could find was the hole that had mysteriously blown into the roof, and some vandalism to the mosaic in the basement beneath Trinity Church. The second time, your friend was attacked — which was horrible, I know — but that doesn't explain the pipes which suddenly burst, shooting scalding hot water, rendering your friend's attackers powerless. Then of course, there is my own partner who lies in a hospital bed even now, in a coma, as his three little kids cry over him every day." Saunders paused for emphasis.

"All of these strange occurrences which seem to be centered increasingly on you. Wouldn't you be suspicious?"

"I am not the one who did anything to Ally!" Tyler cried, feeling herself starting to lose her grip again. "I can't explain those other things, but Ally is in real danger and if you won't do anything about it, then I sure as hell will!"

Fury raged through her as all the hurt and pain cascaded into one giant wave of emotion. Unable to control herself, Tyler felt her magic rise, crackling the air with electricity.

The lights started flashing as Saunders stared at her, wide-eyed.

Suddenly every lamp in the office blew, raining glass over them.

ONE HUNDRED FIFTY-ONE

Saunders cued up the security footage to watch through it for seemingly the hundredth time.

After the lights had blown in her office, Saunders had Tyler placed into a cell for her own safety since the girl was clearly losing all control. Saunders had dealt with enough families of lost children to know that when pushed to the limit, they often became another problem for them to handle.

While she knew Tyler was involved with something, she also felt her pain was genuine. She didn't want anything to happen to another Jones' girl, so despite being the one to push her buttons — without a partner handy, she would have to be both good *and* bad cop — a night cooling down in a cell would probably be the best thing for her.

No phone, no internet, no distractions. Maybe the girl would actually get some sleep.

She had already been planning on holding her for further questioning when she had felt that strange thickness in the air, that same hum that she had felt in the diner only seconds before it had imploded.

Both times she had felt it, it was when she had been with Tyler Jones.

Pressing the play button again, she watched as Tyler grew increasingly more agitated. When she finally lost control, Saunders could see the exact moment.

She could also see what looked like a cloud of fog surrounding the girl.

She had seen this same fog when it had been happening in the office, but here, captured on video, there was proof of it.

"I'm about to head home. Don't push yourself too hard, it's not going to wake him up any faster," a voice spoke from the doorway.

It was her friend Callie, the cop who had been on desk duty when Tyler had burst in. Callie was good friends with Brooks too, maybe even more as Callie was also friends with his wife.

Saunders gave her a grateful smile, gesturing for her to come in for a moment. "Can you look at this video before you go?"

Callie came up to her, peering over her shoulder at her laptop screen. "What am I looking at?"

"Just watch," Saunders replied.

She pressed play and waited for Callie to notice the strange fog but Callie only looked confused. "It's that girl again. She looks pretty upset, but what did you want me to see?"

Saunders pointed at the fog that clearly enveloped Jones with a pen. "You don't see this fog around the girl?"

Callie leaned in closer, squinting at the screen. "No? There's nothing there.

Saunders frowned, wondering how her friend could not see it. "It's right there. Like a thick mist around her."

Callie looked up from the screen, staring at her in puzzlement.

"Dude, there's definitely nothing there."

Saunders felt all the hairs on the back of her arms rising. She could see this thing, had felt it even when Jones lost control, so why then, couldn't her friend see it?

How could she be the only one to see it?

This is the end of IN HER SKIN. Continue the thrilling action now with FIRST DATE JITTERS.

TWISTED MAGIC

10: FIRST DATE JITTERS

JO HO

ONE HUNDRED FIFTY-TWO

The four walls were closing in on her.

Any second now, one of them would come so close, she would feel the painted white brick pushing against her nose as it began its final stone embrace.

At least that's how it felt to Tyler stuck in the cell for close to two hours now.

Saunders had taken her phone — had confiscated everything actually — but Tyler knew she hadn't been left empty-handed.

She still had her powers, and though she didn't know the full extent of what they could do, they were still proving to be a force of nature and her greatest asset.

Which was why she was going to break out of this cell.

A fury burned inside of her, swirling around, an inferno of rage. Not only were the cops not finding Ally, but they had also locked her up as if she were the criminal! After two hours of being stuck here, she knew she'd had enough of this.

Moving to the cell door, she stared through the steel

bars. There were no guards or cops around, only a handful of other undesirables trapped in their own cages, left here to rot for the night.

Her neighbor was a drunk with an injured fist. Blood seeped out of a fresh bandage which was the only thing clean on him. Though she was some eight feet away, his pungent scent of weeks old sweat and urine was impossible to miss.

Recoiling at the acrid smell, Tyler forced herself to focus on the locked steel door that blocked her way to freedom.

Her eyes slid down the cold black metal stopping when they came to the lock. It wasn't much bigger than the one they had come across at the library — which Tyler had easily melted. This then, should not be a problem.

She held her hand over the lock.

With only the slightest effort, Tyler knew she could blast the thing off and get the hell out of there. Her anger was such that it was hard to be cautious when all she wanted was to use her powers to save Ally. Pulling in her magic, she focused on the lock as, conjured by her will, heat began to radiate from it.

"I wouldn't if I were you." The warning came, low and with a slightly mocking tone.

Tyler stopped, snatching her hand away, her eyes darting around to locate the source of the warning.

They landed on the drunk but he was barely able to move without stumbling, so it seemed unlikely that such a statement would have come from him.

Turning slowly she saw a man several cells away. He looked to have been in his thirties. Several day's growth covered the bottom half of his lean face. He wore a long trench coat and couldn't have had an inch of fat on him. Despite how wiry he was there was a quiet power that came off of him. He made no pretense of hiding the fact that he was watching her with a half-amused curl to his lips.

"Whatever you're doing, you should stop. They have cameras everywhere so unless you have a way of taking them out... I'd suggest you settle in for the night."

Tyler's eyes narrowed into slits. "I don't know what you're talking about. I was just stretching my legs."

"You were certainly stretching something, but it wasn't your legs," he replied, a lazy glint to his eyes.

Tyler felt herself grow cold all over. Did he *know* she had been about to use her magic? If he did, would that make him some sort of supernatural being?

Forcing herself to stay cool, even though her pulse began to race, Tyler flicked her eyes up to his face. Other than the slight arch of his brow, however, she couldn't see anything different about him.

"Who are you?" She kept her voice calm. Act natural. Don't give any sign that he knows what he's talking about.

"Just your friendly neighborhood no-one," he drawled, seeming amused by her reaction.

He might have said more but approaching footsteps stopped them short. A uniformed cop came in, marching to his cell with barely concealed irritation.

The prisoner grinned at the cop. "Why Duke, so nice to see you again."

Duke glared at him as he unlocked the door to his cell. "Can it, Tobias. I don't want to deal with any more of your crap tonight."

Tobias — if that was his name — feigned innocence, holding up his hands. "What, I was just being friendly. Shoot me."

Duke might have growled something under his breath that sounded like he wished he could, but he was a little too far away and his voice too low for Tyler to make it out completely. Judging by his very demeanor, however, she figured she had him pegged correctly.

"You're free to go," Duke said, spitting out the words one-by-one. Clearly, he didn't have much love lost for Tobias, not that Tobias cared one bit. Tipping an invisible hat, he emerged from his cell.

As he followed Duke to the exit, he shot one last look at Tyler, pointedly staring up to where a discreet camera was fixed to the ceiling.

"Remember what I said," Tobias warned one last time as he headed off.

Tyler didn't know what to make of him.

She watched as he left, frowning at their encounter when she saw a sudden movement beneath his long trench coat and what looked to be a *furry tail* ducking out of sight.

Startled, Tyler's eyes shot back up but Tobias had already disappeared around the corner.

ONE HUNDRED FIFTY-THREE

The hum of music playing from Cassie's headphones as she worked on coursework provided a welcome backdrop to the noise inside Marley's head.

School had passed uneventfully — which Marley was thankful for. She'd needed one thing to be as it should be, one bit of stability in her life.

Especially now there were so many questions about her dad.

All day, she had found herself unable to concentrate on anything other than that sign Mary had placed over her dad's image. The framed photograph was hidden in the bottom of a drawer now, under layers of her clothes so the others wouldn't find it and ask questions. But for Marley herself, the questions wouldn't quit coming.

Not only had her father lied to her, not only did he know things about her that he shouldn't, but now Mary's ghostly fingers were pointing at him in such a clear manner that their meaning couldn't be ignored.

She knew she had to look into this, confront the issue… but he was her *dad*.

Happy memories of their lives together rushed into her mind. Like a movie of their greatest hits, she saw the two of them at all the birthdays and Christmases. There he was kissing her knee better after she had scraped it along the sidewalk when she'd been learning to cycle at seven. Then again, during her humiliation after the whole sorry Jeffrey incident, when she'd thought she'd been stood up by a boy only to find out that he wasn't even real. Her dad was the first person by her side in any catastrophe, but where once, the thought of him provided a sense of security, now there was only a hollowness she couldn't fill.

She couldn't trust him.

She felt a sense of warmth suddenly, like the gentle heat of a fire that was several feet away, and knew that Christian had arrived. He had appeared leaning against the wall beside the door, his arms folded over his chest, a quizzical expression on his face.

"What's wrong?" He asked.

"Nothing." Marley knew her reply was curt, but there were more things on her mind than her manners.

"So what am I doing here?"

"I don't know, why are you asking me?" Marley shot back defensively. Apparently curt had grown to petulant.

His eyes turned cloudy with confusion. "I sensed you needed me. I'm sorry if I got it wrong. We should probably work on our bat signal or something."

He started to fade, knowing that he wasn't welcome there.

"Wait, don't go." Marley pleaded suddenly. Even though he wasn't really on her plane, Christian could feel her turmoil.

"I've… I've been going through something," she answered, a hesitant tone to her voice.

"Go ahead," he encouraged, unfolding his arms.

She cast a look at Cassie, but she was deep in work mode, paying them no attention whatsoever. Comforted by this, Marley spoke quickly, filling him in on Mary's latest visit. When she was done, he looked as troubled as she felt.

"Have all our leads on that symbol dried up?"

"I think so," Marley said, wishing she had a different answer.

"And you don't feel comfortable asking him about this?"

"My dad won't talk about anything to do with our family history. Ever since my mom walked out on us. I tried asking him about our bloodline when this first started happening but he shut me down and we didn't speak for a while. I'm not sure I can ask again… I'm not really prepared to deal with the fallout." She hugged herself miserably, knowing that she was taking the coward's path yet not able to force herself to do otherwise.

"I didn't know about any of that," Christian replied. He crossed the room to her, taking a seat on the edge of her bed. Marley found herself briefly wondering how that even worked — he wasn't physically there, so how was he able to sit on a bed that he couldn't actually connect with? — before setting the disconcerting thought aside. It was just another question she wouldn't be able to answer.

He was so close to her that if he were anyone else, she would be able to feel their life-force, but other than that psychic connection she had to him, that warm feeling that let her know whenever he was around, there was nothing else there.

She wondered if this was how Christian always felt: without a lifeline, or any real connection to tether him here, was emptiness all there was for him?

"Marley?" Christian's eyes were focused on her as he still waited for a response.

"Sorry, my mind drifted… but, that's about the gist of it. Things haven't been great with him recently."

"You think his reluctance to talk about your family has to do with your mom leaving?" He asked this gently, not wanting to upset her any further. She didn't normally open up like this and Christian knew that the moment was fragile — one wrong step and she might close herself off from him.

"Maybe? It's almost like he holds the family to blame instead of her. I swear he hates them more than he hates her."

"Why do you say that?" Christian asked, trying to make sense of it all.

"He just doesn't seem angry with her… and the few times she has come up in conversation, he gets this almost wistful look in his eyes. He still wears this beaded bracelet she got for him on their first year anniversary. If it were me, I would have burned everything she had given me," Marley revealed in one big outburst.

Her anger simmered beneath the surface though Christian could see a sudden brightness in her eyes. The tears weren't too far away. He felt an overwhelming urge to reach out to her, to smooth back the curtain of almost-black hair that framed her face.

"Time changes things for people. Maybe he's resigned himself to it all… besides, it couldn't have been all bad between them, they made you after all."

She stared deep into his eyes, the corners of her mouth turning up into a small smile. She was so close that Christian felt his heart skip a beat. He wished he could feel her breath on his skin, her heat radiating toward him… instead, there was *nothing*. Only his own conflicting emotions stirring up a whirlwind.

A knock sounded on the door interrupting the moment.

Marley broke away first, calling out. "Come in."

By the easy way she said it, Christian knew Marley was expecting Tyler to walk through the door, so when it opened and Rhett stepped inside, he couldn't say which of them was more surprised.

He knew for sure which of them was more irritated

though. What the hell was up with this guy? Why was he *everywhere*?

Hair still glistening from a recent shower, Rhett looked as if he had stepped out of a preppy college commercial. All that was missing was a glint on his white white teeth and the picture would be perfect. He leaned against the doorframe, juggling two pizza boxes under his arm.

"Oh hey, I thought you were someone else," Marley said, getting up from the bed and crossing to him.

Rhett tossed a glance over his shoulder, but seeing no-one, turned back to her. "Am I intruding?"

"Yes, go away," Christian said at the exact time that Marley replied, "No, I wasn't doing anything important. What's up?"

Hearing Christian's response, she tossed a perplexed look at him before her eyes went back to Rhett.

"I ordered food but they accidentally sent me an extra pizza. There's no way I can eat them both so I wondered if you wanted to join me?" Rhett smiled as he spoke, which only annoyed Christian all the more.

He snorted then laughed. "This guy… Look how hard he's trying. I wonder how times he's pulled this routine before. What a loser."

But Marley wasn't laughing. In fact, she looked to be considering his offer. The laugh died in his throat as another feeling took over.

Panic.

"Well, I guess that depends… what topping did you get?" Marley responded, a playful tone to her voice.

God help him, was she flirting with Rhett?

"Pepperoni of course. This other one's vegetarian which I can't touch for fear of losing my man card. Don't worry, there's nothing weird on it like ham and pineapple or something."

"There's nothing wrong with ham and pineapple!"

Marley exclaimed in mock-annoyance. "Why is everyone so against that?"

Cassie must have heard some conversation as she turned around in her chair. Seeing Rhett with the two pizza boxes, she took stock of the situation and smiled encouragingly.

"Because it literally should be banned. I don't know who came up with that unholy idea, but she needs to be shot," Rhett grinned.

Marley smiled as she looked over his shoulder and across the hall to Tyler's room which was still closed. There was a gap an inch wide from the bottom of the door to the floor through which Marley could see no signs of life. Tyler must have crashed out to the world. A part of her felt that she should wake her so they could all grab food, but she also knew Tyler needed rest.

As if she knew what Marley was thinking, Cassie spoke up from her side of the room. "You should go, Marley. I'm just going to be working the rest of the night and it looks like Tyler's still out for the count. Go eat."

Like Rhett, Cassie had no idea that Christian was in the room though that didn't stop him from giving her a dirty look either.

"Come on," Rhett urged, emboldened by Cassie's blessing. "Save me from the horror that is eggplant on a pizza."

Laughing, Marley rolled her eyes. "I happen to like eggplant too."

Stepping out after him, she gave Cassie and Christian a quick wave. "Thanks for the chat, I'll talk to you later," she said. While Rhett thought the comment was for Cassie, Christian knew it was meant for him though it did nothing to assuage the terrible ache he suddenly felt inside.

"Are you sure you should go…" he managed to ask but Marley had already closed the door leaving him with an oblivious Cassie.

Smiling happily to herself, Cassie turned back to her work as she put the earbuds back into her ears, singing "love is in the air."

Christian had to fight the urge to throw something at her before he realized that he wouldn't be able to, anyway.

Letting out a sigh of frustration, he vanished.

ONE HUNDRED FIFTY-FOUR

Rhett's room was pretty much like the guy himself. Tastefully decorated with things in their rightful place. Coursebooks were stacked neatly on shelves. What furniture that hadn't come with the room had a modern slant to them. There was a round glass table, a reading chair that was made from one piece of curved wood strategically placed by the window where it would get the most light. The bed was perfectly made and covered with striped covers. Though he had the same coffee-colored carpet that she had (each of the residential hall floors had different colored carpet), his was spotless.

Marley felt herself wincing slightly thinking of their own floor which was littered with clothes. Well, her side at least. Cassie — ever the neat freak — her side of the room was as clean as Rhett's.

If only there was a spell that would take care of her messiness.

She gave him an incredulous stare. "Do you have OCD or something? Your room is so clean."

Rhett's cheeks turned a little red as he set the pizzas

onto the table then grabbed plates and a pair of glasses from a shelf.

"My mom had me on a strict cleaning schedule every weekend. Guess it took."

He pulled out a chair for Marley, gesturing to it. It was an old-fashioned move that Marley found herself somewhat charmed by. Everything he did seemed easy and natural.

"Thanks." She sat down on the chair, watching as he brought over a bottle of Evian from a mini-fridge. "We have one of those too, a mini-fridge? Courtesy of Cassie's parents."

"I heard they're famous, one's a TV anchor, right?"

"Her dad. Cassie's mom's a model," Marley answered expecting Rhett to be impressed by the latter; instead, he pulled a face, surprising her with his reaction. "What, you must be the only guy in the world who doesn't like models?"

He poured water into her glass before he poured his own drink. "I just can't imagine what it must be like to only be valued for how you look. What's that saying… beauty fades…" He stopped, racking his brain.

"But a sense of humor remains," Marley finished for him.

"Well, that and intelligence, creativity, skills and so on…" Rhett replied, opening up the pizza boxes.

Marley stared at him until he noticed her scrutiny. "I can't tell if you're trying to impress or if you're just being you."

Rhett stopped what he was doing to flash a sexy grin at her. "Can't I impress by being me? Why's it got to be one or the other?"

Marley laughed, liking how easy it was to be around him. It was almost as if they had known each other before.

Taking a seat opposite her, he gestured to the pizzas as

he grabbed a slice for himself. Marley picked one of the biggest vegetarian slices and took a bite.

"It's good," she nodded approvingly.

"It should be at those prices," Rhett laughed. "Back home you could get five large pizzas for that price."

"Where are you from?" Marley asked.

"Emmettsberg. It's a small town in Iowa," Rhett said. "You've probably never heard of it.

"I'm not that familiar with the Mid-West," Marley answered. "Isn't Iowa all cornfields and flatlands?"

"Mostly, but there's more to us than that. There's just something about the good, honest living back home that I don't feel in a big city like Boston. I mean, I like it here too, but I kinda miss having complete strangers say hi to you on the street. Here, everything's so loud and busy. People are always on the go. Back in Iowa, you end up shooting the breeze with complete strangers. If your car breaks down, every car that comes by stops to help. It's nice." Thinking of home, his eyes had taken on a faraway look.

"I've never really felt that kind of connection with a place before," Marley revealed, chewing another mouthful of pizza. "We've always lived on the West Coast. When I was born, we were in one of the burbs in California. Later, we moved to San Fran where my Dad and I were until I was accepted here."

"What does your mom do?" Rhett asked not realizing what a loaded question that was becoming.

"She's not in our lives," Marley said simply and left it at that. She'd had enough family talk today and just wanted to enjoy this time, where she wouldn't be worrying about her issues.

He didn't push the subject. "Right. Sorry. I didn't know. How's your dad, anyway? I haven't seen him recently."

Something must have flickered over her face as he looked suddenly apologetic.

"He's fine. Already has his favorite students, apparently," Marley answered. "I bet you're teacher's pet too?" She teased, lighting up the mood.

"They do seem to like me," Rhett admitted. "It's partly how I got the RA gig. I get a free dorm room, free food, free parking, discounted tuition plus a small salary."

"Wow, I didn't know the job came with so many perks." If there wasn't that other giant responsibility on her shoulders, she would apply for the gig herself.

"It's not all good though; sometimes you have to deal with difficult situations." Something in his tone made her think he wasn't talking in hypotheticals.

"Like what?"

Rhett lowered his pizza. "I've got this weird problem actually…" he started, but stopped, wondering if he should continue.

Dabbing her mouth with a napkin, Marley set her food down. "I'm good at keeping secrets if you're worried."

He had no idea just how many she was keeping at any one time. Pretty soon she'd need a spreadsheet to keep count.

"It's one of the students in our dorm. His roommate has always been a little off, but lately, he's been getting into more and more freaky stuff. It's really beginning to scare him."

Rhett wasn't the kind to spout hyperbolic gossip so Marley knew this must be pretty serious.

"What kind of freaky stuff? Like drugs?"

"No. Like black magic. He started using an Ouija board lately."

Marley felt a cold shiver take hold. Someone in their dorm was using black magic? If this was true, it was way too close to home. With the protective wards in place now, Marley knew no demons could come into their dorm, but that didn't stop someone from misusing magic.

Had Michael found out about their wards and done something to one of the kids in their dorm?

Whatever was going on, it would have to be investigated.

"Who are they? Just wondering if I know either of them," she asked carefully, hoping she sounded normal.

"Dalton's the one that came to me with this. His roommate's Zack."

Marley shook her head. "I don't think I've met either of them."

"It might be innocent but as RA, it falls on me to check it out, especially when Dalton is having trouble sleeping as he's worried about what his roommate is getting up to."

So many thoughts ran through her head that Marley couldn't think how to respond. Worried what this Zack guy could be doing, she wanted to check up on him though it would be weird for her to leave Rhett now.

And besides, she realized she didn't really want to.

She could lie and say it was all about the pizza, though — good as the pizza was, and it was good — it was more about the company. Rhett was easy on the eye and even easier to like.

She was sure Dalton and Zack could wait until tomorrow.

"I'm weirding you out with this aren't I?" Rhett asked, misreading her expression.

"No… I'm fine," Marley said, but Rhett looked apologetic.

"Some people love hearing this kind of stuff, but others are super turned off. I'm guessing you're in the latter group."

"No, I'm OK with all this, I promise. I'm quite into the supernatural actually," Marley revealed.

Well, not so much into as being forced into it.

"For real?" Rhett asked, looking surprised. "In that case, there's this movie I was planning on seeing tomorrow, it's a supernatural thriller. Did you ever see The Sixth Sense?"

See it? I'm living it, Rhett.

Wisely, she kept the thought to herself.

"Yes. I felt like I was totally emerged in Malcolm's life. Like everything that happened to him was happening to me," Marley replied.

"Do you want to come with me then? Tomorrow night?" Rhett asked, looking winsomely hot as he waited for her answer.

"Like a date?" Marley needed the clarification. Boys could be so confusing she'd found. One minute you'd think you were dating, only to discover that your potential boyfriend actually died several years ago…

Clarification was good as far as Marley was concerned.

Rhett laughed. "Yes. A date with me."

Marley tilted her head at him. "Can you do that? I'm mean, you're my RA?"

Rhett laughed again, a rich, warm sound that filled her up inside. "I'm not a priest, Marley. I can date."

"Well, then, sure. I'd love to."

ONE HUNDRED FIFTY-FIVE

The shop looked about as uninteresting as everything else on this planet.

Old coins littered the dust-covered window display where no one in their right mind would pay the extortionate prices being demanded. It was almost as if the shop didn't want any business. Michael took a moment to focus on the place wondering why it wasn't what it should be yet he knew that he had come to the right address.

And then he saw it.

The faint ebbing at the corners of the shop that revealed a glamor was in place, and which only someone of his vast powers would be able to discern.

Pushing open the door, he stepped inside the shop called Juju.

As he had expected, the glamor faded the instant he crossed the threshold and closed the door behind him.

A woman — the owner — he presumed, assisted a group by the counter. There were around five of them dressed head to toe in black. All had long dark hair, even the men.

He knew what they were immediately.

Vampires.

Blood-sucking fiends and low-lives who had to rely on hypnotizing their prey to get what they wanted. Only one-tier above demons as far as he was concerned.

Michael had dealt with a few of them in his time, and things always went the same. They would assume their superior strength added with supernatural speed made them invincible.

Michael had always liked to prove them wrong in that regard.

Despite his personal feelings towards them, however, he was here to shop like everyone else. Striding toward the counter, he approached, waiting until the woman — a witch — finished serving them. She wore a ring of enchanted butterflies that moved as she moved. It was a subtle form of magic yet not something the average witch would know how to do. Michael found himself wondering about the woman as she dealt with her customers.

The vamps paid for their purchases as she put everything into a shopping bag that was printed with the name of the coin store. Feeling his presence, the vamps shot a look at him. Far from showing any fear, Michael kept his eyes steadily on them which seemed to anger them.

"I've not seen your kind before," one of the vamps said, the one with a mane of the longest hair. It was a sign of their virility, the long hair. They wore it like a modern-day cloak that would flap behind them in the wind.

Just for fun, Michael toyed with the idea of burning the whole thing off.

"What are you?" The vamp asked even though Michael had no inclination of continuing the conversation.

"Impatient," Michael retorted. "I urge you to hasten proceedings so I can go about my day faster. Some of us have things to do."

The witch's dark eyes flicked up at him, showing interest at what she saw. Though she hadn't yet addressed him in any way, hadn't even said anything actually, intelligence shone out of her, of the kind these vamps wished they had. She finished bagging their purchases though she seemed in no hurry to do so.

An animal-like growl came out of a vamp, the one with eyes of an unnatural blue. They glowed with an almost neon-like light.

"Seems to me like you could do with a lesson in manners," he hissed as Michael caught the scent of iron in his breath. Apparently, he'd already drunk quite a bit of blood that morning.

"I don't have time to play with you, low-dweller," Michael responded casually as if he were swatting a fly away. "Be on your way."

But the vamps weren't taking kindly to him. And they weren't in the least bit scared of this man-like creature standing before them.

More fool them.

Opening their mouths, their fangs began to protrude until they were fully exposed. The witch took a step back, but Michael noticed she showed no fear on her face.

"You know the rules. Not in my house," she warned quietly.

"Stay out of this, Helena," the only female in the group warned.

Michael could feel the swirl of magic appearing around them suddenly, but it wasn't coming from her. The shop was enchanted with some kind of spell though these fools either did not know it, or they didn't care.

The vamps circled Michael with an animosity that would have struck fear into most, but Michael felt a brief flash of excitement.

They rushed him as one, a pack descending on their prey as Michael called forth his own magic. Whatever the store was about to do, it never had the chance. Michael mumbled a word under his breath and snapped his fingers.

Suddenly all five vamps had their necks snapped. One by one, they dominoed to the floor until it was littered with their bodies.

Silence fell on the shop until Helena let out an impressed sigh.

"How did you *do* that?" She asked, unable to hide her awe.

"The snapping of their necks? It's a simple matter," Michael replied, somewhat surprised by the lack of fear in her voice. This might be the first human to surprise him.

"Not that. How did you get past the shop's spell? It has protected us for generations. No supernatural entity is able to commit violence here. If they do, the shop takes care of them."

Michael shrugged. "I have no idea how your store's spell works. I only know that those vamps were getting in the way of what I want."

Helena's eyes flew up to his face. "And what is that?"

"I require a very specific object, one which can control a person," Michael replied.

"Freewill can't be taken, you must know that," Helena started to say, but Michael stopped her with a raising of his hand.

"Yes, yes. But if it is given, what cursed objects or spells do you have?" Michael asked, his impatience creeping in again. Must he explain himself? Couldn't she just give him what he wanted?

Helena's expression turned coy. She twisted a lock of her brunette hair around her finger as the enchanted butterflies in her hair flapped their wings.

"Well, that kind of magic isn't really allowed… That's the kind of thing that would get the Guardians after you."

Michael felt the laugh bursting out of him.

"Have you seen any of them around lately? I think you'll find the last of them have all but gone."

At this, Helena's eyes turned shrewd as she pinned them on him. "How do you know that?"

"Because I made sure of it myself," Michael replied, not in the least bit concerned that she would know this. In fact, it would help his case if she did.

As he suspected, Helena didn't shy from the fact. Rather, she seemed encouraged. There was a definite pep in her step as she drew a sigil into the air.

A bookcase full of the usual ingredients one associated with witches — jars of insects and the body parts of animals as well as uncommon herbs — slid open revealing a staircase that led down into a room with a red light.

"In that case, I believe I might have what you want after all…"

ONE HUNDRED FIFTY-SIX

"Do I know you?"

The guy who had asked the question rubbed sleep-filled eyes, though Marley was happy to see that she hadn't woken him up as he was already dressed in jeans and a shirt, though his feet were bare on the carpet.

He had a pinched face which probably wasn't helped by the sleepless nights he'd been experiencing which Marley could see he was suffering from. His eyes were red-rimmed and he could barely hold himself upright. His shoulders sloped to the floor, and a yawn came out of him every few seconds. Dalton, she knew his name was, was giving her a puzzled look.

"No… I live here too. I'm a friend of Rhett's," she replied as her brain reached for the explanation she had rehearsed in her head several times over on her way here.

"Er, congratulations?" He said, scratching at the stubble that covered his chin.

"Sorry, I'm not doing a good job of this. Rhett mentioned to me that you were having some trouble. I have a specific skillset and might be able to help you with that."

She lowered her voice, not wanting to alert the room-mate since he was probably still there. It was only eight in the morning after all. Dalton's eyes went a little wider as he started to understand what she was hinting at.

The door opened wider, and he stepped aside.

"Come in," he said, darting a look into the hallway but no one cared what they were up to: the few students who were awake were busy getting ready for class.

Marley stepped into his room noticing the black sheet that hung suspended from the ceiling, dividing the room in half. Dalton's side of the room, the side closest to the door was pretty much how she expected it — clothes were strewn in a haphazard fashion over every piece of furniture, the bed was still unmade. Dirty plates and glasses were stacked beside course books and papers.

Seeing the mess through her eyes, Dalton suddenly darted toward the bed, hastily straightening the sheets and rearranging the pillows. He shouldn't have bothered though as his efforts just made the whole thing look untidier.

Marley decided to keep that to herself though. She wasn't there to police his cleanliness.

"Sorry. I wasn't expecting anyone," Dalton apolo-gized, grabbing the dirty dishes and dumping them into the sink.

"Don't worry," Marley explained. "You should see the state of mine."

Dalton moved closer to her, lowering his voice to a whisper. "So Rhett told you I was having difficulty with Zack?"

He inclined his head at the black divider.

"Yeah. I wanted to see if I could speak to him, find out what's he's up to?"

Dalton's expression turned wary. "When I woke around an hour ago, I could hear him muttering to him-self, but he's made it clear that he doesn't like his privacy invaded so I left him to it. He went quiet when you knocked though."

Did he now?

Approaching the room divider, Marley reached for the material when she felt a cold that seeped deep into her bones. The chill was so sudden and so intense that she saw her breath mist the air in front of her face.

The temperature had plummeted for no natural reason.

Her heart sped up as she felt the presence of something else in the room with them. Rhett's talk from last night came into her mind, his mention of the occult and black magic in particular.

She felt the first pinprick of fear, but with Dalton standing behind her she couldn't stop. She needed to know what lay behind that curtain.

Shivering from the cold she pulled the divider aside.

Sitting cross-legged on his bed, both hands resting on a planchette on top of an Ouija board, was Zack. Whatever monster Marley had imagined was far worse than the short, underweight guy who sat before her. Despite being the one causing all the trouble, Zack didn't seem better rested than Dalton, in fact, he looked much worse.

If Dalton was at a five, then Zack was sub-zero.

Exhaustion didn't stop his anger from erupting, however. At her appearance, Zack jumped to his feet. "Who the hell are you?" he demanded.

Marley spoke calmly, hoping her unease wouldn't show. "Dalton was getting concerned about you so I came to see if I could offer some assistance."

Instead of answering her, Zack spun around to Dalton. "What have you been saying about me?" he fumed, spitting the words out.

"The truth, Zack. You won't listen to me, so maybe you'll listen to a stranger. Besides, I didn't sign up for this, OK? Your weirdness is freaking me out and I'm not prepared to be another statistic when you suddenly decide to go psycho on me while I'm sleeping," Dalton shot back, tiredness making him lose any last patience.

"You don't have any idea what's going on!" Zack roared, clutching his hands into fists so he wouldn't punch him.

Feeling the violence simmering under the surface, Marley took a step back. "Can you talk to me, Zack? Tell me what's happening."

Zack shot her a look of pure contempt. "I don't know you, so do yourself a favor, and get the hell out of my room."

He moved as if to get in her face but Dalton darted in front of Marley, physically blocking him in case he made a move. "Jesus, man, she's just trying to help you!"

"Neither of you understand and you won't even if I try to explain. Just get out of my face and leave me alone!" Zack dived around Marley, storming out of the room.

In the silence that followed all they could hear was the thumping of their own hearts.

"I'm sorry. I might have made things worse for you." Marley began wishing that she'd given the whole idea more thought before she'd ever knocked on the door.

Dalton ran a hand through his hair, looking as concerned as she felt. "At least you're trying. Most people wouldn't even bother, especially with Zack behaving like that."

"Has he always been this way?" Marley asked.

"Highly strung? No. He was fine at first. We even hung out playing video games. We'd watch a movie if there was a good one on TV, but in the last two weeks, he changed big time. He was always into the occult, the paranormal, stuff like that, but most people are — I love a good horror flick — but Zack started acting weird. He couldn't sleep and I'd find him walking around the room at night, talking to someone only there would never be anyone there."

His eyes turned dark with the memory of it all. "Then things grew stranger. When he realized I'd noticed something was up, he threw up that divider and stopped talking to me. He doesn't leave the room except for class. He used to do martial arts, but that's stopped too. And it's always so frigging cold in here, no matter how sunny and warm it is outside. I don't know what he's messing around with but it isn't good and I don't like being in such proximity to it."

Dalton was on the brink of a meltdown himself. Marley had experienced enough of them to know the signs. Since she didn't want to worry him further, she decided it would be best to keep her suspicions to herself.

"I'd feel the same in your position," Marley agreed.

Dalton's eyes slid up to her face where they held her gaze as he studied her. "Why are you doing this, anyway? What's in this for you?"

"Nothing," Marley shrugged. "I've just helped people with issues like this before. And I'd like to try before the situation gets worse. If you involve the Dean or his parents, he's only going to hate you more. I'm hoping we can figure this out without bringing in the big guns."

She was about to say more when her phone flashed up with a voicemail. The phone had never rung so she must have lost coverage while being in this room.

"Hold up, I have a message. Let me get this," Marley asked. Listening to the voicemail, Marley's face turned white. She couldn't believe what she was hearing.

"I'm sorry, I've got to go!" Grabbing a notebook she found on his table, she scribbled her number inside.

"Call me when he gets back and we'll deal with this OK? I'm sorry, but I've got to go. My friend's in trouble."

With that, she was gone, leaving Dalton to scratch his head wondering what on Earth just happened.

Staring around the room, his eyes landed on the ouija board that still sat on Zack's bed. As the thought came to him that he should just burn the thing, the planchette began to *move*.

Dalton stood frozen in fear, heart thumping a beat inside his chest as the planchette landed on four letters.

D. E. A. D.

By the time it reached the second D, Dalton had grabbed his things and the notebook Marley's number was written on, and raced out of there.

ONE HUNDRED FIFTY-SEVEN

Early morning sunlight bounced off the glass of the rectangular building that housed BPD, Boston's biggest police department.

Approaching quickly, out of breath from rushing here, Marley felt a sense of overwhelming relief when she recognized Eve's black curls, alongside Cassie's smaller frame ahead. Eve must have parked her car nearby as she still carried the car keys in her hand.

"Hey, wait up!" She called out, running to catch up with them as they started to head inside.

"You got the call too?" Eve asked, surprised to see all three of them there.

"From Detective Saunders? Yes. She left a voicemail saying that Tyler had been arrested but she would be released soon if I wanted to come down to pick her up," Marley explained between breaths.

"So Saunders called all three of us?" Cassie reiterated, trying to untangle the thoughts in her mind. "Why would she do that unless she has us down as her emergency contact?"

"Well, she probably does actually," Marley answered.

"She doesn't really have anyone else to put down anymore."

Even as she said the words, she felt a flash of pain in her chest. She couldn't imagine what it must feel like to be so alone in the world, without family to even put down on a list like this except for Ally.

"It's still strange for her to call all three of us. It would usually be the one person," Eve revealed so sure of herself that Marley wondered how Eve seemed to know more about these things than the average person. Did she have history with the police?

"Let's just get inside. I can't believe she's been here the whole night." Cassie shuddered, looking both guilty and ashamed.

"I know. I thought she was getting some sleep. We should have checked on her," Marley lamented, wishing that hindsight wasn't such a bitch. Tyler — with all the terrible things that had recently happened to her — had been in trouble while she had been off eating pizza and checking out their RA. A great friend she was turning out to be.

Hurrying past uniformed cops carrying styrofoam cups of coffee and bagels, the girls reached the information desk. Since both Eve and Cassie hesitated to give their names, Marley volunteered her own before moving across to a waiting area where they sat on plastic seats that were bolted to the walls.

It seemed they were overly concerned with people either stealing them or using them as a weapon. Either way, Marley found the chairs vastly uncomfortable as she shifted in her seat, crossing one leg over the other.

Time crawled almost to a stop, at least, that was how it seemed. Expecting to see Tyler at any second, Marley found herself frowning impatiently when a half hour later they were still sitting on those uncomfortable seats. Cassie had taken to checking out Instagram feeds on her phone, while Eve sat with her back ramrod straight, her eyes scoping out every movement in the place.

Unable to sit silently any longer, Marley turned to face Eve.

"So what did you do last night, after you left us? Anything fun?"

Eve's eyes turned hooded as she turned to look at her. She didn't answer the question straight away, just looked at Marley with an expression she couldn't quite decipher. "No. Nothing eventful," she finally answered.

But there was something about her tone that implied otherwise. Marley picked up on it immediately and would have pried further when Saunders finally appeared, walking toward them in seemingly no hurry whatsoever.

Marley jumped up. Eve and Cassie followed suit.

Saunders looked tired this morning. She was dressed in a pale blue pant suit with leather loafers chosen for comfort rather design. Everything about her was neat and orderly, yet she didn't seem as calm and together as she usually was.

"Thanks for coming," Saunders began, gesturing for them to sit back down. Not knowing what else to do, they sat back into their chairs.

"What happened with Tyler? Is she OK?" Marley asked. "Your voicemail didn't explain anything."

"She's fine, but she had a bit of an episode here last night," Saunders replied as she watched them all carefully.

Marley forced herself to remain calm; the woman was suspicious of them enough as it was. "What kind of episode?"

"She got upset about her sister, turned up here and started yelling at the staff," Saunders replied, her eyes sweeping the three of them, reading their every reaction.

"If my ten-year-old sister had been kidnapped, I would be pretty upset too," Eve responded in her typical she-didn't-give-a-crap tone, but one which always seemed magnified whenever she was speaking to a cop.

"Here's where things got interesting. While she was getting upset, the lights all blew out." Saunders stopped talking, letting her words linger.

"I don't see why that's interesting or relevant," Eve said, looking for all the world as if she was genuinely confused.

"Because it only happened to the lights that were above her. The rest of the lights around the station were fine. It was like she did something to them."

Cassie had yet to say anything. Clearing her throat she tried for a confident tone like Eve's but all she managed was a thin, weedy voice. "You know that sounds crazy, right?"

"Yes," Saunders replied, staring at Cassie now until she turned flustered under her scrutiny. "Almost as crazy as blowing up a diner or the pipes in a laundry block."

She left her sentence hanging, as the girls tried to find something to say that would throw her off this path.

"I thought you called us here to get our friend, not grill us about things that were out of our control," Marley said.

"Yeah. We have classes we need to get to when we get out of here," Eve jumped in, backing her up.

Saunders eyes flashed with something akin to interest before a veil came down over them. "Heaven forbid I distract you from more important things."

Glancing across the room she gave a curt nod to a cop standing in the doorway. He disappeared but returned with Tyler beside him moments later. She looked dishevelled and her clothes were creased from being slept in, but otherwise, she looked as Marley expected her to.

"You guys are here?" Tyler seemed overwhelmed to see them all.

"Didn't Saunders tell you she'd called us?" Eve asked.

"No," Tyler answered, shooting the cop a hard look. "I was just told to wait until she sent for me."

"Sorry," Saunders apologized though her tone revealed she felt anything but.

"So that's it? She can go?" Cassie asked, making sure, beginning to get as flighty as Eve.

Saunders nodded. "I've let you off with a light warning this time, seeing as you are under a tremendous amount of stress, but I won't be able to be as lenient if you cause a scene again."

Tyler thought of several choice things she could say to the cop, but sanity prevailed in the end. Keeping her thoughts to herself, she just nodded.

Saunders turned to the other girls. "You three need to be there for her. Keep her out of trouble, you understand?"

A chorus of "yes's" came out of them.

Finally satisfied that that would be all she would get out of them, Saunders started heading back to her office when Tyler stopped, calling at her.

"Detective Saunders? Remember to keep me in the loop on Ally's progress. Please," she added, needing to know she had at least achieved this one small thing.

"I will," Saunders nodded.

The girls gathered around Tyler protectively as the four hurried away from the station.

ONE HUNDRED FIFTY-EIGHT

S tacks of pancakes, fruit bowls and a plate of bacon were placed around them — courtesy of Cassie and her enormous wallet — as the girls sat around a booth at the IHOP that was only a few blocks away from the BPD.

The place was barely moving at this hour with most people having already broken their fast and gone on their way.

It turned out that, having barely slept a wink at the station (even if her clothes told a different story), Tyler was starving. She spoke between mouthfuls of food, chewing as fast as she talked, explaining all that had gone on the night before.

"She's obviously on to us," Eve commented when Tyler was done, thinking out loud.

"Maybe she's just asking questions. She is a cop after all, though it does seem too much that she would think we caused all those things." As always, Marley tried for the optimistic approach only to be shot down with a look from Eve.

"Oh, she definitely suspects. I mean, she basically said

so. If she can find some kind of proof, we may be in trouble." Eve wasn't trying to guilt Tyler, but her words had the same effect.

Tyler set her fork down, her appetite suddenly vanishing. "I shouldn't have gone there, I've just made things the worse. I'm sorry, this was all me."

"What was all her?" Christian stood behind the row of plants that formed a screen at the back of their seats. If the conversation wasn't so serious, Marley would have laughed at how ludicrous he looked standing between two Swiss Cheese plants.

When he was filled in, his expression became serious and Marley could see how helpless he felt. She wasn't far off from feeling the same.

"I feel kind of responsible, Tyler," Marley began. "I should have checked up on you instead of hanging out with Rhett."

"Thank you! That's what I've been saying all along," Christian couldn't help from cutting in, earning an annoyed glance from Marley. "More saving-the-world, less Rhett. We should make that a group motto."

"What is your problem with him?" Marley demanded suddenly, irritated by his attitude toward Rhett.

"You want me to make a list? Because I can," Christian offered.

Knowing this wasn't getting them anywhere, she ignored him and continued talking to Tyler. "I just thought you were sleeping, and God knows, you've needed the rest."

Tyler gave her a small smile as her eyes softened. There was no hard feeling there. "You weren't to know. I'm just grateful that you are here for me during all of this. You're already helping much more than you know just by being here."

Supportive smiles went around the group as Christian felt a moment of pride. These girls were at each other's throats not that long ago, but they were becoming a family now. They had each other's backs. Maybe they would have a chance to beat Michael after all…

"While I was locked up, I had time to really think and I want to ask Christian something," Tyler said, looking around for him even though she wouldn't be able to see him.

"He's here so ask away," Marley answered as Christian nodded.

"Those artifacts Michael has been after… he uses them to power up, right? So, can't we do the same? Can't I use the stocking to gain more power to find Ally?" Her questions came out in one big jumble having spent all night thinking about this.

Christian's eyes narrowed. He hesitated for only a moment, but Marley caught it, the flicker of doubt that flashed over his face before it vanished.

"Unfortunately, no. That's not how the artifacts can be used. The stocking is only useful to us in that we are stopping Michael from getting stronger. There's nothing you can do with it, so you definitely should not try. Anything that's filled with black magic can be dangerous if you don't know what you are doing, or if it's used in the wrong manner."

Marley repeated him though she didn't quite buy his answer.

And neither did Tyler.

Picking up on Marley's hesitation, she kept her thoughts to herself, the hint of an idea in the back of her mind but one that would have to wait until later.

"Well, artifacts or not, the cops are clearly struggling to find your sister," Eve raised. "We need to do something together."

"But what?" Cassie asked, wringing her hands. "Any of the spells we've tried before either haven't worked, or they've gone wrong in some way."

"Maybe that's because Michael knows it's what we'd do so he's put something in place to stop them?" Tyler supplied even as the thought started to take hold in her mind, growing legs.

"Right, he probably has his own spells to conceal her," Christian agreed.

"In which case," Marley said after she repeated him. "We need to be smarter. Maybe it's not Ally we should be looking for…"

Cassie's eyes grew so wide that they seemed as if they would pop off her face. "Maybe it's Michael himself… or one of his demons!"

"That's a great idea, Cass, but which one do we go for? He's sent a bunch of them after us…" Tyler asked, running their faces through her head.

"But the same two keep cropping up, don't they?" Eve mused. "That first night, the two that attacked me, I've seen them again. They were at the Castle."

"Oh! They were at The Athenaeum too! It was the shorter one who pushed me down the stairs, which the other one didn't seem too happy about. The taller one called all the shots."

"So we should go after the taller one?" Eve asked only to earn a shudder from Cassie.

"I actually think he's the scarier one. There's just something about him. The way he looks at you, like something he wants to devour. He freaks me out way more than the hunchbacked one."

"We only know one of their names, right? Was it Pike?" Marley asked Cassie as she nodded.

"Well if he's the lesser demon, it's likely that he's also less powerful so my vote is for him," Marley replied.

"Me too," Cassie agreed as Tyler and Eve nodded their consent.

"Well, that's decided. Now we have a different problem: I highly doubt Michael would allow us to cast location spells on any of them," Eve said, lines creasing her brow.

"Yeah, he seems too smart not to have considered

that," Tyler conceded, much as she hated to. "So how are we going to find this Pike demon without using any of our magic?"

As the girls racked their brains for ideas, Cassie suddenly looked up and smiled.

A weathered sign with the logo 'REAL MEATS' creaked on a rusty pole as the four girls approached the nondescript building huddled between two factories. It seemed a strange place to house a popular supernatural hangout, yet here it was.

The sun darted behind a cloud, casting the world with a grayness that seemed fitting for a visit to a place named 'Furnace'.

Eve and Cassie were the only ones to have come here before, and even then, they hadn't gotten very far having been stopped by the hulk-sized bouncer who stood before a locked steel door.

The same bouncer was still there now, dressed in jeans and a leather jacket, apparently, it was his uniform. It was only his uncompromising posture and eyes that constantly appraised the area that gave his true purpose away.

Though their previous trip had drawn a blank at the time, they had found one piece of information which they put to good use now. Wearing Christian's face and body, Cassie marched up to the bouncer, the girls in tow.

Seeing him, the bouncer's expression immediately changed. The hardness left his eyes to be replaced with sadness. Before Cassie could even speak, the bouncer greeted her.

"You're Christian, aren't you?" Cassie nodded, slightly taken aback as she had already been warned by the real Christian that Eric had never taken him here, and only ever met his snitch, alone. "I don't believe we've met… have we?" She squeaked out that last part of her question, though luckily, it came out in Christian's voice so it wasn't too noticeable.

The bouncer offered her his giant paw of a hand. "No. I'm Hemingway. I was a friend of Eric's. I'm sorry to hear about your loss."

Cassie wasn't sure what she found more startling — that he had been friends with Christian's mentor, or that his name was Hemingway. Taking his hand, she pumped it up and down.

"Thanks. It's been tough," she managed, hoping that he wouldn't ask anything personal that she wouldn't be able to answer. Christian had wanted to be here, but since the place was frequented by supernaturals, there was no guarantee that they wouldn't be able to see his ghost. It was only this reason that Christian had sat this one out. He wasn't too happy about them walking into the lion's den like this, though, apparently, like Juju, the bar was en-spelled so that magic and violence couldn't be used against the patrons, which might have led to the bar's everlasting popularity as it certainly wasn't due to its location.

"So, you're taking over the Guardian business?" Hemingway asked.

"That's what he wanted," Cassie replied cooly, figuring that would be the right answer based on the things Christian had already told them about himself.

"Good luck with it. I hear there are all sorts of problems now. The Guardians are dropping like flies," Hemingway said without thinking. He looked immediately contrite. "Sorry. I should think before I speak."

Cassie gave him what she hoped was a watery smile. "No problem."

Hemingway finally turned his gaze to Tyler, Eve, and Marley who stood quietly off-side throughout their conversation. When his eyes landed on Eve, they gained a spark of recognition.

"You again," he commented.

"I told you I knew Christian," Eve couldn't help but say, even as she knew it sounded a little childish.

Hemingway didn't bother to reply. Stepping aside, the steel door opened revealing a narrow spiral staircase that led down into the darkness. Cassie didn't want to go first but as Hemingway was still watching, and as she still wore Christian's face, there was no other choice. Squaring her shoulders, she stepped through the doorway and started down the staircase.

The second her foot touched the first step, a candle magically appeared floating by the wall to her left. There wasn't much room between the wall and her, so the candle was only a foot or so from her arm. At that close a distance, she should have felt the heat emanating from the candle however slight — but there was nothing.

Her fingers reached out to the candle until they went through the flame but the flame never wavered. "It's an illusion," Cassie said.

"This is the kind of thing we should learn how to do, it might come in handy one day," Marley commented.

"I'll add it to our To-Do list," Eve said wryly.

They curved downward as music that sounded like upbeat jazz came from within the walls. When they reached the bottom, they found themselves in a circular room with a domed ceiling that was carved out of the ground itself. Plush armchairs and sofas covered with purple velvet were artfully arranged around coffee tables. Each table had its own floral display of neon-colored flowers — flowers that were actually alive, swaying and moving in time to the music.

But it was the patrons themselves that had the girls gaping having never seen such sights before, at least, not to this extent.

Gathered by the bar, there was a group of horned-demons who laughed and joked as they tossed down blue-tinted drinks. Lounging leisurely on one of the sofa sections, was a startlingly handsome man with long, platinum hair. He was shirtless, wearing only black leather pants that clung to him. His skin was so smooth that it seemed almost to shine. A group of admiring young females were draped over him shamelessly. One of them, pulled up the sleeve of her dress to offer him her wrist.

The man smiled as fangs suddenly sprang from his mouth and faster than humanly possible, he sank the fangs into her wrist.

Marley stilled a gasp, even as the girls tensed around her. So vampires were real. If they were all this good-looking, they were going to have a hard time resisting them if one ever came their way.

As if he could sense her inspection, the vamp raised his eyes to Marley's. Electricity shot through her body as she felt herself become mesmerized by his eyes which were the color of fire. Golden flames danced inside.

It wasn't until she felt a hand on her shoulder that she tore her eyes away. Eve was staring at her with some concern. With a start, Marley saw that both Cassie and Tyler had moved and were now several feet away.

"You OK? You were just standing there," Eve said.

"Only for a second though. I was looking at something," Marley replied.

"It was a lot more than a second," Eve replied.

Her reply surprised her. How had time slipped away from her like that? Had the vamp done that to her somehow? Thinking about his little harem, she suddenly realized that maybe that's what he did to get them. She'd read about vampires and the glamor they could do, had seen it on TV shows even. She'd always thought it was made up then again, she'd never believed in vampires either until now.

Even as she came to the conclusion, she could feel his eyes burning into her back. It was all she could do not to look at him again. Focusing on Eve, she urged her forward. "Go on…"

They stopped by the bar and when the bartender — an impossibly svelte nymph-like creature — asked what they wanted to drink, Eve took charge. Lowering her voice, she asked, "I'm looking for a friend of Eric's, the Guardian? I don't suppose you might know who that is, do you?"

The bartender shook her head. "Sorry, I can't help you."

It wasn't clear by her response whether she could help and just wouldn't, or if she didn't know. Either way, they had drawn a blank.

They moved around the private club, making inquiries from any of the crowd who didn't seem too frightening, trying not to stare at the strange goings-on between the patrons. When finally a voice reached out to them.

"Why are you looking for me?"

Eric's snitch, it turned out, was a demon with a very distinct appearance.

From the top of his bald head down to the clawed feet which poked out of the sandals he wore, his skin was a vivid blood red that made the white of his eyes stand out so much as to be comical. He stood quietly, waiting for an answer.

"You're Eric's friend?" Cassie asked.

The demon turned his shrewd eyes on her. "Who are you supposed to be? Another Guardian? It's a serviceable attempt I suppose though I suspect the real one might be somewhat aggrieved by the, how do I say this? Feminine touches you have given him."

The girls shot each other a look. Could he see through Cassie's magic?

"Yes," he answered their unspoken question. Anyone in my line of work would have spotted the inconsistencies straight away."

Cassie blinked at him, startled that her cover had been blown before shooting a resigned look at the others. "Fine. I suppose Christian was right after all. Everyone's a critic," she moaned, feeling she was being treated unfairly.

The demon tilted his head at her, not understanding her comment.

"The Guardian whose appearance she has adopted took umbrage with her interpretation of him. He said, and I'm quoting here, "Why the hell have you given me man boobs?" Marley explained.

Cassie stamped her foot. "They're not boobs! I was trying for pec muscles!"

The demon looked on in amusement. "I think you might need a little more practice, dear. Feel free to come by my office if you ever need instructions in the art of disguise. My name's Esteban and I charge by the hour though I'm assuming you're here for a different reason right now?"

Eve stepped forward. "Yes, we were hoping for some intel on a demon.

"Well, you are certainly in the right place for that," Esteban quipped.

"His name's Pike," Marley explained tentatively.

The only sign that Esteban knew who he was came from a slight narrowing of his eyes. His voice turned bland though Tyler could feel an interest from him that hadn't been there a moment before.

"Describe him for me," Esteban asked.

"About this tall, has a hunchback. Ugly," Eve supplied. She kept Michael's name out of it, knowing that this wasn't a good place to be throwing that around.

"I know the one," Esteban revealed as Tyler felt a burst of excitement in her chest. "What do you need him for?"

"He has something of mine and I want it back," Tyler answered grimly. Esteban considered her answer for a moment, scratching his chin with a gnarly finger.

"Pike plays around with some dangerous people. I wouldn't go messing with him unless it was necessary," Esteban warned.

"It is," Tyler responded, her voice curt, unwillingly to give any more of their reasoning away.

Respecting this, Esteban nodded his head. "Well, I guess if anyone has a chance of doing something, it might be you four," he continued, drawing startled looks from them all.

"I'm sorry, do you know who we are?" Marley asked.

Esteban smiled. "Sweetheart, when four new girls pop up waving the kind of magical powers around that have the supernatural community talking, I make it a point to know more about them. It is, after all, my job."

"People are talking about us?" Cassie asked, not sure whether she wanted this infamy or not.

"Don't worry. They don't know who you are as such, only that you're young girls who are new on the scene, but already, you have the kind of power that others could only dream about." Esteban swallowed down the rest of his drink only for the glass to magically refill itself.

"Can you tell us how we can find Pike?" Eve asked, not at all comfortable with what he was telling them.

"He likes to watch cock-fighting. There's a fight that takes place daily, over by the corner of Lexington and Green Park. If you hurry, you should get there in time."

Marley looked at him with all the puzzlement she felt. "Why would you help us like this? You haven't even asked for anything?"

Esteban's dark eyes flicked over to her. "Because I don't like Pike or the crew he hangs with. I'm hearing bad things about them. They're causing chaos around my city and I don't appreciate that at all. Most of the community are too frightened to go against them, the others are under their pay. You four, however, aren't. And something tells me, you might be able to do something about them."

He stopped, taking a pause. When he continued again, his voice turned serious. "Most important of all, however, I don't call many people a friend, yet Eric was a friend of mine, so, if I can assist you in this matter, I will."

Marley tried to see if he was lying or manipulating them in some way, but he seemed genuine.

"Thank you," Cassie said, not knowing how else they could show their appreciation.

Esteban's attention was taken by a passing demon who didn't have a nose. "Excuse me, but I have business matters to attend to. Good luck," he said, hurrying away. "Carl! I know you can hear me…" He called after the demon.

Marley looked at the others. "I guess we head to the fight then?"

"Yeah," Tyler agreed.

ONE HUNDRED SIXTY

Marley looked across from Eve's parked car.

They had arrived at a rundown area of town that only seemed to be frequented by undesirables. A drunk staggered past, reeking of garbage, pushing a shopping cart with trash bags inside. Normally, Marley would offer money to the homeless but an air of animosity surrounded this man that stopped her from reaching for her purse.

It didn't feel safe to be taking out money here.

Though they stood out in the open, it felt like there were eyes on them. Marley wasn't sure if it was just her mind playing games with her, or if there really were demons hiding around every corner. After their visit at Furnace, they now knew that demons were much more common than they had first realized.

That thought didn't fill her with ease.

"Where do you think this fight might be taking place?" she asked, looking around but not finding anything that seemed suitable. All she could see was a neglected parking lot covered with cracked concrete. Weeds grew out of several potholes that no sane person would ever drive their car into, and certainly not Eve who had opted to park her Corolla by the sidewalk.

"Over in that building I think," Eve said, pointing to a ruined block that overlooked the motorway as she locked her car. "I just saw someone head over there, and since there's nothing around for several blocks, it seems the most likely culprit."

"We shouldn't just march over there though," Cassie said, a nervous edge to her voice.

Tyler scanned the area when her eyes alighted on a flat roof close by. "Let's see if we can get onto the roof. It'd be the perfect spot to scout out the area."

Crossing the street, they stepped into a four-story building that housed a fire station at one point but left neglected for the last few decades. All that remained of its former glory were the poles that were used for quick descents from the upper floors.

The trucks were long gone as were any furniture. Most of the doors and windows had either been stolen or had rotted away. Wind whistled through the building at such a rate that Marley had to tie her long hair back with the band she always kept spare on her wrist.

A pigeon flew overhead in the rafters, disturbed by them as Cassie found herself reflexively ducking, not wanting anything to land on her head.

Getting her bearings, Eve looked around them but when her eyes landed on a broken staircase, she frowned. "The roof that we want is there, but that's the only way to get up to it."

She pointed at the crumbling staircase which had broken away. Tyler became still suddenly, channeling her magic toward the stairs. Right before their eyes, the staircase began to shape itself as broken bricks reformed, and planks of wood unsnapped, becoming whole again. Some of the damage couldn't be healed, but by the time Tyler finished, the staircase was steady enough to be used again.

"That's pretty damn cool," Eve said in admiration.

"Thanks," Tyler acknowledged, feeling pleased with herself. Magic sure made life easier at times like this.

Tyler stepped cautiously forward, testing the step. It bowed a little under her weight but stayed otherwise firm. "It's good," she told the others as she climbed carefully to the top. When she got there safely, the others joined her on the roof.

Suddenly, Cassie ducked down. "Someone's over there!" She hissed through her teeth, grabbing at them to get down.

Across from them a figure in a black coat headed into the building opposite. Like the one they were hiding inside, the other building was equally rundown if not more so. Where glass windows had once stood, only gaping holes remained affording the girls a clear view inside where a crowd gathered.

"But, those aren't demons are they? Aren't most of those just regular people?" There was a twinge inside Cassie's chest which only grew bigger, the more human faces she could make out.

"It's not only demons who are monsters," Eve said quietly. Of all people, she knew this well enough.

"Any of you see him yet?" Tyler asked, scanning the crowd for Pike's face.

"No. It looks like the fight isn't going to start for a while, I don't even see any chickens," Cassie informed them as Marley felt her phone vibrating in the pocket of her jeans.

"One sec," she told them, taking out her phone. She didn't recognize the number but the area code was local. "Hello?"

"Marley?" Asked a frantic male voice.

"Yes, who's this?" Marley asked.

"It's Dalton, from the dorms. I really need your help. Oh God, can you get here?"

Taken aback by the urgency in his voice, Marley tried

to remain calm though a flower of apprehension opened inside her chest. "What's happened?"

"It's Zack! I don't know how, but... I think he's been possessed! He's acting crazy! I'm scared he might do something so I've trapped him in the room, but I don't know what else to do and I can't hold him forever. Please, can you get here?"

Hearing the utter panic in his voice, Marley didn't hesitate.

"Hang tight, Dalton. I'm on my way."

Three heads snapped to her, hearing her comment. She explained quickly, getting up to leave when Eve stopped her. "You can't go alone."

"I'll be fine," Marley started only for Eve to cut her off with one of those stern stares that she seemed so good at.

"You don't have an active power, Marley. Something could happen."

"She's right," Tyler agreed. "Eve should go with you. Cassie can stay here with me that way we're all covered if something goes down."

Seeing Cassie's nod, Marley knew it was useless to argue; besides, she didn't actually want to face whatever was happening alone. Jumping up, she shot Cassie and Tyler a glance.

"The two of you be careful. You're just here for information, understand? Whatever happens, don't start something you can't finish."

"Got it," Cassie agreed.

"Go," Tyler urged. "We'll be fine."

Knowing that time was of the essence, Marley and Eve rushed back to Eve's car.

ONE HUNDRED SIXTY-ONE

"How do you know this Dalton guy, exactly?"

Eve put the pedal to the metal, weaving through the streets as fast as was legally allowed as Marley answered her question, briefing her on her early morning meeting, drawing a concerned look from her.

"I don't get any demon vibes from the roommate," Marley explained. "But he's definitely into the occult from what I could see. It's possible black magic's involved. Either way, he's gotten himself into some kind of mess and since this isn't really in Rhett's wheelhouse, I volunteered to help."

She fell silent as Eve tried unsuccessfully to hide her knowing smile.

"How is our resident advisor, lately?" Eve hoped she wasn't being too intrusive since the two hadn't had many heart-to-hearts before, but it seemed the right time to talk about it.

"He's nice. Really nice, actually. I find him super easy to talk to. I like how assured he seems. He's not cocky, just quietly confident. It's appealing," Marley finished, as a flush began to creep over her cheeks. She paused, biting the corner of her lip. When Eve looked at her encouragingly, she continued.

"The few times I've gotten close to a guy before, things were always fine until they found out about my 'condition.' As soon as that reared its ugly head they would run a mile."

"But your condition wasn't real. It was your power manifesting."

"Well, none of us knew that at the time. It doesn't excuse the fact that when it came down to it, none of the guys cared enough to even discuss the situation with me. They just dropped me like I was contagious." Even now, Marley could feel the bitterness sting.

"A lot of boys are stupid," Eve commented, feeling angry on her behalf. "I should know, I've dated enough of them."

At this revelation, Marley was surprised. "Really? I didn't know that. You never talk much about yourself."

Gripping the wheel, Eve kept her eyes dead ahead, her voice taking on a disconnected tone.

"I try not to think about the past. It's easier that way. But, yeah, I was considered a serial dater. There were so many cute guys at school, I kind of ended up seeing a few. I never cheated on any of them, though. I just found that I grew tired of them pretty fast. I liked the chase. That feeling of things being exciting and new. And Jason… he was the most exciting of them all."

She fell quiet suddenly, as Marley stilled, understanding that this was a difficult conversation for her. She didn't move, barely even breathed not wanting to break the spell.

"He was so different from the other guys. When we first met, it was at a restaurant. I was hanging out with my usual crowd when in roared this smoking hot guy on his Harley. The thing was loud and impossible to miss, announcing him like it was his own fanfare. He passed by my window, our eyes met… and just like that, I was gone. He had these eyes that sent shivers down my spine whenever he looked my way. Later, after we'd been together a while… after things had turned… bad… I used to have nightmares about his eyes."

Eve trailed off, clenching the wheel so tightly that her knuckles turned white.

"In the beginning, I craved having his attention on me. It was like he'd stepped out of a romance flick — the ones I used to roll my eyes at for being so corny. But when it actually happened to me, I lost my head completely."

Streets blurred past but Marley barely noticed a thing, caught up in Eve's tale.

"He'd do all these romantic things like turn up at my place unannounced, with flowers or candy. Other guys, they liked to play it cool, but Jason was so into me and he didn't care who knew it. He would call all the time, message me throughout the day. It was so refreshing and kind of addictive to have this much devotion from one guy."

Outside, the lights flashed to red. Eve stopped the car as they waited. When it changed to green, they moved off again.

"I saw him every day, but it wasn't enough. I found myself breaking dates with family and friends just so I could see him more. He was always so crushed if I had somewhere else to be that I'd end up bailing on everyone to see him. I didn't realize that that's how it starts happening. How they isolate you from those who love you, who might get in their way."

Her voice trembled, the only sign of how this was affecting her. Marley wanted to reach across to touch her hand but knew that it would obstruct her driving so she kept them in her lap.

"After a while, when I finally came up for air, I realized that as much as I loved Jason, I still had family or friends that I wanted to see, who I was missing, but when I tried to arrange dates with them, Jason would mess things up for me. He'd guilt me or turn up when I was with my friends, making everyone feel awkward until I just left with him. After that, it started to get a little suffocating, but that wasn't even the worst of it. He started finding fault with me. Started making digs, and undermining me whenever I tried to do anything. His comments didn't sound too bad at first — he'd help me pick my outfits, tell me how I should wear my hair the way he liked."

Marley knew how beautiful Eve was under those heavy layers of make-up so it struck her as incredulous that any guy would find an issue with Eve's appearance, particularly as that was what had drawn him to her in the first place.

Eve continued talking, her voice becoming strained. "That soon turned into who I could and couldn't talk to, what I could do. Then it got much, much worse."

Her throat felt dry, and she found she had to swallow before she could continue.

"The first time he hit me, I had threatened to leave him. He was so mortified that he started to cry. Seeing him like that, I thought he must be really sorry, that it was a one-off and would never happen again. I made two crucial mistakes that time: I immediately forgave him. But even worse than that, I put my own pain aside, my own feelings to comfort him."

Thinking of that moment again, an incredulous laugh came out of her.

"That's because we're taught that guys don't cry right? So if they do, it must be because they really care about us," Marley supplied, having a good idea where this was leading.

Eve glanced at her, relieved to see the understanding in Marley's eyes.

"Exactly. It didn't happen again for months. We were back to being amazing again, so I thought we were passed it. Then one day, he erupted, and I was the target of his anger. The crazy thing is, I don't even remember what it was that set him off. I don't remember doing anything, he just flew off the handle and laid into me. I tried breaking it off, but a few days later he was back and trying so hard to make it up to me."

Her eyes glistened with tears. "I know it sounds stupid hearing all this, but you don't know what it's like until you're in it… and by then, you're already trapped."

Marley's heart hurt for her friend, not only for the pain and terror she went through but for the shame which even now, Eve still felt. Ignoring her earlier reluctance, Marley laid her hand on Eve's, squeezing it in solidarity. Eve squeezed back.

"But you weren't trapped forever because you got out of it. What happened? How did you get away from him?" Marley asked.

Opening her mouth to speak, Eve felt her body go numb. Her heart started thumping, and she found herself taking shallower breaths in what must be the beginning of a panic attack. Apparently, even though she had opened up about her past relationship, she wasn't quite ready to tell everything just yet.

Sensing her struggle, Marley's face filled with apology. "That's OK, Eve. We don't have to continue. We can talk about something else."

Relief and gratefulness welled up. For the first time in a long while, Eve realized she had found a real friend in Marley. She cared about her, cared about what she had gone through, and most importantly, despite knowing her mistakes, she wasn't judging her. Eve nodded, keeping her eyes up front, unable to look at her knowing that if she did, the sobs would come and might never stop.

Marley knew how big a deal it was that Eve was trusting her like this. Feeling that she needed to reciprocate, she started talking about her own recent discoveries. She opened up about her dad's strange behavior of late, how she'd caught him in an outright lie. Lastly, she reiterated Mary's disturbing warning.

"Does anyone else know about this?" Eve asked in a voice heavy with concern.

"Only Christian," Marley replied. "He doesn't know what to make of it either. You're the only other person I've told."

Guilt rose, a heavy lead stone pressing down onto Eve's chest. It was time to tell Marley about the painting in Paul's office and the symbol that was hidden within it. The only question was, how? Eve was trying to come up with the words when the familiar sight of BU appeared.

"Hey, Marl, I need to tell you something," Eve began, maneuvering the car toward EJ Halls. "One sec, let me park the car first."

"Sure," Marley responded curiously.

This delicate conversation needed her full concentration, which she couldn't do if she was still driving. Finding a space by the dorm's entrance, she parked quickly and turned the engine off.

Turning in her seat, she faced Marley head on when a figure appeared behind Marley's window, drawing her attention. Her thoughts on the conversation ahead, it took a moment before she realized it was a figure she knew well.

She saw the toned chest and broad shoulders that were only emphasized by the black leather jacket and knew without a moment's doubt that below the window, the feet would be encased in those familiar biker's boots that had once kicked her in the stomach so hard that she had thought something inside had burst.

Terror hit like a four-wheel truck, sending her motionless.

As if she were that helpless girl all those times before, Eve couldn't move. Her blood had turned to ice, her fingers numb as pins and needles lanced through them. Marley had her back to him so she couldn't see him, but a desperate fear took hold as Eve worried that Jason would hurt her friend.

Almost without meaning to, Eve summoned her *others* with a simple mental cry. Within moments, faster than Eve could even comprehend, spiders of all sizes began to crawl over Marley's window, covering it in one quivering black mass until all light was obscured from the glass.

Marley must have suddenly noticed how dark it had gotten behind her as she turned around then screamed, lunging away from the window toward Eve.

"Open the door, get out!" Marley cried, instinctively trying to get away from the army she hadn't realized Eve had raised. Still numb with shock, Eve didn't immediately move so Marley leaned over her, throwing open Eve's door.

Marley pushed Eve toward the opening. "Eve, come on!" Marley yelled.

The part of her that was still conscious reacted to Marley's command. Eve got out of the car robotically, as Marley slid across the seats, leaping out after her.

Immediately, Eve raked her eyes to the other side of the car where Jason was — except, there was no one there now. Where he had stood, there was only empty space though her spiders still remained.

"Jesus," Marley said, her face white as a sheet. "What the hell happened there?"

Eve didn't get a chance to answer, however, as something smashed through one of the windows upstairs in the dorm, soaring through the air to land a few feet away from them.

It was the wooden planchette from Zack's ouija board.

Marley's head snapped up to the broken window where she could see Dalton bracing himself against Zack — who looked as if he was trying to kill him.

"Oh no," Marley cried as she sprinted into the dorm.

Rapidly regaining her senses now that Jason had disappeared, Eve shook herself and she hurried after her.

ONE HUNDRED SIXTY-TWO

A big crowd was gathering in the ruined building. Tyler and Cassie lay on the roof, on a box that Cassie had found that they had flattened. It didn't offer much comfort from the cold and hard concrete roof but it was better than nothing.

They had been here a good half hour, maybe even more as they waited for the event to begin, but at this point, there wasn't even any sign of the animals.

Their stakeout had proved pretty uneventful so far; it wasn't anything like how it was in the movies. Tyler wished she'd brought a book with her or something. Having to wait like this pushed the boundaries of what patience she had.

She felt, rather than saw Cassie staring at her. Meeting her eyes, Cassie's cheeks flushed red.

"What?" Tyler asked, wondering what she had been thinking that would have caused a reaction like that.

"I was just thinking… what exactly was your intention when you went to the police?"

Tyler bit her lip, remembering how stupid her actions had been. "I don't know if I had one, to be honest. I just lost it, really. I'd been using my powers to try to find Ally, but everything was going wrong."

She stopped as the familiar pain flared up again whenever Ally was mentioned. "Every day that passes… her life hangs in the balance. Not just because Michael has her, but because of her kidney problems."

She swallowed as a lump formed in her throat. "I can't lose Ally. She's all I have left."

Tyler's pain was so strong that Cassie felt as if it were her own sister that was missing — and she didn't even *have* a sister. A picture of her parents flashed into her mind. Her mom was always smiling, always happy. There she was with her dad, the two of them dancing ballroom style across the living room while Cassie watched and clapped in time. They did this kind of nonsense a lot in their house. Sometimes, Cassie would even dance with her dad though she tended to have two left feet.

Seeing them in her mind, Cassie understood how ungrateful she had been lately. Her parents were wonderful people, but even as she thought this, a shadow fell over them.

As much as she loved them, and they, her, Cassie was only ever comfortable around them when they were at home alone; when no one from the outside was looking.

When it was just their small family, Cassie could relax and be herself. She could know that she wasn't being judged by how she looked. The world didn't hang on her disappointing appearance.

It was only when the rest of the world looked that it all went wrong.

It was actually the reason why Cassie never invited anyone home.

She'd made it a rule never to do so, not after her last attempt had resulted in such an unmitigated disaster — and the horror of it was, her parents didn't even know.

Cassie had been fourteen at the time. Her mom had been bugging her, saying that she never got to meet any of her friends. She wanted to throw her a party to get to know some of them. Cassie had resisted the idea for as long as she could — frankly, though she knew a lot of people, she didn't count any of them as her real friends. All they ever wanted was to talk about her parents. Cassie had yet to meet someone who wanted to talk about *her*, and even then, in a good way.

Despite her every intention, however, Cassie had found herself throwing a party at their home. Edged on by her mother, she invited everyone she knew. The kids at school were delighted and turned up at her house in droves.

Almost as soon as the party had started, Cassie knew she had made a giant mistake.

Though literally, every kid she knew was there, no one was talking to her. If they weren't hanging onto her dad, the boys were lusting after her mom. When she found a group of them in her parents' room, going through her mom's lingerie and discussing what they'd like to do to her mom — in great detail — the boy's had sneered at her, commenting about her own lack of assets and how anyone who ever dated her, would just be trying to get to her mom.

Cut to the quick, Cassie had fled the room to find her parents, but they were so enjoying being worshipped by the masses that neither of them took her complaints seriously, putting it down to her self-consciousness. The only way she would ever make any friends was if she tried, they advised.

After that, Cassie hid away in her room, watching her beloved DVD collection of Buffy the Vampire Slayer until the last guest had left.

Her parents hadn't even noticed that she wasn't present at her own party.

She knew it wasn't their fault, however. Her parents couldn't help being so wonderful that everyone wanted a part of them, but Cassie knew better than to take their advice in the future. Their reality wasn't her reality after all, and they would never understand what it was like for her. After that, she never agreed to a party again. She never invited anyone to her home, no matter how much her parents pleaded or cajoled.

Hearing Tyler speak now, seeing how desperately she missed her sister, Cassie realized she had to step out of her comfort zone. She had to include her parents in her life more, even if that meant inviting people home, especially now she had several who she cared deeply about.

Tyler stiffened beside her, drawing her from her thoughts.

The roosters were finally arriving, but they were in cages that were barely any bigger than them. Seeing the birds in the cages made Tyler's blood run cold as she couldn't help but picture Ally lying in that cage of her own.

A cheer rose as two birds were set into the middle of a ring. A figure in black joined the back of the crowd. He was conspicuous by the hoodie he wore that covered most of his face leaving only his mouth in sight, but Cassie gasped, recognizing him immediately.

"That's him! That's Pike! I'd know his face anywhere," she shuddered.

Blood began to pound inside her head. Tyler's back straightened as all of her senses fired. He was here, their link to Ally! Their idea had worked, they had found him!

Oblivious to their scrutiny, Pike sidled up behind the crowd, handing a wad of bills over to a guy that came around holding out a basket. He took Pike's money, noted how much he had taken from him, writing the amount into a notebook.

And suddenly, with little fanfare, the doors to the cages were flown open as helpers hit the back of the cages with metal baseball bats, sending the terrified birds squawking out of them.

The crowd watched gleefully as the roosters started

attacking each other. The larger of the two stabbed his beak into the head of the other bird, drawing blood as his opponent fought back. Feather's flew into the air, blood spraying onto the concrete. The crowd's chilling joy sent Tyler into a tailspin.

From the moment she had seen the birds in their cages, her traumatized mind had thrown Ally's image at her, until now, staring across at the bloodsport, Tyler couldn't see the birds at all.

In their place was Ally.

And like the birds, she was being torn to pieces while the crowd cheered it on.

Rage boiled inside, turning into a frenzy that she couldn't stop even if she wanted to. She had to stop this awful fight. She had to stop Ally from being tortured like this.

She had to stop it before something terrible happened.

A rumble went through Tyler, surging down the building they lay upon, exploding outward until it reached the building opposite. Beneath the crowd's feet, the ground began to tremble. They didn't notice at first, their attention fixed on that awful fight, but when the ground shook, their cries for blood turned to unease.

The tremors grew until the men stumbled on bent knees, staggering as they tried to keep their balance. The two birds, more frightened of whatever this now was than their hatred of each other, ran off in opposite directions as cracks started appearing on the walls, shooting up in zig-zagging lines.

A few bricks, dislodged by the tremors, fell down, narrowly missing the crowd below, but Tyler didn't care. Her eyes had turned black with hatred and were focused on the row of cages that still contained roosters trapped inside.

One by one, the doors to the cages burst open as the surprised birds made a bid for freedom. When their handlers went after them, they found the ground exploding beneath their feet, sending them flying backward.

Cassie was watching the entire thing with shock. She knew the second the magic had come out of Tyler, that she was the cause of all this. At first, she thought Tyler only meant to scare the crowd and to free the birds, but as more bricks tumbled down, it was only a matter of time before someone was killed.

"Tyler…" she called out cautiously, hoping that her friend would stop now. But Tyler continued as if she couldn't hear her. The magic grew stronger until Cassie saw the cracks growing along the walls had reached the ceiling — which was also beginning to crack.

Cassie's eyes grew wide with horror.

"Stop it, Tyler! That roof is going to kill those men!" Cassie cried, but either Tyler couldn't hear her, or she wasn't listening. Worried for the men, Cassie jumped onto her feet and started waving her arms.

"HEY! THE ROOF IS COMING DOWN! LOOK OUT!" She shouted at them.

But there was so much chaos and noise that they couldn't hear her over the rumbling. Flying back to Tyler's side, Cassie grabbed both of her cold hands.

"Tyler… I know what they were doing is wrong. I know you're under so much stress and grief, but you can't kill them, OK? That won't help get Ally back, and it might make things worse for you when we do find her. Please, Tyler. You've got to listen to me, stop this now before it's too late. Ally needs you. We need you. Don't do this to us. Stop while you still can," Cassie pleaded.

Tyler didn't respond, lost in her dark rage and her thirst for their blood.

Cassie's own desperation caused tears to fall down her cheeks. "Please, Tyler," Cassie sobbed, shaking Tyler's hands, suddenly desperately afraid.

"Stop."

Maybe it was her words or the desperation that

poured out of her, but Tyler suddenly heard her. Cassie knew the moment the light went back into her eyes.

Forcing her emotions to reign back, Tyler screamed as she drew her magic into herself. The tremors died abruptly as all went still, but the roof, having been disturbed too much suddenly craved, crashing to the floor below.

Dust and rubble fogged the air as the girls stared on in horror.

When the dust cloud started to fade, they saw a few of the men had been injured. One limped, dragging his broken ankle behind him, while another pressed his hand against a gash on his head. The rest of men had gotten away, however.

Including Pike.

He was gone, taking the only lead they had on Ally with him.

ONE HUNDRED SIXTY-THREE

The door to Dalton's room was closed but Marley could hear the ruckus inside as she arrived, winded from the run up several flights of stairs to get here.

Flinging open the door, she was immediately hit by the icy cold that sent shivers down her spine. Inside, there were three figures instead of the two she expected.

Zack was trying to escape the room, but Dalton was stopping him… and so was Rhett. The two of them pushed against Zack but he seemed to have gained a supernatural strength as it took every ounce of strength for the other two to keep him inside.

Seeing the door open now, Zack turned his gaze to the doorway as Marley caught her first real look at his face. She gasped in horror.

There was clearly something wrong with him.

Zack's skin was mottled black and blue, his eyes had turned milky white — there was no pupil inside. Black foam bubbled of his mouth.

Zack was definitely possessed, but Marley didn't have a clue what from, this being far out of her wheelhouse.

"What the hell…?" Eve managed to gasp in between breaths as she rounded the hallway behind her.

Hearing her, Rhett spared a glance their way. "Close the door!" he yelled. "He's trying to get outside!" The girls hurried into the room, shutting the door behind them.

"Christian!" Marley called out for him, hoping that he would be able to tell her what to do.

He appeared in a blink of an eye but his usual questioning expression turned alarmed the moment he took stock of the situation.

"This isn't good," he said.

"Oh, you think?" Marley snapped back wondering why he was stating the obvious. "How do we stop this?" Marley asked him, barely able to hear herself over Zack's snarling.

"With an exorcism," Christian replied, drawing an annoyed look from Marley.

"I know that! But how do we do one?"

"Well… you can't. I mean, we need holy water, and a priest who's versed in this sort of thing," Christian managed to splutter.

"But we don't have any of those!" Marley hissed, getting seriously worried at his response, any hope that she'd had for helping Zack fading fast.

Rhett and Dalton dug their heels into the floor, using the full force of their combined weight against Zack. Even then, Zack managed to push them back toward the girls. Gaping at them, Christian's expression turned sick. "I don't know, Marley. That's how we've always dealt with possession before," he admitted.

Zack — or the spirit who had hijacked his body — continued plowing toward them when he noticed Christian standing off to one side. The sight of another spirit seemed to fuel his anger.

The room grew even colder if that was possible as an invisible wind blew around them. Socks, shoes, and books were lifted into its icy embrace, as they hovered into the air before hurling toward them like missiles.

Marley grabbed Eve's hand yanking her down so hard that they fell to the carpet. The books that had been flying their way went soaring over their heads where they smashed harmlessly against the wall. Rhett wasn't so lucky, however, as a metal alarm clock collided with his face. He flinched back, letting go of Zack momentarily, but it was all Zack needed.

With a single swoop of his arm, he knocked Dalton away then sent Rhett flying across the room where he tumbled over the edge of the bed. Free at last, Zack started for the door spewing black spittle and hate, heading straight for Marley and Eve.

"Marley!" Christian cried out just as Zack got within a few feet of her.

Not knowing what else she could do Marley went to stop him, grabbing him around the wrist, she yelled out, "Stop!"

The result was instant.

Like his arm had been welded to her hand, Zack froze dead, unable to move. His cloudy white eyes fixed on Marley with something close to hatred, but then, as he saw her command of him, his animosity faded completely.

As before when she could sense what troubled spirits were feeling, Marley could feel the hope that now flooded out of Zack.

Shaken, yet awed by this new extension of her power, Marley forced herself to speak in a commanding voice. "I'm speaking to the spirit who has Zack. What do you want?"

A mess of images flooded her mind as Zack's spirit took hold of it. She couldn't make much sense of it at first, they seemed composed of a jumble of memories. Then one rose above the others, one thought that seemed more urgent.

Abruptly her mind cleared.

The spirit had left Marley's head.

He still squatted inside Zack's body like an unwanted guest, though the furious rage that had consumed him earlier had vanished.

Marley let go of his hand.

Zack didn't move though he now could. Only those milky eyes of his followed her around as he waited for her next move.

Rhett and Dalton had righted themselves by now and were staring at her with identical expressions of shock.

Marley walked to Zack's wardrobe. "We need to move this," she told them as she went to take hold of it only for Rhett to move her aside, as he took her place.

"I've got it," he said, not having a clue why she was requesting this yet doing it, anyway.

Dalton joined him, grabbing hold of the other end of the wardrobe. At a nod from Rhett, the two wiggled the wardrobe out of the space it sat in.

When there was enough room to see behind it, Marley looked for the item Zack had shown her.

Lying on top of the skirting board where it had been wedged behind the wardrobe for years now, was a few sheets of paper that had been stapled together.

Marley's fingers reached into the gap to retrieve it.

When she held the paper in her hands, she saw the name typed neatly on the top right of the paper.

Jonathan Hamilton.

And immediately the world went black as she was taken to another place.

ONE HUNDRED SIXTY-FOUR

Through the black fog that had appeared around her, Marley knew that she was seeing the world through Jonathan's eyes now, that it was his memories she inhabited.

Arms wrapped around herself, she watched as a young boy of around four appeared, sitting on a threadbare rug playing with two toy trucks. At first she could only see him and that rug, the rest of the world consisted only of that inky black, but after a few moments, the black receded to be replaced by the interior of a mobile home.

His parents were fighting again, but Jonathan tried not to listen as he smashed his trucks together, trying to mask the sound of their voices with the metal of his toys.

Clash. Clash. CLASH, they went until he caught one of his fingers in-between the two trucks.

Tears sprang in his eyes as he shoved the sore finger into his mouth. Wanting his mommy, who always kissed his ills better, Jonathan got up and started for his parent's room when he heard the front door slamming so hard that the walls shook and he thought they would come falling down — just like the London Bridge Mommy liked to sing about.

He saw her outside.

She was crying, trying to get back into their home but Daddy wouldn't let her. He threw her suitcase onto the ground, blocking her way inside. His mommy must have seen him then as she turned her tearful face to him and called out his name, but when she tried to go to him, Daddy slapped her across the face so hard that she fell onto the ground.

Jonathan cried out, hating to see his mommy hurt like that, wishing that he was big enough to protect her. He waited, then, swallowing his cries as he waited for her to get back up and come inside to him.

But Mommy never came back.

And Jonathan never saw her again.

The memory changed, speeding forward several years until Jonathan was a pimply-faced teenager now, who took solace in his lonely life by reading. Unlike everyone else who hated school, Jonathan knew his life would ever only improve if he could educate himself so he spent every moment he could learning, even as his dad sat in the living room in the same worn-out armchair, drinking away his life.

When Jonathan left for BU, his dad never got out of that armchair. Never even took his eyes off the sports game he was watching.

Jonathan didn't care anymore. He was ready to begin his life, to finally make something of himself. In the back of his mind was the hope that when he did, maybe his mom would walk back into his life again.

The memories sped forward yet again.

Now Jonathan was a fully fledged student though life wasn't quite as he had envisioned it.

He wasn't sociable, had no real friends, and his room-mate was an annoying jerk who had apparently come to college to party. He played music and video games late into the night, talking loudly to fellow gamers on his headset, constantly waking Jonathan up.

All Jonathan did was work, spending every moment studying, but life was hard coping on his own. He wished he had friends he could confide in, someone he could talk to, but Jonathan just didn't know how to reach out to anyone.

It was hard to when people had a habit of letting him down.

One night, feeling like he couldn't sit in this small room anymore — his roommate was having a particularly bad time on a game and was spending most of the night cursing out the other players — Jonathan took himself out for a late night walk.

Thanksgiving was two days away, so Jonathan knew he'd get a break from his roommate then when he went back west. At least Jonathan would get a week of quietness. Until then, he had to grab his moments of peace whenever he could, and that was through going out on late-night walks.

This night it was raining though Jonathan had always enjoyed walking in the rain. He only meant to walk a few blocks, but it was so nice out in the fresh night air that he carried on until he eventually reached the reservoir. The moon reflected prettily in the water, dappled by the falling rain.

The sound of both the water and the rain calmed him, filling him with the peace he had been missing.

He was admiring the stars when the heaven's suddenly opened and the rain began to bucket down. Faster than it seemed possible, the ground became slick with wet. Pulling up the collar on his jacket, Jonathan started hurrying back to college when he slipped on a wet patch and went down, hitting his head against the ground.

That was all it took.

An accident. A slip and a fall.

Jonathan blacked out and never recovered. Normally,

it wouldn't have taken long for his body to have been discovered, but after that night, Boston had been besieged by the worst storm in its history. Heavy rains came down continuously for days until the earth loosened around him causing a landslide that covered him completely.

What with the storm and the Thanksgiving holiday, no one thought of Jonathan, especially not his roommate who had never liked how he'd had such a stick up his ass. When he'd returned from the holidays to find Jonathan gone, he'd figured, like many other students who couldn't cope with their first year at school, Jonathan had simply gone home.

The weeks went by yet not a single person thought enough about his disappearance to look into it. Eventually, Jonathan's roommate threw out his things, taking over that side of the room until a new roommate eventually came, a Chinese overseas student who was even more militant about his studies than Jonathan. The only sign that Jonathan had ever been there was the paper he had written, which had slipped off the top of the wardrobe and sat wedged in the gap behind.

But Jonathan wasn't gone entirely.

He had haunted the room ever since, only echoing his lot in life, no one had noticed him in death either. He had been lost in this limbo, without anyone knowing he was there until Zack had come along.

Like Jonathan, Zack was a loner. He was quiet. Identifying with darker things than most, he'd had a fascination with the occult as far back as he could remember.

When Zack had started playing with the Ouija board, it had wakened Jonathan's ghost. Every time Zack used the board, Jonathan's felt as if his soul was being prodded; yet Zack wasn't asking the right questions for Jonathan to be able to explain his story. As Zack messed with him, he grew increasingly more and more frustrated until Jonathan decided to take matters into his own hands

C oming out of her vision, Marley's eyes were bright with tears.

Having felt every bit of pain and the crippling loneliness he had felt, Marley knew what it was he wanted.

"Jonathan," she said his name softly. "People will know your story. People will care that you died."

Jonathan stared at her a moment as Marley felt a rush of energy. A faint white mist left Zack's body as Zack suddenly slumped to the floor, unconscious. A few moments later, when he woke, looking up at them, it was with his own brown eyes.

Over the next hour, Marley explained all that she had learned.

"So you got into his head, somehow? You saw what happened to him?" Dalton asked, trying to get his head around it all.

Marley nodded. "He was only haunting the room because he wants people to know what happened. He needs to know that his life mattered, that it counted."

"But what can we do? We know his story now but only the four of us. It doesn't seem enough," Rhett finished, earning a grateful smile from Marley.

"Thanks, but Eve and I can take it from here," she said.

"Yeah, the girls don't need your help," Christian said to Rhett somewhat petulantly, getting a hard look from Marley as a response.

"You're sure?" Rhett asked. "Not that I can probably be of much help. This is a little out of my league."

She shot him a smile. "We'll be fine. I need to ask a favor from you though. I didn't know about my particular gift until a few weeks ago. Until then, people called me a freak. I was pretty much the school outcast. I really don't want to repeat that experience here so can the three of you promise to keep this secret? I know it's a lot to ask but I just want to have some semblance of a normal life."

"I won't say anything," Dalton agreed in a voice full of sincerity.

"Your secret's safe with me too," Zack nodded. "After all, I owe you for what you've just done. That was… unpleasant, having someone sit inside me, taking over my body while I could do nothing but watch. I don't ever want to go through that again."

Rhett was the last to speak. A soft smile played on his lips though Marley couldn't quite read the expression in his eyes. "Of course," he just said simply, and left it at that. "I'm going to stay and help the guys clear up. Are you and Eve going to do whatever you're going to do now?"

Eve and Marley exchanged a look as they nodded in unison.

"I guess I'll see you later then," he said, already turning to help the others.

A wave of disappointment fell over her. Was Rhett dismissing her? Somehow, she'd thought that he'd be a more talkative about this. She thought he'd have a bigger reaction. Confused, Marley wondered if he was going to run like all the other boys in her life now.

Had she made a big mistake trusting him?

ONE HUNDRED SIXTY-FIVE

"Are you OK?" Cassie's voice asked timidly.

Tyler tore her gaze away from the wreckage of the building which only moments before had still been standing.

There was no sign of Pike now.

He had gone, probably from the moment that Tyler had started her little temper tantrum. Truth be told, she had no idea when he had left, so lost in her rage. She hadn't been watchful and now Pike had gotten away.

She had messed it all up.

Sinking onto her knees, the pent-up emotion she had been holding inside suddenly burst in one big explosion. Tears poured out of her as Tyler wailed, sobbing for every awful thing that had happened to her this year.

All she wanted was her parents to hold her in their arms, to tell her it would all be OK. Instead, the whole world was on her shoulders and here she was, messing up so badly that her only lead on Ally was gone.

Tears streamed down her face, misting her vision so that she couldn't see anymore. Digging her nails into her palms until they hurt, Tyler cried as if she would never stop.

Seeing her friend hurting so much brought tears into Cassie's own eyes. Feeling helpless, she did the only thing she could think of to do. Kneeling beside her, she wrapped her thin arms around Tyler and held on as tightly as she could.

"We'll figure this out, Tyler. You're not alone. You have us. We will do this together," Cassie murmured into the top of Tyler's head, over and over, until her words finally cut through the haze of grief.

Tyler's sobs lessened, as the tears began to dry. When there were only sniffs left, she gave Cassie a watery smile.

"Sorry." She didn't know what else to say. What could she say after a meltdown like that?

"Don't apologize. I don't know how you've kept it together for so long. I would have caved a long time ago," Cassie said, letting her out of her embrace, but she held onto Tyler's hand.

To Cassie's surprise, Tyler didn't let go of it, holding on as if it were a lifeline. They only parted when Cassie's phone started ringing inside her bag. Cassie ignored it, thinking this moment too fragile to break.

"You can answer it," Tyler said with another one of those watery smiles.

Rummaging inside her bag until her fingers felt the protective case on her phone, Cassie took it out it to see "Trip Calling" flashing up on the screen. "I'll only be a moment," Cassie reassured Tyler as she answered. "Hi Trip."

His voice came down the line dripping with warmth. "Oh, hello Cassie. I was just wondering how you were? What are you up to today?"

Ordinarily, Cassie wouldn't have thought anything of answering him, but she wanted to get off the phone quickly. "Nothing much, why?"

Silence sounded, filling the space until Trip cleared his

throat. When he spoke again, there was something different in his voice though she couldn't put her finger on it. "I was just missing you is all. If you tell me where you are, I'll come pick you up. We can grab a coffee or something?"

Looking at Tyler's tear-streaked face she knew that wouldn't be a possibility. "Sorry, I can't. Tyler's upset right now, I need to be with her."

Hearing her response, Tyler couldn't help but feel surprised. This was the girl who not that long ago had been so desperate for male attention that she had worn her friend's face to go cruising. Was she really turning down a date with Trip for her?

More silence came down the line as Cassie wondered if she'd upset him. "Is that OK? I hope you understand."

"Of course I do. Don't worry. I'll be right here when you're done. You can tell me all about it later." That strange tone she had thought was there a moment ago was gone now. She let out a silent sigh of relief. Two upset people was a few more than she knew how to handle.

"Thanks. I'll call you later then," Cassie said, hanging up the call.

"You didn't have to do that for me," Tyler said.

Cassie smiled. "It's fine. I'll just talk to him later. Why don't we go and grab a drink or a snack? We passed by a bunch of places on the way here, we could try one of those. What do you think? It's my treat."

Seeing how much she cared about her, Tyler smiled at her gratefully. "Honestly, Cass, I'm feeling much better now. Seeing Pike get away and knowing it was my fault was too much. I guess I just needed to cry it out. I'd been holding it inside so much… I guess it had to come out."

She stood up, dusting the dirt from her knees as Cassie followed suit.

"Still, I know I could do with a drink," Cassie said causing Tyler to feel a bolt of shock. They were still a few years away from being legal.

Her eyes went wide. She blinked at her. "What, like a real one?"

"No! Of course not," Cassie replied, looking equally shocked that Tyler would even think such a thing. "I meant like a green juice."

Something about her reply tickled Tyler's funny bone, making her laugh.

"Oh, Cassie," she said, hooking her arm in hers. "Come on."

Two green juices later, the two were feeling much better so Cassie had left Tyler to her own devices. She'd wanted to stay with her, just in case, but Tyler had insisted that she was fine. She needed some air, to clear her head, and wanted to go for a walk. Unable to convince her to allow her to accompany her, Cassie made sure Tyler was really OK before she agreed to leave her alone.

She was in an Uber on her way back to the dorm now, making a call. After a few rings, her mom's surprised voice answered.

"Sweetheart! That's two calls in one week! Is everything OK?" Angie asked, suddenly sounding worried.

"I'm fine, Mom," Cassie replied, rolling her eyes though her mom could not see her. "I was just calling to see what you guys were up to. I was thinking I'd bring Trip round for dinner so you can meet him."

Angie went quiet, knowing how out of character this was for her daughter. "Darling, we would be delighted! You just name the day and we'll make it happen. Dad and I don't have anything so important that we can't move it around you."

"OK," Cassie said. "I need to call Trip and work out a date with him, but I'll get back to you on when we can do this."

"No problem, Honey," Angie said, barely able to keep the delight out of her voice. "Was there anything else?"

"No. That was all," Cassie answered.

"Oh," Angie said, sounding disappointed. "I was hoping you'd give me all the gossip about Trip, and your new friends, and school."

Cassie laughed. "I'll be seeing you soon, we can talk about it all then. But you and Dad, you're both OK right?"

Angie paused, startled by the question. "We're great, why, have you heard something? You know better than to believe the tabloids."

"No. I haven't read anything, I just wanted to make sure you were both OK." Cassie knew she was making a mess of this call, but after everything that had happened today, she just needed to know they were alright.

"Everything's great here. The only problem we have is how much we miss you."

"Let me call Trip now to fix up a date. I'll speak to you soon OK?" Cassie said.

"Make it sooner rather than later, please. You know how I'm dying to meet this first beau of yours," Angie pleaded drawing another laugh out of her.

"I know, Mom, I see all the not-so-subtle hints you keep posting up. See you soon. Say hi to Dad."

She hung up the call, quickly searching her recent calls log for Trip's number. He answered after only one ring. "Hello, Cassie."

"Hey. I'm sorry about earlier. I didn't want to blow you off like that but Tyler really was upset."

"I'm fine, Cassie. Honestly. It's not a problem. What had upset her so much?" He asked, sounding genuinely interested.

"Oh, just some stuff that made her think of all that she's lost recently," Cassie answered, not really knowing where she could begin to tell him the truth without revealing all of their secrets.

"That's too bad. It must be hard," he said, oozing sympathy.

"Anyway," Cassie said, changing the conversation before she said something she shouldn't. "Are you free tomorrow night? I was wondering if you'd like to come to my parent's house for dinner?"

Trip gave a sharp indrawn of breath that Cassie caught and felt immediately pleased by. He was nervous about meeting her parents! That was a good sign, wasn't it?

"I'd love to," Trip replied. "What time?"

"I need to call my mom back to work that out, but I'm sure it'll be around eight. You can pick me up at the dorm and we'll go together."

"Sounds like a plan," Trip said.

"How did your day go today?" Cassie asked, conscious that he asked her so many questions about her day that she usually forgot to ask about his.

"Oh, it was good. I went shopping at this cool place and picked up this really neat gift."

"What is it?" Cassie asked.

"Well, that would be telling wouldn't it," Trip laughed. "It's a surprise."

A flush of warmth spread over her as she realized that he must mean that the gift was for her. Was he upgrading from flowers and candy? What could it be?

"So you didn't have any classes today?"

"Oh yeah, that was after. Actually, we had this interesting history assignment today. Did you know that Boston has all this rich and mysterious history? There's this Elm Tree, the one that was found in the street recently? They used it for hanging witches. Isn't that crazy?"

"Uh huh," Cassie replied, uncomfortable by where the conversation had suddenly gone.

"And you know that music festival we're going to? Apparently, the Charles Esplanade where it's being held is known to have been the site of supernatural activity. We found details of events going all the way back to the early 17th century."

Cassie's ears suddenly pricked up. "That's interesting. What time period, exactly?"

Trip laughed down the phone. "Oh, I can't remember, hang on, let me look…" He disappeared only to return a few moments later, rustling some papers. "It says here during the 1690s there was a spate of reports about strange happenings there."

The time period couldn't be a coincidence. The year 1693 was when the Five Seals had been created. Could one of the last two be at the Charles?

Trying to contain her growing excitement, Cassie asked, "Along the whole place?"

"Not exactly. The activity seemed to occur around some of the bridges that lead to it."

Excitement bubbled up inside her as Cassie knew she might have a hit on the next Seal.

"Hey, I should go actually and sort out this dinner with my Mom. I'll message you later with all the details, OK?"

"Sure. I look forward to hearing from you again," Trip said, making her laugh by how formal he just sounded.

"I'll speak to you later," she said, her fingers already opening her phone's web browser to see what information she could find on the Charles Esplanade.

ONE HUNDRED SIXTY-SIX

The late afternoon sun's rays bathed the surrounding area in yellow and gold. There wasn't another soul at the reservoir, thankfully, so it looked as if Marley and Eve would be able to do what they had come here to do. The still waters instilled a calm that Marley knew would not last though she tried to enjoy it while she could.

It was a far cry from the last time Marley had found herself here, alone at the reservoir a little after dark, when Mary had appeared to her in a vision of absolute terror. Marley couldn't believe how long ago that meeting felt now. It had been before she knew Mary was her ancestor and one of the last witches to have been killed at the Salem Witch Trials.

How time flies whether you're having fun or not.

Though Marley had only briefly seen the spot where Jonathan had suffered his untimely death, she knew exactly how to get there as a thin, misty trail hovering a few feet from the ground highlighted the way. She had no idea whether this was Jonathan's doing, or an extension of her own ability, but she was starting to realize how important her gift was. Far from being the useless — and let's face it — the least active power of the four, Marley was beginning to see how much of a difference she could be making to people's lives.

It made her almost grateful for her power.

Almost.

Having watched what she had done back in the dorm, Christian had followed them here. He hung back a ways behind, however, seemingly not wanting to disturb her while she was 'at work.' Actually, he'd been a little strange since she'd stopped Jonathan from hurting anyone, barely saying a word to her. Something was definitely up.

"Do you see that trail?" She asked him, pointing at it.

Christian's eyes followed the line of her finger but they remained confused, unable to see what she could.

"No. I don't see anything. It must just be you," he answered, so quietly that he might as well as not have spoken.

Bringing up the rear, Eve was further back, on the phone checking several voicemails she had received. Her phone had been ringing all day, but she never answered the calls, saying she'll handle whatever it was later. Guess now was that time which gave Marley an opportunity to find out what was bugging Christian.

"What's wrong?" She asked, quietly enough that Eve would not be able to hear her.

"Nothing," Christian replied but he couldn't seem to meet her eyes.

"Did I do something wrong back there?" Marley asked, wondering if that was what was bothering him. It wasn't like she'd had any training in this. They were all winging it so if he was being pissy because she'd made a mistake, well, she'd have some choice words for him.

"No, you were amazing," he finally answered. "It's not anything you did, Marley. It's me."

Marley blinked in confusion, brushing a strand of hair

that had fallen in her eyes and tucking it behind an ear. "What about you?"

Christian fixed his eyes ahead as he spoke in a voice raw with pain. "You're all growing in leaps and bounds, which is amazing. It's how it's supposed to be, but me… I seem to be becoming more and more redundant. I barely know anything, I can't physically assist you. Hell, I can't even touch something, then today, I see how another spirit was able to possess a human without their permission."

"I don't understand. You want to possess someone?" Marley asked, unable to picture this somehow.

"No," Christian exclaimed, gripping his hands in frustration. His head furrowed as lines appeared over them making him seem suddenly much older. "I just want to be able to do it, but I can't seem to do anything. I'm… forget it." He said suddenly, turning away. "I'm just… I'm just having a bad day."

Marley found herself reaching out to comfort him before she knew what she was doing. Her fingers reached his shoulder *then went right through it*. She hadn't meant to do it, hadn't meant to emphasize the very thing Christian was struggling to deal with. When Christian saw her fingers going through him, it must have been too much as a look of tremendous hurt came over him.

Then he disappeared.

Marley felt like she'd been kicked in the stomach. She stopped, wondering if she should summon him back or just give him time to compose himself when she realized the trail had ended.

She was at the right spot.

Eve jogged up beside her. "Hey, sorry about that."

"No worries. We're here by the way," Marley revealed. "He's over there." She pointed to a raised section of the ground that was barely distinguishable from the rest of the area. There wasn't one foot of ground that wasn't sloping or at an angle from the next. It was no wonder that no one had thought anything of this extra bump in the grass.

Eve took a wider stance as her hair began to swim around her face. Calling her *others*, a small gray shape appeared over the crest of the slope. He was quickly joined by another, then more, as squirrels poured out of seemingly every crevice and tree.

Gathering on the mound Marley had pointed to, the squirrels started to dig away at the ground. Dirt went flying, as Eve's little army of diggers worked away at the earth. In no time, piles of the loosened earth littered the ground like molehills. The squirrels stopped digging, chattering in excitement before moving away.

There, finally unearthed, finally found... Jonathan's face protruded from the ground.

Even though this is what they had come here for, seeing the face, half-eaten away by time caused nausea to rise up inside. Beside her, Eve clapped a hand over her mouth but managed to stop herself from being sick.

As Marley fought to control her own nausea, the wispy figure of Jonathan's ghost appeared over his body. He shot her a grateful smile as a brilliant light opened up behind him, so bright that it almost blinded her.

"I'll take care of this, Jonathan," Marley promised. "Your spirit is free now."

Giving her one last smile of gratitude, Jonathan stepped into the light and disappeared.

Marley knew by Eve's reaction that she was the only one to have seen his spirit depart. "He's gone now... Jonathan, he's finally at peace. But we're not done here yet. How are we going to let the authorities know about this?"

Staring across the reservoir, at a lone dog-walker, Eve's expression turned thoughtful as she zeroed in on the dog. "Let me try something," she said.

Marley felt Eve's magic once more as Eve communicated with the dog.

Moments later, safely hidden behind a cluster of bushes far enough away that they could still see where Jonathan's body was located, but would not be seen by anyone who was there, they watched as a dog bounded up to the site. Barking at his discovery, his owner hurried over only to fall back in horror.

When the dog's owner had recovered enough to take out his phone to notify the police, Eve and Marley left.

* * *

With Eve taking off to the library to work on an assignment, Marley made her way back to the dorm when, reaching Rhett's door, she stopped, wondering if she should knock.

The two of them had made plans for a date last night, but Marley only realized when she and Eve were coming back from the reservoir that they'd never actually set up a time, and neither had had the chance to talk about it when they had seen each other earlier.

Glancing down at her phone, she checked for what might have been the twentieth time since she'd left Jonathan's body to see if she'd received a message from Rhett, but her inbox remained empty. Her gut began to churn as she thought that, like all the other guys before him, this was probably too much for Rhett. He was gone, and she'd be surprised if he didn't treat her like a leaper for the rest of her time here.

God, why had she thought it would be a good idea to start something with her RA of all people? Now she was stuck here having to face him every day for a year. Turning away, she started for her room when Rhett's door opened and she found him staring at her in surprise.

Oh, kill me now.

"Hey," she said, turning away so he wouldn't see the humiliation that she knew must be written all over her face.

"Hi! Where are you going? I was just coming to find you," Rhett said, falling into step beside her.

Marley stopped to stare at him. "You were?"

"Yeah," Rhett smiled. It was his usual sexy smile, and not the smile she was expecting: the distant one which screamed 'stay the hell away from me, you freak.'

"I'm so forgetful. You know I never actually set up a time with you for our date tonight? I would have called, but it turns out, I don't have your number either." He smiled ruefully, displaying dimples that she noticed for the first time. "I'm really doing great, right?"

Marley couldn't answer on account of the shock that was slowly spreading all over her body. He wasn't dumping her? Seeing her glazed expression, Rhett waved a hand in front of her eyes. "That bad, huh?"

This jolted her from her stupor. "No! Of course not! I'm mean, you're doing alright, but it would help if we sorted out those things."

His eyes took in her face, noticing the strain of the day taking its toll on her.

"We don't have to go out tonight, if you'd rather not. This morning was a little… insane. I'd understand if you want to reschedule, do this another time?"

At his words, a burst of happiness opened in her chest.

"No, I'm good. I'd still like to go."

"Great," he beamed, looking relieved. "How about I pick you up at eight?"

She nodded, trying not to look too desperate. "Eight it is."

Mirroring his smile, she headed to her room, adding a little sway of her hips, knowing that he was staring after her.

ONE HUNDRED SIXTY-SEVEN

Eve's phone buzzed with another missed call from Si.

Since their argument yesterday, he had been calling every few hours. "Just checking in" he called it though she knew better. Only, stubborn as he was, he never apologized for doubting her. As far as Eve was concerned, she expected a lot more loyalty from him of all people. With neither of them giving in, things were tense between them right now but she didn't have the energy to fix it.

Barely glancing at her phone, she tried to focus on the course books that were fanned out around her. Instead of her usual desk where she could sprawl out with her two laptops, she'd chosen this small corner tucked beneath one of the library's many alcoves.

It afforded privacy so she could finally get done some of the work she had been putting off. Fresh air flowed in from the round window in front of her.

From here, she could see one of those pop-up flower displays that BU prided themselves on, and the entrance to the history block where students rushed to and fro, hurrying to class. Not that she was really paying much attention to them or her coursework for that matter.

She had way too much on her mind.

She'd been *this* close to telling Marley about the symbol in the painting when they'd had to help Dalton. Things had happened so quickly afterward that Eve had completely forgotten about the subject until now, when left to her own devices, the guilt was hitting her hard.

She could just call Marley and tell her right now, but she knew Marley was looking forward to her date with Rhett tonight, and Eve didn't want to spoil that for her.

God knows they could all do with some downtime.

Wanting to do the responsible thing, Eve had come to the library to catch up on work, but she couldn't focus on any of it. Every person that passed by, every shadow that fell over the table made her jump as she would worry that it was Jason, back from the dead to finish what he had started.

Drumming painted black fingernails on the leather tabletop, she grabbed her phone, but not to call her brother back. He could stew for a while longer. Sliding across the screen, her finger stopped over the Facebook icon.

Before *the-thing-that-happened*, when she had been part of the popular clique — scratch that, when she had *thought* she had been part of the clique — a great social media presence had been as crucial as air. A person's popularity was measured by how many likes and comments their posts would garner and managing a successful Facebook profile took as much thought and energy as a part-time job.

In those days, Eve's entire life had been put on display for the world to rate and like though she hadn't opened her Facebook app for months now.

Steeling herself, she clicked on the icon.

The bright blue and white badge flashed up as her profile came onto the screen. With astonishment (and some horror), Eve saw that she had over five thousand notifications in her inbox.

Five *thousand*.

Luckily, she wasn't interested in seeing Yuna's daily self-effacing posts which were only ever put up to gain compliments from the unsuspecting masses or Grace's ones that were thinly veiled attempts at showing off. Eve was searching for one particular profile... one she had thought she would never look at again.

Clicking on his name, Jason's page loaded and his face flooded her screen.

He'd chosen his picture well. The sun had lit up his face and he'd had that sexy smile that had made her weak in the knees whenever he flashed it her way. He sat astride his favorite motorbike (one of four he owned), wind whistling through his thick hair, toned and muscular, looking like a movie star.

She wanted to jab her fingers into his eyes and claw them out.

Tearing herself from his picture, she scrolled through his time bar. As she'd suspected, despite having disappeared for almost a year — missing, presumed dead the cops had said — his page was inundated with posts on an almost daily basis.

"Miss you, Jason" read one from a girl Eve didn't know. "I know you're not dead! I'm praying for you, Buddy," said another from a fellow road hog who did know Jason. She remembered seeing him around although she hadn't thought them very close — more acquaintances than friends.

Certainly not "buddies."

On and on the comments went, mostly from people who didn't know him at all, although interspersed among the nonsense, she found the occasional posts from his family.

Those affected her the most. From what she knew of them, they were good people, nothing at all like their son.

They had no idea what a monster they had created.

She scrolled through, not really sure what she was looking for when her own face flashed up at her. Eve started, and almost dropped her phone, not expecting to be confronted with her past in such a direct way.

There she was hanging off Jason as he took her on a spin on his bike. Another at the local drive-in, sur-rounded by a group of her then friends — none of whom had bothered to speak to her after Jason had disappeared.

Having trusted the girls in her circle, expecting their sympathy and understanding, she had revealed some of what he had done to her. Instead, they had declared her a drama queen who craved attention and was willing to throw the memory of Jason under the bus in order to get it. It was a painful lesson to learn that they cared more about the memory of Jason — who they have only ever known in passing — than their actual relationship with Eve.

They never got it, and they never would.

Then again, how could she really blame them when she was smiling in every one of these pictures looking as if she were having the time of her life? No one would ever know the terror she had gone through or what bruises lay beneath that glossy surface. It had taken a year to recover, a year when drastic new measures had been put into place, but it was all for nothing apparently, as Jason wasn't gone from her life even if he was just a sick trick of Michael's.

The mind wasn't always good at separating fiction from reality, and when PTSD was added to the mix, it was a whole sorry affair.

Two male voices cut into her thoughts, pulling her gaze from her phone. A student stood on the lawn out-side, shooting the breeze with his professor. They were laughing, not talking about much, but it wasn't their con-versation that had caught her attention.

It was who was doing it.

Standing directly in front of her, looking as casual as can be, it was Marley's dad, Paul.

Eve felt herself freezing, wondering if he could see her before realizing that it wouldn't be a problem if he did. He didn't know that she had broken into his office or about her suspicions.

"I'm obviously thrilled you're enjoying the course, it's always nice to know when my hard work is being appreciated," Paul was saying to his student. "But I've actually got to cut this conversation short... I have another class starting in a minute and I can't be late..."

"No problem," the student responded already backing off. "Catch you later, Mr. Gray."

Paul nodded as the student disappeared into the history block. He waited for a few counts before slinging his leather bag onto his shoulder, he went in the *other* direction.

Eve blinked.

He had just said that he had a class to do so why was he was leaving the history block where he taught?

She watched his figure retreating as Marley's earlier revelations reverberated in her mind. There were a few too many questions hanging over his head; yet it was obvious that Marley wasn't ready to deal with them herself.

But that didn't mean Eve couldn't act.

Her spidey senses tingling, Eve didn't think about what she was doing. Trusting her instincts, she grabbed her course books, shoved them into her bag then hurried out of the library after him.

ONE HUNDRED SIXTY-EIGHT

MASSACHUSETTS BAY COLONY, 1693

The birds had only just begun their early morning song when The Four blew open the double doors to the mansion with nothing more than a wave.

Two guards rushed them holding rifles that they barely knew how to use, their expressions stark with terror. They weren't more than farmer's sons, plucked from their homes, swayed by promises of a better life.

Esther offered them a simple way out. They could leave in peace or in various pieces.

They chose wisely, fleeing with their weapons clutched by their chests.

Of course, The Four would not have killed them. They were barely more than boys and not caught up in the Council's evil. Still, since fear was the driving force behind these murders, Tabitha had concluded that it was time to use it to their advantage.

Their findings had pointed them to this place, this expensive house, dripping with luxury fittings and fixtures and which had formed the meeting point for the Salem Council.

Mary took in the lavish decor with distaste. Why was it always the wealthy who persecuted those from more unfortunate backgrounds? What made the rich decide they could take so much from the poor that they could even go after their lives like this?

The questions rolled through her mind against images of the prisoners — poor, young Bridget in particular. She hoped she would have a good life with now; perhaps, in time, she would be able to consider Sofia another mother.

They went cautiously through the house, long skirts swishing over polished floorboards that gleamed in the low evening light, but came across no one else.

Whoever owned this house was not home. How fortunate for them, Tabitha thought grimly, her mind still seething from all that had gone before.

Having learned from their last break-in, their search began on the top floor — if the Council or their men arrived, they would not be trapped several floors above ground where it would be more difficult to escape. They entered into the bedrooms, using their magic to tip the furniture over, letting their contents spill over the floor.

They found mounds of hidden jewels and piles of money, and files of what seemed to be material the Council were using as blackmail. There were documents alluding to rape, and murder, all manner of crime that the Council had somehow uncovered and were using against the town, keeping them silent.

At least, now it was easier to understand where the Council's power had suddenly sprung up from.

They made their way down to the lower floor, searching every nook and cranny until, standing by an antique table, Catherine unearthed a paper that made her gasp.

The others crowded around, looking over her shoulder to see what it was that had caused her reaction.

In her hand, she held a drawing. The artist had an obvious talent for capturing a person's likeness as the ten or so people who sat around an oval table seemed so lifelike that they could have been real.

The picture depicted a meeting of the council which consisted of all men and only one woman of a great if cold beauty. The artist's strokes captured her high cheekbones and regal posture that spoke of aristocratic blood.

But it was her eyes that were chilling. There was something about them that seemed *wrong*.

Still, it wasn't the woman that had captured Catherine's attention, but the man sitting beside her. He wasn't much taller than the woman and did not have her presence, much as he might have liked. Everything about him, from the ill-fitting clothes to the thin mustache that covered his upper lip, reeked of one who was trying hard to fit into this important group, but who would never escape the lowly place he had come from.

Seeing his familiar face, Mary felt herself grow faint and had to be caught by Esther.

"No. It can't be," she cried, her voice trembling with emotion.

Yet it was.

She knew the man in the picture, knew him intimately as originally there had been one more member of their group.

Originally, they had been known as The Five.

The man in this picture, the man who sat at the head of the Salem Council's table and who had been in charge of the Salem Witch Hunts…

…Had been the fifth witch in their coven.

ONE HUNDRED SIXTY-NINE

Rhett turned up at her door at eight pm — sharp.

A smile spread over Marley's face when she saw how punctual he was being. Glancing in the mirror, she gave her appearance one last check.

She was wearing her usual denim jeggings but these were a new pair. The top she had chosen was a figure-hugging and off-the-shoulder thinly knitted number that would keep the late summer evening chill at bay while not at the expense of fashion.

She teamed her outfit with a pair of black ankle boots and simple hoop earrings, brushed her lashes with a coat of mascara, dabbed peach gloss on her lips, and run her brush through her hair to get rid of any tangles.

And then she was done. Marley had a great complexion (apparently one of the things she had inherited from her mom, not that she could remember — it was her dad who told her this) so she never needed foundation. She knew she was lucky — especially after witnessing how long it used to take Cassie to get ready. That time had decreased by half now, though Cassie still spent quite a bit of time in front of her mirror, the only difference being now she would admire instead of berating herself.

One step at a time, she thought.

Opening the door, she was hit with Rhett's deliciously spicy scent. Some kind of aftershave maybe? She wasn't sure, but it made her want to tuck her face under this neck, which surprised her. She hadn't quite realized that she was liking Rhett so much.

His dark eyes ran over her briefly as he gave her a slow smile. "You look great; then again you always do."

"Thanks," she smiled back at him. It was impossible not to really. There was just something so warm about him.

"Are you ready to go?" He asked.

Grabbing her handbag, she slipped it over her shoulder. "Sure. Let's go."

The night was a sea of midnight blue as stars crisscrossed the sky. They walked the seven or so blocks to the theatre, enjoying each other's company as they chatted about school and where they came from. Pretty much everything apart from what had happened earlier that day. Marley appreciated that he was respecting her space by not questioning her, but it was like a shadow hanging over them that she couldn't shake. Finally, she knew she had to break the ice as he would never raise the issue himself.

"I know you must have questions about earlier. It's OK to ask," she offered.

Rhett looked at her. When he saw her calm expression, his eyes became thoughtful. "Well, I do have some, it's true."

"Go ahead."

"So, I get that you must be some sort of medium. But you don't just see spirits, you can touch them, command them?" Rhett asked, shoving his hands into his pockets.

"That was new. I've never been able to touch them like

that before," Marley explained. "I usually just see them, and can talk with them."

"When did this start?"

"When I was young though I didn't know what that was at the time. We thought I was schizophrenic actually until recently. My dad still thinks I am," she revealed.

Rhett looked shocked by this. Sympathy poured off of him. "Wow. That's terrible. You haven't told him?"

"The thing is," Marley answered, biting her lip. "He's super religious, and I think this kind of thing would go against what he believes. He'd think it was a Devil power or something."

"Really? I'd never have thought that about him. He seems so… laid back." Rhett frowned, having trouble aligning the person he knew to what he was hearing about him now.

"Religious people can be laid back, Rhett. I don't know who you've known," Marley frowned at him herself, earning an embarrassed flush from him.

"I know. Sorry, I'm making a mess of this. I just mean to say that, he doesn't seem the type who would label you as one thing or another, without seeing the whole person, especially when you're his only child."

Marley shrugged. "Maybe he wouldn't be. It could just be my own fear talking. I don't know."

The conversation went quiet, both caught up in their thoughts until Marley found herself looking at him through the curtain of her hair.

"Isn't any of this freaking you out?"

An eyebrow arched in surprise. "Not exactly. I actually find it pretty fascinating. I've always believed in ghosts. I'd guess you'd call me a spiritual person, though I don't believe in God. At least, not as it's written in the Bible or how he is viewed in the traditional sense. I think God is more like this universal power, and some of us can tap into this power more than others."

"Like how Zack was sensitive to Jonathan's spirit?"

Marley asked, thinking back to what they had learned about him that morning.

"Yes, but clearly, you are way more connected and powerful than he is. That's why I'm shocked that you think your father would think of your gift in such a negative light, when I actually think it could be a force of good."

Marley blinked, staring at him from beneath her lashes. She had never thought of her powers as coming from the other side before, the side of good, though he could very well be right. While many stories painted witches as being creatures of evil, ugly old hags stirring cauldrons bubbling over with green goo, wasn't there also a part of history that depicted them as spiritual beings of nature. Weren't they known as healers, seers, and such?

"Anyway," Rhett continued, oblivious to the thoughts running through her mind. "Whatever you are, whenever they came from, it's pretty clear to me that you are special, and that's all I care about, really."

He looked at her with that sexy smile of his that sent delicious shivers down her spine. Her cheeks grew warm as a blush began spreading over them.

Marley hadn't expected this.

She hadn't been trying or looking, but somehow, in the middle of all of this madness, she had finally met a guy who had not run the opposite way when he found out who she really was — issues and all — but one who liked her *because* of them.

A river of heat spread inside her as she picked up her step.

Things were finally looking up.

S aunders rubbed her stiff neck, sore from hours sat in front of the computer screen.

She turned down the brightness on the display, hoping that it would stop the migraine that threatened. Already, the edges of her vision had started to turn funny, in that way it had ever since she'd been a young girl.

It must have been around the age of ten when she had first experienced it. Describing it like the static that was often found when tuning a television set for channels, Saunders would find her vision becoming impaired while the world would become too bright as her senses were flooded.

Sometimes pills helped, though usually, her migraines continued on mercilessly.

Having just gotten off the phone to Brooks' wife, she learned that there was still no change in his condition. Initially, when they'd had these calls, the tone — though somber — would have an optimistic edge to it. He was a lion, a hero, and everyone fully expected him to wake up.

But with every passing day, the hope was dying.

She could hear it in his wife's too-bright voice when she called to give his daily report. The woman was hanging on by a thread, determined to stay strong for her kids, but Saunders knew the break was coming. She'd seen it enough times to recognize the signs.

And there wasn't a damn thing she could do about it.

Getting out of her chair, she stormed out of the office. She needed air, a change of scenery. Anything to stop her looking at that screen as she went over the evidence for the millionth time only to come up empty.

Squinting at the overhead lights, she headed down the hall into the break area where a tea and coffee station sat beside a vending machine offering nothing but sugar overdoses and bad carbs. Sliding in a five dollar bill, she pushed the numbers for a Snickers bar. To hell with the healthy eating, she needed to get through the day and this would help for now, until she suffered the inevitable sugar crash later. By then, she'd be passed out in bed with Milo breathing his bad doggy breath all over her.

She couldn't wait.

The machine spat out her change as she picked up the candy bar, tore the wrapper off and took a giant, unlady-like bite. Not ready to sit back at her desk just yet, she took a detour around the office, stretching her legs, drawing out the time.

She passed by cops, heads bent over their desks working on various investigations. Some kind of briefing was taking place in the conference room where aerial pictures of several warehouses highlighted by a dock, were being projected onto the wall. She walked past them all, chewing on her chocolate bar when she approached a large noticeboard with blown-up black and white pictures of suspects.

Almost of their own accord, her eyes scanned the board as they did each time she passed this way. Usually, she found nothing of interest though today, her vision went strange when her eyes passed over a freeze frame of a streetcam.

Like a beacon calling out to her from the darkness, the static was back with a vengeance suddenly, as it was whenever she was about to piece together some crucial piece of information. Saunders' unbeaten success rate at closing cases was due, in no small part, to this uncanny knack that she had for sniffing things out.

And right now, it was telling her to study this particular picture in detail.

Her hand holding the candy bar lowered as she stepped closer to the board. The information printed above the picture mentioned that it was the suspect for a slew of brutal murders inside a local bar downtown known as The Castle. It had happened a few nights ago, but although the suspect had been caught on camera, the cops were having a hard time ID'ing him.

As was the norm for a streetcam, the face of the guy wasn't too clear, not enough on its own to find a match through their system. Though the picture was in black and white, she had seen blood enough times that she knew what those splatters were that covered his white shirt.

But there was something about the blood splatter that bothered her.

Taking out her phone, she took a snapshot of the image, then finding the image in her phone, she blew the picture up even more, sliding across the image until she found the spot that had sent her senses tingling.

The top right corner of the blood splatter covered some kind of logo on the perp's top. It was easy to miss, and Saunders wouldn't have noticed it herself if it wasn't for that strange static that had drawn her attention to it.

No longer interested in her candy bar, she tossed it into a trashcan, hurrying back to her office where, moments later, after running a trace for the logo in the system, she found a match.

Her eyes grew wide with shock.

O n the other side of town, inside Guardian HQ, Tyler sat on the floor of the hidden library having gone there alone after she had finally managed to cut Cassie loose, though she was surprised by how much persuasion it had taken.

What a time for Cassie to suddenly start caring so much about her.

Books were opened all around her, as she read feverishly, devouring the information inside.

It wasn't until she had gotten here and started looking that she'd discovered that she was right — Christian *had* been lying to them.

So long as the person knew how, black magic artifacts

could be used by *anyone*. Not only those who were evil, or demons.

Anyone.

Including her.

And Tyler was determined to play Michael at his own game. She would use the artifact that they had found. She would power up so she could stop him.

She would save her sister.

TWISTED MAGIC

11: GRAVE MATTERS

JO HO

ONE HUNDRED SEVENTY

Vehicles and people littered the streets, spilling out of buildings and stores as they finished work for the day and started for home, many with glazed looks in their eyes. With buds in their ears, listening to music or podcasts, they were zoned out to the world.

Eve couldn't say anything about that having been the same way once before though things had changed after last summer, when she had been forced to take her mortality much more seriously.

She never went anywhere with earbuds anymore, after all, those noise-canceling ones that were all the rage also stopped you from being able to hear if someone was sneaking up behind you.

It was all fun and music until someone knocked you unconscious and shoved you in the trunk of their car.

Dodging traffic like it was her job, Eve tailed Marley's dad keeping several cars behind so he wouldn't suspect that he was being followed.

Not that it seemed he had any idea.

He kept a leisurely pace, cruising around the city as if he had all the time in the world. Stressed-out and second-guessing herself every few minutes, Eve on the other hand, wondered what the hell it was she was doing.

"You have lost it for real this time, Girl," she admonished.

Yet even as the doubts began again, Eve couldn't help feeling that nervous tinge in her stomach, the one that had told her to follow him.

She watched Paul's car signal right at the lights when the car in front of her suddenly collided with another. An airbag exploded out of the wheel of the red Toyota, cushioning the driver from what might have otherwise been a serious blow to her head.

Slamming on the brakes, Eve fought to control her own car and only just managed to get it to stop: her Corolla was now inches from the Toyota.

Smoke blew out of the engine of the Toyota as its driver — a woman of around forty — hunched over the deployed airbag. Someone rushed over to check on her. A man from the crowded sidewalk called for help. Knowing there was no more assistance she could offer, Eve looked for Paul's car.

Too late, she saw the flash of its bumper turning into a side street. She was going to lose him yet there was nothing she could do to get out any faster.

She twisted in her seat, desperately searching for anything that might help when a movement in the sky caught her eye as a flock of birds flew over Paul's car.

If only she could see what they were seeing.

From where they were in the sky, they had the perfect view and would have no problem following him.

No sooner had the thought entered her mind when Eve's magic reached out. She felt the minds of the birds then suddenly, *she was flying with them!*

The city flew by beneath separated by a gulf of nothingness. Wind cushioned her wings as the bird — or was it her? — soared through the skies. Eve could feel every sensation, every ruffling of the bird's feathers as if it were her own. Her body felt so different, so light, yet despite how hollow her bird-bones were now, they were also impossibly strong.

She flew instinctively, swimming in the air as her new eyes picked up the hood of Paul's car as easily as if it were right in front of her. Adjusting her flight, Eve surfed the air riding the currents. Without any concern that he would notice her new form, she was able to fly in any manner that she wished without drawing any attention.

Though she took easily to the actual flying, her new vision would take a while longer to get used to. Her bird eyes were set so widely apart on either side of her face that her view of the world was distorted.

She could see at a much wider circumference like everything was coming at her in Imax vision, but there was also the information overload. Details were flying at her so fast that she struggled to take it all in, and it didn't help that she could see for what seemed like miles with crystal clarity.

She didn't know how long she had been up there when she suddenly noticed Paul's car pulling up outside a building that had seen better days. Among the peeling paint and dirt-encrusted windows, graffiti-covered several of its walls. Attempts had been made at softening the harsh and plain exterior with window boxes, but all that remained of the plants were the shriveled, dried husks.

Despite its outward appearance, people were gathered inside. Watching through the windows, they seemed to be mostly families. Several young kids darted around, playing hide and seek while their parents chatted. A weathered wooden sign half hanging off its hinges declared this the Goodmayes Community Center.

Eve flew onto the roof of the opposite building. Landing gracefully — which must have been due to the bird's talents — Eve watched Paul enter the building.

A horn blasting behind her jolted her from the bird and she found herself abruptly back inside her own body which felt disappointedly heavy and clumsy. Though it was easier to see now with her eyes back in the middle of her face, she was startled by how much less of her environment she could experience.

The horn sounded again, its impatient driver letting known his feelings. Glancing into her rearview mirror, Eve could see the man in the car behind her gesturing rudely.

Sliding her gaze to the front, she saw that the two crashed cars had been moved aside leaving enough space for the traffic to ease through. The only one holding things up now, was her.

Signaling that she was moving out, Eve drove through the gap toward the community center. Though it was a little distance away, Eve had a perfectly clear map of it in her mind: as if her flight had been imprinted inside her head, she could see the route to the center clearly.

Not ten minutes later she found herself pulling up to the curb a few cars down from Paul's.

She slid lower into her seat, waiting and watching.

This was lunacy of the highest order she knew, following her friend's dad halfway across the city because of a small lie he had told a student. If it wasn't for that symbol in the painting she had seen, she'd think this a crazy overreaction.

Round and round the thoughts went through her mind until Paul emerged wearing a pair of paint-splattered overalls. Prying open a can of paint, Eve watched with a sense of growing disappointment as Paul began to cover the graffiti with what looked to be a mural.

She'd followed him all the way across town for this?

She wasn't much of a detective that was for sure. Still, that prickly feeling that she had felt stayed with her. She took in the sight of Marley's dad, seemingly being nothing other than a Good Samaritan as he did his Christian duty when he stopped as a figure approached from the street.

She blinked, not sure if she were seeing things. Maybe her eyes were taking a while to re-adjust being back to her normal vision, but the person who had started talking to Paul looked to be... Trip.

Cassie's Trip.

Carefully winding down the window, Eve tried to hear what they were speaking about but she was too far away to make out the conversation. Whatever they were talking about though, it seemed like an intense conversation: Paul had set down his paintbrush, gesturing passionately.

Even as she wondered if this was one big bizarre coincidence her conversation with Marley came to her mind. There were too many fingers pointing toward Paul, which though even Marley had her own suspicions about her father, she obviously didn't feel right investigating him.

It was lucky then that Marley had friends.

At this point, Eve didn't know if Paul was innocent or completely devious, but she did know one thing... having just started on his mural, and now seemingly engaged in an intense conversation with Trip, he would be busy here a while longer.

Maybe it was time she did some snooping a little closer to home...

***

Usually, a neat-freak, Cassie's side of the room was now a total mess.

Her laptop was open, a million tabs on the screen. Her phone and iPad were also being used with various bits of information that she had deemed relevant sitting on their screens. Color printouts were scattered over the bed with the results of everything she had researched so far on the Charles Esplanade and its history of the supernatural.

Convinced that the next seal was somewhere within

this region — due to the information Trip had unwittingly imparted — Cassie had narrowed her search down to ten or so areas, but it was far too late in the day to start looking for it now.

Barely able to contain herself, Cassie had called Eve to let her know what she had discovered, but the call continued to ring until it had reached her voicemail. Leaving a message, Cassie hadn't bothered to try Marley knowing that she was on her date with Rhett. It could wait until Marley got back.

Tyler, however, she could tell.

Jumping off her bed, careful not to crease the papers covering it, Cassie sprang out of her room and across the hall to Tyler's door. She rapped her knuckles but the door didn't open. Waiting, she tried a few times with the same result. Finally, she pressed her ear on the door but couldn't hear any sounds from inside. From the blackness seeping out beneath the door, she could see that no lights were on either.

It seemed that Tyler wasn't home.

A finger of unease slid along her spine sending chills that made Cassie wrap her arms around herself. Checking her wristwatch, a platinum Rolex encrusted with tiny diamonds that her dad had given her when she'd turned sixteen, Cassie saw that it was almost nine pm.

Shouldn't Tyler be home by now? Thinking of last night, when they hadn't kept a close enough eye on her and she had been subsequently arrested, Cassie felt the first flash of panic. Had she made a mistake? Should she not have left Tyler alone?

Cassie was still second-guessing herself when Tyler came around the corridor.

Seeing Cassie outside her door, Tyler's expression turned guarded for a moment as she clutched her rucksack to her chest more tightly before returning to normal quickly, hoping Cassie hadn't noticed.

But Cassie had.

"There you are! Where have you been?" She asked as Tyler approached.

"Nowhere. I just went for a walk is all."

"For three hours? You must be exhausted," Cassie couldn't imagine walking for that long, especially after the horrible rooster fight they had been forced to endure: she would never unsee the sight of those birds tearing each other to pieces.

"Yeah. Anyway, what's up?" Tyler said, changing the subject before Cassie could ask more questions.

Cassie's eyes sparkled with excitement. "I think I might have a hit on the next seal!"

Despite her own preoccupation, Tyler's own excitement picked up. "What have you found?"

When Cassie was done explaining Tyler congratulated her. "Good work, Cass. We should look for the seal tomorrow, once we've told the others."

Opening her door, Tyler trudged inside though she didn't put her bag down, just kept hugging it to her chest like it was a safety blanket. Seeing how tired she looked, Cassie bottled her own excitement. It had been another rough day for her friend, maybe more talk about work wasn't what she needed right now.

"Hey, do you want to hang out with me? I can order food," she offered.

Tyler felt a wave of gratefulness at Cassie's suggestion: she was proving to be the kindest one of the group.

Tyler wished she could trust her with the truth.

Instead, she shook her head, feigning a yawn. "I'd love to but I'm too tired. I'll just grab a snack and rest up for tomorrow since it looks like there'll be a whole lot more walking involved."

"I'm going to order food anyway, I can drop you off something then leave you alone?" Cassie seemed very concerned that Tyler eat and the truth was, Tyler *was* starving, but there was something more important than food that she needed to attend to.

"By the time food gets here I'll be crashed out. Don't worry about it, Cass. Thank you, but I'll be fine," Tyler said, putting her hand on the door in a conscious move to shut it.

"OK," Cassie answered apparently believing every word of Tyler's excuse. "Get some sleep. We'll knock for you in the morning."

"Night," Tyler said.

"Night," Cassie replied as she finally went back into her own room.

Locking her door, Tyler ran for her bed as she opened her bag, taking out the leather-bound book that she had stolen from the Guardian's secret library.

She ran her finger over the embossed title, THE ART OF BLACK MAGIC and felt a chill envelop her. Pushing the fear to the back of her mind, she settled onto her bed, gulped down half a bottle of her energy potion, and opened the book.

ONE HUNDRED SEVENTY-ONE

Credits rolled as the movie came to an end.

Marley blinked, her eyes adjusting to the lights as they faded back in illuminating the theater.

It was a popular movie she and Rhett had just attended judging by the number of couples she could see. Marley had enjoyed the last hour and a half and had particularly enjoyed being able to switch her mind off recent troubles, though at certain moments in the movie she wasn't able to concentrate. The heat from Rhett's arm had pressed into hers making her very aware of their closeness, to the point where she had started fantasizing about him putting his arm around her, and then wondering how she would react if he did.

Unfortunately, she wouldn't know the answer to that tonight as he was already shifting in his seat to let the couple beside them out of their row. People seemed in such a hurry to leave.

"I'll never get used to city life," Rhett exclaimed as a guy almost trod on his feet, shoving his way to the exit. "I mean, he's not going to get out of here that much faster, would it kill him to have a little patience?"

"You don't know, maybe he's busting for the restroom," Marley mocked, watching the same guy as he pushed rudely past the crowd that had reached the exit before him.

"He's cruising for a bruising is what he is," Rhett said making Marley laugh.

When he turned to her with a raised brow, she asked, "What eighties movie did you steal that line from?"

Rhett looked rueful. "I'm not very cool, am I?"

Marley grinned. "Cool people are the ones who don't care what others think of them."

Rhett thought about her words for a moment before his brow furrowed some more. "Wait, was that an insult?"

Marley laughed harder, unable to contain herself as a smile spread over Rhett's face. She saw his eyes turning dark with intent as they lowered to her lips. Her laughter died as her body tensed in expectation. Slowly, Rhett moved his face closer until she could see the little bronze flecks in his eyes. Lowering his lips to her, he kissed her.

A shiver of delight went through Marley. His lips were warm yet the kiss was so hot. He tasted sweet, like the soda he had been drinking but there was also something spicy about him. Maybe it was that aftershave he wore.

Whatever it was, Marley was filled with a light-headedness as she sank into his kiss.

They only pulled apart when the overhead lights turned overly bright, warning them that it was time to go.

Smiling at her, Rhett offered his hand. She took it as the two of them left the theater.

Neither of them realizing that they had an audience.

Hunkered down in the shadows of the back row, unnoticed by anyone, Christian sat looking lost and alone.

Absolute devastation in his eyes.

The door clicked open as Eve crept into Paul's apartment.

It was lucky that she had picked Marley up here before or she would never have known where it was. Striding confidently up the stairs as if she had every right to be there, she arrived at Paul's second-floor apartment and sent her army of ants into the door where they had climbed inside and unlocked it.

She was beginning to appreciate just how helpful her new friends could be.

Shutting the door behind her, Eve turned on the lights but made sure to keep her distance from the windows. It had been ten or so minutes since she'd left Paul, and she figured she should have at least an hour to look around though that might be pushing it. Setting an alarm for thirty minutes in her phone, she started her search.

She wasn't really sure what she was looking for, maybe more of those symbols? Starting with the paintings that now decorated the walls, she examined each of them though she found nothing of any consequence.

Her eyes took in the living room and the few pieces of furniture that sat around the sofa. They were a mix of old and new. The walnut coffee table she recognized as one that was sold in IKEA, while the leather sofa looked worn but comfortable; it was probably one Paul had owned before, back when he and Marley had lived on the West Coast.

There was a side console that sat before a window which Eve made her way to now. On it was a china dish where some keys and bills were kept. The drawers contained a mish-mash of stationary and leaflets with some of Boston's best-loved tourist sites. A few had red circles marked on them which Eve took to mean Paul was intending to visit those locations.

Interestingly, none of the leaflets were to do with the harbor, yet Paul had somehow found himself there not long after they had lost their last seal.

It was just another one of those mysteries where Paul was concerned.

Finding nothing of interest in the console, Eve searched the two shelving units that flanked the TV where a few collectibles were displayed among various history books. Most noticeably — at least to Eve — was the smiling fat golden Buddha that sat on the top shelf. She knew from various conversations with Marley that her dad was super religious and a Christian, so the Buddha statue must be a throwback to Marley's Asian mom.

Paul must be a very forgiving person to keep those sort of mementos around after the woman he had loved had left them so abruptly. If Eve were in his place, she wouldn't be quite as understanding.

She looked under the sofa in case something was shoved under there but there was only a thin layer of dust and a pen that must have rolled beneath it.

Leaving the living room, she passed by a kitchen and was surprised to see how many gadgets he had. Among them she spotted an Instant Pot, a Nutribullet, a bread maker and the latest Keurig. A large spice rack hung on the side of the refrigerator with a brand of jerk seasoning that she recognized as they used it at home. This surprised her, that Paul would have such wide-ranging tastes… then again, he did have a mixed-race daughter. That kind of thing tended to open a person up to other cultures.

She stepped into the bedroom, noticing immediately that Paul was far neater than Marley was. Dirty clothes sat inside a laundry basket and not, as was often in Marley's case, strewn all over her bed. Even the books he was reading at night formed a neat pile on his bedside table, arranged by ascending size. A walk-in closet took up one wall of space.

Eve approached the closet first, opening the door to see a rail of clothes hanging head height. Above the rail was a shelf where folded towels and bedding were kept. His clothes consisted mostly of similar style shirts, sweaters and the corduroy pants that he wore to school. On his downtime, it looked like he switched it up to jeans.

All in all, it was a boring find.

Eve stepped in to see if there was anything behind the rail when her foot connected with solid metal. If she weren't wearing her Doc Martens she might have stubbed a toe, as it was, she had felt nothing.

Bending down, she slid the hanging clothes away to find a safe sitting on the floor of the closet. She tried the dial but of course, it was locked. Eve frowned, wondering if there was a way she could use her insects to break inside but it didn't seem possible. It seemed she had reached a dead end.

Why did Marley's dad have a safe in the apartment? What did he keep in there?

Examining the safe, Eve suddenly noticed the corner of something white lying beneath it that would have gone unnoticed if she hadn't been so close to it. Reaching down, she retrieved an unopened envelope.

It was addressed to Marley Gray at this new address and was written in a pretty cursive handwriting. The date stamp was only two weeks ago. Curious, Eve turned the envelop over to see the sender had written their name but no return address.

It was from a Lisa Gray.

Eve found it strange that Lisa — whoever she was — would write her name on the back but not an address: didn't that defeat the whole point?

Eve didn't know who Lisa was, but she did what any

person with an internet connection would do — she Googled the name on her phone.

It was a common name as the hundreds of hits that flooded her screen showed until Eve streamlined her search by adding the words 'West Coast' to her search.

Fewer faces popped up this time. As Eve scrolled through them wondering what exactly she was looking for when one particular face stood out among the rest.

It was an Asian woman and she was the spitting image of Marley.

Eve's eyes opened in shock as she studied the photograph and the listing beneath it. The photograph had been taken fifteen years ago, at a local arts and crafts fair. Lisa sat by her stall selling crystals, beaded necklaces, and bracelets that she made. The caption described her as a local artist selling her wares.

Her nerves were shrieking at her, letting her know that her discovery was important, even if she didn't know how. Tucking the letter into her jacket, Eve slid the clothes back into their previous position, shut the closet door and hurried out of the apartment.

All the while, she debated with herself.

If she gave the letter to Marley, she'd have to explain that she broke into her father's apartment, but if she didn't, Marley wouldn't know that her mom had been trying to contact her.

Not sure what to do, Eve got into her car and drove home.

The meatball sub that she had picked up on her way home lay uneaten still in its wrapper as Milo sat beneath it, looking hopeful though Saunders had a strict 'no people food' policy for her dog, much to his perpetual dismay.

Still, he could hope and dream only a few feet away, his giant tongue hanging out.

After rushing home from the station, Saunders had taken Milo for their daily walk. She had even thrown a few balls for him though her heart wasn't in it today. Milo must have sensed that she was troubled as he didn't demand she play as he usually did. Instead, he walked by her side just happy to be with her.

She knelt on the carpet by her home office, papers and printouts spread all around her. Though the casual outsider might think otherwise, Saunders knew exactly what she was doing, mentally taking note as she diligently examined the forty-five current players of Blackville University's football team. The Black Tigers consisted of young men in the peak of their health, with glowing skin and six packs which didn't help her job any, as it made distinguishing them a much tougher task.

Still, having been at it for a while, Saunders had whittled the possible contenders down to five who could match that street cam shot of the person wanted for questioning in The Castle bar murders case that she had seen on the bulletin board at work. Though the picture had been in black and white, Saunders had been able to tell the perp had light hair so that eliminated any of the players with dark or even no hair. Of course, it was possible that the perp might have changed their appearance after their little murder spree, but she would consider that option if these five leads did not get her anywhere.

She checked over the names on her list, reading them twice:

Adam Mead
Bryan Jackson
Trip Rockwell
Taylor Redwood
Mark Gregory
Unlocking the screen saver on her computer, Saunders

typed the first name to see if Mead had any prior convictions.

She would investigate each of these players tonight, compile a profile on them.

Tomorrow morning, she would pay each of them a visit.

ONE HUNDRED SEVENTY-TWO

The sun shone over the Charles Esplanade bursting with excited festival goers. Beside the long stretch of the riverwalk, the water glistened. It was a beautiful morning with the city experiencing an unseasonal late September heatwave, yet the four girls who stood beneath the clock tower at the mouth of the festival couldn't have looked more dismayed.

"I had no idea there would be this many people here," Marley said overwhelmed by the gathering crowd.

"And it's so early too," Cassie filled in staring at the looming clock above them, feeling her same trepidation.

"It's always like this," Eve supplied. "It's the most popular music festival in the city."

Marley's eyes slid over to her. "At least we're here early. If we split up into pairs, we'll cover more ground."

Fidgeting with her bag, Tyler's face became apologetic. "Actually, it looks like I have to go into work for a shift."

"Are you serious? I thought your boss gave you time off," Eve asked.

"He did, but apparently that time is up. If I don't go

in, I'll lose my job and I can't afford that yet. My loan might have finally come through but it's shown me how careful I need to be," Tyler answered, already swinging her bag onto her shoulder. "It's only one short shift though. I'll be back to help you all soon," she promised.

Tilting her head to one side, Cassie looked as confused as she felt. "But if you're going to work, why did you come here with us?"

Tyler blinked, hesitating for only a moment before she answered. "I only just got the message from William. One of the staff members is having car trouble."

"Right," Cassie responded.

"Go to work, we'll be fine," Marley said. "We're only looking for the seal and with so many people here, Michael would be stupid to try anything and that's even if he has figured out the location."

"He's had us followed before. I think he always has someone tailing us." Eve's eyes darted around as she spoke, trying to see if Michael had sent someone after them.

"Well, good luck figuring out what we're up to today since we're just here for a good time," Marley winked, putting on an act in case they were being watched.

"There's Trip," Cassie said suddenly, pointing across from them. "I'd better go, but don't worry, I'll be searching for the seal the whole time I'm with him. He thinks it's a treasure hunt we're doing."

"We'll catch up later?" Eve asked as Cassie nodded, moving away.

"I'll see you guys later too," Tyler said, heading off in the opposite direction.

"Enjoy your shift," Marley called out after her.

Tyler shot her a wry look over her shoulder. "I doubt that, but thanks."

Tyler walked quickly, rounding a corner until she knew the girls couldn't see her anymore.

Then, instead of heading toward her work which

would take her across downtown, she crossed into a park. There was hardly a soul to be seen; it seemed the entire city was at the festival or getting ready to go. Tyler was relieved.

What she wanted to do next, she didn't want an audience for.

A part of her felt bad for lying to the girls; she didn't get any enjoyment from doing it. In fact, it made her feel terrible, but her feelings weren't important. Neither was stopping Michael from locating the seals.

The only thing that was important was finding Ally.

She had barely slept last night, having spent most of it pouring over the book of black magic. She'd read until the words had swum before her eyes and she had passed out, unconscious.

But it was worth it.

Tyler knew what she had to do now.

Hugging her bag to her chest — the book was inside — Tyler made her way to a secluded spot where a bank of bushes obscured her from view. Lowering onto her knees, Tyler took out the book, turning to a page she had marked last night with a folded piece of paper.

She skimmed over the spell again.

Even though she had already memorized it, she needed to make sure that she knew it. God knew what might happen if she made a mistake.

This particular spell was so she could easily spot other magical beings. The text that accompanied the spell wasn't too clear on how far the spell could reach, or even what the result would be, but anything would be better than nothing. Since she had wrecked their last plan, Tyler was determined to find her way to Ally.

She was sure that the others were right that either Michael or his demons would be watching them, but with this spell, she would be able to follow them right back.

Setting the book down, Tyler pulled in her focus.

Feeling the familiar swell of magic, she began to chant the words she had memorized.

The archaic words were tricky to pronounce and she had no idea what they meant, but she knew the spell was working as a sudden wind appeared, swirling like a mini whirlwind around her. Leaves and sticks were lifted in its invisible embrace as Tyler started to feel a power so great that it made her gasp.

It came from all around her, from the trees and the tiny living creatures that inhabited them. She could feel their very lifeforce… and it very nearly overwhelmed her.

Forcing herself to stay in the moment, she continued to chant the words to the spell, repeating them over and over until the wind exploded, sending everything it had picked up flying her way.

They stung her bare arms, leaving her with red welts where they had hit. Tyler flinched and stopped chanting, cradling her hurt arms.

The spell was done but the only difference she felt was in the way she was no longer connected to the living things around her.

Unsure whether the spell had worked, she shoved the book into her bag and left.

Which is how she didn't see the bird fall out of the tree, landing on the ground where she had been only moments before Tyler's spell drained all of its life.

Its glassy eyes stared up at the tree it had been resting in, never to be able to see again.

"I guess it's just the two of us then," Marley said smiling at Eve which only made her feel more terrible.

All night, she had tossed and turned in her bed, questioning her own actions. The unopened letter had sat on her vanity table and was now inside her jacket, seemingly burning a hole to her chest.

Eve needed to tell Marley what she had found and now that they were alone, she had the perfect opportunity... if she could just summon up the courage. She touched Marley on the shoulder.

"I need to talk to you," Eve began. Marley looked up from a map of the festival listing the different stages and acts that were due to perform today.

"One sec," Marley interrupted, her gaze drawn to a figure behind Eve. Her lips curled into an amused smile. "Don't look now but I think you've got yourself an admirer."

Eve was thrown for a loop, not expecting those words to come out of her mouth.

Marley inclined her head toward the general direction of the guy. "Your four 'o' clock but if you turn around now it'll be too obvious."

"What does he look like?" Eve asked, curious in spite of herself. It had been a long time since a guy had shown her any interest, especially covered up under layers of make-up as she was. In fact, she could only think of Darren from the boat tours who had seemed genuinely interested, but look how that had ended.

"White guy, rugged. Very hot, circa Brad Pitt before kids. Obviously works out. It's funny though," Marley said.

"What?" Eve asked.

"Most guys who look like that love to show it all off, but he's covered up in a leather jacket. Isn't he hot wearing that in this weather? I'm just in a T-shirt and I'm still feeling the heat. He must be sweltering."

Eve's blood turned to ice.

Though her first instinct was to grab Marley's hand and run the opposite way, Eve turned slowly around.

She spotted him immediately.

It was hard not to since he was standing stock still

amongst the crowd of people. He still looked like a movie star though there was something very unnatural about him.

Probably because he's dead, Eve thought grimly to herself.

It made sense why Marley could see him being that it was her ability, though she didn't seem to have any idea that the Jason who stood before them was a ghost, which he must have been... she had no idea what he could be otherwise.

"So...?" Marley asked with an impish look. "What do you think?"

Eve couldn't answer her, locked into his gaze. Even from here she could feel the intensity of his hate, several feet away. She felt unsafe, as if he could hurt her again. A whimper left her lips which Marley caught. Her expression became concerned.

"Eve?" She asked, looking back across. Suddenly, the blood drained from her face. "Oh God... is that Jason?"

At his name, something snapped inside. She jolted awake, grabbed Marley's hand and started pulling her away.

"Eve," Marley cried, tossing another look over her shoulder but Jason hadn't moved. He was still there, still glowering after them.

"Answer me. Is that him?"

"Yes." The reply hissed out between her clenched teeth.

Marley suddenly shook Eve's hand off of her. "Stop!"

"We don't have to run away from him. He can't hurt you anymore Eve. You have powers and you have us. There's nothing he can do to you so you don't have to be scared of him." Marley was so sure of herself yet Eve could feel none of her confidence.

"We can fight back. At the very least we can go to the police. In fact, I think we should turn around and face him together. He doesn't get to hurt you any more and we should let him know that," Marley said, already turning back when Eve grabbed her arm, stopping her.

"We can't," Eve said.

"Yes we can, just come with me," Marley said, not understanding Eve's reluctance and mistakenly thinking she just needed a push.

"No, Marley! Listen to me! We can't go to him, and we definitely can't go to the police," Eve cried, setting her straight.

"Why not?" Marley asked, her eyes round with confusion.

"Because Jason's dead. Si and I…. We killed him."

There was a definite pep in her step as she made her way to Trip. Forget being cool, Cassie could barely contain her excitement to see him.

Today Trip would be meeting her parents.

Since she had made the decision to introduce him to them, her usual reluctance at bringing anyone home had turned into excitement. All those other times had ended badly only because those people, those school kids, weren't actually friends of hers, but Trip, not only was he her *boyfriend*, but he was perfect.

She couldn't wait to show him off.

But first, they had to find the next seal.

Reaching Trip, she threw her arms around him as he caught her, looking startled. "Sorry," she smiled, holding onto him. "I'm just so happy to see you."

Trip smiled at her — a little stiffly Cassie thought. Feeling suddenly self-conscious, she let go of him letting her arms fall down to her sides.

"That's nice," he replied. "I'm always happy to see you too."

Leaning in close, he pressed his lips to hers letting

them sit there for a few seconds before moving away again. If Cassie felt a little disappointed by the perfunctory kiss, she didn't show it, they had plenty of time to practice kissing later. Hooking her arm into his, her grin grew brighter.

"Are you as excited as I am about dinner tonight?" She couldn't help asking.

"Of course," Trip replied sounding less thrilled then she had imagined him to be. Then again, not everyone wore their feelings on their sleeve. Cassie had to remind herself that just because she behaved a certain way, she shouldn't expect others to.

"I can't wait to meet the people who raised you," Trip finished.

"Mom's been sending me messages all day. She wants to know if there's anything you can't eat?" Cassie wanted to know. Not that Angie would be cooking — the woman could barely make toast without burning it.

"I eat anything," Trip replied, seeming confused by the question.

"I just meant do you have any allergies?" Cassie clarified.

"Not that I know of," Trip answered.

"Well, I'm sure it won't be a problem. Mom will probably have so much food we won't be able to eat it all." Switching lanes quickly, Cassie brought up their plan for the day. "So I was thinking we could walk along the Esplanade until we get to one of the bridges. I thought we could check them out, get our picture taken on as many of them as we can."

Trip stared at her, his brown eyes penetrating deep into hers. "Sure, we can do that. Any reason why you like these bridges so much?"

Cassie forced her face to stay natural. "I've just always had a thing for them. You must too, right? Have a thing for something random?"

The question seemed to throw him. "I can't think of anything."

Cassie stared up at him with a quizzical expression. "It'll come to you later, I'll bet. Anyways, what did you get up to last night, after we spoke?"

Trip looked like he might be getting whiplash by the fast change of topics but he tried his best to answer. "I had an interesting meeting with someone."

"Who?"

"Just someone who I think might come in handy in the near future," Trip replied cryptically.

"Like how?" Cassie asked, pushing for more information. It wasn't in her DNA to quit, maybe it was something she had inherited from her news anchor father.

Trip didn't answer, staring at her so intensely until her cheeks turned pink.

"Sorry, I'm just full of questions today."

But Trip didn't look insulted, in fact, he seemed quite interested in talking. "No, don't apologize. I'm just not used to talking about myself quite so much."

"Are you kidding? You're the star quarterback. You must get inundated with questions all the time."

Trip shrugged his broad shoulders. "I don't get asked much about personal things."

"I guess that's true. I mean, we've been dating now for a few weeks but I still don't know much — if anything — about your family. Like where do you come from?"

Trip's eyes took on a faraway look. "You wouldn't know it. It's this little hellhole that no one ever wants to live in."

"Do you have any brothers or sisters?"

"No," Trip shook his head. "There's only me."

"So we have that in common," Cassie stated only for Trip to shake his head.

"My upbringing was very different from yours. My parents were very militant... very strict. They didn't have a happy life, and I guess they weren't able to forgive past sins because they are still suffering so much even today."

"It can't all be bad though. They had you," Cassie smiled up at him. "I'm sure they'll move on at some point. Everyone has to. There's no point focusing on the past, not when the future lies ahead of you."

"Wise words from one so young," Trip replied without thinking, making Cassie laugh.

"I'm literally the same age as you!"

Trip didn't reply, knowing that in truth, he was several decades older than her. Back where he was from, time passed at a much slower pace.

"You know, even if they are strict, I'd love to meet them one day," Cassie said.

Trip looked down at the ground as an anxious feeling began to gnaw in the pit of his stomach.

"I'm sure I can arrange that."

ONE HUNDRED SEVENTY-FOUR

Tyler left the park, acutely aware of everything she was feeling.

Her body felt heightened as if every single nerve was working overtime. The wind tickled the little hairs on her arms while the sun's rays danced across the top of her head, worming its warmth inside. Even the ground beneath her feet felt more solid somehow, yet conversely, it seemed as if it was also rising up to meet her steps.

It was an unsettling feeling that she wasn't sure she liked.

Feeling tiredness start creeping in, Tyler took out her trusty Evian bottle and swallowed several mouthfuls of its contents. In just a few seconds, the energy potion kicked in giving her a whole new lease of life — for the next few hours at least. Enough time for her to see if her new spell was working.

"Tyler? Is that you?"

She stopped, her eyes sweeping left to right, recognizing the voice yet not being able to immediately place it when the afro curls suddenly came into view, bobbing up behind a group of girls in skimpy clothing.

Si's welcoming green eyes crinkled as she spotted him coming to her.

"I thought it was you. I'd recognize the back of that cool haircut anywhere."

Ordinarily, Tyler would have welcomed bumping into Si like this but having just cast her spell, she was all geared up to see if it would work. She wasn't prepared to stop and have a conversation even if it was with a guy she liked. She felt a flush of irritation that she had to force herself to hide.

"Oh, hey," she answered then felt immediately guilty for her less than enthusiastic tone. This was the guy who had brought over all those meals for her when he had heard Ally had disappeared. He deserved more than that lame greeting. Forcing a smile on her face, she tried again. "I didn't know you'd given my hair cut much thought?" She asked, genuinely puzzled by his opening.

"It's pretty distinctive, like the girl it belongs to," he smiled.

Tyler wasn't sure what was happening right now and her face must have reflected that uncertainty as Si turned suddenly apologetic.

"Sorry, it's too soon, isn't it? I was trying to lighten the mood," he explained. He ran a hand through his curls and licked his lips. Tyler could see that he wasn't completely comfortable with what he was saying, in fact, it seemed he was making a huge effort just to be there. "There isn't really a handbook for things like this."

"Like this?" Tyler wasn't sure what he was referring to.

"Have you heard anything about Ally?" He finally asked the loaded question that was obviously on his mind.

As usual, the stab of pain was instant. Tyler flinched,

her eyes dropping to the ground. Staring at her feet, she counted slowly in her head before she could reply.

"No. They're still working on it," she managed to mumble back, hating the truth even as she said it.

"I'm so sorry. If there's anything I can do…" Si began then stopped, trailing off. "That's such a ridiculous thing to say, isn't it? There's nothing I can really do to help, but I want you to know that I'm here for you. Anything you need. I know we don't know each other that well, but, you've been kind to Eve, so I appreciate that and want you to know that if there is something I can do to help, you only have to ask."

With growing horror, Tyler realized her eyes were filling with tears. What was it about this guy that he had this effect on her? He was just being nice. Swallowing the lump that had suddenly appeared in her throat she nodded. "Thank you. I appreciate that more than you know."

He must have sensed how she was feeling as he looked away respectfully allowing her a moment to compose herself. When she was ready to move on, he spoke again.

"Are you on your way to the festival?" Si asked, gesturing at the largest of several stages before them.

A stage was being set inside a wooden shell-shaped concert venue known locally as The Hatch Shell which had hosted some of the biggest music acts in the world. It was the most popular stage and although the concert wouldn't be starting until the evening, pockets of people were already camped on the grass before it, making sure they would have the best seats for the night.

"I was actually on my way to work for a shift when I just got a message to say that it's been canceled," Tyler said without missing a beat.

Si let out a breath, his eyes brimming over with respect. "I can't believe you're going to work at a time like this. You're much more composed than I would be in your position."

Tyler hesitated, unsure how to respond. There was a nervous flutter in her stomach caused in no small part to the guilt that was starting to raise its ugly head.

She wasn't brave, far from it.

Her moral compass was so off-kilter right now yet nobody knew. Especially not Si. Here he was thinking she was some kind of hero when the truth was she may have just started something terrible that she couldn't ever take back. And she wouldn't, not if there was any chance that she could save her sister.

Not even if it meant burning the world down.

Ally was all that mattered to her. Without her, there was no world she wanted to live in.

"Well, life has to go on," she continued at a complete opposite to her thoughts. "It's not easy obviously, but I still have responsibilities to take care of and I'm going to try my best to do them even though she isn't here. It's what she would have wanted." At least this last part wasn't a lie; Ally *would* want her to carry on.

"Since you're going to the festival, we might as well head there together," Si suggested surprising her with the invitation. Aside from the one or two times she had met him, Tyler didn't know much about him, but she did know that he was nice. As it looked like her spell hadn't kicked in yet — Tyler had carefully observed everything around her while they had talked and there hadn't been any sight of a demon or magical being — it wouldn't hurt to hang out with Si.

Maybe she'd even enjoy it.

"Sure, that would be nice," she answered giving him a small smile. They started across the street until the gray of the sidewalk turned into the green grass. Feeling the softness beneath her feet, smelling the fresh smell of the grass, Tyler felt a calm come over her that she hadn't felt since maybe from the day Ally had disappeared.

Out here under the open blue sky and sunshine with the comforting aroma of hotdogs and cotton candy that drifted over from various stalls and carts that were lined up on the street, Tyler almost felt as if she wasn't living in a black hole of crushing fear.

She was determined to make the most of this moment knowing that it wouldn't last.

"Have you seen much of Eve lately?" Si asked casually. Though his tone seemed natural, there was something underlying his words that cause Tyler to look at him.

"Yes, maybe not half an hour ago, why?"

Si chewed on the corner of his lip before replying. "I just wondered if she seemed all right to you," he answered carefully. Tyler could feel herself beginning to frown, wondering what he was getting to.

"I haven't noticed anything different, she seems the same as she normally is," Tyler responded. He seemed relieved by her answer. "We had an argument a few days ago and I haven't really seen or heard from her since. It's out of character for her."

And there was that careful tone again.

He looked like he had more he wanted to say but something held him back — probably the thought that he was breaking Eve's confidence. Either way, his questions left Tyler feeling apprehensive.

"What has she been doing that's been worrying you?" she asked.

"Has she said mentioned anything about how she's been... seeing things?"

"No, that's Marley's department," Tyler replied without thinking. As soon as the words left her mouth, she snapped it shut, instantly regretting it. *That was stupid, Tyler! Stupid!*

All hope that he would have missed what she said faded with his next question.

"Marley's department? What do you mean?" His eyes were pinned on her face trying to read her every reaction.

"Never mind, I was making a bad joke. Forget I said

anything. Tell me why you're worried about Eve," Tyler asked quickly hoping that he would lay off the subject of Marley since there was no way that conversation would turn out well.

Si carried on walking, sliding his hands into his pockets looking like he had the weight of the world's problems on his shoulders. "She's just been acting strangely. She's seeing things that aren't there, maybe even creating drama. I'm not sure what to do."

"Why on earth would she do that?" Tyler asked, truly baffled at why the girl she knew would do any of these things.

Si shrugged, his shoulders moving up and down. "Attention? God knows. She went through a rough patch last year, but I thought we were through it. Now I'm wondering if something has kicked it all back up. Whatever is going on, she's sure as hell not telling me."

Tyler could feel the frustration seeping out of him.

"I haven't noticed anything but how about this, if she does anything weird or out of character, do you want me to tell you? Would that put your mind at rest?" She offered this to him before realizing that Eve might take a real issue with it but she could see how hurt Si was. Of all people, she knew how these kinds of concerns could grow. It couldn't hurt to keep him in the loop, after all, he was only concerned about his sister, the same way she was concerned about Ally.

Si shot her relieved smile. "Would you? That would be great a weight off my mind. If you're keeping an eye on her I won't have to worry so much."

Tyler tried to smile reassuringly but a finger of unease danced over her back.

Why did she feel like she was promising way more than she could handle?

ONE HUNDRED SEVENTY-FIVE

Marley grabbed Eve by the arm, pulling her to a quiet spot beneath a tree. Darting a look around them, she didn't speak until she was sure that they wouldn't be overheard.

"What do you mean you and Si *killed* him?" She whispered barely able to get the words out. Her world had been rocked so much that she had to steady herself against the tree.

Eve's eyes were a little wild around the corners. She answered in a low voice heavy with the weight of what they had done. "We had no choice."

Staring at her, her mind reeling, Marley tried to keep her voice stable. "You'd better explain everything to me."

Despite knowing that Marley was her friend, the words were still hard to form. Desperately alarmed, Marley pleaded with her.

"Eve, I can't help you unless you tell me everything, so talk... please."

Seeing how tortured she felt, Eve knew she couldn't keep it a secret any longer. Drawing in her breath she started to speak.

ONE YEAR AGO

The lights above blinked on as Eve stepped into the restroom of Shaken & Stirred wearing the pretty yellow dress with the brown trim that she'd thought Jason would love so much.

Her chest rose and fell quickly as she tried to still the sobs. Her mind went round and round in her perpetually twisted soundtrack of thoughts.

If only she wasn't so stupid. Why couldn't she just keep her big mouth shut instead of making Jason so angry that he had no recourse but to shut her up...

Eve looked warily into the mirror. The wan pinched face staring back at her couldn't be her own, yet she knew it was.

So was that vivid redness that covered her right eye.

Having only been hit moments ago, the swelling was only just starting to appear. She knew from experience that the ugly purple bruise wouldn't fully form until to-morrow, which was something at least.

For now, she could cover up the damage and hurry home. She'd be able to hide in her room for the rest of the night easily enough without Si suspecting a thing. All she'd have to say is that she was having her monthly cramps.

The excuse worked like a charm every time.

Opening up the compact containing her foundation she tried to dab the makeup onto her face, but pain exploded from even her gentlest touch causing tears to sting her eyes.

She blinked them back, determined not to give in to them. Not here, she told herself. Not here where anyone could walk in.

Where they could report back to Si.

God knows what he would do if he knew. She imagined he'd be furious with her. He'd want to know how she'd ever gotten herself into such a mess. Hadn't she seen enough Jerry Springer repeats to know better than to keep walking back into the arms of the man who kept hurting her?

But no one had told her how hard this would be.

And no one understood just how desperately she loved him: she needed him like the air she breathed. The few moments she had when they weren't together, Eve could barely function. Things she had been able to do before, normal, everyday things like grocery shopping and cooking a meal, even deciding what to wear had become impossible to do unless he was with her. She couldn't seem to make decisions anymore, always second-guessing herself. It had got to the point when she just didn't want to, preferring to leave everything up to Jason since he was always right, anyway.

She stayed in the restroom, working away at her face with an expert touch until she'd finally covered up the red with three layers of foundation. The key was to let each layer dry, then covering it with a loose powder before attempting to add the next: the powder gave the foundation something to grip onto.

When she couldn't see the mark on her face anymore, Eve headed back outside expecting Jason to have left by now; he never allowed others to see their fights. Instead, she found him knocking back another beer — his fifth by the look of it. Between swallows, he kept his head bowed, which Eve knew to be a clear sign of trouble. That and he kept glaring across the bar at her oblivious brother — the cause of their fight in the first place.

Jason was always jealous of anyone she had in her life, but since, under much pressure from him, she had done such a good job of cutting everyone out, only her brother was left. Tonight, Jason had wanted to hang out even though Eve had already warned him that they were down one member of staff so she would have to work.

He hadn't bought her excuse apparently as he'd

turned up to the bar to check on her. He was always suspicious of what she was up to when she wasn't with him, constantly imagining that she was cheating on him, which was so ludicrous as when would she have the time? Even when they slept, she sometimes woke to find him staring at her with those dark eyes, accusing her of having dreams about another man. The crunch came when he saw her smiling at a customer and flew into a rage. Waiting until she was out back to refill the bowls of chips that sat at every table, he let her know exactly what he thought of her flirty behavior.

Jason belched, wiping his mouth on the sleeve of his shirt. Finally noticing how much he'd had to drink, Si frowned in his direction and began heading his way.

Eve darted to Jason's side, knowing that she had to distract Si long enough to get Jason away: his rages were ten times worse after he'd been drinking.

"I think I'm going to have to cut you off for the night," Si began before Eve could stop him.

Jason peered up at him from the top of a mug that was almost empty. "I'm not done yet," he said softly, the calm before the storm.

"Yeah, actually, you are," Si answered, folding his arms across his chest and making his meaning known. Despite his sister's apparent infatuation for the guy, Si wasn't sure about Jason. There was something quietly disturbing about him. He seemed too together all the time, too charming. More than that, despite claiming that she was so happy, Eve seemed a shell of her usual self. She'd been jumpy lately and didn't confide in him anymore. Part of that was probably due to her telling all her secrets to Jason, although Eve had many boyfriends before she never acted this way. She'd also never dated someone for so long without Si having had much time with him.

Something stank and it wasn't the home-brew that he'd been fermenting in the basement.

Jason stared him dead in the eyes before sliding them

over to Eve. He laughed though there was no joy in the sound. "Your brother seems to think I can't hold my liquor."

"Why don't I drive you home? We can hang out and watch that movie you wanted," Eve suggested taking hold of his arm.

Jason's eyes turned flat, a clear sign of his inner rage though Eve kept her hand on his, determined to steer him out of there to avoid any trouble.

"I thought you had to work?" He taunted, though only Eve picked up on the tone. He was an expert at hiding his true feelings, something she had learned from him.

"We can handle the bar if you want to go," Si answered, hoping to give his sister a break as she looked so tense suddenly.

"Thanks," she said, dragging Jason with her. She felt a wave of relief when he got off the stool, following her outside. The night air felt humid, with a cloying damp that she could feel deep within her bones. This was the kind of weather that would turn her curls into frizz though that was the least of her concerns.

Heading to the Corolla, she unlocked the doors somewhat surprised when Jason got in without a struggle.

They took off, weaving down the quiet streets. There was a heaviness in the car though Eve wasn't sure if it was just the weather or Jason, stewing silently beside her. Driving on autopilot, Eve could almost feel the animosity pouring off of him. Gritting her teeth, she kept quiet, knowing that if she broke the ice, she'd have to deal with the fallout.

Sometimes it was better not to ask what was wrong.

Just a few more blocks, she thought to herself. She'd drop him off, then go back home. A fat drop of rain landed on the windscreen, making her jump. Realizing how ridiculous she was being, a small laugh burst out at her over-the-top reaction.

Jason's reaction was instant.

Ignoring the fact that she was driving, he flew at her, punching her in the arm so hard that her hand jerked on the wheel. The car swerved, tires screeching on the road as she struggled to straighten up through the blinding pain. The car behind them blared out its horn as it gave them a wide berth. Eve eased up on the gas and the car quickly overtook them as the driver flipped a finger at them.

"What the hell, Jason!" She yelled, her terror at their likelihood of a crash overriding her fear of his pummelling.

"You think this is funny?!" He shrieked into her ear as he hit her once again.

Her side felt like it had exploded. She gasped, tears stinging her eyes. Adrenaline pumped through her veins, the only thing likely keeping them alive right then. Seeing a spot by the curb, she slammed on the brakes, screeching to a stop.

Turning to face Jason, she started to voice her incredulity at him when his fist came flying at her face. The blow sent her reeling. She saw stars swimming before her eyes as more pain came, from everywhere it seemed.

Her shoulders, arms… her face.

Eve's fingers found the door latch and opened the door, but when she tried to jump out of the car, she found herself restrained by the seat belt.

The one thing that was supposed to save her in an emergency was going to be what ultimately killed her.

How ironic, she thought to herself when a blow came to her head so hard that she knocked it against the side of the car.

Then blessedly, all was black.

ONE HUNDRED SEVENTY-SIX

When she woke, Eve couldn't open her eyes. They felt heavy. There was a strange rocking motion like she was in a moving bed. She could smell exhaust fumes close by while the air immediately around her contained a mixture of dirt and dust.

Forcing her eyes open a crack, she saw the ceiling was only a few inches from her face. The frown that observation induced sent more pain to hit as the nerves in her face shrieked out their protests.

What the hell?

Where am I?

Moving her hands up, she pressed against the ceiling to feel cold metal against her fingertips. The truth crashed down on her like a ton of bricks.

She was in the trunk of her car!

Her heart seized in her chest as a fresh wave of panic began to form. Jason must have put her there. This was an absolute new low for him. Pushing against the roof of the trunk did nothing: it might as well have been an impenetrable brick wall.

"Jason!" She yelled out hoarsely, her throat dry from

however long she might have been unconscious for. "Let me out!"

She kicked at the side of the car knowing that he'd probably hear her but the car never faltered for a second. Wherever he was driving them, he wasn't going to stop just because she said so.

Remembering that she usually had her phone in her pocket, Eve reached down for it when she felt the flimsy fabric of the dress she wore. She cursed in disbelief. This was one of those pretty but impractical dresses that didn't have a pocket on them. If her phone was still in the car, it would be inside the main cab.

She was stuck here until Jason decided to finish whatever he was doing.

Crippling fear came over her as she wrapped her arms around herself. This was bad. Really bad. Unable to help herself, tears streamed from her eyes. Sobbing, Eve could only hope that Si would realize something was wrong and come looking for her.

Please, God… Don't let that be the last time I see my brother.

She was still praying that he would come to find her when she drifted into unconsciousness again.

When she woke again, the icy chill made her teeth chatter.

She lay on the freezing cold ground, amongst the dirt and dead branches. The full moon shone down next to its starry neighbors. If it wasn't for them, Eve would barely be able to see more than a few feet in front of her.

Ghostly stick figures created by a forest of trees stretched as far as she could see. She could hear no sound of the city. There was no traffic, or the general noise she'd expect downtown. She knew she must be far from the city, yet she had no recollection of how she had gotten there.

There was a thick fog inside her head. Something flittered at the edge of it, a warning of some kind, but she couldn't make any sense of it.

Pushing herself up, she winced. The pain was everywhere. Along her arms, in her sides, even in her face. Staring down she suddenly saw the ugly finger-shaped marks running down the length of her arms.

Fear ran down her spine, flooding her body with ice.

Getting unsteadily onto her feet, Eve knew she was in terrible danger. She had to get out of there wherever there was. She was just getting her bearings when a stick snapped behind her.

With sudden clarity, Eve knew that it was Jason.

And he meant to finish what he had started.

Terrified, she started running. Her feet hit the ground but far more slowly than she intended them to. Having been out cold for so long, her muscles hadn't woken up yet. Her movements were sluggish as if she were wading through mud. She stumbled through the trees, branches whipping against her arms, cutting them to the quick.

Footsteps thundered behind her, catching up so quickly that Eve whimpered like a distressed animal. Forcing her legs to move faster, she ran, picking up speed when something slashed at her side.

Red blossomed over her dress.

Her blood.

He had cut her with a knife.

Panic renewed, she sprinted as fast as she could, relying on pure adrenaline now. Her pulse pounded in her veins, her heart thumping like a drum. She started making headway when he flew at her, tackling her to the ground.

She landed with a thud, her face pressed into the dirt, Jason's weight lying on top of her.

"No!" She managed to cry out. "Get off me!" She

twisted and bucked, trying to force him off of her but he was twice her weight and seemingly three times as strong.

Grabbing her shoulder, he flipped her onto her back. His face loomed over her, dark and twisted with hate, but it was his eyes that terrified. Those black, empty, lifeless pits — how had she ever found them arresting? There was no soul in them, nothing but a monster left.

A monster who held her in his grasp.

"Did you think you would get away?" Jason taunted, straddling her. Madness shone from him, all vestiges of sanity seemed to have fled. Instinctively, Eve knew that the only chance she had of surviving this, was to placate him. Even as the fear threatened to choke her, Eve forced herself to speak in a soft voice.

"I wasn't trying to get away. I didn't know it was you," she began. Her body stilled, she stopped struggling against him, hoping to lull him into a false sense of security.

"Liar!" Jason roared as he backhanded her across the face. Eve's ears rang from the force of the blow. She tasted blood in her mouth.

"You were going to leave me! You think I don't know that? You think I'm stupid?" He lowered his face so close to her that she could smell the liquor on his breath.

"No… of course not! I would never leave you… I love you," she cried even as her eyes swept the area, hoping for something that would help her.

But Jason saw what she was doing. Enraged, he punched her on the chest then wrapped his hands around her neck.

Pressing down onto her windpipe, he started to squeeze.

"You are never leaving me, Eve. I'll make sure of that. No one will ever have you. You belong to me." He spat out the words, staring grimly down at her as Eve felt her lungs closing.

She slapped at him, tried to poke him in the eyes but he was ready for the move, blocking her hands with his elbows.

Her chest was on fire. She desperately needed air. The edges of her vision started turning fuzzy as black spots obscured what was left that she could see.

This was it.

She was dying.

She knew the moment was close when all the pain faded suddenly away. Closing her eyes so that she wouldn't have to see his hateful face any longer, Eve allowed herself to sink into the ground, allowing the Earth to swallow her in its last embrace.

She was losing consciousness.

In just a moment it would all end. She would never have to deal with Jason and his rage again. The thought made her lips curl until other faces came into her mind.

Her parents, their skin kissed by the Jamaican sun, who she would never see again. Then Si, her brother, who was possibly the best person in the world. She would never see any of them ever again. The thought of this brought a new crushing weight to her chest, but this was different from Jason's blows. The pressure around her neck released, and she found herself reflexively gulping in the air greedily.

Her eyes flew open wondering what miracle had happened that she was still alive.

Something warm trickled onto her chest, running down along her neck until it dripped onto the ground. Jason's prone body lay on top of her.

Realizing that he wasn't moving, Eve pushed him away when she found his body rolling off of her with ease. A shadow fell over her as a new figure blinked into her vision.

One that she recognized straight away.

"Eve…" His tortured voice called out to her. "Are you OK?"

Was that really him?

Was that Si standing above her now, looking like an angel?

"Si?" She croaked, sounding nothing like her usual self. It was the voice of an old woman, but at least she had a voice.

He reached down, pulling her up. Eve staggered to her feet, dazed and confused, her eyes flicking to Jason's still body at her feet.

Why wasn't he moving?

Trying to blink the fog away, she suddenly saw the trail of red that was soaking into the collar of his shirt. Tracing the line backward, it went up his neck all the way to his forehead — where a nasty gash now sat.

Turning to Si, she saw the crowbar he must have dropped onto the ground when he went to help her up. The end of it was darker than the rest. Something glinted in the moonlight, slick with wet.

Jason's blood.

Si's face had grown paler than she'd ever seen it. He kept flinching as his eyes ran over her, checking her injuries.

"I'm sorry it took me so long to find you. I got turned around in the woods," he muttered, hoarse with regret.

"How did you find me?" Eve managed to stutter. It was just one of many questions crowding her head.

"Your phone. I activated the 'Find My Phone' feature," he answered looking back at Jason.

"We need to call the police, tell them what he tried to do," Eve began only for Si to turn even paler.

"We can't."

His answer was quiet but firm.

"He's dead, Eve. I killed him."

ONE HUNDRED SEVENTY-SEVEN

Marley felt her breath leaving her body at Eve's revelation.

"That's what happened to Jason? But why couldn't you go to the police?"

Eve gave her an exasperated look. "They wouldn't have believed us. Even my friends hadn't believed me when I tried to tell them about the abuse. He was so good at hiding what a monster he was; everyone thought he was a rock star. No one had ever seen how cruel he could be. Who was going to side with us over Jason? Besides, they shoot Black kids in the street and in their backyards, what do you think they would have done to us if we had gone to them?"

Marley's head swam yet she heard the truth of her words even if it wasn't something she had ever experienced herself. Stereotypes for Asians were more annoyances than anything else, and in the few times she had experienced them, it was only when they thought she would be good at math (she wasn't) or that she was subservient (she wasn't that either). Eve had obviously lived a much different life than her.

"What did you do with his body?" She kept her voice as low as possible, her eyes darting around to make sure they weren't being overheard.

"We buried him in the woods. Got rid of the evidence. Cleaned out the car inside out using every chemical under the sun. His bike was still at the bar where he'd left it, but plenty of people had seen him leaving with me. When the cops came to ask when I had last seen him, I told them the truth, up until the point when he attacked me in the car. I just said that we'd exchanged words and I'd told him that I was breaking up with him. Then he got out of the car in a fit of rage and I never saw him again."

"And they believed that?" Marley asked.

Eve shrugged. "They came back and grilled me a bunch of times until Si threatened to sue them. They didn't have a case against me: everything I had said was corroborated by witnesses."

Eve's shoulders were hunched as if she were physically trying to protect herself from a blow.

"Was that his ghost?" Eve finally asked.

Marley was troubled. "I don't know. When I see a ghost I can usually feel their presence first, but I didn't feel anything when I saw him."

"But if that wasn't his ghost, what was it? I mean, he can't be back from the dead… can he?" Eve asked.

But Marley didn't have an answer for her. Eve found herself shaking as the horror of it all came rushing back. Seeing her pain, Marley went to hug her at the same time that Eve stepped forward, resulting in Marley bumping into her.

Something fell to the ground.

The envelope Eve had been keeping in her pocket.

Marley bent down to retrieve it before Eve could snatch it out of her hands. "Sorry, you dropped this…" she started but stopped when she took in the name written on the envelope. "What is this?"

Eve looked instantly stricken. Her expression became apologetic as she stammered, reaching for a response.

"It's yours," was all she managed.

"I can see that, but why do you have it?" Marley asked.

Knowing that there wasn't going to be an easy way for her to explain herself, Eve jumped right in. "Turn it over," she said.

Having no idea what this was about, Marley turned it over but when she saw the name written on the back on the envelope, her eyes went wide.

"Lisa Gray," she stammered. "But… that's my mom. Why do you have a letter addressed to me that's written by my mom?"

"I know this is going to sound crazy, but before you even told me about your Dad hiding things from you, I learned something of my own," she started, segueing quickly into how she had gone from finding the symbol in the painting to breaking into his apartment, at which point, Marley held up her hand.

"Are you kidding me? You broke into my dad's apartment?" Her voice had grown louder than she'd intended and several passersby who had overheard their conversation turned to study them with interest. Regaining her composure, Marley lowered her voice to a whisper. "That's insane Eve! I can't believe you did that!"

"Well, apparently I had good reason to. Haven't you always said that your mom left and hasn't been in touch with you since?" Eve asked, desperate to get her side across before their friendship was irreparably broken. "Then why is there a letter addressed to you in his apartment? Look at the date, Marley, that's only a few weeks ago. That letter came for you in Boston, but you've been here less than two months yourself, which means your dad is in regular contact with her."

Marley felt the world spinning. Though she didn't

want to face the fact that her dad would lie about something this big, the truth was sitting in her hands.

"But why? Why would he lie to me?" Her voice sounded small even to her ears.

"I can't answer that, but maybe your mom can," Eve suggested, staring pointedly at the envelope she held.

Before she could second guess herself Marley tore the envelope open. Inside, was a single sheet of paper. The handwriting was neat and flowery. As Marley raised the note to her face, she caught the scent of sandalwood coming off the paper. It had been her mom's favorite scent. She knew it well as her dad still wore the sandalwood bracelet she had given to him when they had first started dating.

Steeling herself, she started to read:

My dearest, Marley,
I hear you are starting college soon, in just a few weeks. I am so thrilled to hear that, yet also filled with such bitterness that I can't be there to see you off.
I always wondered what you would grow up to be. It seems fitting that the curious little girl I knew would strive to become a journalist. You always loved people, loved hearing their stories. I'm glad that hasn't changed.
To think that my little girl is eighteen years old already…
I have missed so much of your life, though I guess that can't be helped. I just hope that one day you will understand.
Don't blame your father. Everything he has done was to protect you.
I'll write again soon.
My love as always,
Mom

Marley felt like her brain was going to explode. Why was Lisa writing to her? Why was she acting as if she always wrote to her, especially when she had been absent from her life for over thirteen years now? How did she know so much about her, and why did it seem as if her dad was in contact with her.

"What does it say?" Eve asked.

But Marley couldn't tell her.

She couldn't deal with any of this. Not the letter, not the questions in her mind, and certainly not Eve. "I can't!" She blurted out as she ran away, desperately looking for answers that she knew would not come.

ONE HUNDRED SEVENTY-EIGHT

Sweaty soaks and steam punctuated the air of the boy's locker room as Saunders wandered inside. She had checked with their coach first, but it was he who suggested that she'd catch them all if she just went into the changing room. She had been quite happy to wait for them until they were done after their practice.

She wasn't sure if he was trying to intimidate her or not, but it was no skin off her nose if she found herself in a room with half-naked footballers, though they were far too young for her taste, so young that anyone of them could have been her kid.

As Saunders strolled inside, several of the boys cat-called to her, but all of the joviality stopped when she flashed her badge at them.

Apparently, her credentials were like an anti-Viagra.

She could see the boys deflating one by one. There was something about a woman in charge that often messed with testosterone filled men. It was as if her own status and power had them quaking which suited her just fine.

"Hello gentleman, now that I seem to have your attention, have any of you seen Trip Rockwell?"

She'd been able to find all the other players on her list but him and this had seemed the most likely place to look.

A player whose chest gleamed from having just stepped out of the shower spoke up, the only thing keeping his nudity in check was the tiny towel wrapped around his waist. "He wasn't at practice today. Hasn't been to practice for the last week or so."

Saunders tilted her head at him. "Why? Is he sick?"

The player shook his head. "No man… sorry, ma'am," he corrected himself before continuing. "He's been preoccupied, ever since he started dating that new girl."

A spark of interest grew in Saunders' chest but she kept it off her face, staying neutral. "What's her name?"

He frowned, trying to see her face in his mind. "Don't know her name, but she's a redhead. Not your type of red," he inclined at Saunders' own mane. "Hers is more ginger. She's not bad looking but she's nothing like his regular type so she must be really great in the sack."

A round of laughter came out of the guys until Saunders' baleful stare had them quieting again. Hearing the description of Trip's new girlfriend made her think. On a hunch, she took out her phone, scrolling through until she found a picture of the four girl's she had taken at the burning diner, when they hadn't been looking. They were huddled around Jones, trying to comfort their friend whose sister had just been taken.

She held her phone up, showing it to him. "Is she any of these girls?"

He looked over the picture then nodded, pointing at Cassie Cuthbert. "Yeah, that's her. Find her, and you'll find him."

Thanks, Saunders thought to herself.

I will do just that.

Faces blurred into one as Marley pushed past them. After the bombshell Eve had just laid — both of them — Marley knew she shouldn't have left her, especially if Jason, or something masquerading as him, was back, but she couldn't face her. She couldn't face anyone.

Her entire world as she had known it was shattered. Everything she knew, that she had counted on was a lie.

Why would her dad lie to her about her mom?

As far as Marley knew, Lisa had left and never looked back. Those initial dark days returned to her now as she thought back to how, as a five-year-old, she had clung to her panda bear, sobbing into its ear until it was soaked with her tears. She had cried rivers of tears for weeks after, wailing for Mommy to come home.

Her dad had been there for every moment of it, hugging her, soothing her pains away. His loving, caring face flashed into her mind.

Those first few nights after Lisa had gone had been the toughest. Marley had made herself physically sick from her despair, so how could her dad have kept her mom from her? Why would he do such a thing?

It just didn't make any sense

Feeling a sob rise in her throat, Marley pushed on blindly, no real destination in mind when a familiar face caught her eye in the crowd.

One whose sexy smile was always a welcoming distraction.

Seeing her, Rhett waved, though his eyes soon crinkled with concern, picking up on her distress. He was with a group of people — friends — though he said something to them, then crossed the distance between them in a few long strides.

"Hey," he asked, his tone uber gentle. "What's the matter?"

To her horror, Marley felt the first tears escape from her eyes. She hated crying in front of people, hated how it made her seem weak, though Rhett only seemed concerned at whatever was troubling her.

"I just got some news that's shocked me," she replied, unsure just how much she could go into right now.

Her shoulders trembled, revealing just what a toll this was having on her. Without thinking, Rhett reached out and enveloped her in his arms. He felt warm and strong, capable of protecting her against the world. Comforted by his strength, she sank into his embrace, closing her eyes, and for just a moment, things didn't feel quite as terrible.

When she opened her eyes again, it was to see Christian's stricken face looking back at her.

She tensed immediately, jerking away from Rhett.

Although she knew she hadn't done anything wrong, it felt as if she had been caught cheating on Christian — which was ridiculous.

"What's wrong," Rhett asked, startled by her pulling away from him so abruptly.

"Sorry. I've just seen someone I need to talk to," she replied knowing immediately that this was true. Looking back at Rhett, she shot him a smile full of apology as she headed to Christian who had turned away from her and was now walking as fast as he could in the opposite direction.

She hurried after him, reaching him fast before he could disappear. "Christian," she called out.

Hearing his name, he froze but didn't turn. His body was tense as if preparing for bad news. Marley reached out to touch him before remembering that it wouldn't be possible. She moved around to face him only to be immediately struck by how stricken he looked.

Her stomach churned knowing that she was the cause of his turmoil. Without knowing why she blurted out the first thing on her mind. "It's not what it looks like."

Christian stared down at her, those green-gold eyes of

his burning with their contempt. "You don't have to explain yourself to me," he began, his tone cutting. "You're a free agent after all."

Something about his answer annoyed her. "Then why do you seem so upset?"

"I'm just wondering how you seem to be doing everything but searching for the seals," he retorted.

Confused by her own emotions, his reaction only made her feel more unsettled. "I actually haven't had much of a chance to look. Things have been crazy this morning."

"Last night too, I'll bet," he said earning a frown from Marley.

"What do you mean?" she asked, but whatever response she might have expected from him, it wasn't the explosive gasp that suddenly burst out of him.

"It's always the same with you, isn't it? You have no time to care about the things that you should be caring about because you're always too busy being with Rhett or having dinner with your dad. The fact that the fate of the world lies in your hands means nothing to you!"

Marley reeled back at the anger in his voice, stunned by his reaction. "That's not fair, of course, I care! Haven't you seen how hard I've been trying?"

"No! All I see is you going out on dates, not giving a damn that you made me like this! You killed me so now I can't do anything but stand and watch from the sidelines!" Christian was waving his arms around now, not caring how he was coming across.

"You know that was an accident, Christian! How many more times are you going to throw that in my face?" The flames of anger were beginning to rise in her now. There was no way Christian was going to talk to her like this, not when she hadn't done anything wrong.

"Until you stop being such a selfish brat!" He yelled, unable to contain everything he was feeling. Deep down, Christian knew he should stop, that he was going too far, but he couldn't stop himself. The sight of Marley in Rhett's arms had filled him with a rage so great, that he wanted to tear them apart. Unable to physically do that, he was left with only his words.

And he intended on her hearing every one of them.

"You don't care about anyone else but yourself. Just how many more people around you have to die before you start taking your responsibilities seriously?"

Before Marley could respond, Christian blinked away.

ONE HUNDRED SEVENTY-NINE

It took everything Eve had not to run back home to hide in her room.

She could still see the shock on Marley's face though even worse than that was the terrible revelation that Paul had been lying to her for her entire life. She had watched Marley's face crumble the moment the truth had sank in. Though she didn't regret Marley learning about the letter, she felt awful with the manner in which she had found out.

Eve should have sat her down, prepared her for that earth-shattering moment; instead, she had been focused on her own issues. After Marley had listened to her own horror story so compassionately, her own heart was broken now and Eve was to blame.

There was a place reserved in hell for people like her.

She clutched the thin hoodie she wore, zipping it closed. Though the sun bore down merrily, Eve couldn't feel its warmth today. There was a chill in the air, a coldness in her bones that made her want to retreat into the safety of her bed. Even more than the cold, however, was the growing fear that had begun to seep in.

A whole year had passed without Eve ever telling anyone the truth about Jason, yet now Marley knew. Would she use it against her? Would she be so upset at what Eve had done that she would turn against her? Eve cupped her numb hands together in an attempt to warm her frozen fingers.

As always, whenever the topic of Jason was raised, Eve's concern wasn't for her own safety but Si's. Her brother had been dragged into this sorry mess because of her failings, but she would die before he would suffer anymore.

Seeing a refreshment area in front of her, Eve started for it when a quartet of girls came into view, lounging on the grass in their short short skirts and revealing tops.

Of course, Eve thought to herself. It had to be The Meantastic Four.

If she had been paying any attention to her where-abouts, Eve would have realized that the girls would be here, after all, this was where their favorite band was due to play. Eve had seen it in the line-up but hadn't paid it enough attention, her mind having been so focused on when to reveal the letter to Marley.

She could continue past, knowing that they would see her and spout whatever spitefulness that they would in-evitably say, or she could use her magic again to move them off.

After all, it had worked pretty well the last time.

She could still hear their delightful screams in her head.

Despite the thoughts racing through her mind Eve knew they were just that — she didn't have the strength to face them today. Knowing this, she felt a swirl of shame that made her bow her head.

With a single command, she could do such damage to those bitches, though it still wouldn't be a match against what they had done to her. They had never cared about her, so their bruises would fade. While Eve's... hers stayed with her, choosing to rise up again and again, seemingly always when she was least prepared.

No. Though she could have died from the shame alone, Eve spun around hurrying back in the direction she had come from when she ran smack into a solid wall of muscle.

"Sorry," she said reflexively to the pumped chest in the leather jacket when she froze.

A tiny gold motorbike hung off the chain around the guy's neck but Eve didn't need to examine it to know that it would have the initials JS engraved on it; she had played with this necklace in her fingers many a time, back when she had lain in its owner's arms.

Back before she had known what a monster Jason would be.

Blood raced through her veins as her heart pounded. She couldn't breathe, afraid that if she did, he would notice her, that he would become real.

This was a dream she knew. It had to be a nightmare or a vision, maybe even a spell. One of Michael's tricks to unnerve her. Jason could not be here. He was not real.

Then Jason grabbed her on either side of her hips.

His fingers burned like fire though Eve didn't know if it was just her nerves shrieking at his familiar touch.

They were real.

Very real.

Desperately afraid yet needing to see it for her own eyes, Eve slid her gaze upward until it settled on those features that she knew only too well.

Jason's cold eyes pinned her in place. He looked much as he had when she had last seen him: his bronzed skin spoke of long days tanning under the sun and not the year-long grave that Eve knew he had lain in. Only the tops of the black veins that she could see peeking out from his shirt showed something unnatural about it.

In short, he was looking pretty good for a dead guy.

He smiled, a gruesome movement to his lips as he

held her in place. Lowering his head closer until Eve could smell the death on him, he spoke.

"Bet you thought you'd never see me again?"

His voice sent shivers down her spine. Though it sounded like him, there was a wrongness with it, like all of the life had gone. Eve tried to tear herself away but it was as if her feet had grown roots.

She couldn't move away from him no matter how desperately she wanted to. Seeming to know this about her, Jason's smile grew wider, stretching the skin on his face with a bizarre slackness.

"Don't worry. I won't be going away this time. I'm going to finish what I came back for." The threat was low, but she caught it clearly.

Terror made her react the only way she knew how.

She felt the rushing of her *others* as they scurried from beneath, faster than she knew it was even possible for them to move. A rat burst out of a nearby drain, racing toward her — toward him. The rodent threw itself up into the air and landed on Jason mid-calf. The creature opened its mouth and sank its teeth into his leg.

Jason barely reacted, apparently not feeling a thing.

Eve watched with growing horror as a black spot blossomed in the leg of Jason's jeans caused by the rat's bite — it was blood but contained none of its usual redness.

Jason's blood was black.

As black as his heart.

More of the rats spilled out of the drain, converging through the panicked crowd's stampeding feet as they sprinted to get away from the horde.

It seemed as if there were hundreds of them, all throwing themselves at Jason, but he only acted as if they were an annoyance, flinging and kicking away as many as he could, but within moments, he was overwhelmed.

His hands finally left Eve's body to swat at the rats.

Free at last, Eve bolted away as fast as her terrified legs could carry her.

ONE HUNDRED EIGHTY

Tyler's head throbbed.

She didn't know if it was the spell she had cast or Si's general chatter which she would normally have enjoyed, but her head ached with a pain that no amount of pills or her energy potion could dull. It got to the point where she wondered if she should make an excuse to search on her own, but she already knew how well that idea would go down.

Si, ever the gentleman, would need more than her thin excuses to leave her alone. He seemed determined to look after her which somewhere in the back of her mind, she found touching.

And it wasn't like his company wasn't easy to like.

He didn't ask stupid questions or pretend to know things that he didn't. He actually made her feel like she mattered, and that was enough to want to stay around him.

"Tyler?" He asked, staring at her with a mildly confused expression as he waited for an answer to a question that she had obviously not heard.

"I'm sorry. I think I checked out for a second," she replied.

He smiled in that easy going way of his. "No problem. It wasn't anything important anyway, I was just wondering if you were hungry. There's a pretzel van over there that's calling my name," he gestured a few feet away from them.

Now that he had mentioned it, Tyler felt a pang in her stomach and couldn't remember when she had last eaten. Was it at the IHOP? With a start, Tyler realized that an entire day might have gone past without her eating anything.

The sweet smell of sugar and cinnamon drifted over making her mouth water. "I'd love one of the sweet ones, actually," she said, sliding her hand into her pocket to fish out her money.

"Don't worry about it," Si said, already heading toward the van. Tyler felt herself relax, enjoying the moment of being looked after. Rolling her neck, she slid her eyes across the crowd, taking in the general ambiance when one of the figures across from her glowed with a magical neon light.

It was as if she were seeing him through thermal glasses: while everyone else was a dull red, the burst of bright neon yellow was impossible to miss.

Tyler knew instantly that it was the spell at work.

Here was her first supernatural!

Any thought of food went immediately out of her mind — as did Si — as she hurried after the person, a man who looked to be in his forties. From where she was, she couldn't see what made him a supernatural: he looked like a normal man. If it wasn't for the spell, she wouldn't have known he was any different.

Which, in her mind, only went to show how right she had been to cast it.

The man who had a middle-Eastern look about him moved through the crowd, ignoring all the sights and sounds around him which only begged the question: if he wasn't here for the festivities, why was he here at all?

Tyler felt a tingle in her bones. She knew, just knew that the guy was up to no good, and if that was the case, she was pretty sure that he would be able to lead her to Ally, after all, demons were nearly always bad weren't they? Esteban, their "friend" at Furnace had proven to be their only demon ally to date, and even then, Tyler wasn't sure how much she would really trust him.

She followed the man, keeping back so that he wouldn't notice her when he suddenly stopped dead. Not knowing what to do, Tyler also stopped.

Which was a big mistake.

The guy took off at a sprint, having somehow sensed her behind him. Tyler didn't hesitate, taking off after him. Running as fast as she could, determined that she wasn't going to lose him like she had lost Pike at that cock-fighting match, Tyler forced herself into high gear. Shoving past startled people, she apologized with breathless sorries but carried on regardless of who she pushed out of the way.

The sea of people was relentless. It didn't matter where he went, he was slowed down by the sheer number of them until he swerved suddenly into a small alley.

Tyler sprinted in behind him only for the man to whirl around.

"Why are you following me, Witch?" He snarled.

If Tyler was startled that he knew what she was, she didn't show it. Play it cool, she told herself, trying to still her racing heart. "I'm looking for someone and I think you might know where he is."

"And why would you think that?" He asked, his voice a low rumble.

"You're some sort of demon aren't you? I know you must know where others like you hang around. I need information and I'm not letting you go until you help me,"

Tyler responded, surprising herself with the force of her conviction.

The man's eyebrows rose an inch. A vivid scar crisscrossed his check at an angle while a pencil-thin mustache covered his upper lip. Tyler took in his general appearance and noticed that he was quite the dandy. His tailored pants went in at the ankles, crocodile skin shoes adorned his feet. There was even a flower pinned to his shirt.

For a demon, he was seriously cool.

He was also seriously pissed at her.

"My, what a little racist we have here." His eyes narrowed into slits as he spat the words at her.

Tyler blinked at him, not understanding his meaning.

"You don't think so?" He taunted, opening his hands wide so that she could see all of him. "You just tarred me with the same brush as the lowliest of the supernatural race and purely because of what? How I look?"

"I'm not actually interested in what you are, only what you know. Do you know where Michael is? Or any of his demon thugs? Tell me what you know!" Tyler demanded, moving closer to him.

"Listen, this was cute at first. Actually, it never was. I suggest you turn away and leave before something happens that you're going to regret," he warned.

But Tyler wasn't scared of him. Pumped up with her potion and the spell, driven by her need to save her sister above all else, she knew she could match anything he threw at her.

"I make it a point never to regret anything," she answered back.

"Fine," he said. "But don't say I didn't warn you."

Quicker than a flash, a ball of energy materialized in his hands which he hurled toward her. Having known something was coming, Tyler dodged easily out of its way. It flew harmlessly past but then a cry of pain sounded behind her.

"Dammit!" She heard the man curse as she spun around to see what had happened.

A guy lay face down on the ground having been hit by the energy ball. He didn't move, obviously hurt badly when Tyler suddenly noticed the two pretzels lying on the tarmac by his hand.

One of them was covered with sugar and cinnamon — just as she had requested.

"Si?" She gasped his name exactly as two things happened.

The demon bolted down the alley, running away as Eve rounded the corner, her phone in her hand. Seeing her brother on the ground, she rushed toward him.

"Si! Are you OK?" She turned him over, but he was out for the count. Scratches covered his face where he had scraped it in the fall. She pressed her face to his chest to check that he was breathing. When she heard his heart-beat and saw the rise and fall of his chest, she felt her initial terror dial down to a dealable amount.

"What happened?" She screamed at Tyler only to hear no answer from her. Looking up, she saw that Tyler wasn't even looking her way — her gaze very much on the guy who was disappearing down the alley.

Tyler's head throbbed wickedly. Dimly, in the back of her mind, she knew that she should be more concerned for Si who had been hurt because of her, but the thought seemed very far away. Mostly, she could only think about the demon or whatever he was, who would get away if she didn't chase after him.

Making her decision, she took off after the guy to Eve's utter shock.

"Tyler!" She yelled after her, but she was already halfway down the alley. Unable to believe that she would leave them like this, that she would show so little concern for her brother, Eve cradled his head into her lap as she prayed for him to wake up.

"Si…. Can you hear me? Please, Si… you need to wake up now…"

Moments passed as the world froze for Eve. When there was still no response from Si, she unlocked her phone, started to dial emergency services when Tyler arrived back.

"What the hell, Tyler! How could you leave us like that?" She screamed.

Tyler stared down at Si with a strange expression. She seemed out of it, almost as if she wasn't concerned.

"I had to go after him. He might know where Ally is," came her wooden response.

"So you just left Si like that? How could you of all people not help him!" Eve cried, demanding an answer. She had to know what could have possessed Tyler to behave like that.

Instead of the regret or apology she was expecting, however, Tyler's face turned hard. "I told you. I had to go after him. It was more important."

"More important than my brother?" Eve yelled, unable to take Tyler's responses anymore. All the hurt and terror that she had felt converged into one mass of emotion. Bubbling over with anger, Eve felt her army of rats materialise again. Coming out from behind boxes and trash, they went for Tyler, not able to distinguish Eve's pain from her fear.

But Tyler wasn't going to let herself be hurt.

Summoning her own magic, she rocked the ground as the pipes attached to the buildings on either side grew so hot that they burst, raining scalding hot water onto the rats who squealed in terror.

Stopping their attack on Tyler, they ran blindly, desperate to escape the boiling water that burnt their little bodies but there was no shelter for them, no place they could escape.

Within moments, the ground was littered by the bodies of the rats.

The water only stopped coming out of the pipes as Tyler regained control of her emotions.

"What have you done?" Eve cried.

Light spilled in through the glass doors leading to the terrace that Michael liked to keep open.

He appreciated the crisp air that drifted through the apartment, particularly as it helped to mask some of the child's awful scent which had been intensifying of late. Like an overripe fruit on the verge of becoming rotten, the girl reeked of nastiness.

He stared at her in the cage which he had placed under direct sunlight since so many creatures of this world seemed to rely on it for their health. The floor of the cage was cluttered now, filled with toys that Pike had gotten for her on his order, but she wasn't playing with them.

She never played with them even though they were provided as a form of comfort for her.

His eyes skimmed over the plastic keys on a giant ring that lay untouched by her feet, still in its original plastic wrapping. Two toy trucks and an electronic reading device that made noises were piled messily next to numerous silver platters of food. There was a lobster still in its shell though the bright red color that it had first arrived with had dulled some. A stack of meat that was one of the hotel's most highly praised dishes that came with its own little white paper socks on its bones attracted nothing but flies.

There were other dishes too, numerous specialties that Michael had ordered in an effort to get her to eat, but the girl refused to touch any of them, choosing instead to either lie blankly, staring at the ceiling or rocking herself to sleep.

Why was feeding a child so difficult?

She looked frail, her skin seemed an odd color: he could swear that with every passing day she was growing more pale. Frankly it was lucky that he didn't need her for too much longer since it looked like she wouldn't last anyway.

Michael's shoes barely made a sound over the deep cream carpet as he approached his room. He needed to get ready for the night's big event. Everything had to be perfect. From the clothes to the way he smelled. He had spent the last few weeks researching his prey, setting the trap.

Tonight, she would walk straight into it.

Thinking of it all, a surge of excitement rushed up that was only dented by the look he caught the child giving him. His throat went dry as Michael felt that strange sensation whenever she looked at him with that particular expression on her face.

Her eyes seemed impossibly round and were bright with unshed tears. Her lips quivered but she would say nothing. She would only stare at him with that face making him so uncomfortable that he felt the need to give her things in an effort to stop her looking at him like that.

Clearing his throat, Michael spoke. "Do you need more toys?"

"No," Ally's voice came back, weak yet forceful at the same time. "I need my sister!"

For some reason that he couldn't fathom her words made him flinch. Her voice seemed much louder than someone of her size should be able to make. Understanding that she needed reassurance, Michael answered, "Don't worry. If everything goes to plan, you'll be seeing her soon."

It was the truth which the girl must have sensed as she seemed suddenly relieved. Turning away from him, she rolled onto her side, curling into a tight ball with her back to him.

Michael breathed out a sigh. Now that he couldn't see

her face with *that* expression, the uncomfortable weight he had felt in his chest was lifting.

Entering his room, he made a beeline for his walk-in closet, which, a few days ago had consisted of only a few things including the clothes he had picked up the jock in. Now the rails were filled with the best the hotel had to offer. There were suits that only came in dark hues, sweaters, shirts, and pants for casual wear. There was even a section of nautical outfits should Michael wish to look like a sailor. As money was of no consequence, he had purchased one of everything the hotel's concierge had recommended for him.

As a result, he knew he would look the part of the perfect boyfriend that night.

Turning on the shower, Michael started undressing as he thought back to the day's progress. He and Cassie had spent hours searching for the next seal though of course, it had been a fruitless task as he had made up the "clues" that Cassie had pieced together. The entire day had been a ploy to separate the girls, to keep them busy while he began his plan in earnest, and Cassie had taken the bait, hook, link, and sinker.

Everything was going exactly as it should.

Pushed to the limit, Tyler was beginning to lose her wits while Cassie was falling deeper for "Trip." He was convinced that she would tip over the edge tonight after he had met and charmed both of her parents. His Jason-sized surprise was sure to take care of Eve. And Marley… her turn was coming soon enough.

All of his preparations were finally coming together. Everything was on time for *His* arrival, which was just as it needed to be. This had all been a very long time in coming.

A very long time…

ONE HUNDRED EIGHTY-ONE

MASSACHUSETTS BAY COLONY, 1693

Mary stared down at the drawing, at the face which she had loved so much only to have been crushed when he had left their coven.

Though it had been two years ago, Mary could remember it as if it were yesterday. After she had welcomed him into their coven, trained and then fell in love with him, Ezekiel had fallen for another.

Putting a brave face on her own heartbreak, Mary had smiled at him, wishing he and his new love all the happiness in the world. She'd had to watch him walking away to begin his new life through her own tears.

For months afterward, she had tortured herself with the thought that had she been brave enough to reveal her true feelings for him, their story might have had a different ending.

Time had erased her pain, to the point where Mary barely thought of him but for a passing moment, so to see his face again — and in this capacity — was an enormous shock.

"Why is Ezekiel in charge of this council?" Asked Esther, her eyes dark and troubled.

"Why would he go after his own?" Catherine echoed all their confusion.

"I do not know, but we must find him if we are to learn the truth," Mary said softly.

It was a simple case to locate his home. They were able to perform a location spell which had led them to the grand estate they now stood outside. It seemed Ezekiel did not bother to conceal himself, so sure was he, that he would not be discovered.

The mansion was larger than any they had seen before. Fit for a Lord, it stood three floors high with towers that curved to the sky on each of its four corners. Rose bushes and flower beds filled with exotically colorful blooms brightened the entrance though many of the flowers were magically enhanced to look the way they did.

Tabitha shuddered at how unnatural that was. It was an unholy waste of the Earth's magic to use it in such a superficial way that she found herself wondering how Ezekiel could have forgotten his training so fast.

Mary was also troubled by what she could see. How could Ezekiel — who had been a penniless beggar when she had found him — amass such wealth in only two years?

Approaching the double height front doors, Mary lifted the heavy brass knocker intending to knock when Tabitha stopped her.

"Wait," she warned. "Something is not right."

Carefully, Mary released her hold on the knocker. "What do you sense?"

Tabitha stared at the door, seeing the flickering cloud of black around the edges of the door. "The door has been enchanted. We cannot enter from here. Follow me."

Turning, she led the way to the back of the building where she came upon a locked cellar door. Touching the lock with her hand, she muttered a word, and the handle fell away with a clang as the door swung inward.

The four descended the six or so stairs into the dark cellar. Aged wine barrels were organized neatly while various sized wheels of cheese lined the shelves that covered the walls. Spices hung from the ceiling, drying in the coolness, but among the commonly used thyme and basil, Mary could see wreaths of the deadly nightshade Belladonna which had no use being near edible herbs as its only use was as a poison.

"Careful of the belladonna," she warned, knowing that every part of the plant was poisonous and could even harm them if they only touched it.

Moving through the room, they headed to the stairs when Mary was floored by a sense of evil so great that she gasped. Her sisters felt it too she knew as they each stopped in the same spot — beside a tall bookshelf that was filled with hams in the process of being cured.

The evil seeped out from behind the bookshelf.

Gesturing to the right with her hand, the bookshelf slid magically aside revealing a hidden room beyond.

The walls and ceiling were draped in a silken black fabric that met at an altar in the back of the room. In front of the altar remnants of blood crusted the edges of a bronze bowl. Beside it lay a collection of horrors. Mary caught a glimpse of chicken heads that seemed as if they had been torn from their bodies; their eyes still reflected the stark terror of their last moments.

She saw the innards of an animal that she couldn't name, even what looked to be a human finger. Marly shuddered as an icy chill bloomed from inside.

"These are all used in the Dark Arts," Catherine cried, the truth sinking like a heavy stone.

"Is this what he has become?" Esther asked to silence. No one wanted to believe the truth even though it was staring them in their faces.

"But he wouldn't, would he?" Tabitha said. "Not when he knows the cost of this."

A movement came from within the black silks, startling them, making Catherine yelp in fright. A chain rattled as it dragged across the stone floor. Esther moved some of the billowing fabric aside to find a straw mat on the ground upon which a black man lay. A thick steel chain was tied around his ankle, securing him to the wall. What little clothing he had was lashed to shreds. Red welts covered his back. His bare feet seeped with infections from the many cuts he had sustained.

It was clear he was a slave that was being kept here against his will.

Catherine lowered onto her knees, feeling his clammy head as he lay, mumbling feverishly. "He is in a bad way. I do not know if he can be saved."

Esther knelt down beside her. "Let us try together," she answered, her mouth set into a tight line.

Whatever Mary wanted to say was stopped by a loud crash behind them.

The Four looked around to see the man they had loved as a brother — and maybe even more in Mary's case — standing behind them, fury seeping from his eyes. The bookshelf that had concealed the room lay behind him, knocked to its side, blocking the only way out.

"Ezekiel," Mary gasped as his eyes found hers. What she saw there only made her fear intensify. Devoid of any warmth, Ezekiel glared at her with all the hate in the world.

"You dare come into my house!" He roared as magic cackled between his fingertips. Mary gaped at it, not having seen this kind of magic before — it certainly wasn't of the sort that they had taught him.

This magic took from life with nothing to give back in return.

"Why are you doing this?" Mary managed to ask as she planted herself in front of her sisters.

"You wouldn't understand," he spat, advancing. "You have never loved another with the kind of all encompassing love, one that hurts your heart and causes sleepless nights. You do not know what it is that I must do to keep that love alive."

There was madness in his eyes now, the kind of madness that came from obsession. She stole a look at Catherine and Esther still kneeling behind her, trying desperately to help the slave.

"I do understand. I have loved another. I know what it is to want them with all my heart," Mary confessed, thinking perhaps that a personal approach would make him calm. Ezekiel's only response was the sneer that now graced his lips.

"You do not know what I speak of. You never did. All this power we had, and the four of you wasted it away on peasants! Do you see what I have achieved without you?" He gestured at the house, his cellar full to the brim with goods.

"Yes," Mary responded quietly. "Only too well." Her tone had none of the awe that Ezekiel craved and in fact only revealed her regret. "If this is how you have used your magic, I wished to the heavens that we had never trained you in the arts."

A laugh came out of Ezekiel even as his eyes hardened. "You think you taught me what I know. Do not flatter yourself, *Sister*. You could only hope of being as powerful as I am. In fact, let me show you what I mean."

With a simple gesture, a barrel flew towards them. Tabitha cried out, gesturing stop with her hand just in time. The barrel exploded as if it had hit an invisible wall, raining red wine over them. The wood barely had time to land onto the stone floor before another barrel hurtled toward them, followed by several more. Each met with the same fate which only incensed Ezekiel all the more.

Screaming incomprehensibly at them, his casting grew out of control as the barrels were now joined by heavy wheels of cheese and whatever else was in the room. The air was an explosion of produce and as Ezekiel threw everything he could at them.

The onslaught was such that Mary and Tabitha had to back away. Tossing a look over her shoulder, Mary was relieved to see the slave beginning to open his eyes: Catherine and Esther were successful in bringing him back to consciousness. Her sisters broke his shackles then rose, ready to join in the fight. With the four against him, Ezekiel could not hope to win this battle.

And he must have known this as he cast a different spell.

Suddenly, the slave charged at Catherine knocking her clear across the room where her body rag-dolled limply in the air before she came crashing down onto the hard floor. Before Esther could react, he went for her, sending her flying onto the altar where she landed awkwardly at an angle.

Tabitha screamed as a wall of brick shot up from the floor, protecting them from being further attacked as Mary focused on knocking him out with a spell, but whatever Ezekiel had done to him, was stronger than Mary's own skill: he was being controlled by Ezekiel and she couldn't stop it.

She suddenly noticed that she had a clear line of sight to Ezekiel, however, who had left himself vulnerable while he compelled the slave to attack. There was a metal rake that hung from a rack of gardening utensils which Mary could impale Ezekiel with. With a simple thought and a word, she could end his life. End this completely.

But looking at his face, at the man she still loved even though it seemed he may have lost his soul, Mary could not do it. She hesitated…

As if he could sense this, Ezekiel turned his gaze to her.

Suddenly the slave changed directions. Instead of running to her as she had thought he would, he barreled toward Ezekiel whose hand flew out, grabbing him by the neck. Uttering words in an archaic tongue that Mary did not understand yet whose meaning she understood, Ezekiel drained the life from the slave, taking in his life-force to become more powerful.

Stunned that he would sacrifice a person like this, Mary froze.

And the world suddenly exploded in a cloud of dust.

Bricks and oak beams fell down over them, too many for Mary to protect them from. She tried casting a protection spell when something struck her on the back of the head. She fell onto her knees, seeing stars amongst the cloud of dust that had appeared in the debris.

Ezekiel had brought the house down on top of them.

When the cloud finally faded away enough for her to see, Mary saw the bodies of her sisters lying broken on the ground.

ONE HUNDRED EIGHTY-TWO

With a dab of pale pink gloss, Cassie was done.

She studied herself critically in the mirror, knowing just how important it was to be looking her best tonight.

Although her closet was filled with designer outfits, many of which had been passed down to her from her mom, Cassie had chosen a pretty olive green A-line dress from a little boutique store downtown. It wasn't somewhere her mom would ever dream of visiting but Cassie loved nearly everything in there: it was classy yet had its own individual taste, something which she would like to think about herself. She loved the way the dress emphasized the redness in her hair and made the most of her milky white skin.

To finish her look, Cassie took out the shoes that had still sat in the box that they had arrived in. She took in the peep toes shoes with the pretty fabric flower on the end as a warmth spread all over her. For the first time in her life, Cassie finally felt ready to wear them. She was ready to carry on the family tradition that had first started with her Grandma.

Her mind went back to all those times when she was a child, sitting on the floor by her Grandma's feet as her hands busily knitted whatever project she was currently working on. Cassie loved to hear the stories her Grandma would tell her, though none were more special than that of the special shoes that she had worn on her first date with the young man who came courting, who would later become her beloved husband. The shoes were worn again at her wedding, then passed on to Angie when she came of age when she had continued on with the tradition wearing them on the most special occasions in her life.

Now, Cassie would be wearing them today.

Slipping them on, she marveled at how they finished off her outfit. Filled with excitement over the night ahead, Cassie twirled, admiring herself in the mirror when her phone beeped with a text.

Trip was outside already, waiting for her with his driver and the car. Beaming with delight, she grabbed her Dior clutch, skipping down the stairs to meet him.

***

The drive had gone by in relative silence.

Now that they were both so close to the dinner, Cassie found herself feeling a little tongue-tied and could only assume that Trip felt the same as he kept looking away from her.

She didn't mind though. It was nice to have a moment to admire the journey to her home, to let herself feel the happy anticipation of what was going to happen though there was still that small part of her that worried about Trip meeting her parents.

As Cassie knew it was perfectly normal to be feeling somewhat apprehensive, she tried not to give it much thought. In no time at all, they pulled into her family's drive.

A stone fountain sat in front of the house. Her mom

had insisted it was modern art yet to Cassie, it was just a slab of marble with water spilling down its side. Still, it gave off a pleasant sound that always filled her with peace whenever she heard it.

Getting out of the car, Trip stared down at her intensely. "You look very beautiful tonight, Cassie."

Cassie smiled back at him, delighted that he was so smitten with her. He suddenly darted to the front passenger seat returning with a pretty white corsage that he handed to her.

"I almost forgot."

Although the flower was very pretty, Cassie wasn't sure what to make of this gift. Seeing her confusion, Trip asked, "What's wrong?"

"This is a corsage," she answered. "But, we're not going to prom?"

Trip dropped his eyes to the flower in her hands then back up to her face. "Have I made a mistake? In my research, it was customary to bring one of these flowers."

"In your research?" Cassie asked, sounding confused.

Trip shook his head. "Wrong word. Sorry. I think I'm just nervous."

Deciding to take pity on him, Cassie let the subject drop as she slipped the corsage onto her wrist. "It's beautiful. I love it. Thank you."

The front door suddenly swung open and Angie stood there in all her stunning glory, a Martini already in her hand. Tonight she wore a shimmering strapless tube dress that clung to her every curve and left nothing to the imagination. From the professionally styled wavy hair to the tip of her French pedicured toes that were balanced in six-inch stilettos, Angie had gone all out leaving Cassie's insecurities to immediately return.

She caught a glimpse of herself in one of the glass panels that flanked the front door. She looked good, better than she'd ever looked actually, but there was just no competing with her mom.

The woman was a model from head to toe while Cassie was just her daughter.

"Honey! Why are you just standing there gaping at me! Give me a hug!" Angie cried, lunging forward to envelop Cassie in her arms, spilling some of her drink in the process.

Cassie was hit with a blast of her mom's favorite perfume. She seemed to have overdosed on it tonight as Cassie felt the back of her throat becoming uncomfortably dry.

"And this must be Trip!" Angie smiled, stretching out her arms at him. "My, if I was younger I would go after you myself..." Angie giggled, waiting for Trip to approach her. Cassie watched like a hawk, uncomfortably aware of the sudden knots in her stomach. She waited in agony as Trip went to greet her. Angie wrapped herself around him, plastering her body to his in such a way that Cassie felt a streak of irritation.

She clung onto him for longer than was necessary Cassie thought, as Trip politely extracted himself from her arms, coming back immediately to Cassie's side. Rather amazingly, it didn't seem like he was lusting after her mom like every other guy on the planet.

In fact, his gaze was already back on her. Giving her a smile, he lifted his arm for her to take.

Angie seemed momentarily startled before she quickly composed herself, taking a sip of her drink. "Come inside you two. Dad's waiting to say hi."

They followed her into the house. Trip gave the place a brief once over but seemed otherwise uninterested in her home: the only interest he had was for her. Cassie felt the corners of her mouth lifting into a big grin as the tension she had felt suddenly melted away.

"Is that my amazing college daughter I see before me?"

Tom, her handsome anchor dad rushed her with a

hug, picking her up and swinging her around until she squealed. "Dad! Put me down!"

Laughing, he set her down. "Sorry, did I mess up your hair. I never learn."

He looked as great as he always did. He oozed warmth as much as her mom oozed sexuality. Striding to Trip, Tom grabbed his hand, pumping it up and down with enthusiasm. "It's so great to finally meet a boyfriend of Cassie's. She has never brought one home before."

Cassie loved that her dad could never believe that boys just weren't interested in her. In his mind, he had made up his own little story, and she was happy to go along with it, seeing as it was so much better than the real one.

Tom slipped his arm around Angie as the two stood there looking like there were in a commercial for a house. Cassie found herself feeling wistful, wondering if she and Trip would look like this in the future.

"This way, we're having drinks on the patio while the table is being set," Angie revealed, leading the way.

They settled on the outside lounges, Cassie beside Trip while Tom poured drinks for everyone. When he got to Angie, he asked whether she'd like to switch to something lighter, but she only laughed at him, requesting another frozen Gin Martini.

Talk turned to school as Cassie duly reported her progress. She might have embellished a little not wanting to worry them, knowing that her extracurricular activities were taking up a lot of time away from her studies. Angie didn't speak much, choosing to listen to the chatter while drinking her cocktail, but she seemed to spend an inordinate amount of time staring at the shoes Cassie was wearing. For some reason, the fact that she had worn them to this dinner was having a real effect on her.

When Tom expertly steered the conversation to Trip, he didn't even know that he was essentially being interrogated, but Cassie recognized the signs — she had been his little helper throughout her life, after all, helping him to compile his interview questions and being the perfect rapt audience when he had to run lines. She didn't mind any of it though as her dad was just showing his interest.

Trip answered as best he could though he continuously deflected the answers, turning attention onto Cassie instead. When she realized that he was trying to make her the center of attention, her heart swelled.

Soon enough one of her parents' staff announced that dinner was ready.

They were now seated around a long glass table with a pure white floral centerpiece. Angie had opted for a monochrome look tonight; everything was white or black barring the silverware. Steaming plates of the first course were set down before them by the help (her parents never did their own cooking).

"We thought we'd start with Italian tonight, a ravioli filled with lobster, langoustine, salmon and sorrel served with a delicate truffle foam," Tom announced.

"Sounds delicious," Cassie said. And it really did. Just smelling the heavenly food brought memories of family vacations by Lake Como in Italy. Taking a bite of the ravioli, Cassie sighed, sitting back in her chair. It tasted as good as it smelled, maybe even better. Looking across at Trip, he also took his first taste. When his eyes flared open with delight, she felt her shoulders relaxing.

A maid arrived with another glass for Angie, which earned a frown from Tom. "Maybe you want to slow down?" he suggested quietly only for Angie to laugh.

"It's just wine now, Dear, plus we're celebrating!"

Cassie shot a look between her parents, picking up on a vibe between them but she wasn't sure what it was. They both liked a drink or two so this wasn't exactly new. Her dad looked as if he wanted to say more but thought better of it. Turning back to them, he asked, "So how was the festival today? I know we're keeping you from it, but we had to take the opportunity to meet you when it was offered since our daughter seems so determined to keep you to herself."

"Oh, it was fun, then again, every day with Cassie is," Trip answered shooting her a besotted smile that Cassie returned. Tom felt his own lips curling into a smile at the blossoming feelings between the two. Only Angie seemed a little preoccupied, holding onto her glass as if it were a lifeline.

"How's work going, Mom?" Cassie asked. "You haven't been posting as much on Instagram lately."

"Oh, busy as always. I have been thinking of expanding my horizons, trying new things," Angie revealed to Cassie's surprise.

"Like what?"

"All sorts of things, really. Maybe I'll even go back to school. Ooh, I could join you, Cassie! Wouldn't that be a blast, the two of us, attending classes together?" Angie seemed suddenly very excited by the idea while Cassie could only feel dread. It would be the worst idea in the world. If Angie turned up to Cassie's college, Cassie would hate every minute of it.

Luckily she was saved from answering by her father. "Don't scare her like that, Dear. No one wants to go to school with their mom, no matter how cool she is."

"If you really wanted to go to school, there are others you could try," Cassie suggested gently, not wanting to rain on her mom's parade.

Angie pouted, seeming to be actually upset that Cassie wouldn't want her there, however hypothetical this all was. "It was just a suggestion."

Cassie shot a startled look at her, hearing the bite in her voice. Setting her glass down, Angie changed the subject.

"Let's not talk about that. Let's talk about something else, like that dress you're wearing, which is very cute, Sweetheart, but didn't you want to have it taken in?" Angie mimed Cassie's chest area, implying that it wasn't big enough to fit into the dress. Feeling mortified, Cassie's cheeks turned bright red.

"I think it looks just perfect on her," Trip chimed in, earning a grateful look from her though Angie's eyes seemed to turn flatter.

"Oh it looks nice, I just mean since she hasn't inherited my curves there are little tricks of the trade that I've taught her," Angie suggested before laughing. "It's funny, I'm reminded of those times when she was little and she used to walk around in my heels, wearing my dresses that would drag across the ground. She looked so adorable."

Cassie stopped eating, having suddenly lost her appetite. She wasn't sure what was happening, but the temperature seemed to have plummeted, or maybe that was just her mood. Was her mom trying to embarrass her because it certainly seemed that way.

Tom must have thought so too as he sent his wife a hard look. "Well, I'm with Trip. Cassie, you have grown into a lovely young woman and I happen to love how you're looking."

"You have definitely grown. It seemed like only last week when I caught you in my closet stuffing socks down your bra. I hope you've grown out of that now, Honey, though I guess Trip will find out soon enough," Angie laughed, her hand to her throat while Cassie sank lower in her chair, unable to look Trip in the face for fear of what she'd find there.

"That's enough!" Trip suddenly snapped, shocking them all. Throwing down his napkin, he pushed his chair back. "Mr. Cuthbert, thank you for the invitation to dinner. I'm sorry that it's not ending on a happier note." To Angie, he said, "Mrs. Cuthbert, I don't want to be rude but I didn't come here to listen to you belittle Cassie like this, so we are leaving. Cassie?" Trip asked, reaching out his hand to her.

Cassie's mouth had opened into a perfect 'o'. Never in

her life had anyone ever stood up for her like this, and certainly not against either of her fabulous parents. She didn't move right away, unsure of what to do, but when Trip sent her an encouraging smile, she got up and ran to his side.

Angie didn't move, shocked at his outburst as the two of them marched through the house. They were moments from walking out of the front door when Tom came rushing up behind them.

"Guys, wait a minute!" He called after them.

They stopped. "I'm so sorry, Sweetheart. You too, Trip. She's not usually like this."

"What is going on with her, Dad?" Cassie demanded, finally speaking up for herself. Now that her initial shock had worn away, anger was simmering close behind.

"She had a really bad day today. She just got replaced by a younger model for this lucrative campaign she was looking forward to doing. And it isn't the first time. It's been happening more and more lately, so I think your mom is having a hard time with it all. I think seeing you so happy and thriving is making her jealous."

"While that might be, it still doesn't excuse her behavior. Parents shouldn't be able to take their insecurities out on the children," Trip said, angrier than Cassie had ever seen him before. "We shouldn't be the ones who get punished."

"I know," Tom agreed. "I'm sorry, Guys. It's wrong and I'll make sure she knows it."

Apparently surprised by his own outburst, Trip caught himself, looking embarrassed. "Yes. Please, make sure she knows."

Giving Cassie a quick hug, Tom went back to deal with his wife as Trip's driver — who had been waiting outside for them — readied the car. All the while, Cassie stared at Trip, overwhelmed by his defense of her.

Her heart felt like it would burst from love.

ONE HUNDRED EIGHTY-THREE

The man who opened the door was an older version of Trip Rockwell.

Saunders took in his eyes, hardened by years of cynical living and the overall air of disdain that he gave off which didn't recede even when she showed him her badge.

After she had explained that she had some questions about his son, he didn't even blink, apparently either used to being questioned by the police about him or half-expecting it to happen every day.

She followed him through a marble foyer that was much too overwrought for her taste. A trio of gold chandeliers was suspended from the ceiling — one would have been too much for Saunders let alone three. She attempted to keep her shudder to herself.

She followed Donald Rockwell into a reception that overlooked the gardens, his arms folded over his chest. It was customary to ask if your guest wanted a drink though Donald was clearly not concerned with such things.

"What is it that has brought you to this neck of the

woods?" He asked, seemingly able to add a slur to the question knowing that Saunders would never have the kind of money it took to live in this neighborhood.

She didn't let it bother her. She knew this jerk's number. Had him pegged as soon as he'd opened the door, actually. Now to see if she had been right about him…

"I need to find your son, Trip. He's wanted in a case we're looking into," Saunders replied, watching him closely. Donald didn't seem the least bit phased by her response, shrugging his wide shoulders impassively.

"Well, if you see him, tell him I said hi," he said blithely. "I haven't seen him in days."

Apparently, this little fact did not bother him in the least. Saunders arched a brow.

"And you're not worried?"

Donald shook his head. "He takes off all the time. We don't police his whereabouts."

"Do you know if he's with his girlfriend?" Saunders asked.

A laugh rumbled out of Donald. "Trip has never stayed with a girl for more than a few nights. If he had a girlfriend, she'd have to be mighty special. I've seen the stunners he brings home. I mean, some of them have made me want to have a go, you know what I mean?"

Saunders gave him a long stare wondering when it was since her arrival that he thought he could talk to her like this, before realizing that he was exactly who she had pegged him for: a loud-mouthed, misogynistic trust-fund baby who was probably the worst kind of father.

It was no wonder that Trip didn't like to hang around here.

Saunders showed him the same photograph of the girls that she had shown the football player. She pointed at Cassie.

"This is his girlfriend. Has he mentioned her? Maybe he's brought her home?"

Donald peered down at her phone, took in Cassie's picture then shook his head.

"You must be mistaken. My son would never be interested in a mousy thing like that."

"That's not what I've been hearing. I have it on good authority that this is his girlfriend."

The frown appeared on Donald's face — his first honest reaction since Saunders had stepped foot into this ugly house. "Well, if that's who he's dating, she must have something on him because I am telling you, not in a million years."

Her phone rang just then, buzzing in her pocket. Fishing it out, she gestured one minute, then took the call as Donald glared at her, not liking how she was calling the shots.

"Detective Saunders?" She answered but at the message she received, she came to attention. "I'll be right there."

Hanging up, she shot Donald a look, giving him her card. "I have to go. If your son comes back or calls, tell him I need to speak to him urgently. I'll see myself out," she finished quickly, knowing that it would infuriate him.

Hurrying to her car, she floored it across the city.

***

The machines connected to her partner beeped slowly — slower in Saunders' mind which she knew wasn't her imagination. His wife had called to give her the bad news: the doctors didn't think Brooks had much time left.

Saunders studied her partner's ashen face. He seemed like a withered version of himself, a shell of the giant she knew him to be.

Outside, his wife and four kids sat, having been prepared for the worst. She could hear the youngest wailing in her mother's arms. Each cry cut into Saunders until she found herself digging her nails into her palms.

Despite all her efforts she had failed him.

She hadn't found the Jones' girl or nailed down how it was that he came to be lying in this terrible state an inch from death.

Outside, as his youngest cried for the impending loss of her father, Saunders felt her own tears streaking down her cheeks.

T rip took off his jacket, taking care to lay it in a particular way on the grass for Cassie to sit on.

Rather than let their less than successful dinner ruin their night, Trip had ordered food from Cassie's favorite restaurant from the car. By the time they had gotten there, the food was ready. They had picked it up and made their way back to the festival where they were camped out behind the Hatch Shell. A silent movie played, projected onto the back of the stage, giving off a romantic ambiance for Cassie and Trip.

Whatever Trip had slipped the bouncer who guarded the stage must have been a lot as they were the only ones there. The whole thing was romantic beyond measure and Cassie couldn't have been happier.

Against the backdrop of the music, Trip fed her a strawberry dipped in chocolate. The sweetness of the strawberry burst in her mouth only for the smoothness of the chocolate to kick in straight after. Cassie almost swooned. She felt like she was floating.

She was feeling a whole lot of other things too.

There was an urgent stirring inside that she couldn't hold back any longer. She didn't want food anymore: she wanted something else. Moving the plastic tubs aside, she knelt before Trip, staring deeply into his eyes. Leaning forward, she kissed him passionately, wrapping her arms around him as their lips sought each other with a hunger that couldn't be abated.

Laying her down, Trip moved on top of her. Cassie stared up at his eyes that had grown so dark in the half-light that they seemed almost black. Reaching up, she pulled his head down as he left a trail of kisses down her neck. His hands roamed her body, sliding down her arms to her waist then lower. They danced over her hips, tracing a pattern that made her shiver.

Slowly, he pulled her dress up, sliding the material across her skin until her legs were bare. His warm hands stroked her legs, moving up until they reached her thighs.

Cassie held her breath as Trip moved his head back until he could stare down at her, an unspoken question in his eyes. She nodding, giving him her consent though Trip did not move.

Reaching down, she slipped her underwear off, settling back onto his jacket, preparing herself for the moment that she had waited for her entire life. Now that it was here, Cassie felt warm and safe. She knew she was with the right person. She knew that she had been right to wait until this very moment to lose her virginity.

Trip started to move his hips. His wonderful face loomed above her, that face that she had grown to love. When it started, Cassie prepared herself for the new feelings.

Trip grunted above her, his expression serious — too serious — showing no enjoyment at all while pain exploded in her lower region making her bite her lip. Where were the nice feelings she was expecting?

Trying to ride the pain away, Cassie focused on Trip's face, hoping that the sight of it would relax her. He pumped away at her, his expression strange when suddenly, his face changed.

His skin turned blue, his lips black. And his eyes… his eyes became a milky white, but it was his flesh that really frightened her, hanging off his protruding cheekbones, rotting away in clumps.

Cassie screamed with terror just as Trip finished.

He rolled off of her, his back to her. Cassie lay there, blindsided, unsure what had just happened. Her pulse raced so fast that she thought she might pass out. The whole act had lasted only seconds, yet Cassie hadn't felt anything but pain.

Was this how her first time was supposed to be?

Feeling suddenly vulnerable and needing reassurance, Cassie called out. "Trip?"

Her voice trembled, she sounded weak as a bird. When he didn't respond Cassie first flush of panic.

Was it that terrible?

Was she that bad?

Crawling over to him, she found him staring down at his phone. "What are you doing?"

He didn't answer her, instead pushing the "send" button on his phone. Cassie heard the familiar sound of something posting to Instagram and felt a chill race down her spine.

"Trip? What's going on?"

He finally looked at her and she was relieved to see his normal face, but there was no hint of the love and care that she usually saw. Trip's face was hard, his eyes seemed dead.

"I thought you might be terrible, Cassie but you exceeded even my expectations. The last few weeks have been hell but I bet the guys that I would be able to do it. And now that I have, the world will see just what I've had to put up with."

She could hear his words but their meaning wasn't sinking in. Cassie blinked at him in a daze. "What are you saying? I don't understand."

"I'm saying it was all for a bet Cassie. Of course, I would never like someone like you. And know everyone will see what I have had to cope with."

His meaning suddenly became clear. Her eyes darted to his phone. "What have you done?" She gasped.

"I recorded the whole sorry act. It's all been uploaded onto Instagram. I'm sure your parents, as well as the rest of the school, will have a great time watching how bad you were."

Snatching up his jacket, Trip left.

ONE HUNDRED EIGHTY-FOUR

The chatter of the Starbucks was like an annoying buzz in Tyler's ears.

Ensconced in a corner booth, a book jacket covering the black magic spell book, Tyler read page after page, memorizing the passages as fast as she could.

Her anger from the fight she had had with Eve had faded as had her initial horror at seeing those rats she had killed.

She wasn't sorry for what she had done though.

It was Eve's fault for attacking her in the first place. She had simply been defending herself.

The buzzing sounded again though much louder than the hum she had been hearing for the last few hours. It took a moment before she realized that she had received a notification on her phone.

It was a video.

Someone with an unknown number had just sent a video to her.

Without thinking anything of it, Tyler hit play. It took a while to understand what it was that she was seeing, but when she did, she clapped her hand over her mouth.

Shoving her book into her bag, she raced outside.

***

Si sat, slumped against the passenger seat in their car.

After the fight, he had come round within moments. Eve had pleaded with him to go to a hospital but he wouldn't hear of it. They couldn't afford it, he'd said, besides, there was only a bump on his head that she pressed a cold can of soda to now.

Blessedly, he couldn't remember what happened, just that he had seen Tyler taking off and followed her, but when he'd come to, Tyler had gone and Eve was there in her place. She'd made a ridiculous excuse as to why they had been surrounded by all those dead rats.

"Where did she go?" Si asked suddenly before flinching at the sound of his own voice which seemed too loud for him.

"Tyler? Don't worry about her," Eve snapped. "She's not worth your concern."

Si lowered his hand, staring at her hard. "She's gone through so much, where is your compassion, Eve? Just what is your problem with her?"

Eve was about to reply with the great many issues she had with Tyler when the video arrived. The phone was sitting on the dashboard, right by their faces, impossible to miss. Reflexively she hit play, but when she understood what its contents contained, the blood drained out of her face.

***

Sitting on a bench overlooking the river, Marley finally summoned up the courage to call Christian and was relieved when he actually appeared.

“Well, you’re not in imminent danger so why have I been summoned?”

By his tone, Marley could see that he had not gotten over their earlier argument. She sighed. “I just need to explain. Will you just listen?”

“Fine,” he said, sitting on the bench beside her.

“I found out some crazy things today, and it just so happened that Rhett was there when I was upset. It wasn’t like I looked for him,” she began.

Something in her voice must have convinced him as Christian dropped the attitude. “What did you find out?”

“That my dad’s been lying to me this whole time. It looks like my mom has been in constant contact with him. She’s been sending me letters, but he’s never given them to me.”

Whatever Christian had expected to hear that wasn’t it. When he thought about the grief he’d been giving her all day, he felt like a serious jerk. “I’m… sorry, Marley. I didn’t know.”

“That makes two of us,” she replied smiling sadly. “I only found out because Eve had some suspicions about him. She broke into his apartment and found the letter.”

“Eve did what?” Christian spluttered, trying to get his head around it all.

“That’s what happened to me today, so you can see why I was pretty upset. I don’t know what to do. Should I search for her, or confront my dad, knowing that he might just lie to me again. He’s apparently very good at that.” She didn’t bother to hide the bitterness in her voice.

“I don’t think you should do anything right now. You’ve had a big shock, so you shouldn’t do anything rash that you might later regret. Sit on it until you’re calm. Decide then.”

Marley stared at him beneath her lashes. “When did you become so insightful?”

“Are you kidding? I was born this way. You should

have seen the kind of advice I dished out in Kinder-garten," he joked.

And just like that, some of her pain seemed to have lessened. Steeling herself to broach the awkward subject of Rhett, her phone beeped with a message. She watched the entire message, feeling sicker by the second.

"What is that?" Christian asked before his eyes went wide with realization. "*Oh*. Oh!"

When it was finally over, her stomach knotted in fear.

She knew what this would mean.

She sprinted down the path as fast as she could, heading to the mouth of the festival, just as Eve and Tyler appeared, both of them as out of breath as she was.

From the stark expressions on their faces, she knew they must have received the same video. "Where is she?" Eve asked.

"I don't know," Tyler responded, wringing her hands.

The girls scanned the crowd but it would be impossible to find her among all the people.

Suddenly, gasps rose from the crowd. People were looking up and pointing.

"Is someone up there?" A bystander asked.

Looking to see where they pointed to, Marley saw a small figure standing at the top of the clock tower that overlooked the Charles River.

Silhouetted against the setting sun, she could just make out the small figure with red hair.

"No… CASSIE!" Marley screamed but there was no response from her.

"Jesus!" She heard Christian cry. "Get up there!"

Eyes darting around the area, Marley shoved through the crowds, sprinting for the clock tower. Bursting into the building, she saw the stairs in the corner and took them, two at a time.

Footsteps thundered behind her and she knew the others were hot on her heels but she couldn't think about them. She had to get to the roof as fast as she could.

She had to stop what was about to happen.

Her lungs were on fire but Marley didn't slow down, not for a moment. Finally, she saw the doors that led to the roof in front of her. Bursting through them, she looked in every direction for Cassie but there was no sign of her.

Staggering forward, Marley searched desperately for her when her eyes found the pair of peep-toes shoes that had been left neatly on the roof — right by the edge of it.

"No…" Marley cried as she sprinted for the edge Eve, Tyler, and Christian right beside her. They got to the edge of the building at the same time and looked down.

There, floating face down in the Charles River, not moving at all…

It was Cassie.

This is the end of GRAVE MATTERS. An enormous thank you for reaching this mid-season finale! The thrilling saga will continue with the next book, due out in the new year (2019). Sign up to Jo's newsletter or Facebook group to be the first to hear when it will be available!

A NOTE FROM THE AUTHOR

If you've got this far then hopefully you've liked this book, maybe even loved it (yay!) in which case can you please take a few minutes to review this book and the series?

I'm an indie author which means I write on my little computer from my little rental home (London is expensive, y'all). The websites, paperbacks, advertising… everything is done by me so if you love my books and would like to see me become successful as an indie author, and you know, maybe finally buy myself and my cats a little home that I own, please help by leaving your reviews.

The more people that know about my books, the better they will do and the more time I will have to write you more books!

And if you haven't signed up to my mailing list yet, what are you waiting for? Be the first to hear Jo's news, book releases, and giveaways. Apply for her ARC teams (she has one for ebooks AND one for audiobooks) to get free, advanced copies of her books to read/listen to and review. Plus, you'll get a free book as a thank you for signing up! What's not to like?

Sign up and join all the cool kids at www.johoscribe.com

SNEAK PEAK AT WANTED, BOOK 1 OF THE CHASE RYDER SERIES

While Jo is busy working on the second half of the Twisted Magic series why not try her other fast-paced YA thriller books, the award-winning Chase Ryder series?

Here's a sneak peak:

NEW YORK CITY, NY

He had been running now for days.

The hot asphalt stung his cracked soles and the burning sun pounded onto his thinning frame, but he knew he couldn't stop. He had to get away.

A battered blue truck thundered past and he flinched. No matter how often it happened, he still wasn't prepared for the rush of sound that roared into his ears. Where he was from, there were no cars. No vehicles of any kind.

He lifted his nose to the wind and welcomed the heady sensation of another new smell to add to his collection. Juicy, with a hint of smoke. He licked his lips, mouth watering in anticipation. Crossing onto the sidewalk, he moved towards the aroma, to where an overweight man in a greasy apron cooked on a stand. Meat patties sizzled on the grill.

He hadn't eaten since the escape, and now his stomach protested painfully. He padded up to the man and gave him a hopeful look, but clapping eyes on him, the vendor grabbed a broom and started shaking it in warning.

"Get lost you filthy beast!"

Red from the heat of the flames, perspiration slid down his wobbly chin and landed with a plop an inch away from the meat. When his target failed to move, he glared down at the optimistic hopeful and--

WHAAM!   Steel-capped boots lashed out onto his rump.

The sharp stabbing pain shocked the brown and white dog who had never felt anything like it in his life.

He blinked back tears and howled.

GREENWICH, FAIRFIELD COUNTY

Everyone loved sunsets. Everyone, that is, but me, Chase Ryder, to whom sunsets signaled that yet another hard night was approaching.

In the leafy upmarket park surrounding a man-made lake, wealthy couples strolled hand-in-hand admiring the mottled orange sky. I stirred, waking from my nap beneath a towering oak. Oaks were best as they provided plenty of foliage to protect against sudden showers and prying eyes. There was also the added bonus of load-bearing lower branches that someone nimble could scramble onto should trouble come calling... and you should know, trouble had me on speed-dial.

I stared at my reflection in the water. The face that stared back at me was fourteen but looked younger. A button nose and blue eyes gave the illusion of innocence. My mouth was plump; a little bigger than I'd like, but at least I'd never need collagen. The shoulder length hair would be a glossy chestnut if it weren't hanging in one big, greasy streak. Despite my current condition, I knew I was above average, but I'm not exactly what you'd call vain, usually choosing to hide my face rather than show it.

My stomach emitted a low rumble. I slipped a hand into a pocket and retrieved the last of my money, a hundred bucks or so. All that's left of my stash. It might seem like a good amount, but I'd already been on the road for eight months. In that time, I learned to only spend when I absolutely had to. *If only I was rich, I wouldn't be in this mess.*

I looked around at my surroundings. Yummy mommies with Pilate's-honed bodies bouncing designer-clad babies on tanned knees. The only hunger they knew was self-inflicted. I compared my figure to that of a passing cyclist, frowning when I realized that the only difference between us was our ages.

Originally from "The Paper City" Holyoke in Hampden County — one of the poorest cities in Massachusetts — I'd come here thinking I would receive more charity in affluent Greenwich, which had seen Mel Gibson and Meryl Streep among its wealthy residents, but these people, so caught up in their self-made dramas, barely noticed me. I'd totaled less here than if I'd stayed home.

I frowned as a shadow fell over the water, obscuring my face. *Strange.* The shadow didn't encompass the whole park, just me. Too late the danger signs came into my head as a hand clamped down on my shoulder. The nails were ripped and blackened with dirt. I noticed the smell next, pungent, like raw sewage mixed with a brewery.

"Spare some change?"

I spun around to find myself gripped, vice-like, in the arms of a guy who was maybe seventeen. His glazed eyes focused on the money in my hands. I looked at his arms — yup, mottled with needle tracks. I scanned the area quickly, searching for help, but help wasn't coming. *Note to self: if trees are leafy enough to shield you from prying eyes, they'll also shield the nasty druggie who has you in his grasp.*

I froze in terror.

The druggie eyeballed the money in my hand and snatched it from me. He hesitated then, doubt clouding his eyes, but when he realized we were isolated from the rest of the park, they narrowed shrewdly.

"That it, or you holding out on me?"

Without waiting for an answer, his hands started patting me down. Here's something you should know about me: no one, but no one touches me without my consent. Instantly a surge of white-hot fury broke through the fear. I screamed into his face.

"Don't you touch me!" and struggled like a wildcat. He was startled but much stronger than he seemed and moved like I was nothing but a mild annoyance. As he reached into my pockets, I saw my opportunity and plunged two fingers into his windpipe, slamming the palm of my other hand under his nose, snapping the weak cartilage there. Eyes wide with shock, he released me instantly.

Groaning in pain, he sank to the ground, hands around his now bloody nose. Fallen, he looked much younger. Not much bigger than me and nothing like the terrifying beast I'd thought he was. I swooped in and snatched my money back.

Shooting a quick prayer to the YouTube gods of Krav Maga,[1] I grabbed my backpack and got the hell out of Dodge.

The sun had barely risen, but I was already on the hunt

for breakfast. Like they say, it's the most important meal of the day.

It had taken me all night to shake off the druggie incident. I knew I was lucky this time, but I couldn't afford another slip-up. In future, I would stay away from trees, bushy or otherwise.

From experience, I knew Monday mornings were the most fruitful, with restaurants tossing whatever hadn't sold from the week before. It was with this promise of delectable treasure that I jogged into the back end of a strip of restaurants and climbed into the dumpster behind The Blessed Palace, a popular Asian establishment. The place was kinda tacky looking, covered with gold and red dragons that looked more like distorted fish than those epic mythological characters, but they do a weekend buffet that never failed to impress, judging by the length of the waiting line that curved around the block on a regular basis.

Sadly for me, Lady Luck hadn't just left the building, she'd taken a slow boat to China, as a deep dumpster dive only delivered some decomposed fish heads *(seriously gross)*, half a fortune cookie *(semi-gross, and empty, so no good fortune for me — figures)* and something I'd prefer not to examine in closer detail. All you need to know is it looked like Swampthing's illegitimate lovechild with a roach.

Enough said.

I sighed with irritation. *Damn greedy staff must have taken the leftovers home with them.* That's the problem with Asians. Never waste a thing.

Shoving the cookie into my mouth, I picked my way over the remaining mess of empty cartons and boxes. As I grabbed hold of the skip to haul myself out, I heard a sound and froze. Someone had just yelped. Loudly. In a that-really-hurt kind of way.

I raised my head and peeked over the edge of the dumpster. A mangy dog, some kind of collie mix, was backing away from a man. There was a bone in his mouth, but the guy had one hand on it. He wore the uniform of The Blessed Palace and struck repeatedly at the dog with a wet dishtowel.

THWACK! The towel made a whipping sound as it connected with the collie's flank. The dog whimpered but didn't let go. He didn't attack either, just kept backing away. It's like the thing didn't know he had two rows of sharp teeth.

My eyes narrowed into slits. From the collie's thin frame, I could tell he was starving, maybe even more so than me. It could have been my own lack of food or the injustice of it all, but I felt a sudden rage building.

Stealthily, I crawled out of the dumpster and dropped silently, landing behind the guy on my Kmart sneakers. He twirled the towel, readying another strike. Neither of them had noticed me yet, so I took full advantage of the situation. I reached for the nearest trashcan, snatched the lid off, and HURLED it at the guy's head. The dull sound it made on contact made us all wince. He dropped like a hot spring roll. I looked at the dog. "RUN MUTT!"

And took off. I only glanced back when I reached the end of the block, so it was a shock to see the dog panting right behind me.

"Shoo! Scram!" I waved my hands at him, but he just cocked his head at me. Seeing that we were alone, I slowed my running to a jog. Clearly Angry Chinese Man wasn't after us. Which, come to think of it, was weird.

I suddenly stopped. What if I'd hit him too hard? Heads are pretty soft and not the best defense against steel. What if I'd... *killed* him? My life didn't flash in front of my eyes so much as my mugshot.

Muttface suddenly dropped his bone. That alone was shocking enough, but then he clamped his jaws around my wrist and started tugging.

"Hey, dufus! I just saved you! What kind of gratitude is that?"

And then I heard it. Furious shouts. Furious *foreign* shouts. I glanced back and saw Angry Chinese Man was not dead after all, but alive and kicking — and he had brought friends. *With cleavers.* The dog and I stared at each other, the same expression mirrored in our eyes... holy crap.

Muttface tore off, stopping a few yards ahead of me. He looked at me and barked once before tearing off again. Didn't need a membership to Mensa to figure out what he meant. Having no plan b, I sprinted after him.

The dog ran fast, but never in a straight line. It was like he had experience evading capture. Already light-headed, I was becoming dizzy with all the twists and turns we were taking. *I* had no idea where we were any more so Angry Chinese Man and chums had no chance. I followed Muttface down a side street.

And suddenly I collapsed.

One minute I was running, the next I tasted tarmac. I felt a wet, sandpapery tongue on my face.

And then there was darkness.

To find out if what happens to Chase and her new four-legged friend, grab your copy of Wanted, The Chase Ryder series, or you can pick up the three-book bundle saving you 20% off the price!

ALSO BY JO HO

SERIES

The Twisted Series, YA Urban Fantasy

(Available as ebook, paperback, audiobook)

Perfect for fans of The Mortal Instruments, The Vampire Diaries, and Pretty Little Liars!

Read it three ways!

As the single editions:

What Doesn't Kill You (Book 1)

Beware The Signs (Book 2)

See No Evil (Book 3)

The Blood That Binds (Book 4)

When Trouble Comes (Book 5)

Bad Habits (Book 6)

Left Behind (Book 7)

Hell Hath No Fury (Book 8)

In Her Skin (Book 9)

First Date Jitters (Book 10)

Grave Matters (Book 11)

Plus lots more to come!

TWISTED MAGIC 1

A specially discounted box set edition containing all 11 of the first Twisted books.

TWISTED SAGAS

Discounted 3 - book box sets of the Twisted series

The Chase Ryder Series, YA Thriller

- Winner of a Readers' Favorite Gold Medal Book Award -

(Available as ebook, paperback, hardcover, large print, audiobook)

Love stories the entire family can enjoy? Love dogs?

Then you'll love this series!

Wanted, Book 1

Haunted, Book 2

Hunted, Book 3

STANDALONES

(Available as ebook and paperback)

A new town, a new place, and a new mystery…

The Boy Next Door (YA Mystery)

Books are available as ebook, paperback, and audiobook

For purchase links please visit Jo's website at
www.johoscribe.com/buy-now

AFTERWORD

Twisted is a television series that I have been trying to make for coming up to eight years now.

I created it soon after my television series Spirit Warriors aired.

At one point I even had one of the producers behind one of the biggest film franchises in the world attached. We were trying to get it set up in the States but for a variety of reasons, it just didn't happen.

In all this time, and after so many other projects, I still haven't been able to let this one go. I believe in these girls and their troubles and I believe there are others out there who want to hear their story. Outside of the supernatural shenanigans are the problems so many girls face today. I know, because each of these girls is a part of me in some way.

I wasn't one of the popular girls at school.

I was very overweight — one of the side effects of coming from a troubled background. I was bullied from students and a staff member who took great joy in belittling me in front of the whole class on a regular basis until I learned to be terrified of attending those classes.

I was also the girl who couldn't bear to look at herself in the mirror as she saw nothing but ugliness, which wasn't surprising as that is what the world repeatedly told me I was.

And I was the girl who looked for validation in all the wrong places.

So this series is important to me as I know there are millions of girls out there who felt the same way I did. The ones who aren't "perfect". The ones who are outcasts, misfits, geeks — to them I say, know that you are unique and special. Stay true to yourself and great things can and will come.

If you'd like to help me make this into a TV series, please *leave your reviews* for these books and help spread the word. The more love there are for these books and the more demand there is for this show, the more likely it is to happen.

My thanks go to my wonderful proof reader and grammar guru, Janice Harris for her support and insightful work. Thank you also to the fabulous Harold Trammel whose notes aren't only perceptive but an utter joy to read. Last but not least, thank you to Dawn C. D. Harrison and Simon Richardson who cast their critical and much-needed eyes over proceedings. I'm so grateful to you all.

And finally as always, to my love Matt who brings joy to each and every day.

- Jo

ABOUT THE AUTHOR

A proud geek and video gamer, and champion of complex female protagonists, Jo brings her page-turning screenwriting style to books to weave well-crafted, suspenseful stories with twists you don't see coming.

A self-taught screenwriter, Jo's writing life began when she created the ground-breaking, critically acclaimed CBBC action fantasy television series, "Spirit Warriors," which introduced leading actress, Jessica Henwick ("Game of Thrones," "Star Wars: The Force Awakes") to the screen. Granted the biggest budget ever given to a CBBC show at the time, it was nominated for "Best Children's Program" at the 2011 Broadcast Awards, with Jo herself, going on to win the Women in Film & Television's "New Talent" Award in 2010. Jo even made history by being the first East Asian person — man or woman — to have created a British television drama series.

Since then, Jo has worked with some of the most acclaimed producers in the world with several television shows and movies currently in development. It is her dream to bring her Twisted series to screen and she believes she can make it happen with her readers' help!

Jo lives in London and hopes one day to travel across America in a super kitted out, Zombie-apocalypse-ready RV, with her lovely fella, Matt, and three equally lovely kitties.

Join Jo's Facebook Reader's Group at www.facebook.com/groups/JoHoAuthor/and interact with her there, as well as to hear the latest news and offers as they are released.

Or you can join Jo's Newsletter if Facebook isn't your thing.

For a complete list of Jo's books, visit her website.

 facebook.com/Johowriter

twitter.com/johoscribe

 instagram.com/johoscribe